THE

CENTENARY EDITION

OF THE WORKS OF

NATHANIEL HAWTHORNE

Volume V

OUR OLD HOME

EDITORS

General Editors

WILLIAM CHARVAT, 1905–1966

ROY HARVEY PEARCE

CLAUDE M. SIMPSON

MATTHEW J. BRUCCOLI

FREDSON BOWERS, *Textual Editor*

L. NEAL SMITH, *Associate Textual Editor*

A PUBLICATION OF

THE OHIO STATE UNIVERSITY CENTER

FOR TEXTUAL STUDIES

NATHANIEL HAWTHORNE

OUR OLD HOME:
A SERIES OF
ENGLISH SKETCHES

Ohio State University Press

Standard Book Number 8142–0002–8
Library of Congress Catalogue Card Number 75–92336
Copyright © 1970 by the Ohio State University Press
All Rights Reserved
Printed in the United States of America

ACKNOWLEDGMENTS

THE EDITORS of the Centenary Hawthorne are grateful for the assistance given by librarians, scholars, and bibliophiles. We are indebted to Ellen B. Ballou, Dublin, New Hampshire; C. Waller Barrett, Charlottesville, Virginia; William H. Bond and Roger E. Stoddard, the Houghton Library, Harvard University; Herbert Cahoon and Douglas Ewing, the Pierpont Morgan Library; C. E. Frazer Clark, Jr., Bloomfield Hills, Michigan; Anne Freudenberg and William H. Runge, the Alderman Library, University of Virginia; Collin B. Hamer, Jr., the New Orleans Public Library; Kenneth A. Lohf, Columbia University Libraries; Charles Mann, the Pennsylvania State University Library; George Monteiro, Brown University; Norman Holmes Pearson, Yale University; the Seven Gables Bookshop, New York City; Lola L. Szladits, the Berg Collection, New York Public Library; and the late John Cook Wyllie, University of Virginia.

Special acknowledgment is made to John Manning, and thanks are due Kathleen Addlesperger, Marianne Bailey, Peggy Bennington, Catherine King, and Kathleen Narcross, of the Ohio State University, and Mrs. F. Russell Hart, of Charlottesville, Virginia.

We thank these libraries for their permission to transcribe and edit the manuscript materials of *Our Old Home*: The Henry W. and Albert A. Berg Collection of the New York Public Library, Astor, Lenox, and Tilden foundations; the

ACKNOWLEDGMENTS

Columbia University Libraries; the Harvard College Library; the Henry E. Huntington Library; the Pierpont Morgan Library; the Ohio State University Libraries; the St. Lawrence University Library; the Stanford University Library; and the Barrett Collection, University of Virginia Library. Our thanks go also to Mr. Robert H. Taylor, Princeton, New Jersey, and to Mr. Walter P. Chrysler, Jr., New York City, for access to and use of manuscript materials in their possession.

We gratefully acknowledge the support of the National Endowment for the Humanities of the National Foundation on the Arts and Humanities.

The support of the following divisions of the Ohio State University has made this project possible: the Department of English, the Graduate School, the University Libraries, the Office of Research, and the Research Foundation.

THE EDITORS

CONTENTS

Introduction to *Our Old Home*   xiii

Textual Introduction: *Our Old Home*   xliii

To a Friend   3

Consular Experiences   6

Leamington Spa   41

About Warwick   65

Recollections of a Gifted Woman   90

Lichfield and Uttoxeter   120

Pilgrimage to Old Boston   139

Near Oxford   167

Some of the Haunts of Burns   193

A London Suburb   213

Up the Thames   243

Outside Glimpses of English Poverty   277

Civic Banquets   310

Textual Notes   349

Editorial Emendations in the Copy-Text   359

CONTENTS

Rejected First-Edition Substantive Variants   393

Word-Division   399

Historical Collation   405

Alterations in the Manuscript   425

Special Appendix: Original 1857 "Uttoxeter"   481

Cross-references with *The English Notebooks*   489

The illustration facing page xliii is folio 4 of the original manuscript of "To a Friend" in the Henry E. Huntington Library, San Marino, California (HM 7173).

OUR OLD HOME

INTRODUCTION TO

OUR OLD HOME

URING Hawthorne's 1853–57 sojourn in England as American consul at Liverpool, he kept a voluminous journal with an eye to its future usefulness. His English notebooks, comprising some 300,000 words,[1] contain detailed accounts of the family's sightseeing, with due attention to nature, architecture, and the whimsicalities of British character. Even in journal form his observations are "worked up," and are not mere jottings; the familiar combination of acceptance and skepticism is here, leading Hawthorne to tell his Boston publishers as early as 1856 that he "could easily make up a couple of nice volumes . . . ; but, unluckily, they would be much too good and true to bear publication. It would bring a terrible hornet's nest about my ears."[2] The next year he announced to Ticknor that his journal filled "hundreds of pages, which I would publish if the least of them were not too spicy."[3] We are not really asked to take the author's disclaimers very seriously: the possibility of eventual publication was more central to his thinking than were the

[1] Randall Stewart (ed.), *The English Notebooks by Nathaniel Hawthorne* (New York and London, 1941). A special appendix to this Centenary Edition lists those passages in *The English Notebooks* that have furnished material for *Our Old Home*.

[2] May 23, 1856, to W. D. Ticknor, MS, Berg Collection, New York Public Library.

[3] June 5, 1857, MS, Berg Collection, New York Public Library.

dangers of publication. In 1857, indeed, he levied upon a journal entry of July 4, 1855, as the basis for a brief piece entitled "Uttoxeter" contributed to an English miscellany *The Keepsake*.[4] But after leaving the consulate late in 1857 Hawthorne was absorbed for almost three years by travel and residence in Italy, together with the writing of *The Marble Faun*.

Early in 1860 Ticknor evidently asked Hawthorne to write something for the *Atlantic Monthly*, then still under the original editorship of J. R. Lowell but owned since 1859 by Ticknor and Fields. Hawthorne, who had just finished reading proofs for *The Marble Faun* and was remaining in England to assure the English copyright of his latest romance, replied that he had "lost the habit of writing magazine articles," but that if "some good idea" came to him he would try to develop it.[5] Soon after he returned to America he wrote to Fields:

> I have been looking at that sketch of Leigh Hunt, and though it has some good things in it, more labour than I am now capable of would be requisite to make it presentable. Perhaps I might find some sketch of rural or town scenery that would do. There is a long account of a visit to places connected with the memory of Burns—not in the least thoughtful or imaginative, but of the photographic kind. How would that answer? [6]

Although he concluded by wondering whether the recent centenary celebrations of Burns's birth had exhausted public interest, he probably did not wait for Fields's reaction, for in less than a week he sent Lowell an article which must have been the Burns piece. "Of course," Hawthorne wrote Lowell on July 24, "if you don't think it worth printing, you will tell me so." [7] Whatever the immediate response, "Some of the

---

[4] See note 28.

[5] February 10, 1860, MS, Berg Collection, New York Public Library.

[6] July 19, 1860, MS, St. Lawrence University Library.

[7] MS, Houghton Library, Harvard University.

Haunts of Burns" appeared in the October, 1860, issue of the *Atlantic,* attributed to "A Tourist Without Imagination or Enthusiasm." Thus began what slowly shaped itself into a series and eventually into the volume *Our Old Home.*[8]

Hawthorne's appearance in the *Atlantic* was not immediately repeated. His Concord home The Wayside was for some months upset by carpenters who were adding several rooms that included a tower study. Equally distracting, perhaps, was the immense effort Hawthorne was making to write several romances. At any rate, no more essays came from his pen for almost a year after the Burns piece. The next we hear, Fields, who had taken over the editorship of the *Atlantic* from Lowell in the spring of 1861, wrote to say that he hoped to begin publishing Hawthorne's prospective "story (about the house)"—*Septimius Felton*—with the issue of January, 1862. A postscript expressed Fields's pleasure over "Near Oxford," which was printed in the *Atlantic* of October, 1861. "Do the Cathedrals at your pleasure," he wrote, "and oblige T & F. The sooner the better." [9]

Hawthorne was, as it happened, represented in the January, 1862, *Atlantic*—not by the beginning of a romance or by the cathedrals article Fields wanted, but by "Pilgrimage to Old Boston," an essay that excited no great comment, despite the local associations which Hawthorne gently pointed out. In the early months of the new year Hawthorne was continuing to produce notes and drafts of the Septimius story, but with-

[8] Much of the story told in the following pages can also be found, with some of the documents, in James T. Fields, *Yesterdays With Authors* (Boston, 1872), pp. 102–11, and James C. Austin, *Fields of the Atlantic Monthly* (San Marino, Calif., 1953), pp. 214–33.

[9] [September 18, 1861], MS, Huntington Library. The germ of *Septimius Felton* was Thoreau's remark to Hawthorne that a man had once occupied Wayside who believed he would never die. The romance, one of several works which Hawthorne was unable to finish, was eventually serialized in the *Atlantic,* January–August, 1872, and was published in book form that year. See Edward H. Davidson, *Hawthorne's Last Phase* (New Haven, 1949), pp. 72 ff.

out satisfaction to himself. On February 20 he appended a postscript to a letter his wife had written to Fields, saying "As to my steady writing, that's all a mistake. Perhaps I will send you an article, but I don't know." [10] Soon thereafter he paid a visit to his old friend Horatio Bridge in Washington, had his portrait painted by Emanuel Leutze, witnessed the progress of hostilities at close range, and was part of a Massachusetts delegation which called on President Lincoln. His Washington impressions were contained in an essay for the July *Atlantic*, "Chiefly About War Matters," with an unflattering description of Lincoln which Fields persuaded him to omit.

Before the middle of the year Hawthorne resumed work on the English sketches. When Fields received "Leamington Spa" in July, he acknowledged it with characteristic enthusiasm: "I don't think even your pen ever did a better thing in its way." And along with the usual check for $100 he broached a fresh idea. "What a delectable *Book* you are building up out of these capital papers. Let us, Author and Publisher, be thinking of a sleek volume, for pretty soon we shall have made one. *We!*" [11] Within a few days after the appearance of "Leamington Spa" in the October *Atlantic*, Fields wrote to congratulate Hawthorne, saying "I am stopped in the street to laugh with friends over your fat dowager; how the papers all praise the article & ask for more of the same sort." Fields, too, asked for more—one for December and yet another for January. [12] Hawthorne responded immediately, promising an article for each issue and rather diffidently accepting praise for the dowager. [13] Despite his mixed feelings about the reception of his articles, he began to devote himself assiduously to them, and between October and the next June

[10] MS, Boston Public Library.
[11] July 24, 1862, MS, Huntington Library.
[12] September 24, 1862, MS, Huntington Library.
[13] September 27, 1862, MS, Berg Collection, New York Public Library.

produced six for the magazine and two others reserved for the book.

As the correspondence shuttled back and forth between Boston and Concord, Hawthorne's obvious pleasure was constantly held in check by a familiar strain of skepticism that is a hallmark of the sketches themselves. On October 5 Hawthorne forwarded his contribution for December. "I hope you will like it," he wrote Fields; "for the subject seemed interesting to me when I was on the spot, but I always feel a singular despondency and heaviness of heart in re-opening these old journals now. However, if I can make readable sketches out of them, it is no matter. I want $100 awfully and immediately." [14] Fields must have expressed dissatisfaction with the title "A Sketch or two in Warwick," for on October 9 Hawthorne wrote him:

> Name it anything you like, provided the title shall promise no more than is to be found in the paper. This is the merit of my title; it expresses just what the article is. But call it "Warwick"—which implies a fuller description than I give—or "An Old English Town"—or "Leycester's Hospital"—which does not cover everything, and yet suggests a detailed description of the Hospital and full account of it, which I do not pretend to—or "About Warwick"—which is unexceptionable, and better than the present title, as being shorter. In a word suit yourself, I wash my hands of it; though I think the title last suggested is the best, on the whole. [15]

Titles had troubled Hawthorne in the past, but he usually hit upon the final choice himself, as he did in this instance. "About Warwick" it was. When it appeared, Fields declared, with pardonable hyperbole, "That absolutely perfect paper is hailed with delight all over the land. Curtis . . . joined the chorus with enthusiasm. Lowell & Longfellow chanted high

[14] MS transcription, Hawthorne-Fields Letter Book, Houghton Library, Harvard University.
[15] MS, Massachusetts Historical Society.

praises to me last night, and Holmes swears you are the Prince of English writers." [16]

The same letter acknowledged "that glorious paper" Hawthorne had sent for the January issue, "Recollections of a Gifted Woman." This piquant essay centering on Shakespeare devotes half its space to Stratford, half to Hawthorne's reminiscences of Delia Bacon. Here the author's gentleness does not hide the fact that Miss Bacon was the victim of delusions; he was indulgent toward her anti-Stratfordian views on the Shakespeare-Bacon controversy, but he did not endorse her theories, even in a preface he wrote for her book. What the essay does not tell us is that Hawthorne's personal sympathies were so engaged that, unknown to Miss Bacon, he supplied the funds for the book's London publication and prevailed upon Ticknor to take half the edition for the American market. As Hawthorne hints, *The Philosophy of the Plays of Shakspere Unfolded* fell dead from the press, but he accepted his financial loss chivalrously.[17]

Up to this time Fields had paid Hawthorne $100 for each essay, regardless of length. Now he set a new schedule: $100 for all articles of ten pages or less, $10 additional for each page over ten. The "Gifted Woman," being fifteen pages, thus brought $150, much to Hawthorne's gratification.[18] Fields continued to press for book publication when sketches should

---

[16] December 4, 1862, MS, Huntington Library.

[17] See *Letters of Hawthorne to . . . Ticknor, 1851–1864* (Newark, N. J., 1910), II, 32–55; Theodore Bacon, *Delia Bacon* (Boston, 1888), pp. 164–317; and Vivian C. Hopkins, *Prodigal Puritan: A Life of Delia Bacon* (Cambridge, Mass., 1959), pp. 200–244.

In acknowledging Harriet Beecher Stowe's praise of his essay, Hawthorne wrote (January 4, 1863, MS copy, Chicago Historical Society) that Delia Bacon deserved "honorable remembrance." His essay, he said, was designed to forestall "the possibility that, in these irreverent days, the subject might be taken up by somebody who had not so genuine a respect for her as I had."

[18] Fields to Hawthorne, December 4, 1862, Hawthorne to Fields, December 6, 1862, MSS, Huntington Library.

have sufficiently accumulated, and Hawthorne's pace quickened to produce about half the volume during his final six months of composition. Illness early in December delayed "A Suburban Residence," intended for the *Atlantic* of February, 1863, but he finished it in time for March publication under the title "A London Suburb." Again the note of diffidence is uppermost in his accompanying letter: "I herewith bore you with another article. I am sorry that it runs to such length but I have left out what would have made a sheet or two more in order to bring it within reasonable compass. Don't read this to Una [Hawthorne's daughter was visiting the Fieldses] nor let her hear it, for it always plagues me to have my wife and children read my productions before they are printed and if I could prevent it afterwards, I would." [19] Fields promptly paid Hawthorne $150 for the essay, and soon thereafter declared that "this last one is so excellent from beginning to end I must roar again. I declare to you it is the best of the series. But this I always say of the last one I read." [20] Hawthorne whimsically accepted Fields's praise: "I am much encouraged by what you say about the English articles—not but what I am sensible that you mollify me with a good deal of soft soap, but it is skilfully applied and effects all that you intend it should." [21]

Hawthorne had meantime announced that he might follow up "A London Suburb" by dipping "into London a little, being so near it in the one just sent you." He foresaw two additional articles necessary "to make up a volume of, say 325 pages. Methinks it would be better to defer publication till the autumn—at least, till summer"; and he went on to proph-

[19] January 4, 1863, to Fields, MS transcription, Hawthorne-Fields Letter Book, Houghton Library, Harvard University.

[20] Hawthorne to Fields, January 8, 1863, MS transcription, Hawthorne-Fields Letter Book, Houghton Library, Harvard University; Fields to Hawthorne, January 26, 1863, MS, Huntington Library.

[21] January 30, 1863, MS transcription, Hawthorne-Fields Letter Book, Houghton Library, Harvard University.

esy gloomily that when the war was over, the country would lie in such ruinous darkness that people would not be able to read, and books would cease to sell. "Not that I really believe this, but I should not wonder if it were true." [22] The London essay, called "Up the Thames," went to Fields on February 22, accompanied by a letter apologizing for the length of the article and authorizing Fields to cut as he pleased. In this mood Hawthorne was convinced that the entire series was "good for nothing; but that is none of my business, provided the public and you are of a different opinion." Although his pages on Leigh Hunt might not reflect the high regard in which Fields held the Englishman, Hawthorne declared that "no more genuine characterization and criticism (so far as the writer's purpose to be true goes) was ever done. . . . I might have made more of it, but should not have improved it." [23] The recent months of concentration had kept him in "nearly solitary imprisonment" and he intended to write only two additional articles (one more than he had announced six weeks earlier).

Fields's response on February 23 was characteristic: the piece was by no means too long; he admired Hawthorne's treatment of Hunt; he would not hear of Hawthorne's stopping with but two more papers.[24] For a time Hawthorne remained firm in his plans. By mid-April he had written "Outside Glimpses of English Poverty" and in a letter acknowledging payment for it he stated: "I shall begin to write the last article (which will come first in the volume) in a day or two. I don't think the public will bear any more of this sort of thing." [25] Despite his momentarily jaundiced feeling, he

[22] January 8, 1863, to Fields. See note 20.
[23] MS, Huntington Library.
[24] MS, Huntington Library.
[25] April 18, 1863, MS transcription, Hawthorne-Fields Letter Book, Houghton Library, Harvard University.

quickly finished "Consular Experiences" and dispatched it to Fields on April 30. In the accompanying letter he proposed, straightforwardly and without alternatives, the title the book was to bear: *"Our Old Home;* a series of English Sketches by &c." But after telling Fields "you can begin printing it whenever you like," he wondered whether there should not be "some novelty in the collected volume, . . . something that may excite a little discussion and remark." Perhaps "Consular Experiences" might be reserved for the book, in which case Hawthorne thought he could "concoct another article" for the August issue. He described the "Consular" paper in terms calculated to whet reader interest:

> The article has some of the features that attract the curiosity of the foolish public, being made up of personal narrative and gossip, with a few pungencies of personal satire, which will not be the less effective because the reader can scarcely find out who was the individual meant.

And as if to suggest that he had a shrewd eye for publicity, he went on:

> I am not without hope of drawing down upon myself a good deal of critical severity on this score, and would gladly incur more of it if I could do so without seriously deserving censure. The story of the Doctor of Divinity, I think, will prove a good card in this way. It is every bit true (like the other anecdotes) only not told so darkly as it might have been for the reverend gentleman. I do not believe there is any danger of his identity being ascertained, and do not care whether it is or no—as it could only be done by the impertinent researches of other people.[26]

[26] MS, Huntington Library. Hawthorne's account of the Reverend Dr. Richards of New Orleans is expanded from journal entries of May 24 and 31, 1855, which are more factual though less evocative. The clergyman, Hawthorne wrote (*English Notebooks,* p. 113), had been brought back to his ship "in a state of delirium tremens, by a woman of the town!" A letter to Ticknor was even blunter and more direct: "I send home by this steamer a Doctor of Divinity who has been out here on a spree, and who was

Fields immediately sent words of praise and evidently agreed with Hawthorne's suggestion that "Consular Experiences" be kept "fresh for the volume"; Hawthorne's letter of acknowledgment on May 3, 1863, repeated the promise of an additional essay for the August *Atlantic*. With the book now definitely in prospect, Hawthorne went on to say that he would gather the articles from unbound issues of the magazine and, making "such corrections as seem desirable," would have them ready for the printer within a few days. He would also rewrite an 1857 essay on Uttoxeter.

The possibility of English publication was also on his mind, but with characteristic gloom he was prepared to accept anything from this source, "even if it were only five pounds."

> I don't see why anybody should give more, or so much, for a book that a dozen pirates will be ready to seize upon, if it prove to have any sellable value. However, it will not take in England, being calculated (by the objects which it describes, and the sentiments it expresses) for the American market only.

He was also beginning to give some thought to a dedication. First there was his Bowdoin classmate Franklin Pierce, whose campaign biography he had written: "he put me into the position where I made all those profound observations of English scenery, life, and character," and "a few pages of friendly and explanatory talk . . . would be very gratifying to

---

brought to my office, destitute, after a week's residence in a brothel! I wish you could have heard the lecture I gave him. He shook in his shoes, I can tell you. Not knowing whether I should ever have another opportunity of preaching to a Doctor of Divinity (an orthodox man, too) I laid it on without mercy; and he promised never to forget it. I don't think he ever will." (May 27, 1855, MS, Berg Collection, New York Public Library.)

The final word in his journal (p. 116) tells us what Hawthorne would not put into print: that he personally advanced passage money for the minister's return to Boston. And in contrast to the severe tone of his letter, the journal entry concludes: "In my opinion, he has incurred sin no further than as a madman may."

my own life-long affection for him." He was also considering
the English merchant Francis Bennoch, whose house in
Blackheath the Hawthornes had occupied during the summer
of 1856 and whose kindnesses Hawthorne wished to recognize. His musings also included the possibility that he might
not inscribe the book to anyone.[27]

During the month of May Hawthorne made an entirely
new essay out of his earlier Uttoxeter piece, which had described his "sentimental pilgrimage" to the spot where Dr.
Johnson did penance for having fifty years earlier refused to
take his father's place at the Uttoxeter bookstall. Hawthorne
broadened the Johnsonian settings as indicated by his own
new title "Lichfield and Uttoxeter." [28] Meantime, compositors
had begun work on *Our Old Home* and Hawthorne was
already receiving proof. His final essay, to be called "Civic
Banquets," he found difficult to write in the "dull weather" of
late spring.[29] But it was finished in early June and dispatched
to Boston. Because Fields was away, Hawthorne sent the

[27] MS, Huntington Library. Although nothing further is heard of
Bennoch as dedicatee, Sophia Hawthorne inscribed her edition of *Passages
from the English Note-Books* (Boston, 1870) to him for having "contributed so largely (as is attested by the book itself) to render Mr. Hawthorne's residence in England agreeable and homelike."

[28] The original "Uttoxeter" essay appeared in *The Keepsake* (London,
1857), pp. 108–13, and was reprinted in *Harper's New Monthly Magazine*, XIV (April, 1857), 639–41. Dr. Johnson's expiation had interested
Hawthorne long before his English sojourn. Two chapters of his *Biographical Stories for Children* (1842) relate the episodes in the life of young
Sam and the great Doctor. And a paragraph in a now lost early journal,
under date of October 24, 1838 (Sophia Hawthorne [ed.], *Passages from
the American Note-Books*), records an idea for a sketch explicitly inspired
by the Uttoxeter penance: "Each circumstance of the career of an apparently successful man to be a penance and torture to him on account of
some fundamental error in early life"—the germ, Mark Van Doren has
suggested, of the Dimmesdale motif in *The Scarlet Letter* (*Nathaniel
Hawthorne* [New York, 1949], p. 33).

[29] May 28, 1863, to Fields, MS transcription, Hawthorne-Fields Letter
Book, Houghton Library, Harvard University. Here Hawthorne asked
further proof change of a correction he had made in a sheet he had just
returned. The passage defends Hawthorne's retention of two experienced
Englishmen on his consular staff despite official preference for American

manuscript to Ticknor, and failing to get the usual acknowledgment, inquired anxiously on June 18, for the piece was to
appear in the *Atlantic* before book publication.[30] The magazine was not Ticknor's responsibility, but he took "Civic
Banquets" in hand and proofs were ready when Fields returned from the country at the end of the month.

Ebullient as always, Fields wrote of his delight in reading
the essay at the printing office, where the workmen "thought
me sun-struck; and I was, but not by the luminary so far away
as they had reckoned." The August *Atlantic* would contain
"Civic Banquets"; meantime, the July issue was just out, and
Holmes had "kept me on his door-step last night half an hour"
discussing Hawthorne's essay, "Outside Glimpses of English
Poverty." In his enthusiasm Fields urged Hawthorne to continue his English sketches even after publication of the book.
Our Old Home was itself going forward. Despite Hawthorne's pessimism about British interest, Smith, Elder & Co.
had offered £150 for English rights, and since the firm required that sheets be "in *their hands* thirty days before the
book is published in the States," Fields now needed the
introductory matter.[31]

On July 1 Hawthorne wrote to express his delight "with
Smith & Elder—or rather with you; for it is you that squeeze

---

citizens. Where the MS had read "possessing a happy faculty of knowing
when I am well off," Hawthorne's letter noted that he had made a proof
correction to "possessing a happy faculty of seeing my own interest"; he
now wanted the words "and the public's" added to the emended reading.
As he told Fields, "the public interest was my sole and undivided
object while I held office," and by the proposed alteration "I only give
myself credit for half the disinterestedness I really felt."

[30] Hawthorne to Ticknor, June 7, 1863, *Complete Writings* (Autograph edition, 1900), XVII, 438; June 18, 1863, MS, Berg Collection,
New York Public Library.

[31] June 30, 1863, MS, Huntington Library. As Fields told Hawthorne,
the English publisher took *Our Old Home* on condition that it be given
"the first offer of your new *Romance*," which Fields had probably described
as in prospect. Contract arrangements were set out in a letter from Smith,
Elder & Co. to Ticknor and Fields, June 4, 1863, MS, Houghton Mifflin
Contract Files, Burlington, Massachusetts.

the English sovereigns out of the poor devils. On my own behalf, I never could have thought of asking more than £50, and should hardly have expected to get £10." As to the prefatory matter, which he would immediately prepare, "It requires some little thought and policy in order to say nothing amiss at this time; for I intend to dedicate the book to Frank Pierce, come what may." [32]

Hawthorne evidently did not expect his dedication to go unchallenged, for Pierce was considered traitorous by Northerners who deplored his Constitutional opposition to the war and his attacks on the Lincoln administration.[33] The first reaction came from Fields, who wrote on July 3: "Your dedication to F. P. has a paragraph in it I shd. be glad to talk over with you when you come here. But it is a charming bit of writing, that same dedication." [34] A few days later, Hawthorne asked to have the dedicatory letter returned to him, so that he might make "some alterations and improvements—that is, if its perfection allows of any." [35] Given his facetious tone, his intentions cannot be easily guessed. But his views crystallized when Fields sent proofs of the preliminary matter along with a letter saying: "It is the opinion of wiser men than I am in the 'Trade' that the Dedn. & Letter to F. P. will ruin the sale of yr. book. I tell you this, in season that you may act upon it if you elect so to do." One dealer was threatening a boycott; a mutual friend called it "the most damaging move you could possibly make." Fields was not insistent, but he marked a passage which might be "omitted with safety." [36]

Hawthorne's reply was carefully meditated and vigorous:

[32] Hawthorne to Fields, MS, Huntington Library.

[33] See Roy F. Nichols, *Franklin Pierce* (rev. ed., Philadelphia, 1958), pp. 516–23, and Randall Stewart's discussion of the dedication and its consequences in "Hawthorne and the Civil War," *Studies in Philology,* XXXIV (1937), 98–106.

[34] MS, Huntington Library.

[35] July 14, 1863, to Fields, MS, Huntington Library.

[36] July 15, 1863, MS, Huntington Library.

I find that it would be a piece of poltroonery in me to with-draw either the dedication or the dedicatory letter. My long and intimate personal relations with Pierce render the dedi-cation altogether proper, especially as regards this book, which would have had no existence without his kindness; and if he is so exceedingly unpopular that his name is enough to sink the volume, there is so much the more need that an old friend should stand by him. I cannot, merely on account of pecuniary profit or literary reputation, go back from what I have deliberately felt and thought it right to do; and if I were to tear out the dedication, I should never look at the volume again without remorse and shame. As for the literary public, it must accept my book precisely as I think fit to give it, or let it alone.

But, because he had no wish for martyrdom "when it is honorably and conscientiously possible to avoid it," he had revised the closing paragraph "in such a way that, while doing what I know to be justice to my friend, it contains not a word that ought to be objectionable to any set of readers." If his Northern audience was alienated, it was "a herd of dolts and mean-spirited scoundrels" to whom he would not bow, even if he should lose "a thousand or two of dollars." [37]

In revising the close of his prefatory letter, Hawthorne tried to detach himself from his immediate disenchantment with the war by writing, "I dedicate my book to the Friend, and shall defer a colloquy with the Statesman till some calmer and sunnier hour." Following a sentence which described the American presidency as "the most august position in the world," he recast the rest of the passage to remove almost all signs of his fears for the nation's future without essentially altering his praise for Pierce's loyalty to principle. [38]

Despite Hawthorne's attempt to make the dedication solely a gesture of personal friendship, it was perforce looked upon

[37] July 18, 1863, MS transcription, Hawthorne-Fields Letter Book, Houghton Library, Harvard University.

[38] For the passage as originally drafted, see Editorial Emendations in the Copy-Text, pp. 360–61 below.

as a political act, at best foolish, at worst disloyal. The solicitude of Emerson, Longfellow, Judge Hoar, and others had caused Fields to write his letter of caution, and he could do no more.[39] But pressures came from other sources. Ellery Channing, though importuned by Fields, could not bring himself to approach Hawthorne, and persuaded Elizabeth Peabody to do so. Hawthorne was distressed to discover the growing awareness of a matter he thought so confidential with his publisher that he had not even shared it with Sophia. He replied forthrightly in one of the lengthiest and strongest letters he ever wrote.[40] About the same time he received from "some spiteful Abolitionist" a packet of newspaper clippings attacking Pierce.[41]

That he reconciled himself to the consequences is evident in his remark to Ticknor that "I must try to get my poor blunted pen at work again pretty soon; especially as Fields threatens me that nobody will buy the new book on account of the dedication." [42] Yet it was possible to sympathize with Hawthorne's steadfastness even if one could not ignore the political contexts of 1863. Mrs. Fields recorded her mixed feelings after a brief visit to The Wayside late that July:

> It is a beautiful incident in Hawthorne's life, the determination at all hazards to dedicate this book to his friend. Mr.

[39] Fields, *Yesterdays With Authors,* p. 107; Annie Fields, *Nathaniel Hawthorne* (Boston, 1899), p. 125.

[40] July 20, 1863, to Elizabeth Peabody, MS, Houghton Library, Harvard University. Her letter to Hawthorne seems not to have been preserved. Years later she rehearsed the circumstances in a letter to Horatio Bridge (June 4, 1887, MS, Bowdoin College), implicating Channing in the request that she write Hawthorne, and insisting that her brother-in-law, who "knew *nothing* about slavery," badly underestimated Union sentiment in the North.

[41] Evidently in reaction to a July 4th speech Pierce had made at Concord, New Hampshire. Hawthorne, who had been present, wrote Pierce that he had destroyed these evidences of "malice" (July 24, 1863, MS, New Hampshire Historical Society).

[42] July 27, 1863, MS, Berg Collection, New York Public Library.

P's politics at present shut him away from the faith of patriots, but Hawthorne has loved him since college days and
he will not relent.[43]

Emerson, on the other hand, could think only of political
obloquy when he noted in his journal:

> Hawthorne unlucky in having for a friend a man who can-
> not be befriended; whose miserable administration admits but
> of one excuse, imbecility. Pierce was either the worst, or he
> was the weakest, of all our Presidents.[44]

When *Our Old Home* was published, Emerson called the
book "pellucid but not deep," according to Mrs. Fields, and he
"cut out the dedication and letter, as others have done." [45] His
final estimate was more judicious. A long journal entry the
day after Hawthorne's funeral included a personal assessment
of his fellow townsman's "painful solitude . . . which, I
suppose, could not longer be endured."

> Lately he had removed himself the more by the indignation
> his perverse politics and unfortunate friendship for that paltry
> Franklin Pierce awakened, though it rather moved pity for
> Hawthorne, and the assured belief that he would outlive it,
> and come right at last.[46]

If the dedication could excite pity, still another reaction was
possible. To Charles Eliot Norton, a vigorous Union man, the
inscription read "like the bitterest of satires . . . what a blow
his friend has dealt to the weakest of ex-Presidents." Norton
found himself "half annoyed, half amused at Hawthorne." [47]

[43] M. A. DeWolfe Howe, *Memories of a Hostess* (Boston, 1922), p. 15.

[44] Recorded between July 24 and August 25, 1863, *Journals* (Boston,
1909–14), IX, 528.

[45] Howe, *Memories of a Hostess*, p. 15 n.

[46] *Journals*, X, 40–41.

[47] To George W. Curtis, September 21, 1863, Sara Norton and M. A.
DeWolfe Howe (eds.), *Letters of Charles Eliot Norton* (Boston, 1913), I,
264–65.

And at least one newspaper echoed this point of view, declaring that the closing paragraph of the dedicatory letter "was either written before the exposure of Pierce's letter to Jeff. Davis, or is to be regarded as a fine bit of ironical writing." [48]

Meantime, prospects for the book proved less gloomy than Fields had anticipated. Replying to a letter of September 16 from Hawthorne, Fields reported that advance sales had been going so "handsomely" that a second printing had been ordered, and response in the West made him confident that another impression would soon be called for. [49] Apparently even notoriety had its uses, and despite the mixed press to be anticipated, the book was creating a stir far beyond what could have been expected from "Consular Experiences" alone.

In accordance with publishing agreements *Our Old Home* was issued simultaneously in England and America on September 19, 1863. [50] The Ticknor and Fields edition was priced at $1.25 and Hawthorne's royalty was 12 per cent, or $.15 per

[48] *New York Evening Post,* October 7, 1863, 1:1. For Hawthorne, perhaps the real irony was that just as *Our Old Home* was being issued, a letter which Pierce had written to Jefferson Davis in 1860 was discovered upon the seizure of Davis's house near Jackson, Mississippi, and was widely circulated by Northern newspapers. Pierce had described the mood of the North as fundamentally divided and prophesied that if the Union were disrupted "through the madness of northern abolitionists . . . , the fighting will not be along Mason & Dixon's line merely. It will be within our own borders, in our own streets . . . " (*Post,* September 19, 1863).
The loyalist press interpreted Pierce's words as encouraging the then Senator Davis to expect popular Northern response to the Southern cause, and in 1863 the letter was often construed as traitorous incitement. Hawthorne's dedication merely compounded the ignominy of Pierce in the public eye.

[49] Undated letter (c. September 18, 1863), MS, Huntington Library.

[50] These plans were announced in a "Literary" paragraph of the *Boston Transcript,* September 8, 2:3. Advertisements of September 19 announced publication "this day" in the *Transcript,* the *Boston Daily Advertiser,* the *Boston Daily Courier,* the *Boston Post,* and the *New York Post.* The same ad appeared on September 21 in the *Transcript,* the *New York Times,* and the *New York Daily Tribune.* Smith, Elder advertisements in the September 12 issue of *Athenæum* and *Saturday Review* announced publication of the English edition on the 19th, followed by "Ready this day" notices in both journals on September 19.

copy. In England the work was issued in two volumes at a guinea, or about $5.25. Although we do not know the size of the British impression, it appears to have sold out quickly, for a second printing (called "edition," as was customary) was listed among new books in the *Athenæum* for October 17. From this point the evidence is conflicting: the *Reader* of October 24 listed a "New Edition" among publications of the week, and seven days later a "Third Edition." Furthermore, the November 28 *Athenæum* listed a new edition. Taken literally, these details would point to four printings within less than three months of publication, even assuming that the October 24 announcement in the *Reader* referred to the second impression which the *Athenæum* had listed a week before. But the Smith, Elder advertisements in the *Athenæum* were still announcing *Our Old Home* as "Now Ready" on October 17, and a one-column advertisement of October 24 quoting reviews—the major promotional effort of the year for the book—made no reference to fresh printings. Nor did subsequent listings of the book in Smith, Elder's *Athenæum* advertisements through December. The negative evidence offered by advertising is of no value in determining the printing history of the book; taken positively, however, the steady promotion in the *Athenæum* (supplemented by one post-publication advertisement per month in the *Saturday Review*) indicates at least a modestly active demand for *Our Old Home*. In 1864 there was no further notice of the work until November, when a new edition in one five-shilling volume was issued.

The American printing history is contained in the Ticknor and Fields Cost Books, which indicate a first impression of 3,500 copies before publication, followed by a second printing of 2,000 copies ordered in September. The third printing which Fields confidently anticipated at the time of publication was not necessary until early in 1864. Thereafter additional impressions, varying in size from as few as 150 copies to as many as 3,000, accounted for a total production of slightly more than 15,000 copies by 1880, including a new edition (Little Classics) in 1876. *Our Old Home* was thus a moderately popular work in the Hawthorne canon, not to be compared with *The Marble Faun* in its immediate appeal. In its first three years it enjoyed American sales just slightly lower than those of the three earlier romances. Thereafter the small but steady demand is probably to be accounted for by en bloc purchase of sets, which Ticknor and Fields began to offer soon after Hawthorne's death in 1864.

By far the most energetic critical responses to *Our Old Home* came from England.[51] In America the reviews were generally slight, except for multi-columned essays in the *New York Tribune* and the *New York Times*. For one thing, the

[51] This discussion of the contemporary reception of *Our Old Home* draws upon the following reviews and notices: *Albion*, XLI (October 10, 1863), 489; *American Publishers' Circular and Literary Gazette*, 3d ser., I (October 15, 1863), 430; *Athenæum*, No. 1875 (October 3, 1863), 428–30; [Edward B. Hamley], "Hawthorne on England," *Blackwood's Magazine*, XCIV (November, 1863), 610–23; *Boston Daily Advertiser*, September 30, 1863, 2:3; *Boston Post*, September 26, 1863, 1:7; *Boston Transcript*, September 28, 1863, 2:2, and October 2, 1863, 1:4–5; *Christian Remembrancer*, XLVII (January, 1864), 165–88; *Continental Monthly*, IV (November, 1863), 595; [Henry Bright], *Examiner*, No. 2907 (October 17, 1863), 662–63; [George W. Curtis (?)], *Harper's Weekly*, VII (November 21, 1863), 739; *Illustrated London News*, XLIII (October 3, 1863), 346; *New York Daily Tribune*, October 3, 1863, 9:1–4; *New York Times*, November 28, 1863, 5:1–4; *North American Review*, XCVII (October, 1863), 588–89; *Punch*, XLV (October 17, 1863), 161; [Gerald Massey], "New Englanders and the Old Home," *Quarterly Review*, CXV (January, 1864), 42–68; "Nathaniel Hawthorne on England and the English," *Reader*, II (September 26, 1863), 336–38; "American Views of the English Character," *ibid.*, II (October 3, 1863), 367–68; *Salem Register*, September 24, 1863, 2:3; *Saturday Review*, XVI (October 10, 1863), 493–94; "Mr. Hawthorne on England," *Spectator*, XXXVI (October 3, 1863), 2578–80; *Times* (London), November 9, 1863, 10:1–3; *Westminster Review*, LXXXI (January, 1864), 238–40.

Six of the English reviews reached an American audience through *Littell's Living Age*, which, between November, 1863, and the following April, reprinted notices from *Blackwood's* (in part), *Christian Remembrancer*, *Punch*, *Quarterly Review*, *Reader* (September 26, 1863), and *Spectator*.

book was substantially a reprint of magazine pieces and could not be expected to have the freshness of an entirely new work. Moreover, American interest in things English invited either conventional endorsement of Hawthorne's views or polite indifference in requital of England's hostility toward the North. American reviews usually found the travel pieces delightful, the author's style pure and graceful. Hawthorne's treatment of English traits seemed fair; the *Boston Transcript* praised the book for its "manly truthfulness," and the *New York Times* reviewer validated Hawthorne's complaint about mercenary guides by reciting his own unhappy experiences. To the *North American Review* Hawthorne's essential kindliness was hidden behind a mask of "roughness and unsociableness" which often dropped away to reveal "a tenderness of human fellow-feeling." The *New York Tribune* saw no malignancy toward John Bull, rather "a resistless desire to laugh at the solemn pomposity and inflated conceit which present such tempting game to the humorist"; and the *Albion* observed that Hawthorne's "pen is much less severe than those of many English satirists of our national character and manners, while it nowhere drips the gall of American Anglophobia." Both the *Transcript* and the *Continental Monthly* were pleased that Hawthorne had cast his experiences into essays instead of the English romance he had originally intended. "Consular Experiences" attracted a gratifying amount of attention for its fresh autobiographic narrative and was often linked with the *Scarlet Letter* Custom-House sketch, in which Hawthorne also revealed engaging aspects of his personality. The Doctor of Divinity episode was oftenest quoted in both American and English reviews, along with Hawthorne's account of importunate Americans who assumed a possessive attitude toward "their" consul, whether to help them to an interview with Queen Victoria or to press their visionary claims to an English estate. "Outside Glimpses of English Poverty" stirred the

Continental to hope that Hawthorne's sordid descriptions might never apply to America, if "constructive thinking" and "Christian love" could help "to bridge the wide chasm almost necessarily dividing rich and poor."

The dedication to Pierce was occasionally defended: the *Boston Post* called it "exceedingly to the point, . . . mellow, kindly, easy, original." Some reviewers passed over it in silence. Generally, however, it proved an irresistible target to the American press. The *New York Tribune* was typical in calling Hawthorne's gesture "an indulgence of pious sentiment, which is no one's business but his own; but the gratuitous affirmation of the loyalty and patriotism of the ex-President is a gush of Quixotic enthusiasm which will expose Mr. Hawthorne to ridicule as mistaking a windmill for a giant." To the *Boston Daily Advertiser* Hawthorne's act was a "hardly pardonable . . . intrusion"; and the *Liberator* quoted a Salem paper's crisp reaction to the "endorsement of Mr. Pierce's thorough loyalty": "Mr. Hawthorne is good at fiction." [52] *Harper's Weekly* devoted a substantial part of its brief notice to an attack on the author's "tone of doubt and indifference" toward the Civil War, a "monstrous" attitude comparable to that of a "most charming companion who should prove to have no objection to infanticide."

Although English critics might not have been expected to concern themselves with American politics, several did so. The *Spectator* quarreled with Hawthorne's judgment in admiring the "statesmanship" of Pierce, whose "only political claim to the Presidency was grounded on his servility to the champions and the cause of slavery, and, as we now know, of secession." *Blackwood's* was shocked that a book about Eng-

[52] October 2, 1863, 2:2, erroneously crediting the *Salem Register*, in whose columns the remark does not appear. The *Register* review, actually quite moderate, called the dedication "more creditable to the strength and endurance of Hawthorne's college friendship than to his political sagacity and associations."

land should contain political talk "in the style of a New York paper," held that for Hawthorne to view the American presidency as "the most august position in the world" was "phantasy," and argued that it "might have occurred to a philosophical mind" that principles for which Pierce's father stood "might not be either so grand or so wise" in Pierce's own time. The *Athenæum* and several other journals, trying to account for the tone of asperity in *Our Old Home,* fell back on the explanation that the war mood that made it impossible for Hawthorne to write his English romance left him generally embittered. The *Quarterly Review* felt that Hawthorne's acrimony went deeper and antedated the war. The *Reader* in a leading article on "American Views of the English Character" suggested that British travelers had set a pattern which justified replies in kind; more immediately, however, American anger (and Hawthorne's) might be explained by English failure to sympathize enthusiastically with Northern views of the Union—and the uncertainty of the war's outcome doubtless accentuated American irritation with the British.

The need to account for Hawthorne's mood arose from a tone which surprised English readers. *Blackwood's,* looking back over Hawthorne's fiction, synthesized a "shy and reserved, . . . gentle and genial man," from whom an indulgent, appreciative series of tributes could be expected; instead, he startled and shocked with his "perpetual carping"—either he must have changed or he had been "hiding his true character under a benignant mask." The *Illustrated London News* prescribed an oculist for the author, so changed from him who "seemed to be a judge of the beautiful" when he wrote *Transformation* three years before. *Punch,* finding Hawthorne "strong enough . . . to bear being supposed a descendant from a gorilla," suggested that he gratify an interest in "the natural history of half-civilised animals" by writing an autobiographical sequel to *Transformation.*

Most of the English notices of *Our Old Home* concentrated on a handful of passages critical of English physique, manners, personality, and institutions—criticisms made no more palatable by comparisons that sometimes denied American superiority. Most offensive was the description of a fat English dowager (in "Leamington Spa"), with its unflattering animal imagery of "solid beef and streaky tallow . . . steaks and sirloins." Quoted in almost every English review, it lent itself to a wide range of response, from heavy irony in *Punch* to earnest refutation in the *Quarterly Review*. By contrast, the critic in the *Saturday Review* conceded that all Hawthorne's strictures were "true, or very nearly true," including his picture of the elephantine woman. And the London *Times,* determined to make light of Hawthorne's views by protesting at their very mildness, called this passage "the best written" in the book—but then went on to compare it with an even more effective sally by the Englishman Sydney Smith.

Hawthorne touched upon other sensitivities in describing the beef-and-ale heaviness of the British male, in making light of English fruit, in remarking on an "insular narrowness" characteristic of all classes. Here, too, many reviewers complained of insults, a few tried to weigh judiciously, and one or two, like the *Times,* refused to quarrel. The *Spectator,* indeed, wished there had been more of his "fair but pungent sarcasms" and cited several of the celebrated passages without taking offense. And the *Westminster Review,* observing the storms of protest from a little distance, was critical of the vituperations against Hawthorne, recognizing that if he wrote of the fat dowager, he also wrote a mitigating paragraph in which he praised English ladies above his own countrywomen. Other attempts to balance the account included the *Athenæum's* amused comment that Hawthorne, despite his national prejudices, refused to replace two of his English consular subordinates with Americans. And the *Christian Remembrancer* noted that the most fascinating example of feminine beauty in *Our Old Home* was not an American but an English "young lady in white" whom Hawthorne saw in London at the Lord Mayor's banquet—she who served as a model for Miriam in *The Marble Faun*. Although the more annoyed critics accused Hawthorne of having abused English hospitality and of flaunting American prejudices, other reviewers were content to explain Hawthorne's reactions as an outgrowth of his background and to concede that he tried to record his impressions exactly and fairly. The *Christian Remembrancer* shrewdly observed that the English were more likely to be offended by Hawthorne's generalizations than by his detailed observations.

Hawthorne's own final assessment of *Our Old Home* came in a letter of October 18, 1863, to Fields. Remarking that he had seen several notices from across the water, he continued:

> The English critics seem to think me very bitter against their countrymen, and it is perhaps natural that they should, because their self-conceit can accept nothing short of indiscriminate adulation; but I really think that Americans have more cause than they to complain of me. Looking over the volume, I am rather surprised to find that, whenever I draw a comparison between the two peoples, I almost invariably cast the balance against ourselves.
>
> It is not a good nor a weighty book, nor does it deserve any great amount either of praise or censure. I don't care about seeing any more notices of it.[53]

He was not, however, to be so insulated from public opinion as he desired. His young friend Henry Bright, who wrote a restrained, well-balanced review for the *Examiner*, justified himself in a personal letter, presumably for calling Hawthorne "cynical and contemptuous":

[53] MS, Huntington Library.

Don't think me very ungrateful for my abuse of your abuse of English ladies. You see I positively could not help it. An inevitable lance had to be broken, both for the fun of it and the truth of it. It really was too bad, some of the things you say. You talk like a cannibal.[54]

Other letters and reviews from England prompted Hawthorne to restate his fundamental position:

It is laughable to see the innocent wonder with which they regard my criticisms, accounting for them by jaundice, insanity, jealousy, hatred, on my part, and never admitting the least suspicion that there may be a particle of truth in them. The monstrosity of their self-conceit is such that anything short of unlimited admiration impresses them as malicious caricature. But they do me great injustice in supposing that I hate them. I would as soon hate my own people.[55]

In the midst of the English stir, Fields was undismayed, even euphoric. *Our Old Home* "continues to sell bravely," he wrote. "You may safely count on a handsome sum out of that book. Make another series. You cannot do better." [56] But there were still complaints in America, focused on politics and the war. Harriet Beecher Stowe shrilly inquired of Fields, "Do tell me if our friend Hawthorn[e] praises that arch traitor Pierce in his preface & your loyal firm publishes it. . . . what! patronise such a traitor to our faces!—I can scarce believe it . . . But I haven't read it." [57] Soon after Hawthorne's death

---

[54] [c. October, 1863], quoted in Julian Hawthorne, *Nathaniel Hawthorne and His Wife* (Boston, 1884), II, 280.

[55] To Fields, November 8, 1863, MS, Huntington Library.

[56] October 28, 1863, MS, Huntington Library. The facts do not quite justify Fields's enthusiasm. The maximum royalty which Hawthorne could have earned on the 6,500 copies of the American edition printed before his death would come to $975. Add to this the English rights, worth approximately $750, and the fees for ten *Atlantic* installments, about $1,300, and the total value of his work on *Our Old Home* amounts to slightly more than three thousand dollars during his lifetime.

[57] November 3, 1863, MS, Huntington Library.

George W. Curtis discussed the book in a retrospective essay which Fields refused to publish because it attacked Hawthorne's politics. After praising the "intimate and explicit chapters of autobiography" in *Our Old Home,* Curtis went on to regret an aloofness he sensed. At a time when "civilization itself" was at stake, Hawthorne saw in the war "only danger or doubt, and not hope for the right." Such detachment Curtis would not condemn morally, believing that to Hawthorne the present was as far away as the creations of his imagination: he was like a Donatello, of whom one asked " 'Is he human? Is he a man?' " [58] Curtis's view of the detached ethereal artist would come to dominate biographical criticism for almost a century, despite its evident oversimplification. A more plausible explanation of Hawthorne's political involvement was offered by Edward Dicey, an Englishman whom Hawthorne had met on his 1862 visit to Washington. The war, he said, deeply conditioned Hawthorne's feelings, and when the English attacked "everything and everybody in the North . . . the native New England blood was roused within that thoughtful nature." [59]

The book, then, enjoyed a certain notoriety on both shores of the Atlantic. Its final standing, divorced from topicalities and nationalistic bias, will probably depend on its quality as personal reportage. A brief comparison with his journal sources, three times as voluminous, should suggest what he chose to include or omit and should tell us how accurately his finished writing reflects his original impressions.

Several sections of *Our Old Home* are primarily travel pieces. Derived from a continuous body of notebook matter, they are organized chronologically and supplemented by Hawthorne's later reflections upon what he had seen. His first

[58] "The Works of Nathaniel Hawthorne," *North American Review,* XCIX (October, 1864), 550–55.

[59] "Nathaniel Hawthorne," *Macmillan's Magazine,* X (July, 1864), 245.

three contributions to the *Atlantic* belong in this category: "Some of the Haunts of Burns," "Near Oxford," and "Pilgrimage to Old Boston." And it looks as if in the beginning Hawthorne, who was, as he said, unused to "magazining," mined his journals straightforwardly. The first paragraph of his Burns piece, for instance, is almost a verbatim transcript from an entry of June 28, 1857, with such trifling substitutions as "mainly" for "greatly" and "probably" for "I suppose." The one significant omission is a notebook phrase characterizing Gretna Green as "a spot which many people have visited to their woe." The entire essay bears a comparable relationship to its original; Hawthorne polished, tightened, and rearranged, added generalized comments here and there, and only rarely softened an overly forthright remark. Changes of the latter kind suggest the difference between his generation's notion of propriety and ours, and we find it easy to be condescending toward such alterations as "stink" to "odor," "louse" to "that unmentionable parasite"; but if Hawthorne softened at one place, he left vigorous language untouched at half a dozen others. And it may not be easy to choose between "infested with unwashed children, and altogether in a state of chronic filth" and the original "dirty, and infested with dirty children."

Other sketches which closely follow the notebooks include "Up the Thames," drawn from the record of Hawthorne's London visit in the autumn of 1855; "Recollections of a Gifted Woman," a composite of a Stratford travelogue and his account of a visit to Delia Bacon, supplemented by information from letters she sent him; and "About Warwick," another sightseeing piece, slightly individualized by recording both his original view of Leycester's Hospital in 1855 and a second glimpse two years later.

The most complex pastiches were those written last, including "A London Suburb," "Outside Glimpses of English Poverty," "Civic Banquets," and "Consular Experiences." Although their language continues to be a slightly paraphrased and refined version of original notebook entries, these essays reflect Hawthorne's increased familiarity with his journals and a willingness to let patterns of association govern the order of parts (he may even have been aided by a handlist such as he drew up for use with these same manuscript volumes in his projected English romance). "Consular Experiences" is perhaps the most conflated of the essays, composed as it is of anecdotal passages scattered through the four-year record but inevitably dominated by his sensitive early impressions. Much of the generalized opinion in the later essays is an integral part of journal entries, but Hawthorne seems to have interpolated fresh comment more freely than in some of the first-written pieces, as witness topical references to the Civil War in "Consular Experiences" and "Civic Banquets."

Because Hawthorne had from the first visualized his English "journalizing" as a later resource, he took pains to balance spontaneity and polish, momentary impulse and reflection. The pages of *Our Old Home* are therefore pardonably close to his original entries. But not slavishly so: Hawthorne seems to have examined every word for tone, every construction for rhythmical and logical fitness. If the substance was seldom altered, the surface texture was worked over until it achieved a degree of polish familiar to Hawthorne's readers and commanding almost universal praise from contemporary critics.

As a record of personal discovery the volume shows Hawthorne's unwillingness to write guidebook puffery. Many obvious setpieces in the journals, such as his excursion through the Oxford colleges, he passed up as evidently trite; and when he approached familiar ground, as in the pages on Westminster Abbey, his anti-romantic, quizzical, skeptical commentary undercut the usual sentimentality of the uncritical sightseer. Conspicuously absent from the volume is any hint that Hawthorne might have enjoyed the society of literary men. And yet Matthew Arnold was only half-right in asserting that Hawthorne had been "perpetually in contact with the British Philistine." [60] Philistines he knew in plenty, but they did not determine the limits of his outlook. Leigh Hunt is the only author whom we meet in print, because Hunt's death in 1859 freed Hawthorne's pen. It was to protect personal privacy that he gave no public hint of his meeting with the Brownings, his acquaintance with Monckton Milnes, his chance glimpse of Tennyson, his failure to meet Dickens and Thackeray. What he often emphasized, however, was the undramatic scene, the uncelebrated individual, the simple delight of fine weather and rustic paths and old trees. "We see," wrote Henry Bright in the *Examiner,* "how much we have in England, little known or thought about by us, which strikes the imagination and warms the heart of so accomplished an American as Mr Hawthorne."

Above all, Hawthorne was an American and made no effort to conceal the point of view from which he wrote. His tone is not original, although it is free from the condescension of British travelers in America who set the fashion. Despite its candor, *Our Old Home* is not without warmth. And it reminded the American public that for all the differences in the two cultures, England was an inescapable part of America's inheritance, to be viewed with critical sympathy.

C. M. S.

[60] "Emerson," *Discourses in America* (London, 1885), p. 173.

over with butter and honey. At any rate, we must not
judge of an Englishman's susceptibilities by our own,
which, likewise, I trust, are of a far less sensitive
texture than formerly.

And now farewell, my dear friend, and excuse,
if you think it needs any excuse, the freedom with
which I thus publicly assert a personal friendship
between a private individual, and a Statesman,
who has filled what was then the most august position in the world! Can it be, that no man shall
hereafter reach that elevated seat! — that its
platform, which we deemed to be so firmly laid,
has crumbled beneath it! — that a chasm has caped
wide asunder, into which the unbalanced Chair of State
is about to fall! In my seclusion, accustomed only
to private thoughts, I can judge little of these matters,
and know not well what to hope, although I can see
much to fear. I might even deem it allowable for myself in
the last resort, to be content with half the territory that
was once our broad inheritance. But you, as all men
may know by the whole record of your life, will hope
stedfastly while there shall be any shadow or
possibility of a country left, continuing faithful
forever to that grand idea, which, as you once told
me, was the earliest that your brave father taught
you; and whether the Union is to be henceforth a
living giant, or a mangled and dismembered corpse,
it will be said of you that this mighty Polity, or this
miserable ruin, had no more loyal, constant, or
single-minded upholder than Franklin Pierce.

The Wayside. July 2d. 1863.   Written by Nath Hawthorne

TEXTUAL INTRODUCTION:

OUR OLD HOME

THE FIRST EDITION of *Our Old Home* was published both in Boston and in London on September 19, 1863. The Boston edition was typeset, stereotyped, and printed by H. O. Houghton at the Riverside Press, Cambridge, Massachusetts. The Ticknor and Fields Cost Books list the first printing as 3,500 copies.[1] Paper was billed on July 1; printing, stereotyping, and binding were billed on July 31. Fourteen and a half hours of extra corrections were charged.[2]

[1] The Ticknor and Fields Cost Books entries show stereotyping and printing by "W. B. & Co." (Welch, Bigelow), but the stereotyper's imprint in the book is Houghton's. The Houghton printing schedule shows that the type was set by Houghton, but it is possible that the plating was jobbed out by Houghton to Welch, Bigelow. (See the Note on the Typesetting in the Centenary Edition of *The House of the Seven Gables,* pp. lxi–lxiii.)

The Ticknor and Fields Cost Books and the Houghton printing schedule are preserved in the Houghton Library, Harvard University.

[2] Three alterations in proof can be established. First, two manuscript pages were added to "Consular Experiences," beginning in the first edition at 17.23 (Centenary 13.19) with "The individual now in question was a mild and patient, but very ragged and pitiable old fellow" and ending at 19.1 (Centenary 14.23) with "He appeared to see that he had moved me, but did not attempt to press his advantage with any new argument or any varied form of entreaty." This extended passage elaborating the incident of the Philadelphia printer expands 145 words on page 9 of the manuscript (for the original text see pp. 361–62, below). That the two manuscript pages of this expansion must have been written after "Consular Experiences" was in type and its first sheet proofread by Hawthorne is evidenced by Hawthorne's head-note: "(I wish to alter this paragraph in

The Houghton printing schedule lists the book as started on May 11 and finished on July 22. At the end of the schedule it is charged as of July 23.[3] On September 16 Hawthorne wrote Fields about presentation copies,[4] and within the next day or two Fields responded, at that time stating that "The book in advance of publication goes handsomely. We are putting a second Ed. to press this week."[5] In the Cost Books, paper for this second printing was billed as of September 15, and press-work and binding as of September 30. The order for the paper indicates that the second printing was of 2,000 copies. The cost of the first printing came to $.52 per copy, for a book selling at $1.25, and that of the second printing to $.50.

The first edition (I), called 16mo in the Cost Books and in the Riverside Press printing schedule (a designation of size, not of format), was signed in 8's to gathering 25, beginning with 2 on the eleventh leaf (the fifth of the text proper); but the gathering formula is [1]^2 [2]^4 [3]^8 [4–18]^{12} [19]^8, pp.

the proof [in the proof *interlined with a caret*] as follows, in accordance with some notes (made at the time) which I have just found.) (Page 17. Consular Experiences)", with the subscription, "(When you send the next proof, I wish you enclose one of the above.)".

It is impossible to know whether this resetting with its consequential repaging, the small change requested on page 42 of "Consular Experiences" (see below) in the second sheet, the addition at 45.32–46.14, and the alterations in the dedicatory letter "To a Friend" amounted to fourteen and a half hours of work: one would suppose not. Thus it would seem that a number of the textual variants in the first edition from the magazine texts (or from manuscript) were made in proof and that by no means every one originated as annotation when the copy was assembled and overseen except probably for the additions or factual changes.

[3] The printing schedule, on p. 98 of a volume of the Ticknor and Fields Cost Books beginning December 17, 1862, seems to be a fair copy from working notes, and it omits detailed information for some of the gatherings. It does, however, illustrate the setting by compositors for the book from the *Atlantic Monthly* (ΛM), and of "Consular Experiences" from MS, with the additional changes necessitated by proof-corrections. See pp. xlix, lxx, and n. 24 for further references to the schedule.

[4] September 16, 1863, MS transcription, Hawthorne-Fields Letter Book, Houghton Library, Harvard University.

[5] Undated MS, Huntington Library, answering Hawthorne's letter of September 16, apparently before publication on September 19.

[i–ix] x–xi [xii] [9] 10–398 [399–400], with pp. 49, 77, 106, 141, 163, 195, 225, 248, 282, 320, 358 unnumbered. The half-title appears on p. i (p. ii blank), the title-page on p. iii with the copyright notice and printer's and stereo-maker's imprint on p. iv, the dedication to Pierce on p. v (p. vi blank), contents on p. vii (p. viii blank), the prefatory letter "To a Friend" on pp. ix–xi (p. xii blank), and text on pp. 9–398; p. 399 holds advertisements and p. 400 is blank. The second printing removes the advertisements and in most copies appends a 22-page catalogue dated November, 1863. The third printing of 1864 restores advertisements on page 399.

The exact method of imposing and machining the first printing is obscure. Presumably the gatherings in 12's (starting with [4]) were printed in a 24-page forme work-and-turn. The difficulty centers on the reason for printing gathering [3], which starts the text with "Consular Experiences," in 8's instead of 12's; the dedication material, including the contents, in 4's; and the half-title and title leaves in 2's. Whatever answer can be suggested follows from what we can reconstruct of the history of the assembling of copy for the book and its printing.

As early as July 24, 1862, Fields broached the subject of making a book from the series at the time that he acknowledged receipt of "Leamington Spa" for the *Atlantic*.[6] Hawthorne appears to have made no immediate answer. On December 4, 1862, in acknowledging receipt of "Recollections of a Gifted Woman," Fields once more inquires about the possibility of a book to collect the pieces: "And when will you like to publish a volume?"[7] In his answer dated December 6 Hawthorne does not mention a book;[8] but in a letter dated January 8, 1863, thanking Fields for the $150 payment for "A

[6] July 24, 1862, MS, Huntington Library.
[7] December 4, 1862, MS, Huntington Library.
[8] December 6, 1862, MS, Huntington Library.

London Suburb" (sent on January 4), he has evidently accepted the proposal, for he writes: "It will require, I believe, as much as three more articles, including 'A London Suburb,' to make up a volume of, say 325 pages.[9] Methinks it would be better to defer publication till the autumn [10]—at least, till summer; though perhaps it may be desirable to make what harvest we can while the war lasts; for when that comes to an end, I look for utter ruin. . . ." In sending the next piece, "Up the Thames," on February 22, 1863, for the *Atlantic Monthly*, Hawthorne announces his intention "to write two more of these articles, and then hold my hand," to which Fields replied on February 23 hoping that Hawthorne would not stop with only two more essays.[11]

A gap in the correspondence then occurs, since the next mention we have is Hawthorne's acknowledgment on April 18, 1863, of a check for "Outside Glimpses of English Poverty," and in the same letter appears the following: "I shall begin to write the last article (which will come first in the volume) in a day or two. I don't think the public will bear any more of this sort of thing." [12] On April 30, when he sends "Consular Experiences" to Fields, he discusses the book's title and suggests a change in plan for its contents:

> I send the article with which the volume is to commence, and you can begin printing it whenever you like.[13] I can

[9] January 8, 1863, MS transcription, Hawthorne-Fields Letter Book, Houghton Library, Harvard University. Actually, three additional papers were written to follow the "Suburb" essay, and then a fourth, "Consular Experiences," to begin the volume. The whole came to 390 pages of text.

[10] This discussion of deferring publication sounds as if some communication not now known had passed between the two about the details of a book.

[11] February 22, 1863, and February 23, 1863, MSS, Huntington Library.

[12] April 18, 1863, MS transcription, Hawthorne-Fields Letter Book, Houghton Library, Harvard University.

[13] April 30, 1863, MS, Huntington Library. The exact meaning of this remark is a trifle unclear; that is, whether Hawthorne means that (in case

think of no better title than this—"*Our Old Home:* a series
of English Sketches by &c." I submit to your judgment
whether it would not be well to print these "Consular
Experiences" in the volume without depriving them of any
freshness they may have, by previous publication in the
Magazine? . . . It seems to me quite essential to have some
novelty in the collected volume, and, if possible, something
that may excite a little discussion and remark. But decide for
yourself and me; and if you conclude not to publish it in the
Magazine, I think I can concoct another article in season for
the August No, if you wish. After the publication of the
volume, it seems to me the public had better have no more
of them.

Evidently, then, we owe "Civic Banquets" to Hawthorne's
recognition that if "Consular Experiences" was to be with-
drawn from the *Atlantic* so near to publication date, he would
need to supply a substitute.

On May 3 (misdated May 30 in the Letter Book), he
responds to a lost letter from Fields agreeing to withhold
"Consular Experiences" from the *Atlantic* by repeating his
promise to write another essay for the August number. For
the first time he raises the question of a dedication to Pierce.
He asks, "How soon do you mean to get the volume out?" and
suggests negotiations for publication in England. He plans to
provide printer's copy shortly: "As I have most or all of the
unbound Nos. of the Magazine containing my articles, I will
look over them and make such corrections as seem desirable,
and send them to you, probably in the course of a week. You
shall likewise have the re-written copy of 'Uttoxeter' with

Fields wants it for the *Atlantic* after all) it can come out in an early
number, or, since the piece will begin the volume, typesetting of the book
with this article can start at Fields's pleasure. The latter is much the more
likely intention, for a few days later, on May 3 (see below), Hawthorne
discusses assembling the rest of the printer's copy from past magazine
appearances. Moreover, plans for the publication of the book would make
it obvious that even if Fields were to insist on printing "Consular
Experiences" in the *Atlantic,* typesetting of the essay could not wait upon
Atlantic proof to serve as printer's copy for the volume.

additions, before the press is ready for it." [14] On May 28 he answers a letter from Fields that had acknowledged receipt of "Lichfield and Uttoxeter" and remarks that he has begun "Civic Banquets." [15] (On May 26 Hawthorne had written Lowell that an article for the magazine and for his volume was weighing upon him, which he ought to have begun and finished long ago, "but I hope to smash it in a day or two.") [16] The essay was not completed and despatched until early June, however, for on June 18 (in Fields's absence) he wrote Ticknor, "I sent you a week ago to-day a sealed package containing an article for the Magazine; and not hearing of its arrival, I deem it possible it may have miscarried—which would be a pity, as I have no other copy. [17] For reasons connected with the publication of my volume, I wanted this article to appear in the Magazine as soon as possible."

We can, then, reconstruct something of a timetable for the assembly and production of the volume. "Consular Experiences" (pages 9–48 of *Our Old Home*) was sent to Fields on April 30, 1863, with the remark that "you can begin printing it whenever you like." [18] On May 3 he promises to correct copies of the magazine articles already printed (these would include, at this time, "Up the Thames" in the May *Atlantic*) and send them off in the course of a week. On May 28 he is still working on "Civic Banquets" but has rewritten "Lichfield

[14] May 3, 1863, MS, Huntington Library.

[15] May 28, 1863, MS transcription, Hawthorne-Fields Letter Book, Houghton Library, Harvard University.

[16] May 26, 1863, MS, Houghton Library, Harvard University.

[17] June 18, 1863, MS, Berg Collection, New York Public Library. We need not take it, on the strength of this statement, that Hawthorne—contrary to his usual custom—had failed to draft the essay and so would have had no copy at all of its contents. The manuscript of "Civic Banquets" does not have more signs of initial composition than do the other manuscripts. Very likely he meant, merely, that he had no copy of the final version. His mild remark, "which would be a pity," does not suggest more than a nuisance if the package has been lost.

[18] April 30, 1863, MS, Huntington Library.

and Uttoxeter" (pages 141–62 of the volume) and sent it off several days previously; and he requests a change in the proof for "Consular Experiences" on page 42 (in the second sheet of the text) which had been mailed back to Fields the previous day, May 27. "Outside Glimpses of English Poverty," pages 320–57 (for which payment was acknowledged on April 18), must have been set up from corrected magazine proof since it did not appear until the July *Atlantic,* issued the last few days of June; but typesetting could not have been started on it until well after the writing of "Lichfield and Uttoxeter" (pages 141–62) in middle to late May; nor could setting of "Pilgrimage to Old Boston," "Near Oxford," "Some of the Haunts of Burns," or "Up the Thames" have preceded May 28. Finally, "Civic Banquets," mailed June 11, was completed on June 29 (set from *Atlantic* proof) when Fields read proof for this final essay in the printing office, according to his letter to Hawthorne of June 30.[19] On the evidence of the Houghton records that give May 11 as the start of typesetting, Fields held "Consular Experiences" until he had received the bulk of the copy from Hawthorne, which would have been about May 10. By May 27 the compositors had progressed only as far as the second sheet, pages 25–48 (completing "Consular Experiences"). Thus the bulk of the text from "Leamington Spa" on page 49 to the end of "Civic Banquets" on page 398 was typeset and proofread in June and July.

This left the preliminaries. On June 30, 1863, after reading the proof of "Civic Banquets" Fields wrote, "If there is to be any Introductory matter to 'O. O. H.' send it please at once as the printer is quite ready for it now." Hawthorne responded on July 1, "I shall think over the prefatory matter for Our Old Home to-day, and will write it tomorrow"; on July 3 Fields informed Hawthorne that he had received the dedica-

---

[19] June 30, 1863, MS, Huntington Library.

tion and preface and indicated that there was a paragraph in it he would like to talk over when Hawthorne was next in town.[20] More than a suggestion that Fields delayed sending the preface to be typeset immediately on receipt may be found in the fact that although the preliminaries arrived on July 3, Fields did not receive proof until July 15 when he mailed it to Hawthorne, who on July 14 had requested the return of the preface for revision.[21] On July 18 Hawthorne returned a rewritten version of the final paragraph, adding, "and shall wish to see a proof of that and the whole dedication. I send the proof-sheet in another enclosure." [22] The requested proof was sent to him on July 22, when Fields wrote, "Houghton has sent the revised proof & you will please return it as soon as you can conveniently." [23]

With this letter all mention of the printing of the book ceases. What seems clear is that the last revised proof could not have been returned to Fields and given to Houghton before July 24 at the earliest. Thus since the billing for the printing was dated July 31 in the Cost Books, machining of the book-sheets could not have waited for the final approval of the preliminaries but must have started earlier.

The original signing in 8's [24] had envisaged four preliminary leaves (the contents at that time, of course, unknown) and four leaves (eight pages) starting "Consular Experi-

[20] July 1, 1863, and July 3, 1863, MSS, Huntington Library.

[21] July 14, 1863, and July 15, 1863, MSS, Huntington Library. "As I am writing comes yr. letter of yesterday. Here are the proof of Dedication & Letter just in from the printer," wrote Fields.

[22] July 18, 1863, MS transcription, Hawthorne-Fields Letter Book, Houghton Library, Harvard University.

[23] July 22, 1863, MS, Huntington Library.

[24] No particular significance would seem to inhere in the fact that when setting and plating the book 8-leaf gatherings were planned whereas the book eventually came to be printed in 12's. Such a discrepancy between signing and actual imposition is by no means unique. The printing schedule for the book lists the gatherings, and the compositors' names, according to a schedule of 16 pages per gathering, which would correspond to the signatures.

ences," and we know from Fields's letter of June 30, 1863, that the introductory material had not at that time been written. Since the half-title and title-leaf take two conjugate leaves, the remaining preliminaries are found in a 4-leaf gathering, followed by the first text gathering, which is in 8's, and the remaining text gatherings in 12's. It may be noticed that the preliminaries (now in 4's) were not gathered in 12's with the first gathering of the text. We cannot tell whether Houghton machined all gatherings except for the first text in 8's and imposed the preliminaries with it when they became available after July 24, though gathering them separately. It is just as possible that he machined the sheets in order and imposed the dedicatory preliminaries in 4's with the final text-sheet in 8's. This would explain why the preliminary gathering is in 4's, but it does not explain why the first text gathering is in 8's. Still a third possibility is present, however. If Houghton had wanted to machine all sheets without waiting for the delayed preliminaries, he could have imposed the text as we have it, with the first and last gatherings conveniently imposed for special printing in formes of 16 pages instead of 24; the preliminaries would then have been machined as an independent operation. Some unrecoverable mechanical reason may have dictated the independent gathering of the preliminaries in 4's, therefore; the only point of real importance is that it is not necessary to suspect an anomaly created deliberately in case Hawthorne were to relent about the controversial Pierce dedication and permit its removal.

No text changes were made in the plates between the first and second printings (indeed, the second must have been ordered before publication date), and the only later alteration in these plates was the correction of the misprint "myterious" to "mysterious" (145.23) in the 1864 third printing.

The English edition (E) in two volumes, brought out on September 19, 1863, by Smith, Elder & Co., was set from the final proofs or early sheets (or a mixture of both) of the Boston edition and no variant reading has any authority. On the evidence of type-movement it seems to have been printed from type-metal, not from plates. English advertisements suggest that there were three and perhaps even four printings.[25] In 1864 a reset "New Edition" appeared in one volume.

In the United States the third Boston printing appeared in 1864; thereupon the book was reprinted in 1865, 1866 (twice), 1868, 1869, and so on through the Illustrated Library Edition of 1871, the Fireside of 1879, the Globe of about 1880, and the New Fireside of 1886.

The Little Classics Edition of 1876, part of a collected edition published by James R. Osgood and Company, introduced a new typesetting (II) derived from the first-edition plates with some corruption as is to be expected in a resetting. Various "editions" (i.e., impressions) were manufactured from these plates, including the Popular Edition (1891), the Salem (1894), and the Concord (1899).

The Riverside Edition of 1883 (III), edited by Hawthorne's son-in-law, George Parsons Lathrop, and published by Houghton, Mifflin and Company, was reset from the Little Classics text and was issued originally both in trade and in

[25] The British Museum deposit copy was received on October 14, 1863, rather late. On October 17 the *Athenæum* advertised a second edition; the *Reader*, on October 31, a third edition; and the *Athenæum*, on November 28, a "new" edition. Of six copies checked or collated, minor variants appear to confirm the fact of more than one printing. In Vol. I at 27.25, for instance, the reading may be "archipelagoes" as in Boston, or "archipelagos". In Vol. II at 18.25 the misprint "trhee" for the correct "three" appears; the final "3" of "133" drops from the page number; at 151.22 in the "trhee" copies the comma after "Englishman" may drop out, accompanied by batter of the final "n" and of the final "h" in "with" below; type may loosen so as to produce "condu cted" and "apart ments" at 13.19,21. Unfortunately, the pattern of variants established in these surveyed copies does not permit of a precise ordering of the printings (and there may have been some mixture of sheets). The British Museum deposit copy (with the spelling "archipelagoes") may as easily be of the second as of the first printing, at least for the second volume.

large-paper form.[26] The text of this edition is notoriously corrupt. Its plates produced, in time, the Wayside Edition (1884), Standard Library (1891), New Wayside (1902), and Fireside (1909).[27]

A new separate resetting of *Our Old Home* was made in two volumes by Houghton, Mifflin dated 1891 (IV). The trade printing was on wove paper and bound in red cloth; a limited impression of 250 numbered copies was printed on laid paper and bound in imitation parchment.[28] These plates were used for a one-volume impression by Houghton, Mifflin in 1901 (the last impression collated for the Centenary records) and again, as part of the "Atlantic Monthly Library of Travel," in one volume, in 1907.

The last of the collected editions collated for the Centenary text is the Autograph Edition of 1900 (V), reset from the Riverside plates (III) and published by Houghton, Mifflin in a white binding with tipped-in signed illustrations, and in a blue binding with unsigned illustrations. Both appear to be bound from sheets of the same impression.[29] The further history of these Autograph plates has not been investigated for the purpose of the Centenary records, although one may note an *Old Manse* impression printed from them in 1904.

[26] Evidence from *The Scarlet Letter* (Centenary Edition, 1962), pp. lix–lx, suggests that the plates for the trade edition were made from the typesetting before printing and were thereupon corrected in a few details before reimpression in a second trade printing, followed by printing of the large-paper copies from type-metal. These details have not been investigated for *Our Old Home*.

[27] Remainder sheets from Riverside-plate printings seem to have been used to make up special two-volume editions combining *Our Old Home* with the *English Notebooks*. These have the Riverside half-titles but are in special binding. The only copy of this form observed, in the collection of C. E. Frazer Clark, Jr., is undated on the Vol. I title-page and the last copyright date is 1898. Vol. II is dated 1900 on the title and the last copyright date is 1891.

[28] What seem to be the same trade sheets were bound up in London by Chatto and Windus with a tipped-in title dated 1890.

[29] The Historical Collation has been prepared from a copy with the blue binding in the Ohio State University Libraries.

Of the twelve sketches that make up *Our Old Home*, manuscripts are preserved for all except "Some of the Haunts of Burns" and "Outside Glimpses of English Poverty," which have not been located, but that for "About Warwick" is seriously incomplete. In addition, the manuscript is preserved for the prefatory letter "To a Friend" and for "Uttoxeter" (described on page lvi, below), the early form of what was to become "Lichfield and Uttoxeter." Supplemented by the printed versions in the *Atlantic Monthly* (AM) and in the first Boston edition of 1863, these constitute the prime textual documents on which the Centenary Edition has been based. All the manuscripts are written on both sides of the leaf, on unwatermarked laid paper that has been folded once along the short axis to form a fold of two leaves. The leaf measurement is 9¾ by 7¾ inches. Although in the description the formula "paged 1–36" will be used, the first page is seldom numbered. The compositorial markings on these manuscripts will be discussed below.

1. *To a Friend:* The manuscript, in the Henry E. Huntington Library, consists of two conjugate leaves paged 1–4. The copy was sent to Fields on July 2, 1863, and was set directly into book pages. No compositorial markings are present.

2. *Consular Experiences:* The manuscript, in the Barrett Collection at the University of Virginia Library, consists of nineteen leaves paged 1–37 plus an insertion written on recto and verso of an unnumbered leaf for addition, in proof, to page 17 of the book. The copy was sent to Fields on May 30, 1863, and by agreement was reserved for the book without prior *Atlantic* publication; hence the manuscript was set directly into the book pages.

3. *Leamington Spa:* The manuscript, in the St. Lawrence University Library, consists of fourteen leaves paged 1–27. Fields acknowledged receipt of the manuscript on July 24,

1862, and it appeared in the *Atlantic Monthly,* VII (October, 1862), 451–62. Printer's copy for the book was the magazine clipping, annotated.

4. *About Warwick:* Fields dismembered this manuscript and presented single leaves to friends. Leaf 1 (pages 1–2) Between . . . ago; (Centenary 65.1–67.1) is in the Barrett Collection of the University of Virginia Library; leaf 2 (pages 3–4) and . . . no (Centenary 67.1–68.29) in the Stanford University Library; leaf 3 (pages 5–6) better . . . an Am- (Centenary 68.29–70.17) *unknown;* leaf 4 (pages 7–8) erican . . . betwixt (Centenary 70.17–72.9) in the Berg Collection of the New York Public Library; leaves 5 and 6 (pages 9–12) a fantasy . . . red- (Centenary 72.9–75.34) *unknown;* leaf 7 (pages 13–14) dened . . . me as (Centenary 75.34–77.27) in the Berg Collection of the New York Public Library; leaf 8 (pages 15–16) deriving . . . type (Centenary 77.27–79.19) *unknown;* leaves 9 and 10 (pages 17–20) for . . . Leycester (Centenary 79.19–83.11) in the Houghton Library at Harvard University; leaf 11 (pages 21–22) in . . . age (Centenary 83.11–85.5) *unknown;* leaf 12 (pages 23–24) the tinge . . . been (Centenary 85.5–87.4) in the collection of Walter P. Chrysler, Jr., New York City; leaves 13 and 14 (pages 25–27) conspicuous . . . spoon! (Centenary 87.4–89.24) in the Barrett Collection of the University of Virginia Library. The title on page 1 in manuscript is "A Sketch or two in Warwick." The copy was sent to Fields on October 5, 1862, and the sketch appeared in the *Atlantic Monthly,* X (December, 1862), 708–20. Copy for the book was the magazine clipping, annotated.

5. *Recollections of a Gifted Woman:* The manuscript, in the Houghton Library at Harvard University, consists of six-

teen leaves paged 1–31. The copy was received by Fields on December 4, 1862, and was published in the *Atlantic Monthly,* XI (January, 1863), 43–58. Copy for the book was the magazine clipping, annotated.

6. *Lichfield and Uttoxeter:* The manuscript, in the collection of Robert Taylor of Princeton, New Jersey, consists of ten leaves paged 1–20 centrally by Hawthorne in his usual fashion, but also foliated 59–68 in the upper right corner, almost certainly not by Hawthorne. The import of this foliation is unknown. A proof change was requested on May 28, 1863; the date at which copy was sent to Fields is not recorded. It was set directly into the book pages since the earlier appearance even of the much briefer version interdicted *Atlantic* publication. This sketch amplifies the original "Uttoxeter" essay, the manuscript of which is in the Pierpont Morgan Library, and which was first published in *The Keepsake* (London: D. Bogue, 1857), pp. 108–13, and then in *Harper's New Monthly Magazine,* XIV (April, 1857), 639–41. The Morgan manuscript consists of four foliated leaves of unwatermarked laid paper measuring 10 by 8⅟₁₆ inches. Two internal pencil brackets correspond to the beginnings of lines in *The Keepsake;* at the head of a paragraph in the manuscript beginning "I stept into" (Centenary 135.15) is the compositor's name, Miller. The same hand that inserted under the title "By Mᵣ Hawthorne, 'author of the Scarlet Letter' &c. &c." adds at the end of the text, "Proof to Author / Mᵣ Hawthorne / American Consul / Liverpool".

7. *Pilgrimage to Old Boston:* The manuscript, in the Special Collections of the Columbia University Libraries, consists of fourteen leaves paged 1–28. The date of submission of the manuscript is not known; the sketch appeared in the *Atlantic Monthly,* IX (January, 1862), 88–101. Copy for the book was the magazine clipping, annotated.

8. *Near Oxford:* The manuscript, in the Berg Collection of the New York Public Library, consists of twelve leaves paged 1–24. The manuscript was received by Fields before September 9, 1861, and was printed in the *Atlantic Monthly,* VIII (October, 1861), 385–97. At the end of the manuscript is this note: "(I have not read this over since writing it out;—so send me a proof-sheet. N. H.)". Copy for the book was the magazine clipping, annotated.

9. *Some of the Haunts of Burns:* The manuscript is not known. Copy was sent to Lowell on July 24, 1860, and was printed in the *Atlantic Monthly,* VI (October, 1860), 385–95. Copy for the book was the magazine clipping, annotated.

10. *A London Suburb:* The manuscript, in the Ohio State University Libraries, consists of sixteen leaves paged 1–31, now mounted and disjunct. The manuscript was sent to Fields on January 4, 1863, proofs were returned to Hawthorne on January 26, and the sketch appeared in the *Atlantic Monthly,* XI (March, 1863), 306–21. Copy for the book was the magazine clipping, annotated.

11. *Up the Thames:* The manuscript, in the Houghton Library at Harvard University, consists of nineteen leaves paged 1–38, each fold numbered in pencil in the lower left corner. The manuscript was sent to Fields on February 22, 1863, and the sketch appeared in the *Atlantic Monthly,* XI (May, 1863), 598–614. Book copy was almost certainly set from a magazine clipping, annotated. Bound in with the manuscript is a leaf on which is written: "This manuscript is in the handwriting of Nathaniel Hawthorne and is one of his papers now printed in 'Our Old Home.' I present it to be sold for the benefit of the Consumptives' Home. It ought to bring at least twenty-five dollars and if not disposed of at the

Fair I wish it returned to me. James T. Fields. 148 Charles St. February 27. 1871."

12. *Outside Glimpses of English Poverty*: The manuscript is not known. Payment for the sketch was acknowledged by Hawthorne on April 18, 1863; it appeared in the *Atlantic Monthly*, XII (July, 1863), 36–51. The book pages were probably set up from corrected proof, further reviewed.

13. *Civic Banquets*: The manuscript, in the Pierpont Morgan Library, consists of nineteen leaves paged 1–38. The manuscript was sent to Fields on June 11, 1863, and appeared in the *Atlantic Monthly*, XII (August, 1863), 195–212. Book copy must have been a corrected proof, further reviewed. Bound in with the manuscript is the library notation: "This is the original manuscript of the article as published in the Atlantic Monthly, August 1863 (copy of which is laid at end of this ms.) The ms. was given to Mr. James T. Fields of Boston who presented it to the N.Y. Sanitary Fair in 1864 for sale there. It was purchased by Mr. Morgan in 1909 as part of the Wakeman collection of manuscripts." On a separate sheet of notepaper is the following: "This Ms. was presented by J. T. Fields to the Sanitary Fair held in 1864 in N.Y. I purchased it of the person who secured it there— SHW [*in another hand* (autog. of Mr. Wakeman)] It appeared first in the Aug. 1863 Atlantic and this is the original ms.—It is decorated with Mr. Hector's (the compositors) autograph,— whom I have already written about— It afterwards formed the concluding article of 'Our Old Home' ".

The earliest preserved manuscript set for the *Atlantic Monthly* (at the Riverside Press in Cambridge, Massachusetts, like the first Boston edition) is "Near Oxford," which came out in October, 1861. The setting seems straightforward. James Hennessy signs the first page and was given a take of three leaves (pages 1–6), which—with the material he sct on page 7—amounted to 324 AM (*Atlantic Monthly*) lines. H. Lyons's name appears in the first paragraph indention of the fourth leaf, page 7. If we may believe the unique signature "W. S. —" (i.e., W. J. A. Sullivan) in blue (not in the otherwise invariable lead pencil) in the first paragraph opening of page 13, Lyons's take had been planned to be three leaves, though only five pages; but on page 11 a bracket appears "of [foaming" (AM 390.35ᵇ; Centenary 178.12), with Thomas Hector's name signed over the bracket. (This is within the paragraph and after the first opening on the page.) It would seem that Lyons stopped before his take was completed (his truncated stint amounts to 237 AM lines) and that Hector was brought in to finish the setting (108 AM lines), up to where Sullivan had started with the first paragraph indention on page 13. Sullivan's take was three leaves, pages 13–18 (336 AM lines), and he presumably ended at the start of M. L. Schubarth's three-leaf take beginning with the first paragraph on page 19 and continuing to the end of the sketch (296 AM lines) on page 24. Typesetting thus was simultaneous according to the takes, each compositor (except for Lyons) completing his stint by setting down to the first paragraph opening on the initial leaf of the next man's take.[30]

"Pilgrimage to Old Boston" appeared in the *Atlantic Monthly* in January, 1862. On the first page of its manuscript the compositor's name has been erased and cannot be deci-

---

[30] For a description of this method of simultaneous typesetting and the assignment of takes, see the Textual Introduction to the Centenary Edition of *The House of the Seven Gables*, pp. xxxviii–xlv. For an alternative method, used occasionally in these manuscripts, in which a compositor set some text above the first line of his marked stint, see the Textual Introduction to the Centenary *The Blithedale Romance*, pp. xxxiv–xxxv, although a brief description is provided in the *Seven Gables* Textual Introduction.

phered,[31] but for reasons noted below it was probably Hennessy. At the top left of the first page, erased, is the notation, "Send proof to Mr. Fields"; and at the top right, erased, is the word "Pilgrim". This initial take was evidently of three leaves (289 AM lines), since at the foot of page 6, in the first paragraph indention, is the name "R. Sev." (i.e., Roswell Severance).[32] On page 5, breaking a word, is the bracket "peculiari[ties" (Centenary 143.11) and above is written the number 3 and then "Hennessy". On the evidence of other manuscripts with somewhat similar markings, this notation is a paging bracket and has nothing to do with a stint or take (see below, "A London Suburb"). This bracket marks the end of line 200 in AM, which is twenty-two lines down in the first column of page 90. Since any paging notation in AM made for proof purposes during the setting of the manuscript and before final make-up of the magazine issue could not be the final paging or numbering (the more especially since AM printed articles continuously), these 200 lines would just about represent two full pages (208 lines at 52 lines per column) if space were allowed for the title. As in other manuscripts, the name of the compositor may be given within whose stint the paging for proof make-up has occurred. Thus with some confidence, Hennessy may be taken as the compositor whose name was erased on page 1. If the partial erasure of

[31] The occasional erasures of a compositor's name on the first page of a manuscript were probably made by an owner, whether or not Fields, tidying up the appearance. They do not seem to reflect any process, like a change of assignment, in the printing shop except when another name has been substituted.

[32] Occasional takes begin on the verso of a leaf, although the assignment would prevent the two compositors from handling the leaf at the same time. In this particular case, however, there appear to be extenuating circumstances. On p. 7, the normal leaf with which to start the second take, the first paragraph opening is only six lines from the foot, giving the preceding compositor an extra number of lines in his stint. We may perhaps conjecture—since the first paragraph on p. 6 begins only two lines from the foot—that Severance took this leaf, set its two lines as the start of his stint, and then turned the leaf back to his predecessor.

Hector's name in the paragraph opening on page 9 is also the owner's intervention, Severance had a take of only one leaf, or two pages (146 AM lines). In the first paragraph indention on page 12 a name has been completely erased. Between the partly erased name of Hector on page 9 and this unknown compositor who starts a take on page 12 were set 143 AM lines. At the end of the line of the first paragraph on page 14 (and thus not only on a verso but also, uniquely, before the second opening on a manuscript page) appears "R. Sev." again, following a bracket. Since this is not a paging bracket, it is unlikely that this workman is the one whose name was erased on page 12 and who set 99 lines to this point. Yet only 30 AM lines later, in the first opening on page 15, is an erased name beginning with "H". This stint, if stint it is, continues for two pages, or 114 AM lines, until in the first indention on page 17 appears the erased name of Hector.[33] If this marks the start of a real take, as likely (or else a continuation), the stint carries on until, after 151 AM lines, in the first paragraph opening on page 20, a pencil slant but no name appears. These slants are frequently found in connection with a compositor's name in a paragraph opening, usually under the name. But the appearance once of a name written below a slant makes one wonder if the mark was put in by the foreman and not by the compositor and thus indicated a proposed and not necessarily an actual take until confirmed by the signature. On the other hand, it is just possible that the compositor assigned to this take forgot to write in his name, although such an occurrence would be unique (so far as we know) in these manuscripts. Thus no way exists to tell whether the 289 AM lines (four pages) that follow the slant are Hector's, carrying on his stint beginning on page 17, or

---

[33] It is possible that this compositor was Hector, even though his erased name begins a take on page 17: it is not unknown to have a compositor continue with a second take immediately, thus signing his name in succession.

another workman's. On page 25 Severance is named in the
first opening. His take of four pages (141 AM lines) brings
the sketch to a close. The erasures and other anomalies make
the compositorial assignments in this piece very uncertain.
The major irregularity is the brief (30 AM lines) stint of
Severance on pages 14–15. On the other hand, if he continued beyond, and the erasure of the name beginning with
"H" on page 17 was a printing-house adjustment, then all the
other erasures except perhaps the first on page 1 would come
under question, and more problems would be raised than
solved. The paging bracket, standing alone, and with a number that bears no relation to the numbers used to page the
Atlantic, is also found in "Up the Thames."

"Leamington Spa," published in the *Atlantic Monthly* in
October, 1862, is relatively uncomplicated in its markings.
Under the title is "(Insert here the note to the Editor)", a
reference to the headnote that appears in the *Atlantic* text but
was removed for the book. At the upper left on page 1 is
Schubarth's name, which has been erased; but since this is the
only erasure in the manuscript, we must suppose that it was
done by an owner in the name of neatness. This take of eight
pages ends after 352 AM lines when Nathaniel Niles's name
is signed to the first opening on page 9. His take of four pages
was to end at William W. Curtis's name in the first opening
at the foot of page 13; but apparently Curtis finished his stint
early and so crossed through his name and set from a bracket
signed with his name in the first line of page 13, which is the
start of the forty-fourth line on AM 456ª, making a total of
173 AM lines for Niles. Curtis's take of two leaves (190 AM
lines) ends on page 17, where Niles resumes at the first
opening and sets 172 AM lines until Hector comes in seven
lines from the foot of page 20, in the first opening, and sets
311 AM lines to the end of the piece. On page 21 a step
bracket without name occurs between "among" and "men"

(Centenary 59.14), and another on page 23 between "the" and "entrance" (Centenary 61.28). The first marks the beginning of line 18 on AM 460ᵃ; the second, the start of line 36 on AM 461ᵃ. The function of these brackets has not been determined: they are 122 AM lines apart (an AM page consists of two columns of fifty-two lines each), and it may be fortuitous that the first is seventeen lines down on 460ᵃ and the second is seventeen lines up on 461ᵃ. However, it seems clear that they bear no relation to Hector's stint.

"About Warwick" appeared in the December, 1862, *Atlantic Monthly*. The fragmentary state of the manuscript makes compositorial assignment impossible. Hennessy's name heads page 1, and his take must have been of two leaves at least, since no markings appear within the first four manuscript pages consisting of 176½ AM lines. Pages 5–6 are wanting; pages 7–8 are without marks; pages 9–12 are wanting; pages 13–14 have no marks; pages 15–16 are wanting; pages 17–20 have a single bracket, on page 19; 21–22 are wanting; page 23 has a single bracket; and pages 24–27 are without markings. The page 19 bracket "The [present" (Centenary 81.34–82.1) begins AM 716.29ᵃ and the page 23 bracket "mur[der" (Centenary 85.32) begins AM 718.25ᵃ; they are apparently not stint markings. It is certainly odd that the preserved leaves record no compositor except for Hennessy on page 1, even within what would have been a five-page take on pages 23–27. The possibility must at least be considered that he alone worked on this sketch, unique as would be this procedure among the present manuscripts.

"Recollections of a Gifted Woman" appeared in the *Atlantic Monthly*, January, 1863. Its assignment of takes is relatively simple. Hennessy starts off on page 1 with a take of four leaves and sets 400 AM lines. Schubarth begins with the first paragraph on page 9, also with a four-leaf take, and sets 417 AM lines until Hector's take is marked in the opening on page 17. A few lines below the start of Schubarth's stint on page 9 is a bracket and the number 47 at the bracket "and [is" (Centenary 97.31). This is accurate for the start of AM 47 with the word "is".[34] Hector's stint begins on page 17 of the manuscript. On page 21 in the first paragraph he places his pencil signature under a slant and also a bracket. This bracket is not a stint but a paging mark, however, for the paragraph marks the start of AM page 53 (Centenary 109.23) and so does not interfere with Hector's normal stint of four leaves, like the rest. On page 22 a bracket separates "have" from "been" (Centenary 110.24), marking the start of the fifth line on AM page 53^b. Its purpose is unknown. Otherwise, Hector's take ends with page 24 plus the few lines on page 25 above Hennessy's name in the opening, for a total of 418 AM lines. Hennessy sets to the end, 349 AM lines.

"A London Suburb" appeared in the *Atlantic Monthly* for March, 1863. It is unusual in three respects: first, in that no compositor's name is written on page 1 for the first take of two leaves; second, in that a number of takes begin on the verso of a leaf; and, third, in that every other page of the *Atlantic,* correctly numbered, is marked in the text. The first take consists of 216 AM lines from the beginning to page 5. On page 5 Schubarth had written his name in the first opening, near the foot, but after finishing he must have deleted his signature and set some lines above, because 14 AM lines above in the text appears a vertical stroke "my | con-science" (Centenary 217.12–13) with Schubarth's signature following. Actually, the mark is one word in error (a not unknown mistake with these brackets) since it is "my" and not "conscience" that begins AM 308.17^b. Schubarth had a three-page take (totaling 239 AM lines) until at the first

[34] "Recollections" had begun in AM on page 43. Hence if the title were set in proof, as almost certain, any provisional paging would have turned out to be final; but the number 47 is wrong and the final numbering must have been substituted after the proof stage.

opening on page 10 he stopped for the beginning of another workman's stint. This compositor, John Leary, also had a three-page take, which amounted to 140 AM lines. On page 13 Hector had written his name in the first indention, but double brackets earlier in the text on page 12 "ones;][and" (Centenary 224.16) with his signature indicate that he had worked back to set some preceding text (14 AM lines) for a total stint of 414 AM lines and an eight-page original take ending on page 21. Here Hennessy's name appears in the first paragraph opening, and he sets a five-page take of 292 AM lines until on page 26 Julius Howard's take (125 AM lines) begins with the first paragraph. Here it is just possible that an anomaly exists. Schubarth had signed the first opening on page 29, at the very foot, for a relatively short take of three pages but in actual text scarcely more than a page and a half to the end. But 43 AM lines above, in the second line of page 29, a bracket appears "desire [above" (Centenary 240.6) which originally had Howard's name written above it; but this was crossed out and Schubarth substituted, making a total stint of 122 AM lines from the bracket to the end. Howard appears nowhere else in these manuscripts, and it is just possible that Schubarth took over his assignment from the paragraph opening on page 26 and forgot to substitute his name. But the fact that he himself signs this bracketed note no doubt means only that he took over from Howard at the beginning of AM 320.31^a, not at the paragraph opening (Centenary 237.25; AM 319.10^a).

On page 5 appears "have [fancied" (Centenary 217.4), with the page number 317 (actually AM 308.3^b); on page 9 "two [away" (Centenary 221.1), numbered 319, which is actually AM 310.3^b; on page 13 "sometimes [preternaturally" (Centenary 224.30–31), numbered 321, which is AM 312.3^b, with Hector's name attached since this is his stint; again within Hector's stint, with his name inserted, on page 17 "en[closing", numbered 323 (Centenary 228.27; AM 314.3 ᵇ), beginning with the complete word spelled "inclosing"; then on page 21 "their [poets", numbered 325 (Centenary 232.25; AM 316.3 ᵇ), without name; and finally on page 25 "la[dies", numbered 327, with Hennessy's name (Centenary 236.22; AM 318.3ᵇ). These are, obviously, paging marks; they are written in the same hand throughout and one that differs from the compositorial signatures; and they must have been made subsequent to all take markings for the typesetting. That they are not accurate for the *Atlantic* pages may perhaps be imputed to some later change in the magazine arrangement. On the other hand, since the page marking is fifty-four AM lines off, and the sketch begins part way down on the page, it follows that if the marking had envisaged "A London Suburb" with the title heading a page it might have been accurate for the paging though not for the numbers. Finally, three brackets of unknown origin are scattered through the text.[35] No name or number appears with these, and though each marks the start of an AM line the position of one differs from that of the others: the first on page 10 as "me; [they" (Centenary 222.27; AM 311.46ᵃ), the next on 17 as "mankind [must" (Centenary 228.21; AM 314.46ᵃ), and the last on 18 as "voyages [under" (Centenary 229.30; AM 315.9ᵃ).

"Up the Thames" was carried in the May, 1863, *Atlantic Monthly*. No compositor's name appears on the first page, and there may have been an unusual take of sixteen pages (703 AM lines) until Severance signed the paragraph opening on page 17. His take appears to have been nine pages (437 AM lines) up to Schubarth's signature in the opening on page 26. In turn, Schubarth would have had a take of seven pages

---

[35] These brackets, which also appear in other manuscripts, bear no relation to stints, apparently, nor to paging. Each one of them, however, marks the beginning of an AM line. It is possible that they represent the compositor's marking when he temporarily left off typesetting for the day, to eat dinner, or the like.

(313 AM lines) before Hennessy came in against the first paragraph on page 33 to complete the piece with a take of six pages and 237 lines. Paging brackets in the usual hand found in the earlier manuscripts with this feature appear on page 19 "and, [without" followed by the figure 9 and "R. Sev."; another comes on page 24 "twigged [something" numbered 11, also assigned to Severance but only after Schubarth's name had first been written in and then deleted. The first occurs at AM 606.51^a and the second at 608.51^a. "Up the Thames" begins halfway down page 598 of AM. Thus if it had been paged from the head of page 1, allowing for the space occupied by the title, these pagination markings would be accurate for the start of pages 9 and 11 of the proofs. Since the pager was working after the typesetting, his initial confusion on page 24 that Schubarth and not Severance was the compositor may have no significance (Schubarth's stint is the next). Finally, brackets of unknown purpose appear on page 3 "the [passage" (Centenary 245.20; AM 599.15^b), page 12 "water-[entrance" (Centenary 252.32–33; AM 603.25^a), and page 15 "the [street-" (Centenary 255.33; AM 604.24^b).

The last of the sketches to be set initially in the *Atlantic* was "Civic Banquets," for August, 1863. Hector signs its first page and has a take of eight pages (388 AM lines), meeting Hennessy who signs the first opening on page 9 for a take of eight pages (395 AM lines), who in turn meets D. Green signing page 17 for another eight-page take (382 AM lines). Schubarth signs the opening on page 25. Hector had originally signed that on page 33; but perhaps to equalize the takes to seven pages each, Hector crossed out his name and moved back to sign the first paragraph indention on page 32. Thus Schubarth set 316 lines and Hector 328 AM lines to the end. On page 35 a paging bracket "chairs [would" with the figure 211 occurs (AM 211.2^a). The figure is one line off as the consequence of the insertion, after the typesetting and its final paging, of a one-line white space below AM 205.30ᵃ (Centenary 330.34) to mark the transition from Liverpool to London events. In the manuscript a long bracket in the left margin stretches from the opening of the paragraph after the white space to the line of text that ends the first AM column on the adjusted page. Normal brackets occur on page 2 "it [with" (Centenary 311.19; AM 195.13ᵇ), page 6 "here [with" (Centenary 314.32; AM 197.36ᵃ), and page 37 "piece [of" (Centenary 344.14; AM 211.42ᵇ), the latter a word off since AM line 42 begins with "piece", not with "of".

Since the manuscripts for "Some of the Haunts of Burns" and "Outside Glimpses of English Poverty" are not known, no information is available about their composition for the *Atlantic*. However, "Lichfield and Uttoxeter" and "Consular Experiences" were set directly from manuscript into book pages for the first edition. James Foynes signs the first page of "Lichfield and Uttoxeter" and starts his four-page stint, which is the length of all the other stints in this sketch. He sets 154 lines to Hennessy's name in the first indention of page 5; Hennessy sets 135 lines to J. N. Babcock on page 9; Babcock sets 134 lines to Foynes on page 13; Foynes sets 144 lines to Babcock on page 17; and Babcock completes the job with 114 lines to the end. Originally, Babcock signed the opening on page 5, but his name was deleted and Hennessy's substituted, perhaps not in his own signature. On pages 5 and 9 Babcock wrote a slant in the paragraph opening but signed his name in the space following the last line of the preceding paragraph (or found the slant there when he came to sign); but on page 17 he placed his name in the opening itself, with the number 158 (his stint here beginning with the last line of page 158). On the final manuscript page 20 a bracket appears in the text before "that" but is deleted and another bracket placed before the preceding word "near". This is a paging bracket, since below the last line of the text in this page the usual hand writes 161 and Babcock's name. Actually, the original bracket was correct, for "near" is the last word of page 161 of the book and "that" the first word on page 162. It is odd, too, that this paging bracket should be numbered 161 and not 162.

"Consular Experiences" poses a problem or two. Thomas Alexander's name is erased on the first page, and a paging bracket on page 4 "alto[gether" with the figure 13, for the start of page 13, may thus be associated with the name Alexander written vertically in the left margin. If this had been the distinctive hand for paging found in the other manuscripts, there would be no difficulty in interpretation, but it is not. However, the total evidence suggests that since this sketch began the book it was set directly into numbered page proof and the paging, therefore, is close to composition. That is, as will be seen, the sketch was paged, so far as the markings go, before the extended substitute passage was inserted on book pages 17–19. Also, the hand that marked page 13 probably wrote "Alexander" in the margin since the inscription differs from Alexander's own signature on page 8. If, as seems probable, this notation on page 4 is that of the man charged with making up the pages, then it confirms Alexander's erased signature beginning the text, and thus his take, of four pages, can be assigned to start with page 1 (9.1 of the first edition) and to continue for a total of 133 lines until Niles's name appears in the first opening on page 5 (13.18). Niles seems to have set an original four-page take up to 17.10 on page 8 for a total of 121 lines; at this point it would appear that he left the job, for a bracket, with the name Alexander vertically in the right margin (in a different hand from the name on page 4), occurs on page 8 where we must suppose that Alexander took over to complete the take. Foynes's name had not originally appeared, as would be expected, in the first opening at the foot of page 9, but he must have set some preceding matter, for above, about a third of the way on the manuscript page, a bracket is inscribed "He [described" and his signature is added. At some point, subsequently, it was decided that Foynes should set the remainder of the sketch. His name is found in the opening on page 17 and later attached to paging brackets on pages 19 and 24 (where, in the latter, the pager spells it "Foines" and writes it vertically in the left margin). His total take, therefore, was twenty-eight pages and the adjusted stint was 956 or more lines.

The account of the physical characteristics of this manuscript in terms of its relation to the first edition is complicated by the fact that, while reading proof, Hawthorne expanded a few lines on manuscript page 9 by almost two full manuscript pages which were to start on book page 17. The paging bracket for Alexander to start page 13 is accurate, but after book page 17 the paging brackets reflect the original, not the paging adjusted for the insertion. Thus on manuscript page 12 we find "but [without" followed by "21" and Foynes's name, but the actual position in the book is 21.29. Again, on manuscript page 19 appear the bracket "future [nobleman's", the figure "29", and Foynes's name; but the actual position is 29.29. Finally, on manuscript page 24 the bracket "because / [they" followed by "34" and Foynes's name occurs at book page 34.29. Paging of the original, then, must have progressed at least to page 34 (the last marking on manuscript page 24) before the revised proof was returned and adjustment could be made. The revision had started with the same words of the original on 17.23 (Centenary 13.19), "The individual now in question was a"; but whereas in the original the sentence ran on after its predecessor, in the manuscript for the inserted text it began a new paragraph. That this paragraphing was ignored in the typesetting appears to stem from the use by the compositor (probably Gourlay, according to the schedule), charged with setting the revision and making adjustments, of at least part of the original line of type so that the final word of the line is "mild" instead of original "patient-" or one or more of its syllables. (The Centenary text, of course, follows the requested paragraphing.) Although the end of the revision then returns to the wording of the original with "He had but scanty and scattered thoughts" (19.1–2; Centenary 14.23–24), it is possible that the type was reset (or at least relined) to the end of the present paragraph at 19.11 (Centenary 14.32). On the evidence of the original paginal markings, the net gain in number of lines in the book was twenty-eight.

Non-paging brackets had, it must be assumed, begun Alexander's stint on page 8 (17.11; Centenary 13.7), and Foynes's on page 9 (17.30 adjusted; Centenary 13.25). A regular bracket appears on page 17 "which [methought" (27.5 adjusted; Centenary 21.25), with the notation above it, "measured to here". The four lines of text on page 27 above the bracket, added to the twenty-eight additional caused by the revision on pages 17–18, add up to thirty-two lines, the length of the book page. This equation may be fortuitous, however, since no pattern seems to align this bracket with the start of a page in either the original or the revised paging. Yet since the bracket also begins a line of book text, it cannot be some rough preliminary casting-off of copy for editorial purposes about midway through the manuscript, and it must have some printing function; but the purpose is no clearer than the similar brackets (though without the note about measurement) that occur in other manuscripts.

Equating the AM text with the lines of the Boston first edition in order to have a norm for reference, we find that Hennessy set 1,871 book lines, Hector 1,619, Schubarth 1,457, Foynes 1,254, Severance 538, Niles 371, Green 272, Babcock 248, Sullivan 243, Lyons 169, Alexander 150, Curtis 136, Leary 96, and Howard 92. Lines that cannot be assigned total 1,485, including 438 lines in "About Warwick" that may well have been set in substantial part by Hennessy.

Of these workmen, Hennessy, Hector, and Schubarth are the usual *Atlantic Monthly* compositors: of the eight sketches with preserved manuscripts all three worked on four of the pieces, two on three, and Hennessy, at least, on the eighth, "About Warwick." Foynes is in fourth place chiefly because he was the major compositor of "Consular Experiences" and contributed to "Lichfield and Uttoxeter," both works set directly into the book from manuscript. The others, with the possible exception of Severance, set too few lines to furnish any basis for analysis.

Three major textual situations exist. The first is the common one, in which the preserved manuscripts were set into type for the *Atlantic Monthly,* mainly by identifiable compositors, with the resulting text serving as printer's copy for the book after being surveyed by Hawthorne. The problem here is to determine which variants in the *Atlantic* from the manuscript represent unauthoritative compositorial departures not corrected in proof, and which represent Hawthorne's own proof-alterations.[36] The problem does not differ for the two essays, "Consular Experiences" and "Lichfield and Uttoxeter," set directly into the book, although the latter sketch has the additional problem of the relation of its early to its late

---

[36] No editorial markings appear in any preserved manuscript. Hence if there were editorial intervention for the *Atlantic* pieces above the level of the correction of typos, it must have come in proof where it would be impossible to distinguish from compositorial styling and sophistication. We have no means of knowing whether this form of intervention existed on any serious scale beyond the correction of mechanical errors: the inference would be that it would be present, if at all, mainly at the level of styling, but we cannot be sure. Moreover, we have no means of knowing whether any such changes would be marked in the proof sent to the author, whether they would be made in preliminary proof of which the author saw only the revises, or whether they might be made without the author's knowledge after he had returned the proofs but before they were transmitted to the printer.

form with particular reference to the effect of the transmission on the final manuscript.

Second, the two sketches "Some of the Haunts of Burns"
and "Outside Glimpses of English Poverty" for which manuscripts are not known must be surveyed in their earliest preserved documents, the *Atlantic* text, with some reference to
their form in *The English Notebooks,* in an attempt to relate
them to their lost manuscripts.

Third, the variant readings between the AM and the book
texts require analysis to determine whether they represent (*a*)
Hawthorne's revisions marked in the AM pages used as printer's copy, (*b*) Hawthorne's revisions marked in the book
proof, (*c*) compositorial departures from copy in setting the
book not detected and altered in proof by the author,[37] or (*d*)
errors in the AM text not weeded out either in (*a*) or in
(*b*).

Eighty-six substantive readings (a few related) differ between AM and the first Boston edition in those ten sketches
set in the book from AM copy. Twelve of these appear to be
more or less obvious printer's errors like "glass" for MS-AM
"grass" (193.21), "alter" for "altar" (101.21), including an
apparent case of eyeskip in "old" for "whole" (200.9); simple
errors from contamination in context, or of sophistication, like
"towers" for "tower" (85.3); misreadings or sophistications
like "earthern" for "earthen" (52.6), "later" for "latter"
(194.25), and "subtle" for "subtile" (250.5); or relatively

[37] Once again, whether any publisher's editor overlooked either the
printer's copy or the book proofs is not to be determined. On the evidence
of the lack of editorial intervention in the manuscripts set directly into the
book, it is perhaps unlikely that the printer's copy composed of AM pages
received special attention not given to the manuscripts; but one would
expect a publisher's reader to go over the book proofs if for no other
purpose than to correct mechanical errors missed by the author. In this
process some styling changes might perhaps be expected. If these took
place, however, they would be fewer than may have occurred in copy set
from manuscript since the AM texts had already received their styling and
would require less attention.

normal house stylings like "around" for "round" (161.11), "toward" for "towards" (67.23, 73.20, and 111.10), and "elegances" for "elegancies" (213.18). These are all paralleled a number of times in the variants of AM from MS.

Of the remaining seventy-three variants that have some chance of being authoritative, certain ones are not above suspicion, but as a group they provide some basis for critical analysis. One of the interesting facts is that the time of writing, whether early or late, seems to have little relation to the number of variants. The earliest, "Some of the Haunts of Burns," calls forth six substantive variants, and the next earliest, "Near Oxford," only six. We then jump to ten in "Pilgrimage to Old Boston" (which was printed in AM shortly after "Near Oxford"), seven in "Leamington Spa," nine in "About Warwick," eight in "Recollections of a Gifted Woman," seven in "A London Suburb," six in "Up the Thames," four in "Outside Glimpses of English Poverty," and ten in "Civic Banquets." In short, a sketch written so late that printer's copy for the book must have been a corrected proof of the *Atlantic* text still calls forth ten further revisions, whereas the early "Near Oxford" and "Some of the Haunts of Burns" required only six each.

In this group, five variants correct AM misprints; [38] the correction of fact accounts for five substituted readings; [39] a common and important class is the addition either of fresh material or of clarifying detail in twenty-one examples, [40] or

[38] Centenary 163.21, 169.24, 190.17, 227.13, 297.29.

[39] Centenary 41.10, 147.15, 157.13, 220.24, 245.34. Typical is 41.10 which corrects Hawthorne's Leamington address from 16 to 10 Lansdowne Circus, or the change at 220.24 from "by policemen" to "by a policeman".

[40] Centenary 45.25–26, 82.9, 86.20, 89.11, 99.32–34, 106.30, 112.9–12, 115.10–12, 157.34 ["he"], 160.6–7, 160.27, 183.4 184.33, 233.4–7, 239.2–7, 244.8–9, 249.27–30, 261.1–2, 308.20–24, 332.6, 343.9. Typical is the addition "(all of which I have seen)" to attest at 89.11 to the wonders of Redfern's antiquarian shop; the softening of Miss Bacon's imagining at 112.9–12 by the added, "It is very possible, moreover, that her acute mind may always have had a lurking and deeply latent

even the condensation of detail in one.[41] A separate class may be made out of twenty-four changes that substitute either qualifying or more exact words or phrases for the originals.[42] We are left, then, with eighteen alterations that may be called purely stylistic.[43]

Of these classifications authorial correction or revision is relatively clearcut except in the last category. Actually, an occasional uncertainty may appear in a few other variants that are so close in their book form to the AM word as to arouse suspicion. Prominent here are book "shuffling" for "scuffling" (60.1), "phases" for "faces" (106.29), "hours" for "hour" (188.16) and "on my memory" for "in my memory" (217.20), especially in view of MS concurrence in each case with AM; but in all but the last two some reasonably plausible argument can be advanced for the probable authority of the change.[44] On the other hand, the eighteen stylistic variants are relatively indifferent in their nature and correspondingly difficult

---

distrust of its own fantasies, and that this now became strong enough to restrain her from a decisive step"; or in the final judgment of Southey's biography of Lord Nelson, 233.4–7, the new "But Southey accomplished his own purpose, which, apparently, was to present his hero as a pattern for England's young midshipmen."

[41] Centenary 320.1–2.

[42] Centenary 45.20–21, 49.7, 60.1, 73.33, 78.11, 89.19, 106.29, 108.29, 119.23–24, 154.27–28, 161.32, 188.16, 196.5–6, 205.6–7, 205.33, 207.21, 208.28, 212.26, 224.11, 289.20, 314.31, 316.1, 330.16, 345.19. Typical are the changes from "Her visage is . . . not always positively forbidding" to "seldom positively forbidding" (49.7) and from "black-letter" to "old English" (73.33), or that denominating London lodging-house keepers as "usually" a savage tribe instead of "actually" (108.29).

[43] Centenary 42.22, 45.15–16, 75.6, 78.22, 81.8, 90.12, 139.18, 147.9, 162.3, 179.3, 217.20, 218.26, 248.15–16, 276.4–5, 303.11, 316.6–8, 320.8, 334.14–15.

[44] For instance, that Shakespeare's works "present many faces of truth" is unexceptionable; but the improvement in the alteration to "phases" is apparent when one reads farther: "each with scope large enough to fill a contemplative mind." A *phase* may have such a scope, but scarcely a *face*. Again, a stone threshold may indeed be worn from the days of the Plantagenets by the "scuffling" of "hob-nailed footsteps"; but "shuffling" is a word more characteristic of gait and one that may be thought to imply a less conscious action. This variant is less certain than the other, of course.

to adjudicate. Only one may be called strictly grammatical: whether at 45.15–16 "person or thing" should carry the AM singular reference "it" governed by "or" or should be thought of as a collective plural reference to "they" as in the book. Syntactical considerations suggest the advisability, though scarcely the necessity, of adding the pronoun "that" at 218.26, a change that may perhaps in some part be associated with the restoration in the book of elided "by" at 42.22 and "I" at 162.3, and perhaps of "and" to introduce the last element of a series at 147.9. Felicity of verbal arrangement doubtless causes a shift to a more natural position of the parenthetical "if I mistake not" at 276.4, the distinction between "now" and "still" at 316.6–8, and the tightening of the loose attachment at 81.8 by the substitution of "that" for "having". A larger group concerns itself with what may be called idiom or usage. Did the Earl of Warwick's hall at 75.6 make a splendid appearance with its decorations "while" King James sat at supper as in AM, or "where" as in I?[45] May one use "uglinesses" and "sulkinesses" in the plural, or should they be pared to the singular (139.18, 179.3)? Is an impression retained "in" one's memory or "on" it (217.20)?[46] When Hawthorne imagines the Thames breaking through the tunnel and choking it with a mixture of sand, mud, and stones, "skeletons of drowned people, the rusty iron-work of sunken vessels, and the great many such precious and curious things as a river always contrives to hide in its bosom" (248.14–17), is the I change of "the great many" from MS-AM "a great many" dictated by a desire for exact parallelism in the series of items each prefaced by "the" or is it simple contamination and compositorial error? Does one prefer to write "live to

[45] That the change of "while" to "where" may be meaningful could be suggested on the analogy of 237.17 in which Hennessy either misread or sophisticated MS "where" as "while" in AM.

[46] For a discussion of this reading and a rejection of the I variant, see below, pages lxxxvii–lxxxviii.

grow up", as in AM (and ENB, 276.27),[47] or the less refined "live and grow up" at 303.11? Were Hawthorne's earliest glimpses "of" Englishmen or "at" Englishmen (320.8)? Does one say "all of which characteristics" or "all which" (334.14–15)? In another classification, is the apparent distinction inadvertent or a conscious attempt at a shade of meaning in the question whether the old pensioners are subject to supervision "as regards their personal freedom or conduct", as in I, or "as regards their personal freedom and conduct" (78.21–22) as in AM? (MS is wanting here, but the journal reads "and" with AM.) Is a legitimate distinction present in "those wayside brooks" of New England, or "the wayside brooks" (90.12)? [48]

These are difficult questions to answer, and some are no doubt impossible, especially since we have no means of knowing what compositors set which first-edition pages from AM copy. Evidence of a sort is not wanting, however, as an occasional guide. In six readings the first edition departs from its AM copy to return to what had been the MS form. Two of these do not signify since they represent only the correction of

[47] All ENB references are to Randall Stewart (ed.), *The English Notebooks* (New York and London, 1941).

[48] "Any landscape in New England . . . would have its blue eyes open in those lakelets that we encounter almost from mile to mile at home, but of which the Old Country is utterly destitute; or it would smile in our faces through the medium of the wayside brooks that vanish under a low stone-arch, on one side of the road, and sparkle out again on the other. Neither of these pretty features is often found in an English scene" (90.7–15). Here in MS-AM "those" wayside brooks balances "those" lakelets, naturally enough. Yet if Hawthorne was the one who in proof or copy marked MS-AM "Neither of these pretty features are" to "is" a few lines earlier, he was doubtless the agent who changed "those" to "the", and vice versa. One may only speculate as to the reason. It may have been that "those" brooks clashed in his mind with "these" pretty features. It may have been a desire for absolute exactness, for it is the brooks alone that properly balance the lakelets, not the special brooks that run under roads—this latter only an added detail applicable to some of the brooks. If the change were to be made in proof, and without extensive rewriting, the substitution of "the" was the simplest means for securing the necessary general reference.

misprints in AM, as readily remarked by the compositor, perhaps, as by the author ("Font" for "Fort" at 163.21; "barrows" for "burrows" at 227.13). The rest may well be authorial, and from them something can be learned of the care that Hawthorne expended, at least from time to time, on certain details of the book proofs. In this respect perhaps the most interesting is his return at 45.15–16 from an AM venture into the singular governed by "or" to the original MS plurals,[49] a change that inclines one to the belief that Hawthorne himself had been responsible for the original AM alteration (as for that immediately above at 45.9) and thus in the book proof recalled it, and his uncertainty, and decided he had been right the first time. But regardless of speculations about the origin of the AM alteration, the fact remains that a most careful change away from a literal and rigid "correctness" was made in the book.[50] If this encourages the hypothesis that Hawthorne in proof could be as concerned about minutiae as about larger questions, we can understand his care to do justice to the rapacity of London lodging-house keepers at 108.29 by returning what may have been an AM misreading "actually" to original MS "usually", and to complete a stylistic revision at 316.6–8 begun in AM but requiring further attention. More important for the purposes of analysis of the indifferent reading is the probability that he was responsible for the tiny idiomatic change at 320.8 whereby AM "glimpses of" was restored to original MS

---

[49] " . . . we should never pass judgment on the merits of any person or thing, unless we behold them in the sphere and circumstances to which they are specially adapted" (45.14–16). Here AM had read "behold it" and "to which it is", a change in AM all the more interesting in that it had been preceded only a few lines earlier by a shift from MS singular in the reading, "the haunt of swans, whose aspect and movement in the water are [MS "is"] most stately" (45.8–10).

[50] Actually, Hawthorne may have been more concerned with the propriety of using "it" for "person" as well as "thing" than he was with the problem of exact reference.

"glimpses at". Although a fortuitous compositorial alteration cannot be entirely overlooked here, the fact remains that "glimpses at" is a good Hawthorne usage.[51]

The evidence of the changes in I from AM, then, breaks down to demonstrate that in every sketch, even those that he had written only a few months earlier, Hawthorne made substantive alterations either in the AM copy or in book proof (or, probably, in both) that added information, sharpened detail, increased stylistic felicity, and—in a number of cases —probably concerned themselves with questions of syntax and usage. On the other hand, a number of AM departures from MS that seem unauthorized were passed over without change, as one would expect. In turn, the compositors of I introduced a few misprints that were not detected, made a few identifiable sophistications, and effected a small amount of identifiable house-styling altering Hawthorne's old-fashioned forms. Generally speaking, however, the compositors seem not to have interfered substantially with their copy, since it was printed and had already been styled once in the same printing house. (A similar conservatism is not to be expected, however, in copy set in their shop from manuscript.) To sum up what can be determined, except in familiar cases of compositorial tinkering with Hawthorne forms such as are encountered throughout his career, the general faithfulness of the book to its printed AM copy seems to be established, and thus the general authority of its variants, even relatively indifferent ones, must be rated as high. Hence, the kind of alterations found in I, and their relative authority, can serve as a form of evidence when one tackles the central problem of the authority of the AM or book variants in text set directly from manuscript.

[51] See 169.6–8: "One of the park-keepers, on horseback, rode beside our carriage, pointing out the choice views, and glimpses at the palace, as we drove through the domain."

Of approximately three hundred variants from MS,[52] an immediate disposition can be made of a considerable number. On the credit side, the nature of the addition or substitution effectively suggests, for 128, that these represent Hawthorne reading proof for the AM appearances or else annotating AM copy or the proofs of the book.[53]

Most of these 128 substantive variants are removed by some form of evidence from suspicion of compositorial intervention. At 35.13, as at 13.19–14.23, documentary proof is available for the authority of the changes in proof in "Consular Experiences." Although AM "ingenuous" might be suspected as a Hennessy misreading of MS "generous" at 114.14, the word "generous" is written with particular clarity in MS and thus seems to authenticate the AM change by making misreading a very difficult conjecture to advance. Only a few variants involve syntax or grammatical forms, like 91.29 where there might be a very slight question whether Hennessy could have changed the superlatives "noblest . . . most" to "nobler . . . more"; or 184.33 where Sullivan could have supplied "monument" in default of a clear reference. But, on the one hand,

[52] The figure will differ according to the method of counting related or consequential changes as one alteration or as multiple; also, the count may differ in relation to repeated similar alteration, such as the four changes within a hundred lines or so of MS "Poet's Corner" to AM "Poets' Corner".

[53] Centenary 3.5, 3.6, 3.20, 4.26, 4.31, 4.35, 5.19–33, 13.19–14.23, 14.26, 15.7, 15.30, 28.1, 29.11, 32.28, 35.13, 35.17, 36.4, 36.14, 36.23, 37.17, 38.6–20, 39.14, 40.9–11, 41.10, 45.15–16, 45.20–21, 45.25–26, 46.19, 49.7, 52.15–16, 53.25, 56.24, 56.25, 56.25–26, 59.18, 61.33, 64.12–13, 64.21, 68.3–4, 81.8, 82.9, 86.13, 86.20, 87.30, 89.11, 89.19, 91.29, 92.4, 93.32, 94.2, 99.32, 99.33–34, 101.28, 103.29–30, 106.30, 107.26, 108.7, 108.29, 112.9–12, 114.14, 115.8, 115.10–12, 119.23–24, 146.28, 147.15, 147.19, 148.29, 150.5, 150.19, 151.28, 153.9, 153.9, 154.27–28, 157.13, 157.34, 157.34, 160.6–7, 160.27, 160.28, 161.13, 161.32, 162.3, 172.20, 173.11, 174.16, 176.18, 180.15–16, 180.16–17, 181.6, 182.25, 183.4, 183.26, 183.31, 184.33, 187.13–14, 188.20, 188.22, 192.9, 220.24, 224.11, 227.20, 230.34, 233.4–7, 239.2–7, 241.17, 241.18, 244.8–9, 245.34, 246.34, 249.10, 249.27–30, 261.1–2, 272.13, 313.12, 314.31, 316.1, 316.6–8, 320.1, 320.2, 324.6, 324.20, 330.16, 332.6, 334.14–15, 340.21, 343.9, 343.29, 345.19.

speculation is idle about Sullivan's characteristics owing to the small number of lines that he set; on the other, Hennessy's only other possible example of a somewhat similar nature (or that of any other compositor) is confined to 119.23–24 where MS "most beautiful" becomes AM "beautifullest" as part of a recasting of an entire sentence that must be authorial.

To these 128 readings may be added the following 21 where AM or I correct obvious MS errors, and one cannot be sure whether the agent was compositor or author: 15.24, 18.5, 21.7, 52.21, 53.12, 80.14, 100.8, 111.9, 112.4, 146.3, 168.4, 173.17, 190.3, 234.2, 237.23, 244.25, 262.14, 315.23, 337.34, 340.20, and 344.17. These 149 variants, then, require no detailed analysis to assign their authority.

At the opposite pole are 65 readings in which the AM or I variants appear to be manifestly unauthoritative.[54] These range widely, as would be expected. Some are simple misreadings of the manuscript, like "cause" for "course" (19.3), "general" for "generic" (22.33), "things" for "stingo" (178.18), "covering" for "awning" (253.34), and "light" for "lights" (334.30). Other variants that may be attributed to misreading of ambiguously formed inscription are 38.22, 94.18, 111.6, 116.15, 134.14, and 184.6. Or they may be simple misprints, like 169.24 and 190.17, or a positive error like the omission of "still" at 316.8. A large number are house-styling changes or modernizations of Hawthorne's characteristics of the kind that appear in all his printed texts and that were introduced by various compositors, whether in AM or I, in *Our Old Home* as well. Prominent is the reduction of his old-fashioned

---

[54] Centenary 4.28, 19.3, 20.8, 22.33, 38.22, 52.3, 52.6, 57.13, 57.33, 67.20, 67.23, 73.20, 90.5, 94.18, 96.7, 101.21, 103.20, 105.16, 111.6, 111.10, 112.13, 114.7, 116.15, 126.6, 134.14, 136.20, 140.31, 151.31, 161.11, 163.21, 163.29, 168.2, 169.24, 174.12, 178.18, 179.31, 180.4, 184.6, 190.17, 213.18, 227.13, 234.4, 237.5, 243.8, 250.5, 253.22, 253.26, 253.34, 254.30, 255.19, 259.15, 259.18–19, 273.30, 275.23, 312.10, 312.21, 312.33, 314.8, 315.11, 316.8, 322.12, 327.7, 330.7, 334.30, 335.8.

-ies endings to *-es* in such words as "extravagancies" (20.8), "subsidencies" (90.5), "excellencies" (312.10), and "imprudencies" (322.12).[55] The MS form "subtle" is changed to "subtile" at 96.7, 105.16, and 140.31, and "subtlety" to "subtilty" at 273.30. Similar is the change to "older" of Hawthorne's almost invariable "elder", as at 52.3 and 136.20, and of the usual MS "round" to "around" (112.13).[56] Hawthorne's "a" before a word beginning with "h" is regularly altered to "an" (151.31, 253.22, 327.7), and there is a general normalizing of MS "further" to "farther" (67.20, 174.12, 254.30, 255.19, 259.15, 314.8).[57] Other fancied normalizations are "his" to "its" at 103.20 and "foods" to "food" at 312.33. Other old-fashioned forms are modernized, like MS "bran-new" (168.2), "gentlefolks" (179.31), "engraven" (180.4), "sewn" (234.4), "sung" (237.5), "dumb-foundered" (330.7), and "plates-full" (335.8). (See, for this last, Centenary *The Marble Faun*, 52.30, "beaksful".) A corrective apostrophe is inserted, though unnecessarily, in "birds-nests" (57.33). Another in "minutes" (57.13), though doubtless the compositor Niles's doing, has been accepted as a normalization agreeing with Hawthorne's usage elsewhere, as in 23.6 and 226.29. Hawthorne's omission of the genitive apostrophe in plurals like these seems to go back to the usage of the eighteenth century and earlier. A typical example is 210.14 "within two or three minutes walk" in ENB (509.43) altered in AM to "minutes' ", though ENB and AM at 212.3 read "within a minute's walk".

---

[55] See also the change in I at 213.18 of MS-AM "elegancies" to "elegances".

[56] See also the change in I to "around" of MS-AM "round" at 161.11.

[57] See also the continuation of this normalization in I from AM at 114.7. That this is true compositorial alteration in AM may be indicated by the fact that four of these appear in "Up the Thames" and one in "Civic Banquets" which were published within a few months of each other, shortly before the book was proofread.

Almost inexplicably, "simulacrum" is altered to "simu-lachre" (259.18–19), and "parti-colored" to "party-colored" (315.11).

The remaining 104 variants constitute generally indifferent readings.[58] An attempt to determine their authority or non-authority should have a double basis: (1) the evidence from classification combined with parallels; and (2) the evidence that may be drawn from a study of compositorial accuracy. Unfortunately, this latter evidence is of little value in these texts, partly because the recoverable number of lines set by each of the three main AM compositors is not very large (in no case over 2,000 lines of book text) and in part because the indisputable substantive departures from copy are in a relatively few categories that furnish insufficient evidence for extrapolation to the wide variety of doubtful readings.

Classification appeals to two main hypotheses. First, if similar changes are made with some consistency in AM throughout the whole range of sketches, it is improbable that Hawthorne was the agent. That is, since he corrected AM proofs for these sketches from before October, 1861, to June or July, 1863, it would be difficult to argue, for example, that if he was so curious as to alter MS "further" in proof to "farther" in "Near Oxford," printed in October, 1861, he would continue to write "further" in all manuscripts and faithfully then to correct each proof to "farther" up through "Civic Banquets,"

[58] Centenary 8.34, 28.26, 42.22, 45.9, 49.24, 51.19, 54.12, 55.31, 58.5, 60.1, 60.27, 88.24, 89.12, 90.12, 90.15, 90.20, 91.21, 93.20, 106.29, 109.34, 115.28, 119.3–4, 134.14 ["the"], 139.18, 140.22, 141.9–11, 144.27, 145.25, 146.7, 146.30, 147.9, 150.6, 151.25, 152.33, 153.6, 153.17, 154.29, 155.13, 156.30–31, 157.16, 161.8, 162.3, 162.5, 162.15, 163.23–24, 165.17, 165.20, 166.8, 166.16, 168.11, 168.27–28, 171.2, 171.22, 173.2, 178.19, 179.3, 183.16, 183.32, 184.30, 187.10, 188.16, 215.11–12, 216.1, 217.12, 217.20, 218.26, 219.10, 222.6, 225.10, 226.27, 230.5, 230.7, 230.15, 231.25, 234.17, 235.25, 236.32, 237.17, 239.8, 248.15–16, 257.4, 260.3, 264.4, 266.14, 266.21, 267.10, 267.33, 268.23, 268.32, 270.11, 273.18–19, 276.4–5, 310.9, 311.4–5, 315.16, 320.8, 329.24, 329.32, 330.18, 335.4, 337.34, 338.7, 344.23, 344.28.

printed in August, 1863. Second, if certain variants appear in part to have been produced by a misreading of Hawthorne's sometimes difficult hand, it is probable that others in parallel were subject to the same misreading.

However, each of these hypotheses needs some discrimination in its application. For instance, the first is certainly applicable with real rigor to the forms of words like "elegancies", "further", or "elder". But when usage is less in question, and the matter is one of minor additions, excisions, or substitutions of relatively neutral words chiefly in a syntactical context, then it is quite possible to take it that Hawthorne may have repeated, say, certain more or less informal constructions in various manuscripts (occasionally but not always under the influence of his journal entries) that on second thought he might each time wish to tighten up when they came to his attention in the proof. Any writer, for instance, may be led at various times into questions of singular and plural subjects that need later reflection for a final decision. Correspondingly, although it is almost positive that the reduction of plural MS "lights" to "light" in AM at 334.30 was a misreading of a particularly ambiguous inscription, other reductions—like MS "characters" to "character" at 115.28—could be argued as being authorial change in a matter of idiom. Whether misreading or sophistication, or even a combination of both, created some AM variants is not always crystal clear.

The question of misreadings may be looked at first. At 28.26 Foynes (who is the most careful of all the workmen who set enough lines to justify an estimate) [59] misread a very imperfectly formed MS "this" as "the", but fortunately the sense indicates that this variant is an error in I. The only

---

[59] In this list of raw and unanalyzed doubtful readings, Foynes has only 3 in his 1,254 lines, as against 10 for Severance in his 538 lines, 19 for Schubarth in 1,457 lines, 21 for Hector in 1,619 lines, and 23 for Hennessy in 1,871 lines. Eighteen appear in 1,485 unassigned lines.

other such variant is Hector's "the" at 225.10 for MS "this",
which is another misreading although the context does not
provide quite such firm support for MS as does that at 28.26.
Both, on the evidence, may be rejected as compositorial error.
At 103.20 an unclear MS "his" misled Schubarth to read
"its", an appropriate enough reference for the marble statue of
John a' Combe, but not what Hawthorne had actually written
either in MS or in the original account in ENB. No other
such confusion appears in the texts. A more troublesome case
is represented by the two alterations of MS "whence" to
"where", the first found in "Lichfield and Uttoxeter" (126.6),
set directly from MS into book form (Hennessy), and the
second in "Pilgrimage to Old Boston" (163.29) between
ENB-MS and the AM text set by an unknown compositor
(Ignoto) who may or may not have been Hector. In each case
although the "whence" is formed with relative clarity for one
who is familiar with Hawthorne's writing, a misreading is
possible owing to the characteristics of Hawthorne's hand.[60] If
we are to suppose that about October or November of 1861,
when Hawthorne must have been reading proofs for the
"Pilgrimage" sketch, he had occasion to revise his idiom, we
must then suppose that in May, 1863, he repeated it (and
how many times intervening?) only to revise it again when
furnished proof within a week or two. This repetition is not
impossible, but it must be remarked that though "where" is
suitable enough in both contexts, "whence" is definitely the
more precise word, particularly at 163.29 where the chance of
misreading is the more probable.[61] Enough chance of misread-

[60] Moreover, the word at 163.29 is squeezed into the right margin.

[61] " . . . and emerged into the loftiest lantern, whence we saw level
Lincolnshire, far and near" at 163.29–30 ("whence" is also the reading of
ENB, 478.42); and 126.5–6, "Everywhere, there were empty niches
whence statues had been thrown down". For a parallel of a sort, in which
"whence" is preserved although "where" would have been appropriate, see
212.19–21: "we returned . . . to Ayr, whence, taking the rail, we soon
beheld Ailsa Craig".

ing exists to reject both variants in the prints, therefore,[62] in view of the lack of other evidence in these texts that Hawthorne was engaged in a stylistic revision of his use of "whence". Other possible misreadings involving the use of "where" occur. The most notable is at 260.3, set by Severance, where the inscription of a word that could be debated in MS as representing either "where" or "when" but on careful scrutiny appears to be the latter is typeset as "where" in AM, a choice that appears to be compositorial. That this is an almost certain case of misreading is of some interest because a question does indeed arise about Hawthorne's distinction between place and time. For example, at 183.16 MS had read "that odd state of mind when we fitfully and teazingly remember some previous scene" but in AM, as set by Sullivan, the "when" appears as "wherein". The word is clearly enough written so that ordinary misreading is not very probable. Since we know so little of the work of Sullivan, "wherein" must be doubtfully accepted as a Hawthorne proof-correction leading to a slightly more specific reference, moving from time to place one might say.[63] This is the direction also found at 75.6 from AM "while" to I "where" ("About Warwick" MS is missing here): ". . . where [AM "while"] King James sat at supper." Almost no basis for judgment is present here, except that the possibility of misreading is absent since I is being set from the AM print. It may just be that contamination has

---

[62] An additional argument may be adduced in favor of the non-authority of the I variant at 126.6. In all of "Lichfield and Uttoxeter" only three other substantive variants exist between MS and I. One of these ("petty" at 134.14) is a demonstrable misreading, and a second is a demonstrable sophistication ("older" for "elder" at 136.20). The third, the addition of "the" at 134.14, is certainly correct but need not be a proof-correction. In short, it seems probable that Hawthorne saw no need to alter any readings in this sketch when it was set into book form.

[63] In the absence of evidence it would be wilful to speculate that Sullivan might have misread "when" as "where", nevertheless, and Hawthorne in reading proof forgot that he had written "when" and, not liking "where", altered it to "wherein".

flowed from the phrase "where King James . . . had once been feasted" at 74.32, although the distance makes such an explanation far from readily acceptable. It seems better to take the variant as a genuine authorial revision (and some fine shade of meaning is certainly involved in that "while"—in combination with the "when" at 75.4—might give a false impression that the decorations were temporary whereas the tapestry must be supposed permanently hung). This being so, one may the more readily label as an error the reverse change at 237.17 from MS "where" to AM "while" in "In the midst of the confusion, where everybody was treading on his neighbor's toes". The word "where" is written clearly, and only a small blob of ink above the first "e" might—though imaginatively—lead to a misreading. On the total evidence it would seem more likely that Hennessy, inadvertently or consciously, is sophisticating the text through a misunderstanding of the author's exact meaning. Hawthorne is here talking about the place where the confusion occurred, not the time, although superficially the latter might seem to be in question.

Given Hawthorne's hand, a confusion between "on" and "in" is always possible since only the dot of an "i" might serve to distinguish between them. At 109.34, MS reads "which did not fail to produce on the listener's mind, something like a temporary faith", but in Hector's setting of AM this becomes "in the listener's mind". In MS the "on" is certain, especially to one accustomed to Hawthorne's hand, but a compositor might mistake the word, even though no dot appears; on the other hand, pure misreading is not entirely required as a hypothesis to account for the variant since the "in" is the more natural idiom. The puzzle seems to be solved by reference to Hawthorne's journal which reads (ENB 388.37–38) "does not fail to produce, on the listener's part, something like a temporary faith in what she believes so strongly." When the whole clause in "Recollections" is read, beginning "and beneath them all, there ran a deep and powerful under-current of earnestness, which did not fail . . .", one can perhaps see that when he copied this passage in MS almost word for word from ENB, and in the key phrase merely substituted "mind" for "part", he may well have inadvertently kept the ENB "on". However, in proof, he was faced with an undercurrent that produced a faith *on* the mind, and he changed the false reading to the proper "in". This seems to be a better hypothesis than to argue that the basic metaphor is that of an impression being made on the mind, especially when this impression must be a temporary faith produced by an undercurrent. If this is so, it is proper to resurvey a curious small change made in I at 217.20, involving an "impression", which reads in MS-AM, "I do not repent of a single wasted hour, and only wish that I could have spent twice as many in the same way; for the impression in my memory is, that I was as happy . . . as the English summer-day was long." Here I changes "in my memory" to "on my memory", but probably in error. It is easy to imagine a compositor setting without a great deal of reflection and taking it at first sight that impressions must be made *on* something. If the verb "impress" were used, the "on" would be appropriate; but Hawthorne is speaking of a memory that emanates from the impression that has long been *in* his mind, not one that is being impressed upon it at the moment. Some small relation does seem to obtain between these two readings at 109.34 and 217.20, in each case leading to the conclusion that "in" is the preferred word. One may also, perhaps, adduce, as a similar usage, at ENB 390.17–18, "a sort of weight or sting in my conscience".

Because Hawthorne's final "s" was not always clearly formed, as in "lights" at 334.30 set by Schubarth as "light", other MS plurals reduced to the singular in AM need inspection. These are "characters" at 115.28, "accounts" at 173.2, "gentlefolks" at 179.31, "parts" at 230.15, and "presences" at 231.25. The first two were set by Hennessy, and the others, including the obvious sophistication of MS "gentlefolks", by Hector.[64] Such a concentration is, of course, suspicious; and it is also suspicious that with the possible exception of "parts" each represents a plural reduced to a collective singular.[65] Since these old-fashioned formal plurals, like "He was a medical man, and wrote both in his official and professional characters" (115.27–28), or "I have observed . . . not only in portraits, but in the actual presences of such renowned people" (231.23–25), are written over the span of these essays and are normally a characteristic of Hawthorne's style,[66] it is relatively simple to assign them all as Hennessy sophistications. This being so, two such readings altered in I from their MS-AM forms are more clearly revealed as sophistications and therefore returnable to their original idiomatic plurals: MS-AM "uglinesses" (139.18) and "sulkinesses" (179.3), the former being in part confirmed by ENB 462.29.

A few readings exist in which the contrary alteration takes

[64] See "holiday-folks" at 225.3.

[65] To these examples should be added I "impression" for MS "impressions" at 4.28, set by an unknown compositor. Unfortunately, ENB furnishes only a single gloss, which confirms "accounts" (ENB 407.29), but that is a useful one. See, also, footnote 66 below. Hennessy's reversal, in which he sets "village-street" for MS "village-streets" at 91.21 does not seem to be a question of idiom but instead a simple misreading or misprint. The only evidence that might be adduced for an authorial proof-alteration is the ENB (57.26–28) remark about the village of Eastham, "It was not merely one long, wide street, as in most New England villages, but several crooked streets". But this is insufficient to justify acceptance of AM, "The Warwickshire elm has not so beautiful a shape as those that overhang our village-street".

[66] One may compare 157.33–158.1 in MS, "He had met with several Americans, who, at various times, have come on pilgrimage to this place, and had been in correspondence with others", which in the course of recasting in AM changes to the plural, "He had met with several Americans, who . . . had come on pilgrimages . . . and he had . . ." (Hector). No reason exists to deny this AM version as part of Hawthorne's rather extensive tinkering with language that is part of the "Pilgrimage to Old Boston" proof-correction, involving as it does two other changes within the sentence.

place: these are headed by the factually wrong change in I (85.3) to "towers" of AM "tower" by an unknown compositor, and include the alteration in I from ENB, MS, and AM "hour" to "hours" at 188.16. Then there is, in AM, the accepted Hector "pilgrimages" for MS "pilgrimage" (157.34; see above, note 66), the rejected Hennessy "village-street" for MS "village-streets" (91.21; see above, note 65), and the Hennessy "kinds" for MS "kind" (239.8). The question of "hour" versus "hours" is not an easy one, but in context the temptation for a compositor to think the original an error might well have proved irresistible. But when ENB (419.21) supports both MS and AM (surveyed in proof), and the change in question is away from an idiom in the compositorial conventionality, the conjecture in favor of compositorial sophistication is certainly the safer. The Hennessy alteration at 239.8 may perhaps pass as a necessary correction, whoever the agent. Grammar requires the plural ("It is one of the simplest kinds of games").

Five alterations take place in the position of "only" as a modifier, in each case the direction of change being toward the exact and formal usage. A typical example occurs in an unknown compositor's stint (just possibly Hennessy if he set all of "About Warwick") at 88.24, in which MS "The shop . . . being only denoted by the name of 'REDFERN,'" (identical with the wording found in ENB at 587.19) is altered in AM to the more formal "being denoted only". Another is in Hennessy's stint at 119.3–4 where AM substitutes "could have been brought about only by" for MS "could only have been"; and the same, again in Hennessy's typesetting, at 273.18–19, "could have been made available only when" for MS "could only have been". In Hector's stint at 311.5 AM reads "confining himself to fruit and vegetables only because . . ." whereas MS has "only confining". The final instance is a shade more grating: in Niles's stint at 49.24 MS reads, "Morally, she is only strong, I suspect, in society", changed in AM to "strong . . . only in society". (Here MS agreed with ENB 28.36.) The authority of these alterations is uncertain, for though they appear in the work of at least three compositors they might well represent conventional house-styling. Hawthorne himself was sometimes loose in his placement of "only" as may be seen at 47.32, "I only wish that my descriptive powers . . .", or 97.24–25, "It only brought human nature . . .", or 217.18–19, "and only wish that", all of which passed unaltered into the AM prints, here in the work of Schubarth, Hennessy and Schubarth respectively.[67] One might speculate that in the passage at 49.24, at least, the real difference in sense attracted the author's revisory eye in proof, or, if not that, perhaps his ear was offended by the jingle "Morally, she is only. . . ." Two slight pieces of evidence suggest the possibility that these changes are of a piece, and are authorial. First, if they were house-styling, then Hennessy, who would have made the alterations at 119.3–4 and 273.18–19 (and just possibly at 88.24), missed a similar opportunity at 97.24 and also at 113.34 ("if she could only find herself"). Such lapses are quite possible, of course. The second piece of evidence may be stronger: in MS at 125.21–22 during the writing (ENB offers no gloss here) Hawthorne at first had "I could only appropriate the minutest portion" but then changed it to read "appropriate only". Insofar as one swallow makes a summer, this piece of evidence may suggest that in proof, as well, Hawthorne was sometimes conscious of the colloquial informality of the loose use of "only" and was concerned to alter it to a syntax more suitable for print. These particular changes, then, may be accepted as presumably authorial even though some doubt must always linger.

[67] In twelve pertinent examples in the *English Notebooks,* seven have the formal usage (4.38, 26.18, 287.34, 329.7, 367.8, 394.21, 502.38) and five the informal (27.4, 28.36, 214.8, 478.27, 587.19). This proportion is revealing since ENB is more informal in style than OOH.

Another question of house style is raised by the two alterations at 144.27 (Hennessy) and 178.19 (Hector) of MS
"were" to "be": "Unless it be Salisbury Close" (here ENB,
467.29, reads "were" like MS), and "unless it be the Trinity
Ale of Cambridge". Since both changes are made in the same
construction, and both occur within the stints of different
workmen and in the proof of very early published sketches,
some ground may be found for viewing them as authoritative.
Changes of "that" to "which" and of "which" to "that" as in
Hector's stint at 156.30–31 and Schubarth's at 266.21 are too
mysterious to adjudicate with confidence; but the double
switch at 156.30–31 may perhaps suggest Hawthorne's own
hand in proof. Troublesome are cases where AM by the
addition of words omitted in MS achieves a formal parallelism. At least two of these represent variants in I from MS-
AM, as when "by" is added at 42.22 (Schubarth) to introduce the series "the cabs, hackney-coaches, and Bath-chairs"
parallel to the preceding "by the grocer and butcher"; and at
162.3 (Ignoto) in which the pronoun subject "I" is added
before "knew" to make an independent clause. Both of these
are so indifferent as to defy assignment of authority but may
perhaps pass provisionally as Hawthorne's. (Unfortunately,
ENB is of no help here.) An exact parallel to the second of
the above is found in Schubarth's stint at 267.10, where the
AM addition of "I" seems acceptable. Perhaps the alteration
that gives one most reason to trust these two pronominal
additions is that at 157.34 where, in the course of recasting
the sentence in other respects, Hawthorne took occasion to
add in AM the repeated pronoun "he" in the same
circumstances.

The other examples have no pattern. From the appearance
of "the" before "sultry" in ENB and the early manuscript and
the *Keepsake* form of "Uttoxeter," it is evident that its omission in MS at 134.14 is in error and restoration by AM

(Foynes) is correct, the more especially since the omission would lead quite wrongly to the personification of "materialism", for which there is no evidence, to correspond to the capitals of "Memory" and "Remorse". At 152.33 (Severance) the AM addition of "of" in "than of a river" (to complete preceding "more the appearance of a canal") is certainly correct (regardless of the agent), on the evidence of the full AM form in ENB (472.39–40). At 60.27 (where ENB is silent), it would seem that the AM addition (Hector) of "the" before "old oaken frame-work" is also correct. Unless this framework were to be associated with the preceding "the quaint gables" (and a comma separates the two), the framework must be an independent unit in the series "the thatch, the quaint gables, and the old oaken frame-work".[68] The slight syntactical rearrangement by which in Hennessy's stint at 236.32 the omission of MS "was" before "followed" tightens the construction seems acceptable, although Hennessy is not a particularly trustworthy witness. Under ordinary circumstances two other such variants might seem to be more suspicious, however. The first is in Hector's stint at 157.16, where *contra* ENB 475.28–29 and MS "the middle channel", AM reads conventionally "the middle of the channel"; in the second, at 166.8 (Severance), ENB (480.11) and MS "bleat" of sheep is changed to "bleating" to be in parallel, "I heard the lowing of cattle, too, and the bleating of sheep". On the other hand, both appear in "Pilgrimage to Old Boston," which, like "Near Oxford," also one of the three earliest sketches, has an unusually high proportion of variation between MS and AM. The association of these two early essays in heavy variation may be fortuitous (since not all of the differences appear to be authorial, and Hennessy's share in

[68] In support of this position, though in a different passage, see ENB 19.5–7: "We saw one cottage which I suppose was several hundred years old; it was of stone, filled into a wooden frame, the black oak of which was visible, like an external skeleton".

"Near Oxford" was a major one whereas many lines in "Pilgrimage" cannot be assigned and evaluated); but it is quite possible that Hawthorne decided in proof that the style he had copied in MS from ENB needed improvement, as apparently happened in "Pilgrimage" at 156.30–31 (ENB 475.14–16). Nevertheless, the drift to conventionality in both of these alterations does not induce confidence; and, in the case of the first, "the middle of the channel" appears to represent a misunderstanding: what Hawthorne seems to have had in mind in ENB and MS was, instead, that the measure was to the channel in the middle of the river.

Although with some doubt, it is possible to think that Hawthorne made the change of "bleat" to "bleating", and this may be tentatively accepted; but the apparent misunderstanding evident at 157.16 forces one to reject the AM variant.

Alterations are comparatively numerous in the forms of verbs. The two changes of "was" to "were" in a conditional clause introduced by "if" are probably authorial since that was Hawthorne's ordinary usage. Both occur in "Pilgrimage to Old Boston," and in the work of two different compositors, Hennessy and Severance respectively, though both are workmen whose alterations need to be viewed with care. The first, at 141.11, is buttressed by the fact that ENB (463.28) reads "were" despite MS "was"; the other, at 165.20, then, should also be approved.

More difficult are some changes in tense. Four of these occur in "Pilgrimage to Old Boston" and two in "Near Oxford," both of which have been remarked as containing an unusual number of minor AM alterations, leaving only one more, in "Civic Banquets"—but that appears to be a misreading. That Hawthorne took some care with tense may be indicated by what seems to be definitely an authorial change at 157.33–158.1, recasting the MS sentence, "He had met with several Americans, who, at various times, have come on pilgrimage to this place, and had been in correspondence . . .", to "He had met . . . had come on pilgrimages . . . and he had been". The origin of MS "have come" is clear from ENB (475.43–44), which is cast throughout in the present and perfect, suitable for a journal but not for the narrative of the sketch, "He has met with several Americans, who have made pilgrimage to the place, and has been in correspondence with others." Similarly, when at 146.29–31 AM (Severance) changes MS "and drove up . . . by a road rather less steep and abrupt than the one we previously climbed" to read "had previously climbed" in the print, the journal narrative had kept the preterite through-out—"drove . . . than that which led us thither"—whereas the sketch requires the distinction between preterite and past perfect. ENB (470.12) is less useful at 150.5–6 where MS remarks "but the old gateway was obstructed" but AM (Hector) returns to the ENB present in "is obstructed" as its version of ENB "is closed". Here Hawthorne seems to be taking great care by the change to indicate (as in the journal) that the obstruction was not merely a temporary one.

Such care gives one confidence in the other tense altera-tions in these sketches, mostly as resulting from the necessity to change the style of the journal, which had been followed too faithfully. The AM change of "striven" for MS "strove" at 154.29 restores Hawthorne's customary usage (see ENB 219.21); moreover, the "strove" of MS seems to be an inad-vertent slip: ENB (474.2–3) reads, "The poor ducklings ut-tered their baby quacks, and strove . . . to escape", whereas MS alters "uttered" to "had uttered" but inadvertently neg-lects to change the preterite "strove" to the past participle. In "Near Oxford" the AM (Hennessy) alteration to the preterite "sat" from the inappropriate MS perfect "have sometimes sat" at 171.2 is certainly required, and it resembles the change at

157.34 remarked above. At 171.22 the AM (Hennessy) change of MS "must inevitably be reminded" to "have been reminded" puts the Duke of Marlborough's wanderings in their proper time relation, as they had, indeed, been in ENB (407.5) "was reminded". Finally, in "Civic Banquets" at 329.24 the partly illegible word in MS, plus some possible sophistication, makes it probable that the compositor Green made an error in setting MS "has been under fire" as "had been".

Less certain is the authority for various changes between the singular and plural. Hawthorne could be misled by false attraction, as when, at 222.5–6, in MS he wrote "Choice of other amusements were at hand", corrected in AM (Hennessy), by whatever agent, to "was". But he seems not to have had entirely fixed principles about double subjects in cases where they might be thought of as collective singulars, at least in his initial composition. Thus MS at 45.9–10 has "whose aspect and movement in the water is most beautiful and stately" (ENB, 567.1, "was"); [69] at 264.3–4 "the English face and form is seldom statuesque"; [70] and at 268.21–23 "the quaintness of the earlier monuments, and the antique beauty of some of them, is what chiefly gives them value." In AM these appear as "are" in the work of Schubarth, Severance, and Schubarth, again, in order. It must be noted, however, that (as at 203.8–9, and in ENB) Hawthorne ordinarily used

[69] At 45.9, at least, it seems clear that the ENB construction encouraged the MS form. ENB (566.42–567.2) reads about the swans, "how beautiful and stately was their aspect and their movement in the water, and how infirm, disjointed, and decrepit was their gait, when they unadvisedly chose to emerge", in which verb precedes subject, whereas in the MS recasting the subject comes first, "the haunt of swans, whose aspect and movement in the water is most beautiful and stately—most infirm, disjointed, and decrepit, when, unadvisedly, they see fit to emerge".

[70] This example may be slightly suspect. In MS "and form" is added by wiping out original "is seldom" after "face", writing over it, and then continuing "is seldom". But since the verb was inscribed again after the addition of the double subject, the odds may favor its being intentional and not a mechanical repetition.

the plural in such circumstances, even to excess as in MS "a pinch or two of wayside dust have been moistened into nutritious soil" where MS reveals that "has" was originally written but then changed to "have". Whether or not he resolved his original uncertainty here in the proof stage (and this sketch "Recollections of a Gifted Woman" was corrected and revised with particular care), AM in a Hennessy section reads "has" (93.20). A more normal example occurs at 215.11–12. Here MS reads "my prime object was to lose my way" but as the result of a proof or copy revision AM provides "my prime purpose and achievement were". Although the absolute authority of each of these changes listed above cannot be demonstrated, it may be a reasonable conjecture that Hawthorne was concerned, in print, to achieve a formal correctness in concord. If so, we may perhaps free from the stigma of a Hennessy sophistication the alteration at 90.14–15 in "Recollections" of MS "Neither of these pretty features are often to be found in an English scene" to "Neither . . . is".[71] And to this may doubtfully (in the lack of evidence) be added the alteration at 226.27 (Hector) by which the "congregation listen" instead of "listens".

As with verbs, so with pronouns. On the evidence at 45.15–16 of what seems to be an authorial change in I back to the pronominal plurals of MS that had been altered in AM to singulars, Hawthorne was concerned with such correctness of reference. However, only one other comparable change appears, at 89.8–12 (Ignoto) where after a list of curiosities in Redfern's shop, Hawthorne remarks, in AM, "I doubt not that the signet-ring of Joseph's friend Pharaoh, or the Duke of Alva's leading-staff, or the dagger that killed the Duke of Buckingham, (all of which I have seen,) or any other almost

[71] The original verb may have been an overscrupulous attempt to achieve concord with two plural antecedents, "lakelets" and "brooks", which together make up the "pretty features". A change of MS "those" to "the" before "brooks" is discussed above, p. lxxvii.

incredible thing, might make its appearance." In MS the phrase is "their appearance", but "its" is accurate, and there is at least a chance that Hawthorne would have written "appearances" if the plural had been more than colloquially intended.

A few additions or omissions of pronouns appear. The addition in AM (Schubarth) at 219.10 of "its" (missing in MS) in "Tomorrow is born before its Yesterday is dead" may seem to be more likely authorial (perhaps repairing a slip in MS) than compositorial since the phrase is quite normal without it. A curious question of idiom arises twice in AM "Civic Banquets" at 329.32 (Green) and 335.4 (Schubarth) involving the omission of MS "it". Centenary 329.28–32 at first read in MS just as it was later to appear in AM: "this was one of the necessities of an office . . . beneath which I might be crushed . . . but could not shirk without cowardice and shame." However, the complete sentence is syntactically by no means so clear as this selection of the key words might suggest, and in MS Hawthorne interlined an "it" after "shirk", which, apparently, he thought better of in proof. For a full discussion, see the Textual Note to this passage; but the conclusion is that the odds favor the authority of the return in AM to the original MS version more than they do compositorial oversight of an interlined word. The case is strengthened, it would seem, by just about the same omission at 335.2–5 in the stint of a different compositor which reads in AM ". . . implored blessing on the food,—a ceremony which the English never omit, at a great dinner or a small one, yet consider, I fear, not so much a religious rite as a sort of preliminary relish before the soup." Here again, it would seem, Hawthorne found himself involved, as at 329.32, in a difficulty in reference. The point may be a small one whether MS "consider it" (for AM "consider") refers back to "blessing" or to "ceremony", but on the evidence Hawthorne seems to have cared enough to excise the word in proof and thereby to align "consider" with "omit" as having "ceremony" as subject. If, then, the omission of "it" in these two cases was not idiomatic, at least in the main, but structural, one may the more readily accept the AM addition of "it" after "to accept" at 162.2–5 (Ignoto) where in MS the sentence closed with "accept": "I had myself received an invitation, but I knew too well the pains and penalties incurred by an invited guest, at public festivals in England, to accept it." Oddly enough, the three cruxes concern the same general subject matter.

Variation in words that are almost doublets always causes problems. For instance, in Foynes's stint at 37.16–18 MS reads "The position is totally beyond the attainment of an American; here to-day . . . and gone tomorrow" where the alteration in AM of "here" to "there" seems justified as an authorial second thought. Foynes, in the first place, is an unusually accurate compositor; and the direction of the change in the word is from the familiar to the unfamiliar. In the second place, the "here" would necessarily be interpreted as referring exclusively to England, whereas Hawthorne was discussing the problem of consular appointments in all foreign countries. In reverse, at 107.25–27 (Hector), the point of view is that of England, from which Hawthorne is writing and hence the change is appropriate from MS "there" to AM "here" in the discussion of Miss Bacon's stay in England: "indeed, the object for which she had come hither, and which had kept her there for three years past". In this sentence MS "there" clashed with "hither", and "here" in AM restores the desired point of view. "These" and "those" changes are more difficult. At 140.21–23 AM (Hennessy) alters MS "those" to "these" in MS "farm-houses, and, once in a while, an old church-tower, were visible, but those are almost too common objects to be noticed in an English landscape." Contrary, at

235.23–25 AM (Hennessy) changes to "those" MS "these" in "I did not at first recognize an old acquaintance, but wondered what those golden crowns and images could be." In each case the AM reading seems more appropriate by a shade to the point of view, and there is perhaps some evidence to support authorial proof-correction when ENB (290.1) buttresses "these" as the point of view for the 235.25 reading, "I did not know what it was—these golden crowns, and glistening figures." It would seem that MS "these" was a slip in the inscription.[72]

Still more difficult is the variation between "in" and "into" since this is so largely indifferent to the sense and a question may well arise whether Hawthorne would trouble to alter one form to another in proof except where some real shade of meaning was involved. Yet, curiously, all three instances of such alteration occur in "Pilgrimage to Old Boston" and "Near Oxford," where, as already remarked, an unusual amount of minor variation exists between MS and AM. In "Near Oxford" at 184.29–30 AM (Sullivan) changes MS "in" to "into" when Hawthorne tears off a small piece of a mouldering banner and, in MS, "put it in my waistcoat pocket". Here ENB (417.18–19) reads "in my waistpocket" and so agrees with MS. In "Pilgrimage" MS "into" is twice changed to "in". At 151.25 MS "the many peaks into which the structure ascends" (ENB, 472.3, "into") becomes in AM (Ignoto) "in which"; and at 153.6 MS "blowing right into our teeth" (ENB, 473.2, "in") becomes AM (Severance) "in". It may be that in the 151.25 passage Hawthorne changed "into" to "in" because of the echo of the various other "to" words in the sentence, "its finer effect is due, I think, to the many peaks into which the structure ascends, and to the pinnacles which, as it were, repeat and re-echo

[72] Somewhat similar, perhaps, although with different motive, is the accepted change in I to "the wayside brooks" from MS-AM "those". See the discussion above, page lxxvii.

them into the sky." More likely, however, he could have become conscious that the "into" of "into the sky" refers to the pinnacles, not to the subsidiary peaks, and that the phrase "into which the structure ascends" gave a false impression of the final height which belonged, instead, to the pinnacles alone. If this is true, the change was indeed a meaningful one and must be accepted. Occurring in the work of a different compositor, and so very shortly after the acceptable 151.25 alteration, the AM change at 153.6 may perhaps be accepted also, though necessarily on different grounds. The earlier reading corrected an inaccuracy that in MS repeated the original infelicity of ENB; in 153.6, however, one would need to suppose that the MS departure from "in our teeth" of ENB, whether conscious or inadvertent, seemed too strong to Hawthorne as he read over the proof, and he came to prefer his original, which did not imply that the wind penetrated his teeth. No discernible cause can be detected in the alteration at 184.30. Of the three this is the most likely to be compositorial. But we have too little of Sullivan's setting to be able to speak with any confidence of his fidelity to copy, and it may just possibly be significant that the change appears in "Near Oxford" which shares various external and internal characteristics with "Pilgrimage to Old Boston." Wanting any criterion at all, we may as well accept AM here on faith but on little else except that, in general, Hawthorne favored "into" even when "in" would be appropriate, as at 202.22–24, "stowed higgledy-piggledy with coarse-natured rustics into this narrowness and filth"; or at 206.24–25, "dwellings that look from their windows directly down into the passing tide".[73] See also 197.29, 199.6, 200.4, 201.26, and especially 204.26, for typical examples.

More closely associated with idiom, perhaps, are four var-

---

[73] ENB, 504.43, "stowed higgledy-piggledy into this narrowness and filth"; and 507.32, "houses that look from their windows directly down into the river".

iants involving the preposition "at". The most unusual is the change in I to "at" at 320.8 when in AM (Hennessy) original MS "glimpses at" had been altered to "glimpses of". Unless this happens to be a compositorial variant (which is possible), we have evidence that even so late as the book proofs Hawthorne was not above making changes that would restore his own usage. The alteration at 183.31–32 of MS "the infernal cauldrons that seethe and bubble at the fires" to AM (Sullivan) "over the fires" seems unexceptionable in its superior accuracy (see also 305.29). The main difficulty comes with two variants in "Leamington Spa," both in the work of Niles, who is an unknown quantity. Although sophistication is possible, at 58.3–5, a superior sense is achieved when MS "small panes of glass . . . through which a by-gone age is peeping at the daylight" becomes in AM "out into the daylight", and an authorial proof-correction may be credited the better to contrast the internal gloom of the church with the daylight outside. This seems to be a matter of the point of view. From the outside in, one takes peeps *at*, as at 206.18–19, "I took peeps at the town"; but from the inside out one peeps *out*, as at 201.10–11 which reads in AM, "another little window that peeps out among the thatch" (ENB, 504.5, "peeps out from"). The case is altered at 55.31–32, however, where MS "I first saw an example of this at Bebington churchyard" is unusual enough, perhaps, to lead a compositor to the normal "in Bebington churchyard". Tentatively, therefore, this latter may be rejected in favor of MS. Unfortunately, ENB offers no gloss on any of these cruxes. Finally, at 168.11–12 the unusual MS phrase "The park-gate of Blenheim stands close at the end of the village-street" is wrongly altered in AM to "close to the end". The Textual Note to the phrase discusses its somewhat complex transmission.

Five other prepositional cruxes occur, in each case very likely authorial. In the first, at 8.34, I (Alexander) alters MS "out of" to "in" in order to avoid the usage "omit out of"; in the second, at 160.27–28, Queen Elizabeth's Secret-Book Hawthorne saw "in manuscript, written, for aught I know, by her own hand" (AM, Ignoto), a more vivid re-creation than "in her own hand" of MS (an apparent parallel being, perhaps, ENB, 421.18–19, "illuminated by the own hand of Raphael himself"). The third appears to correct a lapse in Hawthorne's characteristic use of "so" with the negative instead of "as": at 187.10–11 AM (Schubarth) has it that Pope's "spirit cannot be exorcised so long as the tower stands"; if the phrase had been, for instance, "will be present" then MS "as long as the tower stands" would have followed naturally.[74] Idiom seems to be involved in the AM (Ignoto) substitution of "for" for "of" in the MS phrase at 216.1–2 "facilities of repose". Second thoughts at 310.9–10 may have led to a shift in AM (Hector) from MS "towards" to AM "to" in MS "a slight distaste, at all events, if not an absolute repugnance towards merely spiritual nutriment." Here Hawthorne may have been willing to write "distaste towards" but felt that "repugnance" required "to".

At 166.16–17 the subordinating conjunction "that" of MS is omitted in AM (Severance), "and I fancied it was bidding me farewell"; the only analogue is the change made in I at 218.25–26 in which "that", missing in MS-AM, is restored in "I must needs confess that the noontide sun came down more fervently". The authority of either one is moot since Hawthorne might or might not choose to elide. By a hair one might prefer the directness gained at 166.16 and the better rhythm without "that" as in AM, but this would be much a subjective judgment. More confidence may attend the choice

---

[74] ENB (392.15, 392.40) holds two analogues, though not exact ones. Hawthorne writes of being presented with an edition of Longfellow "incredibly poor, as far as the pictures go"; but in the next entry he writes of "a fine sunny day, though not so very warm as many of the preceding days had been." He seldom deviates from this latter formula.

in another syntactical variation in which AM drops a somewhat loose use of "and". Within a few lines of two other variants that, small as they are, may be authorial (90.12 in I and 90.15 in AM), at 90.20 a very long MS compound sentence of considerable complexity in each clause is broken in AM (Hennessy) into two sentences by the omission of the linking "and" and the start of the second clause with the capital "To". This is a desirable improvement. Different in kind is the tightening at 230.6–8 (also set by Hennessy) in which AM omits "but" in MS "but yet" to read, "All this is but cold comfort for the evening of life, yet may compare rather favorably with the preceding portions of it". Still different is 344.23. In MS a syntactically correct parenthetical balanced phrase joined by "and" intervenes between the two parts of a compound object joined by "and". The result is rather chaotic, and perhaps as a result of the substitution of clarifying dashes for the original parenthetical commas, the "and" in the predicate is dropped so that the two countries join the two persons as part of one long resolution of the meaning of "He meant well by all parties".

Two questions arise of singular or plural with the genitive. At 51.19–20 "Lovers' Grove" in ENB (567.20) becomes "Lover's" in MS but remains "Lovers' " in AM (Niles). Since Hawthorne was secure in the singular of "Lover's Leap" in ENB (514.32) for a different resort, the care taken to restore the ENB plural for "Lovers' Grove" would seem to indicate the authorial touch, although we have no way of knowing, of course, whether Niles had followed MS in the original typesetting. It would be very odd if he had not. At 266.14 and again at 267.33, 268.32, and 270.11, MS (and ENB) "Poet's Corner" [75] becomes AM "Poets' Corner", all in the work of

[75] ENB 213.5, 218.23, 219.4, 220.35, 235.18, 235.33, 247.36, and 594.40.
Although the MS readings of 266.14, 267.33, and 268.32 are clearly in the genitive singular, the apostrophe at 270.11 might be construed as in

Schubarth. Both singular and plural were used interchangeably at the time although modern purists have succeeded in enforcing the plural. It is not impossible that in proof Hawthorne corrected himself, although on the evidence of ENB and of MS he had used the singular for several years preceding. One may guess, however, that under the circumstances the odds favor compositorial or editorial intervention here, and thus the mid-century texture of the sketch is better preserved by the original readings.

The remaining variants are a mixed bag. At 276.4–5 MS confuses the syntax and ends by having Leigh Hunt arm in arm "by" another poet. In AM (Hennessy) the necessary "with" is supplied but in the process the original parenthesis becomes obscured, and it is not until the proof of I that Hawthorne succeeded in saying what he wanted with some ease and grace. These alterations in AM, and again in I, appear to be authorial. The journal entry exposes an AM (Hector?) error at 155.13–14. MS had commented on the grim aspect of the Old Boston waiter, evidently a descendant of the old Puritans, "and quite as sour as those who peopled the daughter-city in New England." The ENB (474.15–16) entry is even more explicit: "and apparently a genuine descendant of the old Puritans of Boston, who peopled their daughter-city in New England." According to this evidence of Hawthorne's intent, the AM "people", which transfers the sourness from the past to the contemporary residents of Boston, is a compositorial slip. In "Civic Banquets" MS enumerates the guests as "three or four noblemen, several baronets, and plenty of knights, generals, members of Parliament, aldermen", whereas AM (Schubarth) omits "knights" at

---

the plural position. Hawthorne was not always careful about the position of his genitive apostrophes, and the present seems to be such a case, for it is not spaced quite so widely after the final "s" as it might be if intended to follow the word and instead seems to represent merely an inscription of the singular somewhat to the right of the customary position.

337.33–338.1. Since ENB (322.6–7) reads, "two or three noblemen, some baronets, members of parliament, aldermen", it is as possible that Hawthorne referred back to his journal in reading proof to check his facts from time to time and make necessary alterations as that we have here an eyeskip on the part of Schubarth. The journal is of some help with another variant only a few lines further at 337.6–8. Both in ENB (320.28–29) and in "Civic Banquets" at 334.30–31 the Lord Mayor of London's banqueting arrangement is described as two long tables extending down the length of the room and a cross-table, presumably at the head. When the time comes for the ceremony of the Lord Mayor's personal toast, MS reads, "And forthwith the Loving Cup—several of them, indeed, one on each side of the tables—came slowly down with all the antique ceremony." If at this point Hawthorne— as conjectured above—was consulting his journal in checking proof, he would have read in ENB (322.10–12), "And forthwith the Loving Cup (or rather two of them, on either side of the table) came slowly down, with all the antique ceremony." At first sight this seems to imply that only two Loving Cups circulated at the long tables (one on each side), and thus were passed from one of the long tables to the other; but since Hawthorne in the journal is writing from his own point of view at the long table at which he was seated, of course only two cups—one on each side—came down his table from the cross-table. Since it is highly probable that to expedite the ceremony two cups for each long table were provided, this would coincide with the MS reading with its plural "tables" and "several" cups. Oddly, perhaps, AM (Schubarth) omits the "one" before "on each side of the tables". Again, this might represent a Schubarth eyeskip, but there seems to be a relation between the change at 337.34 (perhaps triggered by reference to ENB) and here, which may also refer back to the journal. Thus it may be suggested that Hawthorne found his memory was confused about the exact number of cups, and that his journal entry was ambiguous to him seven years later since it referred only to his own table, and thus that he deliberately omitted the "one" in proof in order to be calculatedly vague and thereby escape a possible error.

At 161.8 and again at 162.15 AM (Ignoto) substitutes "antiquary" for MS "antiquarian" in the account of the bookseller of Old Boston. Earlier, at 157.31–32, both ENB (475.43) and MS (repeated by AM, Hector) had called this bookseller "a local antiquary", but in the two later passages MS seems to pick up the word "antiquarian" from ENB, although, in a final passage about Mr. Porter, not reproduced in MS, ENB (477.30) again calls him an antiquary. The evidence suggests that in the journal and MS Hawthorne was using the two words interchangeably as was frequent in his time; that he was not aware of the distinction by which *antiquarian* may be associated with old books and *antiquary* with antiquities in general is clearly indicated by the ENB use of "antiquarian" where "antiquary" would be more suitable, and the reverse. That a compositor would correct an author on this fine point is not impossible of course, but the revision to the more correct word throughout may reasonably be assigned to the author unless we are to conjecture editorial intervention of this nature in the proofs.[76]

For the remaining, criteria are wanting to apply to a differentiation. At 217.12 perhaps the lure of the conventional proved too much for Schubarth when MS "on one hand" becomes AM "on the one hand".[77] For the others an editor

[76] See below for the discussion of whether Hawthorne did or did not read proof on "Pilgrimage to Old Boston."

[77] The parallel is not exact, but one can quote at 66.16–17 MS-AM "here a cottage and there a villa, on one side a wooded plantation, and on the other a rich field of grass".

may as well throw himself on the general authority of AM and trust to the odds—as already established—that the general majority of AM variants from MS seem to be authoritative, by a proportion of at least two to one. Certain of these remaining variants show MS and ENB agreement, but it is always possible, of course, to conceive that Hawthorne found the journal informality less suitable for print when he saw his words in proof; and indeed some examples of this nature have been illustrated above. At 146.7, in this last group, AM (Severance) logically reads "It is vain to attempt" instead of ENB-MS "in vain"; at 153.17–18 ENB-MS "throughout the whole distance" becomes in AM (Hector) "through"; at 163.23–24 ENB-MS "through yet a smaller staircase" becomes in AM (Ignoto) "a yet smaller"; at 168.27–28 "the great, knotted, aslantwise trunks of the old oaks" of ENB-MS reads "slanting trunks" in AM (Hennessy); at 234.17 MS follows ENB in the phrase "the three first days of Easter" whereas AM (Hennessy) reads "the first three days"; the banners in Chelsea Hospital in ENB-MS "rot away from" their staves at 257.4 but "rot from" in AM (Ignoto).[78] The rest have no journal gloss. MS "no more distinguished congregation" at 54.12 reads "distinguished a" in AM (Curtis); at 145.24–25 the doubtful "the spiritual impression of its beauty remains so strongly" is altered in AM (Severance) to "strong"; a useful but not entirely necessary "that" is added in AM (Hennessy) at 230.5–6, missing in MS, in "steamers, which have made the sea another element than that they used to be acquainted with." At 315.16, MS "picture of Countess Godiva" reads in AM (Hector) "the Countess"; and at 330.18 MS quaint "it once or twice times happened" becomes "twice happened" in AM (Green).

---

[78] ENB references: 468.15 "in vain", 473.17 "throughout", 478.37 "yet a", 405.37 "aslantwise", 289.39 "three first", and 250.30 "rot away from".

Two problems remain that concern the editing of *Our Old Home*. The first turns on the question whether Hawthorne ever read proof for "Pilgrimage to Old Boston." On May 7, 1862, he sent Fields an article "Chiefly About War-Matters" for the *Atlantic Monthly* with an accompanying letter that begins: "Here is the article. I had to leave out a great deal; else it would have grown into a book—and it is already too long. You must remember to send me a proof—which you did not do, the last time."

The last article of Hawthorne's to appear in the *Atlantic* before the date of this letter is "Pilgrimage to Old Boston." But it is unlikely that the letter can refer to this sketch. Between the manuscript and the AM text of "Pilgrimage" occur forty substantive variants.[79] One of these can be dismissed immediately as having no bearing on the problem since it corrects in AM what is an obvious MS error at 146.3, the omission of "been". Six more can also be dismissed: the first two merely house-style Hawthorne's "subtle" to "subtile" at 140.31, and "a" to "an" at 151.31; three at 155.13, 163.21, and 163.29 are definitely AM errors; and the sixth at 157.16 is probably an error too. Of the remaining thirty-three, twenty-six are small stylistic changes, whether of syntax, usage, or expression, and may be thought debatable although most have been considered and on the evidence assigned to Hawthorne.[80] Regardless of these, however, there remain seven changes that in ordinary course would be assigned to no other agent than the author. These are the AM sub-

---

[79] Centenary 140.22, 140.31, 141.9–11, 144.27, 145.25, 146.3, 146.7, 146.28, 146.30, 147.19, 148.29, 150.5, 150.6, 150.19, 151.25, 151.31, 152.33, 153.6, 153.9, 153.9, 153.17, 154.29, 155.13, 156.30, 156.31, 157.16, 157.34, 160.28, 161.8, 161.13, 162.3, 162.5, 162.15, 163.21, 163.23–24, 163.29, 165.17, 165.20, 166.8, 166.16.

[80] Centenary 140.22, 141.9–11, 144.27, 145.25, 146.7, 146.30, 148.29, 150.6, 151.25, 152.33, 153.6, 153.9, 153.9, 153.17, 154.29, 156.30, 156.31, 157.34, 160.28, 162.3, 162.5. 163.23–24, 165.17, 165.20, 166.8, 166.16.

stitutions of "term" for "phrase" at 146.28; "now" for "since" (147.19); "proximity" for "vicinity" (150.5); "mould of a decaying" for "decay of a mouldering" (150.19); "the hand" for "the own hand" (161.13); and "antiquary" for "antiquarian" (161.8, 162.15).

If these are, at least in the main, not authorial, then a truly extraordinary attention would have been paid in proof to this sketch by the *Atlantic* editors. What assistance these editors generally gave to the author in other matters than house styling, doubtfully, and the marking of mechanical error by the printer, is unknown of course. But if Hawthorne did not read proof on "Pilgrimage," they were responsible for these seven differences plus whatever ones of the less significant twenty-six that cannot be imputed to the compositors. The indication of a difficulty in the acceptance of such a general proposition is not disproof, however. On the other hand, concrete evidence suggests that the interference of a hypothetical editor is no more to be detected in "Pilgrimage to Old Boston" than in the other sketches. As has been remarked, both "Pilgrimage" and "Near Oxford," the two earliest sketches for which manuscripts are preserved, set themselves apart from the rest of the series, mostly written when Hawthorne had decided on eventual book publication, in the higher proportion of substantive variation found in them between MS and AM. In part one may put this down to Hawthorne's greater care, perhaps, with those later sketches that he knew were to be published between covers. But the main reason seems to be Hawthorne's further experience with the process of turning his journal entries into publishable essays. To be more precise, comparison of the way in which Hawthorne mined his journals for the earliest "Some of the Haunts of Burns" and then for "Near Oxford" and "Pilgrimage to Old Boston" indicates in these sketches a considerably greater reliance on an exact transcript or close paraphrase, whereas the later sketches seem to free themselves progressively from this considerable dependence until in "Outside Glimpses of English Poverty," and to only a slighter extent, perhaps, in "Civic Banquets," Hawthorne becomes relatively free in his treatment of journal entries, not only in respect to the addition of material not present in the journal, but also, very frequently, in the treatment of the material that he was using as a basis for his reworking. Even such an intermediate sketch as "Recollections of a Gifted Woman" shows this progression.

The effect of the less formal journal style, thus, is more prominent in the manuscripts of "Near Oxford" and "Pilgrimage" when Hawthorne was in the earlier stages of learning by experience how best to use his factual records for literary purposes. This stylistic influence, insufficiently felt when writing the manuscripts and thus requiring more attention in proof when the roughnesses were seen in cold type, seems to differentiate these two essays from their successors and to account for the significantly greater number of minor changes that characterize them. The two offer a relatively accurate basis for comparison with one another, therefore; and if "Near Oxford" does not exhibit more evidences of authorial proof-alteration than "Pilgrimage to Old Boston," the inference may be drawn that the circumstances were the same that underlay the proofreading of each.

In contrast to the forty substantive variants between AM and MS of "Pilgrimage," "Near Oxford" has thirty-five.[81] Of these, two correct MS errors (168.4 and 190.3), one (174.12) is a house-styling change of "further" to "farther" as is 180.4 ("engraved" for "engraven"), and eight

---

[81] Centenary 168.2, 168.4, 168.11, 168.27–28, 169.24, 171.2, 171.22, 172.20, 173.2, 173.17, 174.12, 174.16, 176.18, 178.18, 178.19, 179.31, 180.4, 180.15–16, 180.16–17, 181.6, 182.25, 183.16, 183.26, 183.31, 183.32, 184.6, 184.30, 187.10, 187.13–14, 188.16, 188.20, 188.22, 190.3, 190.17, 192.9.

represent AM errors (168.2, 169.24, 173.2, 178.18, 179.31, 184.6, 188.16, 190.17). Of the remaining twenty-three, fourteen are small, stylistic changes.[82] The residue of nine can be attributed to Hawthorne in AM proof: "houses" for "homes" (172.20), "station" for "life" (174.16), "variety capable" (176.18), "gentleman" for "person" (180.15–16), "unpruned" for "untrimmed" (181.6), "wide air-holes" for "apertures" (182.25), "humorous" omitted in MS (183.26), "to inhabit" for "for a study" (187.13–14), and "feature" for "ingredient" (192.9).

When one considers that these sketches are similar in length (1,009 book lines for "Pilgrimage" and 940 for "Near Oxford" [including a six-line footnote]), these statistics show essentially the same number of proofreading changes, and the kind does not materially differ. Indeed, if a discrepancy occurs it is that rather more variants appear in "Pilgrimage" than in "Near Oxford" if the proofreading had been exclusively editorial in the former. The eight changes in "Near Oxford" (as against seven in "Pilgrimage") which seem almost certainly non-editorial are not so remarkably different in their nature as to lead to any serious suspicion that a different agent was responsible for each. Finally, sufficient evidence seems to exist, first, to explain the peculiarity of the amount of proofreading change in "Near Oxford" (and by extension in "Pilgrimage") and, second, to suggest that Hawthorne went over "Near Oxford" in proof so that the two sketches cannot be associated as both untouched by the author. At the foot of the last page of the Oxford manuscript appears the following note: "(I have not read this over since writing it out;—so send me a proof-sheet. N. H.)." Except for the apparent need for a special request for a proof-sheet, which is rather odd, the fact

---

[82] Centenary 168.11, 168.27–28, 171.2, 171.22, 173.17, 178.19, 180.16–17, 183.16, 183.31, 183.32, 184.30, 187.10, 188.16, 188.22.

that Hawthorne particularly wanted to review the sketch in proof, because he had not gone over it thoroughly in manuscript, is significant and may apply as well to the next essay, "Pilgrimage to Old Boston."

Only one conclusion can be drawn, therefore. The evidence in the comparison of the number and the nature of the variants not only in "Near Oxford" but also in the other sketches does not offer grounds for believing that any difference existed in the proofreading of "Pilgrimage" from that of the others, various of which have external evidence for the receipt of proofs. In some manner Hawthorne must have been mistaken in his letter to Fields, if he was actually referring to "Pilgrimage" as the piece that was not sent in proof "the last time".

The transmission of the text of "Lichfield and Uttoxeter" has had an effect on the editorial procedure that has been adopted. The original manuscript of "Uttoxeter" (described above, page lvi) preserved in the Pierpont Morgan Library shows printer's markings that relate it to its first publication in the English gift annual *The Keepsake* (1857), pages 108–13. Collation discloses that the text in *Harper's New Monthly Magazine*, XIV (April, 1857), 639–41, was set from that in *The Keepsake* with no authorial correction in the copy. For instance the error originating in *The Keepsake* at Centenary 482.35 of "market-days" for manuscript "market-day" was faithfully transmitted to *Harper's*. Although *Harper's* corrected the finicky *Keepsake* error of "Bulls' Heads" at 484.6 for manuscript "Bull's Heads," it created several new wrong readings and restyled the text. It is not likely that Hawthorne saw the proof for the *Harper's* publication. At any rate, when Hawthorne revised his sketch for the book, he added the extensive early section on Lichfield; but when he came to Uttoxeter he had the *Keepsake* (not the *Harper's*) pages before him.[83] In some part, therefore, the manuscript for *Our Old Home* in this section either copies, or is influenced by, the texture of the *Keepsake* styling so that it inadvertently departs from the more authoritative original accidentals of the "Uttoxeter" manuscript. Hence although the 1863 MS of "Lichfield and Uttoxeter" is the prime authority for the new material in the final form of the sketch, and is the copy-text for the present edition throughout, the contamination from the *Keepsake* text that was produced in it when Hawthorne was writing the Uttoxeter section gives it only secondary authority in respect to the accidentals when the two texts coincide. Under these conditions, the Centenary text restores the purity of Hawthorne's original accidentals from the Pierpont Morgan "Uttoxeter" manuscript in all cases when the 1863 MS repeats the *Keepsake* accidentals that depart from the Morgan manuscript. This manuscript alone can represent his true intentions and usage.

In "Lichfield and Uttoxeter" we have perhaps the most complex of the copy-text problems in that emendation in the Taylor MS copy-text can come from the Morgan manuscript as well as from the *Keepsake* version (although actually Hawthorne seems not to have changed a reading in its proof) and also from the book text.

The remaining copy-text procedures call for standard treatment. In all sketches where manuscripts are preserved, these manuscripts are made the copy-text and are emended in respect to the substantives only by the substitution of revisions and corrections that Hawthorne may be conjectured to have added both in the proof of the *Atlantic Monthly*[84] and in the

---

[83] The main evidence is the perpetuation in MS of the *Keepsake* error "Bulls' Heads" at 135.3; but the relation of the accidentals in MS and *Keepsake* is much closer than in MS and *Harper's*.

[84] "Consular Experiences" and "Lichfield and Uttoxeter" did not appear in the *Atlantic* before book publication, and for these Hawthorne's proof-revisions can be drawn only from the first edition.

marked AM pages sent to the book printer or in the book proof itself. The MSS, of course, are the major authority for the Centenary accidentals. These have been altered only when MS seems to be in error or else in need of such styling for consistency as marks the editorial procedures for the Centenary Edition explained in the statement of textual principles printed in the first four volumes of romances. Two sketches— "Some of the Haunts of Burns" and "Outside Glimpses of English Poverty"—are not known to be preserved in manuscript. For these the *Atlantic Monthly* versions are the copytext with such revisions from the book as appear to be made by Hawthorne in the marked printer's copy or in proof. In addition, the *English Notebooks* have been used for emendation of the AM accidentals when the journals appear to preserve Hawthorne's usual characteristics more faithfully than the print and may be presumed to represent what would have stood in the lost manuscripts. The material for "Outside Glimpses" in the journal is so sparse and scattered that not a great deal of use could be made of the *Notebooks* evidence; but the Burns sketch has benefited materially from the references to the accidentals of the journals. Finally, those parts of "About Warwick" for which the manuscript has not been preserved have utilized the *Atlantic Monthly* as copy-text, supplemented by the evidence of the journal accidentals, the parallels with the accidentals in the extant parts of the manuscript, and the revisions in the book substantives.

The text of the early essay "Uttoxeter" is edited from the manuscript as copy-text with reference to the printed versions in *The Keepsake* and in *Harper's Magazine,* and is printed in an appendix with its own apparatus.

F. B.

OUR OLD HOME

To

FRANKLIN PIERCE,

AS A SLIGHT MEMORIAL OF A COLLEGE FRIENDSHIP, PROLONGED
THROUGH MANHOOD, AND RETAINING ALL ITS VITALITY
IN OUR AUTUMNAL YEARS,

This Volume is Inscribed

By NATHANIEL HAWTHORNE.

TO A FRIEND

I HAVE NOT ASKED your consent, my dear General, to the foregoing inscription, because it would have been no inconsiderable disappointment to me had you withheld it; for I have long desired to connect your name with some book of mine in commemoration of an early friendship that has grown old between two individuals of widely dissimilar pursuits and fortunes. I only wish that the offering were a worthier one than this volume of sketches, which certainly are not of a kind likely to prove interesting to a Statesman in retirement, inasmuch as they meddle with no matters of policy or government, and have very little to say about the deeper traits of national character. In their humble way, they belong entirely to aesthetic literature, and can achieve no higher success than to represent to the American reader a few of the external aspects of English scenery and life, especially those that are touched with the antique charm to which our countrymen are more susceptible than are the people among whom it is of native growth.

I once hoped, indeed, that so slight a volume would not be all that I might write. These and other sketches, with which, in a somewhat rougher form than I have given them here, my Journal was copiously filled, were intended for the side-scenes, and back-grounds, and exterior adornment, of a work of fiction, of which the plan had imperfectly developed itself in my mind, and into which I ambitiously proposed to convey more of various modes of truth than I could have grasped by a direct effort. Of course, I should not mention this abortive project, only that it has been utterly thrown aside, and will never now be accomplished. The Present, the Immediate, the Actual, has proved too potent for me. It takes away not only my scanty faculty, but even my desire for imaginative composition, and leaves me sadly content to scatter a thousand peaceful fantasies upon the hurricane that is sweeping us all along with it, possibly, into a Limbo where our nation and its polity may be as literally the fragments of a shattered dream as my unwritten Romance. But I have far better hopes for our dear country; and for my individual share of the catastrophe I afflict myself little, or not at all, and shall easily find room for the abortive work on a certain ideal shelf, where are reposited many other shadowy volumes of mine, more in number, and very much superior in quality, to those which I have succeeded in rendering actual.

To return to these poor sketches, some of my friends have told me that they evince an asperity of sentiment towards the English people which I ought not to feel, and which it is highly inexpedient to express. The charge surprises me, because, if it be true, I have written from a shallower mood than I supposed. I seldom came into personal relations with an Englishman without beginning to like him, and feeling my favorable impressions wax stronger with the progress of the acquaintance. I never stood in an English crowd without being conscious of hereditary sympathies. Nevertheless, it is undeniable that an American is continually thrown upon his national antagonism by some acrid quality in the moral atmosphere of England. These people think so loftily of themselves, and so contemptuously of everybody else, that it requires more generosity than I possess to keep always in perfectly good humor with them. Jotting down the little acrimonies of the moment in my Journal, and transferring them thence (when they happened to be tolerably well expressed) to these pages, it is very possible that I may have said things which a profound observer of national character would hesitate to sanction, though never any, I verily believe, that had not more or less of truth. If they be true, there is no reason in the world why they should not be said. Not an Englishman of them all ever spared America, for courtesy's sake or kindness; nor, in my opinion, would it contribute in the least to our mutual advantage and comfort if we were to besmear one another all over with butter and honey. At any rate, we must not judge of an Englishman's susceptibilities by our own, which, likewise, I trust, are of a far less sensitive texture than formerly.

And now farewell, my dear friend, and excuse, if you think it needs any excuse, the freedom with which I thus publicly assert a personal friendship between a private individual, and a Statesman, who has filled what was then the most august position in the world. But I dedicate my book to the Friend, and shall defer a colloquy with the Statesman till some calmer and sunnier hour. Only this let me say, that, with the record of your life in my memory, and with a sense of your character in my deeper consciousness as among the few things that time has left as it found them, I need no assurance that you continue faithful forever to that grand idea of an irrevocable Union, which, as you once told me, was the earliest that your brave father taught you. For other men there may be a choice of paths—for you, but one; and it rests among my certainties that no man's loyalty is more stedfast, no man's hopes or apprehensions on behalf of our national existence more deeply heartfelt, or more closely intertwined with his possibilities of personal happiness, than those of FRANKLIN PIERCE.

THE WAYSIDE, July 2ᵈ, 1863.

· 5 ·

OUR OLD HOME

CONSULAR EXPERIENCES

THE CONSULATE of the United States, in my day, was located in Washington Buildings, (a shabby and smoke-stained edifice of four stories high, thus illustriously named in honor of our national establishment,) at the lower corner of Brunswick-street, contiguous to the Goree Arcade, and in the neighborhood of some of the oldest docks. This was by no means a polite or elegant portion of England's great commercial city, nor were the apartments of the American official so splendid as to indicate the assumption of much consular pomp on his part. A narrow and ill-lighted staircase gave access to an equally narrow and ill-lighted passage-way on the first-floor, at the extremity of which, surmounting a door-frame, appeared an exceedingly stiff pictorial representation of the Goose and Gridiron, according to the English idea of those ever-to-be-honored symbols. The staircase and passage-way were often thronged, of a morning, with a set of beggarly and piratical-looking scoundrels, (I do no wrong to our own countrymen in styling them so, for not one in twenty was a genuine American,) purporting to belong to our mercantile marine, and chiefly composed of Liverpool Blackballers and the scum of every maritime nation on earth; such being the seamen by whose assistance we then disputed the navigation of the world with England. These specimens of a most unfortunate class of people were shipwrecked crews in quest of bed, board, and clothing, invalids asking permits for the hospital, bruised and bloody wretches complaining of ill-treatment by their officers, drunkards, desperadoes, vagabonds, and cheats, perplexingly intermingled with an uncertain proportion of reasonably honest men. All of them (save here and there a poor devil of a kidnapped landsman in his shore-going rags) wore red flannel shirts, in which they had sweltered or shivered throughout the voyage, and all required consular assistance in one form or another.

Any respectable visitor, if he could make up his mind to elbow a passage among these sea-monsters, was admitted into an outer office, where he found more of the same species, explaining their respective wants or grievances to the Vice-Consul and clerks, while their shipmates awaited their turn outside the door. Passing through this exterior court, the stranger was ushered into an inner privacy, where sat the Consul himself, ready to give personal attention to such peculiarly difficult and more important cases as might demand the exercise of (what we will courteously suppose to be) his own higher judicial or administrative sagacity.

It was an apartment of very moderate size, painted in imitation of oak, and duskily lighted by two windows looking across a by-street at the rough brick-side of an immense cotton ware-house, a plainer and uglier structure than ever was built in America. On the walls of the room hung a large map of the United States, (as they were, twenty years ago, but seem little likely to be, twenty years hence,) and a similar one of Great Britain, with its territory so provokingly compact that we may expect it to sink sooner than sunder. Farther adornments were some rude engravings of our naval victories in the war of 1812, together with the Tennessee State House, and a Hudson river steamer, and a colored, life-size lithograph of General Taylor, with an honest hideousness of aspect, occupying the place of honor above the mantel-piece. On the top of a book-case stood a fierce and terrible bust of General Jackson, pilloried in a military collar which rose above his ears, and frowning forth immitigably at any Englishman who might happen to cross the threshold. I am afraid, however, that the truculence of the old General's expression was utterly thrown away on this stolid and obdurate race of men; for, when they occasionally inquired whom this work of art represented, I was mortified to find that the younger ones had never heard of the battle of New Orleans, and that their elders had either forgotten it altogether, or contrived to mis-remember, and twist it wrong end foremost into something like an English victory! They have caught from the old Romans (whom they resemble in so many other characteristics) this excellent method of keeping the national glory intact by sweeping all defeats and humiliations clean out of their memory. Nevertheless, my patriotism forbade me to take down either the bust or the pictures, both because it seemed no more than right that an American Consulate (being a little patch of our nationality imbedded into the soil and institutions of England) should fairly represent the American taste in the fine arts, and because these decorations reminded me so delightfully of an old-fashioned American barber's shop.

One truly English object was a barometer hanging on the wall, generally indicating one or another degree of disagreeable weather, and so seldom pointing to Fair, that I began to consider that portion of its circle as made superfluously. The deep chimney, with its grate of bituminous coal, was English too, as was also the chill temperature that sometimes called for a fire at mid-summer, and the foggy or smoky atmosphere which often, between November and March, compelled me to set the gas a-flame at noon-day. I am not aware of omitting anything important in the above descriptive inventory, unless it be some book-shelves filled with octavo volumes of the American Statutes, and a good many pigeon-holes stuffed with dusty communications from former Secretaries of State, and other official documents of similar value, constituting part of the archives of the Consulate, which I might have done my successor a favor by flinging into the coal-grate. Yes; there was one other article demanding prominent notice—the consular copy of the New Testament, bound in black morocco, and greasy, I fear, with a daily succession of perjured kisses; at least, I can hardly hope that all the ten thousand oaths, administered by me between two breaths, to all sorts of people and on all manner of worldly business, were reckoned by the swearer as if taken at his soul's peril.

Such, in short, was the dusky and stifled chamber in which I spent wearily a considerable portion of more than four good years of my existence. At first, to be quite frank with the reader, I looked upon it as not altogether fit to be tenanted by the commercial representative of so great and prosperous a country as the United States then were; and I should speedily have transferred my head-quarters to airier and loftier apartments, except for the prudent consideration that my Government would have left me thus to support its dignity at my own personal expense. Besides, a long line of distinguished predecessors, of whom the latest is now a gallant general under the Union banner, had found the locality good enough for them; it might certainly be tolerated, therefore, by an individual so little ambitious of external magnificence as myself. So I settled quietly down, striking some of my roots into such soil as I could find, adapting myself to circumstances, and with so much success, that, though from first to last I hated the very sight of the little room, I should yet have felt a singular kind of reluctance in changing it for a better.

Hither, in the course of my incumbency, came a great variety of visitors, principally Americans, but including almost every other nationality on earth, especially the distressed and downfallen ones like those of Poland and Hungary. Italian bandits, (for so they looked,) proscribed conspirators from Old Spain, Spanish Americans, Cubans who professed to have stood by Lopez and narrowly escaped his fate, scarred French soldiers of the second Republic—in a word, all sufferers, or pretended ones, in the cause of Liberty, all people homeless in the widest sense, those who never had a country or had lost it, those whom their native land had impatiently flung off for planning a better system of things than they were born to—a multitude of these, and, doubtless, an equal number of jail-birds outwardly of the same feather, sought the American Consulate, in hopes of at least a bit of bread, and perhaps to beg a passage to the blessed shores of Freedom. In most cases there was nothing, and in any case distressingly little, to be done for them; neither was I of a proselyting disposition, nor desired to make my Consulate a nucleus for the vagrant discontents of other lands. And yet it was a proud thought, a forcible appeal to the sympathies of an American, that these unfortunates claimed the privileges of citizenship in our Republic on the strength of the very same noble misdemeanors that had rendered them outlaws to their native despotisms. So I gave them what small help I could. Methinks the true patriots and martyr-spirits of the whole world should have been conscious of a pang near the heart, when a deadly blow was aimed at the vitality of a country, which they have felt to be their own in the last resort.

As for my countrymen, I grew better acquainted with many of our national characteristics, during those four years, than in all my preceding life. Whether brought more strikingly out by the contrast with English manners, or that my Yankee friends assumed an extra peculiarity from a sense of defiant patriotism, so it was that their tones, sentiments, and behavior, even their figures and cast of countenance, all seemed chiselled in sharper angles than ever I had imagined them to be, at home. It impressed me with an odd idea of having some-how lost the property of my own person, when I occasionally heard one of them speaking of me as "my Consul"! They often came to the Consulate in parties of half-a-dozen or more, on no business whatever, but merely to subject their public servant to a rigid examination, and see how he was getting on with his duties. These interviews were rather formidable, being characterized by a certain stiffness which I felt to be sufficiently irksome at the moment, though it looks laughable enough in the retrospect. It is my firm belief that these fellow-citizens, possessing a native tendency to organization, generally halted outside of the door to elect a speaker, chair-man, or moderator, and thus approached me with all the formalities of a deputation from the American people. After salutations on both sides—abrupt, awful, and severe on their part, and deprecatory on mine—and the national ceremony of shaking hands being duly gone through with, the interview proceeded by a series of calm and well-considered questions or remarks from the spokesman, (no other of the guests vouch-safing to utter a word,) and diplomatic responses from the Consul, who sometimes found the investigation a little more searching than he liked. I flatter myself, however, that, by much practice, I attained considerable skill in this kind of intercourse, the art of which lies in passing off common-places for new and valuable truths, and talking trash and emptiness in such a way that a pretty acute auditor might mistake it for something solid. If there be any better method of dealing with such junctures—when talk is to be created out of nothing, and within the scope of several minds at once, so that you cannot apply yourself to your interlocutor's individuality—I have not learned it.

Sitting, as it were, in the gateway between the old world and the new, where the steamers and packets landed the greater part of our wandering countrymen, and received them again when their wanderings were done, I saw that no people on earth have such vagabond habits as ourselves. The Continental races never travel at all, if they can help it; nor does an Englishman ever think of stirring abroad unless he has the money to spare, or proposes to himself some definite advantage from the journey; but it seemed to me that nothing was more common than for a young American deliberately to spend all his resources in an aesthetic peregrination about Europe, returning with pockets nearly empty to begin the world in earnest. It happened, indeed, much oftener than was at all agreeable to myself, that their funds held out just long enough to bring them to the door of my Consulate, where they entered, as if with an undeniable right to its shelter and protection, and required at my hands to be sent home again. In my first simplicity—finding them gentlemanly in manners, passably educated, and only tempted a little beyond their means by a laudable desire of improving and refining themselves, or, perhaps, for the sake of getting better artistic instruction in music, painting, or sculpture, than our country could supply—I sometimes took charge of them on my private responsibility, since our Government gives itself no trouble about its stray children, except the seafaring class. But after a few such experiments, discovering that none of these estimable and ingenuous young men, however trustworthy they might appear, ever dreamed of re-imbursing the Consul, I deemed it expedient to take another course with them. Applying myself to some friendly shipmaster, I engaged homeward passages on their behalf, with the understanding that they were to make themselves serviceable on shipboard; and I remember several very pathetic appeals from painters and musicians, touching the damage which their artistic fingers were likely to incur from handling the ropes. But my observation of so many heavier troubles left me very little tenderness for their finger-ends. In time, I grew to be reasonably hard-hearted, though it never was quite possible to leave a countryman with no shelter save an English poor-house, when, as he invariably averred, he had only to set foot on his native soil to be possessed of ample funds. It was my ultimate conclusion, however, that American ingenuity may be pretty safely left to itself, and that, one way or another, a Yankee vagabond is certain to turn up at his own threshold, if he has any, without help of a Consul, and perhaps be taught a lesson of foresight that may profit him hereafter.

Among these stray Americans, I met with no other case so remarkable as that of an old man, who was in the habit of visiting me once in a few months, and soberly affirmed that he had been wandering about England more than a quarter of a century, (precisely twenty-seven years, I think,) and all the while doing his utmost to get home again. Herman Melville, in his excellent novel or biography of "Israel Potter," has an idea somewhat similar to this.

The individual now in question was a mild and patient, but very ragged and pitiable old fellow, shabby beyond description, lean and hungry-looking, but with a large and somewhat red nose. He made no complaint of his ill-fortune, but only repeated in a quiet voice, with a pathos of which he was himself evidently unconscious—"I want to get home to Ninety-second street, Philadelphia." He described himself as a printer by trade, and said that he had come over, when he was a younger man, in the hope of bettering himself, and for the sake of seeing the Old Country, but had never since been rich enough to pay his homeward passage. His manner and accent did not quite convince me that he was an American, and I told him so; but he stedfastly affirmed—"Sir, I was born and have lived in Ninety-second street, Philadelphia," and then went on to describe some public edifices and other local objects with which he used to be familiar, adding, with a simplicity that touched me very closely—"Sir, I had rather be there than here!" Though I still manifested a lingering doubt, he took no offence, replying with the same mild depression as at first, and insisting again and again on Ninety-second street. Up to the time when I saw him, he still got a little occasional job-work at his trade, but subsisted mainly on such charity as he met with in his wanderings, shifting from place to place continually, and asking assistance to convey him to his native land. Possibly, he was an impostor, one of the multitudinous shapes of English vagabondism, and told his falsehood with such powerful simplicity because, by many repetitions, he had convinced himself of its truth. But if, as I believe, the tale was fact, how very strange and sad was this old man's fate! Homeless on a foreign shore, looking always towards his country, coming again and again to the point whence so many were setting sail for it—so many who would soon tread in Ninety-second street—losing, in this long series of years, some of the distinctive characteristics of an American, and at last dying and surrendering his clay to be a portion of the soil whence he could not escape in his lifetime!

He appeared to see that he had moved me, but did not attempt to press his advantage with any new argument or any varied form of entreaty. He had but scanty and scattered thoughts in his gray head, and in the intervals of those, like the refrain of an old ballad, came in the monotonous burden of his appeal—"If I could only find myself in Ninety-second street, Philadelphia!" But even his desire of getting home had ceased to be an ardent one, (if, indeed, it had not always partaken of the dreamy sluggishness of his character,) although it remained his only locomotive impulse, and perhaps the sole principle of life that kept his blood from actual torpor.

The poor old fellow's story seemed to me almost as worthy of being chanted in immortal song as that of Odysseus or

Evangeline. I took his case into deep consideration, but dared not incur the moral responsibility of sending him across the sea, at his age, after so many years of exile, when the very tradition of him had passed away, to find his friends dead, or forgetful, or irretrievably vanished, and the whole country become more truly a foreign land to him than England was now, and even Ninety-second street, in the weed-like decay and growth of our localities, made over anew and grown unrecognizable by his old eyes. That street, so patiently longed for, had transferred itself to the New Jerusalem, and he must seek it there, contenting his slow heart, meanwhile, with the smoke-begrimed thoroughfares of English towns, or the green country-lanes and by-paths with which his wanderings had made him familiar; for doubtless he had a beaten track and was the "long-remembered beggar" now, with food and a roughly hospitable greeting ready for him at many a farm-house door, and his choice of lodging under a score of haystacks. In America, nothing awaited him but that worst form of disappointment which comes under the guise of a long-cherished and late-accomplished purpose, and then a year or two of dry and barren sojourn in an almshouse, and death among strangers, at last, where he had imagined a circle of familiar faces. So I contented myself with giving him alms, which he thankfully accepted, and went away with bent shoulders and an aspect of gentle forlornness, returning upon his orbit, however, after a few months, to tell the same sad and quiet story of his abode in England for more than twenty-seven years, in all which time he had been endeavoring, and still endeavored as patiently as ever, to find his way home to Ninety-second street, Philadelphia.

I recollect another case, of a more ridiculous order, but still with a foolish kind of pathos entangled in it, which impresses me now more forcibly than it did at the moment. One day, a queer, stupid, good-natured, fat-faced individual came into my private room, dressed in a sky-blue, cut-away coat and mixed trowsers, both garments worn and shabby, and rather too small for his overgrown bulk. After a little preliminary talk, he turned out to be a country shopkeeper, (from Connecticut, I think,) who had left a flourishing business, and come over to England purposely and solely to have an interview with the Queen. Some years before, he had named his two children, one for Her Majesty and the other for Prince Albert, and had transmitted photographs of the little people, as well as of his wife and himself, to the illustrious godmother. The Queen had gratefully acknowledged the favor in a letter under the hand of her private secretary. Now the shopkeeper, like a great many other Americans, had long cherished a fantastic notion that he was one of the rightful heirs of a rich English estate; and on the strength of Her Majesty's letter and the hopes of royal patronage which it inspired, he had shut up his little country-store and come over to claim his inheritance. On the voyage, a German fellow-passenger had relieved him of his money on pretence of getting it favorably exchanged, and had disappeared immediately on the ship's arrival; so that the poor fellow was compelled to pawn all his clothes except the remarkably shabby ones in which I beheld him, and in which (as he himself hinted, with a melancholy, yet good-natured smile) he did not look altogether fit to see the Queen. I agreed with him that the bob-tailed coat and mixed trowsers constituted a very odd-looking court-dress, and suggested that it was doubtless his present purpose to get back to Connecticut as fast as possible. But no! The resolve to see the Queen was as strong in him as ever; and it was marvellous the pertinacity with which he clung to it, amid raggedness and starvation, and the earnestness of his supplication that I would supply him with funds for a suitable appearance at Windsor Castle.

I never had so satisfactory a perception of a complete booby before in my life; and it caused me to feel kindly towards him, and yet impatient and exasperated on behalf of common sense, which could not possibly tolerate that such an unimaginable donkey should exist. I laid his absurdity before him in the very plainest terms, but without either exciting his anger or shaking his resolution. "Oh my dear man," quoth he, with good-natured, placid, simple, and tearful stubbornness, "if you could but enter into my feelings, and see the matter from beginning to end as I see it!" To confess the truth, I have since felt that I was hard-hearted to the poor simpleton, and that there was more weight in his remonstrance than I chose to be sensible of, at the time; for, like many men who have been in the habit of making playthings or tools of their imagination and sensibility, I was too rigidly tenacious of what was reasonable in the affairs of real life. And even absurdity has its rights, when, as in this case, it has absorbed a human being's entire nature and purposes. I ought to have transmitted him to Mr. Buchanan, in London, who, being a good-natured old gentleman, and anxious, just then, to gratify the universal Yankee nation, might, for the joke's sake, have got him admittance to the Queen, who had fairly laid herself open to his visit, and has received hundreds of our countrymen on infinitely slighter grounds. But I was inexorable, being turned to flint by the insufferable proximity of a fool, and refused to interfere with his business in any way except to procure him a passage home. I can see his face of mild, ridiculous despair, at this moment, and appreciate, better than I could then, how awfully cruel he must have felt my obduracy to be. For years and years, the idea of an interview with Queen Victoria had haunted his poor, foolish mind; and now, when he really stood on English ground, and the palace-door was hanging a-jar for him, he was expected to turn back, a pennyless and bamboozled simpleton, merely because an iron-hearted Consul refused to lend him thirty shillings (so low had his demand ultimately sunk) to buy a second-class ticket on the rail for London!

He visited the Consulate several times afterwards, subsisting on a pittance that I allowed him in the hope of gradually starving him back to Connecticut, assailing me with the old petition at every opportunity, looking shabbier at every visit, but still thoroughly good-tempered, mildly stubborn, and smiling through his tears, not without a perception of the ludicrousness of his own position. Finally, he disappeared altogether, and whither he had wandered, and whether he ever saw the Queen, or wasted quite away in the endeavor, I never knew; but I remember unfolding the "Times," about that period, with a daily dread of reading an account of a ragged Yankee's attempt to steal into Buckingham palace, and how he smiled tearfully at his captors and besought them to introduce him to Her Majesty. I submit to Mr. Secretary Seward that he ought to make diplomatic remonstrances to the British ministry, and require them to take such order that the Queen shall not any longer bewilder the wits of our poor compatriots by responding to their epistles and thanking them for their photographs.

One circumstance in the foregoing incident—I mean the unhappy storekeeper's notion of establishing his claim to an English estate—was common to a great many other applications, personal or by letter, with which I was favored by my countrymen. The cause of this peculiar insanity lies deep in the Anglo-American heart. After all these bloody wars and vindictive animosities, we have still an unspeakable yearning towards England. When our forefathers left the old home, they pulled up many of their roots, but trailed along with them others, which were never snapt asunder by the tug of such a lengthening distance, nor have been torn out of the original soil by the violence of subsequent struggles, nor severed by the edge of the sword. Even so late as these days, they remain entangled with our heart-strings, and might often have influenced our national course like the tiller-ropes of a ship, if the rough gripe of England had been capable of managing so sensitive a kind of machinery. It has required nothing less than the boorishness, the stolidity, the self-sufficiency, the contemptuous jealousy, the half-sagacity, invariably blind of one eye and often distorted of the other, that characterize this strange people, to compel us to be a great nation in our own right, instead of continuing virtually, if not in name, a province of their small island. What pains did they take to shake us off, and have ever since taken to keep us wide apart from them! It might seem their folly, but was really their fate, or, rather, the Providence of God, who has doubtless a work for us to do, in which the massive materiality of the English character would have been too ponderous a dead-weight upon our progress. And, besides, if England had been wise enough to twine our new vigor roundabout her ancient strength, her power would have been too firmly established ever to yield, in its due season, to the otherwise immutable law of imperial vicissitude. The earth might then have beheld the intolerable spectacle of a sovereignty and institutions, imperfect, but indestructible.

Nationally, there has ceased to be any peril of so inauspicious and yet outwardly attractive an amalgamation. But, as an individual, the American is often conscious of the deep-rooted sympathies that belong more fitly to times gone by, and feels a blind, pathetic tendency to wander back again, which makes itself evident in such wild dreams as I have alluded to above, about English inheritances. A mere coincidence of names, (the Yankee one, perhaps, having been assumed by legislative permission,) a supposititious pedigree, a silver mug on which an anciently engraved coat-of-arms has been half scrubbed out, a seal with an uncertain crest, an old yellow letter or document, in faded ink, the more scantily legible the better—rubbish of this kind, found in a neglected drawer, has been potent enough to turn the brain of many an honest Republican, especially if assisted by an advertisement for lost heirs, cut out of a British newspaper. There is no estimating or believing, till we come into a position to know it, what foolery lurks latent in the breasts of very sensible people. Remembering such sober extravagancies, I should not be at all surprised to find that I am myself guilty of some unsuspected absurdity, that may appear to me the most substantial trait in my character.

I might fill many pages with instances of this diseased American appetite for English soil. A respectable-looking woman, well-advanced in life, of sour aspect, exceedingly homely, but decidedly New Englandish in figure and manners, came to my office with a great bundle of documents, at the very first glimpse of which I apprehended something terrible. Nor was I mistaken. The bundle contained evidences of her indubitable claim to the site on which Castle-street, the Town Hall, the Exchange, and all the principal business part of Liverpool, have long been situated; and with considerable peremptoriness, the good lady signified her expectation that I should take charge of her suit and prosecute it to judgment; not, however, on the equitable condition of receiving half the value of the property recovered, (which, in case of complete success, would have made both of us ten or twentyfold millionaires,) but without recompense, or re-imbursement of legal expenses, solely as an incident of my official duty. Another time came two ladies, bearing a letter of emphatic introduction from his Excellency the Governor of their native State, who testified in most satisfactory terms to their social respectability. They were claimants of a great estate in Cheshire, and announced themselves as blood-relatives of Queen Victoria—a point, however, which they deemed it expedient to keep in the back-ground until their territorial rights should be established, apprehending that the Lord High Chancellor might otherwise be less likely to come to a fair decision in respect to them, from a probable disinclination to admit new members into the royal kin. Upon my honor, I imagine that they had an eye to the possibility of the eventual succession of one or both of them to the crown of Great Britain, through superiority of title over the Brunswick line although, being maiden ladies, like their predecessor Elizabeth, they could hardly have hoped to establish a lasting dynasty upon the throne. It proves, I trust, a certain disinterestedness on my part, that, encountering them thus in the dawn of their fortunes, I forbore to put in a plea for a future dukedom.

Another visitor of the same class was a gentleman of refined manners, handsome figure, and remarkably intellectual aspect. Like many men of an adventurous cast, he had so quiet a deportment, and such an apparent disinclination to general sociability, that you would have fancied him moving always along some peaceful and secluded walk of life. Yet, literally from his first hour, he had been tossed upon the surges of a most varied and tumultuous existence, having been born at sea, of American parentage, but on board of a Spanish vessel, and spending many of the subsequent years in voyages, travels, and outlandish incidents and vicissitudes, which, methought, had hardly been paralleled since the days of Gulliver or De Foe. When his dignified reserve was overcome, he had the faculty of narrating these adventures with wonderful eloquence, working up his descriptive sketches with such intuitive perception of the picturesque points that the whole was thrown forward with a positively illusive effect, like matters of your own visual experience. In fact, they were so admirably done that I could never more than half believe them, because the genuine affairs of life are not apt to transact themselves so

artistically. Many of his scenes were laid in the East, and
among those seldom visited archipelagoes of the Indian ocean,
so that there was an Oriental fragrance breathing through his
talk and an odor of the Spice Islands still lingering in his
garments. He had much to say of the delightful qualities of
the Malay pirates, who, indeed, carry on a predatory warfare
against the ships of all civilized nations, and cut every Christian throat among their prisoners, but, (except for deeds of
that character, which are the rule and habit of their life, and
matter of religion and conscience with them,) they are a
gentle-natured people, of primitive innocence and integrity.

But his best story was about a race of men (if men they
were) who seemed so fully to realize Swift's wicked fable of
the Yahoos, that my friend was much exercised with psycho-
logical speculations whether or no they had any souls. They
dwelt in the wilds of Ceylon, like other savage beasts, hairy,
and spotted with tufts of fur, filthy, shameless, weaponless,
(though warlike in their individual bent,) tool-less, houseless,
language-less, except for a few guttural sounds, hideously
dissonant, whereby they held some rudest kind of communication among themselves. They lacked both memory and
foresight, and were wholly destitute of government, social
institutions, or law or rulership of any description, except the
immediate tyranny of the strongest; radically untameable,
moreover, save that the people of the country managed to
subject a few of the less ferocious and stupid ones to out-door
servitude among their other cattle. They were beastly in
almost all their attributes, and that to such a degree that the
observer, losing sight of any link betwixt them and manhood,
could generally witness their brutalities without greater horror than at those of some disagreeable quadruped in a menag-
erie. And yet, at times, comparing what were the lowest
generic traits in his own race with what was highest in these

abominable monsters, he found a ghastly similitude that half-compelled him to recognize them as human brethren.

After these Gulliverian researches, my agreeable acquaintance had fallen under the ban of the Dutch government, and had suffered (this, at least, being matter of fact) nearly two years' imprisonment with confiscation of a large amount of property, for which Mr. Belmont, our minister at the Hague, had just made a peremptory demand of re-imbursement and damages. Meanwhile, since arriving in England on his way to the United States, he had been providentially led to inquire into the circumstances of his birth on shipboard, and had discovered that not himself alone, but another baby, had come into the world during the same voyage of the prolific vessel, and that there were almost irrefragable reasons for believing that these two children had been assigned to the wrong mothers. Many reminiscences of his early days confirmed him in the idea that his nominal parents were aware of the exchange. The family to which he felt authorized to attribute his lineage was that of a nobleman, in the picture-gallery of whose country-seat (whence, if I mistake not, our adventurous friend had just returned) he had discovered a portrait bearing a striking resemblance to himself. As soon as he should have reported the outrageous action of the Dutch government to President Pierce and the Secretary of State, and recovered the confiscated property, he purposed to return to England and establish his claim to the nobleman's title and estate.

I had accepted his Oriental fantasies (which, indeed, to do him justice, have been recorded by scientific societies among the genuine phenomena of natural history) not as matters of indubitable credence, but as allowable specimens of an imaginative traveller's vivid coloring and rich embroidery on the coarse texture and dull neutral tints of truth. The English

romance was among the latest communications that he entrusted to my private ear; and as soon as I heard the first
chapter—so wonderfully akin to what I might have wrought
out of my own head, not unpractised in such figments—I
began to repent having made myself responsible for the future
nobleman's passage homeward in the next Collins steamer.
Nevertheless, should his English rent-roll fall a little behind-
hand, his Dutch claim for a hundred thousand dollars was
certainly in the hands of our Government, and might at least
be valuable to the extent of thirty pounds, which I had
engaged to pay on his behalf. But I have reason to fear that
his Dutch riches turned out to be Dutch gilt or fairy gold,
and his English country-seat a mere castle in the air—which I
exceedingly regret; for he was a delightful companion and a
very gentlemanly man.

A Consul, in his position of universal responsibility, the
general adviser and helper, sometimes finds himself compelled
to assume the guardianship of personages who, in their own
sphere, are supposed capable of superintending the highest
interests of whole communities. An elderly Irishman, a natu-
ralized citizen, once put the desire and expectation of all our
pennyless vagabonds into a very suitable phrase, by patheti-
cally entreating me to be a "father to him"; and, simple as I sit
scribbling here, I have acted a father's part not only by scores
of such unthrifty old children as himself, but by a progeny of
far loftier pretensions. It may be well for persons who are
conscious of any radical weakness in their character, any
besetting sin, any unlawful propensity, any unhallowed impulse, which (while surrounded with the manifold restraints
that protect a man from that treacherous and life-long enemy,
his lower self, in the circle of society where he is at home)
they may have succeeded in keeping under the lock and key
of strictest propriety—it may be well for them, before seeking
the perilous freedom of a distant land, released from the

watchful eyes of neighborhoods and coteries, lightened of that wearisome burden, an immaculate name, and blissfully obscure after years of local prominence—it may be well for such individuals to know that, when they set foot on a foreign shore, the long-imprisoned Evil, scenting a wild license in the unaccustomed atmosphere, is apt to grow riotous in its iron cage. It rattles the rusty barriers with gigantic turbulence, and if there be an infirm joint anywhere in the frame-work, it breaks madly forth, compressing the mischief of a lifetime into a little space.

A parcel of letters had been accumulating at the Consulate for two or three weeks, directed to a certain Doctor of Divinity, who had left America by a sailing packet and was still upon the sea. In due time, the vessel arrived, and the reverend Doctor paid me a visit. He was a fine-looking middle-aged gentleman, a perfect model of clerical propriety, scholar-like, yet with the air of a man of the world rather than a student, though overspread with the graceful sanctity of a popular metropolitan Divine, a part of whose duty it might be to exemplify the natural accordance between Christianity and good-breeding. He seemed a little excited, as an American is apt to be on first arriving in England, but conversed with intelligence as well as animation, making himself so agreeable that his visit stood out in considerable relief from the monotony of my daily common-place. As I learned from authentic sources, he was somewhat distinguished in his own region for fervor and eloquence in the pulpit, but was now compelled to relinquish it temporarily for the purpose of renovating his impaired health by an extensive tour in Europe. Promising to dine with me, he took up his bundle of letters and went away.

The Doctor, however, failed to make his appearance at dinner-time, or to apologize the next day for his absence; and in the course of a day or two more, I forgot all about him, concluding that he must have set forth on his Continental

travels, the plan of which he had sketched out at our interview. But, by-and-by, I received a call from the master of the
vessel in which he had arrived. He was in some alarm about
his passenger, whose luggage remained on shipboard, but of
whom nothing had been heard or seen since the moment of
his departure from the Consulate. We conferred together, the
Captain and I, about the expediency of setting the police on
the traces (if any were to be found) of our vanished friend;
but it struck me that the good Captain was singularly reticent,
and that there was something a little mysterious in a few
points that he hinted at, rather than expressed; so that, scrutinizing the affair carefully, I surmised that the intimacy of life
on shipboard might have taught him more about the reverend
gentleman than, for some reason or other, he deemed it prudent to reveal. At home, in our native country, I would have
looked to the Doctor's personal safety and left his reputation
to take care of itself, knowing that the good fame of a thousand saintly clergymen would amply dazzle out any lamentable spot on a single brother's character. But in scornful and
invidious England, on the idea that the credit of the sacred
office was measurably entrusted to my discretion, I could not
endure, for the sake of American Doctors of Divinity generally, that this particular Doctor should cut an ignoble figure in
the police-reports of the English newspapers, except at the last
necessity. The clerical body, I flatter myself, will acknowledge
that I acted on their own principle. Besides, it was now too
late; the mischief and violence, if any had been impending,
were not of a kind which it requires the better part of a week
to perpetrate; and to sum up the entire matter, I felt certain,
from a good deal of somewhat similar experience, that, if the
missing Doctor still breathed this vital air, he would turn up
at the Consulate as soon as his money should be stolen or
spent.

Precisely a week after this reverend person's disappearance, there came to my office a tall, middle-aged gentleman in a blue military surtout, braided at the seams, but out at elbows, and as shabby as if the wearer had been bivouacking in it throughout a Crimean campaign. It was buttoned up to the very chin, except where three or four of the buttons were lost; nor was there any glimpse of a white shirt-collar illuminating the rusty black cravat. A grisly moustache was just beginning to roughen the stranger's upper lip. He looked disreputable to the last degree, but still had a ruined air of good society glimmering about him, like a few specks of polish on a sword-blade that has lain corroding in a mud-puddle. I took him to be some American marine officer, of dissipated habits, or perhaps a cashiered British major, stumbling into the wrong quarters through the unrectified bewilderment of last night's debauch. He greeted me, however, with polite familiarity, as though we had been previously acquainted; whereupon I drew coldly back (as sensible people naturally do, whether from strangers or former friends, when too evidently at odds with fortune) and requested to know who my visitor might be, and what was his business at the Consulate. "Am I then so changed!" he exclaimed with a vast depth of tragic intonation; and after a little blind and bewildered talk, behold! the truth flashed upon me. It was the Doctor of Divinity! If I had meditated a scene or a *coup de théâtre,* I could not have contrived a more effectual one than by this simple and genuine difficulty of recognition. The poor Divine must have felt that he had lost his personal identity through the misadventures of one little week. And, to say the truth, he did look as if, like Job, on account of his especial sanctity, he had been delivered over to the direst temptations of Satan, and proving weaker than the Man of Uz, the Arch Enemy had been empowered to drag him through Tophet, transforming him, in the process, from the most decorous of metropolitan clergymen into the rowdiest and dirtiest of disbanded officers. I never fathomed the mystery of his military costume, but conjectured that a lurking sense of fitness had induced him to exchange his clerical garments for this habit of a sinner; nor can I tell precisely into what pitfall, not more of vice than terrible calamity, he had precipitated himself,—being more than satisfied to know that the outcasts of society can sink no lower than this poor, desecrated wretch had sunk.

The opportunity, I presume, does not often happen to a layman of administering moral and religious reproof to a Doctor of Divinity; but finding the occasion thrust upon me, and the hereditary Puritan waxing strong in my breast, I deemed it a matter of conscience not to let it pass entirely unimproved. The truth is, I was unspeakably shocked and disgusted. Not, however, that I was then to learn that clergymen are made of the same flesh and blood as other people, and perhaps lack one small safeguard which the rest of us possess, because they are aware of their own peccability, and therefore cannot look up to the clerical class for the proof of the possibility of a pure life on earth, with such reverential confidence as we are prone to do. But I remembered the innocent faith of my boyhood, and the good old, silver-headed clergyman, who seemed to me as much a Saint then on earth as he is now in Heaven, and partly for whose sake, through all these darkening years, I retain a devout, though not intact nor unwavering respect for the entire fraternity. What a hideous wrong, therefore, had this backslider inflicted on his brethren, and still more on me, who much needed whatever fragments of broken reverence (broken, not as concerned religion, but its earthly institutions and professors) it might yet be possible to patch into a sacred image! Should all pulpits and communion-tables have thenceforth a stain upon them, and the guilty one go unrebuked for it? So I spoke to the unhappy man as I never thought myself warranted in speaking to any other mortal, hitting him hard, doing my utmost to find out his vulnerable part and prick him into the depths of it. And not without more effect than I had dreamed of, or desired!

No doubt, the novelty of the Doctor's reversed position, thus standing up to receive such a fulmination as the clergy have heretofore arrogated the exclusive right of inflicting, might give additional weight and sting to the words which I found utterance for. But there was another reason (which, had I in the least suspected it, would have closed my lips at once) for his feeling morbidly sensitive to the cruel rebuke that I administered. The unfortunate man had come to me, laboring under one of the consequences of his riotous outbreak in the shape of delirium tremens; he bore a hell within the compass of his own breast, all the torments of which blazed up with tenfold inveteracy when I thus took upon myself the devil's office of stirring up the red-hot embers. His emotions, as well as the external movement and expression of them by voice, countenance, and gesture, were terribly exaggerated by the tremendous vibration of nerves resulting from the disease. It was the deepest tragedy I ever witnessed. I know sufficiently, from that one experience, how a condemned soul would manifest its agonies; and for the future, if I have anything to do with sinners, I mean to operate upon them through sympathy, and not rebuke. What had I to do with rebuking him? The disease, long latent in his heart, had shown itself in a frightful eruption on the surface of his life. That was all! Is it a thing to scold the sufferer for?

To conclude this wretched story, the poor Doctor of Divinity, having been robbed of all his money in this little airing beyond the limits of propriety, was easily persuaded to give up the intended tour and return to his bereaved flock, who, very probably, were thereafter conscious of an increased unction in his soul-stirring eloquence, without suspecting the awful depths into which their pastor had dived in quest of it. His voice is now silent. I leave it to members of his own profession to decide whether it was better for him thus to sin outright, and so to be let into the miserable secret what manner of man he was, or to have gone through life outwardly unspotted, making the first discovery of his latent evil at the judgment-seat. It has occurred to me that his dire calamity, as both he and I regarded it, might have been the only method by which precisely such a man as himself, and so situated, could be redeemed. He has learned, ere now, how that matter stood.

For a man with a natural tendency to meddle with other people's business, there could not possibly be a more congenial sphere than the Liverpool Consulate. For myself I had never been in the habit of feeling that I could sufficiently comprehend any particular conjunction of circumstances with human character, to justify me in thrusting in my awkward agency among the intricate and unintelligible machinery of Providence. I have always hated to give advice, especially when there is a prospect of its being taken. It is only one-eyed people who love to advise, or have any spontaneous promptitude of action. When a man opens both his eyes, he generally sees about as many reasons for acting in any one way as in any other, and quite as many for acting in neither, and is therefore likely to leave his friends to regulate their own conduct, and also to remain quiet as regards his especial affairs till necessity shall prick him onward. Nevertheless, the world, and individuals, flourish upon a constant succession of blunders. The secret of English practical success lies in their characteristic faculty of shutting one eye, whereby they get so distinct and decided a view of what immediately concerns them that they go stumbling towards it over a hundred insurmountable obstacles, and achieve a magnificent triumph without ever being aware of half its difficulties. If General McClellan could but have shut his left eye, the right one would long ago have guided us into Richmond. Meanwhile, I have strayed far away from the Consulate, where, as I was about to say, I was compelled, in spite of my disinclination, to impart both advice and assistance in multifarious affairs that did not personally concern me, and presume that I effected about as little mischief as other men in similar contingencies. The duties of the office carried me to prisons, police-courts, hospitals, lunatic asylums, coroner's inquests, death-beds, funerals, and brought me in contact with insane people, criminals, ruined speculators, wild adventurers, diplomatists, brother-consuls, and all manner of simpletons and unfortunates, in greater number and variety than I had ever dreamed of as pertaining to America; in addition to whom there was an equivalent multitude of English rogues, dexterously counterfeiting the genuine Yankee article. It required great discrimination not to be taken in by these last-mentioned scoundrels; for they knew how to imitate our national traits, had been at great pains to instruct themselves as regarded American localities, and were not readily to be caught by a cross-examination as to the topographical features, public institutions, or prominent inhabitants, of the places where they pretended to belong. The best shibboleth I ever hit upon lay in the pronunciation of the word "been," which the English invariably make to rhyme with "green," and we Northerners, at least, (in accordance, I think, with the custom of Shakspere's time,) universally pronounce "bin."

All the matters that I have been treating of, however, were merely incidental, and quite distinct from the real business of the office. A great part of the wear and tear of mind and temper resulted from the bad relations between the seamen and officers of American ships. Scarcely a morning passed, but that some sailor came to show the marks of his ill-usage on shipboard. Often, it was a whole crew of them, each with his broken head or livid bruise, and all testifying with one voice to a constant series of savage outrages during the voyage; or, it might be, they laid an accusation of actual murder, perpetrated by the first or second officers with many blows of steel knuckles, a rope's end, or a marline-spike, or by the Captain, in the twinkling of an eye, with a shot of his pistol. Taking the seamen's view of the case, you would suppose that the gibbet was hungry for the murderers. Listening to the Captain's defence, you would seem to discover that he and his officers were the humanest of mortals, but were driven to a wholesome severity by the mutinous conduct of the crew, who, moreover, had themselves slain their comrade in the drunken riot and confusion of the first day or two after they were shipped. Looked at judicially, there appeared to be no right side to the matter, nor any right side possible in so thoroughly vicious a system as that of the American mercantile marine. The Consul could do little, except to take depositions, hold forth the greasy Testament to be prophaned anew with perjured kisses, and, in a few instances of murder or manslaughter, carry the case before an English magistrate, who generally decided that the evidence was too contradictory to authorize the transmission of the accused for trial in America. The newspapers all over England contained paragraphs, inveighing against the cruelties of American shipmasters. The British parliament took up the matter (for nobody is so humane as John Bull, when his benevolent propensities are to be gratified by finding fault with his neighbor) and caused Lord John Russell to remonstrate with our Government on the outrages for which it was responsible before the world, and which it failed to prevent or punish. The American Secretary of State, old General Cass, responded, with perfectly astounding ignorance of the subject, to the effect that the statements of outrages had probably been exaggerated, that the present laws of the United States were quite adequate to deal with them, and that the interference of the British minister was uncalled for.

The truth is, that the state of affairs was really very horrible, and could be met by no laws at that time (or, I presume, now) in existence. I once thought of writing a pamphlet on the subject, but quitted the Consulate before finding time to effect my purpose, and all that phase of my life immediately assumed so dreamlike a consistency that I despaired of making it seem solid or tangible to the public. And now it looks distant and dim, like troubles of a century ago. The origin of the evil lay in the character of the seamen, scarcely any of whom were American, but the off-scourings and refuse of all the sea-ports of the world, such stuff as piracy is made of, together with a considerable intermixture of returning emigrants, and a sprinkling of absolutely kidnapped American citizens. Even with such material, the ships were very inadequately manned. The shipmaster found himself upon the deep, with a vast responsibility of property and human life upon his hands, and no means of salvation except by compelling his inefficient and demoralized crew to heavier exertions than could reasonably be required of the same number of able seamen. By law he had been entrusted with no discretion of judicious punishment; he therefore habitually left the whole matter of discipline to his irresponsible mates, men often of scarcely a superior quality to the crew. Hence ensued a great mass of petty outrages, unjustifiable assaults, shameful indignities, and nameless cruelty, demoralizing alike to the perpetrators and the sufferers; these enormities fell into the ocean between the two countries, and could be punished in neither. Many miserable stories come back upon my memory as I write; wrongs that were immense, but for which nobody could be held responsible, and which, indeed, the closer you looked into them, the more they lost the aspect of wilful misdoing and assumed that of an inevitable calamity. It was the fault of a system, the misfortune of an individual. Be that as it may, however, there will be no possibility of dealing effectually with these troubles as long as we deem it inconsistent with our national dignity or interests to allow the English courts, under such restrictions as may seem fit, a jurisdiction over offences perpetrated on board our vessels in mid-ocean.

In such a life as this, the American shipmaster developes himself into a man of iron energies, dauntless courage, and inexhaustible resource, at the expense, it must be acknowledged, of some of the higher and gentler traits which might do him excellent service in maintaining his authority. The class has deteriorated of late years, on account of the narrower field of selection, owing chiefly to the diminution of that excellent body of respectably educated New England seamen, from the flower of whom the officers used to be recruited. Yet I found them, in many cases, very agreeable and intelligent companions, with less nonsense about them than landsmen usually have, eschewers of fine-spun theories, delighting in square and tangible ideas, but occasionally infested with prejudices that stuck to their brains like barnacles to a ship's bottom. I never could flatter myself that I was a general favorite with them. One or two, perhaps, even now, would scarcely meet me on amicable terms. Endowed universally with a great pertinacity of will, they especially disliked the interference of a Consul with their management on shipboard; notwithstanding which, I thrust in my very limited authority at every available opening, and did the utmost that lay in my power, though with lamentably small effect, towards enforcing a better kind of discipline. They thought, no doubt, (and on plausible grounds enough, but scarcely appreciating just that one little grain of hard New England sense, oddly thrown in among the flimsier composition of the Consul's character,) that he, a landsman, a bookman, and, as people said of him, a fanciful recluse, could not possibly understand anything of the difficulties or the necessities of a shipmaster's position. But their cold regards were rather acceptable than otherwise; for it is exceedingly awkward to assume a judicial austerity, in the morning, towards a man with whom you have been hob-nobbing over night.

With the technical details of the business of that great Consulate, (for great it then was, though now, I fear, woefully fallen off, and perhaps never to be revived in anything like its former extent,) I did not much interfere. They could safely be left to the treatment of two as faithful, upright, and competent subordinates, both Englishmen, as ever a man was fortunate enough to meet with, in a line of life altogether new and strange to him. I had come over with instructions to supply both their places with Americans, but, possessing a happy faculty of knowing my own interest and the public's, I quietly kept hold of them; being little inclined to open the consular doors to a spy of the State Department or an intriguer for my own office. The venerable Vice-Consul, Mr. Pearce, had witnessed the successive arrivals of a score of newly appointed Consuls, shadowy and short-lived dignitaries, and carried his reminiscences back to the epoch of Consul Maury, who was appointed by Washington, and has acquired almost the grandeur of a mythical personage in the annals of the Consulate. The principal clerk, Mr. Wilding, who has since succeeded to the Vice-Consulship, was a man of English integrity—not that the English are more honest than ourselves, but only there is a certain sturdy reliableness common among them, which we do not quite so invariably manifest in just these subordinate positions—of English integrity, combined with American acuteness of intellect, quick-wittedness, and diversity of talent. It seemed an immense pity that he should wear out his life at a desk, without a step in advance from year's end to year's end, when, had it been his luck to be born on our side of the water, his bright faculties and clear probity would have ensured him eminent success in whatever path he might adopt. Meanwhile, it would have been a sore mischance to me, had any better fortune on his part deprived me of Mr. Wilding's services.

A fair amount of common sense, some acquaintance with the United States Statutes, an insight into character, a tact of management, a general knowledge of the world, and a reasonable, but not too inveterately decided preference for his own will and judgment over those of interested people—these natural attributes and moderate acquirements will enable a Consul to perform many of his duties respectably, but not to dispense with a great variety of other qualifications, only attainable by long experience. Yet, I think, few Consuls are so well accomplished. An appointment of whatever grade, in the Diplomatic or Consular service of America, is too often what the English call a "job"; that is to say, it is made on private and personal grounds, without a paramount eye to the public good or the gentleman's especial fitness for the position. It is not too much to say, (of course, allowing for a brilliant exception, here and there,) that an American never is thoroughly qualified for a foreign post, nor has time to make himself so, before the revolution of the political wheel discards him from his office. Our country wrongs itself by permitting such a system of unsuitable appointments, and, still more, of removals for no cause, just when the incumbent might be beginning to ripen into usefulness. Mere ignorance of official detail is of comparatively small moment; though it is considered indispensable, I presume, that a man in any private capacity shall be thoroughly acquainted with the machinery and operation of his business, and shall not necessarily lose his position on having attained such knowledge. But there are so many more important things to be thought of, in the qualifications of a foreign resident, that his technical dexterity or clumsiness is hardly worth mentioning.

One great part of a Consul's duty, for example, should

consist in building up for himself a recognized position in the society where he resides, so that his local influence might be felt in behalf of his own country, and, so far as they are compatible (as they generally are to the utmost extent) for the interests of both nations. The foreign city should know that it has a permanent inhabitant and a hearty well-wisher in him. There are many conjunctures (and one of them is now upon us) where a long-established, honored, and trusted American citizen, holding a public position under our Government in such a town as Liverpool, might go far towards swaying and directing the sympathies of the inhabitants. He might throw his own weight into the balance against mischief-makers; he might have set his foot on the first little spark of malignant purpose, which the next wind may blow into a national war. But we wilfully give up all advantages of this kind. The position is totally beyond the attainment of an American; there to-day, bristling all over with the porcupine-quills of our Republic, and gone tomorrow, just as he is becoming sensible of the broader and more generous patriotism which might almost amalgamate with that of England, without losing an atom of its native force and flavor. In the changes that appear to await us, and some of which, at least, can hardly fail to be for good, let us hope for a reform in this matter.

For myself, as the gentle reader would spare me the trouble of saying, I was not at all the kind of man to grow into such an ideal Consul as I have here suggested. I never in my life desired to be burdened with public influence. I disliked my office from the first, and never came into any good accordance with it. Its dignity, so far as it had any, was an incumbrance; the attentions it drew upon me (such as invitations to Mayor's banquets and public celebrations of all kinds, where, to my horror, I found myself expected to stand up and speak) were —as I may say without incivility or ingratitude, because there

is nothing personal in that sort of hospitality—a bore. The
official business was irksome, and often painful. There was
nothing pleasant about the whole affair except the emoluments; and even those, never too bountifully reaped, were
diminished by more than half in the second or third year of
my incumbency. All this being true, I was quite prepared, in
advance of the inauguration of Mr. Buchanan, to send in my
resignation. When my successor arrived, I drew the long,
delightful breath, which first made me thoroughly sensible
what an unnatural life I had been leading, and compelled me
to admire myself for having battled with it so sturdily. The
new-comer proved to be a very genial and agreeable gentleman, an F. F. V., and, as he pleasantly acknowledged, a
Southern Fire-Eater—an announcement to which I responded, with similar good humor and self-complacency, by
parading my descent from an ancient line of Massachusetts
Puritans. Since our brief acquaintanceship, my fire-eating
friend has had ample opportunities to banquet on his favorite
diet, hot and hot, in the Confederate service. For myself, as
soon as I was out of office, the retrospect began to look unreal.
I could scarcely believe that it was I, that figure whom they
called a Consul, but a sort of Double Ganger, who had been
permitted to assume my aspect, under which he went through
his shadowy duties with a tolerable show of efficiency, while
my real self had lain, as regarded my proper mode of being
and acting, in a state of suspended animation.

The same sense of illusion still pursues me. There is some
mistake in this matter. I have been writing about another
man's consular experiences, with which, through some mysterious medium of transmitted ideas, I find myself intimately
acquainted, but in which I cannot possibly have had a personal interest. Is it not a dream altogether? The figure of that
poor Doctor of Divinity looks wonderfully life-like; so do
those of the Oriental adventurer with the visionary coronet

above his brow, and the moon-struck visitor of the Queen, and the poor old wanderer, seeking his native country through English highways and by-ways for almost thirty years; and so would a hundred others that I might summon up with similar distinctness. But were they more than shadows? Surely, I think not. Nor are these present pages a bit of intrusive autobiography. Let not the reader wrong me by supposing it. I never should have written with half such unreserve, had it been a portion of this life congenial with my nature, which I am living now, instead of a series of incidents and characters entirely apart from my own concerns, and on which the qualities personally proper to me could have had no bearing. Almost the only real incidents, as I see them now, were the visits of a young English friend, a scholar and a literary amateur, between whom and myself there sprung up an affectionate, and, I trust, not transitory regard. He used to come and sit or stand by my fireside, talking vivaciously and eloquently with me about literature and life, his own national characteristics and mine, with such kindly endurance of the many rough republicanisms wherewith I assailed him, and such frank and amiable assertion of all sorts of English prejudices and mistakes, that I understood his countrymen infinitely the better for him, and was almost prepared to love the intensest Englishman of them all, for his sake. It would gratify my cherished remembrance of this dear friend, if I could manage, without offending him, or letting the public know it, to introduce his name upon my page. Bright was the illumination of my dusky little apartment, as often as he made his appearance there!

The English sketches, which I have been offering to the public, comprise a few of the more external and therefore more readily manageable things that I took note of, in many escapes from the imprisonment of my consular servitude. Liverpool, though not very delightful as a place of residence, is a most convenient and admirable point to get away from. London is only five hours off by the fast train. Chester, the most curious town in England, with its encompassing wall, its ancient Rows, and its venerable Cathedral, is close at hand. North Wales, with all its hills and ponds, its noble sea-scenery, its multitude of gray castles and strange old villages, may be glanced at in a summer-day or two. The lakes and mountains of Cumberland and Westmoreland may be reached before dinner-time. The haunted and legendary Isle of Man, a little kingdom by itself, lies within the scope of an afternoon's voyage. Edinburgh or Glasgow are attainable over night, and Loch Lomond betimes in the morning. Visiting these famous localities, and a great many others, I hope that I do not compromise my American patriotism by acknowledging that I was often conscious of a fervent hereditary attachment to the native soil of our forefathers, and felt it to be our own Old Home.

LEAMINGTON SPA

IN THE COURSE of several visits, and stays of considerable length, we acquired a homelike feeling towards
Leamington, and came back thither again and again,
chiefly because we had been there before. Wandering and
wayside-people, such as we had long since become, retain a
few of the instincts that belong to a more settled way of life,
and often prefer familiar and common-place objects (for the
very reason that they are so) to the dreary strangeness of scenes
that might be thought much better worth the seeing. There is
a small nest of a place in Leamington—at No. 10 Lansdowne
Circus—upon which, to this day, my reminiscences are apt to
settle as one of the cosiest nooks in England or in the world;
not that it had any special charm of its own, but only that we
staid long enough to know it well, and even to grow a little
tired of it. In my opinion, the very tediousness of home and
friends makes a part of what we love them for; if it be not
mixed in sufficiently with the other elements of life, there
may be mad enjoyment, but no happiness.

The modest abode, to which I have alluded, forms one of a
circular range of pretty, moderate-sized, two-story houses, all
built on nearly the same plan, and each provided with its little
grass-plot, its flowers, its tufts of box, trimmed into globes and

other fantastic shapes, and its verdant hedges, shutting the house in from the common drive and dividing it from its equally cosey neighbors. Coming out of the door, and taking a turn round the circle of sister-dwellings, it is difficult to find your way back by any distinguishing individuality of your own habitation. In the centre of the Circus is a space fenced in with iron railing, a small play-place and sylvan retreat for the children of the precinct, permeated by brief paths through the fresh English grass, and shadowed by various shrubbery; amid which, if you like, you may fancy yourself in a deep seclusion, though probably the mark of eye-shot from the windows of all the surrounding houses. But, in truth, with regard to the rest of the town and the world at large, an abode here is a genuine seclusion; for the ordinary stream of life does not run through this little, quiet pool, and few or none of the inhabitants seem to be troubled with any business or outside activities. I used to set them down as half-pay officers, dowagers of narrow income, elderly maiden-ladies, and other people of respectability, but small account, such as hang on the world's skirts rather than actually belong to it. The quiet of the place was seldom disturbed except by the grocer and butcher, who came to receive orders, or by the cabs, hackney coaches, and Bath-chairs, in which the ladies took an infrequent airing, or the livery-steed which the retired captain sometimes bestrode for a morning-ride, or by the red-coated postman who went his rounds twice a day to deliver letters, and again in the evening, ringing a hand-bell, to take letters for the mail. In merely mentioning these slight interruptions of its sluggish stillness, I seem to myself to disturb too much the atmosphere of quiet that brooded over the spot; whereas, its impression upon me was, that the world had never found the way hither, or had forgotten it, and that the fortunate inhabitants were the only ones who possessed the spell-word of admittance. Nothing could have suited me better, at the time; for I had been holding a position of public servitude, which imposed upon me (among a great many lighter duties) the ponderous necessity of being universally civil and sociable.

Nevertheless, if a man were seeking the bustle of society, he might find it more readily in Leamington than in most other English towns. It is a permanent watering-place, a sort of institution to which I do not know any close parallel in American life; for such places as Saratoga bloom only for the summer-season, and offer a thousand dissimilitudes, even then; while Leamington seems to be always in flower, and serves as a home to the homeless, all the year round. Its original nucleus, the plausible excuse for the town's coming into prosperous existence, lies in the fiction of a chalybeate well, which, indeed, is so far a reality that out of its magical depths have gushed streets, groves, gardens, mansions, shops, and churches, and spread themselves along the banks of the little river Leam. This miracle accomplished, the beneficent fountain has retired beneath a pump-room, and appears to have given up all pretensions to the remedial virtues formerly attributed to it. I know not whether its waters are ever tasted now-a-days; but not the less does Leamington—in pleasant Warwickshire, at the very midmost point of England, in a good hunting neighborhood, and surrounded by country-seats and castles—continue to be a resort of transient visitors, and the more permanent abode of a class of genteel, unoccupied, well-to-do, but not very wealthy people, such as are hardly known among ourselves. Persons who have no country-houses, and whose fortunes are inadequate to a London expenditure, find here, I suppose, a sort of town and country life in one.

In its present aspect, the town is of no great age. In contrast with the antiquity of many places in its neighborhood, it has a bright, new face, and seems almost to smile even amid the sombreness of an English autumn. Nevertheless, it is hundreds upon hundreds of years old, if we reckon up that sleepy lapse of time during which it existed as a small village of thatched houses, clustered round a Priory; and it would still have been precisely such a rural village, but for a certain Doctor Jephson, who lived within the memory of man, and who found out the magic well, and foresaw what fairy wealth might be made to flow from it. A public garden has been laid out along the margin of the Leam, and called the Jephson Garden, in honor of him who created the prosperity of his native spot.—A little way within the garden-gate, there is a circular temple of Grecian architecture, beneath the dome of which stands a marble statue of the good Doctor, very well executed, and representing him with a face of fussy activity and benevolence; just the kind of man, if luck favored him, to build up the fortunes of those about him, or, quite as probably, to blight his whole neighborhood by some disastrous speculation.

The Jephson Garden is very beautiful, like most other English pleasure-grounds; for, aided by their moist climate and not too fervid sun, the landscape-gardeners excel in converting flat or tame surfaces into attractive scenery, chiefly through the skilful arrangement of trees and shrubbery. An Englishman aims at this effect even in the little patches under the windows of a suburban villa, and achieves it on a larger scale in a tract of many acres. The Garden is shadowed with trees of a fine growth, standing alone, or in dusky groves and dense entanglements, pervaded by woodland paths; and emerging from these pleasant glooms we come upon a breadth of sunshine, where the green sward—so vividly green that it has a kind of lustre in it—is spotted with beds of gem-like flowers. Rustic chairs and benches are scattered about, some of them ponderously fashioned out of the stumps of obtruncated trees, and others more artfully made with intertwining branches, or perhaps an imitation of such frail handiwork in iron. In a central part of the Garden is an archery-ground, where laughing maidens practise at the butts, generally missing their ostensible mark, but, by the mere grace of their action, sending an unseen shaft into some young man's heart. There is space, moreover, within these precincts, for an artificial lake, with a little green island in the midst of it; both lake and island being the haunt of swans, whose aspect and movement in the water are most beautiful and stately—most infirm, disjointed, and decrepit, when, unadvisedly, they see fit to emerge, and try to walk upon dry land. In the latter case, they look like a breed of uncommonly ill-contrived geese; and I record the matter here for the sake of the moral—that we should never pass judgment on the merits of any person or thing, unless we behold them in the sphere and circumstances to which they are specially adapted. In still another part of the Garden, there is a labyrinthine Maze, formed of an intricacy of hedge-bordered walks, involving himself in which, a man might wander for hours, inextricably, within a circuit of only a few yards. It seemed to me a sad emblem of the mental and moral perplexities in which we sometimes go astray, petty in scope, yet large enough to entangle a lifetime, and bewilder us with a weary movement, but no genuine progress.

The Leam—the "high complectioned Leam," as Drayton calls it—after drowsing across the principal street of the town beneath a handsome bridge, skirts along the margin of the Garden without any perceptible flow. Heretofore, I had fancied the Concord the laziest river in the world, but now assign that amiable distinction to the little English stream. Its water is by no means transparent, but has a greenish, goose-puddly hue, which, however, accords well with the other coloring and characteristics of the scene, and is disagreeable neither to sight nor smell. Certainly, this river is a perfect feature of that gentle picturesqueness in which England is so rich, sleeping, as it does, beneath a margin of willows that droop into its bosom, and other trees, of deeper verdure than our own country can boast, inclining lovingly over it. On the garden-side, it is bordered by a shadowy, secluded grove, with winding paths among its boskiness, affording many a peep at the river's imperceptible lapse and tranquil gleam; and, on the opposite shore, stands the priory-church, with its churchyard full of shrubbery and tombstones.

The business-portion of the town clusters about the banks of the Leam, and is naturally densest around the well, to which the modern settlement owes its existence. Here are the commercial inns, the post-office, the furniture-dealers, the iron-mongers, and all the heavy and homely establishments that connect themselves even with the airiest modes of human life; while upward from the river, by a long and gentle ascent, rises the principal street, which is very bright and cheerful in its physiognomy, and adorned with shop-fronts almost as splendid as those of London, though on a diminutive scale. There are likewise side-streets and cross-streets, many of which are bordered with the beautiful Warwickshire elm, a most unusual kind of adornment for an English town; and spacious avenues, wide enough to afford room for stately groves, with foot-paths running beneath the lofty shade, and rooks cawing and chattering so high in the tree-tops that their voices get musical before reaching the earth. The houses are mostly built in blocks and ranges, in which every separate tenement is a repetition of its fellow, though the architecture of the different ranges is sufficiently various. Some of them are almost palatial in size and sumptuousness of arrangement. Then, on the outskirts of the town, there are detached villas, enclosed within that separate domain of high stone-fence and embowered shrubbery, which an Englishman so loves to build and plant around his abode, presenting to the public only an iron-gate, with a gravelled carriage-drive winding away towards the half-hidden mansion. Whether in street or suburb, Leamington may fairly be called beautiful, and, at some points, magnificent; but, by-and-by, you become doubtfully suspicious of a somewhat unreal finery; it is pretentious, though not glaringly so; it has been built with malice aforethought as a place of gentility and enjoyment. Moreover, splendid as the houses look, and comfortable as they often are, there is a nameless something about them, betokening that they have not grown out of human hearts, but are the creations of a skilfully applied human intellect; no man has reared any one of them, whether stately or humble, to be his life-long residence, wherein to bring up his children, who are to inherit it as a home. They are nicely contrived lodging-houses, one and all—the best as well as the shabbiest of them—and therefore inevitably lack some nameless property that a home should have. This was the case with our own little snuggery in Lansdowne Circus, as with all the rest; it had not grown out of anybody's individual need, but was built to let or sell, and was therefore like a ready-made garment—a tolerable fit, but only tolerable.

All these blocks, ranges, and detached villas, are adorned with the finest and most aristocratic names that I have found anywhere in England, except perhaps in Bath, which is the great metropolis of that second-class gentility with which watering-places are chiefly populated. Lansdowne Crescent, Lansdowne Circus, Lansdowne Terrace, Regent-street, Warwick-street, Clarendon-street, the Upper and Lower Parade; such are a few of the designations. Parade, indeed, is a well-chosen name for the principal street, along which the population of the idle town draws itself out for daily review and display. I only wish that my descriptive powers would enable me to throw off a picture of the scene, at a sunny noontide, individualizing each character with a touch; the great people alighting from their carriages at the principal shop-doors; the elderly ladies and infirm Indian officers, drawn along in Bath-chairs; the comely, rather than pretty, English girls, with their deep, healthy bloom, which an American taste is apt to deem fitter for a milkmaid than for a lady; the moustached gentle-men with frogged surtouts and a military air; the nurse-maids and chubby children, but no chubbier than our own, and scampering on slenderer legs;—the sturdy figure of John Bull, in all varieties, and of all ages, but ever with the stamp of authenticity somewhere about him.

To say the truth, I have been holding the pen over my paper, purposing to write a descriptive paragraph or two about the throng on the principal Parade of Leamington, so arrang-ing it as to present a sketch of the British out-of-door aspect on a morning walk of gentility; but I find no personages quite sufficiently distinct and individual in my memory to supply the materials of such a panorama. Oddly enough, the only figure that comes fairly forth to my mind's eye, is that of a dowager, one of hundreds whom I used to marvel at, all over England, but who have scarcely a representative among our own ladies of autumnal life, so thin, care-worn, and frail, as age usually makes the latter.

I have heard a good deal of the tenacity with which Eng-lish ladies retain their personal beauty to a late period of life; but (not to suggest that an American eye needs use and cultivation before it can quite appreciate the charm of English beauty, at any age) it strikes me that an English lady of fifty is apt to become a creature less refined and delicate, so far as her physique goes, than anything that we Western people class under the name of woman. She has an awful ponderos-ity of frame, not pulpy, like the looser development of our few fat women, but massive with solid beef and streaky tallow; so that (though struggling manfully against the idea) you inevi-tably think of her as made up of steaks and sirloins. When she walks, her advance is elephantine. When she sits down, it is on a great round space of her Maker's footstool where she looks as if nothing could ever move her. She imposes awe and respect by the muchness of her personality, to such a degree that you probably credit her with far greater moral and intellectual force than she can fairly claim. Her visage is usually grim and stern, seldom positively forbidding, yet calmly terrible, not merely by its breadth and weight of feature, but because it seems to express so much well-founded self-reliance, such acquaintance with the world, its toils, troubles, and dangers, and such sturdy capacity for trampling down a foe. Without anything positively salient, or actively offensive, or, indeed, unjustly formidable to her neighbors, she has the effect of a seventy-four gun ship in time of peace; for, while you assure yourself that there is no real danger, you cannot help thinking how tremendous would be her onset, if pugnaciously inclined, and how futile the effort to inflict any counter-injury. She certainly looks tenfold—nay, a hundredfold—better able to take care of herself than our slender-framed and haggard womankind; but I have not found reason to suppose that the English dowager of fifty has actually greater courage, fortitude, and strength of character, than our women of similar age, or even a tougher physical endurance than they. Morally, she is strong, I suspect, only in society, and in the common routine of social affairs, and would be found powerless and timid in an exceptional strait, that might call for energy outside of the conventionalities amid which she has grown up.

You can meet this figure in the street, and live, and even smile at the recollection. But conceive of her in a ball-room, with the bare, brawny arms that she invariably displays there, and all the other corresponding development, such as is beautiful in the maiden blossom, but a spectacle to howl at in such an overblown cabbage-rose as this.

Yet, somewhere in this enormous bulk, there must be hidden the modest, slender, violet-nature of a girl, whom an alien mass of earthliness has unkindly overgrown; for an English maiden in her teens, though very seldom so pretty as our own damsels, possesses, to say the truth, a certain charm of half-blossom, and delicately folded leaves, and tender womanhood shielded by maidenly reserves, with which, somehow or other, our American girls often fail to adorn themselves during an appreciable moment. It is a pity that the English violet should grow into such an outrageously developed peony as I have attempted to describe. I wonder whether a middle-aged husband ought to be considered as legally married to all the accretions that have overgrown the slenderness of his bride, since he led her to the altar, and which make her so much more than he ever bargained for! Is it not a sounder view of the case, that the matrimonial bond cannot be held to include the three-fourths of the wife that had no existence when the ceremony was performed? And, as a matter of conscience and good morals, ought not an English married pair to insist upon the celebration of a Silver Wedding, at the end of twenty-five years, in order to legalize and mutually appropriate that corporeal growth, of which both parties have individually come into possession, since they were pronounced one flesh?

The chief enjoyment of my several visits to Leamington lay in rural walks about the neighborhood, and in jaunts to places of note and interest, which are particularly abundant in that region. The high-roads are made pleasant to the traveller by a border of trees, and often afford him the hospitality of a wayside-bench beneath a comfortable shade. But a fresher delight is to be found in the foot-paths, which go wandering away from stile to stile, along hedges, and across broad fields, and through wooded parks, leading you to little hamlets of thatched cottages, ancient, solitary farm-houses, picturesque old mills, streamlets, pools, and all those quiet, secret, unexpected, yet strangely familiar features of English scenery, that Tennyson shows us in his idylls and eclogues. These by-paths admit the wayfarer into the very heart of rural life, and yet do not burden him with a sense of intrusiveness. He has a right to go whithersoever they lead him; for, with all their shaded privacy, they are as much the property of the public as the dusty high-road itself, and even by an older tenure. Their antiquity probably exceeds that of the Roman ways; the footsteps of the aboriginal Britons first wore away the grass, and the natural flow of intercourse between village and village has kept the track bare ever since. An American farmer would plough across any such path, and obliterate it with his hills of potatoes and Indian corn; but, here, it is protected by law, and still more by the sacredness that inevitably springs up, in this soil, along the well-defined footprints of centuries. Old associations are sure to be fragrant herbs in English nostrils; we pull them up as weeds.

I remember such a path, the access to which is from Lovers' Grove, a range of tall old oaks and elms, on a high hill-top, whence there is a view of Warwick Castle, and a wide extent of landscape, beautiful, though bedimmed with English mist. This particular foot-path, however, is not a remarkably good specimen of its kind, since it leads into no hollows and seclusions, and soon terminates in a high-road. It connects Leamington by a short cut with the small, neighboring village of Lillington, a place which impresses an American observer with its many points of contrast to the rural aspects of his own country. The village consists chiefly of one row of contiguous dwellings, separated only by party-walls, but ill-matched among themselves, being of different heights and apparently of various ages, though all are of an antiquity which we should call venerable. Some of the windows are leaden-framed lattices, opening on hinges. These houses are mostly built of gray stone, but others, in the same range, are of brick, and one or two are in a very old fashion—Elizabethan, or still elder—having a ponderous frame-work of oak, painted black, and filled in with plastered stone or bricks. Judging by the patches of repair, the oak seems to be the more durable part of the structure. Some of the roofs are covered with earthen tiles; others (more decayed and poverty-stricken) with thatch, out of which sprouts a luxurious vegetation of grass, house-leeks, and yellow flowers. What especially strikes an American is the lack of that insulated space—the intervening gardens, grass-plots, orchards, broad-spreading shade-trees—which occur between our own village-houses. These English dwellings have no such separate surroundings; they all grow together, like the cells of a honey-comb.

Beyond the first row of houses, and hidden from it by a turn of the road, there was another row (or block, as we should call it) of small, old cottages, stuck one against another, with their thatched roofs forming a single contiguity. These, I presume, were the habitations of the poorest order of rustic laborers; and the narrow precincts of each cottage, as well as the close neighborhood of the whole, gave the impression of a stifled, unhealthy atmosphere among the occupants. It seemed impossible that there should be a cleanly reserve, a proper self-respect among individuals, or a wholesome unfamiliarity between families, where human life was crowded and massed into such intimate communities as these. Nevertheless, not to look beyond the outside, I never saw a prettier rural scene than was presented by this range of contiguous huts; for in front of the whole row was a luxuriant and well-trimmed hawthorn-hedge, and belonging to each cottage was a little square of garden-ground, separated from its neighbors by a line of the same verdant fence. The gardens were chock-full, not of esculent vegetables, but of flowers, familiar ones, but very bright-colored, and shrubs of box, some of which were trimmed into artistic shapes; and I remember, before one door, a representation of Warwick Castle, made of oyster-shells. The cottagers evidently loved the little nests in which they dwelt, and did their best to make them beautiful, and succeeded more than tolerably well; so kindly did Nature help their humble efforts with its verdure, flowers, moss, lichens, and the green things that grew out of the thatch. Through some of the open door-ways, we saw plump children, rolling about on the stone-floors, and their mothers, by no means very pretty, but as happy-looking as mothers generally are; and while we gazed at these domestic matters, an old woman rushed wildly out of one of the gates, upholding a shovel, on which she clanged and clattered with a key. At first, we fancied that she intended an onslaught against ourselves, but soon discovered that a more dangerous enemy was abroad; for the old lady's bees had swarmed, and the air was full of them, whizzing by our heads like bullets.

Not far from these two rows of houses and cottages, a green lane, overshadowed with trees, turned aside from the main-road, and tended towards a square, gray tower, the battlements of which were just high enough to be visible above the foliage. Wending our way thitherward, we found the very picture and ideal of a country-church and churchyard. The tower seemed to be of Norman architecture, low, massive, and crowned with battlements. The body of the church was of very modest dimensions, and the eaves so low that I could touch them with my walking-stick. We looked into the windows, and beheld the dim and quiet interior, a narrow space, but venerable with the consecration of many centuries, and keeping its sanctity as entire and inviolate as that of a vast cathedral. The nave was divided from the side-aisles of the church by pointed arches, resting on very sturdy pillars; it was good to see how solemnly they held themselves to their age-long task of supporting that lowly roof. There was a small organ, suited in size to the vaulted hollow, which it weekly filled with religious sound. On the opposite wall of the church, between two windows, was a mural tablet of white marble, with an inscription in black letters—the only such memorial that I could discern, although many dead people doubtless lay beneath the floor, and had paved it with their ancient tombstones, as is customary in old English churches. There were no modern painted windows, flaring with raw colors, nor other gorgeous adornments, such as the present taste for mediæval restoration often patches upon the decorous simplicity of the gray village-church. It is probably the worshipping-place of no more distinguished a congregation than the farmers and peasantry, who inhabit the houses and cottages which I have just described. Had the lord of the manor been one of the parishioners, there would have been an eminent pew near the chancel, walled high about, curtained, and softly cushioned, warmed by a fire-place of its own, and distinguished by hereditary tablets and escutcheons on the enclosed stone-pillar.

A well-trodden path led across the churchyard; and the gate being on the latch, we entered, and walked round among the graves and monuments. The latter were chiefly headstones, none of which were very old, so far as was discoverable by the dates; some, indeed, in so ancient a cemetery, were disagreeably new, with inscriptions glittering like sunshine, in gold letters. The ground must have been dug over and over again, innumerable times, until the soil is made up of what was once human clay, out of which have sprung successive crops of grave-stones, that flourish their allotted time, and disappear, like the weeds and flowers in their briefer period. The English climate is very unfavorable to the endurance of memorials in the open air. Twenty years of it suffice to give as much antiquity of aspect, whether to tombstone or edifice, as a hundred years of our own drier atmosphere; so soon do the drizzly rains and constant moisture corrode the surface of marble or freestone. Sculptured edges lose their sharpness in a year or two; yellow lichens overspread a beloved name, and obliterate it while it is yet fresh upon some survivor's heart. Time gnaws an English grave-stone with wonderful appetite; and when the inscription is quite illegible, the Sexton takes the useless slab away, and perhaps makes a hearthstone of it, and digs up the unripe bones which it ineffectually tried to memorialize, and gives the bed to another sleeper. In the Charter-street burial-ground at Salem, and in the old grave-yard on the hill, at Ipswich, I have seen more ancient grave-stones, with legible inscriptions on them, than in any English churchyard.

And yet this same ungenial climate, hostile as it generally is to the long remembrance of departed people, has sometimes a lovely way of dealing with the records on certain monuments, that lie horizontally in the open air. The rain falls into the deep incisions of the letters, and has scarcely time to be dried away before another shower sprinkles the flat stone again, and replenishes those little reservoirs. The unseen, mysterious seeds of mosses find their way into the lettered furrows, and are made to germinate by the continual moisture and watery sunshine of the English sky; and by-and-by, in a year, or two years, or many years, behold the complete inscription—

Here Lyeth the Body,

and all the rest of the tender falsehood—beautifully embossed in raised letters of living green, a bas-relief of velvet moss on the marble slab! It becomes more legible under the skyey influences after the world has forgotten the deceased than when it was fresh from the stone-cutter's hands. It outlives the grief of friends. I first saw an example of this at Bebington churchyard, in Cheshire, and thought that Nature must needs have had a special tenderness for the person (no noted man, however, in the world's history) so long ago laid beneath that stone, since she took such wonderful pains to 'keep his memory green.' Perhaps the proverbial phrase, just quoted, may have had its origin in the natural phenomenon here described.

While we rested ourselves on a horizontal monument, which was elevated just high enough to be a convenient seat, I observed that one of the grave-stones lay very close to the church; so close that the droppings of the eaves would fall upon it. It seemed as if the inmate of that grave had desired to creep under the church-wall. On closer inspection, we found an almost illegible epitaph on the stone, and with difficulty made out this forlorn verse:—

> 'Poorly lived,
> And poorly died,
> Poorly buried,
> And no one cried.'

It would be hard to compress the story of a cold and luckless life, death, and burial, into fewer words, or more impressive ones; at least, we found them impressive, perhaps because we had to re-create the inscription by scraping away the lichens from the faintly traced letters. The grave was on the shady and damp side of the church, endwise towards it, the headstone being within about three feet of the foundation-wall; so that, unless the poor man was a dwarf, he must have been doubled up to fit him into his final resting-place. No wonder that his epitaph murmured against so poor a burial as this! His name, as well as I could make it out, was Treeo—John Treeo, I think—and he died in 1810, at the age of seventy-four. The grave-stone is so overgrown with grass and weeds, so covered with unsightly lichens, and so crumbly with time and foul weather, that it is questionable whether anybody will ever be at the trouble of decyphering it again. But there is a quaint and sad kind of enjoyment in defeating (to such slight degree as my pen may do it) the probabilities of oblivion for poor John Treeo, and asking a little sympathy for him, half-a-century after his death, and making him better and more widely known, at least, than any other slumberer in Lillington churchyard; he having been, as appearances go, the outcast of them all.

You find similar old churches and villages in all the neighboring country, at the distance of every two or three miles; and I describe them, not as being rare, but because they are so common and characteristic. The village of Whitnash, within twenty minutes' walk of Leamington, looks as secluded, as rural, and as little disturbed by the fashions of to-day, as if Doctor Jephson had never developed all those Parades and Crescents out of his magic well. I used to wonder whether the inhabitants had ever yet heard of railways, or, at their slow rate of progress, had even reached the epoch of stage-coaches. As you approach the village, while it is yet unseen, you observe a tall, overshadowing canopy of elm-tree tops, beneath which you almost hesitate to follow the public road, on account of the remoteness that seems to exist between the precincts of this old-world community and the thronged modern street, out of which you have so recently emerged. Venturing onward, however, you soon find yourself in the heart of Whitnash, and see an irregular ring of ancient, rustic dwellings, surrounding the village-green, on one side of which stands the church, with its square Norman tower and battlements, while close adjoining is the vicarage, made picturesque by peaks and gables. At first glimpse, none of the houses appear to be less than two or three centuries old, and they are of the ancient, wooden-framed fashion, with thatched roofs, which give them the air of birds-nests, thereby assimilating them closely to the simplicity of nature.

The church-tower is mossy and much gnawed by time; it has narrow loop-holes up and down its front and sides, and an arched window over the low portal, set with small panes of glass, cracked, dim, and irregular, through which a by-gone age is peeping out into the daylight. Some of those old, grotesque faces, called gargoyles, are seen on the projections of the architecture. The churchyard is very small, and is encompassed by a gray stone-fence that looks as ancient as the church itself. In front of the tower, on the village-green, is a yew-tree of incalculable age, with a vast circumference of trunk, but a very scanty head of foliage; though its boughs still keep some of the vitality which perhaps was in its early prime when the Saxon invaders founded Whitnash. A thousand years is no extraordinary antiquity in the lifetime of a yew. We were pleasantly startled, however, by discovering an exuberance of more youthful life than we had thought possible, in so old a tree; for the faces of two children laughed at us out of an opening in the trunk, which had become hollow with long decay. On one side of the yew stood a frame-work of worm-eaten timber, the use and meaning of which puzzled me exceedingly, till I made it out to be the village-stocks; a public institution that, in its day, had doubtless hampered many a pair of shank-bones, now crumbling in the adjacent churchyard. It is not to be supposed, however, that this old-fashioned mode of punishment is still in vogue among the good people of Whitnash. The vicar of the parish has antiquarian propensities, and had probably dragged the stocks out of some dusty hiding-place, and set them up on their former site as a curiosity.

I disquiet myself in vain with the effort to hit upon some characteristic feature, or assemblage of features, that shall convey to the reader the influence of hoar antiquity lingering into the present daylight, as I so often felt it in these old English scenes. It is only an American who can feel it, and even he begins to find himself growing insensible to its effect, after a long residence in England. But, while you are still new in the Old Country, it thrills you with strange emotion to think that this little church of Whitnash, humble as it seems, stood for ages under the Catholic faith, and has not materially changed since Wickliffe's days, and that it looked as gray as now in Bloody Mary's time, and that Cromwell's troopers broke off the stone noses of those same gargoyles that are now grinning in your face. So, too, with the immemorial yew-tree; you see its great roots grasping hold of the earth, like gigantic claws, clinging so sturdily that no effort of time can wrench them away; and, there being life in the old tree, you feel all the more as if a contemporary witness were telling you of the things that have been. It has lived among men, and been a familiar object to them, and seen them brought to be christened and married and buried in the neighboring church and churchyard, through so many centuries, that it knows all about our race, so far as fifty generations of the Whitnash people can supply such knowledge.

And, after all, what a weary life it must have been for the old tree! Tedious beyond imagination! Such, I think, is the final impression on the mind of an American visitor, when his delight at finding something permanent begins to yield to his Western love of change, and he becomes sensible of the heavy air of a spot where the forefathers and fore-mothers have grown up together, intermarried, and died, through a long succession of lives, without any intermixture of new elements, till family features and character are all run in the same inevitable mould. Life is there fossilized in its greenest leaf. The man who died yesterday, or ever so long ago, walks the village-street to-day, and chooses the same wife that he married a hundred years since, and must be buried again, tomorrow, under the same kindred dust that has already covered him half a score of times. The stone threshold of his cottage is

worn away with his hob-nailed footsteps, shuffling over it from
the reign of the first Plantagenet to that of Victoria. Better
than this is the lot of our restless countrymen, whose modern
instinct bids them tend always towards 'fresh woods and
pastures new.' Rather than such monotony of sluggish ages,
loitering on a village-green, toiling in hereditary fields, listening to the parson's drone lengthened through centuries in the
gray Norman church, let us welcome whatever change may
come—change of place, social customs, political institutions,
modes of worship—trusting that, if all present things shall
vanish, they will but make room for better systems, and for a
higher type of man to clothe his life in them, and to fling
them off in turn.

Nevertheless, while an American willingly accepts growth
and change as the law of his own national and private existence, he has a singular tenderness for the stone-encrusted
institutions of the mother-country. The reason may be
(though I should prefer a more generous explanation) that he
recognizes the tendency of these hardened forms to stiffen her
joints and fetter her ancles, in the race and rivalry of improvement. I hated to see so much as a twig of ivy wrenched away
from an old wall, in England. Yet change is at work, even in
such a village as Whitnash. At a subsequent visit, looking
more critically at the irregular circle of dwellings that surround the yew-tree and confront the church, I perceived that
some of the houses must have been built within no long time,
although the thatch, the quaint gables, and the old oaken
frame-work of the others, diffused an air of antiquity over the
whole assemblage. The church itself was undergoing repair
and restoration, which is but another name for change. Ma-
sons were making patchwork on the front of the tower, and
were sawing a slab of stone and piling up bricks, to strengthen
the side-wall, or possibly to enlarge the ancient edifice by an
additional aisle. Moreover, they had dug an immense pit in

the churchyard, long, and broad, and fifteen feet deep, two thirds of which profundity were discolored by human decay and mixed up with crumbly bones. What this excavation was intended for, I could nowise imagine, unless it were the very pit in which Longfellow bids the 'Dead Past bury its Dead,' and Whitnash, of all places in the world, were going to avail itself of our poet's suggestion. If so, it must needs be confessed that many picturesque and delightful things would be thrown into the hole, and covered out of sight forever.

The article which I am writing has taken its own course, and occupied itself almost wholly with country churches; whereas, I had purposed to attempt a description of some of the many old towns—Warwick, Coventry, Kenilworth, Stratford-on-Avon—which lie within an easy scope of Leamington. And still another church presents itself to my remembrance. It is that of Hatton, on which I stumbled in the course of a forenoon's ramble, and paused a little while to look at it for the sake of old Doctor Parr, who was once its vicar. Hatton, so far as I could discover, has no public house, no shop, no contiguity of roofs, (as in most English villages, however small,) but is merely an ancient neighborhood of farm-houses, spacious, and standing wide apart, each within its own precincts, and offering a most comfortable aspect of orchards, harvest-fields, barns, stacks, and all manner of rural plenty. It seemed to be a community of old settlers, among whom everything had been going on prosperously since an epoch beyond the memory of man; and they kept a certain privacy among themselves, and dwelt on a cross-road at the entrance of which was a barred gate, hospitably open, but still impressing me with a sense of scarcely warrantable intrusion. After all, in some shady nook of those gentle Warwickshire slopes, there may have been a denser and more populous settlement, styled Hatton, which I never reached.

Emerging from the by-road, and entering upon one that

crossed it at right angles and led to Warwick, I espied the church of Doctor Parr. Like the others which I have described, it had a low stone tower, square, and battlemented at its summit; for all these little churches seem to have been built on the same model, and nearly at the same measurement, and have even a greater family-likeness than the cathedrals. As I approached, the bell of the tower (a remarkably deep-toned bell, considering how small it was) flung its voice abroad, and told me that it was noon. The church stands among its graves, a little removed from the wayside, quite apart from any collection of houses, and with no signs of a vicarage; it is a good deal shadowed by trees, and not wholly destitute of ivy. The body of the edifice, unfortunately, (and it is an outrage which the English churchwardens are fond of perpetrating,) has been newly covered with a yellowish plaster or wash, so as quite to destroy the aspect of antiquity except upon the tower, which wears the dark gray hue of many centuries. The chancel-window is painted with a representation of Christ upon the Cross, and all the other windows are full of painted or stained glass, but none of it ancient, nor (if it be fair to judge from without of what ought to be seen within) possessing any of the tender glory that should be the inheritance of this branch of Art, revived from mediæval times. I stepped over the graves, and peeped in at two or three of the windows, and saw the snug interior of the church, glimmering through the many-colored panes, like a show of common-place objects under the fantastic influence of a dream; for the floor was covered with modern pews, very like what we may see in a New England meeting-house, though, I think, a little more favorable than those would be to the quiet slumbers of the Hatton farmers and their families. Those who slept under Doctor Parr's preaching now prolong their nap, I suppose, in the churchyard roundabout, and can scarcely have drawn much spiritual benefit from any truths that he contrived to tell them, in their lifetime. It struck me as a rare example (even where examples are numerous) of a man utterly misplaced, that this enormous scholar, great in the classic tongues, and inevitably converting his own simplest vernacular into a learned language, should have been set up in this homely pulpit and ordained to preach salvation to a rustic audience, to whom it is difficult to imagine how he could ever have spoken one available word.

Almost always, in visiting such scenes as I have been attempting to describe, I had a singular sense of having been there before. The ivy-grown English churches (even that of Bebington, the first that I beheld) were quite as familiar to me, when fresh from home, as the old wooden meeting-house in Salem, which used, on wintry Sabbaths, to be the frozen purgatory of my childhood. This was a bewildering, yet very delightful emotion, fluttering about me like a faint summer-wind, and filling my imagination with a thousand half-remembrances, which looked as vivid as sunshine, at a side-glance, but faded quite away whenever I attempted to grasp and define them. Of course, the explanation of the mystery was, that history, poetry, and fiction, books of travel, and the talk of tourists, had given me pretty accurate pre-conceptions of the common objects of English scenery, and these, being long ago vivified by a youthful fancy, had insensibly taken their places among the images of things actually seen. Yet the illusion was often so powerful, that I almost doubted whether such airy remembrances might not be a sort of innate idea, the print of a recollection in some ancestral mind, transmitted with fainter and fainter impress through several descents, to my own. I felt, indeed, like the stalwart progenitor in person, returning to the hereditary haunts after more than two hundred years, and finding the church, the hall, the farm-house, the cottage, hardly changed during his long absence—the same shady by-paths and hedge-lanes—the same veiled sky, and green lustre of the lawns and fields—while his own affinities for these things, a little obscured by disuse, were reviving at every step.

An American is not very apt to love the English people, as a whole, on whatever length of acquaintance. I fancy that they would value our regard, and even reciprocate it in their ungracious way, if we could give it to them in spite of all rebuffs; but they are beset by a curious and inevitable infelicity, which compels them, as it were, to keep up what they seem to consider a wholesome bitterness of feeling between themselves and all other nationalities, especially that of America. They will never confess it;—nevertheless, it is as essential a tonic to them as their bitter ale. Therefore—and possibly, too, from a similar narrowness in his own character—an American seldom feels quite as if he were at home among the English people. If he do so, he has ceased to be an American. But it requires no long residence to make him love their island, and appreciate it as thoroughly as they themselves do. For my part, I used to wish that we could annex it, transferring their thirty millions of inhabitants to some convenient wilderness in the great West, and putting half or a quarter as many of ourselves into their places. The change would be beneficial to both parties. We, in our dry atmosphere, are getting too nervous, haggard, dyspeptic, extenuated, unsubstantial, theoretic, and need to be made grosser. John Bull, on the other hand, has grown bulbous, long-bodied, short-legged, heavy-witted, material, and, in a word, too intensely English. In a few more centuries, he will be the earthliest creature that ever the earth saw. Heretofore, Providence has obviated such a result by timely intermixtures of alien races with the old English stock; so that each successive conquest of England has proved a victory, by the revivification and improvement of its native manhood. Cannot America and England hit upon some scheme to secure even greater advantages to both nations?

ABOUT WARWICK

BETWEEN bright, new Leamington, the growth of the present century, and rusty Warwick, (founded by King Cymbeline in the twilight ages, a thousand years before the mediæval darkness,) there are two roads, either of which may be measured by a sober-paced pedestrian in less than half-an-hour.

One of these avenues flows out of the midst of the smart parades and crescents of the former town—along by hedges and beneath the shadow of great elms, past stuccoed Elizabethan villas and wayside ale-houses, and through a hamlet of modern aspect—and runs straight into the principal thoroughfare of Warwick. The battlemented turrets of the Castle, embowered half-way up in foliage, and the tall, slender tower of Saint Mary's church rising from among clustered roofs, have been visible almost from the commencement of the walk. Near the entrance of the town stands Saint John's school-house, a picturesque old edifice of stone, with four peaked gables in a row, alternately plain and ornamented, and wide, projecting windows, and a spacious and venerable porch, all overgrown with moss and ivy, and shut in from the world by a high stone-fence, not less mossy than the gabled front. There is an iron-gate, through the rusty open-work of which you see a grassy lawn, and almost expect to meet the shy, curious eyes of the little boys of past generations, peeping forth from their infantile antiquity into the strangeness of our present life. I find a peculiar charm in these long-established English schools, where the schoolboy of to-day sits side by side, as it were, with his great grandsire, on the same old benches, and often, I believe, thumbs a later, but unimproved edition of the same old grammar or arithmetic. The new-fangled notions of a Yankee school-committee would madden many a pedagogue, and shake down the roof of many a time-honored seat of learning, in the mother-country.

At this point, however, we will turn back, in order to follow up the other road from Leamington, which was the one that I loved best to take. It pursues a straight and level course, bordered by wide gravel walks and overhung by the frequent elm, with here a cottage and there a villa, on one side a wooded plantation, and on the other a rich field of grass or grain; until, turning at right angles, it brings you to an arched bridge over the Avon. Its parapet is a balustrade carved out of freestone, into the soft substance of which a multitude of persons have engraved their names or initials, many of them now illegible, while others, more deeply cut, are illuminated with fresh green moss. These tokens indicate a famous spot; and casting our eyes along the smooth gleam and shadow of the quiet stream, through a vista of willows that droop on either side into the water, we behold the gray magnificence of Warwick Castle, uplifting itself among stately trees, and rearing its turrets high above their loftiest branches. We can scarcely think the scene real; so completely do those machicolated towers, the long line of battlements, the massive buttresses, the high-windowed walls, shape out our indistinct ideas of the antique time. It might rather seem as if the sleepy river (being Shakspere's Avon, and often no doubt the mirror of his gorgeous visions) were dreaming now of a lordly residence that stood here many centuries ago; and this fantasy is strengthened, when you observe that the image in the tranquil water has all the distinctness of the actual structure. Either might be the reflection of the other. Wherever Time has gnawed one of the stones, you see the mark of his tooth just as plainly in the sunken reflection. Each is so perfect, that the upper vision seems a castle in the air, and the lower one, an old strong-hold of feudalism, miraculously kept from decay in an enchanted river.

A ruinous and ivy-grown bridge, that projects from the bank a little on the hither side of the castle, has the effect of making the scene appear more entirely apart from the every-day world, for it ends abruptly in the middle of the stream; so that if a cavalcade of the knights and ladies of romance should issue from the old walls, they could never tread on earthly ground, any more than we, approaching from the side of modern realism, can overleap the gulf between our domain and theirs. Yet, if we seek to disenchant ourselves, it may readily be done. Crossing the bridge on which we stand, and passing a little further on, we come to the entrance of the castle, abutting on the highway, and hospitably open, at certain hours, to all curious pilgrims who choose to disburse half-a-crown or so towards the support of the Earl's domestics. The sight of that long series of historic rooms, full of such splendors and rarities as a great English family necessarily gathers about itself, in its hereditary abode, and in the lapse of ages, is well-worth the money, or ten times as much, if indeed the value of the spectacle could be reckoned in money's worth. But after the attendant has hurried you from end to end of the edifice, repeating a guide-book by rote, and exorcising each successive hall of its poetic glamour and witchcraft by the mere tone in which he talks about it, you will make the doleful discovery that Warwick Castle has ceased to be a dream. It is better, methinks, to linger on the bridge, gazing at

Cæsar's tower and Guy's tower in the dim English sunshine above, and in the placid Avon below, and still keep them as thoughts in your own mind, than climb to their summits, or touch even a stone of their actual substance. They will have all the more reality for you, as stalwart relics of immemorial time, if you are reverent enough to leave them in the intangible sanctity of a poetic vision.

From the bridge over the Avon, the road passes in front of the castle-gate, and soon enters the principal street of Warwick, a little beyond Saint John's school-house, already described. Chester itself, most antique of English towns, can hardly show quainter architectural shapes than many of the buildings that border this street. They are mostly of the timber-and-plaster kind, with bowed and decrepit ridge-poles, and a whole chronology of various patchwork in their walls; their low-browed door-ways open upon a sunken floor; their projecting stories peep, as it were, over one another's shoulders, and rise into a multiplicity of peaked gables; they have curious windows, breaking out irregularly all over the house, some even in the roof, set in their own little peaks, opening lattice-wise, and furnished with twenty small panes of lozenge-shaped glass. The architecture of these edifices (a visible oaken frame-work, showing the whole skeleton of the house, as if a man's bones should be arranged on his outside, and his flesh seen through the interstices) is often imitated by modern builders, and with sufficiently picturesque effect. The objection is, that such houses, like all imitations of by-gone styles, have an air of affectation; they do not seem to be built in earnest; they are no better than playthings, or overgrown baby-houses, in which nobody should be expected to encounter the serious realities of either birth or death. Besides, originating nothing, we leave no fashions for another age to copy, when we ourselves shall have grown antique.

Old as it looks, all this portion of Warwick has over-

brimmed, as it were, from the original settlement, being outside of the ancient wall. The street soon runs under an arched
gateway, with a church or some other venerable structure
above it, and admits us into the heart of the town. At one of
my first visits, I witnessed a military display. A regiment of
Warwickshire militia, probably commanded by the Earl, was
going through its drill in the market-place; and on the collar
of one of the officers was embroidered the Bear and Ragged
Staff, which has been the cognizance of the Warwick earldom
from time immemorial. The soldiers were sturdy young men,
with the simple, stolid, yet kindly, faces of English rustics,
looking exceedingly well in a body, but slouching into a
yeomanlike carriage and appearance, the moment they were
dismissed from drill. Squads of them were distributed everywhere about the streets, and sentinels were posted at various
points; and I saw a sergeant, with a great key in his hand, (big
enough to have been the key of the castle's main entrance
when the gate was thickest and heaviest,) apparently setting a
guard. Thus, centuries after feudal times are past, we find
warriors still gathering under the old castle-walls, and commanded by a feudal lord, just as in the days of the King-
Maker, who, no doubt, often mustered his retainers in the
same market-place where I beheld this modern regiment.

The interior of the town wears a less old-fashioned aspect
than the suburbs through which we approach it; and the
High-street has shops with modern plate-glass, and buildings
with stuccoed fronts, exhibiting as few projections to hang a
thought or sentiment upon as if an architect of to-day had
planned them. And, indeed, so far as their surface goes, they
are perhaps new enough to stand unabashed in an American
street; but behind these renovated faces, with their monotonous lack of expression, there is probably the substance of the
same old town that wore a Gothic exterior in the middle ages.
The street is an emblem of England itself. What seems new

in it is chiefly a skilful and fortunate adaptation of what such a people as ourselves would destroy. The new things are based and supported on sturdy old things, and derive a massive strength from their deep and immemorial foundations, though with such limitations and impediments as only an Englishman could endure. But he likes to feel the weight of all the past upon his back; and, moreover, the antiquity that overburdens him has taken root in his being, and has grown to be rather a hump than a pack, so that there is no getting rid of it without tearing his whole structure to pieces. In my judgment, as he appears to be sufficiently comfortable under the mouldy accretion, he had better stumble on with it as long as he can. He presents a spectacle which is by no means without its charm for a disinterested and unencumbered observer.

When the old edifice, or the antiquated custom or institution, appears in its pristine form, without any attempt at intermarrying it with modern fashions, an American cannot but admire the picturesque effect produced by the sudden cropping up of an apparently dead and buried state of society into the actual present, of which he is himself a part. We need not go far in Warwick without encountering an instance of the kind. Proceeding westward through the town, we find ourselves confronted by a huge mass of natural rock, hewn into something like architectural shape, and penetrated by a vaulted passage, which may well have been one of King Cymbeline's original gateways; and on the top of the rock, over the archway, sits a small, old church, communicating with an ancient edifice, or assemblage of edifices, that look down from a similar elevation on the side of the street. A range of trees half hides the latter establishment from the sun. It presents a curious and venerable specimen of the timber-and-plaster style of building, in which some of the finest old houses in England are constructed; the front projects into porticoes and vestibules, and rises into many gables, some in a

row, and others crowning semi-detached portions of the structure; the windows mostly open on hinges, but show a delightful irregularity of shape and position; a multiplicity of chimneys break through the roof at their own will, or, at least,
without any settled purpose of the architect. The whole affair
looks very old; so old, indeed, that the front bulges forth, as if
the timber frame-work were a little weary, at last, of standing
erect so long; but the state of repair is so perfect, and there is
such an indescribable aspect of continuous vitality within the
system of this aged house, that you feel confident that there
may be safe shelter yet, and perhaps for centuries to come,
under its time-honored roof. And on a bench, sluggishly enjoying the sunshine, and looking into the street of Warwick
as from a life apart, a few old men are generally to be seen,
wrapped in long cloaks, on which you may detect the glistening of a silver badge, representing the Bear and Ragged Staff.
These decorated worthies are some of the twelve brethren of
Leycester's Hospital; a community which subsists to-day
under the identical modes that were established for it in the
reign of Queen Elizabeth, and of course retains many features
of a social life that has vanished almost everywhere else.

The edifice itself dates from a much older period than the
charitable institution of which it is now the home. It was the
seat of a religious fraternity, far back in the middle ages, and
continued so till Henry the Eighth turned all the priesthood
of England out of doors, and put the most unscrupulous of his
favorites into their vacant abodes. In many instances, the old
monks had chosen the sites of their domiciles so well, and built
them on such a broad system of beauty and convenience, that
their lay occupants found it easy to convert them into stately
and comfortable homes; and as such they still exist, with
something of the antique reverence lingering about them.
The structure now before us seems to have been first granted
to Sir Nicholas Lestrange, who perhaps intended, like other

men, to establish his household gods in the niches whence he
had thrown down the images of Saints, and to lay his hearth
where an altar had stood. But there was probably a natural
reluctance, in those days (when Catholicism, so lately repu-
diated, must needs have retained an influence over all but the
most obdurate characters) to bring one's hopes of domestic
prosperity and a fortunate lineage into direct hostility with
the awful claims of the ancient religion. At all events, there is
still a superstitious idea, betwixt a fantasy and a belief, that
the possession of former Church-property has drawn a curse
along with it, not only among the posterity of those to whom
it was originally granted, but wherever it has subsequently
been transferred, even if honestly bought and paid for. There
are families, now inhabiting some of the beautiful old abbeys,
who appear to indulge a species of pride in recording the
strange deaths and ugly shapes of misfortune that have occurred among their predecessors, and may be supposed likely
to dog their own pathway down the ages of futurity. Whether
Sir Nicholas Lestrange, in the beef-eating days of Old Harry
and Elizabeth, was a nervous man, and subject to apprehensions of this kind, I cannot tell; but it is certain that he
speedily rid himself of the spoils of the Church, and that,
within twenty years afterwards, the edifice became the property of the famous Dudley, Earl of Leycester, brother of the
Earl of Warwick. He devoted the ancient religious precinct to
a charitable use, endowing it with an ample revenue, and
making it the perpetual home of twelve poor, honest, and
war-broken soldiers, mostly his own retainers, and natives
either of Warwickshire or Gloucestershire. These veterans, or
others wonderfully like them, still occupy their monkish dor-
mitories and haunt the time-darkened corridors and galleries
of the Hospital, leading a life of old-fashioned comfort, wearing the old-fashioned cloaks, and burnishing the identical
silver badges which the Earl of Leycester gave to the original

twelve. He is said to have been a bad man in his day; but he has succeeded in prolonging one good deed into what was to him a distant future.

On the projecting story, over the arched entrance, there is the date, 1571, and several coats-of-arms, either the Earl's or those of his kindred, and immediately above the door-way a stone sculpture of the Bear and Ragged Staff.

Passing through the arch, we find ourselves in a quadrangle, or enclosed court, such as always formed the central part of a great family residence in Queen Elizabeth's time, and earlier. There can hardly be a more perfect specimen of such an establishment than Leycester's Hospital. The quadrangle is a sort of sky-roofed hall, to which there is convenient access from all parts of the house. The four inner fronts, with their high, steep roofs and sharp gables, look into it from antique windows, and through open corridors and galleries along the sides; and there seems to be a richer display of architectural devices and ornaments, quainter carvings in oak, and more fantastic shapes of the timber frame-work, than on the side towards the street. On the wall opposite the arched entrance are the following inscriptions, comprising such moral rules, I presume, as were deemed most essential for the daily observance of the community:

"𝕳onor all 𝕸en"—"𝕱ear 𝕲od"—"𝕳onor the 𝕶ing"— "𝕷ove the 𝕭rotherhood";

and again, as if this latter injunction needed emphasis and repetition among a household of aged people soured with the hard fortune of their previous lives—

"𝕭e kindly affectioned one to another."

One sentence, over a door communicating with the Master's side of the house, is addressed to that dignitary—

"𝕳e that ruleth over men must be just."

All these are charactered in old English letters, and form part of the elaborate ornamentation of the house. Everywhere—on the walls, over windows and doors, and at all points where there is room to place them—appear escutcheons of arms, cognizances, and crests, emblazoned in their proper colors, and illuminating the ancient quadrangle with their splendor. One of these devices is a large image of a porcupine on an heraldic wreath, being the crest of the Lords de Lisle. But especially is the cognizance of the Bear and Ragged Staff repeated over and over, and over again and again, in a great variety of attitudes, at full-length and half-length, in paint and in oaken sculpture, in bas-relief and rounded image. The founder of the Hospital was certainly disposed to reckon his own beneficence as among the hereditary glories of his race; and had he lived and died a half-century earlier, he would have kept up an old Catholic custom by enjoining the twelve bedesmen to pray for the welfare of his soul.

At my first visit, some of the brethren were seated on the bench outside of the edifice, looking down into the street; but they did not vouchsafe me a word, and seemed so estranged from modern life, so enveloped in antique customs and old-fashioned cloaks, that to converse with them would have been like shouting across the gulf between our age and Queen Elizabeth's. So I passed into the quadrangle, and found it quite solitary, except that a plain and neat old woman happened to be crossing it, with an aspect of business and carefulness that bespoke her a woman of this world, and not merely a shadow of the past. Asking her if I could come in, she answered very readily and civilly that I might, and said that I was free to look about me, hinting a hope, however, that I would not open the private doors of the brotherhood, as some visitors were in the habit of doing. Under her guidance, I went into what was formerly the great hall of the establishment, where King James the First had once been feasted by an Earl of Warwick, as is commemorated by an inscription on the cobwebbed and dingy wall. It is a very spacious and barnlike apartment, with a brick-floor, and a vaulted roof, the rafters of which are oaken beams, wonderfully carved, but hardly visible in the duskiness that broods aloft. The hall may have made a splendid appearance, when it was decorated with rich tapestry, and illuminated with chandeliers, cressets, and torches glistening upon silver dishes, where King James sat at supper among his brilliantly dressed nobles; but it has come to base uses in these latter days—being improved, in Yankee phrase, as a brewery and wash-room, and as a cellar for the brethren's separate allotments of coal.

The old lady here left me to myself, and I returned into the quadrangle. It was very quiet, very handsome, in its own obsolete style, and must be an exceedingly comfortable place for the old people to lounge in, when the inclement winds render it inexpedient to walk abroad. There are shrubs against the wall, on one side; and on another is a cloistered walk, adorned with stags' heads and antlers, and running beneath a covered gallery, up to which ascends a balustraded staircase. In the portion of the edifice opposite the entrance-arch are the apartments of the Master; and looking into the window, (as the old woman, at no request of mine, had specially informed me that I might,) I saw a low, but vastly comfortable parlor, very handsomely furnished, and altogether a luxurious place. It had a fire-place with an immense arch, the antique breadth of which extended almost from wall to wall of the room, though now fitted up in such a way that the modern coal-grate looked very diminutive in the midst. Gazing into this pleasant interior, it seemed to me, that, among these venerable surroundings, availing himself of whatever was good in former things, and eking out their imperfection with the results of modern ingenuity, the Master might lead a not unenviable life. On the cloistered side of the quadrangle, where the dark oak panels made the enclosed space dusky, I beheld a curtained window reddened by a great blaze from within, and heard the bubbling and squeaking of something—doubtless very nice and succulent—that was being cooked at the kitchen-fire. I think, indeed, that a whiff or two of the savory fragrance reached my nostrils; at all events, the impression grew upon me that Leycester's Hospital is one of the jolliest old domiciles in England.

I was about to depart, when another old woman, very plainly dressed, but fat, comfortable, and with a cheerful twinkle in her eyes, came in through the arch, and looked curiously at me. This repeated apparition of the gentle sex (though by no means under its loveliest guise) had still an agreeable effect in modifying my ideas of an institution, which I had supposed to be of a stern and monastic character. She asked whether I wished to see the Hospital, and said that the Porter, whose office it was to attend to visitors, was dead, and would be buried that very day; so that the whole establishment could not conveniently be shown me. She kindly invited me, however, to visit the apartment occupied by her husband and herself; so I followed her up the antique staircase, along the gallery, and into a small, oak-panelled parlor, where sat an old man in a long blue garment, who arose and saluted me with much courtesy. He seemed a very quiet person, and yet had a look of travel and adventure, and gray experience, such as I could have fancied in a Palmer of ancient times, who might likewise have worn a similar costume. The little room was carpeted and neatly furnished; a portrait of its occupant was hanging on the wall; and on a table were two swords crossed—one probably his own battle-weapon; and the other, which I drew half out of the scabbard, had an inscription on the blade, purporting that it had been taken from the field of Waterloo. My kind old hostess was anxious to exhibit all the particulars of their housekeeping, and led me into the bedroom, which was in the nicest order, with a snow-white quilt upon the bed; and in a little interven-

ing room was a washing and bathing apparatus—a convenience (judging from the personal aspect and atmosphere of
such parties) seldom to be met with in the humbler ranks of
British life.

The old soldier and his wife both seemed glad of somebody
to talk with; but the good woman availed herself of the
privilege far more copiously than the veteran himself, insomuch that he felt it expedient to give her an occasional nudge
with his elbow in her well-padded ribs. "Don't you be so
talkative!" quoth he; and indeed he could hardly find space
for a word, and quite as little after his admonition as before.
Her nimble tongue ran over the whole system of life in the
Hospital. The brethren, she said, had a yearly stipend, (the
amount of which she did not mention,) and such decent
lodgings as I saw, and some other advantages, free; and instead of being pestered with a great many rules, and made to
dine together at a great table, they could manage their little
household matters as they liked, buying their own dinners,
and having them cooked in the general kitchen, and eating
them snugly in their own parlors. "And," added she, rightly
deeming this the crowning privilege, "with the Master's permission, they can have their wives to take care of them; and
no harm comes of it; and what more can an old man desire!" It
was evident enough that the good dame found herself in what
she considered very rich clover, and, moreover, had plenty of
small occupations to keep her from getting rusty and dull; but
the veteran impressed me as deriving far less enjoyment from
the monotonous ease, without fear of change or hope of
improvement, that had followed upon thirty years of peril and
vicissitude. I fancied, too, that, while pleased with the novelty
of a stranger's visit, he was still a little shy of becoming a
spectacle for the stranger's curiosity; for, if he chose to be
morbid about the matter, the establishment was but an almshouse, in spite of its old-fashioned magnificence, and his fine

blue cloak only a pauper's garment, with a silver badge on it that perhaps galled his shoulder. In truth, the badge and the peculiar garb, though quite in accordance with the manners of the Earl of Leycester's age, are repugnant to modern prejudices, and might fitly and humanely be abolished.

A year or two afterwards I paid another visit to the Hospital, and found a new Porter established in office, and already capable of talking like a guide-book about the history, antiquities, and present condition of the charity. He informed me that the twelve brethren are selected from among old soldiers of good character, whose other resources must not exceed an income of five pounds; thus excluding all commissioned officers, whose half-pay would of course be more than that amount. They receive from the Hospital an annuity of eighty pounds each, besides their apartments, a garment of fine blue cloth, an annual abundance of ale, and a privilege at the kitchen-fire; so that, considering the class from which they are taken, they may well reckon themselves among the fortunate of the earth. Furthermore, they are invested with political rights, acquiring a vote for member of Parliament in virtue either of their income or brotherhood. On the other hand, as regards their personal freedom or conduct, they are subject to a supervision which the Master of the Hospital might render extremely annoying, were he so inclined; but the military restraint under which they have spent the active portion of their lives makes it easier for them to endure the domestic discipline here imposed upon their age. The Porter bore his testimony (whatever were its value) to their being as contented and happy as such a set of old people could possibly be, and affirmed that they spent much time in burnishing their silver badges, and were as proud of them as a nobleman of his star. These badges, by-the-by, except one that was stolen and replaced in Queen Anne's time, are the very same that decorated the original twelve brethren.

I have seldom met with a better guide than my friend the Porter. He appeared to take a genuine interest in the peculiarities of the establishment, and yet had an existence apart from them, so that he could the better estimate what those peculiarities were. To be sure, his knowledge and observation were confined to external things, but, so far, had a sufficiently extensive scope. He led me up the staircase and exhibited portions of the timber frame-work of the edifice that are reckoned to be eight or nine hundred years old, and are still neither worm-eaten nor decayed; and traced out what had been a great hall, in the days of the Catholic fraternity, though its area is now filled up with the apartments of the twelve brethren; and pointed to ornaments of sculptured oak, done in an ancient religious style of art, but hardly visible amid the vaulted dimness of the roof. Thence we went to the Chapel—the Gothic church which I noted several pages back —surmounting the gateway that stretches half across the street. Here the brethren attend daily prayer, and have each a prayer-book of the finest paper, with a fair, large type for their old eyes. The interior of the Chapel is very plain, with a picture of no merit for an altar-piece, and a single old pane of painted glass in the great eastern window, representing—no Saint nor Angel, as is customary in such cases—but that grim sinner, the Earl of Leycester. Nevertheless, amid so many tangible proofs of his human sympathy, one comes to doubt whether the Earl could have been such a hardened reprobate, after all.

We ascended the tower of the Chapel, and looked down between its battlements into the street, a hundred feet below us; while clambering half-way up were fox-glove flowers, weeds, small shrubs, and tufts of grass, that had rooted themselves into the roughnesses of the stone-foundation. Far around us lay a rich and lovely English landscape, with many a church-spire and noble country-seat, and several objects of high historic interest. Edge Hill, where the Puritans defeated Charles the First, is in sight on the edge of the horizon, and much nearer, stands the house where Cromwell lodged on the night before the battle. Right under our eyes, and half-enveloping the town with its high-shouldering wall, so that all the closely compacted streets seemed but a precinct of the estate, was the Earl of Warwick's delightful park, a wide extent of sunny lawns, interspersed with broad contiguities of forest-shade. Some of the cedars of Lebanon were there; a growth of trees in which the Warwick family take an hereditary pride. The two highest towers of the Castle heave themselves up out of a mass of foliage, and look down in a lordly manner upon the plebeian roofs of the town; a part of which are slate-covered, (these are the modern houses,) and a part are coated with old red tiles, denoting the more ancient edifices. A hundred and sixty or seventy years ago, a great fire destroyed a considerable portion of the town, and doubtless annihilated many structures of a remote antiquity; at least, there was a possibility of very old houses in the long Past of Warwick, which King Cymbeline is said to have founded in the year ONE of the Christian era!

And this historic fact or poetic fiction, whichever it may be, brings to mind a more indestructible reality than anything else that has occurred within the present field of our vision; though this includes the scene of Guy of Warwick's legendary exploits, and some of those of the Round Table, to say nothing of the battle of Edge Hill. For perhaps it was in the landscape now under our eyes that Posthumus wandered with the King's daughter, the sweet, chaste, faithful, and courageous Imogen, the tenderest and womanliest woman that Shakspere ever made immortal in the world. The silver Avon, which we see flowing so quietly by the gray Castle, may have held their images in its bosom.

The day, though it began brightly, had long been overcast,

and the clouds now spat down a few spiteful drops upon us, besides that the east-wind was very chill; so we descended the winding tower-stair, and went next into the garden, one side of which is shut in by almost the only remaining portion of the old city-wall. A part of the garden-ground is devoted to grass and shrubbery, and permeated by gravel walks, in the centre of one of which is a beautiful stone vase of Egyptian sculpture, that formerly stood on the top of a Nilometer, or graduated pillar for measuring the rise and fall of the river Nile. On the pedestal is a Latin inscription by Doctor Parr, who (his vicarage of Hatton being so close at hand) was probably often the Master's guest, and smoked his interminable pipe along these garden-walks. Of the vegetable garden, which lies adjacent, the lion's share is appropriated to the Master, and twelve small, separate patches to the individual brethren, who cultivate them at their own judgment and by their own labor; and their beans and cauliflowers have a better flavor, I doubt not, than if they had received them directly from the dead hand of the Earl of Leycester, like the rest of their food. In the farther part of the garden is an arbor for the old men's pleasure and convenience, and I should like well to sit down among them there, and find out what is really the bitter and the sweet of such a sort of life. As for the old gentlemen themselves, they put me queerly in mind of the Salem Custom-House, and the venerable personages whom I found so quietly at anchor there.

The Master's residence, forming one entire side of the quadrangle, fronts on the garden, and wears an aspect at once stately and homely. It can hardly have undergone any perceptible change within three centuries; but the garden, into which its old windows look, has probably put off a great many eccentricities and quaintnesses, in the way of cunningly clipt shrubbery, since the gardener of Queen Elizabeth's reign threw down his rusty shears and took his departure. The present Master's name is Harris; he is a descendant of the founder's family, a gentleman of independent fortune, and a clergyman of the established church, as the regulations of the Hospital require him to be. I know not what are his official emoluments; but, according to all English precedent, an ancient charitable fund is certain to be held directly for the behoof of those who administer it, and perhaps incidentally, in a moderate way, for the nominal beneficiaries; and, in the case before us, the twelve brethren being so comfortably provided for, the Master is likely to be at least as comfortable as all the twelve together. Yet I ought not, even in a distant land, to fling an idle gibe against a gentleman of whom I really know nothing; except that the people under his charge bear all possible tokens of being tended and cared for as sedulously as if each of them sat by a warm fireside of his own, with a daughter bustling round the hearth to make ready his porridge and his tit-bits. It is delightful to think of the good life which a suitable man, in the Master's position, has an opportunity to lead; linked to time-honored customs, welded in with an ancient system, never dreaming of radical change, and bringing all the mellowness and richness of the past down into these railway days, which do not compel him or his community to move a whit quicker than of yore. Everybody can appreciate the advantages of going ahead; it might be well, sometimes, to think whether there is not a word or two to be said in favor of standing still, or going to sleep.

From the garden we went into the kitchen, where the fire was burning hospitably, and diffused a genial warmth far and wide, together with the fragrance of some old English roast-beef, which, I think, must at that moment have been done nearly to a turn. The kitchen is a lofty, spacious, and noble room, partitioned off round the fire-place, by a sort of semi-circular oaken screen, or, rather, an arrangement of heavy and high-backed settles, with an ever-open entrance between them, on either side of which is the omnipresent image of the Bear and Ragged Staff, three feet high, and excellently carved in oak, now black with time and unctuous kitchen-smoke. The ponderous mantel-piece, likewise of carved oak, towers high towards the dusky ceiling, and extends its mighty breadth to take in a vast area of hearth; the arch of the fire-place being positively so immense that I could compare it to nothing but the city-gateway. Above its cavernous opening were crossed two ancient halberds, the weapons, possibly, of soldiers who had fought under Leycester in the Low Countries; and elsewhere on the walls were displayed several muskets, which some of the present inmates of the Hospital may have levelled against the French. Another ornament of the mantel-piece was a square of silken needle-work or embroidery, faded nearly white, but dimly representing that wearisome Bear and Ragged Staff, which we should hardly look twice at, only that it was wrought by the fair fingers of poor Amy Robsart, and beautifully framed in oak from Kenilworth Castle at the expense of a Mr. Conner, a countryman of our own. Certainly, no Englishman would be capable of this little bit of enthusiasm. Finally, the kitchen-firelight glistens on a splendid display of copper flagons, all of generous capacity, and one of them about as big as a half-barrel; the smaller vessels contain the customary allowance of ale, and the larger one is filled with that foaming liquor on four festive occasions of the year, and emptied amain by the jolly brotherhood. I should be glad to see them do it; but it would be an exploit fitter for Queen Elizabeth's age than these degenerate times.

The kitchen is the social hall of the twelve brethren. In the daytime, they bring their little messes to be cooked here, and eat them in their own parlors; but after a certain hour, the great hearth is cleared and swept, and the old men assemble round its blaze, each with his tankard and his pipe, and hold high converse through the evening. If the Master be a fit man for his office, methinks he will sometimes sit down sociably among them; for there is an elbow-chair by the fireside which it would not demean his dignity to fill, since it was occupied by King James at the great festival of nearly three centuries ago. A sip of the ale and a whiff of the tobacco-pipe would put him in friendly relations with his venerable household; and then we can fancy him instructing them by pithy apothegms and religious texts which were first uttered here by some Catholic priest and have impregnated the atmosphere ever since. If a joke goes round, it shall be of an elder coinage than Joe Miller's, as old as Lord Bacon's collection, or as the jest-book that Master Slender asked for when he lacked small-talk for sweet Anne Page. No news shall be spoken of, later than the drifting ashore, on the northern coast, of some stern-post or figure-head, a barnacled fragment of one of the great galleons of the Spanish Armada. What a tremor would pass through the antique group, if a damp newspaper should suddenly be spread to dry before the fire! They would feel as if either that printed sheet or they themselves must be an unreality. What a mysterious awe, if the shriek of the railway-train, as it reaches the Warwick station, should ever so faintly invade their ears! Movement of any kind seems inconsistent with the stability of such an institution. Nevertheless, I trust that the ages will carry it along with them; because it is such a pleasant kind of dream for an American to find his way thither, and behold a piece of the sixteenth century set into our prosaic times, and then to depart, and think of its arched door-way as a spell-guarded entrance which will never be accessible or visible to him any more.

Not far from the market-place of Warwick stands the great church of Saint Mary's; a vast edifice, indeed, and almost worthy to be a cathedral. People who pretend to skill in such matters say that it is in a poor style of architecture, though de-

signed (or, at least, extensively restored) by Sir Christopher
Wren; but I thought it very striking, with its wide, high, and
elaborate windows, its tall tower, its immense length, and (for
it was long before I outgrew this Americanism, the love of an
old thing merely for the sake of its age) the tinge of gray
antiquity over the whole. Once, while I stood gazing up at the
tower, the clock struck twelve with a very deep intonation,
and immediately some chimes began to play, and kept up
their resounding music for five minutes, as measured by the
hand upon the dial. It was a very delightful harmony, as airy
as the notes of birds, and seemed a not unbecoming freak of
half-sportive fancy in the huge, ancient, and solemn church;
although I have seen an old-fashioned parlor-clock that did
precisely the same thing, in its small way.

The great attraction of this edifice is the Beauchamp (or, as
the English, who delight in vulgarizing their fine old Norman
names, call it, the Beechum) chapel, where the Earls of
Warwick and their kindred have been buried, from four
hundred years back till within a recent period. It is a stately
and very elaborate chapel, with a large window of ancient
painted glass, as perfectly preserved as any that I remember
seeing in England, and remarkably vivid in its colors. Here
are several monuments with marble figures recumbent upon
them, representing the earls in their knightly armor and their
dames in the ruffs and court-finery of their day, looking
hardly stiffer in stone than they must needs have been in their
starched linen and embroidery. The renowned Earl of Leycester of Queen Elizabeth's time, the benefactor of the Hospital,
reclines at full length on the tablet of one of these tombs, side
by side with his Countess—not Amy Robsart, but a lady who
(unless I have confused the story with some other mouldy
scandal) is said to have avenged poor Amy's murder by poi-
soning the Earl himself. Be that as it may, both figures, and
especially the Earl, look like the very types of ancient Honor

and Conjugal Faith. In consideration of his long-enduring kindness to the twelve brethren, I cannot consent to believe him as wicked as he is usually depicted; and it seems a marvel, now that so many well-established historical verdicts have been reversed, why some enterprising writer does not make out Leycester to have been the pattern nobleman of his age.

In the centre of the chapel is the magnificent memorial of its founder, Richard Beauchamp, Earl of Warwick in the time of Henry the Sixth. On a richly ornamented altar-tomb of gray marble lies the bronze figure of a knight in gilded armor, most admirably executed; for the sculptors of those days had wonderful skill in their own style, and could make so life-like an image of a warrior, in brass or marble, that, if a trumpet were sounded over his tomb, you would expect him to start up and handle his sword. The Earl whom we now speak of, however, has slept soundly in spite of a more serious disturbance than any blast of a trumpet, unless it were the final one. Some centuries after his death, the floor of the chapel fell down and broke open the stone-coffin in which he was buried; and among the fragments appeared the anciently entombed Earl of Warwick with the color scarcely faded out of his cheeks, his eyes a little sunken, but in other respects looking as natural as if he had died yesterday. But exposure to the atmosphere appeared to begin and finish the long-delayed process of decay in a moment, causing him to vanish like a bubble; so that, almost before there had been time to wonder at him, there was nothing left of the stalwart Earl save his hair. This sole relic the ladies of Warwick made prize of, and braided it into rings and brooches for their own adornment; and thus, with a chapel and a ponderous tomb built on purpose to protect his remains, this great nobleman could not help being brought untimely to the light of day, nor even keep his love-locks on his skull, after he had so long done with love. There seems to be a fatality that disturbs people in their sepulchres, when they have been over-careful to render them magnificent and impregnable; as witness the builders of the Pyramids, and Hadrian, Augustus, and the Scipios, and most other personages whose mausoleums have been conspicuous enough to attract the violator; and as for dead men's hair, I have seen a lock of King Edward the Fourth's, of a reddish brown color, which perhaps was once twisted round the delicate forefinger of Mistress Shore.

The direct lineage of the renowned characters, that lie buried in this splendid chapel, has long been extinct. The earldom is now held by the Grevilles, descendants of the Lord Brooke who was slain in the Parliamentary War; and they have recently (that is to say, within a century) built a burial vault on the other side of the church, calculated (as the Sexton assured me, with a nod as if he were pleased) to afford suitable and respectful accommodation to as many as fourscore coffins. Thank Heaven, the old man did not call them 'CASKETS'!—a vile modern phrase, which compels a person of sense and good taste to shrink more disgustfully than ever before from the idea of being buried at all. But, as regards those eighty coffins, only sixteen have as yet been contributed; and it may be a question with some minds, not merely whether the Grevilles will hold the Earldom of Warwick until the full number shall be made up, but whether earldoms and all manner of lordships will not have faded out of England, long before those many generations shall have passed from the castle to the vault. I hope not. A titled and landed aristocracy, if anywise an evil and an incumbrance, is so only to the nation which is doomed to bear it on its shoulders; and an American, whose sole relation to it is to admire its picturesque effect upon society, ought to be the last man to quarrel with what affords him so much gratuitous enjoyment. Nevertheless, conservative as England is, and though I scarce ever found an Englishman who seemed really to desire change, there was continually a dull sound in my ears as if the old foundations of things were crumbling away. Some time or other—by no irreverent effort of violence, but, rather, in spite of all pious efforts to uphold a heterogeneous pile of institutions that will have outlasted their vitality—at some unexpected moment, there must come a terrible crash. The sole reason why I should desire it to happen in my day is, that I might be there to see! But the ruin of my own country is perhaps all that I am destined to witness; and that immense catastrophe (though I am strong in the faith that there is a national lifetime of a thousand years in us yet) would serve any man well enough as his final spectacle on earth.

If the visitor is inclined to carry away any little memorial of Warwick, he had better go to an Old Curiosity Shop in the High-street, where there is a vast quantity of obsolete gewgaws, great and small, and many of them so pretty and ingenious that you wonder how they came to be thrown aside and forgotten. As regards its minor tastes, the world changes, but does not improve; it appears to me, indeed, that there have been epochs of far more exquisite fancy than the present one, in matters of personal ornament, and such delicate trifles as we put upon a drawing-room table, a mantel-piece, or a what-not. The shop in question is near the East-gate, but is hardly to be found without careful search, being denoted only by the name of 'REDFERN,' painted not very conspicuously in the top-light of the door. Immediately on entering we find ourselves among a confusion of old rubbish and valuables, ancient armor, historic portraits, ebony cabinets, inlaid with pearl, tall, ghostly clocks, hideous old china, dim looking-glasses in frames of tarnished magnificence; a thousand objects of strange aspect, and others that almost frighten you by their likeness in unlikeness to things now in use. It is impossible to give an idea of the variety of articles, so thickly strewn about that we can scarcely move without overthrowing some great curiosity with a crash, or sweeping away some small one hitched to our sleeves. Three stories of the entire house are crowded in like manner. The collection, even as we see it exposed to view, must have been got together at great cost; but the real treasures of the establishment lie in secret repositories, whence they are not likely to be drawn forth at an ordinary summons; though, if a gentleman with a competently long purse should call for them, I doubt not that the signet-ring of Joseph's friend Pharaoh, or the Duke of Alva's leading-staff, or the dagger that killed the Duke of Buckingham, (all of which I have seen,) or any other almost incredible thing, might make its appearance. Gold snuff-boxes, antique gems, jewelled goblets, Venetian wine-glasses, (which burst when poison is poured into them, and therefore must not be used for modern wine-drinking,) jasper-handled knives, painted Sèvres tea-cups; in short, there are all sorts of things that a virtuoso ransacks the world to discover.

It would be easier to spend a hundred pounds in Mr. Redfern's shop than to keep the money in one's pocket; but for my part, I contented myself with buying a little old spoon of silver-gilt, and fantastically shaped, and got it at all the more reasonable rate because there happened to be no legend attached to it. I could supply any deficiency of that kind at much less expense than re-gilding the spoon!

RECOLLECTIONS OF A GIFTED WOMAN

FROM Leamington to Stratford-on-Avon the distance is eight or nine miles, over a road that seemed to me most beautiful. Not that I can recall any memorable peculiarities; for the country, most of the way, is a succession of the gentlest swells and subsidencies, affording wide and far glimpses of champaign-scenery, here and there, and sinking almost to a dead level as we draw near Stratford. Any landscape in New England, even the tamest, has a more striking outline, and besides would have its blue eyes open in those lakelets that we encounter almost from mile to mile at home, but of which the Old Country is utterly destitute; or it would smile in our faces through the medium of the wayside brooks that vanish under a low stone-arch, on one side of the road, and sparkle out again on the other. Neither of these pretty features is often to be found in an English scene. The charm of the latter consists in the rich verdure of the fields, in the stately wayside trees and carefully kept plantations of wood, and in the old and high cultivation that has humanized the very sods by mingling so much of man's toil and care among them. To an American there is a kind of sanctity even in an English turnip-field, when he thinks how long that small square of ground has been known and recognized as a possession, transmitted from father to son, trodden often by memorable feet, and utterly redeemed from savagery by old acquaintanceship with civilized eyes. The wildest things in England are more than half-tame. The trees, for instance, whether in hedge-row, park, or what they call forest, have nothing wild about them. They are never ragged; there is a certain decorous restraint in the freest outspread of their branches, though they spread wider than any self-nurturing tree; they are tall, vigorous, bulky, with a look of age-long life, and a promise of more years to come, all of which will bring them into closer kindred with the race of man. Somebody or other has known them from the sapling upward; and if they endure long enough, they grow to be traditionally observed and honored, and connected with the fortunes of old families, till, like Tennyson's Talking Oak, they babble with a thousand leafy tongues to ears that can understand them.

An American tree, however, if it could grow in fair competition with an English one of similar species, would probably be the more picturesque object of the two. The Warwickshire elm has not so beautiful a shape as those that overhang our village-streets; and as for the redoubtable English oak, there is a certain John Bullism in its figure, a compact rotundity of foliage, a lack of irregular and various outline, that make it look wonderfully like a gigantic cauliflower. Its leaf, too, is much smaller than that of most varieties of American oak; nor do I mean to doubt that the latter, with free leave to grow, reverent care and cultivation, and immunity from the axe, would live out its centuries as sturdily as its English brother, and prove far the nobler and more majestic specimen of a tree, at the end of them. Still, however one's Yankee patriotism may struggle against the admission, it must be owned that the trees and other objects of an English landscape take hold of the observer by numberless minute tendrils, as it were, which, look as closely as we choose, we never find in an American scene. The parasitic growth is so luxuriant, that the trunk of the tree, so gray and dry in our climate, is better worth observing than the boughs and foliage; a verdant mossiness coats it all over, so that it looks almost as green as the leaves; and often, moreover, the stately stem is clustered about, high upward, with creeping and twining shrubs, the ivy, and sometimes the misletoe, close, clinging friends, nurtured by the moisture and never too fervid sunshine, and supporting themselves by the old tree's abundant strength. We call it a parasitical vegetation, but if the phrase imply any reproach, it is unkind to bestow it on this beautiful affection and relationship which exist in England between one order of plants and another; the strong tree being always ready to give support to the trailing shrub, lift it to the sun, and feed it out of its own heart, if it crave such food; and the shrub, on its part, repaying its foster-father with an ample luxuriance of beauty, and adding Corinthian grace to the tree's lofty strength. No bitter winter nips these tender little sympathies, no hot sun burns the life out of them, and therefore they outlast the longevity of the oak, and, if the woodman permitted, would bury it in a green grave when all is over.

Should there be nothing else along the road to look at, an English hedge might well suffice to occupy the eyes, and, to a depth beyond what he would suppose, the heart of an American. We often set out hedges in our own soil, but might as well set out figs or pine-apples and expect to gather fruit of them. Something grows, to be sure, which we choose to call a hedge; but it lacks the dense, luxuriant variety of vegetation that is accumulated into the English original, in which a botanist would find a thousand shrubs and gracious herbs that the hedge-maker never thought of planting there. Among them, growing wild, are many of the kindred blossoms of the very flowers which our pilgrim-fathers brought from England, for the sake of their simple beauty and homelike associations, and which we have ever since been cultivating in gardens. There is not a softer trait to be found in the character of those stern men than that they should have been sensible of these flower-roots clinging among the fibres of their rugged hearts, and have felt the necessity of bringing them over sea and making them hereditary in the new land, instead of trusting to what rarer beauty the wilderness might have in store for them.

Or, if the roadside has no hedge, the ugliest stone-fence (such as, in America, would keep itself bare and unsympathizing till the end of time) is sure to be covered with the small handiwork of Nature; that careful mother lets nothing go naked there, and if she cannot provide clothing, gives at least embroidery. No sooner is the fence built, than she adopts and adorns it as a part of her original plan, treating the hard, uncomely construction as if it had all along been a favorite idea of her own. A little sprig of ivy may be seen creeping up the side of the low wall, and clinging fast with its many feet to the rough surface; a tuft of grass roots itself between two of the stones, where a pinch or two of wayside dust has been moistened into nutritious soil for it; a small bunch of fern grows in another crevice; a deep, soft, verdant moss spreads itself along the top and over all the available inequalities of the fence; and where nothing else will grow, lichens stick tenaciously to the bare stones and variegate the monotonous gray with hues of yellow and red. Finally, a great deal of shrubbery clusters along the base of the stone-wall, and takes away the hardness of its outline; and in due time, as the upshot of these apparently aimless or sportive touches, we recognize that the beneficent Creator of all things, working through His handmaiden whom we call Nature, has deigned to mingle a charm of divine gracefulness even with so earthly an institution as a boundary-fence. The clown who wrought at it little dreamed what fellow-laborer he had.

The English should send us photographs of portions of the trunks of trees, the tangled and various products of a hedge, and a square foot of an old wall. They can hardly send anything else so characteristic. Their artists, especially of the later school, sometimes toil to depict such subjects, but are apt to stiffen the lithe tendrils in the process. The poets succeed better, with Tennyson at their head, and often produce ravishing effects by dint of a tender minuteness of touch, to which the genius of the soil and climate artfully impels them; for, as regards grandeur, there are loftier scenes in many countries than the best that England can show; but, for the picturesqueness of the smallest object that lies under its gentle gloom and sunshine, there is no scenery like it anywhere.

In the foregoing paragraphs, I have strayed away to a long distance from the road to Stratford-on-Avon; for I remember no such stone-fences as I have been speaking of in Warwickshire, nor elsewhere in England except among the Lakes, or in Yorkshire and the rough and hilly counties to the north of it. Hedges there were along my road, however, and broad, level fields, rustic hamlets, and cottages of ancient date, from the roof of one of which the occupant was tearing away the thatch, and showing what an accumulation of dust, dirt, mouldiness, roots of weeds, families of mice, swallows' nests, and hordes of insects, had been deposited there since that old straw was new. Estimating its antiquity from these tokens, Shakspere, himself, in one of his morning rambles out of his native town, might have seen the thatch laid on; at all events, the cottage-walls were old enough to have known him as a guest. A few modern villas were also to be seen, and perhaps there were mansions of old gentility at no great distance, but hidden among trees; for it is a point of English pride that such houses seldom allow themselves to be visible from the high-road. In short, I recollect nothing specially remarkable along the way, nor in the immediate approach to Stratford; and yet the picture of that June morning has a glory in my memory, owing chiefly, I believe, to the charm of the English summer-weather, the really good days of which are the most delightful that mortal man can ever hope to be favored with. Such a genial warmth! A little too warm, it might be, yet only to such a degree as to assure an American (a certainty to which he seldom attains till attempered to the customary austerity of an English summer-day) that he was quite warm enough. And after all, there was an unconquerable freshness in the atmosphere, which every little movement of a breeze shook over me like a dash of the ocean-spray. Such days need bring us no other happiness than their own light and temperature. No doubt, I could not have enjoyed it so exquisitely, except that there must be still latent in us Western wanderers (even after an absence of two centuries and more) an adaptation to the English climate which makes us sensible of a motherly kindness in its scantiest sunshine, and overflows us with delight at its more lavish smiles.

The spire of Shakspere's church—the Church of the Holy Trinity—begins to show itself among the trees at a little distance from Stratford. Next we see the shabby old dwellings, intermixed with mean-looking houses of modern date; and the streets being quite level, you are struck and surprised by nothing so much as the tameness of the general scene; as if Shakspere's genius were vivid enough to have wrought pictorial splendors in the town where he was born. Here and there, however, a queer edifice meets your eye, endowed with the individuality that belongs only to the domestic architecture of times gone by; the house seems to have grown out of some odd quality in its inhabitant, as a sea-shell is moulded from within by the character of its inmate; and having been built in a strange fashion, generations ago, it has ever since been growing stranger and quainter, as old humorists are apt to do. Here too, (as so often impressed me in decayed English towns,) there appeared to be a greater abundance of aged people wearing small-clothes, and leaning on sticks, than you could assemble on our side of the water by sounding a trumpet and proclaiming a reward for the most venerable. I tried to account for this phenomenon by several theories; as, for example, that our new towns are unwholesome for age and kill it off unseasonably; or that our old men have a subtle sense of fitness, and die of their own accord rather than live in an unseemly contrast with youth and novelty; but the secret may be, after all, that hair-dyes, false teeth, modern arts of dress, and other contrivances of a skin-deep youthfulness, have not crept into these antiquated English towns, and so people grow old without the weary necessity of seeming younger than they are.

After wandering through two or three streets, I found my way to Shakspere's birth-place, which is almost a smaller and humbler house than any description can prepare the visitor to expect; so inevitably does an august inhabitant make his abode palatial to our imaginations, receiving his guests, indeed, in a castle in the air, until we unwisely insist on meeting him among the sordid lanes and alleys of lower earth. The portion of the edifice with which Shakspere had anything to do is hardly large enough, in the basement, to contain the butcher's stall that one of his descendants kept, and that still remains there, windowless, with the cleaver-cuts in its hacked counter, which projects into the street under a little pent-house roof, as if waiting for a new occupant. The upper half of the door was open, and on my rapping at it, a young person in black made her appearance and admitted me; she was not a menial, but remarkably genteel (an American characteristic) for an English girl, and was probably the daughter of the old gentlewoman who takes care of the house. This lower room has a pavement of gray slabs of stone, which may have been rudely squared when the house was new, but are now all cracked, broken, and disarranged in a most unaccountable way. One does not see how any ordinary usage, for whatever length of time, should have so smashed these heavy stones; it is as if an earthquake had burst up through the floor, which afterwards had been imperfectly trodden down again. The room is white-washed and very clean, but woefully shabby and dingy, coarsely built, and such as the most poetical imagination would find it difficult to idealize. In the rear of this apartment is the kitchen, a still smaller room of a similar rude aspect; it has a great, rough fire-place, with space for a large family under the blackened opening of the chimney, and an immense passage-way for the smoke, through which Shakspere may have seen the blue sky by day and the stars glimmering down at him by night. It is now a dreary spot where the long-extinguished embers used to be. A glowing fire, even if it covered only a quarter part of the hearth, might still do much towards making the old kitchen cheerful; but we get a depressing idea of the stifled, poor, sombre kind of life that could have been lived in such a dwelling, where this room seems to have been the gathering-place of the family, with no breadth or scope, no good retirement, but old and young huddling together cheek by jowl! What a hardy plant was Shakspere's genius, how fatal its development, since it could not be blighted in such an atmosphere! It only brought human nature the closer to him, and put more unctuous earth about his roots.

Thence I was ushered up stairs to the room in which Shakspere is supposed to have been born; though, if you peep too curiously into the matter, you may find the shadow of an ugly doubt on this, as well as most other points of his mysterious life. It is the chamber over the butcher's shop, and is lighted by one broad window containing a great many small, irregular panes of glass. The floor is made of planks, very rudely hewn and fitting together with little neatness; the naked beams and rafters, at the sides of the room and over-head, bear the original marks of the builder's broad axe, with no evidence of an attempt to smooth off the job. Again we have to reconcile ourselves to the smallness of the space enclosed by these illustrious walls—a circumstance more difficult to accept, as regards places that we have heard, read, thought, and dreamed much about, than any other disenchanting particular of a mistaken ideal. A few paces—perhaps seven or eight—take us from end to end of it. So low it is, that I could easily touch the ceiling, and might have done so without a tiptoe-stretch, had it been a good deal higher; and this humility of the chamber has tempted a vast multitude of people to write their names overhead in pencil. Every inch of the side-walls, even into the obscurest nooks and corners, is covered with a similar record; all the window-panes, moreover, are scrawled with diamond-signatures, among which is said to be that of Walter Scott; but so many persons have sought to immortalize themselves in close vicinity to his name that I really could not trace him out. Methinks it is strange that people do not strive to forget their forlorn little identities, in such situations, instead of thrusting them forward into the dazzle of a great renown, where, if noticed, they cannot but be deemed impertinent.

This room, and the entire house, so far as I saw it, are white-washed and exceedingly clean; nor is there the aged, musty smell with which old Chester first made me acquainted, and which goes far to cure an American of his excessive predilection for antique residences. An old lady, who took charge of me upstairs, had the manners and aspect of a gentlewoman, and talked with somewhat formidable knowledge and appreciative intelligence about Shakspere. Arranged on a table and in chairs were various prints, views of houses and scenes connected with Shakspere's memory, together with editions of his works and local publications about his home and haunts, from the sale of which this respectable lady perhaps realizes a handsome profit. At any rate, I bought a good many of them, conceiving that it might be the civillest way of requiting her for her instructive conversation and the trouble she took in showing me the house. It cost me a pang (not a curmudgeonly, but a gentlemanly one) to offer a downright fee to the ladylike girl who had admitted me; but I swallowed my delicate scruples with some little difficulty, and she digested hers, so far as I could observe, with no difficulty at all. In fact, nobody need fear to hold out half-a-crown to any person with whom he has occasion to speak a word in England.

I should consider it unfair to quit Shakspere's house without the frank acknowledgement that I was conscious of not the slightest emotion while viewing it, nor any quickening of the imagination. This has often happened to me in my visits to memorable places. Whatever pretty and apposite reflections I may have made upon the subject had either occurred to me before I ever saw Stratford, or have been elaborated since. It is pleasant, nevertheless, to think that I have seen the place; and I believe that I can form a more sensible and vivid idea of Shakspere as a flesh-and-blood individual now that I have stood on the kitchen-hearth and in the birth-chamber; but I am not quite certain that this power of realization is altogether desirable in reference to a great poet. The Shakspere whom I met there took various guises, but had not his laurel on. He was successively the roguish boy; the youthful deer-stealer; the comrade of players; the too familiar friend of Davenant's mother; the careful, thrifty, thriven man of property, who came back from London to lend money on bond and occupy the best house in Stratford; the mellow, red-nosed, autumnal boon-companion of John a' Combe; and finally, (or else the Stratford gossips belied him,) the victim of convivial habits who met his death by tumbling into a ditch on his way home from a drinking-bout, and left his second-best bed to his poor wife. I feel, as sensibly as the reader can, what horrible impiety it is to remember these things, be they true or false. In either case, they ought to vanish out of sight on the distant ocean-line of the past, leaving a pure, white memory, even as a sail, though perhaps darkened with many stains, looks snowy white on the far horizon. But I draw a moral from these unworthy reminiscences and this embodiment of the poet, as suggested by some of the grimy actualities of his life. It is for the high interests of the world not to insist upon finding out that its greatest men are, in a certain lower sense, very much the same kind of men as the rest of us, and often a little worse; because a common mind cannot properly digest such a discovery, nor ever know the true proportion of the great man's good and evil, nor how small a part of him it was that touched our muddy or dusty earth. Thence comes moral bewilderment, and even intellectual loss in regard to what is best of him. When Shakspere invoked a curse on the man who should stir his bones, he perhaps meant the larger share of it for him or them who should pry into his perishing earthliness, the defects or even the merits of the character that he wore in Stratford, when he had left mankind so much to muse upon that was imperishable and divine. Heaven keep me from incurring any part of the anathema in requital for the irreverent sentences above written!

From Shakspere's house, the next step, of course, is to visit his burial-place. The appearance of the church is most venerable and beautiful, standing amid a great green shadow of lime-trees, above which rises the spire, while the Gothic battlements and buttresses and vast arched windows are obscurely seen through the boughs. The Avon loiters past the churchyard, an exceedingly sluggish river, which might seem to have been considering which way it should flow ever since

Shakspere left off paddling in it, and gathering the large forget-me-nots that grow among its flags and water-weeds.

An old man in small-clothes was waiting at the gate; and inquiring whether I wished to go in, he preceded me to the church-porch, and rapped. I could have done it quite as effectually for myself; but, it seems, the old people of the neighborhood haunt about the churchyard, in spite of the frowns and remonstrances of the sexton, who grudges them the half-eleemosynary sixpence which they sometimes get from visitors. I was admitted into the church by a respectable-looking and intelligent man in black, the parish-clerk, I suppose, and probably holding a richer incumbency than his vicar, if all the fees which he handles remain in his own pocket. He was already exhibiting the Shakspere monuments to two or three visitors, and several other parties came in while I was there.

The poet and his family are in possession of what may be considered the very best burial-places that the church affords. They lie in a row, right across the breadth of the chancel, the foot of each grave-stone being close to the elevated floor on which the altar stands. Nearest to the side-wall, beneath Shakspere's bust, is a slab bearing a Latin inscription addressed to his wife, and covering her remains; then his own slab, with the old anathematizing stanza upon it; then that of Thomas Nash, who married his granddaughter; then that of Doctor Hall, the husband of his daughter Susannah; and, lastly, Susannah's own. Shakspere's is the commonest-looking slab of all, being just such a flag-stone as Essex-street in Salem used to be paved with, when I was a boy. Moreover, unless my eyes or recollection deceive me, there is a crack across it, as if it had already undergone some such violence as the inscription deprecates. Unlike the other monuments of the family, it bears no name, nor am I acquainted with the grounds or

authority on which it is absolutely determined to be Shakspere's; although, being in a range with those of his wife and
children, it might naturally be attributed to him. But then
why does his wife, who died afterwards, take precedence of
him and occupy the place next his bust? And where are the
graves of another daughter and a son, who have a better right
in the family-row than Thomas Nash, his grandson-in-law?
Might not one or both of them have been laid under the
nameless stone? But it is dangerous trifling with Shakspere's
dust; so I forbear to meddle further with the grave (though
the prohibition makes it tempting) and shall let whatever
bones be in it rest in peace. Yet I must needs add that the
inscription on the bust seems to imply that Shakspere's grave
was directly underneath it.

The poet's bust is affixed to the northern wall of the
church, the base of it being about a man's height, or rather
more, above the floor of the chancel. The features of this
piece of sculpture are entirely unlike any portrait of Shakspere that I have ever seen, and compel me to take down the
beautiful, lofty-browed, and noble picture of him which has
hitherto hung in my mental portrait-gallery. The bust cannot
be said to represent a beautiful face or an eminently noble
head, but it clutches firmly hold of one's sense of reality and
insists upon your accepting it, if not as Shakspere the poet, yet
as the wealthy burgher of Stratford, the friend of John a'
Combe who lies yonder in the corner. I know not what the
phrenologists say to the bust. The forehead is but moderately
developed, and retreats somewhat, the upper part of the skull
rising pyramidally; the eyes are prominent almost beyond the
pent-house of the brow; the upper lip is so long that it must
have been almost a deformity, unless the sculptor artistically
exaggerated its length, in consideration that, on the pedestal,
it must be foreshortened by being looked at from below. On
the whole, Shakspere must have had a singular rather than a

prepossessing face; and it is wonderful how, with this bust before its eyes, the world has persisted in maintaining an erroneous notion of his appearance, allowing painters and sculptors to foist their idealized nonsense on us all, instead of the genuine man. For my part, the Shakspere of my mind's eye is henceforth to be a personage of a ruddy English complexion, with a reasonably capacious brow, intelligent and quickly observant eyes, a nose curved slightly outward, a long, queer upper lip, with the mouth a little unclosed beneath it, and cheeks considerably developed in the lower part and beneath the chin. But when Shakspere was himself (for nine-tenths of the time, according to all appearances, he was but the burgher of Stratford) he doubtless shone through this dull mask and transfigured it into the face of an angel.

Fifteen or twenty feet behind the row of Shakspere grave-stones is the great east-window of the church, now brilliant with stained glass of recent manufacture. On one side of this window, under a sculptured arch of marble, lies a full-length marble figure of John a' Combe, clad in what I take to be a robe of municipal dignity and holding his hands devoutly clasped. It is a sturdy English figure, with coarse features, a type of ordinary man whom we smile to see immortalized in the sculpturesque material of poets and heroes; but the prayer-ful attitude encourages us to believe that the old usurer may not, after all, have had that grim reception in the other world which Shakspere's squib foreboded for him. By-the-by, till I grew somewhat familiar with Warwickshire pronunciation, I never understood that the point of those ill-natured lines was a pun. 'Oho!' quoth the Devil, ' 'tis my John a' Combe!'—that is, 'My John has come!'

Close to the poet's bust is a nameless, oblong, cubic tomb, supposed to be that of a clerical dignitary of the fourteenth century. The church has other mural monuments and altar-tombs, one or two of the latter upholding the recumbent figures of knights in armor and their dames, very eminent and worshipful personages in their day, no doubt, but doomed to appear forever intrusive and impertinent within the precincts which Shakspere has made his own. His renown is tyrannous, and suffers nothing else to be recognized within the scope of its material presence, unless illuminated by some side ray from himself. The clerk informed me that interments no longer take place in any part of the church. And it is better so; for methinks a person of delicate individuality, curious about his burial-place, and desirous of six feet of earth for himself alone, could never endure to lie buried near Shakspere, but would rise up at midnight and grope his way out of the church-door, rather than sleep in the shadow of so stupendous a memory.

I should hardly have dared to add another to the innumerable descriptions of Stratford-on-Avon, if it had not seemed to me that this would form a fitting frame-work to some reminiscences of a very remarkable woman. Her labor, while she lived, was of a nature and purpose outwardly irreverent to the name of Shakspere, yet, by its actual tendency, entitling her to the distinction of being that one of all his worshippers who sought, though she knew it not, to place the richest and stateliest diadem upon his brow. We Americans, at least, in the scanty annals of our literature, cannot afford to forget her high and conscientious exercise of noble faculties, which, indeed, if you look at the matter in one way, evolved only a miserable error but, more fairly considered, produced a result worth almost what it cost her. Her faith in her own ideas was so genuine that, erroneous as they were, it transmuted them to gold, or, at all events, interfused a large proportion of that precious and indestructible substance among the waste material from which it can readily be sifted.

The only time I ever saw Miss Bacon was in London, where she had lodgings in Spring-street, Sussex Gardens, at the house of a grocer, a portly, middle-aged, civil, and friendly man, who, as well as his wife, appeared to feel a personal kindness towards their lodger. I was ushered up two (and, I rather believe, three) pair of stairs into a parlor somewhat humbly furnished, and told that Miss Bacon would come soon. There were a number of books on the table; and looking into them, I found that every one had some reference, more or less immediate, to her Shaksperian theory; a volume of Raleigh's History of the World, a volume of Montaigne, a volume of Lord Bacon's letters, a volume of Shakspere's plays; and on another table lay a large roll of manuscript, which I presume to have been a portion of her work. To be sure, there was a pocket-Bible among the books, but everything else referred to the one despotic idea that had got possession of her mind; and as it had engrossed her whole soul as well as her intellect, I have no doubt that she had established subtle connections between it and the Bible likewise. As is apt to be the case with solitary students, Miss Bacon probably read late and rose late; for I took up Montaigne (it was Hazlitt's translation) and had been reading his Journey to Italy a good while, before she appeared.

I had expected (the more shame for me, having no other ground of such expectation than that she was a literary woman) to see a very homely, uncouth, elderly personage, and was quite agreeably disappointed by her aspect. She was rather uncommonly tall, and had a striking and expressive face; dark hair, dark eyes, which shone with an inward light as soon as she began to speak; and, by-and-by, a color came into her cheeks and made her look almost young. Not that she really was so; she must have been beyond middle age; and there was no unkindness in coming to that conclusion, because, making allowance for years and ill-health, I could suppose her to have been handsome and exceedingly attractive once. Though wholly estranged from society, there was little or no restraint or embarrassment in her manner; lonely people are generally glad to give utterance to their pent-up ideas, and often bubble over with them as freely as children with their new-found syllables. I cannot tell how it came about, but we immediately found ourselves taking a friendly and familiar tone together, and began to talk as if we had known one another a very long while. A little preliminary correspondence had indeed smoothed the way, and we had a definite topic in the contemplated publication of her book.

She was very communicative about her theory, and would have been much more so had I desired it; but being conscious within myself of a sturdy unbelief, I deemed it fair and honest rather to repress than draw her out upon the subject. Unquestionably, she was a monomaniac; these overmastering ideas about the authorship of Shakspere's plays, and the deep political philosophy concealed beneath the surface of them, had completely thrown her off her balance; but at the same time they had wonderfully developed her intellect, and made her what she could not otherwise have become. It was a very singular phenomenon; a system of philosophy growing up in this woman's mind without her volition—contrary, in fact, to the determined resistance of her volition—and substituting itself in the place of everything that originally grew there. To have based such a system on fancy, and unconsciously elabo-rated it for herself, was almost as wonderful as really to have found it in the plays. But, in a certain sense, she did actually find it there. Shakspere has surface beneath surface, to an immeasurable depth, adapted to the plummet-line of every reader; his works present many phases of truth, each with scope large enough to fill a contemplative mind. Whatever you seek in him you will surely discover, provided you seek truth. There is no exhausting the various interpretation of his symbols, and a thousand years hence, a world of new readers will possess a whole library of new books, as we ourselves do, in these volumes old already. I had half a mind to suggest to Miss Bacon this explanation of her theory, but forbore, because (as I could readily perceive) she had as princely a spirit as Queen Elizabeth herself, and would at once have motioned me from the room.

I had heard, long ago, that she believed that the material evidences of her dogma as to the authorship, together with the key of the new philosophy, would be found buried in Shakspere's grave. Recently, as I understood her, this notion had been somewhat modified, and was now accurately defined and fully developed in her mind, with a result of perfect certainty. In Lord Bacon's letters, on which she laid her finger as she spoke, she had discovered the key and clue to the whole mystery. There were definite and minute instructions how to find a will and other documents relating to the conclave of Elizabethan philosophers, which were concealed (when and by whom she did not inform me) in a hollow space in the under surface of Shakspere's grave-stone. Thus the terrible prohibition to remove the stone was accounted for. The directions, she intimated, went completely and precisely to the point, obviating all difficulties in the way of coming at the treasure, and even, if I remember right, were so contrived as to ward off any troublesome consequences likely to ensue from the interference of the parish-officers. All that Miss Bacon now remained in England for—indeed, the object for which she had come hither, and which had kept her here for three years past—was to obtain possession of these material and unquestionable proofs of the authenticity of her theory.

She communicated all this strange matter in a low, quiet tone, while, on my part, I listened as quietly, and without any expression of dissent. Controversy against a faith so settled would have shut her up at once, and that, too, without in the least weakening her belief in the existence of those treasures of the tomb; and had it been possible to convince her of their intangible nature, I apprehend that there would have been nothing left for the poor enthusiast save to collapse and die. She frankly confessed that she could no longer bear the society of those who did not at least lend a certain sympathy to her views, if not fully share in them; and meeting little sympathy or none, she had now entirely secluded herself from the world. In all these years, she had seen Mrs. Farrar a few times, but had long ago given her up; Carlyle once or twice, but not of late, although he had received her kindly; Mr. Buchanan, while minister in England, had once called on her, and General Campbell, our Consul in London, had met her two or three times on business. With these exceptions, which she marked so scrupulously that it was perceptible what epochs they were in the monotonous passage of her days, she had lived in the profoundest solitude. She never walked out; she suffered much from ill-health; and yet, she assured me, she was perfectly happy.

I could well conceive it; for Miss Bacon imagined herself to have received (what is certainly the greatest boon ever assigned to mortals) a high mission in the world with adequate powers for its accomplishment, and lest even these should prove insufficient, she had faith that special interpositions of Providence were forwarding her human efforts. This idea was continually coming to the surface, during our interview. She believed, for example, that she had been providentially led to her lodging-house and put in relations with the good-natured grocer and his family; and to say the truth, considering what a savage and stealthy tribe the London lodging-house keepers usually are, the honest kindness of this man and his household appeared to have been little less than miraculous. Evidently, too, she thought that Providence had brought me forward—a man somewhat connected with literature—at the critical juncture when she needed a negotiator with the booksellers; and on my part, though little accustomed to regard

myself as a divine minister, and though I might even have
preferred that Providence should select some other instrument, I had no scruple in undertaking to do what I could for
her. Her book, as I could see by turning it over, was a very
remarkable one, and worthy of being offered to the public,
which, if wise enough to appreciate it, would be thankful for
what was good in it and merciful to its faults. It was founded
on a prodigious error, but was built up from that foundation
with a good many prodigious truths. And, at all events,
whether I could aid her literary views or no, it would have
been both rash and impertinent in me to attempt drawing
poor Miss Bacon out of her delusions, which were the condition on which she lived in comfort and joy, and in the exercise
of great intellectual power. So I left her to dream as she
pleased about the treasures of Shakspere's tombstone, and to
form whatever designs might seem good to herself for obtaining possession of them. I was sensible of a ladylike feeling of
propriety in Miss Bacon, and a New England orderliness in
her character, and, in spite of her bewilderment, a sturdy
common sense, which, I trusted, would begin to operate at the
right time, and keep her from any actual extravagance. And as
regarded this matter of the tombstone, so it proved.

The interview lasted above an hour, during which she
flowed out freely, as to the sole auditor, capable of any degree
of intelligent sympathy, whom she had met with in a very
long while. Her conversation was remarkably suggestive, al-
luring forth one's own ideas and fantasies from the shy places
where they usually haunt. She was indeed an admirable
talker, considering how long she had held her tongue for lack
of a listener—pleasant, sunny and shadowy, often piquant,
and giving glimpses of all a woman's various and readily
changeable moods and humors; and beneath them all, there
ran a deep and powerful under-current of earnestness, which
did not fail to produce, in the listener's mind, something like a

temporary faith in what she herself believed so fervently. But the streets of London are not favorable to enthusiasms of this kind, nor, in fact, are they likely to flourish anywhere in the English atmosphere; so that, long before reaching Paternoster Row, I felt that it would be a difficult and doubtful matter to advocate the publication of Miss Bacon's book. Nevertheless, it did finally get published.

Months before that happened, however, Miss Bacon had taken up her residence at Stratford-on-Avon, drawn thither by the magnetism of those rich secrets which she supposed to have been hidden by Raleigh, or Bacon, or I know not whom, in Shakspere's grave, and protected there by a curse, as pirates used to bury their gold in the guardianship of a fiend. She took a humble lodging and began to haunt the church like a ghost. But she did not condescend to any stratagem or under-hand attempt to violate the grave, which, had she been capable of admitting such an idea, might possibly have been accomplished by the aid of a resurrection-man. As her first step, she made acquaintance with the clerk, and began to sound him as to the feasibility of her enterprise and his own willingness to engage in it. The clerk apparently listened with not unfavorable ears, but as his situation (which the fees of pilgrims, more numerous than at any Catholic shrine, render lucrative) would have been forfeited by any malfeasance in office, he stipulated for liberty to consult the vicar. Miss Bacon requested to tell her own story to the reverend gentle-man, and seems to have been received by him with the utmost kindness, and even to have succeeded in making a certain impression on his mind as to the desirability of the search. As their interview had been under the seal of secrecy, he asked permission to consult a friend, who, as Miss Bacon either found out or surmised, was a practitioner of the law. What the legal friend advised, she did not learn; but the negotiation continued, and certainly was never broken off by an absolute refusal on the vicar's part. He perhaps was kindly temporizing with our poor countrywoman, whom an Englishman of ordinary mould would have sent to a lunatic asylum at once. I cannot help fancying, however, that her familiarity with the events of Shakspere's life, and of his death and burial, (of which she could speak as if she had been present at the edge of the grave,) and all the history, literature, and personalities of the Elizabethan age, together with the prevailing power of her own belief, and the eloquence with which she knew how to enforce it, had really gone some little way towards making a convert of the good clergyman. If so, I honor him above all the hierarchy of England.

The affair certainly looked very hopeful. However erroneously, Miss Bacon had understood from the vicar that no obstacles would be interposed to the investigation, and that he himself would sanction it with his presence. It was to take place after nightfall; and all preliminary arrangements being made, the vicar and clerk professed to wait only her word in order to set about lifting the awful stone from the sepulchre. So, at least, Miss Bacon believed, and as her bewilderment was entirely in her own thoughts, and never disturbed her perception or accurate remembrance of external things, I see no reason to doubt it except it be the tinge of absurdity in the fact. But, in this apparently prosperous state of things, her own convictions began to falter. A doubt stole into her mind whether she might not have mistaken the depository and mode of concealment of those historic treasures; and after once admitting the doubt, she was afraid to hazard the shock of uplifting the stone and finding nothing. She examined the surface of the grave-stone, and endeavored, without stirring it, to estimate whether it were of such thickness as to be capable of containing the archives of the Elizabethan club. She went over anew the proofs, the clues, the enigmas, the pregnant sentences, which she had discovered in Bacon's letters and elsewhere, and now was frightened to perceive that they did not point so definitely to Shakspere's tomb as she had heretofore supposed. There was an unmistakably distinct reference to a tomb, but it might be Bacon's, or Raleigh's, or Spenser's; and instead of the 'Old Player,' as she profanely called him, it might be either of those three illustrious dead, poet, warrior, or statesman, whose ashes, in Westminster Abbey or the Tower burial-ground or wherever they sleep, it was her mission to disturb. It is very possible, moreover, that her acute mind may always have had a lurking and deeply latent distrust of its own fantasies, and that this now became strong enough to restrain her from a decisive step.

But she continued to hover round the church, and seems to have had full freedom of entrance in the daytime, and special license, on one occasion at least, at a late hour of the night. She went thither with a dark lantern, which could but twinkle like a glow-worm through the volume of obscurity that filled the great dusky edifice. Groping her way up the aisle and towards the chancel, she sat down on the elevated part of the pavement above Shakspere's grave. If the divine poet really wrote the inscription there, and cared as much about the quiet of his bones as its deprecatory earnestness would imply, it was time for those crumbling relics to bestir themselves under her sacrilegious feet. But they were safe. She made no attempt to disturb them; though, I believe, she looked narrowly into the crevices between Shakspere's and the two adjacent stones, and in some way satisfied herself that her single strength would suffice to lift the former, in case of need. She threw the feeble ray of her lantern up towards the bust, but could not make it visible beneath the darkness of the vaulted roof. Had she been subject to superstitious terrors, it is impossible to conceive of a situation that could better entitle her to feel them, for if Shakspere's ghost would rise at any provocation, it must have shown itself then; but it is my sincere belief that, if his figure had appeared within the scope of her dark lantern, in his slashed doublet and gown, and with his eyes bent on her beneath the high, bald forehead, just as we see him in the bust, she would have met him fearlessly and controverted his claims to the authorship of the plays, to his very face. She had taught herself to contemn 'Lord Leicester's groom' (it was one of her disdainful epithets for the world's incomparable poet) so thoroughly, that even his disembodied spirit would hardly have found civil treatment at Miss Bacon's hands.

Her vigil, though it appears to have had no definite object, continued far into the night. Several times, she heard a low movement in the aisles; a stealthy, dubious footfall prowling about in the darkness, now here, now there, among the pillars and ancient tombs, as if some restless inhabitant of the latter had crept forth to peep at the intruder. By-and-by, the clerk made his appearance, and confessed that he had been watching her ever since she entered the church.

About this time it was that a strange sort of weariness seems to have fallen upon her; her toil was all but done, her great purpose, as she believed, on the very point of accomplishment, when she began to regret that so stupendous a mission had been imposed on the fragility of a woman. Her faith in the new philosophy was as mighty as ever, and so was her confidence in her own adequate development of it, now about to be given to the world; yet she wished, or fancied so, that it might never have been her duty to achieve this unparalleled task, and to stagger feebly forward under her immense burthen of responsibility and renown. So far as her personal concern in the matter went, she would gladly have forfeited the reward of her patient study and labor for so many years, her exile from her country and estrangement from her family and friends, her sacrifice of health and all other interests to this one pursuit, if she could only find herself free to dwell in

Stratford and be forgotten. She liked the old, slumberous town, and awarded the only praise that ever I knew her to bestow on Shakspere, the individual man, by acknowledging that his taste in a residence was good, and that he knew how to choose a suitable retirement for a person of shy, but genial temperament. And, at this point, I cease to possess the means of tracing her vicissitudes of feeling any further. In consequence of some advice which I fancied it my duty to tender, as being the only confidant whom she now had in the world, I fell under Miss Bacon's most severe and passionate displeasure, and was cast off by her in the twinkling of an eye. It was a misfortune to which her friends were always particularly liable; but I think that none of them ever loved, or even respected, her most ingenuous and noble, but likewise most sensitive and tumultuous character, the less for it.

At that time, her book was passing through the press. Without prejudice to her literary ability, it must be allowed that Miss Bacon was wholly unfit to prepare her own work for publication, because, among many other reasons, she was too thoroughly in earnest to know what to leave out. Every leaf and line was sacred, for all had been written under so deep a conviction of truth as to assume, in her eyes, the aspect of inspiration. A practised book-maker, with entire control of her materials, would have shaped out a duodecimo volume full of eloquent and ingenious dissertation—criticisms which quite take the color and pungency out of other people's critical remarks on Shakspere—philosophic truths which she imagined herself to have found at the roots of his conceptions, and which certainly come from no inconsiderable depth somewhere. There was a great amount of rubbish, which any competent editor would have shovelled out of the way. But Miss Bacon thrust the whole bulk of inspiration and nonsense into the press in a lump; and there tumbled out a ponderous octavo volume, which fell with a dead thump at the feet of the public and has never been picked up. A few persons turned over one or two of the leaves as it lay there, and essayed to kick the volume deeper into the mud; for they were the hack-critics of the minor periodical press in London, than whom, I suppose, though excellent fellows in their way, there are no gentlemen in the world less sensible of any sanctity in a book, or less likely to recognize an author's heart in it, or more utterly careless about bruising, if they do recognize it. It is their trade. They could not do otherwise. I never thought of blaming them. It was not for such an Englishman as one of these to get beyond the idea that an assault was meditated on England's greatest poet. From the scholars and critics of her own country, indeed, Miss Bacon might have looked for a worthier appreciation, because many of the best of them have higher cultivation and finer and deeper literary sensibilities than all but the very profoundest and brightest of Englishmen. But they are not a courageous body of men; they dare not think a truth that has an odor of absurdity, lest they should feel themselves bound to speak it out. If any American ever wrote a word in her behalf, Miss Bacon never knew it, nor did I. Our journalists at once republished some of the most brutal vituperations of the English press, thus pelting their poor countrywoman with stolen mud, without even waiting to know whether the ignominy was deserved! And they never have known it, to this day, nor ever will.

The next intelligence that I had of Miss Bacon was by a letter from the Mayor of Stratford-on-Avon. He was a medical man, and wrote both in his official and professional characters, telling me that an American lady, who had recently published what the Mayor called a 'Shakspere book,' was afflicted with insanity. In a lucid interval she had referred to me, as a person who had some knowledge of her family and affairs. What she may have suffered before her intellect gave way, we had better not try to imagine. No author had ever hoped so confidently as she; none ever failed more utterly. A superstitious fancy might suggest that the anathema on Shakspere's tombstone had fallen heavily on her head in requital of even the unaccomplished purpose of disturbing the dust beneath, and that the 'Old Player' had kept so quietly in his grave, on the night of her vigil, because he foresaw how soon and terribly he would be avenged. But if that benign spirit takes any care or cognizance of such things now, he has surely requited the injustice that she sought to do him—the high justice that she really did—by a tenderness of love and pity of which only he could be capable. What matters it though she called him by some other name! He had wrought a greater miracle on her than on all the world besides. This bewildered enthusiast had recognized a depth in the man whom she denied, which scholars, critics, and learned societies, devoted to the elucidation of his unrivalled scenes, had never imagined to exist there. She had paid him the loftiest honor that all these ages of renown have been able to accumulate upon his memory. And when, not many months after the outward failure of her life-long object, she passed into the better world, I know not why we should hesitate to believe that the immortal poet may have met her on the threshold and led her in, re-assuring her with friendly and comfortable words, and thanking her (yet with a smile of gentle humor in his eyes at the thought of certain mistaken speculations) for having interpreted him to mankind so well.

I believe that it has been the fate of this remarkable book never to have had more than a single reader. I myself am acquainted with it only in insulated chapters and scattered pages and paragraphs. But, since my return to America, a young man of genius and enthusiasm has assured me that he has positively read the book from beginning to end, and is completely a convert to its doctrines. It belongs to him, therefore, and not to me—whom, in almost the last letter that I received from her, she declared unworthy to meddle with her work—it belongs surely to this one individual who has done her so much justice as to know what she wrote, to place Miss Bacon in her due position before the public and posterity.

This has been too sad a story. To lighten the recollection of it, I will think of my stroll homeward past Charlecote Park, where I beheld the most stately elms, singly, in clumps, and in groves, scattered all about in the sunniest, shadiest, sleepiest fashion; so that I could not but believe in a lengthened, loitering, drowsy enjoyment, which these trees must have in their existence. Diffused over slow-paced centuries, it need not be keen nor bubble into thrills and ecstasies, like the momentary delights of short-lived human beings. They were civilized trees, known to man and befriended by him for ages past. There is an indescribable difference—as, I believe, I have heretofore endeavored to express—between the tamed, but by no means effete (on the contrary, the richer and more luxuriant) Nature of England, and the rude, shaggy, barbarous Nature, which offers us its racier companionship in America. No less a change has been wrought among the wildest creatures that inhabit what the English call their forests. By-and-by, among those refined and venerable trees, I saw a large herd of deer, mostly reclining, but some standing in picturesque groups, while the stags threw their large antlers aloft as if they had been taught to make themselves tributary to the scenic effect. Some were running fleetly about, vanishing from light into shadow and glancing forth again, with here and there a little fawn careering at its mother's heels. These deer are almost in the same relation to the wild, natural state of their kind that the trees of an English park hold to the rugged growth of an American forest. They have held a certain intercourse with man for immemorial years; and, most probably, the stag that Shakspere killed was one of the progenitors of this very herd, and may himself have been a partly civilized and humanized deer, though in a less degree than these remote posterity. They are a little wilder than sheep; but they do not snuff the air at the approach of human beings, nor evince much alarm at their pretty close proximity; although, if you continue to advance, they toss their heads and take to their heels in a kind of mimic terror, or something akin to feminine skittishness, with a dim remembrance or tradition, as it were, of their having come of a wild stock. They have so long been fed and protected by man, that they must have lost many of their native instincts, and, I suppose, could not live comfortably through even an English winter without human help. One is sensible of a gentle scorn at them for such dependency, but feels none the less kindly disposed towards the half-domesticated race; and it may have been his observation of these tamer characteristics in the Charlecote herd that suggested to Shakspere the tender and pitiful description of a wounded stag, in As You Like It.

At a distance of some hundreds of yards from Charlecote Hall, and almost hidden by the trees between it and the roadside, is an old brick archway and porter's lodge. In connection with this entrance there appears to have been a wall and an ancient moat, the latter of which is still visible, a shallow, grassy scoop along the base of an embankment of the lawn. About fifty yards within the gateway stands the house, forming three sides of a square, with three gables in a row on the front and on each of the two wings; and there are several towers and turrets at the angles, together with projecting windows, antique balconies, and other quaint ornaments suitable to the half-Gothic taste in which the edifice was built. Over the gateway is the Lucy coat-of-arms, emblazoned in its proper colors. The mansion dates from the early days of Elizabeth, and probably looked very much the same as now when Shakspere was brought before Sir Thomas Lucy for outrages among his deer. The impression is not that of gray antiquity, but of stable and time-honored gentility, still as vital as ever.

It is a most delightful place. All about the house and domain, there is a perfection of comfort and domestic taste, an amplitude of convenience, which could have been brought about only by the slow ingenuity and labor of many successive generations, intent upon adding all possible improvement to the home where years gone by, and years to come, give a sort of permanence to the intangible present. An American is sometimes tempted to fancy that only by this long process can real homes be produced. One man's lifetime is not enough for the accomplishment of such a work of Art and Nature, almost the greatest merely temporary one that is confided to him; too little at any rate—yet perhaps too long, when he is discouraged by the idea that he must make his house warm and delightful for a miscellaneous race of successors, of whom the one thing certain is, that his own grandchildren will not be among them. Such repinings as are here suggested, however, come only from the fact that, bred in English habits of thought, as most of us are, we have not yet modified our instincts to the necessities of our new forms of life. A lodging in a wigwam or under a tent has really as many advantages, when we come to know them, as a home beneath the roof-tree of Charlecote Hall. But alas! our philosophers have not yet taught us what is best, nor have our poets sung us what is beautifullest, in the kind of life that we must lead; and therefore we still read the old English wisdom, and harp upon the ancient strings. And thence it happens that, when we look at a time-honored hall, it seems more possible for men who inherit such a home, than for ourselves, to lead noble and graceful lives, quietly doing good and lovely things as their daily work, and achieving deeds of simple greatness when circumstances require them. I sometimes apprehend that our institutions may perish before we shall have discovered the most precious of the possibilities which they involve.

LICHFIELD AND UTTOXETER

AFTER my first visit to Leamington Spa, I went by an in-
direct route to Lichfield, and put up at the Black
Swan. Had I known where to find it, I would much
rather have established myself at the inn formerly kept by the
worthy Mr. Boniface, so famous for his ale in Farquhar's time.
The Black Swan is an old-fashioned hotel, its street-front
being penetrated by an arched passage, in either side of which
is an entrance-door to the different parts of the house, and
through which, and over the large stones of its pavement, all
vehicles and horsemen rumble and clatter into an enclosed
court-yard, with a thunderous uproar among the contiguous
rooms and chambers. I appeared to be the only guest of the
spacious establishment, but may have had a few fellow-lodg-
ers hidden in their separate parlors, and utterly eschewing
that community of interests which is the characteristic feature
of life in an American hotel. At any rate, I had the great, dull,
dingy, and dreary coffee-room, with its heavy old mahogany
chairs and tables, all to myself, and not a soul to exchange a
word with, except the waiter, who, like most of his class in
England, had evidently left his conversational abilities uncul-
tivated. No former practice of solitary living, nor habits of
reticence, nor well-tested self-dependence for occupation of

mind and amusement, can quite avail, as I now proved, to
dissipate the ponderous gloom of an English coffee-room
under such circumstances as these, with no book at hand save
the county-directory, nor any newspaper but a torn local
journal of five days ago. So I buried myself, betimes, in a huge
heap of ancient feathers, (there is no other kind of bed in
these old inns,) let my head sink into an unsubstantial pillow,
and slept a stifled sleep, infested with such a fragmentary
confusion of dreams that I took them to be a medley, compounded of the night-troubles of all my predecessors in that
same unrestful couch. And when I awoke, the musty odor of a
by-gone century was in my nostrils—a faint, elusive smell, of
which I never had any conception before crossing the Atlantic.

In the morning, after a mutton-chop and a cup of chiccory
in the dusky coffee-room, I went forth and bewildered myself
a little while among the crooked streets, in quest of one or two
objects that had chiefly attracted me to the spot. The city is of
very ancient date, and its name, in the old Saxon tongue, has
a dismal import that would apply well, in these days and
forever henceforward, to many an unhappy locality in our
native land. Lichfield signifies "The Field of the Dead Bodies"—an epithet, however, which the town did not assume in
remembrance of a battle, but which probably sprung up by a
natural process, like a sprig of rue or other funereal weed, out
of the graves of two princely brothers, sons of a pagan King of
Mercia, who were converted by Saint Chad, and afterwards
martyred for their Christian faith. Nevertheless, I was but
little interested in the legends of the remote antiquity of
Lichfield, being drawn thither partly to see its beautiful Cathedral, and still more, I believe, because it was the birth-
place of Dr. Johnson, with whose sturdy English character I
became acquainted, at a very early period of my life, through
the good offices of Mr. Boswell. In truth, he seems as familiar

to my recollection, and almost as vivid in his personal aspect
to my mind's eye, as the kindly figure of my own grandfather.
It is only a solitary child—left much to such wild modes of
culture as he chooses for himself while yet ignorant what
culture means, standing on tiptoe to pull down books from no
very lofty shelf, and then shutting himself up, as it were,
between the leaves, going astray through the volume at his
own pleasure, and comprehending it rather by his sensibilities
and affections than his intellect—that child is the only student that ever gets the sort of intimacy which I am now
thinking of, with a literary personage. I do not remember,
indeed, ever caring much about any of the stalwart Doctor's
grandiloquent productions, except his two stern and masculine poems, "London," and "The Vanity of Human Wishes";
it was as a man, a talker, and a humorist, that I knew and
loved him, appreciating many of his qualities perhaps more
thoroughly than I do now, though never seeking to put my
instinctive perception of his character into language.

Beyond all question, I might have had a wiser friend than
he. The atmosphere in which alone he breathed was dense;
his awful dread of death showed how much muddy imperfection was to be cleansed out of him, before he could be capable
of spiritual existence; he meddled only with the surface of
life, and never cared to penetrate farther than to plough-share
depth; his very sense and sagacity were but a one-eyed clear-
sightedness. I laughed at him, sometimes, standing beside his
knee. And yet, considering that my native propensities were
towards Fairy Land, and also how much yeast is generally
mixed up with the mental sustenance of a New Englander, it
may not have been altogether amiss, in those childish and
boyish days, to keep pace with this heavy-footed traveller and
feed on the gross diet that he carried in his knapsack. It is
wholesome food even now. And, then, how English! Many of
the latent sympathies that enabled me to enjoy the Old Coun-

try so well, and that so readily amalgamated themselves with the American ideas that seemed most adverse to them, may have been derived from, or fostered and kept alive by, the great English Moralist. Never was a descriptive epithet more nicely appropriate than that! Dr. Johnson's morality was as English an article as a beef-steak.

The city of Lichfield (only the Cathedral-towns are called cities, in England) stands on an ascending site. It has not so many old gabled-houses as Coventry, for example, but still enough to gratify an American appetite for the antiquities of domestic architecture. The people, too, have an old-fashioned way with them, and stare at the passing visitor, as if the railway had not yet quite accustomed them to the novelty of strange faces moving along their ancient side-walks. The old women whom I met, in several instances, dropt me a courtesy; and as they were of decent and comfortable exterior, and kept quietly on their way without pause or further greeting, it certainly was not allowable to interpret their little act of respect as a modest method of asking for sixpence; so that I had the pleasure of considering it a remnant of the reverential and hospitable manners of elder times, when the rare presence of a stranger might be deemed worth a general acknowledgement. Positively, coming from such humble sources, I took it all the more as a welcome on behalf of the inhabitants, and would not have exchanged it for an invitation from the mayor and magistrates to a public dinner. Yet I wish, merely for the experiment's sake, that I could have emboldened myself to hold out the aforesaid sixpence to at least one of the old ladies.

In my wanderings about town, I came to an artificial piece of water, called the Minster Pool. It fills the immense cavity in a ledge of rock, whence the building materials of the Cathedral were quarried out, a great many centuries ago. I should never have guessed the little lake to be of man's creation, so very pretty and quietly picturesque an object has it grown to be, with its green banks, and the old trees hanging over its glassy surface, in which you may see reflected some of the battlements of the majestic structure that once lay here in unshaped stone. Some little children stood on the edge of the Pool, angling with pin-hooks; and the scene reminded me (though really, to be quite fair with the reader, the gist of the analogy has now escaped me) of that mysterious lake in the Arabian Nights which had once been a palace and a city, and where a fisherman used to pull out the former inhabitants in the guise of enchanted fishes. There is no need of fanciful associations to make the spot interesting. It was in the porch of one of the houses, in the street that runs beside the Minster Pool, that Lord Brooke was slain, in the time of the Parliamentary War, by a shot from the battlements of the Cathedral, which was then held by the Royalists as a fortress. The incident is commemorated by an inscription on a stone, inlaid into the wall of the house.

I know not what rank the Cathedral of Lichfield holds among its sister-edifices in England, as a piece of magnificent architecture. Except that of Chester, (the grim and simple nave of which stands yet unrivalled in my memory,) and one or two small ones in North Wales, hardly worthy of the name of Cathedrals, it was the first that I had seen. To my uninstructed vision, it seemed the object best worth gazing at in the whole world; and now, after beholding a great many more, I remember it with less prodigal admiration only because others are as magnificent as itself. The traces remaining in my memory represent it as airy rather than massive. A multitude of beautiful shapes appeared to be comprehended within its single outline; it was a kind of kaleidoscopic mystery, so rich a variety of aspects did it assume from each altered point of view, through the presentation of a different face, and the re-arrangement of its peaks and pinnacles and the three battlemented towers, with the spires that shot heavenward from all three, but one loftier than its fellows. Thus it impressed you, at every change, as a newly created structure of the passing moment, in which yet you lovingly recognized the half-vanished structure of the instant before, and felt, moreover, a joyful faith in the indestructible existence of all this cloudlike vicissitude. A Gothic Cathedral is surely the most wonderful work which mortal man has yet achieved, so vast, so intricate, and so profoundly simple, with such strange, delightful recesses in its grand figure, so difficult to comprehend within one idea, and yet all so consonant that it ultimately draws the beholder and his universe into its harmony. It is the only thing in the world that is vast enough and rich enough.

Not that I felt, or was worthy to feel, an unmingled enjoyment in gazing at this wonder. I could not elevate myself to its spiritual height, any more than I could have climbed from the ground to the summit of one of its pinnacles. Ascending but a little way, I continually fell back and lay in a kind of despair, conscious that a flood of uncomprehended beauty was pouring down upon me, of which I could appropriate only the minutest portion. After a hundred years, incalculably as my higher sympathies might be invigorated by so divine an employment, I should still be a gazer from below and at an awful distance, as yet remotely excluded from the interior mystery. But it was something gained, even to have that painful sense of my own limitations, and that half-smothered yearning to soar beyond them. The Cathedral showed me how earthly I was, but yet whispered deeply of immortality. After all, this was probably the best lesson that it could bestow, and, taking it as thoroughly as possible home to my heart, I was fain to be content. If the truth must be told, my ill-trained enthusiasm soon flagged, and I began to lose the vision of a spiritual or ideal edifice behind the time-worn and weather-stained front of the

actual structure. Whenever that is the case, it is most reverential to look another way; but the mood disposes one to minute
investigation, and I took advantage of it to examine the intricate and multitudinous adornment that was lavished on the
exterior wall of this great church. Everywhere, there were
empty niches whence statues had been thrown down, and
here and there a statue still lingered in its niche; and over the
chief entrance, and extending across the whole breadth of the
building, was a row of angels, sainted personages, martyrs,
and kings, sculptured in reddish stone. Being much corroded
by the moist English atmosphere, during four or five hundred
winters that they had stood there, these benign and majestic
figures perversely put me in mind of the appearance of a
sugar-image, after a child has been holding it in his mouth.
The venerable infant, Time, has evidently found them sweet
morsels.

Inside of the Minster, there is a long and lofty nave,
transepts of the same height, and side-aisles and chapels, dim
nooks of holiness, where, in Catholic times, the lamps were
continually burning before the richly decorated shrines of
saints. In the audacity of my ignorance, as I humbly acknowledge it to have been, I criticized this great interior as too much
broken into compartments, and shorn of half its rightful
impressiveness by the interposition of a screen betwixt the
nave and chancel. It did not spread itself in breadth but
ascended to the roof in lofty narrowness. One large body of
worshippers might have knelt down in the nave, others in
each of the transepts, and smaller ones in the side-aisles,
besides an indefinite number of esoteric enthusiasts in the
mysterious sanctities beyond the screen. Thus it seemed to
typify the exclusiveness of sects rather than the world-wide
hospitality of genuine religion. I had imagined a Cathedral
with a scope more vast. These Gothic aisles, with their
groined arches overhead, supported by clustered pillars in

long vistas up and down, were venerable and magnificent, but included too much of the twilight of that monkish gloom out of which they grew. It is no matter whether I ever came to a more satisfactory appreciation of this kind of architecture; the only value of my strictures being to show the folly of looking at noble objects in the wrong mood, and the absurdity of a new visitant pretending to hold any opinion whatever on such subjects, instead of surrendering himself to the old builder's influence with childlike simplicity.

A great deal of white marble decorates the old stone-work of the aisles, in the shape of altars, obelisks, sarcophagi, and busts. Most of these memorials are commemorative of people locally distinguished, especially the deans and canons of the Cathedral, with their relatives and families; and I found but two monuments of personages whom I had ever heard of, one being Gilbert Walmesley, and the other Lady Mary Wortley Montague, a literary acquaintance of my boyhood. It was really pleasant to meet her there; for after a friend has lain in the grave far into the second century, she would be unreasonable to require any melancholy emotions in a chance-interview at her tombstone. It adds a rich charm to sacred edifices, this time-honored custom of burial in churches, after a few years, at least, when the mortal remains have turned to dust beneath the pavement, and the quaint devices and inscriptions still speak to you above. The statues, that stood or reclined in several recesses of the Cathedral, had a kind of life, and I regarded them with an odd sort of deference, as if they were privileged denizens of the precinct. It was singular, too, how the memorial of the latest buried person, the man whose features were familiar in the streets of Lichfield only yesterday, seemed precisely as much at home here as his mediæval predecessors. Henceforward he belonged to the Cathedral like one of its original pillars. Methought this impression in my fancy might be the shadow of a spiritual fact. The dying melt into the great multitude of the Departed as quietly as a drop of water into the ocean, and, it may be, are conscious of no unfamiliarity with their new circumstances, but immediately become aware of an insufferable strangeness in the world which they have quitted. Death has not taken them away, but brought them home.

The vicissitudes and mischances of sublunary affairs, however, have not ceased to attend upon these marble inhabitants; for I saw the upper fragment of a sculptured lady, in a very old-fashioned garb, the lower half of whom had doubtless been demolished by Cromwell's soldiers when they took the Minster by storm. And there lies the remnant of this devout lady on her slab, ever since the outrage, as for centuries before, with a countenance of divine serenity and her hands clasped in prayer, symbolizing a depth of religious faith which no earthly turmoil or calamity could disturb. Another piece of sculpture (apparently a favorite subject in the middle ages, for I have seen several like it in other Cathedrals) was a reclining skeleton, as faithfully representing an open-work of bones as could well be expected in a solid block of marble, and at a period, moreover, when the mysteries of the human frame were rather to be guessed at than revealed. Whatever the anatomical defects of his production, the old sculptor had succeeded in making it ghastly beyond measure. How much mischief has been wrought upon us by this invariable gloom of the Gothic imagination, flinging itself like a death-scented pall over our conceptions of the future state, smothering our hopes, hiding our sky, and inducing dismal efforts to raise the harvest of immortality out of what is most opposite to it—the grave!

The Cathedral service is performed twice every day, at ten o'clock and at four. When I first entered, the choristers (young and old, but mostly, I think, boys, with voices inexpressibly sweet and clear, and as fresh as bird-notes) were just winding up their harmonious labors, and soon came thronging through a side-door from the chancel into the nave. They were all dressed in long white robes, and looked like a peculiar order of beings, created on purpose to hover between the roof and pavement of that dim, consecrated edifice, and illuminate it with divine melodies, reposing themselves, meanwhile, on the heavy grandeur of the organ-tones like cherubs on a golden cloud. All at once, however, one of the cherubic multitude pulled off his white gown, thus transforming himself before my very eyes into a common-place youth of the day, in modern frock-coat and trowsers of a decidedly provincial cut. This absurd little incident, I verily believe, had a sinister effect in putting me at odds with the proper influences of the Cathedral, nor could I quite recover a suitable frame of mind during my stay there. But, emerging into the open air, I began to be sensible that I had left a magnificent interior behind me, and I have never quite lost the perception and enjoyment of it in these intervening years.

A large space in the immediate neighborhood of the Cathedral is called the Close, and comprises beautifully kept lawns and a shadowy walk, bordered by the dwellings of the ecclesiastical dignitaries of the Diocese. All this row of episcopal, canonical, and clerical residences, has an air of the deepest quiet, repose, and well-protected, though not inaccessible seclusion. They seemed capable of including everything that a Saint could desire, and a great many more things than most of us sinners generally succeed in acquiring. Their most marked feature is a dignified comfort, looking as if no disturbance or vulgar intrusiveness could ever cross their thresholds, encroach upon their ornamented lawns, or straggle into the beautiful gardens that surround them with flower-beds and rich clumps of shrubbery. The episcopal palace is a stately mansion of stone, built somewhat in the Italian style, and bearing on its front the figures 1687, as the date of its erection. A large edifice of brick, which, if I remember, stood next to the palace, I took to be the residence of the second dignitary of the Cathedral; and, in that case, it must have been the youthful home of Addison, whose father was Dean of Lichfield. I tried to fancy his figure on the delightful walk that extends in front of those priestly abodes, from which and the interior lawns it is separated by an open-work iron fence, lined with rich old shrubbery, and over-arched by a minster-aisle of venerable trees. This path is haunted by the shades of famous personages who have formerly trodden it. Johnson must have been familiar with it, both as a boy, and in his subsequent visits to Lichfield, an illustrious old man. Miss Seward, connected with so many literary reminiscences, lived in one of the adjacent houses. Tradition says that it was a favorite spot of Major André, who used to pace to-and-fro under these trees, waiting, perhaps, to catch a last angel-glimpse of Honoria Sneyd, before he crossed the ocean to encounter his dismal doom from an American court-martial. David Garrick, no doubt, scampered along the path in his boyish days, and, if he was an early student of the drama, must often have thought of those two airy characters of the Beaux' Stratagem, Archer and Aimwell, who, on this very ground, after attending service at the Cathedral, contrive to make acquaintance with the ladies of the comedy. These creatures of mere fiction have as positive a substance now as the sturdy old figure of Johnson himself. They live, while realities have died. The shadowy walk still glistens with their gold-embroidered memories.

Seeking for Johnson's birth-place, I found it in Saint Mary's Square, which is not so much a square as the mere widening of a street. The house is tall and thin, of three stories, with a square front and a roof rising steep and high. On a side-view, the building looks as if it had been cut in two in the midst, there being no slope of the roof on that side. A ladder slanted against the wall, and a painter was giving a livelier hue to the plaster. In a corner-room of the basement, where old Michael Johnson may be supposed to have sold books, is now what we should call a dry-goods store, or, according to the English phrase, a mercer's and haberdasher's shop. The house has a private entrance on a cross-street, the door being accessible by several much worn stone-steps, which are bordered by an iron balustrade. I set my foot on the steps and laid my hand on the balustrade, where Johnson's hand and foot must many a time have been, and ascending to the door, I knocked once, and again, and again, and got no admittance. Going round to the shop-entrance, I tried to open it, but found it as fast bolted as the gate of Paradise. It is mortifying to be so baulked in one's little enthusiasms; but looking round in quest of somebody to make inquiries of, I was a good deal consoled by the sight of Dr. Johnson himself, who happened, just at that moment, to be sitting at his ease nearly in the middle of Saint Mary's Square, with his face turned towards his father's house.

Of course, it being almost fourscore years since the Doctor laid aside his weary bulk of flesh, together with the ponderous melancholy that had so long weighed him down, the intelligent reader will at once comprehend that he was marble in his substance, and seated in a marble chair, on an elevated stone-pedestal. In short, it was a statue, sculptured by Lucas, and placed here in 1838, at the expense of Dr. Law, the reverend Chancellor of the Diocese.

The figure is colossal (though perhaps not much more so than the mountainous Doctor himself) and looks down upon the spectator from its pedestal of ten or twelve feet high, with a broad and heavy benignity of aspect, very like in feature to Sir Joshua Reynolds's portrait of Johnson, but calmer and sweeter in expression. Several big books are piled up beneath his chair, and, if I mistake not, he holds a volume in his hand, thus blinking forth at the world out of his learned abstraction, owl-like, yet benevolent at heart. The statue is immensely massive, a vast ponderosity of stone, not finely spiritualized, nor, indeed, fully humanized, but rather resembling a great stone-boulder than a man. You must look with the eyes of faith and sympathy, or, possibly, you might lose the human being altogether, and find only a big stone within your mental grasp. On the pedestal, are three bas-reliefs. In the first, Johnson is represented as hardly more than a baby, bestriding an old man's shoulders, resting his chin on the bald head which he embraces with his little arms, and listening earnestly to the high-church eloquence of Dr. Sacheverell. In the second tablet, he is seen riding to school on the shoulders of two of his comrades, while another boy supports him in the rear.

The third bas-relief possesses, to my mind, a great deal of pathos, to which my appreciative faculty is probably the more alive because I have always been profoundly impressed by the incident here commemorated, and long ago tried to tell it for the behoof of childish readers. It shows Johnson in the market-place of Uttoxeter, doing penance for an act of disobedience to his father, committed fifty years before. He stands bareheaded, a venerable figure, and a countenance extremely sad and woe-begone, with the wind and rain driving hard against him, and thus helping to suggest to the spectator the gloom of his inward state. Some market-people and children gaze awe-stricken into his face, and an aged man and woman, with clasped and uplifted hands, seem to be praying for him. These latter personages (whose introduction by the artist is none the less effective, because, in queer proximity, there are some commodities of market-day in the shape of living ducks and dead poultry) I interpreted to represent the spirits of Johnson's father and mother, lending what aid they could to lighten his half-century's burthen of remorse.

I had never heard of the above described piece of sculpture before; it appears to have no reputation as a work of art, nor am I at all positive that it deserves any. For me, however, it did as much as sculpture could, under the circumstances, even if the artist of the Libyan Sybil had wrought it, by reviving my interest in the sturdy old Englishman, and particularly by freshening my perception of a wonderful beauty and pathetic tenderness in the incident of the penance. So, the next day, I left Lichfield for Uttoxeter, on one of the few purely sentimental pilgrimages that I ever undertook, to see the very spot where Johnson had stood. Boswell, I think, speaks of the town (its name is pronounced Yute-oxeter) as being about nine miles off from Lichfield; but the county-map would indicate a greater distance, and, by rail, passing from one line to another, it is as much as eighteen miles. I have always had an idea of old Michael Johnson sending his literary merchandize by carrier's wagon, journeying to Uttoxeter a-foot on market-day morning, selling books through the busy-hours, and returning to Lichfield at night. This could not possibly have been the case.

Arriving at the Uttoxeter station, the first objects that I saw, with a green field or two between them and me, were the tower and gray steeple of a church, rising among red-tiled roofs and a few scattered trees. A very short walk takes you from the station up into the town. It had been my previous impression that the market-place of Uttoxeter lay immediately roundabout the church; and, if I remember the narrative aright, Johnson, or Boswell in his behalf, describes his father's bookstall as standing in the market-place, close beside the sacred edifice. It is impossible for me to say what changes may have occurred in the topography of the town, during almost a century and a half since Michael Johnson retired from business, and ninety years, at least, since his son's penance was performed. But the church has now merely a street of ordinary width passing around it; while the market-place, though near at hand, neither forms a part of it nor is really contiguous, nor would its throng and bustle be apt to overflow their boundaries and surge against the churchyard and the old gray tower. Nevertheless, a walk of a minute or two brings a person from the centre of the market-place to the church-door; and Michael Johnson might very conveniently have located his stall and laid out his literary ware in the corner, at the tower's base; better there, indeed, than in the busy centre of an agricultural market. But the picturesque arrangement and full impressiveness of the story absolutely require that Johnson shall not have done his penance in a corner, ever so little retired, but shall have been the very nucleus of the crowd—the midmost man of the market-place—a central image of Memory and Remorse, contrasting with, and overpowering the sultry materialism around him. He himself, having the force to throw vitality and truth into what persons differently constituted might reckon a mere external ceremony, and an absurd one, could not have failed to see this necessity. I am resolved, therefore, that the true site of Dr. Johnson's penance was in the middle of the market-place.

That important portion of the town is a rather spacious and irregularly shaped vacuity, surrounded by houses and shops, some of them old, with red-tiled roofs, others wearing a pretence of newness, but probably as old in their inner substance as the rest. The people of Uttoxeter seemed very idle in the warm summer-day, and were scattered in little groups along the side-walks, leisurely chatting with one another, and often turning about to take a deliberate stare at my humble self; insomuch that I felt as if my genuine sympathy for the illustrious penitent, and my many reflections about him, must have imbued me with some of his own singularity of mien. If their great-grandfathers were such redoubtable starers in the Doctor's day, his penance was no light one. This curiosity indicates a paucity of visitors to the little town, except for market purposes, and I question if Uttoxeter ever saw an

American before. The only other thing that greatly impressed me was the abundance of public houses, one at every step or two, Red Lions, White Harts, Bull's Heads, Mitres, Cross Keys, and I know not what besides. These are probably for the accommodation of the farmers and peasantry of the neighborhood on market-day, and content themselves with a very meagre business on other days of the week. At any rate, I was the only guest in Uttoxeter at the period of my visit, and had but an infinitesimal portion of patronage to distribute among such a multitude of inns. The reader, however, will possibly be scandalized to learn what was the first, and, indeed, the only important affair that I attended to, after coming so far to indulge a solemn and high emotion, and standing now on the very spot where my pious errand should have been consummated. I stept into one of the rustic hostelries and got my dinner—bacon and greens, some mutton-chops, juicier and more delectable than all America could serve up at the President's table, and a gooseberry pudding—a sufficient meal for six yeomen, and good enough for a prince, besides a pitcher of foaming ale, the whole at the pitiful small charge of eighteenpence!

Dr. Johnson would have forgiven me, for nobody had a heartier faith in beef and mutton than himself. And, as regards my lack of sentiment in eating my dinner, it was the wisest thing I had done that day. A sensible man had better not let himself be betrayed into these attempts to realize the things which he has dreamed about, and which, when they cease to be purely ideal in his mind, will have lost the truest of their truth, the loftiest and profoundest part of their power over his sympathies. Facts, as we really find them, whatever poetry they may involve, are covered with a stony excrescence of prose, resembling the crust on a beautiful sea-shell, and they never show their most delicate and divinest colors, until we shall have dissolved away their grosser actualities by steeping them long in a powerful menstruum of thought. And, seeking to actualize them again, we do but renew the crust. If this were otherwise—if the moral sublimity of a great fact depended in any degree on its garb of external circumstances, things which change and decay—it could not itself be immortal and ubiquitous, and only a brief point of time and a little neighborhood would be spiritually nourished by its grandeur and beauty.

Such were a few of the reflections which I mingled with my ale, as I remember to have seen an old quaffer of that excellent liquor stir up his cup with a sprig of some bitter and fragrant herb. Meanwhile, I found myself still haunted by a desire to get a definite result out of my visit to Uttoxeter. The hospitable inn was called the Nag's Head, and, standing beside the market-place, was as likely as any other to have entertained old Michael Johnson, in the days when he used to come hither to sell books. He, perhaps, had dined on bacon and greens, and drunk his ale, and smoked his pipe, in the very room where I now sat, which was a low, ancient room, certainly much elder than Queen Anne's time, with a red brick floor, and a white-washed ceiling traversed by bare, rough beams, the whole in the rudest fashion, but extremely neat. Neither did it lack ornament, the walls being hung with colored engravings of prize oxen, and other pretty prints, and the mantel-piece adorned with earthen-ware figures of shepherdesses in the Arcadian taste of long ago. Michael Johnson's eyes might have rested on that self-same earthen image, to examine which more closely I had just crossed the brick pavement of the room. And, sitting down again, still, as I sipped my ale, I glanced through the open window into the sunny market-place, and wished that I could honestly fix on one spot rather than another, as likely to have been the holy site where Johnson stood to do his penance.

How strange and stupid it is, that tradition should not have marked and kept in mind the very place! How shameful (nothing less than that) that there should be no local memorial of this incident, as beautiful and touching a passage as can be cited out of any human life; no inscription of it, almost as sacred as a verse of Scripture, on the wall of the church; no statue of the venerable and illustrious penitent in the market-place to throw a wholesome awe over its earthliness, its frauds and petty wrongs of which the benumbed fingers of Conscience can make no record, its selfish competition of each man with his brother or his neighbor, its traffic of soul-substance for a little worldly gain! Such a statue, if the piety of the people did not raise it, might almost have been expected to grow up out of the pavement, of its own accord, on the spot that had been watered by the rain that dript from Johnson's garments, mingled with his remorseful tears.

Long after my visit to Uttoxeter, I was told that there were individuals in the town who could have shown me the exact, indubitable spot where Johnson performed his penance. I was assured, moreover, that sufficient interest was felt in the subject to have induced certain local discussions as to the expediency of erecting a memorial. With all deference to my polite informant, I surmise that there is a mistake, and decline, without further and precise evidence, giving credit to either of the above statements. The inhabitants know nothing, as a matter of general interest, about the penance, and care nothing for the scene of it. If the clergyman of the parish, for example, had ever heard of it, would he not have used the theme, time and again, wherewith to work tenderly and profoundly on the souls committed to his charge? If parents were familiar with it, would they not teach it to their young ones at the fireside, both to ensure reverence to their own gray hairs, and to protect the children from such unavailing regrets as Johnson bore upon his heart for fifty years? If the site were ascertained, would not the pavement thereabouts be worn with reverential footsteps? Would not every town-born child be able to direct the pilgrim thither? While waiting at the station, before my departure, I asked a boy who stood near me —an intelligent and gentlemanly lad, twelve or thirteen years old, whom I should take to be a clergyman's son—I asked him if he had ever heard the story of Dr. Johnson, how he stood an hour doing penance near that church, the spire of which rose before us. The boy stared, and answered, "No!"—"Were you born in Uttoxeter?"—"Yes."—I inquired if no circumstance such as I had mentioned was known or talked about among the inhabitants. "No," said the boy; "not that I ever heard of!"

Just think of the absurd little town, knowing nothing of the only memorable incident which ever happened within its boundaries since the old Britons built it, this sad and lovely story, which consecrates the spot (for I found it holy to my contemplation, again, as soon as it lay behind me) in the heart of a stranger from three thousand miles over the sea! It but confirms what I have been saying, that sublime and beautiful facts are best understood when etherealized by distance.

PILGRIMAGE TO OLD BOSTON

W E SET OUT at a little past eleven, and made our
first stage to Manchester. We were by this time
sufficiently anglicized to reckon the morning a
bright and sunny one; although the May sunshine was mingled with water, as it were, and distempered with a very bitter
east-wind.

Lancashire is a dreary county, (all, at least, except its hilly
portions,) and I have never passed through it without wishing
myself anywhere but in that particular spot where I then
happened to be. A few places along our route were historically
interesting; as, for example, Bolton, which was the scene of
many remarkable events in the Parliamentary War, and in the
market-square of which, one of the Earls of Derby was be-
headed. We saw, along the wayside, the never-failing green
fields, hedges, and other monotonous features of an ordinary
English landscape. There were little factory villages, too, or
larger towns, with their tall chimneys, and their pennons of
black smoke, their uglinesses of brick-work, and their heaps of
refuse matter from the furnace, which seems to be the only
kind of stuff which Nature cannot take back to herself and
resolve into the elements, when man has thrown it aside.
These hillocks of waste and effete mineral always disfigure

the neighborhood of iron-mongering towns, and, even after a considerable antiquity, are hardly made decent with a little grass.

At a quarter to two, we left Manchester by the Sheffield and Lincoln railway. The scenery grew rather better than that through which we had hitherto passed, though still by no means very striking; for (except in the show-districts, such as the Lake country, or Derbyshire) English scenery is not particularly well-worth looking at, considered as a spectacle or a picture. It has a real, homely charm of its own, no doubt; and the rich verdure, and the thorough finish added by human art, are perhaps as attractive to an American eye as any stronger feature could be. Our journey, however, between Manchester and Sheffield, was not through a rich tract of country, but along a valley walled in by bleak, ridgy hills, extending straight as a rampart, and across black moor-lands, with here and there a plantation of trees. Sometimes, there were long and gradual ascents, bleak, windy, and desolate, conveying the very impression which the reader gets from many passages of Miss Brontë's novels, and still more from those of her two sisters. Old stone or brick farm-houses, and, once in a while, an old church-tower, were visible, but these are almost too common objects to be noticed in an English landscape.

On a railway, I suspect, what little we do see of the country is seen quite amiss, because it was never intended to be looked at from any point of view in that straight line; so that it is like looking at the wrong side of a piece of tapestry. The old highways and foot-paths were as natural as brooks and rivulets, and adapted themselves by an inevitable impulse to the physiognomy of the country; and, furthermore, every object within view of them had some subtle reference to their curves and undulations; but the line of a railway is perfectly artificial, and puts all precedent things at sixes and sevens. At any rate, be the cause what it may, there is seldom anything worth seeing within the scope of a railway traveller's eye, and, if there were, it requires an alert marksman to take a flying shot at the picturesque.

At one of the stations, (it was near a village of ancient aspect, nestling round a church, on a wide Yorkshire moor,) I saw a tall old lady in black, who seemed to have just alighted from the train. She caught my attention by a singular movement of the head, not once only, but continually repeated, and at regular intervals, as if she were making a stern and solemn protest against some action that developed itself before her eyes, and were foreboding terrible disaster, if it should be persisted in. Of course, it was nothing more than a paralytic or nervous affection; yet one might fancy that it had its origin in some unspeakable wrong, perpetrated half a lifetime ago in this old gentlewoman's presence, either against herself or somebody whom she loved still better. Her features had a wonderful sternness, which, I presume, was caused by her habitual effort to compose and keep them quiet, and thereby counteract the tendency to paralytic movement. The slow, regular, and inexorable character of the motion—her look of force and self-control, which had the appearance of rendering it voluntary, while yet it was so fateful—have stamped this poor lady's face and gesture into my memory; so that, some dark day or other, I am afraid she will re-produce herself in a dismal Romance.

The train stopped a minute or two, to allow the tickets to be taken, just before entering the Sheffield station, and thence I had a glimpse of the famous town of razors and pen knives, enveloped in a cloud of its own diffusing. My impressions of it are extremely vague and misty—or, rather, smoky:—for Sheffield seems to me smokier than Manchester, Liverpool, or Birmingham; smokier than all England besides, unless New-castle be the exception. It might have been Pluto's own metropolis, shrouded in sulphurous vapor; and, indeed, our approach to it had been by the Valley of the Shadow of Death, through a tunnel three miles in length, quite traversing the breadth and depth of a mountainous hill.

After passing Sheffield, the scenery became softer, gentler, yet more picturesque. At one point, we saw what I believe to be the utmost northern verge of Sherwood Forest; not consisting, however, of thousand-year oaks, extant from Robin Hood's days, but of young and thriving plantations which will require a century or two of slow English growth to give them much breadth of shade. Earl Fitzwilliam's property lies in this neighborhood, and probably his castle was hidden among some soft depth of foliage, not far off. Farther onward, the country grew quite level around us, whereby I judged that we must now be in Lincolnshire; and shortly after six o'clock, we caught the first glimpse of the Cathedral towers, though they loomed scarcely huge enough for our pre-conceived idea of them. But, as we drew nearer, the great edifice began to assert itself, making us acknowledge it to be larger than our receptivity could take in.

At the railway-station, we found no cab, (it being an unknown vehicle in Lincoln,) but only an omnibus belonging to the Saracen's Head, which the driver recommended as the best hotel in the city, and took us thither accordingly. It received us hospitably, and looked comfortable enough, though, like the hotels of most old English towns, it had a musty fragrance of antiquity, such as I have smelt in a seldom-opened London church, where the broad-aisle is paved with tombstones. The house was of an ancient fashion, the entrance into its interior court-yard being through an arch, in the side of which is the door of the hotel. There are long corridors, an intricate arrangement of passages, and an up-and-down meandering of staircases, amid which it would be no marvel to encounter some forgotten guest who had gone astray a hundred years ago, and was still seeking for his bedroom while the rest of his generation were in their graves. There is no exaggerating the confusion of mind that seizes upon a stranger in the bewildering geography of a great, old-fashioned English inn.

This hotel stands in the principal street of Lincoln, and within a very short distance of one of the ancient city-gates, which is arched across the public way, with a smaller arch for foot-passengers on either side; the whole, a gray, time-gnawn, ponderous, shadowy structure, through the dark vista of which you look into the middle ages. The street is narrow, and retains many antique peculiarities; though, unquestionably, English domestic architecture has lost its most impressive features, in the course of the last century. In this respect, there are finer old towns than Lincoln; Chester, for instance, and Shrewsbury, which last is unusually rich in those quaint and stately edifices, where the gentry of the shire used to make their winter-abodes, in a provincial metropolis. Almost everywhere, now-a-days, there is a monotony of modern brick or stuccoed fronts, hiding houses that are older than ever, but obliterating the picturesque antiquity of the street.

Between seven and eight o'clock, (it being still broad daylight in these long English days,) we set out to pay a preliminary visit to the exterior of the Cathedral. Passing through the Stone Bow, as the city-gate close by is called, we ascended a street which grew steeper and narrower as we advanced, till at last it got to be the steepest street I ever climbed; so steep that any carriage, if left to itself, would rattle downward much faster than it could possibly be drawn up. Being almost the only hill in Lincolnshire, the inhabitants seem disposed to make the most of it. The houses on each side had no very remarkable aspect, except one with a stone-portal and carved ornaments, which is now a dwelling-place for poverty-stricken people, but may have been an aristocratic abode in the days of the Norman kings, to whom its style of architecture dates back. This is called the Jewess's house, having been inhabited by a woman of that faith, who was hanged six hundred years ago.

And still the street grew steeper and steeper. Certainly, the Bishop and clergy of Lincoln ought not to be fat men, but of very spiritual, saint-like, almost angelic habit, if it be a frequent part of their ecclesiastical duty to climb this hill; for it is a real penance, and was probably performed as such, and groaned over accordingly, in monkish times. Formerly, on the day of his installation, the Bishop used to ascend the hill barefoot, and was doubtless cheered and invigorated by looking upward to the grandeur that was to console him for the humility of his approach. We, likewise, were beckoned onward by glimpses of the Cathedral towers, and, finally, attaining an open square on the summit, we saw an old Gothic gateway to the left hand, and another to the right. The latter had apparently been a part of the exterior defences of the Cathedral, at a time when the edifice was fortified. The West Front rose behind. We passed through one of the side-arches of the Gothic portal, and found ourselves in the Cathedral Close, a wide, level space, where the great old Minster has fair room to sit, looking down on the ancient structures that surround it, all of which, in former days, were the habitations of its dignitaries and officers. Some of them are still occupied as such, though others are in too neglected and dilapidated a state to seem worthy of so splendid an establishment. Unless it be Salisbury Close, however, (which is incomparably rich as regards the old residences that belong to it,) I remember no more comfortably picturesque precincts round any other Cathedral. But, in truth, almost every Cathedral Close, in turn, has seemed to me the loveliest, cosiest, safest, least wind-shaken, most decorous, and most enjoyable shelter, that ever the thrift and selfishness of mortal man contrived for himself.

How delightful, to combine all this with the service of the temple!

Lincoln Cathedral is built of a yellowish brown stone, which appears either to have been largely restored, or else does not assume the hoary, crumbly surface that gives such a venerable aspect to most of the ancient churches and castles in England. In many parts, the recent restorations are quite evident, but other, and much the larger portions, can scarcely have been touched for centuries; for there are still the gargoyles, perfect, or with broken noses, as the case may be, but showing that variety and fertility of grotesque extravagance which no modern imitation can effect. There are innumerable niches, too, up the whole height of the towers, above and around the entrance, and all over the walls; most of them empty, but a few containing the lamentable remnants of headless saints and angels. It is singular, what a native animosity lives in the human heart against carved images, insomuch that, whether they represent Christian saint or Pagan deity, all unsophisticated men seize the first safe opportunity to knock off their heads! In spite of all dilapidations, however, the effect of the West Front of the Cathedral is still exceedingly rich, being covered from massive base to airy summit with the minutest details of sculpture and carving; at least, it was so once, and even now, the spiritual impression of its beauty remains so strong, that we have to look twice to see that much of it has been obliterated. I have seen a cherrystone carved all over, by a monk, so minutely that it must have cost him half a lifetime of labor; and this Cathedral front seems to have been elaborated in a monkish spirit, like that cherry-stone. Not that the result is in the least petty, but miraculously grand, and all the more so for the faithful beauty of the smallest details.

An elderly man, seeing us looking up at the West Front,

came to the door of an adjacent house, and called to inquire if we wished to go into the Cathedral; but as there would have been a dusky twilight beneath its roof, like the antiquity that has sheltered itself within, we declined for the present. So we merely walked round the exterior, and thought it more beautiful than that of York; though, on recollection, I hardly deem it so majestic and mighty as that. It is vain to attempt a description, or seek even to record the feeling which the edifice inspires. It does not impress the beholder as an inanimate object, but as something that has a vast, quiet, long-enduring life of its own; a creation which man did not build, though in some way or other it is connected with him, and kindred to human nature. In short, I fall straightway to talking nonsense, when I try to express my inner sense of this and other Cathedrals.

While we stood in the Close, at the eastern end of the Minster, the clock chimed the quarters; and then Great Tom, who hangs in the Rood Tower, told us it was eight o'clock, in far the sweetest and mightiest accents that I ever heard from any bell; slow, and solemn, and allowing the profound reverberations of each stroke to die away before the next one fell. It was still broad daylight in that upper region of the town, and would be so for some time longer, but the evening atmosphere was getting sharp and cool. We therefore descended the steep street; our younger companion running before us, and gathering such headway that I fully expected him to break his head against some projecting wall.

In the morning, we took a fly, (an English term for an exceedingly sluggish vehicle,) and drove up to the Minster by a road rather less steep and abrupt than the one we had previously climbed. We alighted before the West Front, and sent our charioteer in quest of the verger; but, as he was not immediately to be found, a young girl let us into the nave. We found it very grand, it is needless to say, but not so grand, methought, as the vast nave of York Cathedral, especially beneath the great central tower of the latter. Unless a writer intends a professedly architectural description, there is but one set of phrases in which to talk of all the Cathedrals in England, and elsewhere. They are alike in their great features;—an acre or two of stone-flags for a pavement; rows of vast columns supporting a vaulted roof at a dusky height; great windows, sometimes richly bedimmed with ancient or modern stained glass; and an elaborately carved screen between the nave and chancel, breaking the vista that might else be of such glorious length, and which is further choked up by a massive organ; in spite of which obstructions you catch the broad, variegated glimmer of the painted east-window, where a hundred Saints wear their robes of transfiguration. Behind the screen are the carved oaken stalls of the Chapter and Prebendaries, the Bishop's throne, the pulpit, the altar, and whatever else may furnish out the Holy of Holies. Nor must we forget the range of chapels, (once dedicated to Catholic saints, but which have now lost their individual consecration,) nor the old monuments of kings, warriors, and prelates, in the side-aisles of the chancel. In close contiguity to the main body of the Cathedral is the Chapter House, which, here at Lincoln, as at Salisbury, is supported by one central pillar rising from the floor, and putting forth branches like a tree, to hold up the roof. Adjacent to the Chapter House are the cloisters, extending round a quadrangle, and paved with lettered tombstones, the more antique of which have had their inscriptions half-obliterated by the feet of monks, taking their noontide exercise in these sheltered walks, five hundred years ago. Some of these old burial stones, although with ancient crosses engraved upon them, have been made to serve as memorials to dead people of very recent date.

In the chancel, among the tombs of forgotten Bishops and knights, we saw an immense slab of stone, purporting to be the monument of Catherine Swineford, wife of John of Gaunt; also, here was the shrine of the little Saint Hugh, that Christian child who was fabled to have been crucified by the Jews of Lincoln. The Cathedral is not particularly rich in monuments; for it suffered grievous outrage and dilapidation, both at the Reformation and in Cromwell's time. This latter iconoclast is in especially bad odor with the sextons and vergers of most of the old churches which I have visited. His soldiers stabled their steeds in the nave of Lincoln Cathedral, and hacked and hewed the monkish sculptures, and the ancestral memorials of great families, quite at their wicked and plebeian pleasure. Nevertheless, there are some most exquisite and marvellous specimens of flowers, foliage, and grape-vines, and miracles of stone-work twined about arches, as if the material had been as soft as wax in the cunning sculptor's hands; the leaves being represented with all their veins, so that you would almost think it petrified Nature, for which he sought to steal the praise of Art. Here, too, were those grotesque faces which always grin at you from the projections of monkish architecture, as if the builders had gone mad with their own deep solemnity, or dreaded such a catastrophe, unless permitted to throw in something ineffably absurd.

Originally, it is supposed, all the pillars of this great edifice, and all these magic sculptures, were polished to the utmost degree of lustre; nor is it unreasonable to think that the artists would have taken these further pains, when they had already bestowed so much labor in working out their conceptions to the extremest point. But, at present, the whole interior of the Cathedral is smeared over with a yellowish wash, the very meanest hue imaginable, and for which somebody's soul has a bitter reckoning to undergo.

In the centre of the grassy quadrangle, about which the cloisters perambulate, is a small, mean, brick building, with a locked door. Our guide—I forgot to say that we had been captured by a verger, in black, and with a white tie, but of a lusty and jolly aspect—our guide unlocked this door, and disclosed a flight of steps. At the bottom appeared what I should have taken to be a large square of dim, worn, and faded oil-carpeting, which might originally have been painted of a rather gaudy pattern. This was a Roman tessellated pavement, made of small, colored bricks, or pieces of burnt clay. It was accidentally discovered here, and has not been meddled with, further than by removing the superincumbent earth and rubbish.

Nothing else occurs to me, just now, to be recorded about the interior of the Cathedral, except that we saw a place where the stone pavement had been worn away by the feet of ancient pilgrims, scraping upon it as they knelt down before a shrine of the Virgin.

Leaving the Minster, we now went along a street of more venerable appearance than we had heretofore seen, bordered with houses, the high, peaked roofs of which were covered with red earthen tiles. It led us to a Roman arch, which was once the gateway of a fortification, and has been striding across the English street ever since the latter was a faint village-path, and for centuries before. The arch is about four hundred yards from the Cathedral; and it is to be noticed that there are Roman remains in all this neighborhood, some above ground, and doubtless innumerable more beneath it; for, as in ancient Rome itself, an inundation of accumulated soil seems to have swept over what was the surface of that earlier day. The gateway, which I am speaking about, is probably buried to a third of its height, and perhaps has as perfect a Roman pavement (if sought for at the original depth) as that which runs beneath the Arch of Titus. It is a rude and massive structure, and seems as stalwart now as it could have been, two thousand years ago; and though Time has gnawed it externally, he has made what amends he could by crowning its rough and broken summit with grass and weeds, and planting tufts of yellow flowers on the projections up and down the sides.

There are the ruins of a Norman castle, built by the Conqueror, in pretty close proximity to the Cathedral; but the old gateway is obstructed by a modern door of wood, and we were denied admittance, because some part of the precincts are used as a prison. We now rambled about on the broad back of the hill, which, besides the Minster and ruined castle, is the site of some stately and queer old houses, and of many mean little hovels. I suspect that all, or most of the life of the present day has subsided into the lower town, and that only priests, poor people, and prisoners, dwell in these upper regions. In the wide, dry moat, at the base of the castle-wall, are clustered whole colonies of small houses, some of brick, but the larger portion built of old stones which once made part of the Norman keep, or of Roman structures that existed before the Conqueror's castle was ever dreamed about. They are like toadstools that spring up from the mould of a decaying tree. Ugly as they are, they add wonderfully to the picturesqueness of the scene, being quite as valuable, in that respect, as the great, broad, ponderous ruin of the Castle Keep, which rose high above our heads, heaving its huge, gray mass out of a bank of green foliage and ornamental shrubbery, such as lilacs and other flowering plants, in which its foundations were completely hidden.

After walking quite round the castle, I made an excursion through the Roman gateway, along a pleasant and level road, bordered with dwellings of various character. One or two were houses of gentility, with delightful and shadowy lawns before them; many had those high, red-tiled roofs, ascending into acutely pointed gables, which seem to belong to the same epoch as some of the edifices in our own earlier towns; and there were pleasant-looking cottages, very sylvan and rural, with hedges so dense and high, fencing them in, as almost to hide them up to the eaves of their thatched roofs. In front of one of these, I saw various images, crosses, and relics of antiquity, among which were fragments of old Catholic tomb-stones, disposed by way of ornament.

We now went home to the Saracen's Head; and as the weather was very unpropitious, and it sprinkled a little, now and then, I would gladly have felt myself released from further thraldom to the Cathedral. But it had taken possession of me, and would not let me be at rest; so at length I found myself compelled to climb the hill again, between daylight and dusk. A mist was now hovering about the upper height of the great central tower, so as to dim and half-obliterate its battlements and pinnacles, even while I stood in the Close, beneath it. It was the most impressive view that I had had. The whole lower part of the structure was seen with perfect distinctness, but, at the very summit, the mist was so dense as to form an actual cloud, as well defined as ever I saw resting on a mountain-top. Really and literally, here was a 'cloud-capt tower.'

The entire Cathedral, too, transfigured itself into a richer beauty and more imposing majesty than ever. The longer I looked, the better I loved it. Its exterior is certainly far more beautiful than that of York Minster; and its finer effect is due, I think, to the many peaks in which the structure ascends, and to the pinnacles which, as it were, repeat and re-echo them into the sky. York Cathedral is comparatively square and angular in its general effect; but in this at Lincoln there is a continual mystery of variety, so that, at every glance, you are aware of a change, and a disclosure of something new, yet working a harmonious development of what you have hereto-fore seen. The West Front is unspeakably grand, and may be read over and over again, forever, and still show undetected meanings, like a great, broad page of marvellous writing in black-letter; so many sculptured ornaments there are, blossoming out before your eyes, and gray statues that have grown there since you looked last, and empty niches, and a hundred airy canopies beneath which carved images used to be, and where they will show themselves again, if you gaze long enough.—But I will not say another word about the Cathedral.

We spent the rest of the day within the sombre precincts of the Saracen's Head, reading yesterday's Times, the guide-book of Lincoln, and the Directory of the Eastern Counties. Dismal as the weather was, the street beneath our window was enlivened with a great bustle and turmoil of people, all the evening, because it was Saturday night, and they had accomplished their week's toil, received their wages, and were making their small purchases against Sunday, and enjoying themselves as well as they knew how. A band of music passed to-and-fro, several times, with the rain-drops falling into the mouth of the brazen trumpet and pattering on the bass-drum; a spirit-shop, opposite the hotel, had a vast run of custom; and a coffee-dealer, in the open air, found occasional vent for his commodity, in spite of the cold water that dripped into the cups. The whole breadth of the street, between the Stone Bow and the bridge across the Witham, was thronged to overflowing, and humming with human life.

Observing in the guide-book that a steamer runs on the river Witham, between Lincoln and Boston, I inquired of the waiter, and learned that she was to start on Monday, at ten o'clock. Thinking it might be an interesting trip, and a pleasant variation of our customary mode of travel, we determined to make the voyage. The Witham flows through Lincoln, crossing the main street under an arched bridge of Gothic construction, a little below the Saracen's Head. It has more the appearance of a canal than of a river, in its passage through the town, being bordered with hewn stone mason-work on each side, and provided with one or two locks. The steamer proved to be small, dirty, and altogether inconvenient. The early morning had been bright; but the sky now lowered upon us with a sulky English temper, and we had not long put off before we felt an ugly wind from the German Ocean blowing right in our teeth. There were a number of passengers on board, country-people, such as travel by third-class on the railway; for, I suppose, nobody but ourselves ever dreamt of voyaging by the steamer, for the sake of what he might happen upon in the way of river-scenery.

We bothered a good while about getting through a preliminary lock; nor, when fairly under way, did we ever accomplish, I think, six miles an hour. Constant delays were caused, moreover, by stopping to take up passengers and freight, not at regular landing-places, but anywhere along the green banks. The scenery was identical with that of the railway, because the latter runs along by the river-side, through the whole distance, or nowhere departs from it except to make a short cut across some sinuosity; so that our only advantage lay in the drawling, snail-like slothfulness of our progress, which allowed us time enough and to spare for the objects along the shore. Unfortunately, there was nothing, or next to nothing, to be seen; the country being one unvaried level over the whole thirty miles of our voyage; not a hill in sight, either near or far, except that solitary one on the summit of which we had left Lincoln Cathedral. And the Cathedral was our landmark for four hours, or more, and at last rather faded out, than was hidden by any intervening object.

It would have been a pleasantly lazy day enough, if the rough and bitter wind had not blown directly in our faces, and chilled us through, in spite of the sunshine that soon succeeded a sprinkle or two of rain. These English east-winds, which prevail from February till June, are greater nuisances than the east-wind of our own Atlantic coast, although they do not bring mist and storm, as with us, but some of the sunniest weather that England sees. Under their influence, the sky smiles and is villainous.

The landscape was tame, to the last degree, but had an English character that was abundantly worth our looking at. A green luxuriance of early grass; old, high-roofed farm-houses, surrounded by their stone-barns, and ricks of hay and grain; ancient villages, with the square, gray tower of a church seen afar over the level country, amid the cluster of red roofs; here and there, a shadowy grove of venerable trees, surrounding what was perhaps an Elizabethan hall, though it looked more like the abode of some rich yeoman. Once, too, we saw the tower of a mediæval castle, that of Tattershall, built by a Cromwell, but whether of the Protector's family I cannot tell. But the gentry do not appear to have settled multitudinously in this tract of country; nor is it to be won-dered at, since a lover of the picturesque would as soon think of settling in Holland. The river retains its canal-like aspect all along; and only in the latter part of its course does it become more than wide enough for the little steamer to turn itself round;—at broadest, not more than twice that width. The only memorable incident of our voyage happened when a mother-duck was leading her little fleet of five ducklings across the river, just as our steamer went swaggering by, stirring the quiet stream into great waves that lashed the banks on either side. I saw the imminence of the catastrophe, and hurried to the stern of the boat to witness its consumma-tion, since I could not possibly avert it. The poor ducklings had uttered their baby-quacks, and striven with all their tiny might to escape;—four of them, I believe, were washed aside and thrown off unhurt from the steamer's prow;—but the fifth must have gone under the whole length of the keel, and never could have come up alive.

At last, in mid-afternoon, we beheld the tall tower of Saint

Botolph's church, (three hundred feet high, the same elevation as the tallest tower of Lincoln Cathedral,) looming in the
distance. At about half-past four, we reached Boston—which
name has been shortened in the course of ages, by the quick
and slovenly English pronunciation, from Botolph's town—
and were taken by a cab to the Peacock, in the market-place.
It was the best hotel in town, though a poor one enough; and
we were shown into a small, stifled parlor, dingy, musty, and
scented with stale tobacco-smoke—tobacco-smoke two days
old, for the waiter assured us that the room had not more
recently been fumigated. An exceedingly grim waiter he was,
apparently a genuine descendant of the old Puritans of this
English Boston, and quite as sour as those who peopled the
daughter-city in New England. Our parlor had the one rec-
ommendation of looking into the market-place, and affording
a side-long glimpse of the tall spire and noble old church.

In my first ramble about the town, chance led me to the
river-side, at that quarter where the port is situated. Here
were long buildings of an old-fashioned aspect, seemingly
ware-houses, with windows in the high, steep roofs. The
Custom House found ample accommodation within an ordinary dwelling-house. Two or three large schooners were
moored along the river's brink, which had here a stone margin; another large and handsome schooner was evidently just
finished, rigged, and equipped for her first voyage; the rudi-
ments of another were on the stocks, in a ship-yard bordering
on the river. Still another, while I was looking on, came up
the stream, and lowered her mainsail, from a foreign voyage.
An old man, on the bank, hailed her and inquired about her
cargo; but the Lincolnshire people have such a queer way of
talking English that I could not understand the reply. Farther
down the river, I saw a brig, approaching rapidly under sail.
The whole scene made an odd impression of bustle, and
sluggishness, and decay, and a remnant of wholesome life;

and I could not but contrast it with the mighty and populous activity of our own Boston, which was once the feeble infant of this old English town;—the latter, perhaps, almost stationary ever since that day, as if the birth of such an offspring had taken away its own principle of growth. I thought of Long Wharf, and Faneuil Hall, and Washington-street, and the Great Elm, and the State House, and exulted lustily, but yet began to feel at home in this good old town, for its very name's sake, as I never had before felt, in England.

The next morning, we came out in the early sunshine, (the sun must have been shining nearly four hours, however, for it was after eight o'clock,) and strolled about the streets, like people who had a right to be there. The market-place of Boston is an irregular square, into one end of which the chancel of the church slightly projects. The gates of the churchyard were open and free to all passengers, and the common footway of the townspeople seems to lie to-and-fro across it. It is paved, according to English custom, with flat tombstones, and there are also raised, or altar-tombs, some of which have armorial bearings on them. One clergyman has caused himself and his wife to be buried right in the middle of the stone-bordered path that traverses the churchyard; so that not an individual of the thousands, who pass along this public way, can help trampling over him or her. The scene, nevertheless, was very cheerful in the morning sun; people going about their business in the day's primal freshness, which was just as fresh here as in younger villages; children, with milk-pails, loitering over the burial-stones; schoolboys playing leap-frog with the altar-tombs; the simple old town preparing itself for the day, which would be like myriads of other days that had passed over it, but yet would be worth living through. And down on the churchyard, where were buried many generations whom it remembered in their time, looked the stately tower of Saint Botolph; and it was good to see and think of such an age-long giant, intermarrying the present epoch with a distant past, and getting quite imbued with human nature by being so immemorially connected with men's familiar knowledge and homely interests. It is a noble tower; and the jackdaws evidently have pleasant homes in their hereditary nests, among its topmost windows, and live delightful lives, flitting and cawing about its pinnacles and flying buttresses. I should almost like to be a jackdaw myself, for the sake of living up there.

In front of the church, not more than twenty yards off, and with a low brick-wall between, flows the river Witham. On the hither bank, a fisherman was washing his boat; and another skiff, with her sail lazily half-twisted, lay on the opposite strand. The stream, at this point, is about of such width that, if the tall tower were to tumble over flat on its face, its top-stone might perhaps reach to the middle channel. On the farther shore, there is a line of antique-looking houses, with roofs of red tile, and windows opening out of them; some of these dwellings being so ancient that the Reverend Mr. Cotton, subsequently our first Boston minister, must have seen them with his own bodily eyes, when he used to issue from the front-portal, after service. Indeed, there must be very many houses here, and even some streets, that bear much the aspect that they did when the Puritan divine paced solemnly among them.

In our rambles about town, we went into a bookseller's shop to inquire if he had any description of Boston for sale. He offered me (or, rather, produced for inspection, not supposing that I would buy it) a quarto history of the town, published by subscription, nearly forty years ago. The book-seller showed himself a well-informed and affable man, and a local antiquary, to whom a party of inquisitive strangers were a god-send. He had met with several Americans, who, at various times, had come on pilgrimages to this place, and he had been in correspondence with others. Happening to have heard the name of one member of our party, he showed us great courtesy and kindness, and invited us into his inner domicile, where, as he modestly intimated, he kept a few articles which it might interest us to see. So we went with him through the shop, up stairs, into the private part of his establishment; and, really, it was one of the rarest adventures I ever met with, to stumble upon this treasure of a man, with his treasury of antiquities and curiosities, veiled behind the unostentatious front of a bookseller's shop, in a very moderate line of village-business. The two up-stair rooms, into which he introduced us, were so crowded with inestimable articles, that we were almost afraid to stir, for fear of breaking some fragile thing that had been accumulating value for unknown centuries.

The apartment was hung round with pictures and old engravings, many of which were extremely rare. Premising that he was going to show us something very curious, Mr. Porter went into the next room and returned with a counterpane of fine linen, elaborately embroidered with silk, which so profusely covered the linen that the general effect was as if the main texture were silken. It was stained, and seemed very old, and had an ancient fragrance. It was wrought all over with birds and flowers, in a most delicate style of needle-work, and among other devices, more than once repeated, was the cypher, M. S.; being the initials of one of the most unhappy names that ever a woman bore. This quilt was embroidered by the hands of Mary Queen of Scots, during her imprisonment at Fotheringay Castle; and having evidently been a work of years, she had doubtless shed many tears over it, and wrought many doleful thoughts and abortive schemes into its texture, along with the birds and flowers. As a counterpart to this most precious relic, our friend produced some of the handiwork of a former Queen of Otaheite, presented by her to Captain

Cook; it was a bag, cunningly made of some delicate vegetable stuff, and ornamented with feathers. Next, he brought out a green silk waistcoat of very antique fashion, trimmed about the edges and pocket-holes with a rich and delicate embroidery of gold and silver. This (as the possessor of the treasure proved, by tracing its pedigree till it came into his hands) was once the vestment of Queen Elizabeth's Lord Burleigh; but that great statesman must have been a person of very moderate girth in the chest and waist; for the garment was hardly more than a comfortable fit for a boy of eleven, the smallest American of our party, who tried on the gorgeous waistcoat. Then, Mr. Porter produced some curiously engraved drinking-glasses, with a view of Saint Botolph's steeple on one of them, and other Boston edifices, public or domestic, on the remaining two, very admirably done. These crystal goblets had been a present, long ago, to an old master of the Free School from his pupils; and it is very rarely, I imagine, that a retired schoolmaster can exhibit such trophies of gratitude and affection, won from the victims of his birch rod.

Our kind friend kept bringing out one unexpected and wholly unexpectable thing after another, as if he were a magician, and had only to fling a private signal into the air, and some attendant imp would hand forth any strange relic we might choose to ask for. He was especially rich in drawings by the Old Masters, producing two or three, of exquisite delicacy, by Raphael, one by Salvator, a head by Rembrandt, and others, in chalk or pen-and-ink, by Giordano, Benvenuto Cellini, and hands almost as famous; and, besides what were shown us, there seemed to be an endless supply of these art-treasures in reserve. On the wall, hung a crayon-portrait of Sterne, never engraved, representing him as a rather young man, blooming, and not uncomely; it was the worldly face of a man fond of pleasure, but without that ugly, keen, sarcastic, odd expression that we see in his only engraved portrait. The picture is an original, and must needs be very valuable; and we wish it might be prefixed to some new and worthier biography of a writer whose character the world has always treated with singular harshness, considering how much it owes him. There was likewise a crayon-portrait of Sterne's wife, looking so haughty and unamiable, that the wonder is, not that he ultimately left her, but how he ever contrived to live a week with such an awful woman.

After looking at these, and a great many more things than I can remember, above stairs, we went down to a parlor, where this wonderful bookseller opened an old cabinet, containing numberless drawers, and looking just fit to be the repository of such knick-knacks as were stored up in it. He appeared to possess more treasures than he himself knew of, or knew where to find; but rummaging here and there, he brought forth things new and old:—rose-nobles, Victoria crowns, gold angels, double-sovereigns of George the Fourth, two-guinea pieces of George the Second;—a marriage-medal of the first Napoleon, only forty-five of which were ever struck off, and of which even the British Museum does not contain a specimen like this, in gold;—a brass medal, three or four inches in diameter, of a Roman emperor;—together with buckles, bracelets, amulets, and I know not what besides. There was a green silk tassel from the fringe of Queen Mary's bed at Holyrood Palace. There were illuminated missals, antique Latin Bibles, and (what may seem of especial interest to the historian) a Secret-Book of Queen Elizabeth, in manuscript, written, for aught I know, by her own hand. On examination, however, it proved to contain, not secrets of state, but recipes for dishes, drinks, medicines, washes, and all such matters of housewifery, the toilet, and domestic quackery, among which we were horrified by the title of one of the nostrums—"How to kill a Fellow quickly"! We never doubted that bloody Queen Bess might often have had occasion for such a recipe, but wondered at her frankness, and at her attending to these anomalous necessities in such a methodical way. The truth is, we had read amiss, and the Queen had spelt amiss; the word was 'Fellon' —a sort of whitlow—not 'Fellow.'

Our hospitable friend now made us drink a glass of wine, as old and genuine as the curiosities of his cabinet; and while sipping it we ungratefully tried to excite his envy, by telling of various things, interesting to an antiquary and virtuoso, which we had seen in the course of our travels about England. We spoke, for instance, of a Missal, bound in solid gold and set round with jewels, but of such intrinsic value as no setting could enhance, for it was exquisitely illuminated, throughout, by the hand of Raphael himself. We mentioned a little silver case, which once contained a portion of the heart of Louis the Fourteenth, nicely done up in spices; but, to the owner's horror and astonishment, Dean Buckland popt the kingly morsel into his mouth, and swallowed it. We told about the black-letter prayer-book of King Charles the Martyr, used by him upon the scaffold, taking which into our hands, it opened of itself at the Communion Service; and there, on the left hand page, appeared a spot about as large as a sixpence, of a yellowish or brownish hue. A drop of the King's blood had fallen there.

Mr. Porter now accompanied us to the church, but first leading us to a vacant spot of ground where old John Cotton's vicarage had stood, till a very short time since. According to our friend's description, it was a humble habitation of the cottage-order, built of brick, with a thatched roof. The site is now rudely fenced in, and cultivated as a vegetable garden. In the right hand aisle of the church, there is an ancient chapel, which, at the time of our visit, was in process of restoration, and was to be dedicated to Mr. Cotton, whom these English people consider as the founder of our American Boston. It would contain a painted memorial window, in honor of the old Puritan minister. A festival, in commemoration of the event, was to take place in the ensuing July, to which I had myself received an invitation, but I knew too well the pains and penalties incurred by an invited guest, at public festivals in England, to accept it. It ought to be recorded, (and it seems to have made a very kindly impression on our kinsfolk here,) that five hundred pounds had been contributed by persons in the United States, principally in Boston, towards the cost of the memorial window, and the repair and restoration of the chapel.

After we emerged from the chapel, Mr. Porter approached us with the vicar, to whom he kindly introduced us, and then took his leave. May a stranger's benediction rest upon him! He is a most pleasant man; rather, I imagine, a virtuoso than an antiquary; for he seemed to value the Queen of Otaheite's bag as highly as Queen Mary's embroidered quilt, and to have an omnivorous appetite for everything strange and rare. Would that we could fill up his shelves and drawers (if there are any vacant spaces left) with the choicest trifles that have dropt out of Time's carpet-bag, or give him the carpet-bag itself, to take out what he will!

The vicar looked about thirty years old, a gentleman, evidently assured of his position, (as clergymen of the established church invariably are,) comfortable and well-to-do, a scholar, and a Christian, and fit to be a Bishop, knowing how to make the most of life, without prejudice to the life to come. I was glad to see such a model English priest so suitably accommodated with an old English church. He kindly and courteously did the honors, showing us quite round the interior, giving us all the information that we required, and then leaving us to the quiet enjoyment of what we came to see. The interior of Saint Botolph's is very fine and satisfactory, as stately, almost, as a Cathedral, and has been repaired—so far as repairs were necessary—in a chaste and noble style. The great eastern window is of modern painted glass, but is the richest, mellowest, and tenderest modern window, that I have ever seen; the art of painting these glowing transparencies, in pristine perfection, being one that the world has lost. The vast, clear space of the interior church delighted me. There was no screen; nothing between the vestibule and the altar, to break the long vista; even the organ stood aside, though it by-and-by made us aware of its presence by a melodious roar. Around the walls, there were old engraved brasses, and a stone-coffin, and an alabaster knight of Saint John, and an alabaster lady, each recumbent at full length, as large as life, and in perfect preservation, except for a slight modern touch at the tips of their noses. In the chancel, we saw a great deal of oaken work, quaintly and admirably carved, especially about the seats formerly appropriated to the monks, which were so contrived as to tumble down, with a tremendous crash, if the occupant happened to fall asleep.

We now essayed to climb into the upper regions. Up we went, winding, and still winding, round the circular stairs, till we came to the gallery beneath the stone-roof of the tower, whence we could look down, and see the raised Font, and my Talma lying on one of the steps, and looking about as big as a pocket-handkerchief. Then up again, up, up, up, through a yet smaller staircase, till we emerged into another stone-gallery, above the jackdaws, and far above the roof, beneath which we had before made a halt. Then up another flight, which led us into a pinnacle of the temple, but not the highest; so, re-tracing our steps, we took the right turret, this time, and emerged into the loftiest lantern, whence we saw level Lincolnshire, far and near, though with a haze on the distant horizon. There were dusty roads, a river, and canals, converging towards Boston, which—a congregation of red-tiled roofs—lay beneath our feet, with pigmy people creeping about its narrow streets. We were three hundred feet aloft, and the pinnacle, on which we stood, is a landmark, forty miles at sea.

Content, and weary of our elevation, we descended the cork-screw stairs, and left the church; the last object that we noticed in the interior being a bird, which appeared to be at home there, and responded with its cheerful notes to the swell of the organ. Pausing on the church-steps, we observed that there were formerly two statues, one on each side of the door-way; the canopies still remaining, and the pedestals being about a yard from the ground. Some of Mr. Cotton's Puritan parishioners are probably responsible for the disappearance of these stone-saints. This door-way, at the base of the tower, is now much dilapidated, but must once have been very rich, and of a peculiar fashion. It opens its arch through a great, square tablet of stone, reared against the front of the tower. On most of the projections, whether on the tower or about the body of the church, there are gargoyles of genuine Gothic grotesqueness, fiends, beasts, angels, and combinations of all three; and where portions of the edifice are restored, the modern sculptors have tried to imitate these wild fantasies, but with very poor success. Extravagance and absurdity have still their law, and should pay as rigid obedience to it as the primmest things on earth.

In our further rambles about Boston, we crossed the river by a bridge, and observed that the larger part of the town seems to lie on that side of its navigable stream. The crooked streets and narrow lanes reminded me much of Hanover-street, Ann-street, and other portions of the North End of our American Boston, as I remember that picturesque region in my boyish days. It is not unreasonable to suppose that the local habits and recollections of the first settlers may have had some influence on the physical character of the streets and houses, in the New England metropolis; at any rate, here is a similar intricacy of bewildering lanes, and numbers of old, peaked and projecting-storied dwellings, such as I used to see there. It is singular what a home-feeling, and sense of kindred, I derived from this hereditary connection and fancied physiognomical resemblance between the old town and its well-grown daughter, and how reluctant I was, after chill years of banishment, to leave this hospitable place, on that account. Moreover, it recalled some of the features of another American town, my own dear native place, when I saw the seafaring people leaning against posts, and sitting on planks, under the lee of ware-houses, or lolling on long-boats, drawn up high and dry, as sailors and old wharf-rats are accustomed to do, in sea-ports of little business. In other respects, the English town is more village-like than either of the American ones. The women and budding girls chat together at their doors, and exchange merry greetings with young men; children chase one another in the summer-twilight; schoolboys sail little boats in the river, or play at marbles across the flat tombstones in the churchyard; and ancient men, in breeches and long waistcoats, wander slowly about the streets, with a certain familiarity of deportment, as if each one were everybody's grandfather. I have frequently observed, in old English towns, that Old-Age comes forth more cheerfully and genially into the sunshine, than among ourselves, where the rush, stir, bustle, and irreverent energy of youth are so preponderant, that the poor forlorn grandsires begin to doubt whether they have a right to breathe in such a world any longer, and so hide their silvery heads in solitude. Speaking of old men, I am reminded of the scholars of the Boston charity-school, who walk about in antique, long-skirted blue coats, and knee-breeches, and with bands at their necks, perfect and grotesque pictures of the costume of three centuries ago.

On the morning of our departure, I looked from the parlor-window of the Peacock into the market-place, and beheld its irregular square already well-covered with booths, and more in process of being put up, by stretching tattered sail-cloth on poles. It was market-day. The dealers were arranging their commodities, consisting chiefly of vegetables, the great bulk of which seemed to be cabbages. Later in the forenoon, there was a much greater variety of merchandize; basket-work, both for fancy and use; twig-brooms, beehives, oranges, rustic attire; all sorts of things, in short, that are commonly sold at a rural fair. I heard the lowing of cattle, too, and the bleating of sheep, and found that there was a market for cows, oxen, and pigs, in another part of the town. A crowd of townspeople and Lincolnshire yeomen elbowed one another in the square; Mr. Punch was squeaking in one corner, and a vagabond juggler tried to find space for his exhibition in another; so that my final glimpse of Boston was calculated to leave a livelier impression than my former ones. Meanwhile, the tower of Saint Botolph's looked benignantly down; and I fancied it was bidding me farewell, as it did Mr. Cotton, two or three hundred years ago, and telling me to describe its venerable height, and the town beneath it, to the people of the American city, who are partly akin, if not to the living inhabitants of Old Boston, yet to some of the dust that lies in its churchyard.

One thing more;—they have a Bunker Hill in the vicinity of their town; and (what could hardly be expected of an English community) seem proud to think that their neighborhood has given name to our first, and most widely celebrated, and best-remembered battle-field.

NEAR OXFORD

O N A FINE MORNING in September, we set out on
an excursion to Blenheim; the sculptor and myself
being seated on the box of our four-horse carriage,
two more of the party in the dicky, and the others less
agreeably accommodated inside. We had no coachman, but
two postillions in short scarlet jackets and leather breeches,
with top-boots, each astride of a horse; so that, all the way
along, when not otherwise attracted, we had the interesting
spectacle of their up-and-down bobbing in the saddle. It was a
sunny and beautiful day, a specimen of the perfect English
weather; just warm enough for comfort—indeed, a little too
warm, perhaps, in the noontide sun—yet retaining a mere
spice or suspicion of austerity, which made it all the more
enjoyable.

The country between Oxford and Blenheim is not particularly interesting, being almost level, or undulating very
slightly; nor is Oxfordshire, agriculturally, a rich part of England. We saw one or two hamlets, and I especially remember
a picturesque old gabled house, at a turnpike-gate, and, altogether, the wayside scenery had an aspect of old-fashioned
English life; but there was nothing very memorable till we
reached Woodstock, and stopt to water our horses at the Black

Bear. This neighborhood is called New Woodstock, but has by no means the bran-new appearance of an American town, being a large village of stone-houses, most of them pretty well time-worn and weather-stained. The Black Bear is an ancient inn, large and respectable, with balustraded staircases, and intricate passages and corridors, and queer old pictures and engravings hanging in the entries and apartments. We ordered a lunch (the most delightful of English institutions, next to dinner) to be ready against our return, and then resumed our drive to Blenheim.

The park-gate of Blenheim stands close at the end of the village-street of Woodstock. Immediately on passing through its portals, we saw the stately palace, in the distance, but made a wide circuit of the park before approaching it. This noble park contains three thousand acres of land, and is fourteen miles in circumference. Having been, in part, a royal domain before it was granted to the Marlborough family, it contains many trees of unsurpassed antiquity, and has doubtless been the haunt of game and deer for centuries. We saw pheasants in abundance, feeding in the open lawns and glades; and the stags tossed their antlers and bounded away, not affrighted, but only shy and gamesome, as we drove by. It is a magnificent pleasure-ground, not too tamely kept, nor rigidly subjected within rule, but vast enough to have lapsed back into Nature again, after all the pains that the landscape-gardeners of Queen Anne's time bestowed on it, when the domain of Blenheim was scientifically laid out. The great, knotted, slanting trunks of the old oaks do not now look as if man had much intermeddled with their growth and postures. The trees of later date, that were set out in the Great Duke's time, are arranged on the plan of the order of battle in which the illustrious commander ranked his troops at Blenheim; but the ground covered is so extensive, and the trees now so luxuriant, that the spectator is not disagreeably conscious of their standing in military array, as if Orpheus had summoned them together by beat of drum. The effect must have been very formal, a hundred and fifty years ago, but has ceased to be so; although the trees, I presume, have kept their ranks with even more fidelity than Marlborough's veterans did.

One of the park-keepers, on horseback, rode beside our carriage, pointing out the choice views, and glimpses at the palace, as we drove through the domain. There is a very large artificial lake (to say the truth, it seemed to me fully worthy of being compared with the Welsh lakes, at least, if not with those of Westmoreland) which was created by Capability Brown, and fills the basin that he scooped for it, just as if Nature had poured these broad waters into one of her own vallies. It is a most beautiful object at a distance, and not less so on its immediate banks; for the water is very pure, being supplied by a small river, of the choicest transparency, which was turned thitherward for the purpose. And Blenheim owes not merely this water-scenery, but almost all its other beauties, to the contrivance of man. Its natural features are not striking; but Art has effected such wonderful things that the uninstructed visitor would never guess that nearly the whole scene was but the embodied thought of a human mind. A skilful painter hardly does more for his blank sheet of canvass, than the landscape-gardener, the planter, the arranger of trees, has done for the monotonous surface of Blenheim; making the most of every undulation; flinging down a hillock, a big lump of earth out of a giant's hand, wherever it was needed; putting in beauty as often as there was a niche for it; opening vistas to every point that deserved to be seen, and throwing a veil of impenetrable foliage around what ought to be hidden;—and then, to be sure, the lapse of a century has softened the harsh outline of man's labors, and has given the place back to Nature again with the addition of what consummate science could achieve.

After driving a good way, we came to a battlemented tower and adjoining house, which used to be the residence of the Ranger of Woodstock Park, who held charge of the property for the King before the Duke of Marlborough possessed it. The keeper opened the door for us; and, in the entrance-hall, we found various things that had to do with the chase and woodland-sports. We mounted the staircase, through several stories, up to the top of the tower, whence there was a view of the spires of Oxford, and of points much farther off; very indistinctly seen, however, as is usually the case with the misty distances of England. Returning to the ground-floor, we were ushered into the room in which died Wilmot, the wicked Earl of Rochester, who was Ranger of the Park in Charles the Second's time. It is a low and bare little room, with a window in front, and a smaller one behind; and, in the contiguous entrance-room, there are the remains of an old bedstead, beneath the canopy of which, perhaps, Rochester may have made the penitent end that Bishop Burnet attributes to him. I hardly know what it is, in this poor fellow's character, which affects us with greater tenderness on his behalf than for all the other profligates of his day, who seem to have been neither better nor worse than himself. I rather suspect that he had a human heart, which never quite died out of him, and the warmth of which is still faintly perceptible amid the dissolute trash which he left behind.

Methinks, if such good fortune ever befel a bookish man, I should choose this lodge for my own residence, with the topmost room of the tower for a study, and all the seclusion of cultivated wildness, beneath, to ramble in. There being no such possibility, we drove on, catching glimpses of the palace in new points of view, and, by-and-by, came to Rosamond's Well. The particular tradition, that connects Fair Rosamond with it, is not now in my memory; but if Rosamond ever lived and loved, and ever had her abode in the maze of

Woodstock, it may well be believed that she and Henry sometimes sat beside this spring. It gushes out from a bank, through some old stone-work, and dashes its little cascade (about as abundant as one might turn out of a large pitcher) into a pool, whence it steals away towards the lake, which is not far removed. The water is exceedingly cold, and as pure as the legendary Rosamond was not, and is fancied to possess medicinal virtues, like springs at which Saints have quenched their thirst. There were two or three old women and some children in attendance, with tumblers which they present to visitors, full of the consecrated water; but most of us filled the tumblers for ourselves, and drank.

Thence we drove to the Triumphal Pillar which was erected in honor of the Great Duke, and on the summit of which he stands, in a Roman garb, holding a winged figure of Victory in his hand, as an ordinary man might hold a bird. The column is I know not how many feet high, but lofty enough, at any rate, to elevate Marlborough far above the rest of the world, and to be visible a long way off; and it is so placed, in reference to other objects, that wherever the hero wandered about his grounds, and especially as he issued from his mansion, he must inevitably have been reminded of his glory. In truth, until I came to Blenheim, I never had so positive and material an idea of what Fame really is—of what the admiration of his country can do for a successful warrior —as I carry away with me and shall always retain. Unless he had the moral force of a thousand men together, his egotism (beholding himself everywhere, imbuing the entire soil, grow- ing in the woods, rippling and gleaming in the water, and pervading the very air with his greatness) must have been swollen within him like the liver of a Strasbourg goose. On the huge tablets, inlaid into the pedestal of the column, the entire Act of Parliament, bestowing Blenheim on the Duke of Marlborough and his posterity, is engraved in deep letters, painted black on the marble ground. The pillar stands exactly a mile from the principal front of the palace, in a straight line with the precise centre of its entrance-hall; so that, as already said, it was the Duke's principal object of contemplation.

We now proceeded to the palace-gate, which is a great pillared archway, of wonderful loftiness and state, giving admittance into a spacious quadrangle. A stout, elderly, and rather surly footman in livery appeared at the entrance, and took possession of whatever canes, umbrellas, and parasols, he could get hold of, in order to claim sixpence on our departure. This had a somewhat ludicrous effect. There is much public outcry against the meanness of the present Duke in his arrangements for the admission of visitors (chiefly, of course, his native countrymen) to view the magnificent palace which their forefathers bestowed upon his own. In many cases, it seems hard that a private abode should be exposed to the intrusion of the public, merely because the proprietor has inherited or created a splendor which attracts general curiosity; insomuch that his home loses its sanctity and seclusion, for the very reason that it is better than other men's houses. But, in the case of Blenheim, the public have certainly an equitable claim to admission, both because the fame of its first inhabitant is a national possession, and because the mansion was a national gift, one of the purposes of which was to be a token of gratitude and glory to the English people themselves. If a man chooses to be illustrious, he is very likely to incur some little inconveniences himself, and entail them on his posterity. Nevertheless, his present Grace of Marlborough absolutely ignores the public claim above suggested, and (with a thrift of which even the hero of Blenheim himself did not set the example) sells tickets, admitting six persons, at ten shillings; if only one person enters the gate, he must pay for six, and if there are seven in company, two tickets are required to admit them. The attendants, who meet you everywhere in the park and palace, expect fees on their own private accounts; their noble master pocketing the ten shillings. But, to be sure, the visitor gets his money's worth, since it buys him the right to speak just as freely of the Duke of Marlborough as if he were the keeper of the Cremorne Gardens.*

Passing through a gateway on the opposite side of the quadrangle, we had before us the noble, classic front of the palace, with its two projecting wings. We ascended the lofty steps of the portal, and were admitted into the entrance-hall, the height of which, from floor to ceiling, is not much less than seventy feet, being the entire elevation of the edifice. The hall is lighted by windows in the upper story, and, it being a clear, bright day, was very radiant with lofty sunshine, amid which a swallow was flitting to-and-fro. The ceiling was painted by Sir James Thornhill in some allegorical design (doubtless commemorative of Marlborough's victories) the purport of which I did not take the trouble to make out,— contenting myself with the general effect, which was most splendidly and effectively ornamental.

We were guided through the show-rooms by a very civil person, who allowed us to take pretty much our own time in looking at the pictures. The collection is exceedingly valuable; many of these works of art having been presented to the Great Duke by the crowned heads of England or the continent. One room was all a-glow with pictures by Rubens; and there were works of Raphael, and many other famous painters, any one of which would be sufficient to illustrate the meanest house that might contain it. I remember none of them, however, (not being in a picture-seeing mood,) so well as Vandyke's large and familiar picture of Charles the First on horseback,

---

* The above was written two or three years ago, or more; and the Duke of that day has since transmitted his coronet to his successor, who, we understand, has adopted much more liberal arrangements. There is seldom anything to criticize or complain of, as regards the facility of obtaining admission to interesting private houses in England.

with a figure and face of melancholy dignity, such as never by any other hand was put on canvass. Yet, on considering this face of Charles, (which I find often repeated in half-lengths,) and translating it from the ideal into literalism, I doubt whether the unfortunate King was really a handsome or impressive-looking man; a high, thin-ridged nose, a meagre, hatchet face, and reddish hair and beard—these are the literal facts. It is the painter's art that has thrown such pensive and shadowy grace around him.

On our passage through this beautiful suite of apartments, we saw, through the vista of open door-ways, a boy of ten or twelve years old coming towards us from the further rooms. He had on a straw hat, a linen sack that had certainly been washed and re-washed for a summer or two, and gray trowsers a good deal worn—a dress, in short, which an American mother, in middle station, would have thought too shabby for her darling schoolboy's ordinary wear. This urchin's face was rather pale, (as those of English children are apt to be, quite as often as our own,) but he had pleasant eyes, an intelligent look, and an agreeable, boyish manner. It was Lord Sunderland, grandson of the present Duke, and heir—though not, I think, in the direct line—of the blood of the great Marlborough, and of the title and estate.

After passing through the first suite of rooms, we were conducted through a corresponding suite on the opposite side of the entrance-hall. These latter apartments are most richly adorned with tapestries, wrought and presented to the first Duke by a sisterhood of Flemish nuns; they look like great, glowing pictures, and completely cover the walls of the rooms. The designs purport to represent the Duke's battles and sieges; and everywhere we see the hero himself, as large as life, and as gorgeous in scarlet and gold as the holy sisters could make him, with a three-cornered hat and flowing wig, reining in his horse, and extending his leading-staff in the attitude of command. Next to Marlborough, Prince Eugene is the most prominent figure. In the way of upholstery, there can never have been anything more magnificent than these tapestries; and, considered as works of art, they have quite as much merit as nine pictures out of ten.

One whole wing of the palace is occupied by the library, a most noble room, with a vast perspective length from end to end. Its atmosphere is brighter and more cheerful than that of most libraries—a wonderful contrast to the old college-libraries of Oxford, and perhaps less sombre and suggestive of thoughtfulness than any large library ought to be; inasmuch as so many studious brains, as have left their deposit on the shelves, cannot have conspired without producing a very serious and ponderous result. Both walls and ceiling are white, and there are elaborate door-ways and fire-places of white marble. The floor is of oak, so highly polished that our feet slipt upon it as if it had been New England ice. At one end of the room stands a statue of Queen Anne, in her royal robes, which are so admirably designed and exquisitely wrought, that the spectator certainly gets a strong conception of her royal dignity; while the face of the statue, fleshy and feeble, doubtless conveys a suitable idea of her personal character. The marble of this work, long as it has stood there, is as white as snow just fallen, and must have required most faithful and religious care to keep it so. As for the volumes of the library, they are wired within the cases and turn their gilded backs upon the visitor, keeping their treasures of wit and wisdom just as intangible as if still in the unwrought mines of human thought.

I remember nothing else in the palace, except the chapel, to which we were conducted last, and where we saw a splendid monument to the first Duke and Duchess, sculptured by Rysbrach, at the cost, it is said, of forty thousand pounds. The design includes the statues of the deceased dignitaries, and various allegorical flourishes, fantasies, and confusions; and beneath sleep the Great Duke and his proud wife, their veritable bones and dust, and probably all the Marlboroughs that have since died. It is not quite a comfortable idea, that these mouldy ancestors still inhabit, after their fashion, the house where their successors spend the passing day; but the adulation lavished upon the hero of Blenheim could not have been consummated, unless the palace of his lifetime had become likewise a stately mausoleum over his remains—and such we felt it all to be, after gazing at his tomb.

The next business was to see the private gardens. An old Scotch under-gardener admitted us, and led the way, and seemed to have a fair prospect of earning the fee all by himself; but, by-and-by, another respectable Scotchman made his appearance and took us in charge, proving to be the head-gardener in person. He was extremely intelligent and agreeable, talking both scientifically and lovingly about trees and plants, of which there is every variety capable of English cultivation. Positively, the garden of Eden cannot have been more beautiful than this private garden of Blenheim. It contains three hundred acres, and, by the artful circumlocution of the paths, and the undulations, and the skilfully interposed clumps of trees, is made to appear limitless. The sylvan delights of a whole country are compressed into this space, as whole fields of Persian roses go to the concoction of an ounce of precious attar. The world, within that garden-fence, is not the same weary and dusty world with which we outside mortals are conversant; it is a finer, lovelier, more harmonious Nature; and the great Mother lends herself kindly to the gardener's will, knowing that he will make evident the half-obliterated traits of her pristine and ideal beauty, and allow her to take all the credit and praise to herself. I doubt whether there is ever any winter within that precinct—any clouds, except the fleecy ones of summer. The sunshine, that I saw there, rests upon my recollection of it as if it were eternal. The lawns and glades are like the memory of places where one has wandered, when first in love.

What a good and happy life might be spent in a Paradise like this! And yet, at that very moment, the besotted Duke (ah! I have let out a secret which I meant to keep to myself; but the ten shillings must pay for all) was in that very garden, (for the guide told us so, and cautioned our young people not to be uproarious,) and, if in a condition for arithmetic, was thinking of nothing nobler than how many ten-shilling tickets had that day been sold. Republican as I am, I should still love to think that noblemen lead noble lives, and that all this stately and beautiful environment may serve to elevate them a little way above the rest of us. If it fail to do so, the disgrace falls equally upon the whole race of mortals as on themselves; because it proves that no more favorable conditions of exist-ence would eradicate our vices and weaknesses. How sad, if this be so! Even a herd of swine, eating the acorns under those magnificent oaks of Blenheim, would be cleanlier and of better habits than ordinary swine.

Well: all that I have written is pitifully meagre, as a description of Blenheim; and I hate to leave it without some more adequate expression of the noble edifice, with its rich domain, all as I saw them in that beautiful sunshine; for if a day had been chosen out of a hundred years, it could not have been a finer one. But I must give up the attempt; only further remarking that the finest trees here were cedars, of which I saw one—and there may have been many such—immense in girth, and not less than three centuries old. I likewise saw a vast heap of laurel, two hundred feet in circumference, all growing from one root; and the gardener offered to show us another growth of twice that stupendous size. If the Great

Duke himself had been buried in that spot, his heroic heart could not have been the seed of a more plentiful crop of laurels.

We now went back to the Black Bear, and sat down to a cold collation, of which we ate abundantly, and drank (in the good old English fashion) a due proportion of various delightful liquors. A stranger in England, in his rambles to various quarters of the country, may learn little in regard to wines, (for the ordinary English taste is simple, though sound, in that particular,) but he makes acquaintance with more varieties of hop and malt-liquor than he previously supposed to exist. I remember a sort of foaming stuff, called hop-champagne, which is very vivacious, and appears to be a hybrid between ale and bottled cider. Another excellent tipple for warm weather is concocted by mixing brown-stout or bitter ale with ginger-beer, the foam of which stirs up the heavier liquor from its depths, forming a compound of singular vivacity and sufficient body. But of all stingo ever brewed from malt, (unless it be the Trinity Ale of Cambridge, which I drank long afterwards, and which Barry Cornwall has celebrated in immortal verse,) commend me to the Arch Deacon, as the Oxford scholars call it, in honor of the jovial dignitary who first taught these erudite worthies how to brew their favorite nectar. John Barleycorn has given his very heart to this admirable liquor; it is a superior kind of ale, the Prince of Ales, with a richer flavor and a mightier spirit than you can find elsewhere in this weary world. Much have we been strengthened and encouraged by the potent blood of the Arch Deacon!

A few days after our excursion to Blenheim, the same party set forth, in two flies, on a tour to some other places of interest, in the neighborhood of Oxford. It was again a delightful day; and, in truth, every day, of late, had been so pleasant that it seemed as if each must be the very last of such perfect weather; and yet the long succession had given us confidence in as many more to come. The climate of England has been shamefully maligned; its sulkinesses and asperities are not nearly so offensive as Englishmen tell us, (their climate being the only attribute of their country which they never overvalue,) and the really good summer-weather is the very kindest and sweetest that the world knows.

We first drove to the village of Cumnor, about six miles from Oxford, and alighted at the entrance of the church. Here, while waiting for the keys, we looked at an old wall of the churchyard, piled up of loose gray stones which are said to have once formed a portion of Cumnor Hall, celebrated in Mickle's ballad and Scott's romance. The Hall must have been in very close vicinity to the church—not more than twenty yards off;—and I waded through the long, dewy grass of the churchyard, and tried to peep over the wall, in hopes to discover some tangible and traceable remains of the edifice. But the wall was just too high to be overlooked, and difficult to clamber over without tumbling down some of the stones; so I took the word of one of our party who had been here before, that there is nothing interesting on the other side. The churchyard is in rather a neglected state, and seems not to have been mown for the benefit of the parson's cow; it contains a good many grave-stones, of which I remember only some upright memorials of slate to individuals of the name of Tabbs.

Soon, a woman arrived with a key of the church-door, and we entered the simple old edifice, which has the pavement of lettered tombstones, the sturdy pillars and low arches, and other ordinary characteristics of an English country-church. One or two pews, probably those of the gentlefolks of the neighborhood, were better furnished than the rest, but all in a modest style. Near the high altar, in the holiest place, there is an oblong, angular, ponderous tomb of blue marble, built against the wall, and surmounted by a carved canopy of the same material; and over the tomb, and beneath the canopy, are two monumental brasses, such as we oftener see inlaid into a church-pavement. On these brasses are engraven the figures of a gentleman in armor and a lady in an antique garb, each about a foot high, devoutly kneeling in prayer; and there is a long Latin inscription likewise cut into the enduring brass, bestowing the highest eulogies on the character of Anthony Forster, who, with his virtuous dame, lies buried beneath this tombstone. His is the knightly figure that kneels above; and if Sir Walter Scott ever saw this tomb, he must have had an even greater than common disbelief in laudatory epitaphs, to venture on depicting Anthony Forster in such hues as blacken him in the romance. For my part, I read the inscription in full faith, and believe the poor deceased gentleman to be a much wronged individual, with good grounds for bringing an action of slander in the courts above.

But the circumstance, lightly as we treat it, has its serious moral. What nonsense it is, this anxiety, which so worries us, about our good fame, or our bad fame, after death! If it were of the slightest real moment, our reputations would have been placed by Providence more in our own power, and less in other people's, than we now find them to be. If poor Anthony Forster happens to have met Sir Walter, in the other world, I doubt whether he has ever thought it worth while to complain of the latter's misrepresentations.

We did not remain long in the church, as it contains nothing else of interest; and driving through the village, we passed a pretty large and rather antique-looking inn, bearing the sign of the Bear and Ragged Staff. It could not be so old, however, by at least a hundred years, as Giles Gosling's time; nor is there any other object to remind the visitor of the Elizabethan age, unless it be a few ancient cottages, that are perhaps of still earlier date. Cumnor is not nearly so large a village, nor a place of such mark, as one anticipates from its romantic and legendary fame; but, being still inaccessible by railway, it has retained more of a sylvan character than we often find in English country-towns. In this retired neighborhood, the road is narrow, and bordered with grass, and sometimes interrupted by gates; the hedges grow in unpruned luxuriance; there is not that close-shaven neatness and trimness that characterize the ordinary English landscape. The whole scene conveys the idea of seclusion and remoteness. We met no travellers, whether on foot or otherwise.

I cannot very distinctly trace out this day's peregrinations; but, after leaving Cumnor a few miles behind us, I think we came to a ferry over the Thames, where an old woman served as ferryman, and pulled a boat across by means of a rope stretching from shore to shore. Our two vehicles being thus placed on the other side, we resumed our drive; first glancing, however, at the old woman's antique cottage, with its stone-floor, and the circular settle round the kitchen fire-place, which was quite in the mediæval English style. We next stopt at Stanton Harcourt, where we were received at the parsonage with a hospitality which we should take delight in describing, if it were allowable to make public acknowledgement of the private and personal kindnesses, which we never failed to find ready for our needs. An American, in an English house, will soon adopt the opinion that the English are the very kindest people on earth, and will retain that idea as long, at least, as he remains on the inner side of the threshold. Their magnetism is of a kind that repels strongly, while you keep beyond a certain limit, but attracts as forcibly if you get within the magic line.

It was at this place, if I remember right, that I heard a gentleman ask a friend of mine whether he was the author of "The Red Letter A"; and, after some consideration, (for he did not seem to recognize his own book, at first, under this improved title,) our countryman responded, doubtfully, that he believed so. The gentleman proceeded to inquire whether our friend had spent much time in America; evidently thinking that he must have been caught young, and have had a tincture of English breeding, at least, if not birth, to speak the language so tolerably, and appear so much like other people. This insular narrowness is exceedingly queer, and of very frequent occurrence, and is quite as much a characteristic of men of education and culture, as of clowns.

Stanton Harcourt is a very curious old place. It was formerly the seat of the ancient family of Harcourt, which now has its principal abode at Nuneham Courtenay, a few miles off. The parsonage is a relic of the family mansion, or castle, other portions of which are close at hand; for, across the garden, rise two gray towers, both of them picturesquely venerable, and interesting for more than their antiquity. One of these towers, in its entire capacity, from height to depth, constituted the kitchen of the ancient castle, and is still used for domestic purposes, although it has not, nor ever had, a chimney; or we might rather say, it is itself one vast chimney, with a hearth of thirty feet square, and a flue and aperture of the same size. There are two huge fire-places within, and the interior walls of the tower are blackened with the smoke that, for centuries, used to gush forth from them, and climb upward, seeking an exit through some wide air-holes in the conical roof, full seventy feet above. These lofty openings were capable of being so arranged, with reference to the wind, that the cooks are said to have been seldom troubled by the smoke; and here, no doubt, they were accustomed to roast oxen whole, with as little fuss and ado as a modern cook would roast a fowl. The inside of the tower is very dim and sombre, (being nothing but rough stone-walls, lighted only from the apertures above mentioned,) and has still a pungent odor of smoke and soot, the reminiscence of the fires and feasts of generations that have passed away. Methinks the extremest range of domestic economy lies between an American cooking-stove and the ancient kitchen, seventy dizzy feet in height, and all one fire-place, of Stanton Harcourt.

Now—the place being without a parallel in England, and therefore necessarily beyond the experience of an American —it is somewhat remarkable, that, while we stood gazing at this kitchen, I was haunted and perplexed by an idea, that, somewhere or other, I had seen just this strange spectacle before. The height, the blackness, the dismal void, before my eyes, seemed as familiar as the decorous neatness of my grandmother's kitchen; only, my unaccountable memory of the scene was lighted up with an image of lurid fires, blazing all round the dim interior circuit of the tower. I had never before had so pertinacious an attack, as I could not but suppose it, of that odd state of mind wherein we fitfully and teazingly remember some previous scene or incident, of which the one now passing appears to be but the echo and reduplication. Though the explanation of the mystery did not, for some time, occur to me, I may as well conclude the matter here. In a letter of Pope's, addressed to the Duke of Buckingham, there is an account of Stanton Harcourt, (as I now find, although the name is not mentioned,) where he resided while translating a part of the Iliad. It is one of the most admirable pieces of description in the language—playful, and picturesque, with fine touches of humorous pathos—and conveys as perfect a picture as ever was drawn of a decayed English country-house; and among other rooms, most of which have since crumbled down and disappeared, he dashes off the grim aspect of this kitchen—which, moreover, he peoples with witches, engaging Satan himself as head-cook, who stirs the infernal cauldrons that seethe and bubble over the fires. This letter, and others relative to his abode here, were very familiar to my earlier reading, and remaining still fresh at the bottom of my memory, caused the weird and ghostly sensation that came over me on beholding the real spectacle, that had formerly been made so vivid to my imagination.

Our next visit was to the church, which stands close by, and is quite as ancient as the remnants of the castle. In a chapel or side-aisle, dedicated to the Harcourts, we found some very interesting family monuments; and among them, recumbent on a tombstone, the figure of an armed knight of the Lancastrian party, who was slain in the wars of the Roses. His features, dress, and armor, are painted in colors, still wonderfully fresh, and there still blushes the symbol of the Red Rose, denoting the faction for which he fought and died. His head rests on a marble or alabaster helmet; and on the tomb lies the veritable helmet, it is to be presumed, which he wore in battle —a ponderous iron case, with the visor complete, and remnants of the gilding that once covered it. The crest is a large peacock, not of metal, but of wood. Very possibly, this helmet was but an heraldic adornment of his tomb; and, indeed, it seems strange that it has not been stolen before now, especially in Cromwell's time, when knightly tombs were little respected, and when armor was in request. However, it is needless to dispute with the dead knight about the identity of his iron pot, and we may as well allow it to be the very same that so often gave him the headache in his lifetime. Leaning against the wall, at the foot of the tomb, is the shaft of a spear, with a woefully tattered and utterly faded banner appended to it; the knightly banner, beneath which he marshalled his followers in the field. As it was absolutely falling to pieces, I tore off one little bit, no bigger than a finger-nail, and put it into my waistcoat pocket; but seeking it subsequently, it was not to be found.

On the opposite side of the little chapel, two or three yards from this tomb, is another monument, on which lie, side by side, one of the same knightly race of Harcourts and his lady.

The tradition of the family is, that this knight was the stand-ard-bearer of Henry of Richmond in the battle of Bosworth-field; and a banner, supposed to be the same that he carried, now droops over his effigy. It is just such a colorless silk rag as the one already described. The knight has the order of the Garter on his knee, and the lady wears it on her left arm—an odd place enough for a garter; but, if worn in its proper locality, it could not be decorously visible. The complete preservation and good condition of these statues, even to the minutest adornment of the sculpture, and their very noses—the most vulnerable part of a marble man, as of a living one—are miraculous. Except in Westminster Abbey, among the chapels of the Kings, I have seen none so well preserved. Perhaps they owe it to the loyalty of Oxfordshire, diffused throughout its neighborhood by the influence of the University, during the great Civil War and the rule of the Parliament. It speaks well, too, for the upright and kindly character of this old family, that the peasantry, among whom they had lived for ages, did not desecrate their tombs, when it might have been done with impunity.

There are other and more recent memorials of the Harcourts, one of which is the tomb of the last lord, who died about a hundred years ago. His figure, like those of his ancestors, lies on the top of his tomb, clad, not in armor, but in his robes as a peer. The title is now extinct, but the family survives in a younger branch, and still holds this patrimonial estate, though they have long since quitted it as a residence.

We next went to see the ancient fish-ponds, appertaining to the mansion, and which used to be of vast dietary importance to the family, in Catholic times, and when fish was not otherwise attainable. There are two or three, or more, of these reservoirs, one of which is of very respectable size; large enough, indeed, to be really a picturesque object, with its grass-green borders, and the trees drooping over it, and the towers of the castle and the church reflected within the weed-grown depths of its smooth mirror. A sweet fragrance, as it were, of ancient time and present quiet and seclusion, was breathing all around; the sunshine of to-day had a mellow charm of antiquity in its brightness. These ponds are said still to breed abundance of such fish as love deep and quiet waters; but I saw only some minnows, and one or two snakes, which were lying among the weeds on the top of the water, sunning and bathing themselves at once.

I mentioned that there were two towers remaining of the old castle; the one containing the kitchen we have already visited; the other, still more interesting, is next to be described. It is some seventy feet high, gray and reverend, but in excellent repair, though I could not perceive that anything had been done to renovate it. The basement story was once the family-chapel, and is, of course, still a consecrated spot. At one corner of the tower is a circular turret, within which a narrow staircase, with worn steps of stone, winds round and round as it climbs upward, giving access to a chamber on each floor, and finally emerging on the battlemented roof. Ascending this turret-stair, and arriving at the third story, we entered a chamber, not large, though occupying the whole area of the tower, and lighted by a window on each side. It was wainscotted from floor to ceiling with dark oak, and had a little fire-place in one of the corners. The window-panes were small, and set in lead. The curiosity of this room is, that it was once the residence of Pope, and that he here wrote a considerable part of the translation of Homer, and likewise, no doubt, the admirable letters to which I have referred above. The room once contained a record by himself, scratched with a diamond on one of the window-panes, (since removed for safe-keeping to Nuneham Courtenay, where it was shown me,) purporting that he had here finished the fifth book of the Iliad, on such a day.

A poet has a fragrance about him, such as no other human being is gifted withal; it is indestructible, and clings forevermore to everything that he has touched. I was not impressed, at Blenheim, with any sense that the mighty Duke still haunted the palace that was created for him; but here, after a century and a half, we are still conscious of the presence of that decrepit little figure of Queen Anne's time, although he was merely a casual guest in the old tower, during one or two summer months. However brief the time, and slight the connection, his spirit cannot be exorcised so long as the tower stands. In my mind, moreover, Pope, or any other person with an available claim, is right in adhering to the spot, dead or alive; for I never saw a chamber that I should like better to inhabit—so comfortably small, in such a safe and inaccessible seclusion, and with a varied landscape from each window. One of them looks upon the church, close at hand, and down into the green churchyard, extending almost to the foot of the tower; the others have views wide and far, over a gently undulating tract of country. If desirous of a loftier elevation, about a dozen more steps of the turret-stair will bring the occupant to the summit of the tower; where Pope used to come, no doubt, in the summer evenings, and peep—poor little shrimp that he was!—through the embrasures of the battlement.

From Stanton Harcourt we drove—I forget how far—to a point where a boat was waiting for us upon the Thames, or some other stream; for I am ashamed to confess my ignorance of the precise geographical whereabout. We were, at any rate, some miles above Oxford, and, I should imagine, pretty near one of the sources of England's mighty river. It was little more than wide enough for the boat, with extended oars, to pass; shallow, too, and bordered with bull-rushes and water-weeds, which, in some places, quite overgrew the surface of the river from bank to bank. The shores were flat and meadowlike, and

sometimes, the boatman told us, are overflowed by the rise of
the stream. The water looked clean and pure, but not particularly transparent, though enough so to show us that the
bottom is very much weed-grown; and I was told that the
weed is an American production, brought to England with
importations of timber, and now threatening to choke up the
Thames and other English rivers. I wonder it does not try its
obstructive powers upon the Merrimack, the Connecticut, or
the Hudson—not to speak of the St. Lawrence or the Mississippi!

It was an open boat, with cushioned seats astern, comfortably accommodating our party; the day continued sunny and
warm, and perfectly still; the boatman, well trained to his
business, managed the oars skilfully and vigorously; and we
went down the stream quite as swiftly as it was desirable to
go, the scene being so pleasant, and the passing hour so
thoroughly agreeable. The river grew a little wider and
deeper, perhaps, as we glided on, but was still an inconsiderable stream; for it had a good deal more than a hundred miles
to meander through, before it should bear fleets on its bosom,
and reflect palaces, and towers, and parliament-houses, and
dingy and sordid piles of various structure, as it rolled to-and-
fro with the tide, dividing London asunder. Not, in truth,
that I ever saw any edifice whatever reflected in its turbid
breast, when the sylvan stream, as we beheld it now, is
swollen into the Thames at London.

Once, on our voyage, we had to land, while the boatman
and some other persons drew our skiff round some rapids,
which we could not otherwise have passed; another time, the
boat went through a lock. We, meanwhile, stept ashore to
examine the ruins of the old nunnery of Godstowe, where
Fair Rosamond secluded herself, after being separated from
her royal lover. There is a long line of ruinous wall, and a
shattered tower at one of the angles; the whole much ivy-

grown—brimming over, indeed, with clustering ivy, which is rooted inside of the walls. The nunnery is now, I believe, held in lease by the city of Oxford, which has converted its precincts into a barn-yard. The gate was under lock and key; so that we could merely look at the outside, and soon resumed our places in the boat.

At three o'clock, or thereabouts, (or sooner or later; for I took little heed of time, and only wished that these delightful wanderings might last forever,) we reached Folly Bridge, at Oxford. Here we took possession of a spacious barge, with a house in it, and a comfortable dining-room, or drawing-room, within the house, and a level roof on which we could sit at ease, or dance, if so inclined. These barges are common at Oxford; some very splendid ones being owned by the students of the different colleges, or by clubs. They are drawn by horses, like canal-boats; and a horse being attached to our own barge, he trotted off at a reasonable pace, and we slipped through the water behind him, with a gentle and pleasant motion, which, save for the constant vicissitude of cultivated scenery, was like no motion at all. It was life without the trouble of living; nothing was ever more quietly agreeable. In this happy state of mind and body, we gazed at Christ Church meadows, as we passed, and at the receding spires and towers of Oxford, and on a good deal of pleasant variety along the banks; young men rowing or fishing; troops of naked boys bathing, as if this were Arcadia, in the simplicity of the Golden Age; country-houses, cottages, water-side inns, all with something fresh about them, as not being sprinkled with the dust of the highway. We were a large party now; for a number of additional guests had joined us at Folly Bridge, and we comprised poets, novelists, scholars, sculptors, painters, architects, men and women of renown, dear friends, genial, outspoken, open-hearted Englishmen; all voyaging onward together, like the wise ones of Gotham in a bowl. I remember not a single annoyance; except, indeed, that a swarm of wasps came aboard of us and alighted on the head of one of our young gentlemen, attracted by the scent of the pomatum which he had been rubbing into his hair. He was the only victim, and his small trouble the one little flaw in our day's felicity, to put us in mind that we were mortal.

Meanwhile, a table had been laid in the interior of our barge, and spread with cold ham, cold fowl, cold pigeon-pie, cold beef, and other substantial cheer, such as the English love, and Yankees too; besides tarts, and cakes, and pears, and plums; not forgetting, of course, a goodly provision of port, sherry, and champagne, and bitter ale, which is like mother's milk to an Englishman, and soon grows equally acceptable to his American cousin. By the time these matters had been properly attended to, we had arrived at that part of the Thames which passes by Nuneham Courtenay, a fine estate belonging to the Harcourts, and the present residence of the family. Here, we landed, and climbing a steep slope from the river-side, paused, a moment or two, to look at an architectural object, called the Carfax, the purport of which I do not well understand. Thence we proceeded onward, through the loveliest park and woodland scenery I ever saw, and under as beautiful a declining sunshine as Heaven ever shed over earth, to the stately mansion-house.

As we here cross a private threshold, it is not allowable to pursue my feeble narrative of this delightful day, with the same freedom as heretofore; so perhaps I may as well bring it to a close. I may mention, however, that I saw the library, a fine, large apartment, hung round with portraits of eminent literary men, principally of the last century, most of whom were familiar guests of the Harcourts. The house itself is about eighty years old, and is built in the classic style; as if the family had been anxious to diverge as far as possible from the Gothic picturesqueness of their old abode at Stanton Harcourt. The grounds were laid out, in part, by Capability Brown, and seemed to me even more beautiful than those of Blenheim. Mason, the poet, a friend of the house, gave the design of a portion of the garden. Of the whole place, I will not be niggardly of my rude, transatlantic praise, but be bold to say, that it appeared to me as perfect as anything earthly can be;—utterly and entirely finished;—as if the years and generations had done all that the hearts and minds of the successive owners could contrive, for a spot they dearly loved. Such homes as Nuneham Courtenay are among the splendid results of long hereditary possession; and we Republicans, whose households melt away like new-fallen snow in a spring morning, must content ourselves with our many counterbalancing advantages;—for this one, so apparently desirable to the far-projecting selfishness of our nature, we are certain never to attain.

It must not be supposed, nevertheless, that Nuneham Courtenay is one of the great show-places of England; it is merely a fair specimen of the better class of country-seats, and has a hundred rivals, and many superiors, in the features of beauty, and expansive, manifold, redundant comfort, which most impressed me. A moderate man might be content with such a home—that is all.

And, now, I take leave of Oxford without even an attempt to describe it; there being no literary faculty, attainable or conceivable by me, which can avail to put it adequately, or even tolerably, upon paper. It must remain its own sole expression; and those, whose sad fortune it may be never to behold it, have no better resource than to dream about gray, weather-stained, ivy-grown, edifices, wrought with quaint Gothic ornament, and standing around grassy quadrangles, where cloistered walks have echoed to the quiet footsteps of twenty generations; lawns and gardens of luxurious repose, shadowed with canopies of foliage, and lit up with sunny glimpses through archways of great boughs; spires, towers, and turrets, each with its history and legend; dimly magnificent chapels, with painted windows of rare beauty and brilliantly diversified hues, creating an atmosphere of richest gloom; vast college-halls, high-windowed, oaken-panelled, and hung round with portraits of the men, in every age, whom the University has nurtured to be illustrious; long vistas of al-coved libraries, where the wisdom and learned folly of all time is shelved; kitchens, (we throw in this feature by way of ballast, and because it would not be English Oxford without its beef and beer,) with huge fire-places, capable of roasting a hundred joints at once, and cavernous cellars, where rows of piled-up hogsheads seethe and fume with that mighty malt-liquor, which is the true milk of Alma Mater;—make all these things vivid in your dream; and you will never know nor believe how inadequate is the result, to represent even the merest outside of Oxford.

We feel a genuine reluctance to conclude this article with-out making our grateful acknowledgements, by name, to a gentleman whose overflowing kindness was the main condi-tion of all our sight-seeings and enjoyments. Delightful as will always be our recollection of Oxford and its neighborhood, we partly suspect that it owes much of its happy coloring to the genial medium through which the objects were presented to us—to the kindly magic of a hospitality, unsurpassed, within our experience, in the quality of making the guest contented with his host, with himself, and everything about him. He has inseparably mingled his image with our remembrance of the Spires of Oxford.

SOME OF THE HAUNTS OF BURNS

WE LEFT Carlisle at a little past eleven, and within the half-hour were at Gretna Green. Thence we rushed onward into Scotland, through a flat and dreary tract of country, consisting mainly of desert and bog, where probably the moss-troopers were accustomed to take refuge after their raids into England. Anon, however, the hills hove themselves up to view, occasionally attaining a height which might almost be called mountainous. In about two hours we reached Dumfries, and alighted at the station there.

Chill as the Scottish summer is reputed to be, we found it an awfully hot day, not a whit less so than the day before; but we sturdily adventured through the burning sunshine up into the town, inquiring our way to the residence of Burns. The street leading from the station is called Shakspere-street; and at its farther extremity we read "Burns Street" on a corner-house—the avenue thus designated having been formerly known as "Mill Hole Brae." It is a vile lane, paved with small, hard stones from side to side, and bordered by cottages or mean houses of white-washed stone, joining one to another along the whole length of the street. With not a tree, of course, or a blade of grass between the paving-stones, the narrow lane was as hot as Tophet, and reeked with a genuine

Scotch odor, being infested with unwashed children, and altogether in a state of chronic filth; although some women seemed to be hopelessly scrubbing the thresholds of their wretched dwellings. I never saw an outskirt of a town less fit for a poet's residence, or in which it would be more miserable for any man of cleanly predilections to spend his days.

We asked for Burns's dwelling; and a woman pointed across the street to a two-story house, built of stone, and white-washed, like its neighbors, but perhaps of a little more respectable aspect than most of them, though I hesitate in saying so. It was not a separate structure, but under the same continuous roof with the next. There was an inscription on the door, bearing no reference to Burns, but indicating that the house was now occupied by a ragged or industrial school. On knocking, we were instantly admitted by a servant-girl, who smiled intelligently when we told our errand, and showed us into a low and very plain parlor, not more than twelve or fifteen feet square. A young woman, who seemed to be a teacher in the school, soon appeared, and told us that this had been Burns's usual sitting-room, and that he had written many of his songs here.

She then led us up a narrow staircase into a little bed-chamber, over the parlor. Connecting with it, there is a very small room, or windowed closet, which Burns used as a study; and the bed-chamber itself was the one where he slept in his latter lifetime, and in which he died at last. Altogether, it is an exceedingly unsuitable place for a pastoral and rural poet to live or die in—even more unsatisfactory than Shakspere's house, which has a certain homely picturesqueness that contrasts favorably with the suburban sordidness of the abode before us. The narrow lane, the paving-stones, and the contiguity of wretched hovels are depressing to remember; and the steam of them (such is our human weakness) might almost make the poet's memory less fragrant.

As already observed, it was an intolerably hot day. After leaving the house, we found our way into the principal street of the town, which, it may be fair to say, is of very different aspect from the wretched outskirt above described. Entering a hotel, (in which, as a Dumfries guide-book assured us, Prince Charles Edward had once spent a night,) we rested and refreshed ourselves, and then set forth in quest of the Mausoleum of Burns.

Coming to Saint Michael's church, we saw a man digging a grave; and, scrambling out of the hole, he let us into the churchyard, which was crowded full of monuments. Their general shape and construction are peculiar to Scotland, being a perpendicular tablet of marble or other stone, within a frame-work of the same material, somewhat resembling the frame of a looking-glass; and, all over the churchyard, these sepulchral memorials rise to the height of ten, fifteen, or twenty feet, forming quite an imposing collection of monuments, but inscribed with names of small general significance. It was easy, indeed, to ascertain the rank of those who slept below; for in Scotland it is the custom to put the occupation of the buried personage (as "Skinner," "Shoemaker," "Flesher") on his tombstone. As another peculiarity, wives are buried under their maiden names, instead of those of their husbands; thus giving a disagreeable impression that the married pair have bidden each other an eternal farewell on the edge of the grave.

There was a foot-path through this crowded churchyard, sufficiently well-worn to guide us to the grave of Burns; but a woman followed behind us, who, it appeared, kept the key of the mausoleum, and was privileged to show it to strangers. The monument is a sort of Grecian temple, with pilasters and a dome, covering a space of about twenty feet square. It was formerly open to all the inclemencies of the Scotch atmosphere, but is now protected and shut in by large squares of rough glass, each pane being of the size of one whole side of the structure. The woman unlocked the door, and admitted us into the interior. Inlaid into the floor of the mausoleum is the grave-stone of Burns—the very same that was laid over his grave by Jean Armour, before this monument was built. Displayed against the surrounding wall is a marble statue of Burns at the plough, with the Genius of Caledonia summoning the ploughman to turn poet. Methought it was not a very successful piece of work; for the plough was better sculptured than the man, and the man, though heavy and cloddish, was more effective than the goddess. Our guide informed us that an old man of ninety, who knew Burns, certifies this statue to be very like the original.

The bones of the poet, and of Jean Armour, and of some of their children, lie in the vault over which we stood. Our guide (who was intelligent, in her own plain way, and very agreeable to talk withal) said that the vault was opened, about three weeks ago, on occasion of the burial of the eldest son of Burns. The poet's bones were disturbed, and the dry skull, once so brimming over with powerful thought and bright and tender fantasies, was taken away, and kept for several days by a Dumfries doctor. It has since been deposited in a new leaden coffin, and restored to the vault. We learned that there is a surviving daughter of Burns's eldest son, and daughters likewise of the two younger sons—and, besides these, an illegitimate posterity by the eldest son, who appears to have been of disreputable life in his younger days. He inherited his father's failings, with some faint shadow, I have also understood, of the great qualities which have made the world tender of his father's vices and weaknesses.

We listened readily enough to this paltry gossip, but found that it robbed the poet's memory of some of the reverence that was its due. Indeed, this talk over his grave had very much the same tendency and effect as the home-scene of his life, which we had been visiting just previously. Beholding his poor, mean dwelling and its surroundings, and picturing his outward life and earthly manifestations from these, one does not so much wonder that the people of that day should have failed to recognize all that was admirable and immortal in a disreputable, drunken, shabbily clothed and shabbily housed man, consorting with associates of damaged character, and, as his only ostensible occupation, gauging the whiskey which he too often tasted. Siding with Burns, as we needs must, in his plea against the world, let us try to do the world a little justice too. It is far easier to know and honor a poet when his fame has taken shape in the spotlessness of marble than when the actual man comes staggering before you, besmeared with the sordid stains of his daily life. For my part, I chiefly wonder that his recognition dawned so brightly while he was still living. There must have been something very grand in his immediate presence, some strangely impressive characteristic in his natural behavior, to have caused him to seem like a demi-god so soon.

As we went back through the churchyard, we saw a spot where nearly four hundred inhabitants of Dumfries were buried during the cholera-year; and also some curious old monuments, with raised letters, the inscriptions on which were not sufficiently legible to induce us to puzzle them out; but, I believe, they mark the resting-places of old Covenanters, some of whom were killed by Claverhouse and his fellow-ruffians.

Saint Michael's church is of red freestone, and was built about a hundred years ago, on an old Catholic foundation. Our guide admitted us into it, and showed us, in the porch, a very pretty little marble figure of a child asleep, with a drapery over the lower part, from beneath which appeared its two baby-feet. It was truly a sweet little statue; and the woman told us that it represented a child of the sculptor, and that the baby (here still in its marble infancy) had died more than twenty-six years ago. "Many ladies," she said, "especially such as had ever lost a child, had shed tears over it." It was very pleasant to think of the sculptor bestowing the best of his genius and art to re-create his tender child in stone, and to make the representation as soft and sweet as the original; but the conclusion of the story has something that jars with our awakened sensibilities. A gentleman from London had seen the statue, and was so much delighted with it that he bought it of the father-artist, after it had lain above a quarter of a century in the church-porch. So this was not the real, tender image that came out of the father's heart; he had sold that truest one for a hundred guineas, and sculptured this mere copy to replace it. The first figure was entirely naked in its earthly and spiritual innocence. The copy, as I have said above, has a drapery over the lower limbs. But, after all, if we come to the truth of the matter, the sleeping baby may be as fitly reposited in the drawing-room of a connoisseur as in a cold and dreary church-porch.

We went into the church, and found it very plain and naked, without altar-decorations, and having its floor quite covered with unsightly wooden pews. The woman led us to a pew cornering on one of the side-aisles, and, telling us that it used to be Burns's family-pew, showed us his seat, which is in the corner by the aisle. It is so situated, that a sturdy pillar hid him from the pulpit, and from the minister's eye; "for Robin was no great friends with the ministers," said she. This touch —his seat behind the pillar, and Burns himself nodding in sermon-time, or keenly observant of profane things—brought him before us to the life. In the corner-seat of the next pew, right before Burns, and not more than two feet off, sat the young lady on whom the poet saw that unmentionable parasite which he has immortalized in song. We were ungenerous enough to ask the lady's name, but the good woman could not tell it. This was the last thing which we saw in Dumfries, worthy of record; and it ought to be noted that our guide refused some money which my companion offered her, because I had already paid her what she deemed sufficient.

At the railway-station we spent more than a weary hour, waiting for the train, which at last came up, and took us to Mauchline. We got into an omnibus, the only conveyance to be had, and drove about a mile to the village, where we established ourselves at the Loudoun Hotel, one of the veriest country-inns which we have found in Great Britain. The town of Mauchline, a place more redolent of Burns than almost any other, consists of a street or two of contiguous cottages, mostly white-washed, and with thatched roofs. It has nothing sylvan or rural in the immediate village, and is as ugly a place as mortal man could contrive to make, or to render uglier through a succession of untidy generations. The fashion of paving the village-street, and patching one shabby house on the gable-end of another, quite shuts out all verdure and pleasantness; but, I presume, we are not likely to see a more genuine old Scotch village, such as they used to be in Burns's time, and long before, than this of Mauchline. The church stands about mid-way up the street, and is built of red freestone, very simple in its architecture, with a square tower and pinnacles. In this sacred edifice, and its churchyard, was the scene of one of Burns's most characteristic productions—"The Holy Fair."

Almost directly opposite its gate, across the village-street, stands Posie Nansie's inn, where the "Jolly Beggars" congregated. The latter is a two-story, red-stone, thatched house, looking old, but by no means venerable, like a drunken patriarch. It has small, old-fashioned windows, and may well have stood for centuries—though, seventy or eighty years ago, when Burns was conversant with it, I should fancy it might have been something better than a beggar's ale-house. The whole town of Mauchline looks rusty and time-worn—even the newer houses, of which there are several, being shadowed and darkened by the general aspect of the place. When we arrived, all the wretched little dwellings seemed to have belched forth their inhabitants into the warm summer evening; everybody was chatting with everybody, on the most familiar terms; the bare-legged children gambolled or quarrelled uproariously, and came freely, moreover, and looked into the window of our parlor. When we ventured out, we were followed by the gaze of the whole town; people standing in their door-ways, old women popping their heads from the chamber-windows, and stalwart men—idle on Saturday at e'en, after their week's hard labor—clustering at the street-corners, merely to stare at our unpretending selves. Except in some remote little town of Italy, (where, besides, the inhabitants had the intelligible stimulus of beggary,) I have never been honored with nearly such an amount of public notice.

The next forenoon my companion put me to shame by attending church, after vainly exhorting me to do the like; and, it being Sacrament Sunday, and my poor friend being wedged into the farther end of a closely filled pew, he was forced to stay through the preaching of four several sermons, and came back perfectly exhausted and desperate. He was somewhat consoled, however, on finding that he had witnessed a spectacle of Scotch manners identical with that of Burns's "Holy Fair," on the very spot where the poet located that immortal description. By way of further conformance to the customs of the country, we ordered a sheep's head and the broth, and did penance accordingly; and at five o'clock we took a fly, and set out for Burns's farm of Moss Giel.

Moss Giel is not more than a mile from Mauchline, and the road extends over a high ridge of land, with a view of far hills and green slopes on either side. Just before we reached the farm, the driver stopt to point out a hawthorn, growing by the wayside, which he said was Burns's "Lousie Thorn"; and I devoutly plucked a branch, although I have really forgotten where or how this illustrious shrub has been celebrated. We then turned into a rude gateway, and almost immediately came to the farm-house of Moss Giel, standing some fifty yards removed from the high-road, behind a tall hedge of hawthorn, and considerably overshadowed by trees. The house is a white-washed stone cottage, like thousands of others in England and Scotland, with a thatched roof, on which grass and weeds have intruded a picturesque, though alien growth. There is a door and one window in front, besides another little window that peeps out among the thatch. Close by the cottage, and extending back at right angles from it, so as to enclose the farm-yard, are two other buildings of the same size, shape, and general appearance as the house; any one of the three looks just as fit for a human habitation as the two others, and all three look still more suitable for donkey-stables and pig-sties. As we drove into the farm-yard, bounded on three sides by these three hovels, a large dog began to bark at us; and some women and children made their appearance, but seemed to demur about admitting us, because the master and mistress were very religious people, and had not yet come back from the Sacrament at Mauchline.

However, it would not do to be turned back from the very threshold of Robert Burns; and as the women seemed to be merely straggling visitors, and nobody, at all events, had a right to send us away, we went into the back-door, and, turning to the right, entered a kitchen. It showed a deplorable lack of housewifely neatness, and in it there were three or four children, one of whom, a girl eight or nine years old, held a baby in her arms. She proved to be the daughter of the people of the house, and gave us what leave she could to look about us. Thence we stept across the narrow mid-passage of the cottage, into the only other apartment below-stairs, a sitting-room, where we found a young man eating bread and cheese. He informed us that he did not live there, and had only called in to refresh himself on his way home from church. This room, like the kitchen, was a noticeably poor one, and, besides being all that the cottage had to show for a parlor, it was a sleeping apartment, having two beds, which might be curtained off on occasion. The young man allowed us liberty (so far as in him lay) to go up stairs. Up we crept, accordingly; and a few steps brought us to the top of the staircase, over the kitchen, where we found the wretchedest little sleeping-chamber in the world, with a sloping roof under the thatch, and two beds spread upon the bare floor. This, most probably, was Burns's chamber; or, perhaps, it may have been that of his mother's servant-maid; and, in either case, this rude floor, at one time or another, must have creaked beneath the poet's midnight tread. On the opposite side of the passage was the door of another attic-chamber, opening which, I saw a considerable number of cheeses on the floor.

The whole house was pervaded with a frowzy smell, and also a dunghill-odor; and it is not easy to understand how the atmosphere of such a dwelling can be any more agreeable or salubrious morally than it appeared to be physically. No virgin, surely, could keep a holy awe about her while stowed higgledy-piggledy with coarse-natured rustics into this narrowness and filth. Such a habitation is calculated to make beasts of men and women; and it indicates a degree of barbarism which I did not imagine to exist in Scotland, that a tiller of broad fields, like the farmer of Mauchline, should have his abode in a pig-sty. It is sad to think of anybody—not to say a poet, but any human being—sleeping, eating, thinking, praying, and spending all his home-life in this miserable hovel; but, methinks, I never in the least knew how to estimate the miracle of Burns's genius, nor his heroic merit for being no worse man, until I thus learned the squalid hindrances amid which he developed himself. Space, a free atmosphere, and cleanliness have a vast deal to do with the possibilities of human virtue.

The biographers talk of the farm of Moss Giel as being damp and unwholesome; but I do not see why, outside of the cottage-walls, it should possess so evil a reputation. It occupies a high, broad ridge, enjoying, surely, whatever benefit can come of a breezy site, and sloping far downward before any marshy soil is reached. The high hedge, and the trees that stand beside the cottage, give it a pleasant aspect enough, to one who does not know the grimy secrets of the interior; and the summer afternoon was now so bright that I shall remember the scene with a great deal of sunshine over it.

Leaving the cottage, we drove through a field, which the driver told us was that in which Burns turned up the mouse's nest. It is the enclosure nearest to the cottage, and seems now to be a pasture, and a rather remarkably unfertile one. A little farther on, the ground was whitened with an immense number of daisies—daisies, daisies, everywhere—and in answer to my inquiry, the driver said that this was the field where Burns ran his plough-share over the daisy. If so, the soil seems to have been consecrated to daisies by the song which he bestowed on that first immortal one. I alighted, and plucked a whole handful of these "wee, modest, crimson-tipped flowers," which will be precious to many friends in our own country as coming from Burns's farm, and being of the same race and lineage as that daisy which he turned into an amaranthine flower, while seeming to destroy it.

From Moss Giel we drove through a variety of pleasant scenes, some of which were familiar to us by their connection with Burns. We skirted, too, along a portion of the estate of Auchinleck, which still belongs to the Boswell family—the present possessor being Sir James Boswell,* a grandson of Johnson's friend, and son of the Sir Alexander who was killed

* Sir James Boswell is now dead.

in a duel. Our driver spoke of Sir James as a kind, free-hearted man, but addicted to horse-races and similar pastimes, and a little too familiar with the wine-cup; so that poor Bozzy's booziness would appear to have become hereditary in his ancient line. There is no male heir to the estate of Auchinleck. The portion of the lands which we saw is covered with wood and much undermined with rabbit-warrens; nor, though the territory extends over a large number of acres, is the income very considerable.

By-and-by we came to the spot where Burns saw Miss Alexander, the Lass of Ballochmyle. It was on a bridge, which (or, more probably, a bridge that has succeeded to the old one, and is made of iron) crosses from bank to bank, high in air, over a deep gorge of the road; so that the young lady may have appeared to Burns like a creature between earth and sky, and compounded chiefly of celestial elements. But, in honest truth, the great charm of a woman, in Burns's eyes, was always her womanhood, and not the angelic mixture which other poets find in her.

Our driver pointed out the course taken by the Lass of Ballochmyle, through the shrubbery, to a rock on the banks of the Lugar, where it seems to be the tradition that Burns accosted her. The song implies no such interview. Lovers, of whatever condition, high or low, could desire no lovelier scene in which to breathe their vows; the river flowing over its pebbly bed, sometimes gleaming into the sunshine, sometimes hidden deep in verdure, and here and there eddying at the foot of high and precipitous cliffs. This beautiful estate of Ballochmyle is still held by the family of Alexanders, to whom Burns's song has given renown on cheaper terms than any other set of people ever attained it. How slight the tenure seems! A young lady happened to walk out, one summer afternoon, and crossed the path of a neighboring farmer, who celebrated the little incident in four or five warm, rude—at least, not refined, though rather ambitious—and somewhat ploughman-like verses. Burns has written hundreds of better things; but henceforth, for centuries, that maiden has free admittance into the dream-land of Beautiful Women, and she and all her race are famous! I should like to know the present head of the family, and ascertain what value, if any, the members of it put upon the celebrity thus won.

We passed through Catrine, known hereabouts as "the clean village of Scotland." Certainly, as regards the point indicated, it has greatly the advantage of Mauchline, whither we now returned without seeing anything else worth writing about.

There was a rain-storm during the night, and, in the morning, the rusty, old, sloping street of Mauchline was glistening with wet, while frequent showers came spattering down. The intense heat of many days past was exchanged for a chilly atmosphere, much more suitable to a stranger's idea of what Scotch temperature ought to be. We found, after breakfast, that the first train northward had already gone by, and that we must wait till nearly two o'clock for the next. I merely ventured out once, during the forenoon, and took a brief walk through the village, in which I have left little to describe. Its chief business appears to be the manufacture of snuff-boxes. There are perhaps five or six shops, or more, including those licensed to sell only tea and tobacco; the best of them have the characteristics of village-stores in the United States, dealing in a small way with an extensive variety of articles. I peeped into the open gateway of the churchyard, and saw that the ground was absolutely stuffed with dead people, and the surface crowded with grave-stones, both perpendicular and horizontal. All Burns's old Mauchline acquaintance are doubtless there, and the Armours among them, except Bonny Jean, who sleeps by her poet's side. The family of Armour is now extinct in Mauchline.

Arriving at the railway-station, we found a tall, elderly, comely gentleman, walking to-and-fro, and waiting for the train. He proved to be a Mr. Alexander—it may fairly be presumed the Alexander of Ballochmyle, a blood-relation of the lovely lass. Wonderful efficacy of a poet's verse, that could shed a glory from Long Ago on this old gentleman's white hair! These Alexanders, by-the-by, are not an old family on the Ballochmyle estate; the father of the lass having made a fortune in trade, and established himself as the first landed proprietor of his name in these parts. The original family was named Whitefoord.

Our ride to Ayr presented nothing very remarkable; and, indeed, a cloudy and rainy day takes the varnish off the scenery, and causes a woeful diminution in the beauty and impressiveness of every thing we see. Much of our way lay along a flat, sandy level, in a southerly direction. We reached Ayr in the midst of hopeless rain, and drove to the King's Arms Hotel. In the intervals of showers I took peeps at the town, which appeared to have many modern, or modern-fronted, edifices; although there are likewise tall, gray, gabled, and quaint-looking houses in the by-streets, here and there, betokening an ancient place. The town lies on both sides of the Ayr, which is here broad and stately, and bordered with dwellings that look from their windows directly down into the passing tide.

I crossed the river by a modern and handsome stone-bridge, and recrossed it, at no great distance, by a venerable structure of four gray arches, which must have bestridden the stream ever since the early days of Scottish history. These are the "Two Briggs of Ayr," whose midnight conversation was over-heard by Burns, while other auditors were aware only of the rush and rumble of the wintry stream among the arches. The ancient bridge is steep and narrow, and paved like a street, and defended by a parapet of red freestone, except at the two ends, where some mean old shops allow scanty room for the pathway to creep between. Nothing else impressed me hereabouts, unless I mention, that, during the rain, the women and girls went about the streets of Ayr barefooted to save their shoes.

The next morning wore a lowering aspect, as if it felt itself destined to be one of many consecutive days of storm. After a good Scotch breakfast, however, of fresh herrings and eggs, we took a fly, and started at a little past ten for the banks of the Doon. On our way, at about two miles from Ayr, we drew up at a road-side cottage, on which was an inscription to the effect that Robert Burns was born within its walls. It is now a public house; and, of course, we alighted and entered its little sitting-room, which, as we at present see it, is a neat apartment, with the modern improvement of a ceiling. The walls are much over-scribbled with names of visitors, and the wooden door of a cupboard in the wainscot, as well as all the other wood-work of the room, is cut and carved with initial letters. So, likewise, are two tables, which, having received a coat of varnish over the inscriptions, form really curious and interesting articles of furniture. I have seldom (though I do not personally adopt this mode of illustrating my humble name) felt inclined to ridicule the natural impulse of most people thus to record themselves at the shrines of poets and heroes.

On a panel, let into the wall in a corner of the room, is a portrait of Burns, copied from the original picture by Nasmyth. The floor of this apartment is of boards, which are probably a recent substitute for the ordinary flag-stones of a peasant's cottage. There is but one other room pertaining to the genuine birth-place of Robert Burns; it is the kitchen, into which we now went. It has a floor of flag-stones, even ruder than those of Shakspere's house—though, perhaps, not so strangely cracked and broken as the latter, over which the hoof of Satan himself might seem to have been trampling. A new window has been opened through the wall, towards the road; but on the opposite side is the little original window, of only four small panes, through which came the first daylight that shone upon the Scottish poet. At the side of the room, opposite the fire-place, is a recess, containing a bed, which can be hidden by curtains. In that humble nook, of all places in the world, Providence was pleased to deposit the germ of the richest human life which mankind then had within its circumference.

These two rooms, as I have said, make up the whole sum and substance of Burns's birth-place; for there were no chambers, nor even attics; and the thatched roof formed the only ceiling of kitchen and sitting-room, the height of which was that of the whole house. The cottage, however, is attached to another edifice of the same size and description, as these little habitations often are; and, moreover, a splendid addition has been made to it, since the poet's renown began to draw visitors to the wayside ale-house. The old woman of the house led us through an entry, and showed a vaulted hall, of no vast dimensions, to be sure, but marvellously large and splendid as compared with what might be anticipated from the outward aspect of the cottage. It contained a bust of Burns, and was hung round with pictures and engravings, principally illustrative of his life and poems. In this part of the house, too, there is a parlor, fragrant with tobacco-smoke; and, no doubt, many a noggin of whiskey is here quaffed to the memory of the bard, who professed to draw so much inspiration from that potent liquor.

We bought some engravings of Kirk Alloway, the Bridge of Doon, and the monument, and gave the old woman a fee besides, and took our leave. A very short drive farther brought us within sight of the monument, and to the hotel, situated close by the entrance of the ornamental grounds within which the former is enclosed. We rang the bell at the gate of the enclosure, but were forced to wait a considerable time; because the old man, the regular superintendent of the spot, had gone to assist at the laying of the corner-stone of a new kirk. He appeared anon, and admitted us, but immediately hurried away to be present at the concluding ceremonies, leaving us locked up with Burns.

The enclosure around the monument is beautifully laid out as an ornamental garden, and abundantly provided with rare flowers and shrubbery, all tended with loving care. The monument stands on an elevated site, and consists of a massive basement story, three-sided, above which rises a light and elegant Grecian temple—a mere dome, supported on Corinthian pillars, and open to all the winds. The edifice is beautiful in itself; though I know not what peculiar appropriateness it may have, as the memorial of a Scottish rural poet.

The door of the basement story stood open; and, entering, we saw a bust of Burns in a niche, looking keener, more refined, but not so warm and whole-souled as his pictures usually do. I think the likeness cannot be good. In the centre of the room stood a glass case, in which were reposited the two volumes of the little pocket-Bible that Burns gave to Highland Mary, when they pledged their troth to one another. It is poorly printed, on coarse paper. A verse of scripture, referring to the solemnity and awfulness of vows, is written within the cover of each volume, in the poet's own hand; and fastened to one of the covers is a lock of Highland Mary's golden hair. This Bible had been carried to America by one of her relatives, but was sent back to be fitly treasured here.

There is a staircase within the monument, by which we ascended to the top, and had a view of both Briggs of Doon; the scene of Tam O'Shanter's misadventure being close at hand. Descending, we wandered through the enclosed garden, and came to a little building in a corner, on entering

which, we found the two statues of Tam and Sutor Wat—
ponderous stone-work enough, yet permeated in a remarkable
degree with living warmth and jovial hilarity. From this part
of the garden, too, we again beheld the old Brigg of Doon,
over which Tam galloped in such imminent and awful peril.
It is a beautiful object in the landscape, with one high,
graceful arch, ivy-grown, and shadowed all over and around
with foliage.

When we had waited a good while, the old gardener came,
telling us that he had heard an excellent prayer at laying the
corner-stone of the new kirk. He now gave us some roses and
sweet-briar, and let us out from his pleasant garden. We
immediately hastened to Kirk Alloway, which is within two or
three minutes' walk of the monument. A few steps ascend
from the road-side, through a gate, into the old grave-yard, in
the midst of which stands the kirk. The edifice is wholly
roofless, but the side-walls and gable-ends are quite entire,
though portions of them are evidently modern restorations.
Never was there a plainer little church, or one with smaller
architectural pretension; no New England meeting-house has
more simplicity in its very self, though poetry and fun have
clambered and clustered so wildly over Kirk Alloway that it is
difficult to see it as it actually exists. By-the-by, I do not
understand why Satan and an assembly of witches should
hold their revels within a consecrated precinct; but the weird
scene has so established itself in the world's imaginative faith
that it must be accepted as an authentic incident, in spite of
rule and reason to the contrary. Possibly, some carnal minister, some priest of pious aspect and hidden infidelity, had
dispelled the consecration of the holy edifice by his pretence
of prayer, and thus made it the resort of unhappy ghosts and
sorcerers and devils.

The interior of the kirk, even now, is applied to quite as
impertinent a purpose as when Satan and the witches used it

as a dancing-hall; for it is divided in the midst by a wall of stone-masonry, and each compartment has been converted into a family burial-place. The name on one of the monuments is Crawfurd; the other bore no inscription. It is impossible not to feel that these good people, whoever they may be, had no business to thrust their prosaic bones into a spot that belongs to the world, and where their presence jars with the emotions, be they sad or gay, which the pilgrim brings thither. They shut us out from our own precincts, too—from that inalienable possession which Burns bestowed in free gift upon mankind, by taking it from the actual earth and annexing it to the domain of imagination. And here these wretched squatters have lain down to their long sleep, after barring each of the two door-ways of the kirk with an iron grate! May their rest be troubled, till they rise and let us in!

Kirk Alloway is inconceivably small, considering how large a space it fills in our imagination before we see it. I paced its length, outside of the wall, and found it only seventeen of my paces, and not more than ten of them in breadth. There seem to have been but very few windows, all of which, if I rightly remember, are now blocked up with mason-work of stone. One mullioned window, tall and narrow, in the eastern gable, might have been seen by Tam O'Shanter, blazing with devilish light, as he approached along the road from Ayr; and there is a small and square one, on the side nearest the road, into which he might have peered, as he sat on horseback. Indeed, I could easily have looked through it, standing on the ground, had not the opening been walled up. There is an odd kind of belfry at the peak of one of the gables, with the small bell still hanging in it. And this is all that I remember of Kirk Alloway, except that the stones of its material are gray and irregular.

The road from Ayr passes Alloway Kirk, and crosses the Doon by a modern bridge, without swerving much from a straight line. To reach the old bridge, it appears to have made a bend, shortly after passing the kirk, and then to have turned sharply towards the river. The new bridge is within a minute's walk of the monument; and we went thither, and leaned over its parapet to admire the beautiful Doon, flowing wildly and sweetly between its deep and wooded banks. I never saw a lovelier scene; although this might have been even lovelier, if a kindly sun had shone upon it. The ivy-grown, ancient bridge, with its high arch, through which we had a picture of the river and the green banks beyond, was absolutely the most picturesque object, in a quiet and gentle way, that ever blessed my eyes. Bonny Doon, with its wooded banks, and the boughs dipping into the water! The memory of them, at this moment, affects me like the song of birds, and Burns crooning some verses, simple and wild, in accordance with their native melody.

It was impossible to depart without crossing the very bridge of Tam's adventure; so we went thither, over a now disused portion of the road, and, standing on the centre of the arch, gathered some ivy-leaves from that sacred spot. This done, we returned as speedily as might be to Ayr, whence, taking the rail, we soon beheld Ailsa Craig rising like a pyramid out of the sea. Drawing nearer to Glasgow, Ben Lomond hove in sight, with a dome-like summit, supported by a shoulder on each side. But a man is better than a mountain; and we had been holding intercourse, if not with the reality, at least with the stalwart ghost of one of Earth's memorable sons, amid the scenes where he lived and sung. We shall appreciate him better as a poet, hereafter; for there is no writer whose life, as a man, has so much to do with his fame, and throws such a necessary light upon whatever he has produced. Henceforth, there will be a personal warmth for us in everything that he wrote; and, like his countrymen, we shall know him in a kind of personal way, as if we had shaken hands with him, and felt the thrill of his actual voice.

A LONDON SUBURB

ONE OF OUR English summers looks, in the retrospect, as if it had been patched with more frequent sunshine than the sky of England ordinarily affords; but I believe that it may be only a moral effect—a 'light that never was on sea nor land'—caused by our having found a particularly delightful abode in the neighborhood of London. In order to enjoy it, however, I was compelled to solve the problem of living in two places at once;—an impossibility which I so far accomplished as to vanish, at frequent intervals, out of men's sight and knowledge on one side of England, and take my place in a circle of familiar faces on the other, so quietly that I seemed to have been there all along. It was the easier to get accustomed to our new residence, because it was not only rich in all the material properties of a home, but had also the homelike atmosphere, the household element, which is of too intangible a character to be let even with the most thoroughly furnished lodging-house. A friend had given us his suburban residence, with all its conveniences, elegancies, and snuggeries—its drawing-rooms and library, still warm and bright with the recollection of the genial presences that we had known there—its closets, chambers, kitchen, and even its wine-cellar, if we could have availed ourselves of so dear and

delicate a trust—its lawn and cosey garden-nooks, and whatever else makes up the multitudinous idea of an English home
—he had transferred it all to us, pilgrims and dusty wayfarers,
that we might rest and take our ease during his summer's
absence on the continent. We had long been dwelling in
tents, as it were, and morally shivering by hearths which,
heap the bituminous coal upon them as we might, no blaze
could render cheerful. I remember, to this day, the dreary
feeling with which I sat by our first English fireside, and
watched the chill and rainy twilight of an autumn day darkening down upon the garden; while the portrait of the
preceding occupant of the house (evidently a most unamiable
personage in his lifetime) scowled inhospitably from above
the mantel-piece, as if indignant that an American should try
to make himself at home there. Possibly it may appease his
sulky shade to know that I quitted his abode as much a
stranger as I entered it. But now, at last, we were in a genuine
British home, where refined and warm-hearted people had
just been living their daily life, and had left us a summer's
inheritance of slowly ripened days such as a stranger's hasty
opportunities so seldom permit him to enjoy.

Within so trifling a distance of the central spot of all the
world (which, as Americans have at present no centre of their
own, we may allow to be somewhere in the vicinity, we will
say, of Saint Paul's Cathedral) it might have seemed natural
that I should be tossed about by the turbulence of the vast
London whirlpool. But I had drifted into a still eddy, where
conflicting movements made a repose, and, wearied with a
good deal of uncongenial activity, I found the quiet of my
temporary haven more attractive than anything that the great
town could offer. I already knew London well; that is to say, I
had long ago satisfied (so far as it was capable of satisfaction)
that mysterious yearning—the magnetism of millions of
hearts operating upon one—which impels every man's indi-

viduality to mingle itself with the immensest mass of human
life within his scope. Day after day, at an earlier period, I had
trodden the thronged thoroughfares, the broad, lonely
squares, the lanes, alleys, and strange, labyrinthine courts, the
parks, the gardens and enclosures of ancient studious societies,
so retired and silent amid the city-uproar, the markets, the
foggy streets along the river-side, the bridges—I had sought
all parts of the metropolis, in short, with an unweariable and
indiscriminating curiosity; until few of the native inhabitants,
I fancy, had turned so many of its corners as myself. These
aimless wanderings (in which my prime purpose and achievement were to lose my way, and so to find it the more surely)
had brought me, at one time or another, to the sight and
actual presence of almost all the objects and renowned localities that I had read about, and which had made London the
dream-city of my youth. I had found it better than my dream;
for there is nothing else in life comparable (in that species of
enjoyment, I mean) to the thick, heavy, oppressive, sombre
delight which an American is sensible of, hardly knowing
whether to call it a pleasure or a pain, in the atmosphere of
London. The result was, that I acquired a home-feeling there,
as nowhere else in the world; though afterwards I came to
have a somewhat similar sentiment in regard to Rome; and as
long as either of those two great cities shall exist, the cities of
the Past and of the Present, a man's native soil may crumble
beneath his feet without leaving him altogether homeless
upon earth.

Thus, having once fully yielded to its influence, I was in a
manner free of the city, and could approach or keep away
from it as I pleased. Hence it happened, that, living within a
quarter-of-an hour's rush of the London Bridge Terminus, I
was oftener tempted to spend a whole summer-day in our
garden, than to seek anything new or old, wonderful or common-place, beyond its precincts. It was a delightful garden, of

no great extent, but comprising a good many facilities for repose and enjoyment, such as arbors and garden-seats, shrubbery, flower-beds, rose-bushes in a profusion of bloom, pinks, poppies, geraniums, sweet-peas, and a variety of other scarlet, yellow, blue, and purple blossoms, which I did not trouble myself to recognize individually, yet had always a vague sense of their beauty about me. The dim sky of England has a most happy effect on the coloring of flowers, blending richness with delicacy in the same texture; but in this garden, as everywhere else, the exuberance of English verdure had a greater charm than any tropical splendor or diversity of hue. The hunger for natural beauty might be satisfied with grass and green leaves forever. Conscious of the triumph of England in this respect, and loyally anxious for the credit of my own country, it gratified me to observe what trouble and pains the English gardeners are fain to throw away in producing a few sour plums, and abortive pears and apples; as, for example, in this very garden, where a row of unhappy trees were spread out perfectly flat against a brick-wall; looking as if impaled alive, or crucified, with a cruel and unattainable purpose of compelling them to produce rich fruit by torture. For my part, I never ate an English fruit, raised in the open air, that could compare in flavor with a Yankee turnip.

The garden included that prime feature of English domestic scenery, a lawn. It had been levelled, carefully shorn, and converted into a bowling-green, on which we sometimes essayed to practise the time-honored game of bowls, most unskilfully, yet not without a perception that it involves a very pleasant mixture of exercise and ease, as is the case with most of the old English pastimes. Our little domain was shut in by the house on one side, and in other directions by a hedge-fence and a brick-wall, which last was concealed or softened by shrubbery and the impaled fruit-trees already mentioned. Over all the outer region, beyond our immediate precincts, there was an abundance of foliage, tossed aloft from the near or distant trees with which that agreeable suburb is adorned. The effect was wonderfully sylvan and rural, insomuch that we might have fancied ourselves in the depths of a wooded seclusion; only that, at brief intervals, we could hear the galloping sweep of a railway-train passing within a quarter of a mile, and its discordant screech, moderated by a little farther distance, as it reached the Blackheath station. That harsh, rough sound, seeking me out so inevitably, was the voice of the great world summoning me forth. I know not whether I was the more pained or pleased to be thus constantly put in mind of the neighborhood of London; for, on one hand, my conscience stung me a little for reading a book, or playing with children in the grass, when there were so many better things for an enlightened traveller to do; while, at the same time, it gave a deeper delight to my luxurious idleness, to contrast it with the turmoil which I escaped. On the whole, however, I do not repent of a single wasted hour, and only wish that I could have spent twice as many in the same way; for the impression in my memory is, that I was as happy in that hospitable garden as the English summer-day was long.

One chief condition of my enjoyment was the weather. Italy has nothing like it, nor America. There never was such weather except in England, where, in requital of a vast amount of horrible east-wind between February and June, and a brown October and black November, and a wet, chill, sunless winter, there are a few weeks of incomparable summer, scattered through July and August, and the earlier portion of September, small in quantity, but exquisite enough to atone for the whole year's atmospherical delinquencies. After all, the prevalent sombreness may have brought out those sunny intervals in such high relief that I see them, in my recollection, brighter than they really were; a little light makes a glory for people who live habitually in a gray gloom.

The English, however, do not seem to know how enjoyable the momentary gleams of their summer are; they call it broiling weather, and hurry to the seaside with red, perspiring faces, in a state of combustion and deliquescence; and I have observed that even their cattle have similar susceptibilities, seeking the deepest shade or standing mid-leg deep in pools and streams to cool themselves, at temperatures which our own cows would deem little more than barely comfortable. To myself, after the summer heats of my native land had somewhat effervesced out of my blood and memory, it was the weather of Paradise itself. It might be a little too warm, but it was that modest and inestimable superabundance which constitutes a bounty of Providence, instead of just a niggardly Enough. During my first year in England, residing in perhaps the most ungenial part of the kingdom, I could never be quite comfortable without a fire on the hearth; in the second twelvemonth, beginning to get acclimatized, I became sensible of an austere friendliness, shy, but sometimes almost tender, in the veiled, shadowy, seldom smiling summer; and in the succeeding years—whether that I had renewed my fibre with English beef and replenished my blood with English ale, or whatever were the cause—I grew content with winter and especially in love with summer, desiring little more for happiness than merely to breathe and bask. At the mid-summer which we are now speaking of, I must needs confess that the noontide sun came down more fervently than I found altogether tolerable; so that I was fain to shift my position with the shadow of the shrubbery, making myself the moveable index of a sun-dial that reckoned up the hours of an almost interminable day.

For each day seemed endless, though never wearisome. As far as your actual experience is concerned, the English summer-day has positively no beginning, and no end. When you awake, at any reasonable hour, the sun is already shining

through the curtains; you live through unnumbered hours of
Sabbath quietude, with a calm variety of incident softly
etched upon their tranquil lapse; and at length you become
conscious that it is bedtime again, while there is still enough
daylight in the sky to make the pages of your book distinctly
legible. Night, if there be any such season, hangs down a
transparent veil through which the by-gone day beholds its
successor; or, if not quite true of the latitude of London, it
may be soberly affirmed of the more northern parts of the
island, that Tomorrow is born before its Yesterday is dead.
They exist together in the golden twilight, where the decrepit
old day dimly discerns the face of the ominous infant; and
you, though a mere mortal, may simultaneously touch them
both, with one finger of recollection and another of prophecy.
I cared not how long the day might be, nor how many of
them. I had earned this repose by a long course of irksome
toil and perturbation, and could have been content never to
stray out of the limits of that suburban villa and its garden. If
I lacked anything beyond, it would have satisfied me well
enough to dream about it, instead of struggling for its actual
possession. At least, this was the feeling of the moment;
although the transitory, flitting, and irresponsible character of
my life there was perhaps the most enjoyable element of all,
as allowing me much of the comfort of house and home
without any sense of their weight upon my back. The no-
madic life has great advantages, if we can find tents ready
pitched for us at every stage.

So much for the interior of our abode—a spot of deepest
quiet, within reach of the intensest activity. But, even when
we stept beyond our own gate, we were not shocked with any
immediate presence of the great world. We were dwelling in
one of those oases that have grown up (in comparatively
recent years, I believe) on the wide waste of Blackheath,
which otherwise offers a vast extent of unoccupied ground in

singular proximity to the metropolis. As a general thing, the proprietorship of the soil seems to exist in everybody and nobody; but exclusive rights have been obtained, here and there, chiefly by men whose daily concerns link them with London, so that you find their villas or boxes standing along village-streets, which have often more of an American aspect than the elder English settlements. The scene is semi-rural. Ornamental trees overshadow the side-walks, and grassy margins border the wheel-tracks. The houses, to be sure, have certain points of difference from those of an American village, bearing tokens of architectural design though seldom of individual taste; and as far as possible, they stand aloof from the street, and separated each from its neighbor by hedge or fence, in accordance with the careful exclusiveness of the English character, which impels the occupant, moreover, to cover the front of his dwelling with as much concealment of shrubbery as his limits will allow. Through the interstices, you catch glimpses of well-kept lawns, generally ornamented with flowers, and with what the English call rock-work, being heaps of ivy-grown stones and fossils, designed for romantic effect in a small way. Two or three of such village-streets as are here described take a collective name—as, for instance, Blackheath Park—and constitute a kind of community of residents, with gateways kept by a policeman, and a semi-privacy, stepping beyond which, you find yourself on the breezy heath.

On this great, bare, dreary common, I often went astray, as I afterwards did on the Campagna of Rome, and drew the air (tainted with London-smoke though it might be) into my lungs by deep inspirations, with a strange and unexpected sense of desert-freedom. The misty atmosphere helps you to fancy a remoteness that perhaps does not quite exist. During the little time that it lasts, the solitude is as impressive as that of a Western prairie or forest; but, soon, the railway-shriek, a mile or two away, insists upon informing you of your whereabout; or you recognize in the distance some landmark that you may have known—an insulated villa, perhaps, with its garden-wall around it, or the rudimental street of a new settlement which is sprouting on this otherwise barren soil. Half-a-century ago, the most frequent token of man's beneficent contiguity might have been a gibbet, and the creak, like a tavern-sign, of a murderer swinging to-and-fro in irons. Blackheath, with its highwaymen and footpads, was dangerous in those days; and even now, for aught I know, the Western prairie may still compare favorably with it as a safe region to go astray in. When I was acquainted with Blackheath, the ingenious device of garrotting had recently come into fashion, and I can remember, while crossing those waste places at midnight and hearing footsteps behind me, to have been sensibly encouraged by also hearing, not far off, the clinking hoof-tramp of one of the horse-patroles who do regular duty there. About sunset, or a little later, was the time when the broad and somewhat desolate peculiarity of the heath seemed to me to put on its utmost impressiveness. At that hour, finding myself on elevated ground, I once had a view of immense London, four or five miles off, with the vast Dome in the midst, and the towers of the two Houses of Parliament rising up into the smoky canopy, the thinner substance of which obscured a mass of things and hovered about the objects that were most distinctly visible—a glorious and sombre picture, dusky, awful, but irresistibly attractive, like a young man's dream of the great world, foretelling at that distance a grandeur never to be fully realized.

While I lived in that neighborhood, the tents of two or three sets of cricket-players were constantly pitched on Blackheath, and matches were going forward that seemed to involve the honor and credit of communities or counties, exciting an interest in everybody but myself, who cared not what part of England might glorify itself at the expense of another. It is necessary to be born an Englishman, I believe, in order to enjoy this great national game;—at any rate, as a spectacle for an outside observer, I found it lazy, lingering, tedious, and utterly devoid of pictorial effects. Choice of other amusements was at hand. Butts for archery were established and bows and arrows were to be let, at so many shots for a penny; there being abundance of space for a farther flight-shot than any modern archer can lend to his shaft. Then there was an absurd game of throwing a stick at crockery-ware, which I have witnessed a hundred times, and personally engaged in once or twice, without ever having the satisfaction to see a bit of broken crockery. In other spots, you found donkies for children to ride, and ponies of a very meek and patient spirit, on which the cockney pleasure-seekers of both sexes rode races and made wonderful displays of horsemanship. By way of refreshment there was gingerbread, (but, as a true patriot, I must pronounce it greatly inferior to our native dainty,) and ginger-beer, and probably stauncher liquor among the booth-keeper's hidden stores. The frequent railway-trains, as well as the numerous steamers to Greenwich, have made the vacant portions of Blackheath a play-ground and breathing-place for the Londoners, readily and very cheaply accessible; so that, in view of this broader use and enjoyment, I a little grudged the tracts that have been filched away, so to speak, and individualized by thriving citizens. One sort of visitors especially interested me; they were schools of little boys or girls, under the guardianship of their instructors—charity-schools, as I often surmised from their aspect, collected among dark alleys and squalid courts; and hither they were brought to spend a summer afternoon, these pale little progeny of the sunless nooks of London, who had never known that the sky was any broader than that narrow and vapoury strip above their native lane. I fancied that they took but a doubtful pleasure, being

half-affrighted at the wide, empty space overhead and roundabout them, finding the air too little medicated with smoke,
soot, and grave-yard exhalations, to be breathed with comfort,
and feeling shelterless and lost because grimy London, their
slatternly and disreputable mother, had suffered them to stray
out of her arms.

Passing among these holiday-people, we come to one of the
gateways of Greenwich Park, opening through an old brick-
wall. It admits us from the bare heath into a scene of antique
cultivation and woodland ornament, traversed in all directions
by avenues of trees, many of which bear tokens of a venerable
age. These broad and well-kept pathways rise and decline
over the elevations and along the bases of gentle hills, which
diversify the whole surface of the Park. The loftiest and most
abrupt of them (though but of very moderate height) is one
of the earth's noted summits and may hold up its head with
Mont Blanc and Chimborazo, as being the site of Greenwich
Observatory, where, if all nations will consent to say so, the
longitude of our great globe begins. I used to regulate my
watch by the broad dial-plate against the observatory-wall,
and felt it pleasant to be standing at the very centre of Time
and Space.

There are lovelier parks than this in the neighborhood of
London, richer scenes of green sward and cultivated trees; and
Kensington, especially, in a summer afternoon, has seemed to
me as delightful as any place can or ought to be, in a world
which, sometime or other, we must quit. But Greenwich,
too, is beautiful—a spot where the art of man has conspired
with Nature, as if he and the great mother had taken counsel
together how to make a pleasant scene, and the longest liver
of the two had faithfully carried out their mutual design. It
has likewise an additional charm of its own, because, to all
appearance, it is the people's property and play-ground in a
much more genuine way than the aristocratic resorts in closer

vicinity to the metropolis. It affords one of the instances in which the monarch's property is actually the people's, and shows how much more natural is their relation to the sovereign than to the nobility, which pretends to hold the intervening space between the two; for a nobleman makes a paradise only for himself, and fills it with his own pomp and pride; whereas the people are sooner or later the legitimate inheritors of whatever beauty kings and queens create, as now of Greenwich Park. On Sundays, when the sun shone, and even on those grim and sombre days when, if it do not actually rain, the English persist in calling it fine weather, it was too good to see how sturdily the plebeians trod under their own oaks, and what fulness of simple enjoyment they evidently found there. They were the people—not the populace—specimens of a class whose Sunday clothes are a distinct kind of garb from their week-day ones; and this, in England, implies wholesome habits of life, daily thrift, and a rank above the lowest. I longed to be acquainted with them, in order to investigate what manner of folks they were, what sort of households they kept, their politics, their religion, their tastes, and whether they were as narrow-minded as their betters. There can be very little doubt of it; an Englishman is English, in whatever rank of life, though no more intensely so, I should imagine, as an artizan or petty shopkeeper than as a member of Parliament.

The English character, as I conceive it, is by no means a very lofty one; they seem to have a great deal of earth and grimy dust clinging about them, as was probably the case with the stalwart and quarrelsome people who sprouted up out of the soil, after Cadmus had sown the dragon's teeth. And yet, though the individual Englishman is sometimes preternaturally disagreeable, an observer standing aloof has a sense of natural kindness towards them in the lump. They adhere closer to the original simplicity in which mankind was created, than we ourselves do; they love, quarrel, laugh, cry, and turn their actual selves inside out, with greater freedom than any class of Americans would consider decorous. It was often so with these holiday-folks in Greenwich Park; and ridiculous as it may sound, I fancy myself to have caught very satisfactory glimpses of Arcadian life among the cockneys there, hardly beyond the scope of Bow-bells, picnicking in the grass, uncouthly gambolling on the broad slopes, or straying in motley groups or by single pairs of love-making youths and maidens, along the sun-streaked avenues. Even the omnipresent policemen or park-keepers could not disturb this beatific impression on my mind. One feature, at all events, of the Golden Age, was to be seen in the herds of deer that encountered you in the somewhat remoter recesses of the Park, and were readily prevailed upon to nibble a bit of bread out of your hand. But, though no wrong had ever been done them, and no horn had sounded nor hound bayed at the heels of themselves or their antlered progenitors, for centuries past, there was still an apprehensiveness lingering in their hearts; so that a slight movement of the hand or a step too near would send a whole squadron of them scampering away, just as a breath scatters the winged seeds of a dandelion.

The aspect of Greenwich Park, with all those festal people wandering through it, resembled that of the Borghese gardens under the walls of Rome, on a Sunday or Saint's day; but, I am not ashamed to say, it a little disturbed whatever grimly ghost of Puritanic strictness might be lingering in the sombre depths of a New England heart, among severe and sunless remembrances of the Sabbaths of childhood, and pangs of remorse for ill-gotten lessons in the catechism, and for erratic fantasies or hardly suppressed laughter in the middle of long sermons. Occasionally, I tried to take the long-hoarded sting out of these compunctious smarts by attending divine service in the open air. On a cart outside of the park-wall, (and, if I mistake not, at two or three corners and secluded spots within the Park itself,) a Methodist preacher uplifts his voice and speedily gathers a congregation, his zeal for whose religious welfare impels the good man to such earnest vociferation and toilsome gesture that his perspiring face is quickly in a stew. His inward flame conspires with the too fervid sun and makes a positive martyr of him, even in the very exercise of his pious labor; insomuch that he purchases every atom of spiritual increment to his hearers by loss of his own corporeal solidity, and, should his discourse last long enough, must finally exhale before their eyes. If I smile at him, be it understood, it is not in scorn; he performs his sacred office more acceptably than many a prelate. These wayside services attract numbers who would not otherwise listen to prayer, sermon, or hymn, from one year's end to another, and who, for that very reason, are the auditors most likely to be moved by the preacher's eloquence. Yonder Greenwich pensioner, too—in his costume of three-cornered hat, and old-fashioned, brass-buttoned blue coat with ample skirts, which makes him look like a contemporary of Admiral Benbow—that tough old mariner may hear a word or two which will go nearer his heart than anything that the chaplain of the Hospital can be expected to deliver. I always noticed, moreover, that a considerable proportion of the audience were soldiers, who came hither with a day's leave from Woolwich—hardy veterans in aspect, some of whom wore as many as four or five medals, Crimean or East Indian, on the breasts of their scarlet coats. The miscellaneous congregation listen with every appearance of heart-felt interest; and, for my own part, I must frankly acknowledge that I never found it possible to give five minutes' attention to any other English preaching; so cold and common-place are the homilies that pass for such, under the aged roofs of churches. And as for cathedrals, the sermon is an exceedingly diminutive and unimportant part of the religious services—if, indeed, it be considered a part—among the pompous ceremonies, the intonations, and the resounding and lofty-voiced strains of the choristers. The magnificence of the setting quite dazzles out what we Puritans look upon as the jewel of the whole affair; for I presume that it was our forefathers, the dissenters in England and America, who gave the sermon its present prominence in the Sabbath exercises.

The Methodists are probably the first and only Englishmen who have worshipped in the open air since the ancient Britons listened to the preaching of the Druids; and it reminded me of that old priesthood, to see certain memorials of their dusky epoch—not religious, however, but warlike—in the neighborhood of the spot where the Methodist was holding forth. These were some ancient barrows, beneath or within which are supposed to lie buried the slain of a forgotten or doubtfully remembered battle, fought on the site of Greenwich Park as long ago as two or three centuries after the birth of Christ. Whatever may once have been their height and magnitude, they have now scarcely more prominence in the actual scene than the battle, of which they are the sole monuments, retains in history; being only a few mounds side by side, elevated a little above the surface of the ground, ten or twelve feet in diameter, with a shallow depression in their summits. When one of them was opened, not long since, no bones, nor armor, nor weapons were discovered, nothing but some small jewels, and a tuft of hair—perhaps from the head of a valiant general, who, dying on the field of his victory, bequeathed this lock, together with his indestructible fame, to after ages. The hair and jewels are probably in the British Museum, where the potsherds and rubbish of innumerable generations make the visitor wish that each passing century could carry off all its fragments and relics along with it, instead of adding them to the continually accumulating burthen which human knowledge is compelled to lug upon its back. As for the fame, I know not what has become of it.

After traversing the Park, we come into the neighborhood of Greenwich Hospital, and will pass through one of its spacious gateways for the sake of glancing at an establishment which does more honor to the heart of England than anything else that I am acquainted with, of a public nature. It is very seldom that we can be sensible of anything like kindliness in the acts or relations of such an artificial thing as a national government. Our own government, I should conceive, is too much an abstraction ever to feel any sympathy for its maimed sailors and soldiers, though it will doubtless do them a severe kind of justice, as chilling as the touch of steel. But it seemed to me that the Greenwich pensioners are the petted children of the nation and that the government is their dry-nurse, and that the old men themselves have a childlike consciousness of their position. Very likely, a better sort of life might have been arranged, and a wiser care bestowed on them; but such as it is, it enables them to spend a sluggish, careless, comfortable old age, grumbling, growling, gruff, as if all the foul weather of their past years were pent up within them, yet not much more discontented than such weather-beaten and battle-battered fragments of humankind must inevitably be. Their home, in its outward form, is on a very magnificent plan. Its germ was a royal palace, the full expansion of which has resulted in a series of edifices externally more beautiful than any English palace that I have seen, consisting of several quadrangles of stately architecture, united by colonnades and gravel walks, and enclosing grassy squares, with statues in the centre, the whole extending along the Thames. It is built of marble or very light-colored stone, in the classic style, with pillars and porticoes, which (to my own taste, and, I fancy, to that of the old sailors) produce but a cold and shivery effect in the English climate. Had I been the architect, I would have studied the characters, habits, and predilections of nautical people in Wapping, Rotherhithe, and the neighborhood of the Tower, (places which I visited in affectionate remembrance of Captain Lemuel Gulliver, and other actual or mythological navigators,) and would have built the Hospital in a kind of ethereal similitude to the narrow, dark, ugly, and inconvenient, but snug and cosey homeliness of the sailor boarding-houses there. There can be no question that all the above attributes, or enough of them to satisfy an old sailor's heart, might be reconciled with architectural beauty and the wholesome contrivances of modern dwellings, and thus a novel and genuine style of building be given to the world.

But their countrymen meant kindly by the old fellows in assigning them the ancient royal site where Elizabeth held her court and Charles the Second began to build his palace. So far as the locality went, it was treating them like so many kings; and, with a discreet abundance of grog, beer, and tobacco, there was perhaps little more to be accomplished in behalf of men whose whole previous lives have tended to unfit them for old age. Their chief discomfort is probably for lack of something to do or think about. But, judging by the few whom I saw, a listless habit seems to have crept over them, a dim dreaminess of mood, in which they sit between asleep and awake, and find the long day wearing towards bedtime without its having made any distinct record of itself upon their consciousness. Sitting on stone-benches in the sunshine, they subside into slumber, or nearly so, and start at the approach of footsteps echoing under the colonnades, ashamed to be caught napping, and rousing themselves in a hurry, as formerly on the midnight watch at sea. In their brightest moments, they gather in groups and bore one another with endless sea-yarns about their voyages under famous Admirals, and about gale and calm, battle and chase, and all that class of incident that has its sphere on the deck and in the hollow interior of a ship, where their world has exclusively been. For other pastime, they quarrel among themselves, comrade with comrade, and perhaps shake paralytic fists in furrowed faces. If inclined for a little exercise, they can bestir their wooden legs on the long esplanade that borders by the Thames, criticizing the rig of passing ships, and firing off vollies of malediction at the steamers, which have made the sea another element than that they used to be acquainted with. All this is but cold comfort for the evening of life, yet may compare rather favorably with the preceding portions of it, comprising little save imprisonment on shipboard, in the course of which they have been tossed all about the world and caught hardly a glimpse of it, forgetting what grass and trees are, and never finding out what woman is, though they may have encountered a painted spectre which they took for her. A country owes much to human beings whose bodies she has worn out and whose immortal parts she has left undeveloped or debased, as we find them here; and having wasted an idle paragraph upon them, let me now suggest that old men have a kind of susceptibility to moral impressions, and even (up to an advanced period) a receptivity of truth, which often appears to come to them after the active time of life is past. The Greenwich pensioners might prove better subjects for true education now than in their schoolboy days; but, then, where is the Normal School that could educate instructors for such a class!

There is a beautiful chapel for the pensioners, in the classic style, over the altar of which hangs a picture by West. I never could look at it long enough to make out its design; for this artist (though it pains me to say it of so respectable a countryman) had a gift of frigidity, a knack of grinding ice into his paint, a power of stupefying the spectator's perceptions and quelling his sympathy, beyond any other limner that ever handled a brush. In spite of many pangs of conscience, I seize this opportunity to wreak a life-long abhorrence upon the poor, blameless man, for the sake of that dreary picture of Lear, an explosion of frosty fury, that used to be a bugbear to me in the Athenaeum Exhibition. Would fire burn it, I wonder!

The principal thing that they have to show you, at Greenwich Hospital, is the Painted Hall. It is a splendid and spacious room, at least a hundred feet long and half as high, with a ceiling painted in fresco by Sir James Thornhill. As a work of art, I presume, this frescoed canopy has little merit, though it produces an exceedingly rich effect by its brilliant coloring and as a specimen of magnificent upholstery. The walls of the grand apartment are entirely covered with pictures, many of them representing battles and other naval incidents that were once fresher in the world's memory than now, but chiefly portraits of old Admirals, comprising the whole line of heroes who have trod the quarter-decks of British ships for more than two hundred years back. Next to a tomb in Westminster Abbey, which was Nelson's most elevated object of ambition, it would seem to be the highest meed of a naval warrior to have his portrait hung up in the Painted Hall; but, by dint of victory upon victory, these illustrious personages have grown to be a mob, and by no means a very interesting one so far as regards the character of the faces here depicted. They are generally common-place, and often singularly stolid; and I have observed (both in the Painted Hall and elsewhere, and not only in portraits, but in the actual presences of such renowned people as I have caught glimpses of) that the countenances of heroes are not nearly so impressive as those of statesmen; except, of course, in the rare instances where warlike ability has been but the one-sided manifestation of a profound genius for managing the world's affairs. Nine-tenths of these distinguished Admirals, for instance, if their faces tell truth, must needs have been blockheads, and might have served better, one would imagine, as wooden figure-heads for their own ships than to direct any difficult and intricate scheme of action from the quarter-deck. It is doubtful whether the same kind of men will hereafter meet with a similar degree of success; for they were victorious chiefly through the old English hardihood, exercised in a field of which modern science had not yet got possession. Rough valor has lost something of its value, since their days, and must continue to sink lower and lower in the comparative estimate of warlike qualities. In the next naval war, as between England and France, I would bet, methinks, upon the Frenchman's head.

It is remarkable, however, that the great naval hero of England—the greatest, therefore, in the world, and of all time—had none of the stolid characteristics that belong to his class, and cannot fairly be accepted as their representative man. Foremost in the roughest of professions, he was as delicately organized as a woman, and as painfully sensitive as a poet. More than any other Englishman, he won the love and admiration of his country, but won them through the efficacy of qualities that are not English, or, at all events, were intensified in his case and made poignant and powerful by something morbid in the man, which put him otherwise at cross-purposes with life. He was a man of genius; and genius in an Englishman (not to cite the good old simile of a pearl in the oyster) is usually a symptom of a lack of balance in the general making up of the character; as we may satisfy ourselves by running over the list of their poets, for example, and observing how many of them have been sickly or deformed, and how often their lives have been darkened by insanity. An ordinary Englishman is the healthiest and wholesomest of human beings; an extraordinary one is almost always, in one way or another, a sick man. It was so with Lord Nelson. The wonderful contrast or relation between his personal qualities, the position which he held, and the life that he lived, makes him as interesting a personage as all history has to show; and it is a pity that Southey's biography—so good in its superficial way, and yet so inadequate as regards any real delineation of the man—should have taken the subject out of the hands of some writer, endowed with more delicate appreciation and deeper insight than that genuine Englishman possessed. But Southey accomplished his own purpose, which, apparently, was to present his hero as a pattern for England's young midshipmen.

But the English capacity for hero-worship is full to the brim with what they are able to comprehend of Lord Nelson's character. Adjoining the Painted Hall is a smaller room, the walls of which are completely and exclusively adorned with pictures of the great Admiral's exploits. We see the frail, ardent man in all the most noted events of his career, from his encounter with a polar bear to his death at Trafalgar, quivering here and there about the room like a blue, lambent flame. No Briton ever enters that apartment without feeling the beef and ale of his composition stirred to its depths, and finding himself changed into a hero for the nonce, however stolid his brain, however tough his heart, however unexcitable his ordinary mood. To confess the truth, I myself, though belonging to another parish, have been deeply sensible to the sublime recollections there aroused, acknowledging that Nelson expressed his life in a kind of symbolic poetry which I had as much right to understand as these burly islanders. Cool and critical observer as I sought to be, I enjoyed their burst of honest indignation when a visitor (not an American, I am glad to say) thrust his walking-stick almost into Nelson's face, in one of the pictures, by way of pointing a remark; and the bystanders immediately glowed like so many hot coals, and would probably have consumed the offender in their wrath, had he not effected his retreat. But the most sacred object of all are two of Nelson's coats, under separate glass-cases. One is that which he wore at the battle of the Nile, and it is now sadly injured by moths, which will quite destroy it in a few years, unless its guardians preserve it as we do Washington's military suit, by occasionally baking it in an oven. The other is the coat in which he received his death-wound at Trafalgar. On its breast are sewn three or four stars and orders of knighthood, now much dimmed by time and damp, but which glittered brightly enough on the battle-day to draw the fatal aim of a French marksman. The bullet-hole is visible on the shoulder, as well as a part of the golden tassels of an epaulet, the rest of which was shot away. Over the coat is laid a white waistcoat with a great bloodstain on it, out of which all the redness has utterly faded, leaving it of a dingy yellow hue, in the threescore years since that blood gushed out. Yet it was once the reddest blood in England—Nelson's blood!

The Hospital stands close adjacent to the town of Greenwich, which will always retain a kind of festal aspect in my memory in consequence of my having first become acquainted with it on Easter Monday. Till a few years ago, the first three days of Easter were a carnival-season in this old town, during which the idle and disreputable part of London poured itself into the streets like an inundation of the Thames—as unclean as that turbid mixture of the offscourings of the vast city, and overflowing with its grimy pollution whatever rural innocence, if any, might be found in the suburban neighborhood. This festivity was called Greenwich Fair, the final one of which, in an immemorial succession, it was my fortune to behold.

If I had bethought myself of going through the Fair with a note-book and pencil, jotting down all the prominent objects, I doubt not that the result might have been a sketch of English life, quite as characteristic and worthy of historical preservation as an account of the Roman Carnival. Having neglected to do so, I remember little more than a confusion of unwashed and shabbily dressed people, intermixed with some smarter figures, but, on the whole, presenting a mobbish appearance such as we never see in our own country. It taught me to understand why Shakspere, in speaking of a crowd, so often alludes to its attribute of evil odor. The common people of England, I am afraid, have no daily familiarity with even so necessary a thing as a wash-bowl, not to mention a bathing-tub; and, furthermore, it is one mighty difference between them and us, that every man and woman, on our side of the water, has a working-day suit and a holiday-suit, and is occasionally as fresh as a rose, whereas, in the good old country, the griminess of his labor or squalid habits clings forever to the individual, and gets to be a part of his personal substance. These are broad facts, involving great corollaries and dependencies. There are really, if you stop to think about it, few sadder spectacles in the world than a ragged coat or a soiled and shabby gown, at a festival.

This unfragrant crowd was exceedingly dense, being welded together, as it were, in the street through which we strove to make our way. On either side were oyster-stands, stalls of oranges, (a very prevalent fruit in England, where they give the withered ones a guise of freshness by boiling them,) and booths covered with old sail-cloth, in which the commodity that most attracted the eye was gilt gingerbread. It was so completely enveloped in Dutch gilding, that I did not at first recognize an old acquaintance, but wondered what those golden crowns and images could be. There were likewise drums and other toys for small children, and a variety of showy and worthless articles for children of a larger growth; though it perplexed me to imagine who, in such a mob, could have the innocent taste to desire playthings, or the money to pay for them. Not that I have a right to accuse the mob, on my own knowledge, of being any less innocent than a set of cleaner and better dressed people might have been; for though one of them stole my pocket-handkerchief, I could not but consider it fair game, under the circumstances, and was grateful to the thief for sparing me my purse. They were quiet, civil, and remarkably good-humored, making due allowance for the national gruffness; there was no riot, no tumultuous swaying to-and-fro of the mass, such as I have often noted in an American crowd; no noise of voices, except frequent bursts of laughter, hoarse or shrill, and a widely diffused, inarticulate murmur, resembling nothing so much as the rumbling of the tide among the arches of London Bridge. What immensely perplexed me was a sharp, angry sort of rattle, in all quarters, far off and close at hand, and sometimes right at my own back, where it sounded as if the stout fabric of my English surtout had been ruthlessly rent in twain; and everybody's clothes, all over the Fair, were evidently being torn asunder in the same way. By-and-by, I discovered that this strange noise was produced by a little instrument called the Fun of the Fair—a sort of rattle, consisting of a wooden wheel, the cogs of which turn against a thin slip of wood, and so produce a rasping sound when drawn smartly against a person's back. The ladies draw their rattles against the backs of their male friends, (and everybody passes for a friend at Greenwich Fair,) and the young men return the compliment on the broad British backs of the ladies; and all are bound by immemorial custom to take it in good part and be merry at the joke. As it was one of my prescribed official duties to give an account of such mechanical contrivances as might be unknown in my own country, I have thought it right to be thus particular in describing the Fun of the Fair.

But this was far from being the sole amusement. There were theatrical booths, in front of which were pictorial representations of the scenes to be enacted within; and, anon, a drummer emerged from one of them, thumping on a terribly lax drum, and followed by the entire dramatis personae, who ranged themselves on a wooden platform in front of the theatre. They were dressed in character, but woefully shabby, with very dingy and wrinkled white tights, threadbare cotton-velvets, crumpled silks, and crushed muslin, and all the gloss and glory gone out of their aspect and attire, seen thus in the broad daylight and after a long series of performances. They sung a song together, and withdrew into the theatre, whither the public were invited to follow them at the inconsiderable cost of a penny a ticket. Before another booth stood a pair of brawny fighting-men, displaying their muscle, and soliciting patronage for an exhibition of the noble British art of pugilism. There were pictures of giants, monsters, and outlandish beasts, most prodigious, to be sure, and worthy of all admiration, unless the artist had gone incomparably beyond his subject. Jugglers proclaimed aloud the miracles which they were prepared to work; and posture-makers dislocated every joint of their bodies and tied their limbs into inextricable knots, wherever they could find space to spread a little square of carpet on the ground. In the midst of the confusion, where everybody was treading on his neighbor's toes, some little boys were very solicitous to brush your boots. These lads, I believe, are a product of modern society—at least, no older than the time of Gay, who celebrates their origin in his "Trivia";—but, in most other respects, the scene reminded me of Bunyan's description of Vanity Fair; nor is it at all improbable that the Pilgrim may have been a merry-maker here, in his wild youth.

It seemed very singular—though, of course, I immediately classified it as an English characteristic—to see a great many portable weighing-machines, the owners of which cried out continually and amain—"Come, know your weight! Come, come, know your weight to-day! Come, know your weight!" —and a multitude of people, mostly large in the girth, were moved by this vociferation to sit down in the machines. I know not whether they valued themselves on their beef, and estimated their standing, as members of society, at so much a pound; but I shall set it down as a national peculiarity, and a symbol of the prevalence of the earthly over the spiritual element, that Englishmen are wonderfully bent on knowing how solid and physically ponderous they are.

On the whole, having an appetite for the brown bread and the tripe and sausages of life, as well as for its nicer cates and dainties, I enjoyed the scene, and was amused at the sight of a gruff old Greenwich pensioner, who, forgetful of the sailor-frolics of his young days, stood looking with grim disapproval at all these vanities. Thus we squeezed our way through the mob-jammed town, and emerged into the Park, where, likewise, we met a great many merry-makers, but with freer space for their gambols than in the streets. We soon found ourselves the targets for a cannonade with oranges, (most of them in a decayed condition,) which went humming past our ears from the vantage-ground of neighboring hillocks, sometimes hitting our sacred persons with an inelastic thump. This was one of the privileged freedoms of the time, and was nowise to be resented except by returning the salute. Many persons were running races, hand in hand, down the declivities, especially that steepest one, on the summit of which stands the world-central Observatory; and (as in the race of life) the partners were usually male and female, and often caught a tumble together before reaching the bottom of the hill. Hereabouts, we were pestered and haunted by two young girls, the eldest not more than thirteen, teazing us to buy matches; and finding no market for their commodity, the taller one suddenly turned a somerset before our faces, and rolled heels over head from top to bottom of the hill on which we stood. Then, scrambling up the acclivity, the topsy-turvy trollop offered us her matches again, as demurely as if she had never flung aside her equilibrium; so that, dreading a repetition of the feat, we gave her sixpence and an admonition, and enjoined her never to do so any more.

The most curious amusement that we witnessed here—or

anywhere else, indeed—was an ancient and hereditary pastime called Kissing in the Ring. I shall describe the sport exactly as I saw it, although an English friend assures me that there are certain ceremonies with a handkerchief, which make it much more decorous and graceful. A handkerchief, indeed! There was no such thing in the crowd, except it were the one which they had just filched out of my pocket. It is one of the simplest kinds of games, needing little or no practice to make the player altogether perfect; and the manner of it is this. A ring is formed, (in the present case, it was of large circumference and thickly gemmed around with faces, mostly on the broad grin,) into the centre of which steps an adventurous youth, and looking round the circle, selects whatever maiden may most delight his eye. He presents his hand, (which she is bound to accept,) leads her into the centre, salutes her on the lips, and retires, taking his stand in the expectant circle. The girl, in her turn, throws a favorable regard on some fortunate young man, offers her hand to lead him forth, makes him happy with a maidenly kiss, and withdraws to hide her blushes, if any there be, among the simpering faces in the ring; while the favored swain loses no time in transferring her salute to the prettiest and plumpest among the many mouths that are primming themselves in anticipation. And thus the thing goes on, till all the festive throng are enwreathed and intertwined into an endless and inextricable chain of kisses; though, indeed, it smote me with compassion to reflect that some forlorn pair of lips might be left out, and never know the triumph of a salute after throwing aside so many delicate reserves for the sake of winning it. If the young men had any chivalry, there was a fair chance to display it by kissing the homeliest damsel in the circle.

To be frank, however—at the first glance, and to my American eye, they looked all homely alike, and the chivalry that I suggest is more than I could have been capable of, at any period of my life. They seemed to be country-lasses, of sturdy and wholesome aspect, with coarse-grained, cabbage-rosy cheeks, and, I am willing to suppose, a stout texture of moral principle, such as would bear a good deal of rough usage without suffering much detriment. But how unlike the trim little damsels of my native land! I desire above all things to be courteous, but, since the plain truth must be told, the soil and climate of England produce feminine beauty as rarely as they do delicate fruit, and though admirable specimens of both are to be met with, they are the hot-house ameliorations of refined society, and apt, moreover, to relapse into the coarseness of the original stock. The men are manlike, but the women are not beautiful though the female Bull be well enough adapted to the male. To return to the lasses of Greenwich Fair, their charms were few and their behavior, perhaps, not altogether commendable; and yet it was impossible not to feel a degree of faith in their innocent intentions, with such a half-bashful zest and entire simplicity did they keep up their part of the game. It put the spectator in good humor to look at them, because there was still something of the old Arcadian life, the secure freedom of the antique age, in their way of surrendering their lips to strangers as if there were no evil or impurity in the world. As for the young men, they were chiefly specimens of the vulgar sediment of London life, often shabbily genteel, rowdyish, pale, wearing the unbrushed coat, unshifted linen, and unwashed faces of yesterday, as well as the haggardness of last night's jollity in a gin-shop. Gathering their character from these tokens, I wondered whether there were any reasonable prospect of their fair partners returning to their rustic homes with as much innocence (whatever were its amount or quality) as they brought to Greenwich Fair, in spite of the perilous familiarity established by Kissing in the Ring!

The manifold disorders resulting from the Fair, at which a

vast city was brought into intimate relations with a comparatively rural district, have at length led to its suppression; this was the very last celebration of it, and brought to a close the broad-mouthed merriment of many hundred years. Thus my poor sketch, faint as its colors are, may acquire some little value in the reader's eyes from the consideration that no observer of the coming time will ever have an opportunity to give a better. I should find it difficult to believe, however, that the queer pastime just described, or any moral mischief to which that and other customs might pave the way, can have led to the overthrow of Greenwich Fair; for it has often seemed to me that Englishmen of station and respectability, unless of a peculiarly philanthropic turn, have neither any faith in the feminine purity of the lower orders of their countrywomen, nor the slightest value for it, allowing its possible existence. The distinction of ranks is so marked, that the English cottage-damsel holds a position somewhat analogous to that of the negro girl in our Southern states. Hence comes inevitable detriment to the moral condition of those men themselves, who forget that the humblest woman has a right and a duty to hold herself in the same sanctity as the highest. The subject cannot well be discussed in these pages; but I offer it as a serious conviction from what I have been able to observe, that the England of to-day is the unscrupulous old England of Tom Jones and Joseph Andrews, Humphrey Clinker and Roderick Random; and in our refined era, just the same as at that more free-spoken epoch, this singular people has a certain contempt for any fine-strained purity, any special squeamishness, as they consider it, on the part of an ingenuous youth. They appear to look upon it as a suspicious phenomenon in the masculine character.

Nevertheless, I by no means take upon me to affirm that English morality, as regards the phase here alluded to, is really at a lower point than our own. Assuredly I hope so, because, making a higher pretension, or, at all events, more carefully hiding whatever may be amiss, we are either better than they, or necessarily a great deal worse. It impressed me that their open avowal and recognition of immoralities served to throw the disease to the surface, where it might be more effectually dealt with, and leave a sacred interior not utterly prophaned, instead of turning its poison back among the inner vitalities of the character at the imminent risk of corrupting them all. Be that as it may, these Englishmen are certainly a franker and simpler people than ourselves, from peer to peasant; but if we can take it as compensatory on our part (which I leave to be considered) that they owe those noble and manly qualities to a coarser grain in their nature, and that, with a finer one in ours, we shall ultimately acquire a marble-polish of which they are unsusceptible—I believe that this may be the truth.

UP THE THAMES

THE UPPER PORTION of Greenwich (where my last article left me loitering) is a cheerful, comely, old-fashioned town, the peculiarities of which, if there be any, have passed out of my remembrance. As you descend towards the Thames, the streets get meaner, and the shabby and sunken houses, elbowing one another for frontage, bear the sign-boards of beer-shops and eating-rooms, with especial promises of white-bait and other delicacies in the fishy line. You observe, also, a frequent announcement of 'Tea Gardens' in the rear; although, estimating the capacity of the premises by their external compass, the entire sylvan charm and shadowy seclusion of such blissful resorts must be limited within a small back-yard. These places of cheap sustenance and recreation depend for support upon the innumerable pleasure-parties who come from London Bridge by steamer, at a fare of a few pence, and who get as enjoyable a meal for a shilling a head as the Ship Hotel would afford a gentleman for a guinea.

The steamers, which are constantly smoking their pipes up and down the Thames, offer much the most agreeable mode of getting to London. At least, it might be exceedingly agreeable, except for the myriad floating particles of soot from the stove-pipe, and the heavy heat of mid-summer sunshine on the unsheltered deck, or the chill, misty air-draft of a cloudy day, and the spiteful little showers of rain that may spatter down upon you at any moment, whatever the promise of the sky; besides which there is some slight inconvenience from the inexhaustible throng of passengers, who scarcely allow you standing-room, nor so much as a breath of unappropriated air, and never a chance to sit down. If these difficulties, added to the possibility of getting your pocket picked, weigh little with you, the panorama along the shores of the memorable river, and the incidents and shows of passing life upon its bosom, render the trip far preferable to the brief, yet tiresome shoot along the railway-track. On one such voyage, a Regatta of wherries raced past us, and at once involved every soul on board our steamer in the tremendous excitement of the struggle. The spectacle was but a moment within our view, and presented nothing more than a few light skiffs, in each of which sat a single rower, bare-armed, and with little apparel save a shirt and drawers, pale, anxious, with every muscle on the stretch, and plying his oars in such fashion that the boat skimmed along with the aerial celerity of a swallow. I wondered at myself for so immediately catching an interest in the affair, which seemed to contain no very exalted rivalship of manhood; but, whatever the kind of battle or the prize of victory, it stirs one's sympathy immensely, and is even awful, to behold the rare sight of a man thoroughly in earnest, doing his best, putting forth all there is in him, and staking his very soul (as these rowers appeared willing to do) on the issue of the contest. It was the seventy-fourth annual Regatta of the Free Watermen of Greenwich, and announced itself as under the patronage of the Lord Mayor and other distinguished individuals, at whose expense, I suppose, a prize-boat was offered to the conqueror and some small amounts of money to the inferior competitors.

The aspect of London along the Thames, below Bridge, as it is called, is by no means so impressive as it ought to be, considering what peculiar advantages are offered for the display of grand and stately architecture by the passage of a river through the midst of a great city. It seems, indeed, as if the heart of London had been cleft open for the mere purpose of showing how rotten and drearily mean it had become. The shore is lined with the shabbiest, blackest, and ugliest buildings that can be imagined, decayed ware-houses, with blind windows, and wharves that look ruinous; insomuch that, had I known nothing more of the world's metropolis, I might have fancied that it had already experienced the downfal which I have heard commercial and financial prophets predict for it, within the century. And the muddy tide of the Thames, reflecting nothing, and hiding a million of unclean secrets within its breast—a sort of guilty conscience, as it were, unwholesome with the rivulets of sin that constantly flow into it—is just the dismal stream to glide by such a city. The surface, to be sure, displays no lack of activity, being fretted by the passage of a hundred steamers and covered with a good deal of shipping, but mostly of a clumsier build than I had been accustomed to see in the Mersey; a fact which I complacently attributed to the smaller number of American clippers in the Thames, and the less prevalent influence of American example in refining away the broad-bottomed capacity of the old Dutch or English models.

About midway between Greenwich and London Bridge, at a rude landing-place on the left bank of the river, the steamer rings its bell and makes a momentary pause in front of a large circular structure, where it may be worth our while to scramble ashore. It indicates the locality of one of those prodigious practical blunders that would supply John Bull with a topic of inexhaustible ridicule, if his cousin Jonathan had committed them, but of which he himself perpetrates ten to our one in the mere wantonness of wealth that lacks better employment. The circular building covers the entrance to the Thames Tunnel, and is surmounted by a dome of glass, so as to throw daylight down into the great depth at which the passage of the river commences. Descending a wearisome succession of staircases, we at last find ourselves, still in the broad noon, standing before a closed door, on opening which, we behold the vista of an arched corridor that extends into everlasting midnight. In these days, when glass has been applied to so many new purposes, it is a pity that the architect had not thought of arching portions of his abortive tunnel with immense blocks of the lucid substance, over which the dusky Thames would have flowed like a cloud, making the sub-fluvial avenue only a little gloomier than a street of upper London. At present, it is illuminated at regular intervals by jets of gas, not very brilliantly, yet with lustre enough to show the damp plaster of the ceiling and walls, and the massive stone pavement, the crevices of which are oozy with moisture, not from the incumbent river, but from hidden springs in the earth's deeper heart. There are two parallel corridors, with a wall between, for the separate accommodation of the double throng of foot-passengers, equestrians, and vehicles of all kinds, which was expected to roll and reverberate continually through the Tunnel. Only one of them has ever been opened, and its echoes are but feebly awakened by infrequent footfalls.

Yet there seem to be people who spend their lives here, and who probably blink like owls when, once or twice a year, perhaps, they happen to climb into the sunshine. All along the corridor, which I believe to be a mile in extent, we see stalls or shops, in little alcoves, kept principally by women; they were of a ripe age, I was glad to observe, and certainly robbed England of none of its very moderate supply of feminine loveliness by their deeper than tomb-like interment. As

you approach, (and they are so accustomed to the dusky
gas-light that they read all your characteristics afar off,) they
assail you with hungry entreaties to buy some of their merchandize, holding forth views of the Tunnel put up in cases
of Derbyshire spar, with a magnifying-glass at one end to
make the vista more effective. They offer you, besides, cheap
jewelry, sunny topazes and resplendent emeralds for sixpence,
and diamonds as big as the Koh-i-noor at a not much heavier
cost, together with a multifarious trumpery which has died
out of the upper world to re-appear in this tartarean bazaar.
That you may fancy yourself still in the realms of the living,
they urge you to partake of cakes, candy, ginger-beer, and
such small refreshment, more suitable, however, for the shadowy appetite of ghosts than for the sturdy stomachs of Englishmen. The most capacious of the shops contains a dioramic
exhibition of cities and scenes in the daylight world, with a
dreary glimmer of gas among them all; so that they serve well
enough to represent the dim, unsatisfactory remembrances
that dead people might be supposed to retain from their past
lives, mixing them up with the ghastliness of their unsubstantial state. I dwell the more upon these trifles, and do my best
to give them a mockery of importance, because, if these are
nothing, then all this elaborate contrivance and mighty piece
of work has been wrought in vain. The Englishman has
burrowed under the bed of his great river, and set ships of two
or three thousand tons a-rolling over his head, only to provide
new sites for a few old women to sell cakes and ginger-beer!

Yet the conception was a grand one; and though it has
proved an absolute failure, swallowing an immensity of toil
and money, with annual returns hardly sufficient to keep the
pavement free from the ooze of subterranean springs, yet it
needs, I presume, only an expenditure three or four (or, for
aught I know, twenty) times as large, to make the enterprise
brilliantly successful. The descent is so great from the bank of

the river to its surface, and the Tunnel dips so profoundly
under the river's bed, that the approaches on either side must
commence a long way off, in order to render the entrance
accessible to horsemen or vehicles; so that the larger part of
the cost of the whole affair should have been expended on its
margins. It has turned out a sublime piece of folly; and when
the New Zealander of distant ages shall have moralized sufficiently among the ruins of London Bridge, he will bethink
himself that somewhere thereabout was the marvellous Tunnel, the very existence of which will seem to him as incredible
as that of the hanging gardens of Babylon. But the Thames
will long ago have broken through the massive arch and
choked up the corridors with mud and sand, and with the
large stones of the structure itself, intermixed with skeletons
of drowned people, the rusty iron-work of sunken vessels, and
the great many such precious and curious things as a river
always contrives to hide in its bosom; the entrance will have
been obliterated and its very site forgotten beyond the memory of twenty generations of men, and the whole neighborhood be held a dangerous spot on account of the malaria;
insomuch that the traveller will make but a brief and careless
inquisition for the traces of the old wonder, and will stake his
credit before the public, in some Pacific Monthly of that day,
that the story of it is but a myth, though enriched with a
spiritual profundity which he will proceed to unfold.

Yet it is impossible, (for a Yankee, at least,) to see so much
magnificent ingenuity thrown away, without trying to endow
the unfortunate result with some kind of usefulness, though
perhaps widely different from the purpose of its original
conception. In former ages, the mile-long corridors with their
numerous alcoves might have been utilized as a series of
dungeons, the fittest of all possible receptacles for prisoners of
state. Dethroned monarchs and fallen statesmen would not
have needed to remonstrate against a domicile so spacious, so

deeply secluded from the world's scorn, and so admirably in
accordance with their thenceforward sunless fortunes. An
alcove here might have suited Sir Walter Raleigh better than
that darksome hiding-place, communicating with the great
chamber in the Tower, pacing from end to end of which, he
meditated upon his History of the World. His track would
here have been straight and narrow, indeed, and would therefore have lacked somewhat of the freedom that his intellect
demanded; and yet the length to which his footsteps might
have travelled forth and re-traced themselves would partly
have harmonized his physical movement with the grand
curves and planetary returns of his thought, through cycles of
majestic periods. Having it in his mind to compose the world's
history, methinks he could have asked no better retirement
than such a cloister as this, insulated from all the seductions
of mankind and womankind, deep beneath their mysteries
and motives, down into the heart of things, full of personal
reminiscences in order to the comprehensive measurement
and verification of historic records, seeing into the secrets of
human nature—secrets that daylight never yet revealed to
mortal—but detecting their whole scope and purport with the
infallible eyes of unbroken solitude and night. And then the
shades of the old mighty men might have risen from their still
profounder abodes and joined him in the dim corridor, treading beside him with an antique stateliness of mien, telling him
in melancholy tones, grand, but always melancholy, of the
greater ideas and purposes which their most renowned performances so imperfectly carried out, that, magnificent suc-
cesses in the view of all posterity, they were but failures to
those who planned them. As Raleigh was a navigator, Noah
would have explained to him the peculiarities of construction
that made the ark so seaworthy; as Raleigh was a statesman,
Moses would have discussed with him the principles of laws
and government; as Raleigh was a soldier, Caesar and Hanni-

bal would have held debate in his presence, with this martial student for their umpire; as Raleigh was a poet, David, or whatever most illustrious bard he might call up, would have touched his harp, and made manifest all the true significance of the Past by means of song and the subtile intelligences of music.

Meanwhile, I had forgotten that Sir Walter Raleigh's century knew nothing of gas-light, and that it would require a prodigious and wasteful expenditure of tallow-candles to illuminate the Tunnel sufficiently to discern even a ghost. On this account, however, it would be all the more suitable place of confinement for a metaphysician, to keep him from bewildering mankind with his shadowy speculations; and, being shut off from external converse, the dark corridor would help him to make rich discoveries in those cavernous regions and mysterious by-paths of the intellect, which he had so long accustomed himself to explore. But how would every successive age rejoice in so secure a habitation for its reformers, and especially for each best and wisest man that happened to be then alive! He seeks to burn up our whole system of society, under pretence of purifying it from its abuses! Away with him into the Tunnel, and let him begin by setting the Thames on fire, if he is able! If not precisely these, yet akin to these were some of the fantasies that haunted me as I passed under the river; for the place is suggestive of such idle and irresponsible stuff by its own abortive character, its lack of whereabout on upper earth, or any solid foundation of realities. Could I have looked forward a few years, I might have regretted that American enterprise had not provided a similar Tunnel, under the Hudson or the Potomac, for the convenience of our National Government in times hardly yet gone by. It would be delightful to clap up all the enemies of our peace and union in the dark together, and there let them abide, listening to the monotonous roll of the river above their heads, or perhaps in a state of miraculously suspended animation, until—be it after months, years, or centuries—when the turmoil shall be all over, the Wrong washed away in blood, (since that must needs be the cleansing fluid,) and the Right firmly rooted in the soil which that blood will have enriched, they might crawl forth again and catch a single glimpse at their redeemed country, and feel it to be a better land than they deserve, and die!

I was not sorry when the daylight reached me after a much briefer abode in the nether regions than, I fear, would await the troublesome personages just hinted at. Emerging on the Surrey side of the Thames, I found myself in Rotherhithe, a neighborhood not unfamiliar to the readers of old books of maritime adventure. There being a ferry hard by the mouth of the Tunnel, I recrossed the river in the primitive fashion of an open boat, which the conflict of wind and tide, together with the swash and swell of the passing steamers, tossed high and low rather tumultuously. This inquietude of our frail skiff (which, indeed, bobbed up and down like a cork) so much alarmed an old lady, the only other passenger, that the boatmen essayed to comfort her. "Never fear, mother!" grumbled one of them. "We'll make the river as smooth as we can for you. We'll get a plane and plane down the waves!" The joke may not read very brilliantly; but I make bold to record it as the only specimen that reached my ears of the old, rough water-wit, for which the Thames used to be so celebrated. Passing directly along the line of the sunken Tunnel, we landed in Wapping, which I should have pre-supposed to be the most tarry and pitchy spot on earth, swarming with old salts, and full of warm, bustling, coarse, homely, and cheerful life. Nevertheless, it turned out to be a cold and torpid neighborhood, mean, shabby, and unpicturesque, both as to its buildings and inhabitants; the latter comprising (so far as was visible to me) not a single unmistakeable sailor, though plenty of land-sharks who get a half-dishonest livelihood by business connected with the sea. Ale-and-spirit vaults (as petty drinking-establishments are styled in England, pretending to contain vast cellars full of liquor within the compass of ten-feet square above-ground) were particularly abundant, together with apples, oranges, and oysters, the stalls of fish-mongers and butchers, and slop-shops, where blue jackets and duck trowsers swung and capered before the doors. Everything was on the poorest scale, and the place bore an aspect of unredeemable decay. From this remote point of London, I strolled leisurely towards the heart of the city, while the streets, at first but thinly occupied by man or vehicle, got more and more thronged with foot-passengers, carts, drays, cabs, and the all-pervading and all-accommodating omnibus. But I lack courage, and feel that I should lack perseverance, as the gentlest reader would lack patience, to undertake a descriptive stroll through London-streets; more especially as there would be a volume ready for the printer before we could reach a mid-way resting-place at Charing Cross. It will be the easier course to step aboard another passing steamer, and continue our trip up the Thames.

The next notable group of objects is an assemblage of ancient walls, battlements, and turrets, out of the midst of which rises prominently one great square tower, of a grayish hue bordered with white stone, and having a small turret at each corner of the roof. This central structure is the White Tower, and the whole circuit of ramparts and enclosed edifices constitutes what is known in English history, and still more widely and impressively in English poetry, as the Tower. A crowd of river-craft are generally moored in front of it; but, if we look sharply at the right moment under the base of the rampart, we may catch a glimpse of an arched water-entrance, half-submerged, past which the Thames glides as indifferently as if it were the mouth of a city-kennel. Never-

theless, it is the Traitor's Gate, a dreary kind of triumphal passage-way (now supposed to be shut up and barred forever)
through which a multitude of noble and illustrious personages have entered the Tower and found it a brief resting-place
on their way to Heaven. Passing it many times, I never
observed that anybody glanced at this shadowy and ominous
trap-door, save myself. It is well that America exists, if it were
only that her vagrant children may be impressed and affected
by the historical monuments of England in a degree of which
the native inhabitants are evidently incapable. These matters
are too familiar, too real, and too hopelessly built in amongst
and mixed up with the common objects and affairs of life, to
be easily susceptible of imaginative coloring in their minds;
and even their poets and romancers feel it a toil, and almost a
delusion, to extract poetic material out of what seems embodied poetry itself to an American. An Englishman cares nothing about the Tower, which to us is a haunted castle in
dream-land. That honest and excellent gentleman, the late
Mr. G. P. R. James, (whose mechanical ability, one might
have supposed, would nourish itself by devouring every old
stone of such a structure,) once assured me that he had never
in his life set eyes upon the Tower, though for years a historic
novelist in London.

Not to spend a whole summer's day upon the voyage, we
will suppose ourselves to have reached London Bridge, and
thence to have taken another steamer for a further passage up
the river. But here the memorable objects succeed each other
so rapidly that I can spare but a single sentence even for the
great Dome, though I deem it more picturesque, in that dusky
atmosphere, than Saint Peter's in its clear blue sky. I must
mention, however, (since everything connected with royalty
is especially interesting to my dear countrymen,) that I once
saw a large and beautiful barge, splendidly gilded and ornamented, and overspread with a rich awning, lying at the pier

nearest to Saint Paul's Cathedral; it had the royal banner of Great Britain displayed, besides being decorated with a number of other flags; and many footmen (who are universally the grandest and gaudiest objects to be seen in England at this day—and these were regal ones, in a bright scarlet livery, bedizened with gold lace, and white silk stockings) were in attendance. I know not what festive or ceremonial occasion may have drawn out this pageant; after all, it might have been merely a city-spectacle appertaining to the Lord Mayor; but the sight had its value in bringing vividly before me the grand old times, when the sovereign and nobles were accustomed to use the Thames as the high street of the metropolis and join in pompous processions upon it; whereas, the desuetude of such customs, now-a-days, has caused the whole show of river-life to consist in a multitude of smoke-begrimed steamers. An analogous change has taken place in the streets, where cabs and the omnibus have crowded out a rich variety of vehicles; and thus life gets more monotonous in hue from age to age, and appears to seize every opportunity to strip off a bit of its gold lace among the wealthier classes, and to make itself decent in the lower ones.

Yonder is Whitefriars, the old rowdy Alsatia, now wearing as decorous a face as any other portion of London; and, adjoining it, the avenues and brick squares of the Temple, with that historic garden, close upon the river-side and still rich in shrubbery and flowers, where the partizans of York and Lancaster plucked the fatal roses, and scattered their pale and bloody petals over so many English battle-fields. Hard by, we see the long white front or rear of Somerset House, and, further on, rise the two new Houses of Parliament, with a huge unfinished tower already hiding its imperfect summit in the smoky canopy—the whole vast and cumbrous edifice a specimen of the best that modern architecture can effect, elaborately imitating the master-pieces of those simple ages when men "builded better than they knew." Close by it, we have a glimpse of the roof and upper towers of the holy Abbey; while that gray, ancestral pile, on the opposite side of the river, is Lambeth palace, a venerable group of halls and turrets, chiefly built of brick, but with at least one large tower of stone. In our course, we have passed beneath half-a-dozen bridges, and emerging out of the black heart of London, shall soon reach a cleanly suburb, where old Father Thames, if I remember, begins to put on an aspect of unpolluted innocence. And now we look back upon the mass of innumerable roofs, out of which rise steeples, towers, columns, and the great crowning Dome—look back, in short, upon that mystery of the world's proudest city, amid which a man so longs and loves to be; not, perhaps, because it contains much that is positively admirable and enjoyable, but because at all events the world has nothing better, the cream of external life is there, and whatever merely intellectual or material good we fail to find perfect in London, we may as well content ourselves to seek that unattainable thing no further on this earth.

The steamer terminates its trip at Chelsea, an old town endowed with a prodigious number of pot-houses, and some famous gardens, called the Cremorne, for public amusement. The most noticeable thing, however, is Chelsea Hospital, which, like that of Greenwich, was founded, I believe, by Charles the Second, (whose bronze statue in the guise of an old Roman, stands in the centre of the quadrangle,) and appropriated as a home for aged and infirm soldiers of the British army. The edifices are of three stories with windows in the high roofs, and are built of dark, sombre brick, with stone edgings and facings. The effect is by no means that of grandeur, (which is somewhat disagreeably an attribute of Greenwich Hospital,) but a quiet and venerable neatness. At each extremity of the street-front there is a spacious and hospitably open gateway, lounging about which I saw some gray veterans in long scarlet coats, of an antique fashion, and the cocked hats of a century ago, or occasionally a modern foraging cap. Almost all of them moved with a rheumatic gait; two or three stumped on wooden legs, and here and there an arm was missing. Inquiring of one of these fragmentary heroes whether a stranger could be admitted to see the establishment, he replied most cordially—"Oh yes, Sir, anywhere! Walk in and go where you please—up stairs or anywhere!" So I entered, and passing along the inner side of the quadrangle, came to the door of the Chapel, which forms a part of the contiguity of edifices next the street. Here another pensioner, an old warrior of exceedingly peaceable and Christian demeanor, touched his three-cornered hat and asked if I wished to see the interior; to which I assenting, he unlocked the door, and we went in.

The Chapel consists of a great hall with a vaulted roof, and over the altar is a large painting in fresco, the subject of which I did not trouble myself to make out. More appropriate adornments of the place, dedicated as well to martial reminiscences as religious worship, are the long ranges of dusty and tattered banners that hang from their staves all round the ceiling of the Chapel. They are trophies of battles fought and won in every quarter of the world, comprising the captured flags of all the nations with whom the British lion has waged war since James the Second's time—French, Dutch, East Indian, Prussian, Russian, Chinese, and American—collected together in this consecrated spot, not to symbolize that there shall be no more discord upon earth, but drooping over the aisle in sullen, though peaceable humiliation. Yes; I said "American," among the rest; for the good old pensioner mistook me for an Englishman, and failed not to point out (and, methought, with an especial emphasis of triumph) some flags that had been taken at Bladensburgh and Washington. I fancied, indeed, that they hung a little higher and drooped a little lower than any of their companions in disgrace. It is a comfort, however, that their proud devices are already indistinguishable, or nearly so, owing to dust and tatters, and the kind offices of the moths, and that they will soon rot from the banner-staves and be swept out in unrecognized fragments from the chapel-door.

It is a good method of teaching a man how imperfectly cosmopolitan he is, to show him his country's flag occupying a position of dishonor in a foreign land. But, in truth, the whole system of a people crowing over its military triumphs had far better be dispensed with, both on account of the ill-blood that it helps to keep fermenting among the nations, and because it operates as an accumulative inducement to future generations to aim at a kind of glory, the gain of which has generally proved more ruinous than its loss. I heartily wish that every trophy of victory might crumble away, and that every reminiscence or tradition of a hero, from the beginning of the world to this day, could pass out of all men's memories at once and forever. I might feel very differently, to be sure, if we Northerners had anything especially valuable to lose by the fading of those illuminated names.

I gave the pensioner (but I am afraid there may have been a little affectation in it) a magnificent guerdon of all the silver I had in my pocket, to requite him for having unintentionally stirred up my patriotic susceptibilities. He was a meek-looking, kindly old man, with a humble freedom and affability of manner that made it pleasant to converse with him. Old soldiers, I know not why, seem to be more accostable than old sailors. One is apt to hear a growl beneath the smoothest courtesy of the latter. The mild veteran, with his peaceful voice and gentle, reverend aspect, told me that he had fought at a cannon all through the battle of Waterloo, and escaped unhurt; he had now been in the Hospital four or five years, and was married, but necessarily underwent a separation from his wife, who lived outside of the gates. To my inquiry whether his fellow-pensioners were comfortable and happy, he answered with great alacrity—"Oh, yes, Sir!"—qualifying his evidence, after a moment's consideration, by saying in an undertone—"There are some people, your Honor knows, who could not be comfortable anywhere." I did know it, and fear that the system of Chelsea Hospital allows too little of that wholesome care and regulation of their own occupations and interests, which might assuage the sting of life to those naturally uncomfortable individuals by giving them something external to think about. But my old friend here was happy in the Hospital, and by this time, very likely, is happy in Heaven, in spite of the bloodshed that he may have caused by touching off a cannon at Waterloo.

Crossing Battersea Bridge, in the neighborhood of Chelsea, I remember seeing a distant gleam of the Crystal Palace, glimmering afar in the afternoon sunshine like an imaginary structure—an air-castle by chance descended upon earth and resting there one instant before it vanished, as we sometimes see a soap-bubble touch unharmed on the carpet—a thing of only momentary visibility and no substance, destined to be overburdened and crushed down by the first cloud-shadow that might fall upon that spot. Even as I looked, it disappeared. Shall I attempt a picture of this exhalation of modern ingenuity, or what else shall I try to paint? Everything in London and its vicinity, has been depicted innumerable times, but never once translated into intelligible images; it is an 'Old, old Story,' never yet told, nor to be told. While writing these reminiscences, I am continually impressed with the futility of the effort to give any creative truth to my sketch, so that it might produce such pictures in the reader's mind as would cause the original scenes to appear familiar, when afterwards beheld. Nor have other writers often been more successful in representing definite objects prophetically to my own mind.

In truth, I believe that the chief delight and advantage of this kind of literature is not for any real information that it supplies to untravelled people, but for reviving the recollections and re-awakening the emotions of persons already acquainted with the scenes described. Thus I found an exquisite pleasure, the other day, in reading Mr. Tuckerman's "Month in England"—a fine example of the way in which a refined and cultivated American looks at the Old Country, the things that he naturally seeks there, and the modes of feeling and reflection which they excite. Correct outlines avail little or nothing, though truth of coloring may be somewhat more efficacious. Impressions, however, states of mind produced by interesting and remarkable objects, these, if truthfully and vividly recorded, may work a genuine effect, and, though but the result of what we see, go further towards representing the actual scene than any direct effort to paint it. Give the emotions that cluster about it, and, without being able to analyze the spell by which it is summoned up, you get something like a simulacrum of the object in the midst of them. From some of the above reflections, I draw the comfortable inference, that the longer and better known a thing may be, so much the more eligible is it as the subject of a descriptive sketch.

On a Sunday afternoon, I passed through a side-entrance in the time-blackened wall of a place of worship, and found myself among a congregation assembled in one of the transepts and the immediately contiguous portion of the nave. It was a vast old edifice, spacious enough, within the extent covered by its pillared roof and overspread by its stone pavement, to accommodate the whole of church-going London, and with a far wider and loftier concave than any human power of lungs could fill with audible prayer. Oaken benches were arranged in the transept, on one of which I seated myself, and joined, as well as I knew how, in the sacred business that was going forward. But, when it came to the sermon, the voice of the preacher was puny, and so were his thoughts, and both seemed impertinent at such a time and place, when he and all of us were bodily included within a sublime act of religion which could be seen above and around us, and felt beneath our feet. The structure itself was the worship of the devout men of long ago, miraculously preserved in stone without losing an atom of its fragrance and fervor; it was a kind of anthem-strain that they had sung and poured out of the organ in centuries gone by, and being so grand and sweet, the Divine benevolence had willed it to be prolonged for the behoof of auditors unborn. I therefore came to the conclusion, that, in my individual case, it would be better and more reverent to let my eyes wander about the edifice, than to fasten them and my thoughts on the evidently uninspired mortal who was venturing—and felt it no venture at all—to speak here above his breath.

The interior of Westminster Abbey (for the reader recognized it, no doubt, the moment we entered) is built of rich brown stone, and the whole of it—the lofty roof, the tall clustered pillars, and the pointed arches—appears to be in consummate repair. At all points where decay has laid its finger, the structure is clamped with iron or otherwise carefully protected; and being thus watched over—whether as a place of ancient sanctity, a noble specimen of Gothic art, or an object of national interest and pride—it may reasonably be expected to survive for as many ages as have passed over it already. It was sweet to feel its venerable quietude, its long-enduring peace, and yet to observe how kindly and even cheerfully it received the sunshine of to-day, which fell from the great windows into the fretted aisles and arches that laid aside somewhat of their aged gloom to welcome it. Sunshine always seems friendly to old abbeys, churches, and castles, kissing them, as it were, with a more affectionate, though still reverential familiarity, than it accords to edifices of later date.

A square of golden light lay on the sombre pavement of the nave, afar off, falling through the grand western entrance, the folding leaves of which were wide open and afforded glimpses of people passing to-and-fro in the outer world, while we sat dimly enveloped in the solemnity of antique devotion. In the south transept, separated from us by the full breadth of the minster, there were painted glass windows, of which the uppermost appeared to be a great orb of many-colored radiance, being, indeed, a cluster of Saints and Angels whose glorified bodies formed the rays of an aureole emanating from a cross in the midst. These windows are modern, but combine softness with wonderful brilliancy of effect. Through the pillars and arches, I saw that the walls, in that distant region of the edifice, were almost wholly encrusted with marble, now grown yellow with time, no blank, unlettered slabs, but memorials of such men as their respective generations deemed wisest and bravest. Some of them were commemorated merely by inscriptions on mural tablets, others by sculptured bas-reliefs, others (once famous but now forgotten generals or admirals, these) by ponderous tombs that aspired towards the roof of the aisle or partly curtained the immense arch of a window. These mountains of marble were peopled with the sisterhood of Allegory, winged trumpeters, and classic figures in full-bottomed wigs; but it was strange to observe how the old Abbey melted all such absurdities into the breadth of its own grandeur, even magnifying itself by what would elsewhere have been ridiculous. Methinks it is the test of Gothic sublimity to overpower the Ridiculous without deigning to hide it; and these grotesque monuments of the last century answer a similar purpose with the grinning faces which the old architects scattered among their most solemn conceptions.

From these distant wanderings, (it was my first visit to Westminster Abbey, and I would gladly have taken it all in at a glance,) my eyes came back and began to investigate what

was immediately about me in the transept. Close at my elbow
was the pedestal of Canning's statue. Next beyond it was a
massive tomb, on the spacious tablet of which reposed the full-
length figures of a marble lord and lady whom an inscription
announced to be the Duke and Duchess of Newcastle; the
historic Duke of Charles the First's time, and the fantastic
Duchess, traditionally remembered by her poems and plays.
She was of a family, as the record on her tomb proudly
informed us, of which all the brothers had been valiant, and
all the sisters virtuous. A recent statue of Sir John Malcolm,
the new marble as white as snow, held the next place; and
near by was a mural monument and bust of Sir Peter Warren.
The round visage of this old British admiral has a certain
interest for a New Englander, because it was by no merit of
his own, (though he took care to assume it as such,) but by
the valor and warlike enterprise of our colonial forefathers,
especially the stout men of Massachusetts, that he won rank
and renown, and a tomb in Westminster Abbey. Lord Mans-
field, a huge mass of marble done into the guise of a judicial
gown and wig, with a stern face in the midst of the latter, sat
on the other side of the transept; and on the pedestal beside
him was a figure of Justice, holding forth, instead of the
customary grocer's scales, an actual pair of brass steelyards. It
is an ancient and classic instrument, undoubtedly, but I had
supposed that Portia (when Shylock's pound of flesh was to
be weighed) was the only judge that ever really called for it
in a court of justice. Pitt and Fox were in the same distinguished company; and John Kemble, in Roman costume,
stood not far off, but strangely shorn of the dignity that is said
to have enveloped him like a mantle in his lifetime. Perhaps
the evanescent majesty of the stage is incompatible with the
long endurance of marble and the solemn reality of the tomb;
though, on the other hand, almost every illustrious personage,
here represented, has been invested with more or less of

stage-trickery by his sculptor. In truth, the artist (unless there be a divine efficacy in his touch making evident a heretofore hidden dignity in the actual form) feels it an imperious law to remove his subject as far from the aspect of ordinary life as may be possible, without sacrificing every trace of resemblance. The absurd effect of the contrary course is very remarkable in the statue of Mr. Wilberforce, whose actual self save for the lack of color, I seemed to behold, seated just across the aisle.

This excellent man appears to have sunk into himself in a sitting posture, with a thin leg crossed over his knee, a book in one hand, and a finger of the other under his chin, I believe, or applied to the side of his nose, or to some equally familiar purpose; while his exceedingly homely and wrinkled face, held a little on one side, twinkles at you with the shrewdest complacency, as if he were looking right into your eyes and twigged something there which you had half a mind to conceal from him. He keeps this look so pertinaciously that you feel it to be insufferably impertinent, and bethink yourself what common ground there may be between yourself and a stone image, enabling you to resent it. I have no doubt that the statue is as like Mr. Wilberforce as one pea to another; and you might fancy that, at some ordinary moment, when he least expected it, and before he had time to smoothe away his knowing complication of wrinkles, he had seen the Gorgon's head and whitened into marble—not only his personal self but his coat and small-clothes, down to a button and the minutest crease of the cloth. The ludicrous result marks the impropriety of bestowing the age-long duration of marble upon small, characteristic individualities, such as might come within the province of waxen imagery. The sculptor should give permanence to the figure of a great man in his mood of broad and grand composure which would obliterate all mean peculiarities; for, if the original were unaccustomed to such a mood, or if his features were incapable of assuming the guise, it seems questionable whether he could really have been entitled to a marble immortality. In point of fact, however, the English face and form are seldom statuesque, however illustrious the individual.

It ill becomes me, perhaps, to have lapsed into this mood of half-jocose criticism in describing my first visit to Westminster Abbey, a spot which I had dreamed about more reverentially, from my childhood upward, than any other in the world, and which I then beheld, and now look back upon, with profound gratitude to the men who built it, and a kindly interest, I may add, in the humblest personage that has contributed his little all to its impressiveness, by depositing his dust or his memory there. But it is a characteristic of this grand edifice that it permits you to smile as freely under the roof of its central nave as if you stood beneath the yet grander canopy of heaven. Break into laughter if you feel inclined, provided the vergers do not hear it echoing among the arches. In an ordinary church, you would keep your countenance for fear of disturbing the sanctities or proprieties of the place; but you need leave no honest and decorous portion of your human nature outside of these benign and truly hospitable walls. Their mild awfulness will take care of itself. Thus it does no harm to the general impression, when you come to be sensible that many of the monuments are ridiculous, and commemorate a mob of people who are mostly forgotten in their graves, and few of whom ever deserved any better boon from posterity. You acknowledge the force of Sir Godfrey Kneller's objection to being buried in Westminster Abbey, because "they do bury fools there!" Nevertheless, these grotesque carvings of marble, that break out in dingy-white blotches on the old freestone of the interior walls, have come there by as natural a process as might cause mosses and ivy to cluster about the external edifice; for they are the historical and biographical record of each successive age, written with its own hand, and all the truer for the inevitable mistakes, and none the less solemn for the occasional absurdity. Though you entered the Abbey expecting to see the tombs only of the illustrious, you are content, at last, to read many names both in literature and history that have now lost the reverence of mankind, if indeed they ever really possessed it. Let these men rest in peace. Even if you miss a name or two that you hoped to find there, they may well be spared. It matters little a few more or less, or whether Westminster Abbey contains or lacks any one man's grave, so long as the Centuries, each with the crowd of personages that it deemed memorable, have chosen it as their place of honored sepulture and laid themselves down under its pavement. The inscriptions and devices on the walls are rich with evidences of the fluctuating tastes, fashions, manners, opinions, prejudices, follies, wisdoms of the Past, and thus they combine into a more truthful memorial of their dead times than any individual epitaph-maker ever meant to write.

When the services were over, many of the audience seemed inclined to linger in the nave or wander away among the mysterious aisles; for there is nothing in this world so fascinating as a Gothic minster, which always invites you deeper and deeper into its heart both by vast revelations and shadowy concealments. Through the open-work screen that divides the nave from the chancel and choir, we could discern the gleam of a marvellous window, but were debarred from entrance into that more sacred precinct of the Abbey by the vergers. These vigilant officials (doing their duty all the more strenuously because no fees could be exacted from Sunday visitors) flourished their staves and drove us towards the grand entrance like a flock of sheep. Lingering through one of the aisles, I happened to look down and found my foot upon a stone, inscribed with this familiar exclamation—O RARE BEN

JONSON!—and remembered the story of stout old Ben's burial in that spot, standing upright;—not, I presume, on account of any unseemly reluctance on his part to lie down in the dust, like other men, but because standing-room was all that could reasonably be demanded for a poet, among the slumberous notabilities of his age. It made me weary to think of it!—such a prodigious length of time to keep one's feet!—apart from the honor of the thing, it would certainly have been better for Ben to stretch himself at ease in some country-churchyard. To this day, however, I fancy that there is a contemptuous alloy mixed up with the admiration, which the higher classes of English society profess for their literary men.

Another day—in truth, many other days—I sought out Poet's Corner, and found a sign-board and pointed finger, directing the visitor to it, on the corner-house of a little lane leading towards the rear of the Abbey. The entrance is at the south-eastern end of the south transept, and it is used, on ordinary occasions, as the only free mode of access to the building. It is no spacious arch, but a small, lowly door, passing through which, and pushing aside an inner screen that partly keeps out an exceedingly chill wind, you find yourself in a dim nook of the Abbey, with the busts of poets gazing at you from the otherwise bare stone-work of the walls. Great poets, too; for Ben Jonson is right behind the door, and Spenser's tablet is next, and Butler's on the same side of the transept, and Milton's (whose bust you know at once by its resemblance to one of his portraits, though older, more wrinkled, and sadder, than that) is close by, and a profile medallion of Gray beneath it. A window high aloft sheds down a dusky daylight on these and many other sculptured marbles, now as yellow as old parchment, that cover the three walls of the nook up to an elevation of about twenty feet above the pavement. It seemed to me that I had always been familiar with the spot. Enjoying a humble intimacy—and how much of my life had else been a dreary solitude!—with many of its inhabitants, I could not feel myself a stranger there. It was delightful to be among them. There was a genial awe, mingled with a sense of kind and friendly presences about me; and I was glad, moreover, at finding so many of them there together, in fit companionship, mutually recognized and duly honored, all reconciled now, whatever distant generations, whatever personal hostility or other miserable impediment, had divided them far asunder while they lived. I have never felt a similar interest in any other tombstones, nor have I ever been deeply moved by the imaginary presence of other famous dead people. A poet's ghost is the only one that survives for his fellow-mortals, after his bones are in the dust—and he not ghostly, but cherishing many hearts with his own warmth in the chillest atmosphere of life. What other fame is worth aspiring for? Or, let me speak it more boldly, what other long-enduring fame can exist! We neither remember nor care anything for the past, except as the poet has made it intelligibly noble and sublime to our comprehension. The shades of the mighty have no substance; they flit ineffectually about the darkened stage where they performed their momentary parts, save when the poet has thrown his own creative soul into them, and imparted a more vivid life than ever they were able to manifest to mankind, while they dwelt in the body. And therefore—though he cunningly disguises himself in their armor, their robes of state, or kingly purple—it is not the statesman, the warrior, or the monarch that survives, but the despised poet whom they may have fed with their crumbs, and to whom they owe all that they now are or have—a name!

In the foregoing paragraph, I seem to have been betrayed into a flight above or beyond the customary level that best agrees with me, but it represents fairly enough the emotions with which I passed from Poet's Corner into the chapels, which contain the sepulchres of Kings and great people. They are magnificent, even now, and must have been inconceivably so when the marble slabs and pillars wore their new polish, and the statues retained the brilliant colors with which they were originally painted, and the shrines their rich gilding, of which the sunlight still shows a glimmer or a streak, though the sunbeam itself looks tarnished with antique dust. Yet this recondite portion of the Abbey presents few memorials of personages whom we care to remember. The shrine of Edward the Confessor has a certain interest, because it was so long held in religious reverence, and because the very dust that settled upon it was formerly worth gold. The helmet and war-saddle of Henry the Fifth, worn at Azincourt and now suspended above his tomb, are memorable objects, but more for Shakspere's sake than the victor's own. Rank has been the general passport to admission here. Noble and regal dust is as cheap as dirt under the pavement. I am glad to recollect, indeed, (and it is too characteristic of the right English spirit not to be mentioned,) one or two gigantic statues of great mechanicians who contributed largely to the material welfare of England, sitting familiarly in their marble chairs among forgotten Kings and Queens. Otherwise, the quaintness of the earlier monuments, and the antique beauty of some of them, are what chiefly gives them value. Nevertheless, Addison is buried among the men of rank; not on the plea of his literary fame, however, but because he was connected with nobility by marriage and had been a Secretary of State. His gravestone is inscribed with a resounding verse from Tickell's lines to his memory, the only lines by which Tickell himself is now remembered, and which (as I discovered, a little while ago) he mainly filched from an obscure versifier of somewhat earlier date.

Returning to Poet's Corner, I looked again at the walls, and wondered how the requisite hospitality can be shown to poets of our own and the succeeding ages. There is hardly a foot of space left, although room has lately been found for a bust of Southey and a full-length statue of Campbell. At best, only a little portion of the Abbey is dedicated to poets, literary men, musical composers, and others of the gentle artist-breed, and even into that small nook of sanctity, men of other pursuits have thought it decent to intrude themselves. Methinks the tuneful throng, being at home here, should recollect how they were treated in their lifetime, and turn the cold shoulder, looking askance at nobles and official personages, however worthy of honorable interment elsewhere. Yet it shows aptly and truly enough what portion of the world's regard and honor has heretofore been awarded to literary eminence in comparison with other modes of greatness—this dimly lighted corner (nor even that quietly to themselves) in the vast Minster, the walls of which are sheathed and hidden under marble that has been wasted upon the illustrious obscure. Nevertheless, it may not be worth while to quarrel with the world on this account; for, to confess the very truth, their own little nook contains more than one poet whose memory is kept alive by his monument, instead of imbuing the senseless stone with a spiritual immortality—men of whom you do not ask, 'Where is he?'—but 'Why is he here?' I estimate that all the literary people who really make an essential part of one's inner life, including the period since English literature first existed, might have ample elbow-room to sit down and quaff their draughts of Castaly round Chaucer's broad, horizontal tombstone. These divinest poets consecrate the spot and throw a reflected glory over the humblest of their companions. And as for the latter, it is to be hoped that they may have long outgrown the characteristic jealousies and morbid sensibilities of their craft, and have found out the little value (probably not amounting to sixpence in immortal currency) of the posthumous renown which they once aspired to win. It would be a poor compliment to a dead poet to fancy him leaning out of the sky, and snuffing up the impure breath of earthly praise.

Yet we cannot easily rid ourselves of the notion that those, who have bequeathed us the inheritance of an undying song, would fain be conscious of its endless reverberations in the hearts of mankind, and would delight, among sublimer enjoyments, to see their names emblazoned in such a treasure-place of great memories as Westminster Abbey. There are some men, at all events—true and tender poets, moreover, and fully deserving of the honor—whose spirits, I feel certain, would linger a little while about Poet's Corner for the sake of witnessing their own apotheosis among their kindred. They have had a strong natural yearning, not so much for applause as sympathy, which the cold fortune of their lifetime did but scantily supply; so that this unsatisfied appetite may make itself felt upon sensibilities at once so delicate and retentive, even a step or two beyond the grave. Leigh Hunt, for example, would be pleased, even now, if he could learn that his bust had been reposited in the midst of the old poets whom he admired and loved; though there is hardly a man among the authors of to-day and yesterday, whom the judgment of Englishmen would be less likely to place there. He deserves it, however, if not for his verse, (the value of which I do not estimate, never having been able to read it,) yet for his delightful prose, his unmeasured poetry, the inscrutable happiness of his touch, working soft miracles by a life-process like the growth of grass and flowers. As with all such gentle writers, his page sometimes betrayed a vestige of affectation, but, the next moment, a rich natural luxuriance overgrew and buried it out of sight. I knew him a little, and (since, Heaven be praised, few English celebrities, whom I chanced to meet, have enfranchised my pen by their decease, and as I assume no liberties with living men) I will conclude this

rambling article by sketching my first interview with Leigh
Hunt.

He was then at Hammersmith, occupying a very plain and
shabby little house, in a contiguous range of others like it,
with no prospect but that of an ugly village-street, and certainly nothing to gratify his craving for a tasteful environment, inside or out. A slatternly maid-servant opened the door
for us, and he himself stood in the entry, a beautiful and
venerable old man, buttoned to the chin in a black dress-coat,
tall and slender, with a countenance quietly alive all over, and
the gentlest and most naturally courteous manner. He ushered us into his little study, or parlor, or both—a very forlorn
room, with poor paper-hangings and carpet, few books, no
pictures that I remember, and an awful lack of upholstery. I
touch distinctly upon these external blemishes and this nudity
of adornment, not that they would be worth mentioning in a
sketch of other remarkable persons, but because Leigh Hunt
was born with such a faculty of enjoying all beautiful things
that it seemed as if Fortune did him as much wrong in not
supplying them, as in withholding a sufficiency of vital breath
from ordinary men. All kinds of mild magnificence, tempered
by his taste, would have become him well, but he had not the
grim dignity that assumes nakedness as the better robe.

I have said that he was a beautiful old man. In truth, I
never saw a finer countenance, either as to the mould of
features or the expression, nor any that showed the play of
feeling so perfectly without the slightest theatrical emphasis.
It was like a child's face in this respect. At my first glimpse of
him, when he met us in the entry, I discerned that he was old,
his long hair being white and his wrinkles many; it was an
aged visage, in short, such as I had not at all expected to see,
in spite of dates, because his books talk to the reader with the
tender vivacity of youth. But when he began to speak, and as

he grew more earnest in conversation, I ceased to be sensible of his age; sometimes, indeed, its dusky shadow darkened through the gleam which his sprightly thoughts diffused about his face, but then another flash of youth came out of his eyes and made an illumination again. I never witnessed such a wonderfully illusive transformation, before or since; and, to this day, trusting only to my recollection, I should find it difficult to decide which was his genuine and stable predicament—youth or age. I have met no Englishman whose manners seemed to me so agreeable—soft, rather than polished, wholly unconventional, the natural growth of a kindly and sensitive disposition without any reference to rule, or else obedient to some rule so subtile that the nicest observer could not detect the application of it.

His eyes were dark and very fine, and his delightful voice accompanied their visible language like music. He appeared to be exceedingly appreciative of whatever was passing among those who surrounded him, and especially of the vicissitudes in the consciousness of the person to whom he happened to be addressing himself at the moment. I felt that no effect upon my mind of what he uttered, no emotion however transitory in myself, escaped his notice, though not from any positive vigilance on his part, but because his faculty of observation was so penetrative and delicate; and to say the truth, it a little confused me to discern always a ripple on his mobile face, responsive to any slightest breeze that passed over the inner reservoir of my sentiments, and seemed thence to extend to a similar reservoir within himself. On matters of feeling, and within a certain depth, you might spare yourself the trouble of utterance, because he already knew what you wanted to say, and perhaps a little more than you would have spoken. His figure was full of gentle movement, though, somehow, without disturbing its quietude; and as he talked, he kept folding his hands nervously, and betokened in many ways a fine and immediate sensibility, quick to feel pleasure or pain, though scarcely capable, I should imagine, of a passionate experience in either direction. There was not an English trait in him from head to foot, morally, intellectually, or physically. Beef, ale, or stout, brandy, or port-wine, entered not at all into his composition. In his earlier life, he appears to have given evidences of courage and sturdy principle, and of a tendency to fling himself into the rough struggle of humanity on the liberal side. It would be taking too much upon myself to affirm that this was merely a projection of his fancy-world into the actual, and that he never could have hit a downright blow, and was altogether an unsuitable person to receive one. I beheld him not in his armor, but in his peacefullest robes. Nevertheless, drawing my conclusion merely from what I saw, it would have occurred to me that his main deficiency was a lack of grit. Though anything but a timid man, the combative and defensive elements were not prominently developed in his character, and could have been made available only when he put an unnatural force upon his instincts. It was on this account, and also because of the fineness of his nature generally, that the English appreciated him no better, and left this sweet and delicate poet poor, and with scanty laurels in his declining age.

It was not, I think, from his American blood that Leigh Hunt derived either his amiability or his peaceful inclinations; at least, I do not see how we can reasonably claim the former quality as a national characteristic, though the latter might have been fairly inherited from his ancestors on the mother's side, who were Pennsylvania Quakers. But the kind of excellence that distinguished him—his fineness, subtlety, and grace—was that which the richest cultivation has heretofore tended to develope in the happier examples of American genius, and which (though I say it a little reluctantly) is perhaps what our future intellectual advancement may make general among us. His person, at all events, was thoroughly American, and of the best type, as were likewise his manners; for we are the best as well as the worst-mannered people in the world.

Leigh Hunt loved dearly to be praised. That is to say, he desired sympathy as a flower seeks sunshine, and perhaps profited by it as much in the richer depth of coloring that it imparted to his ideas. In response to all that we ventured to express about his writings, (and, for my part, I went quite to the extent of my conscience, which was a long way, and there left the matter to a lady and a young girl, who happily were with me,) his face shone and he manifested great delight, with a perfect and yet delicate frankness for which I loved him. He could not tell us, he said, the happiness that such appreciation gave him; it always took him by surprise, he remarked, for—perhaps because he cleaned his own boots, and performed other little ordinary offices for himself—he never had been conscious of anything wonderful in his own person. And then he smiled, making himself and all the poor little parlor about him beautiful thereby. It is usually the hardest thing in the world to praise a man to his face; but Leigh Hunt received the incense with such gracious satisfaction, (feeling it to be sympathy, not vulgar praise,) that the only difficulty was to keep the enthusiasm of the moment within the limit of permanent opinion. A storm had suddenly come up while we were talking; the rain poured, the lightning flashed, and the thunder broke; but I hope, and have great pleasure in believing, that it was a sunny hour for Leigh Hunt. Nevertheless, it was not to my voice that he most favorably inclined his ear, but to those of my companions. Women are the fit ministers at such a shrine.

He must have suffered keenly in his lifetime, and enjoyed keenly, keeping his emotions so much upon the surface as he seemed to do, and convenient for everybody to play upon.

Being of a cheerful temperament, happiness had probably the upper hand. His was a light, mildly joyous nature, gentle, graceful, yet seldom attaining to that deepest grace which results from power; for beauty, like Woman, its human representative, dallies with the gentle, but yields its consummate favor only to the strong. I imagine that Leigh Hunt may have been more beautiful when I met him, both in person and character, than in his earlier days. As a young man, I could conceive of his being finical in certain moods, but not now, when the gravity of age shed a venerable grace about him. I rejoiced to hear him say that he was favored with most confident and cheering anticipations in respect to a future life; and there were abundant proofs, throughout our interview, of an unrepining spirit, resignation, quiet relinquishment of the worldly benefits that were denied him, thankful enjoyment of whatever he had to enjoy, and piety, and hope shining onward into the dusk—all of which gave a reverential cast to the feeling with which we parted from him. I wish that he could have had one full draught of prosperity before he died. As a matter of artistic propriety, it would have been delightful to see him inhabiting a beautiful house of his own, in an Italian climate, with all sorts of elaborate upholstery and minute elegancies about him, and a succession of tender and lovely women to praise his sweet poetry from morning to night. I hardly know whether it is my fault, or the effect of a weakness in Leigh Hunt's character, that I should be sensible of a regret of this nature, when, at the same time, I sincerely believe that he has found an infinity of better things in the world whither he has gone.

At our leave-taking, he grasped me warmly by both hands, and seemed as much interested in our whole party as if he had known us for years. All this was genuine feeling, a quick, luxuriant growth out of his heart, which was a soil for flower-seeds of rich and rare varieties, not acorns—but a true heart, nevertheless. Several years afterwards, I met him for the last time at a London dinner-party, looking sadly broken down by infirmities; and my final recollection of the beautiful old man presents him arm in arm with, nay, if I mistake not, partly embraced and supported by, another beloved and honored poet, whose minstrel name, since he has a week-day one for his personal occasions, I will venture to speak. It was Barry Cornwall, whose kind introduction had first made me known to Leigh Hunt.

OUTSIDE GLIMPSES OF ENGLISH POVERTY

BECOMING an inhabitant of a great English town, I often turned aside from the prosperous thoroughfares, (where the edifices, the shops, and the bustling crowd differed not so much from scenes with which I was familiar in my own country,) and went designedly astray among precincts that reminded me of some of Dickens's grimiest pages. There I caught glimpses of a people and a mode of life that were comparatively new to my observation, a sort of sombre phantasmagoric spectacle, exceedingly undelightful to behold, yet involving a singular interest and even fascination in its ugliness.

Dirt, one would fancy, is plenty enough all over the world, being the symbolic accompaniment of the foul encrustation which began to settle over and bedim all earthly things as soon as Eve had bitten the apple; ever since which hapless epoch, her daughters have chiefly been engaged in a desperate and unavailing struggle to get rid of it. But the dirt of a poverty-stricken English street is a monstrosity unknown on our side of the Atlantic. It reigns supreme within its own limits, and is inconceivable everywhere beyond them. We enjoy the great advantage, that the brightness and dryness of our atmosphere keep everything clean that the sun shines upon, converting the larger portion of our impurities into transitory dust which the next wind can sweep away, in contrast with the damp, adhesive grime that incorporates itself with all surfaces (unless continually and painfully cleansed) in the chill moisture of the English air. Then the all-pervading smoke of the city, abundantly intermingled with the sable snow-flakes of bituminous coal, hovering overhead, descending, and alighting on pavements and rich architectural fronts, on the snowy muslin of the ladies, and the gentlemen's starched collars and shirt-bosoms, invests even the better streets in a half-mourning garb. It is beyond the resources of Wealth to keep the smut away from its premises or its own fingers' ends; and as for Poverty, it surrenders itself to the dark influence without a struggle. Along with disastrous circumstances, pinching need, adversity so lengthened out as to constitute the rule of life, there comes a certain chill depression of the spirits which seems especially to shudder at cold water. In view of so wretched a state of things, we accept the ancient Deluge not merely as an insulated phenomenon, but as a periodical necessity, and acknowledge that nothing less than such a general washing-day could suffice to cleanse the slovenly old world of its moral and material dirt.

Gin-shops, or what the English call spirit-vaults, are numerous in the vicinity of these poor streets, and are set off with the magnificence of gilded door-posts, tarnished by contact with the unclean customers who haunt there. Ragged children come thither with old shaving-mugs, or broken-nosed tea-pots, or any such make-shift receptacle, to get a little poison or madness for their parents, who deserve no better requital at their hands for having engendered them. Inconceivably sluttish women enter at noon-day and stand at the counter among boon-companions of both sexes, stirring up misery and jollity in a bumper together, and quaffing off the mixture with a relish. As for the men, they lounge there continually, drinking till they are drunken—drinking as long as they have a half-penny left, and then, as it seemed to me, waiting for a sixpenny miracle to be wrought in their pockets, so as to enable them to be drunken again. Most of these establishments have a significant advertisement of "Beds," doubtless for the accommodation of their customers in the interval between one intoxication and the next. I never could find it in my heart, however, utterly to condemn these sad revellers, and should certainly wait till I had some better consolation to offer before depriving them of their dram of gin, though death itself were in the glass; for methought their poor souls needed such fiery stimulant to lift them a little way out of the smothering squalor of both their outward and interior life, giving them glimpses and suggestions, even if bewildering ones, of a spiritual existence that limited their present misery. The temperance-reformers unquestionably derive their commission from the Divine Beneficence, but have never been taken fully into its counsels. All may not be lost, though those good men fail.

Pawn-brokers' establishments, distinguished by the mystic symbol of the three golden balls, were conveniently accessible; though what personal property these wretched people could possess, capable of being estimated in silver or copper, so as to afford a basis for a loan, was a problem that still perplexes me. Old clothesmen, likewise, dwelt hard by, and hung out ancient garments to dangle in the wind. There were butchers' shops, too, of a class adapted to the neighborhood, presenting no such generously fattened carcasses as Englishmen love to gaze at in the market, no stupendous halves of mighty beeves, no dead hogs or muttons ornamented with carved bas-reliefs of fat on their ribs and shoulders, in a peculiarly British style of art—not these, but bits and gobbets of lean meat, selvages snipt off from steaks, tough and stringy morsels, bare bones smitten away from joints by the cleaver, tripe, liver, bullocks' feet, or whatever else was cheapest and divisible into the smallest lots. I am afraid that even such delicacies came to many of their tables hardly oftener than Christmas. In the windows of other little shops you saw half-a-dozen wizened herrings, some eggs in a basket, looking so dingily antique that your imagination smelt them, fly-speckled biscuits, segments of a hungry cheese, pipes and papers of tobacco. Now and then a sturdy milk-woman passed by with a wooden yoke over her shoulders, supporting a pail on either side, filled with a whitish fluid, the composition of which was water and chalk and the milk of a sickly cow, who gave the best she had, poor thing! but could scarcely make it rich or wholesome, spending her life in some close city-nook and pasturing on strange food. I have seen, once or twice, a donkey coming into one of these streets with panniers full of vegetables, and departing with a return cargo of what looked like rubbish and street-sweepings. No other commerce seemed to exist, except, possibly, a girl might offer you a pair of stockings or a worked collar, or a man whisper something mysterious about wonderfully cheap cigars. And yet I remember seeing female hucksters in those regions, with their wares on the edge of the side-walk and their own seats right in the carriage-way, pretending to sell half-decayed oranges and apples, toffy, Ormskirk cakes, combs and cheap jewelry, the coarsest kind of crockery, and little plates of oysters—knitting patiently all day long, and removing their undiminished stock in trade at nightfall. All indispensable importations from other quarters of the town were on a remarkably diminutive scale; for example, the wealthier inhabitants purchased their coal by the wheelbarrow-load, and the poorer ones by the peck-measure. It was a curious and melancholy spectacle, when an overladen coal-cart happened to pass through the street and drop a handful or two of its burthen in the mud, to see half-a-dozen women and children scrambling for the treasure-trove, like a flock of hens and chickens gobbling up some spilt corn. In this connection I may as well mention a commodity of boiled snails (for such they appeared to me, though probably a marine production) which used to be peddled from door to door, piping hot, as an article of cheap nutriment.

The population of these dismal abodes appeared to consider the side-walks and middle of the street as their common hall. In a drama of low life, the unity of place might be arranged rigidly according to the classic rule, and the street be the one locality in which every scene and incident should occur. Courtship, quarrels, plot and counterplot, conspiracies for robbery and murder, family difficulties or agreements—all such matters, I doubt not, are constantly discussed or transacted in this sky-roofed saloon, so regally hung with its sombre canopy of coal-smoke. Whatever the disadvantages of the English climate, the only comfortable or wholesome part of life, for the city-poor, must be spent in the open air. The stifled and squalid rooms where they lie down at night, whole families and neighborhoods together, or sulkily elbow one another in the daytime, when a settled rain drives them within doors, are worse horrors than it is worth while (without a practical object in view) to admit into one's imagination. No wonder that they creep forth from the foul mystery of their interiors, stumble down from their garrets, or scramble up out of their cellars, on the upper step of which you may see the grimy housewife, before the shower is ended, letting the rain-drops gutter down her visage; while her children (an impish progeny of cavernous recesses below the common sphere of humanity) swarm into the daylight and attain all that they know of personal purification in the nearest mud-puddle. It might almost make a man doubt the existence of his own soul, to observe how Nature has flung these little wretches into the street and left them there, so evidently regarding them as nothing worth, and how all mankind acquiesce in the great mother's estimate of her offspring. For, if they are to have no immortality, what superior claim can I assert for mine? And how difficult to believe that anything so precious as a germ of immortal growth can have been buried under this dirt-heap, plunged into this cesspool of misery and vice! As often as I beheld the scene, it affected me with surprise and loathsome interest, much resembling, though in a far intenser degree, the feeling with which, when a boy, I used to turn over a plank or an old log that had long lain on the damp ground, and found a vivacious multitude of unclean and devilish-looking insects scampering to-and-fro beneath it. Without an infinite faith, there seemed as much prospect of a blessed futurity for those hideous bugs and many-footed worms as for these brethren of our humanity and co-heirs of all our heavenly inheritance. Ah, what a mystery! Slowly, slowly, as after groping at the bottom of a deep, noisome, stagnant pool, my hope struggles upward to the surface, bearing the half-drowned body of a child along with it, and heaving it aloft for its life, and my own life, and all our lives. Unless these slime-clogged nostrils can be made capable of inhaling celestial air, I know not how the purest and most intellectual of us can reasonably expect ever to taste a breath of it. The whole question of eternity is staked there. If a single one of those helpless little ones be lost, the world is lost!

The women and children greatly preponderate in such places; the men probably wandering abroad in quest of that daily miracle, a dinner and a drink, or perhaps slumbering in the daylight that they may the better follow out their cat-like rambles through the dark. Here are women with young figures, but old, wrinkled, yellow faces, tanned and blear-eyed with the smoke which they cannot spare from their scanty fires—it being too precious for its warmth to be swallowed by the chimney. Some of them sit on the door-steps, nursing their unwashed babies at bosoms which we will glance aside from, for the sake of our mothers and all womanhood, because the fairest spectacle is here the foulest. Yet motherhood, in these dark abodes, is strangely identical with what we have all known it to be in the happiest homes. Nothing, as I remember, smote me with more grief and pity (all the more poignant because perplexingly entangled with an inclination to smile) than to hear a gaunt and ragged mother priding herself on the pretty ways of her ragged and skinny infant, just as a young matron might, when she invites her lady-friends to admire her plump,white-robed darling in the nursery. Indeed, no womanly characteristic seemed to have altogether perished out of these poor souls. It was the very same creature whose tender torments make the rapture of our young days, whom we love, cherish, and protect, and rely upon in life and death, and whom we delight to see beautify her beauty with rich robes and set it off with jewels, though now fantastically masquerading in a garb of tatters, wholly unfit for her to handle. I recognized her, over and over again, in the groups round a door-step or in the descent of a cellar, chatting with prodigious earnestness about intangible trifles, laughing for a little jest, sympathizing at almost the same instant with one neighbor's sunshine and another's shadow, wise, simple, sly, and patient, yet easily perturbed, and breaking into small feminine ebullitions of spite, wrath, and jealousy, tornadoes of a moment, such as vary the social atmosphere of her silken-skirted sisters, though smothered into propriety by dint of a well-bred habit. Not that there was an absolute deficiency of good-breeding, even here. It often surprised me to witness a courtesy and deference among these ragged folks, which, having seen it, I did not thoroughly believe in, wondering whence it should have come. I am persuaded, however, that there were laws of intercourse which they never violated—a code of the cellar, the garret, the common staircase, the door-step, and the pavement, which perhaps had as deep a foundation in natural fitness as the code of the drawing-room.

Yet again I doubt whether I may not have been uttering folly in the last two sentences, when I reflect how rude and rough these specimens of feminine character generally were. They had a readiness with their hands that reminded me of Molly Seagrim and other heroines in Fielding's novels. For example, I have seen a woman meet a man in the street, and, for no reason perceptible to me, suddenly clutch him by the hair and cuff his ears—an infliction which he bore with exemplary patience, only snatching the very earliest opportunity to take to his heels. Where a sharp tongue will not serve the purpose, they trust to the sharpness of their finger-nails, or incarnate a whole vocabulary of vituperative words in a re-sounding slap, or the downright blow of a doubled fist. All English people, I imagine, are influenced in a far greater degree than ourselves by this simple and honest tendency, in cases of disagreement, to batter one another's persons; and whoever has seen a crowd of English ladies (for instance, at the door of the Sistine Chapel, in Holy Week) will be satisfied that their belligerent propensities are kept in abeyance only by a merciless rigor on the part of society. It requires a vast deal of refinement to spiritualize their large physical endowments. Such being the case with the delicate ornaments of the drawing-room, it is the less to be wondered at that women who live mostly in the open air, amid the coarsest kind of companionship and occupation, should carry on the intercourse of life with a freedom unknown to any class of American females, though still, I am resolved to think, compatible with a generous breadth of natural propriety. It shocked me, at first, to see them (of all ages, even elderly, as well as infants that could just toddle across the street alone) going about in the mud and mire, or through the dusky snow and slosh of a severe week in winter, with petticoats high uplifted above bare, red feet and legs; but I was comforted by observing that both shoes and stockings generally re-appeared with better weather, having been thriftily kept out of the damp for the convenience of dry feet within doors. Their hardihood was wonderful, and their strength greater than could have been expected from such spare diet as they probably lived upon. I have seen them carrying on their heads great burthens under which they walked as freely as if they were fashionable bonnets; or sometimes the burthen was huge enough almost to cover the whole person, looked at from behind—as in Tuscan villages you may see the girls coming in from the country with great bundles of green twigs upon their backs, so that they resemble locomotive masses of verdure and fragrance. But these poor English women seemed to be laden with rubbish, incongruous and indescribable, such as bones and rags, the sweepings of the house and of the street, a merchandize gathered up from what poverty itself had thrown away, a heap of filthy stuff analogous to Christian's bundle of sin.

Sometimes, though very seldom, I detected a certain gracefulness among the younger women that was altogether new to my observation. It was a charm proper to the lowest class. One girl I particularly remember, in a garb none of the cleanest and nowise smart, and herself exceedingly coarse in all respects, but yet endowed with a sort of witchery, a native charm, a robe of simple beauty and suitable behavior that she was born in and had never been tempted to throw off, because she had really nothing else to put on. Eve herself could not have been more natural. Nothing was affected, nothing imitative; no proper grace was vulgarized by an effort to assume the manners or adornments of another sphere. This kind of beauty, arrayed in a fitness of its own, is probably vanishing out of the world, and will certainly never be found in America, where all the girls, whether daughters of the upper-ten-dom, the mediocrity, the cottage, or the kennel, aim at one standard of dress and deportment, seldom accomplishing a perfectly triumphant hit or an utterly absurd failure. Those words, "genteel" and "ladylike," are terrible ones and do us infinite mischief, but it is because (at least, I hope so) we are in a transition state, and shall emerge into a higher mode of simplicity than has ever been known to past ages.

In such disastrous circumstances as I have been attempting to describe, it was beautiful to observe what a mysterious efficacy still asserted itself in character. A woman, evidently poor as the poorest of her neighbors, would be knitting or sewing on the door-step, just as fifty other women were; but round about her skirts (though woefully patched) you would be sensible of a certain sphere of decency, which, it seemed to me, could not have been kept more impregnable in the cosiest little sitting-room, where the tea-kettle on the hob was humming its good old song of domestic peace. Maidenhood had a similar power. The evil habit that grows upon us in this harsh world makes me faithless to my own better perceptions; and yet I have seen girls in these wretched streets, on whose virgin purity, judging merely from their impression on my instincts as they passed by, I should have deemed it safe, at the moment, to stake my life. The next moment, however, as the surrounding flood of moral uncleanness surged over their footsteps, I would not have staked a spike of thistle-down on the same wager. Yet the miracle was within the scope of Providence, which is equally wise and equally beneficent, (even to those poor girls, though I acknowledge the fact without the remotest comprehension of the mode of it,) whether they were pure or what we fellow-sinners call vile. Unless your faith be deep-rooted and of most vigorous growth, it is the safer way not to turn aside into this region so suggestive of miserable doubt. It was a place "with dreadful faces thronged," wrinkled and grim with vice and wretchedness; and, thinking over the line of Milton here quoted, I come to the conclusion that those ugly lineaments which startled Adam and Eve, as they looked backward to the closed gate of Paradise, were no fiends from the pit, but the more terrible foreshadowings of what so many of their descendants were to be. God help them, and us likewise, their brethren and sisters! Let me add, that, forlorn, ragged, care-worn, hopeless, dirty, haggard, hungry, as they were, the most pitiful thing of all was to see the sort of patience with which they accepted their lot, as if they had been born into the world for that and nothing else. Even the little children had this characteristic in as perfect development as their grandmothers.

The children, in truth, were the ill-omened blossoms from which another harvest of precisely such dark fruitage as I saw ripened around me was to be produced. Of course, you would imagine these to be lumps of crude iniquity, tiny vessels as full as they could hold of naughtiness; nor can I say a great deal to the contrary. Small proof of parental discipline could I discern, save when a mother (drunken, I sincerely hope) snatched her own imp out of a group of pale, half-naked, humor-eaten abortions that were playing and squabbling together in the mud, turned up its tatters, brought down her heavy hand on its poor little tenderest part, and let it go again with a shake. If the child knew what the punishment was for, it was wiser than I pretend to be. It yelled, and went back to its playmates in the mud. Yet let me bear testimony to what was beautiful, and more touching than anything that I ever witnessed in the intercourse of happier children. I allude to the superintendence which some of these small people (too small, one would think, to be sent into the street alone, had there been any other nursery for them) exercised over still smaller ones. Whence they derived such a sense of duty, unless immediately from God, I cannot tell; but it was wonderful to observe the expression of responsibility in their deportment, the anxious fidelity with which they discharged their unfit office, the tender patience with which they linked their less pliable impulses to the wayward footsteps of an infant, and let it guide them whithersoever it liked. In the hollow-cheeked, large-eyed girl of ten, whom I saw giving a cheerless oversight to her baby-brother, I did not so much marvel at it. She had merely come a little earlier than usual to the perception of what was to be her business in life. But I admired the sickly-looking little boy, who did violence to his boyish nature by making himself the servant of his little sister —she too small to walk, and he too small to take her in his arms—and therefore working a kind of miracle to transport her from one dirt-heap to another. Beholding such works of love and duty, I took heart again, and deemed it not so impossible, after all, for these neglected children to find a path through the squalor and evil of their circumstances up to the gate of Heaven. Perhaps there was this latent good in all of them, though generally they looked brutish, and dull even in their sports; there was little mirth among them, nor even a fully awakened spirit of blackguardism. Yet sometimes, again, I saw, with surprise and a sense as if I had been asleep and dreaming, the bright, intelligent, merry face of a child whose dark eyes gleamed with vivacious expression through the dirt that encrusted its skin, like sunshine struggling through a very dusty window-pane.

In these streets the belted and blue-coated policeman appears seldom in comparison with the frequency of his occurrence in more reputable thoroughfares. I used to think that the inhabitants would have ample time to murder one another, or any stranger, like myself, who might violate the filthy sanctities of the place, before the law could bring up its lumbering assistance. Nevertheless, there is a supervision; nor does the watchfulness of authority permit the populace to be tempted to any outbreak. Once, in a time of dearth, I noticed a ballad-singer going through the street hoarsely chanting some discordant strain in a provincial dialect, of which I could only make out that it addressed the sensibilities of the auditors on the score of starvation; but by his side stalked the policeman, offering no interference, but watchful to hear what this rough minstrel said or sang, and silence him, if his effusion threatened to prove too soul-stirring. In my judgment, however, there is little or no danger of that kind; they starve patiently, sicken patiently, die patiently, not through resignation, but a diseased flaccidity of hope. If ever they should do mischief to those above them, it will probably be by the communication of some destructive pestilence; for, so the medical men affirm, they suffer all the ordinary diseases with a degree of virulence elsewhere unknown, and keep among themselves traditionary plagues that have long ceased to afflict more fortunate societies. Charity herself gathers her robe about her to avoid their contact. It would be a dire revenge, indeed, if they were to prove their claims to be reckoned of one blood and nature with the noblest and wealthiest by compelling them to inhale death through the diffusion of their own poverty-poisoned atmosphere.

A true Englishman is a kind man at heart, but has an unconquerable dislike to poverty and beggary. Beggars have heretofore been so strange to an American that he is apt to become their prey, being recognized through his national peculiarities, and beset by them in the streets. The English smile at him, and say that there are ample public arrangements for every pauper's possible need, that street-charity promotes idleness and vice, and that yonder personification of misery on the pavement will lay up a good day's profit, besides supping more luxuriously than the dupe who gives him a shilling. By-and-by the stranger adopts their theory and begins to practise upon it, much to his own temporary freedom from annoyance, but not entirely without moral detriment or sometimes a too late contrition. Years afterwards, it may be, his memory is still haunted by some vindictive wretch whose cheeks were pale and hunger-pinched, whose rags fluttered in the east-wind, whose right arm was paralyzed and his left leg shrivelled into a mere nerveless stick, but whom he passed by remorselessly because an Englishman chose to say that the fellow's misery looked too perfect, was too artistically got up, to be genuine. Even allowing this to be true, (as, a hundred chances to one, it was,) it would still have been a clear case of economy to buy him off with a little loose silver, so that his lamentable figure should not limp at the heels of your conscience all over the world. To own the truth, I provided myself with several such imaginary persecutors in England, and recruited their number with at least one sickly-looking wretch whose acquaintance I first made at Assisi, in Italy, and, taking a dislike to something sinister in his aspect, permitted him to beg early and late, and all day long, without getting a single baiòcco. At my latest glimpse of him, the villain avenged himself, not by a volley of horrible curses, as any other Italian beggar would, but by taking an expression so grief-stricken, want-wrung, hopeless, and withal resigned, that I could paint his life-like portrait at this moment. Were I to go over the same ground again, I would listen to no man's theories, but buy the little luxury of beneficence at a cheap rate, instead of doing myself a moral mischief by exuding a stony encrustation over whatever natural sensibility I might possess.

On the other hand, there were some mendicants whose utmost efforts I even now felicitate myself on having withstood. Such was a phenomenon abridged of his lower half, who beset me for two or three years together, and, in spite of his deficiency of locomotive members, had some supernatural method of transporting himself (simultaneously, I believe) to all quarters of the city. He wore a sailor's jacket, (possibly, because skirts would have been a superfluity to his figure,) and had a remarkably broad-shouldered and muscular frame, surmounted by a large, fresh-colored face, which was full of power and intelligence. His dress and linen were the perfection of neatness. Once a day, at least, wherever I went, I suddenly became aware of this trunk of a man on the path before me, resting on his base, and looking as if he had just sprouted out of the pavement, and would sink into it again and re-appear at some other spot the instant you left him behind. The expression of his eye was perfectly respectful, but terribly fixed, holding your own as by fascination, never once winking, never wavering from its point-blank gaze right into your face, till you were completely beyond the range of his battery of one immense rifled cannon. This was his mode of soliciting alms; and he reminded me of the old beggar who appealed so touchingly to the charitable sympathies of Gil Blas, taking aim at him from the roadside with a long-barrelled musket. The intentness and directness of his silent appeal, his close and unrelenting attack upon your individuality, respectful as it seemed, was the very flower of insolence; or, if you give it a possibly truer interpretation, it was the tyrannical effort of a man endowed with great natural force of character to constrain your reluctant will to his purpose. Apparently, he had staked his salvation upon the ultimate success of a daily struggle between himself and me, the triumph of which would compel me to become a tributary to the hat that lay on the pavement beside him. Man or fiend, however, there was a stubbornness in his intended victim which this massive fragment of a mighty personality had not altogether reckoned upon, and by its aid I was enabled to pass him at my customary pace hundreds of times over, quietly meeting his terribly respectful eye, and allowing him the fair chance which I felt to be his due, to subjugate me, if he really had the strength for it. He never succeeded, but, on the other hand, never gave up the contest; and should I ever walk those streets again, I am certain that the truncated tyrant will sprout up through the pavement and look me fixedly in the eye, and perhaps get the victory.

I should think all the more highly of myself, if I had shown equal heroism in resisting another class of beggarly depredators, who assailed me on my weaker side and won an easy spoil. Such was the sanctimonious clergyman, with his white cravat, who visited me with a subscription-paper, which he himself had drawn up, in a case of heart-rending distress;—the respectable and ruined tradesman, going from door to door, shy and silent in his own person, but accompanied by a sympathizing friend, who bore testimony to his integrity, and stated the unavoidable misfortunes that had crushed him down;—or the delicate and prettily dressed lady, who had been bred in affluence, but was suddenly thrown upon the perilous charities of the world by the death of an indulgent, but secretly insolvent father, or the commercial catastrophe and simultaneous suicide of the best of husbands;—or the gifted, but unsuccessful author, appealing to my fraternal sympathies, generously rejoicing in some small prosperities which he was kind enough to term my own triumphs in the field of letters, and claiming to have largely contributed to them by his unbought notices in the public journals. England is full of such people, and a hundred other varieties of peripatetic tricksters, higher than these, and lower, who act their parts tolerably well, but seldom with an absolutely illusive effect. I knew at once, raw Yankee as I was, that they were humbugs, almost without an exception—rats that nibble at the honest bread and cheese of the community, and grow fat by their petty pilferings—yet often gave them what they asked, and privately owned myself a simpleton. There is a decorum which restrains you (unless you happen to be a police-constable) from breaking through a crust of plausible respectability, even when you are certain that there is a knave beneath it.

After making myself as familiar as I decently could with the poor streets, I became curious to see what kind of a home was provided for the inhabitants at the public expense, fearing that it must needs be a most comfortless one, or else their choice (if choice it were) of so miserable a life outside was truly difficult to account for. Accordingly, I visited a great almshouse, and was glad to observe how unexceptionably all the parts of the establishment were carried on, and what an orderly life, full-fed, sufficiently reposeful, and undisturbed by the arbitrary exercise of authority, seemed to be led there. Possibly, indeed, it was that very orderliness, and the cruel necessity of being neat and clean, and even the comfort resulting from these and other Christian-like restraints and regulations, that constituted the principal grievance on the part of the poor, shiftless inmates, accustomed to a life-long luxury of dirt and harum-scarumness. The wild life of the streets has perhaps as unforgettable a charm, to those who have once thoroughly imbibed it, as the life of the forest or the prairie. But I conceive rather that there must be insuperable difficulties, for the majority of the poor, in the way of getting admittance to the almshouse, than that a merely aesthetic preference for the street would incline the pauper-class to fare scantily and precariously, and expose their raggedness to the rain and snow, when such a hospitable door stood wide-open for their entrance. It might be that the roughest and darkest side of the matter was not shown me, there being persons of eminent station and of both sexes in the party which I accompanied; and, of course, a properly trained public functionary would have deemed it a monstrous rudeness, as well as a great shame, to exhibit anything to people of rank that might too painfully shock their sensibilities.

The women's ward was the portion of the establishment which we especially examined. It could not be questioned that they were treated with kindness as well as care. No doubt, as has been already suggested, some of them felt the irksomeness of submission to general rules of orderly behavior, after being accustomed to that perfect freedom from the minor proprieties, at least, which is one of the compensations of absolutely hopeless poverty, or of any circumstances that set us fairly below the decencies of life. I asked the governor of the house whether he met with any difficulty in keeping peace and order among his inmates; and he informed me that his troubles among the women were incomparably greater than with the men. They were freakish, and apt to be quarrelsome, inclined to plague and pester one another in ways that it was impossible to lay hold of, and to thwart his own authority by the like intangible methods. He said this with the utmost good nature, and quite won my regard by so placidly resigning himself to the inevitable necessity of letting the women throw dust into his eyes. They certainly looked peaceable and sisterly enough, as I saw them, though still it might be faintly perceptible that some of them were consciously playing their parts before the governor and his distinguished visitors.

This governor seemed to me a man thoroughly fit for his position. An American, in an office of similar responsibility, would doubtless be a much superior person, better educated, possessing a far wider range of thought, more naturally acute, with a quicker tact of external observation and a readier faculty of dealing with difficult cases. The women would not succeed in throwing half so much dust into his eyes. Moreover, his black coat, and thin, sallow visage, would make him look like a scholar, and his manners would indefinitely approximate to those of a gentleman. But I cannot help questioning, whether, on the whole, these higher endowments would produce decidedly better results. The Englishman was thoroughly plebeian both in aspect and behavior, a bluff, ruddy-faced, hearty, kindly, yeomanlike personage, with no refinement whatever, nor any superfluous sensibility, but gifted with a native wholesomeness of character which must have been a very beneficial element in the atmosphere of the almshouse. He spoke to his pauper family in loud, good-humored, cheerful tones, and treated them with a healthy free-dom that probably caused the forlorn wretches to feel as if they were free and healthy likewise. If he had understood them a little better, he would not have treated them half so wisely. We are apt to make sickly people more morbid, and unfortunate people more miserable, by endeavoring to adapt our deportment to their especial and individual needs. They eagerly accept our well-meant efforts; but it is like returning their own sick breath back upon themselves, to be breathed over and over again, intensifying the inward mischief at every repetition. The sympathy that would really do them good is of a kind that recognizes their sound and healthy parts, and ignores the part affected by disease, which will thrive under the eye of a too close observer like a poisonous weed in the sunshine. My good friend the governor had no tendencies in the latter direction, and abundance of them in the former, and was consequently as wholesome and invigorating as the west-wind with a little spice of the north in it, brightening the dreary visages that encountered us as if he had carried a sunbeam in his hand. He expressed himself by his whole being and personality, and by works more than words, and had the not unusual English merit of knowing what to do much better than how to talk about it.

The women, I imagine, must have felt one imperfection in their state, however comfortable otherwise. They were forbid-den, or, at all events, lacked the means, to follow out their **natural instinct** of adorning themselves; all were dressed in one homely uniform of blue-checked gowns, with such caps upon their heads as English servants wear. Generally, too, they had one dowdy English aspect, and a vulgar type of features so nearly alike that they seemed literally to constitute a sisterhood. We have few of these absolutely unilluminated faces among our native American population, individuals of whom must be singularly unfortunate, if, mixing as we do, no drop of gentle blood has contributed to refine the turbid element, no gleam of hereditary intelligence has lighted up the stolid eyes, which their forefathers brought from the Old Country. Even in this English almshouse, however, there was at least one person who claimed to be intimately connected with rank and wealth. The governor, after suggesting that this person would probably be gratified by our visit, ushered us into a small parlor, which was furnished a little more like a room in a private dwelling than others that we entered, and had a row of religious books and fashionable novels on the mantel-piece. An old lady sat at a bright coal-fire, reading a romance, and rose to receive us with a certain pomp of manner and elaborate display of ceremonious courtesy, which, in spite of myself, made me inwardly question the genuineness of her aristocratic pretensions. But, at any rate, she looked like a respectable old soul, and was evidently gladdened to the very core of her frost-bitten heart by the awful punctiliousness with which we responded to her gracious and hospitable, though unfamiliar welcome. After a little polite conversation, we retired; and the governor, with a lowered voice and an air of deference, told us that she had been a lady of quality, and had ridden in her own equipage, not many years before, and now lived in continual expectation that some of her rich relatives would drive up in their carriages to take her away. Meanwhile, he added, she was treated with great respect by her fellow-paupers. I could not help thinking, from a few criticizable peculiarities in her talk and manner, that there might have been a mistake on the governor's part, and perhaps a venial exaggeration on the old lady's, concerning her former position in society; but what struck me was the forcible instance of that most prevalent of English vanities, the pretension to aristocratic connection, on one side, and the submission and reverence with which it was accepted by the governor and his household, on the other. Among ourselves, I think, when wealth and eminent position have taken their departure, they seldom leave a pallid ghost behind them—or, if it sometimes stalks abroad, few recognize it.

We went into several other rooms, at the doors of which, pausing on the outside, we could hear the volubility, and sometimes the wrangling, of the female inhabitants within, but invariably found silence and peace when we stepped over the threshold. The women were grouped together in their sitting-rooms, sometimes three or four, sometimes a larger number, classified by their spontaneous affinities, I suppose, and all busied, so far as I can remember, with the one occupation of knitting coarse yarn stockings. Hardly any of them, I am sorry to say, had a brisk or cheerful air, though it often stirred them up to a momentary vivacity to be accosted by the governor, and they seemed to like being noticed, however slightly, by the visitors. The happiest person whom I saw there (and, running hastily through my experiences, I hardly recollect to have seen a happier one in my life, if you take a careless flow of spirits as happiness) was an old woman that lay in bed among ten or twelve heavy-looking females, who plied their knitting-work roundabout her. She laughed, when we entered, and immediately began to talk to us, in a thin, little, spirited quaver, claiming to be more than a century old; and the governor (in whatever way he happened to be cognizant of the fact) confirmed her age to be a hundred and four. Her jauntiness and cackling merriment were really wonderful. It was as if she had got through with all her actual business in life two or three generations ago, and now, freed from every responsibility for herself or others, had only to keep up a mirthful state of mind till the short time, or long time, (and, happy as she was, she appeared not to care whether it were long or short,) before Death, who had misplaced her name in his list, might remember to take her away. She had gone quite round the circle of human existence, and come back to the play-ground again. And so she had grown to be a kind of miraculous old pet, the plaything of people seventy or eighty years younger than herself, who talked and laughed with her as if she were a child, finding great delight in her wayward and strangely playful responses, into some of which she cunningly conveyed a gibe that caused their ears to tingle a little. She had done getting out of bed in this world, and lay there to be waited upon like a queen or a baby.

In the same room sat a pauper who had once been an actress of considerable repute, but was compelled to give up her profession by a softening of the brain. The disease seemed to have stolen the continuity out of her life, and disturbed all healthy relationship between the thoughts within her and the world without. On our first entrance, she looked cheerfully at us, and showed herself ready to engage in conversation; but suddenly, while we were talking with the century-old crone, the poor actress began to weep, contorting her face with extravagant stage-grimaces, and wringing her hands for some inscrutable sorrow. It might have been a reminiscence of actual calamity in her past life, or, quite as probably, it was but a dramatic woe, beneath which she had staggered and shrieked and wrung her hands with hundreds of repetitions in the sight of crowded theatres, and been as often comforted by thunders of applause. But my idea of the mystery was, that she had a sense of wrong in seeing the aged woman (whose empty vivacity was like the rattling of dry peas in a bladder) chosen as the central object of interest to the visitors, while she herself, who had agitated thousands of hearts with a breath, sat starving for the admiration that was her natural food. I appeal to the whole society of artists of the Beautiful and the Imaginative—poets, romancers, painters, sculptors, actors—whether or no this is a grief that may be felt even amid the torpor of a dissolving brain!

We looked into a good many sleeping-chambers, where were rows of beds, mostly calculated for two occupants, and provided with sheets and pillow-cases that resembled sack-cloth. It appeared to me that the sense of beauty was insufficiently regarded in all the arrangements of the almshouse; a little cheap luxury for the eye, at least, might do the poor folks a substantial good. But, at all events, there was the beauty of perfect neatness and orderliness, which, being heretofore known to few of them, was perhaps as much as they could well digest in the remnant of their lives. We were invited into the laundry, where a great washing and drying were in process, the whole atmosphere being hot and vaporous with the steam of wet garments and bedclothes. This atmosphere was the pauper-life of the past week or fortnight resolved into a gaseous state, and breathing it, however fastidiously, we were forced to inhale the strange element into our inmost being. Had the Queen been there, I know not how she could have escaped the necessity. What an intimate brotherhood is this in which we dwell, do what we may to put an artificial remoteness between the high creature and the low one! A poor man's breath, borne on the vehicle of tobacco-smoke, floats into a palace-window and reaches the nostrils of a monarch. It is but an example, obvious to the sense, of the innumerable and secret channels by which, at every moment of our lives, the flow and reflux of a common humanity pervade us all. How superficial are the niceties of such as pretend to keep aloof! Let the whole world be cleansed, or not a man or woman of us all can be clean.

By-and-by we came to the ward where the children were kept, on entering which, we saw, in the first place, several unlovely and unwholesome little people lazily playing together in a court-yard. And here a singular incommodity befel one member of our party. Among the children was a wretched, pale, half-torpid little thing, (about six years old, perhaps, but I know not whether a girl or a boy,) with a humor in its eyes and face, which the governor said was the scurvy, and which appeared to bedim its powers of vision, so that it toddled about gropingly, as if in quest of it did not precisely know what. This child—this sickly, wretched, humor-eaten infant, the offspring of unspeakable sin and sorrow, whom it must have required several generations of guilty progenitors to render so pitiable an object as we beheld it—immediately took an unaccountable fancy to the gentleman just hinted at. It prowled about him like a pet kitten, rubbing against his legs, following everywhere at his heels, pulling at his coat-tails, and, at last, exerting all the speed that its poor limbs were capable of, got directly before him and held forth its arms, mutely insisting on being taken up. It said not a word, being perhaps underwitted and incapable of prattle. But it smiled up in his face—a sort of woeful gleam was that smile, through the sickly blotches that covered its features—and found means to express such a perfect confidence that it was going to be fondled and made much of, that there was no possibility in a human heart of baulking its expectation. It was as if God had promised the poor child this favor on behalf of that individual, and he was bound to fulfil the contract, or else no longer call himself a man among men. Nevertheless, it could be no easy thing for him to do, he being a person burthened with more than an Englishman's customary reserve, shy of actual contact with human beings, afflicted with a peculiar distaste for whatever was ugly, and, furthermore, accustomed to that habit of observation from an insulated stand-point which is said (but, I hope, erroneously) to have the tendency of putting ice into the blood.

So I watched the struggle in his mind with a good deal of interest, and am seriously of opinion that he did an heroic act, and effected more than he dreamed of towards his final salvation, when he took up the loathsome child and caressed it as tenderly as if he had been its father. To be sure, we all smiled at him, at the time, but doubtless would have acted pretty much the same in a similar stress of circumstances. The child, at any rate, appeared to be satisfied with his behavior; for when he had held it a considerable time, and set it down, it still favored him with its company, keeping fast hold of his forefinger till we reached the confines of the place. And on our return through the court-yard, after visiting another part of the establishment, here again was this same little Wretchedness waiting for its victim, with a smile of joyful, and yet dull recognition about its scabby mouth and in its rheumy eyes. No doubt, the child's mission in reference to our friend was to remind him that he was responsible, in his degree, for all the sufferings and misdemeanors of the world in which he lived, and was not entitled to look upon a particle of its dark calamity as if it were none of his concern; the offspring of a brother's iniquity being his own blood-relation, and the guilt, likewise, a burthen on him, unless he expiated it by better deeds.

All the children in this ward seemed to be invalids, and, going up stairs, we found more of them in the same or a worse condition than the little creature just described, with their mothers (or more probably other women, for the infants were mostly foundlings) in attendance as nurses. The matron of the ward, a middle-aged woman, remarkably kind and motherly in aspect, was walking to-and-fro across the chamber—on that weary journey in which careful mothers and nurses travel so continually and so far, and gain never a step of

progress—with an unquiet baby in her arms. She assured us
that she enjoyed her occupation, being exceedingly fond of
children; and, in fact, the absence of timidity in all the little
people was a sufficient proof that they could have had no
experience of harsh treatment, though, on the other hand,
none of them appeared to be attracted to one individual more
than another. In this point they differed widely from the poor
child below-stairs. They seemed to recognize a universal
motherhood in womankind, and cared not which individual
might be the mother of the moment. I found their tameness as
shocking as did Alexander Selkirk that of the brute subjects
of his else solitary kingdom. It was a sort of tame familiarity, a
perfect indifference to the approach of strangers, such as I
never noticed in other children. I accounted for it partly by
their nerveless, unstrung state of body, incapable of the quick
thrills of delight and fear which play upon the lively harp-
strings of a healthy child's nature, and partly by their woeful
lack of acquaintance with a private home, and their being
therefore destitute of the sweet homebred shyness, which is
like the sanctity of Heaven about a mother-petted child.
Their condition was like that of chickens hatched in an oven,
and growing up without the especial guardianship of a
matron-hen; both the chicken and the child, methinks, must
needs want something that is essential to their respective
characters.

In this chamber (which was spacious, containing a large
number of beds) there was a clear fire burning on the hearth,
as in all the other occupied rooms; and directly in front of the
blaze sat a woman holding a baby, which, beyond all reach of
comparison, was the most horrible object that ever afflicted my
sight. Days afterwards—nay, even now, when I bring it up
vividly before my mind's eye—it seemed to lie upon the floor
of my heart, polluting my moral being with the sense of

something grievously amiss in the entire conditions of humanity. The holiest man could not be otherwise than full of wickedness, the chastest virgin seemed impure, in a world where such a babe was possible. The governor whispered me, apart, that, like nearly all the rest of them, it was the child of unhealthy parents. Ah, yes! There was the mischief. This spectral infant, a hideous mockery of the visible link which Love creates between man and woman, was born of disease and sin. Diseased Sin was its father, and Sinful Disease its mother, and their offspring lay in the woman's arms like a nursing Pestilence, which, could it live and grow up, would make the world a more accursed abode than ever heretofore. Thank Heaven, it could not live! This baby, if we must give it that sweet name, seemed to be three or four months old, but, being such an unthrifty changeling, might have been considerably older. It was all covered with blotches, and preternaturally dark and discolored; it was withered away, quite shrunken and fleshless; it breathed only amid pantings and gaspings, and moaned painfully at every gasp. The only comfort in reference to it was the evident impossibility of its surviving to draw many more of those miserable, moaning breaths; and it would have been infinitely less heart-depressing to see it die, right before my eyes, than to depart and carry it alive in my remembrance, still suffering the incalculable torture of its little life. I can by no means express how horrible this infant was, neither ought I to attempt it. And yet I must add one final touch. Young as the poor little creature was, its pain and misery had endowed it with a premature intelligence, insomuch that its eyes seemed to stare at the bystanders out of their sunken sockets knowingly and appealingly, as if summoning us one and all to witness the deadly wrong of its existence. At least, I so interpreted its look, when it positively met and responded to my own awe-stricken gaze, and therefore I lay the case, as far as I am able, before mankind, on whom God has imposed the necessity to suffer in soul and body till this dark and dreadful wrong be righted.

Thence we went to the school-rooms, which were underneath the chapel. The pupils, like the children whom we had just seen, were, in large proportion, foundlings. Almost without exception, they looked sickly, with marks of eruptive trouble in their doltish faces, and a general tendency to diseases of the eye. Moreover, the poor little wretches appeared to be uneasy within their skins, and screwed themselves about on the benches in a disagreeably suggestive way, as if they had inherited the evil habits of their parents as an innermost garment of the same texture and material as the shirt of Nessus, and must wear it with unspeakable discomfort as long as they lived. I saw only a single child that looked healthy; and on my pointing him out, the governor informed me that this little boy, the sole exception to the miserable aspect of his school-fellows, was not a foundling, nor properly a work-house child, being born of respectable parentage, and his father one of the officers of the institution. As for the remainder—the hundred pale abortions to be counted against one rosy-cheeked boy—what shall we say or do? Depressed by the sight of so much misery, and uninventive of remedies for the evils that force themselves on my perception, I can do little more than recur to the idea already hinted at in the early part of this article, regarding the speedy necessity of a new Deluge. So far as these children are concerned, at any rate, it would be a blessing to the human race, which they will contribute to enervate and corrupt—a greater blessing to themselves, who inherit no patrimony but disease and vice, and in whose souls if there be a spark of God's life, this seems the only possible mode of keeping it a-glow—if every one of them could be drowned to-night, by their best friends, instead of being put tenderly to bed. This heroic method of treating human maladies, moral and material, is certainly beyond the scope of man's discretionary rights, and probably will not be adopted by Divine Providence until the opportunity of milder reformation shall have been offered us, again and again, through a series of future ages.

It may be fair to acknowledge that the humane and excellent governor, as well as other persons better acquainted with the subject than myself, took a less gloomy view of it, though still so dark a one as to involve scanty consolation. They remarked that individuals of the male sex, picked up in the streets and nurtured in the work-house, sometimes succeed tolerably well in life, because they are taught trades before being turned into the world, and, by dint of immaculate behavior and good luck, are not unlikely to get employment and earn a livelihood. The case is different with the girls. They can only go to service, and are invariably rejected by families of respectability on account of their origin, and for the better reason of their unfitness to fill satisfactorily even the meanest situations in a well-ordered English household. Their resource is to take service with people only a step or two above the poorest class, with whom they fare scantily, endure harsh treatment, lead shifting and precarious lives, and finally drop into the slough of evil, through which, in their best estate, they do but pick their slimy way on stepping-stones.

From the schools we went to the bake-house, and the brew-house, (for such cruelty is not harbored in the heart of a true Englishman as to deny a pauper his daily allowance of beer,) and through the kitchens, where we beheld an immense pot over the fire, surging and walloping with some kind of a savory stew that filled it up to its brim. We also visited a tailor's shop and a shoemaker's shop, in both of which a number of men, and pale, diminutive apprentices, were at work, diligently enough, though seemingly with small heart in the business. Finally, the governor ushered us into a shed, inside of which was piled up an immense quantity of new coffins. They were of the plainest description, made of pine-boards, probably of American growth, not very nicely smoothed by the plane, neither painted nor stained with black, but provided with a loop of rope at either end for the convenience of lifting the rude box and its inmate into the cart that shall carry them to the burial-ground. There, in holes ten feet deep, the paupers are buried one above another, mingling their relics indistinguishably. In another world may they resume their individuality, and find it a happier one than here!

As we departed, a character came under our notice which I have met with in all almshouses, whether of the city or village, or in England or America. It was the familiar simpleton, who shuffled across the court-yard, clattering his wooden-soled shoes, to greet us with a howl or a laugh, I hardly know which, holding out his hand for a penny, and chuckling grossly when it was given him. All underwitted persons, so far as my experience goes, have this craving for copper coin, and appear to estimate its value by a miraculous instinct, which is one of the earliest gleams of human intelligence while the nobler faculties are yet in abeyance. There may come a time, even in this world, when we shall all understand that our tendency to the individual appropriation of gold and broad acres, fine houses, and such good and beautiful things as are equally enjoyable by a multitude, is but a trait of imperfectly developed intelligence, like the simpleton's cupidity of a penny. When that day dawns—and probably not till then—I imagine that there will be no more poor streets nor need of almshouses.

I was once present at the wedding of some poor English people, and was deeply impressed by the spectacle, though by no means with such proud and delightful emotions as seem to have affected all England on the recent occasion of the marriage of its Prince. It was in the Cathedral at Manchester, a particularly black and grim old structure, into which I had stepped to examine some ancient and curious wood-carvings within the choir. The woman in attendance greeted me with a smile, (which always glimmers forth on the feminine visage, I know not why, when a wedding is in question,) and asked me to take a seat in the nave till some poor parties were married, it being the Easter holidays, and a good time for them to marry, because no fees would be demanded by the clergyman. I sat down accordingly, and soon the parson and his clerk appeared at the altar, and a considerable crowd of people made their entrance at a side-door, and ranged themselves in a long, huddled line across the chancel. They were my acquaintances of the poor streets, or persons in a precisely similar condition of life, and were now come to their marriage-ceremony in just such garbs as I had always seen them wear; the men in their loafers' coats, out at elbows, or their laborers' jackets, defaced with grimy toil; the women drawing their shabby shawls tighter about their shoulders, to hide the raggedness beneath; all of them unbrushed, unshaven, unwashed, uncombed, and wrinkled with penury and care; nothing virgin-like in the brides, nor hopeful or energetic in the bridegrooms;—they were, in short, the mere rags and tatters of the human race, whom some east-wind of evil omen, howling along the streets, had chanced to sweep together into an unfragrant heap. Each and all of them, conscious of his or her individual misery, had blundered into the strange miscalculation of supposing that they could lessen the sum of it by multiplying it into the misery of another person. All the couples (and it was difficult, in such a confused crowd, to compute exactly their number) stood up at once, and had execution done upon them in the lump, the clergyman addressing only small parts of the service to each individual pair, but so managing the larger portion as to include the whole

company without the trouble of repetition. By this compen-
dious contrivance, one would apprehend, he came danger-
ously near making every man and woman the husband or
wife of every other; nor, perhaps, would he have perpetrated
much additional mischief by the mistake; but, after receiving
a benediction in common, they assorted themselves in their
own fashion, as they only knew how, and departed to the
garrets, or the cellars, or the unsheltered street-corners, where
their honeymoon and subsequent lives were to be spent. The
parson smiled decorously, the clerk and the sexton grinned
broadly, the female attendant tittered almost aloud, and even
the married parties seemed to see something exceedingly
funny in the affair; but for my part, though generally apt
enough to be tickled by a joke, I laid it away in my memory as
one of the saddest sights I ever looked upon.

Not very long afterwards, I happened to be passing the
same venerable Cathedral, and heard a clang of joyful bells,
and beheld a bridal party coming down the steps towards a
carriage and four horses, with a portly coachman and two
postillions, that waited at the gate. One parson and one service
had amalgamated the wretchedness of a score of paupers; a
Bishop and three or four clergymen had combined their spiritual might to forge the golden links of this other marriage-
bond. The bridegroom's mien had a sort of careless and kindly
English pride; the bride floated along in her white drapery, a
creature so nice and delicate that it was a luxury to see her,
and a pity that her silk slippers should touch anything so
grimy as the old stones of the churchyard avenue. The crowd
of ragged people, who always cluster to witness what they
may of an aristocratic wedding, broke into audible admiration
of the bride's beauty and the bridegroom's manliness, and
uttered prayers and ejaculations (possibly paid for in alms)
for the happiness of both. If the most favorable of earthly
conditions could make them happy, they had every prospect

of it. They were going to live on their abundance in one of those stately and delightful English homes, such as no other people ever created or inherited, a hall set far and safe within its own private grounds, and surrounded with venerable trees, shaven lawns, rich shrubbery, and trimmest pathways, the whole so artfully contrived and tended that summer rendered it a paradise, and even winter would hardly disrobe it of its beauty; and all this fair property seemed more exclusively and inalienably their own, because of its descent through many forefathers, each of whom had added an improvement or a charm, and thus transmitted it with a stronger stamp of rightful possession to his heir. And is it possible, after all, that there may be a flaw in the title-deeds? Is, or is not, the system wrong that gives one married pair so immense a superfluity of luxurious home, and shuts out a million others from any home whatever? One day or another, safe as they deem themselves, and safe as the hereditary temper of the people really tends to make them, the gentlemen of England will be compelled to face this question.

CIVIC BANQUETS

IT HAS OFTEN PERPLEXED me to imagine how an Englishman will be able to reconcile himself to any future state of existence, from which the earthly institution of Dinner shall be excluded. Even if he fail to take his appetite along with him, (which it seems to me hardly possible to believe, since this endowment is so essential to his composition,) the immortal day must still admit an interim of two or three hours during which he will be conscious of a slight distaste, at all events, if not an absolute repugnance to merely spiritual nutriment. The idea of Dinner has so embedded itself among his highest and deepest characteristics, so illuminated itself with intellect and softened itself with the kindest emotions of his heart, so linked itself with Church and State, and grown so majestic with long hereditary customs and ceremonies, that, by taking it utterly away, Death, instead of putting the final touch to his perfection, would leave him infinitely less complete than we have already known him. He could not be roundly happy. Paradise, among all its enjoyments, would lack one daily felicity which his sombre little island possessed. Perhaps it is not irreverent to conjecture that a provision may have been made, in this particular, for the Englishman's exceptional necessities. It strikes me that Milton was of the opinion here suggested, and may have intended to throw out a delightful and consolatory hope for his country-men, when he represents the genial Archangel, as playing his part with such excellent appetite at Adam's dinner-table, and confining himself to fruit and vegetables only because, in those early days of her housekeeping, Eve had no more accept-able viands to set before him. Milton, indeed, had a true English taste for the pleasures of the table, though refined by the lofty and poetic discipline to which he had subjected himself. It is delicately implied in the refection in Paradise, and more substantially, though still elegantly betrayed in the sonnet proposing to "Lawrence, of virtuous father virtuous son," a series of nice little dinners in mid-winter; and it blazes fully out in that untasted banquet which, elaborate as it was, Satan tossed up in a trice from the kitchen-ranges of Tartarus.

Among this people, indeed, so wise in their generation, Dinner has a kind of sanctity quite independent of the dishes that may be set upon the table; so that, if it be only a mutton-chop, they treat it with due reverence, and are re-warded with a degree of enjoyment which such reckless de-vourers as ourselves do not often find in our richest abun-dance. It is good to see how staunch they are after fifty or sixty years of heroic eating, still relying upon their digestive powers and indulging a vigorous appetite; whereas an Ameri-can has generally lost the one and learned to distrust the other long before reaching the earliest decline of life; and thence-forward he makes little account of his dinner, and dines at his peril if at all. I know not whether my countrymen will allow me to tell them, though I think it scarcely too much to affirm, that, on this side of the water, people never dine. At any rate, abundantly as Nature has provided us with most of the mate-rial requisites, the highest possible dinner has never yet been eaten in America. It is the consummate flower of civilization and refinement; and our inability to produce it, or to appreciate its admirable beauty if a happy inspiration should bring it into bloom, marks fatally the limit of culture which we have attained.

It is not to be supposed, however, that the mob of cultivated Englishmen know how to dine in this elevated sense. The unpolishable ruggedness of the national character is still an impediment to them, even in that particular line where they are best qualified to excel. Though often present at good men's feasts, I remember only a single dinner, which, while lamentably conscious that many of its higher excellencies were thrown away upon me, I yet could feel to be a perfect work of art. It could not, without unpardonable coarseness, be styled a matter of animal enjoyment, because, out of the very perfection of that lower bliss, there had arisen a dreamlike development of spiritual happiness. As in the master-pieces of painting and poetry, there was a something intangible, a final deliciousness that only fluttered about your comprehension, vanishing whenever you tried to detain it, and compelling you to recognize it by faith rather than sense. It seemed as if a diviner set of senses were requisite, and had been partly supplied, for the especial fruition of this banquet, and that the guests around the table (only eight in number) were becoming so educated, polished, and softened, by the delicate influences of what they ate and drank, as to be now a little more than mortal for the nonce. And there was that gentle, delicious sadness, too, which we find in the very summit of our most exquisite enjoyments, and feel it a charm beyond all the gaiety through which it keeps breathing its undertone. In the present case, it was worth a heavier sigh, to reflect that such a festal achievement—the production of so much art, skill, fancy, invention, and perfect taste—the growth of all the ages, which appeared to have been ripening for this hour, since man first began to eat and to moisten his foods with wine—must lavish its happiness upon so brief a moment, when other beautiful things can be made a joy forever. Yet a dinner like this is no better than we can get, any day, at the rejuvenescent Cornhill Coffee-house, unless the whole man, with soul, intellect, and stomach, is ready to appreciate it, and unless, moreover, there is such a harmony in all the circumstances and accompaniments, and especially such a pitch of well-according minds, that nothing shall jar rudely against the guest's thoroughly awakened sensibilities. The world, and especially our part of it, being the rough, ill-assorted, and tumultuous place we find it, a beef-steak is about as good as any other dinner.

The foregoing reminiscence, however, has drawn me aside from the main object of my sketch, in which I purposed to give a slight idea of those public, or partially public banquets, the custom of which so thoroughly prevails among the English people, that nothing is ever decided upon, in matters of peace or war, until they have chewed upon it in the shape of roast-beef, and talked it fully over in their cups. Nor are these festivities merely occasional, but of stated recurrence in all considerable municipalities and associated bodies. The most ancient times appear to have been as familiar with them as the Englishmen of to-day. In many of the old English towns, you find some stately Gothic hall or chamber, in which the Mayor and other authorities of the place have long held their sessions; and always, in convenient contiguity, there is a dusky kitchen, with an immense fire-place where an ox might lie roasting at his ease, though the less gigantic scale of modern cookery may now have permitted the cobwebs to gather in its chimney. Saint Mary's Hall, in Coventry, is so good a specimen of an ancient banquetting-room that perhaps I may profitably devote a page or two to the description of it.

In a narrow street, opposite to Saint Michael's church, one of the three famous spires of Coventry, you behold a mediæval edifice, in the basement of which is such a venerable and now deserted kitchen as I have above alluded to, and, on the same level, a cellar, with low stone-pillars and intersecting arches like the crypt of a cathedral. Passing up a well-worn staircase, the oaken balustrade of which is as black as ebony, you enter the fine old hall, some sixty feet in length, and broad and lofty in proportion. It is lighted by six windows of modern stained glass, on one side, and by the immense and magnificent arch of another window at the further end of the room, its rich and ancient panes constituting a genuine historical piece, in which are represented some of the kingly personages of old times, with their heraldic blazonries. Notwithstanding the colored light thus thrown into the hall, and though it was noon-day when I last saw it, the panelling of black oak, and some faded tapestry that hung round the walls, together with the cloudy vault of the roof above, made a gloom, which the richness only illuminated into more appreciable effect. The tapestry is wrought with figures in the dress of Henry the Sixth's time, (which is the date of the hall,) and is regarded by antiquaries as authentic evidence both for the costume of that epoch, and, I believe, for the actual portraiture of men known in history. They are as colorless as ghosts, however, and vanish drearily into the old stitch-work of their substance when you try to make them out. Coats-of-arms were formerly emblazoned all round the hall, but have been almost rubbed out by people hanging their overcoats against them, or by women with dishclouts and scrubbing-brushes, obliterating hereditary glories in their blind hostility to dust and spiders' webs. Full-length portraits of several English Kings, Charles the Second being the earliest, hang on the walls; and on the dais, or elevated part of the floor, stands an antique chair of state, which several royal characters are traditionally said to have occupied, while feasting here with their loyal subjects of Coventry. It is roomy enough for a person of kingly bulk, or even two such, but angular and uncomfortable, reminding me of the oaken settles which used to be seen in old-fashioned New England kitchens.

Overhead, supported by a self-sustaining power, without the aid of a single pillar, is the original ceiling of oak, precisely similar in shape to the roof of a barn, with all the beams and rafters plainly to be seen. At the remote height of sixty feet, you hardly discern that they are carved with figures of angels and doubtless many other devices, of which the admirable Gothic art is wasted in the duskiness that has so long been brooding there. Over the entrance of the hall, opposite the great arched window, the parti-colored radiance of which glimmers faintly through the interval, is a gallery for minstrels; and a row of ancient suits of armor is suspended from its balustrade. It impresses me, too, (for, having gone so far, I would fain leave nothing untouched upon,) that I remember, somewhere about these venerable precincts, a picture of the Countess Godiva on horseback, in which the artist has been so niggardly of that illustrious lady's hair, that, if she had no ampler garniture, there was certainly much need for the good people of Coventry to shut their eyes. After all my pains, I fear that I have made but a poor hand at the description, as regards a transference of the scene from my own mind to the reader's. It gave me a most vivid idea of antiquity that had been very little tampered with; insomuch that, if a group of steel-clad knights had come clanking through the door-way, and a bearded and be-ruffed old figure had handed in a stately dame, rustling in gorgeous robes of a long-forgotten fashion, unveiling a face of beauty somewhat tarnished in the mouldy tomb, yet stepping majestically to the trill of harp and viol from the minstrels' gallery, while the rusty armor responded with a hollow ringing sound beneath—why, I should have felt that these shadows, once so familiar with the spot, had a better right in Saint Mary's Hall than I, a stranger from a far country which has no Past. But the moral of the foregoing description is to show how tenaciously this love of pompous dinners, this reverence for Dinner as a sacred institution, has caught hold of the English character; since, from the earliest recognizable period, we find them building their civic banquetting-halls as magnificently as their palaces or cathedrals.

I know not whether the hall just described is now used for festive purposes, but others of similar antiquity and splendor still are. For example, there is Barber Surgeons' Hall, in London, a very fine old room, adorned with admirably carved wood-work on the ceiling and walls. It is also enriched with Holbein's master-piece, representing a grave assemblage of Barbers and Surgeons, all portraits (with such extensive beards that methinks one half of the company might have been profitably occupied in trimming the other) kneeling before King Henry the Eighth. Sir Robert Peel is said to have offered a thousand pounds for the liberty of cutting out one of the heads from this picture, he conditioning to have a perfect fac-simile painted in. The room has many other pictures of distinguished members of the company in long-past times, and of some of the monarchs and statesmen of England, all darkened with age, but darkened into such ripe magnificence as only age could bestow. It is not my design to inflict any more specimens of ancient hall-painting on the reader, but it may be worth while to touch upon other modes of stateliness that still survive in these time-honored civic-feasts, where there appears to be a singular assumption of dignity and solemn pomp by respectable citizens, who would never dream of claiming any privilege of rank outside of their own sphere. Thus, I saw two caps of state for the Warden and Junior Warden of the Company, caps of silver (real coronets or crowns, indeed, for these city-grandees) wrought in open-work and lined with crimson velvet. In a strong-closet, opening from the hall, there was a great deal of rich plate to furnish forth the banquet-table, comprising hundreds of forks and spoons, a vast silver punch-bowl, the gift of some jolly king or other, and, besides a multitude of less noticeable vessels, two Loving Cups, very elaborately wrought in silver-gilt, one presented by Henry the Eighth, the other by Charles the Second. These cups, including the covers and pedestals, are very large and weighty, although the bowl-part would hardly contain more than half a pint of wine, which, when the custom was first established, each guest was probably expected to drink off at a draught. In passing them from hand to hand a-down a long table of compotators, there is a peculiar ceremony which I may hereafter have occasion to describe. Meanwhile, if I might assume such a liberty, I should be glad to invite the reader to the official dinner-table of his Worship, the Mayor, at a large English sea-port where I spent several years.

The Mayor's dinner-parties occur as often as once a fort-night, and inviting his guests by fifty or sixty at a time, his Worship probably assembles at his board most of the eminent citizens and distinguished personages of the town and neigh-borhood, more than once during his year's incumbency, and very much, no doubt, to the promotion of good feeling among individuals of opposite parties and diverse pursuits in life. A miscellaneous party of Englishmen can always find more com-fortable ground to meet upon than as many Americans, their differences of opinion being incomparably less radical than ours, and it being the sincerest wish of all their hearts, whether they call themselves Liberals or what not, that noth-ing in this world shall ever be greatly altered from what it has been and is. Thus there is seldom such a virulence of political hostility that it may not be dissolved in a glass or two of wine, without making the good liquor any more dry or bitter than accords with English taste.

The first dinner of this kind, at which I had the honor to be present, took place during assize-time, and included among the guests the Judges and the prominent members of the bar. Reaching the Town Hall at seven o'clock, I communicated my name to one of several splendidly dressed footmen, and he repeated it to another on the first staircase, by whom it was passed to a third, and thence to a fourth at the door of the reception-room, losing all resemblance to the original sound in the course of these transmissions; so that I had the advantage of making my entrance in the character of a stranger, not only to the whole company, but to myself as well. His Worship, however, kindly recognized me, and put me on speaking terms with two or three gentlemen whom I found very affable, and all the more hospitably attentive on the score of my nationality. It is very singular how kind an Englishman will almost invariably be to an individual American, without ever bating a jot of his prejudice against the American character in the lump. My new acquaintances took evident pains to put me at my ease; and, in requital of their good nature, I soon began to look round at the general company in a critical spirit, making my crude observations apart, and drawing silent inferences, of the correctness of which I should not have been half so well satisfied a year afterwards, as at that moment.

There were two Judges present, a good many lawyers, and a few officers of the army in uniform. The other guests seemed to be principally of the mercantile class, and among them was a ship-owner from Nova Scotia, with whom I coalesced a little, inasmuch as we were born with the same sky over our heads, and an unbroken continuity of soil between his abode and mine. There was one old gentleman, whose character I never made out, with powdered hair, clad in black breeches and silk stockings, and wearing a rapier at his side; otherwise, with the exception of the military uniforms, there was little or no pretence of official costume. It being the first considerable assemblage of Englishmen that I had seen, my honest impression about them was, that they were a heavy and homely set of people, with a remarkable roughness of aspect and behavior, not repulsive, but beneath which it required more familiarity with the national character than I then possessed, always to detect the good-breeding of a gentleman. Being generally middle-aged, or still farther advanced, they were by no means graceful in figure; for the comeliness of the youthful Englishman rapidly diminishes with years, his body appearing to grow longer, his legs to abbreviate themselves, and his stomach to assume the dignified prominence which justly belongs to that metropolis of his system. His face (what with the acridity of the atmosphere, ale at lunch, wine at dinner, and a well-digested abundance of succulent food) gets red and mottled, and developes at least one additional chin, with a promise of more; so that, finally, a stranger recognizes his animal part at the most superficial glance, but must take time and a little pains to discover the intellectual. Comparing him with an American, I really thought that our national paleness and lean habit of flesh gave us greatly the advantage in an aesthetic point of view. It seemed to me, moreover, that the English tailor had not done so much as he might and ought for these heavy figures, but had gone on wilfully exaggerating their uncouthness by the roominess of their garments; he had evidently no idea of accuracy of fit, and smartness was entirely out of his line. But, to be quite open with the reader, I afterwards learned to think that this aforesaid tailor has a deeper art than his brethren among ourselves, knowing how to dress his customers with such individual propriety that they look as if they were born in their clothes, the fit being to the character rather than the form. If you make an Englishman smart, (unless he be a very exceptional one, of whom I have seen a few,) you make him a monster; his best aspect is that of ponderous respectability.

To make an end of these first impressions, I fancied that not merely the Suffolk bar, but the bar of any inland county in New England, might show a set of thin-visaged men, looking wretchedly worn, sallow, deeply wrinkled across the forehead and grimly furrowed about the mouth, with whom these heavy-cheeked English lawyers, slow-paced and fat-witted as they must needs be, would stand very little chance in a professional contest. How that matter might turn out, I am unqualified to decide. But I state these results of my earliest glimpses at Englishmen, not for what they are worth, but because I ultimately gave them up as worth little or nothing. In course of time, I came to the conclusion that Englishmen of all ages are a rather good-looking people, dress in admirable taste from their own point of view, and under a surface never silken to the touch, have a refinement of manners too thorough and genuine to be thought of as a separate endowment —that is to say, if the individual himself be a man of station, and has had gentlemen for his father and grandfather. The sturdy Anglo-Saxon nature does not refine itself short of the third generation. The tradesmen, too, and all other classes, have their own proprieties. The only value of my criticisms, therefore, lay in their exemplifying the proneness of a travel-ler, to measure one people by the distinctive characteristics of another, as English writers invariably measure us, and take upon themselves to be disgusted accordingly, instead of trying to find out some principle of beauty with which we may be in conformity.

In due time, we were summoned to the table, and went thither in no solemn procession, but with a good deal of jostling, thrusting behind, and scrambling for places when we reached our destination. The legal gentlemen, I suspect, were responsible for this indecorous zeal, which I never afterwards remarked in a similar party. The dining-hall was of noble size, and like the other rooms of the suite, was gorgeously painted and gilded and brilliantly illuminated. There was a splendid table-service, and a noble array of footmen, some of them in

plain clothes, and others wearing the town-livery richly decorated with gold-lace, and themselves excellent specimens of
the blooming young manhood of Britain. When we were
fairly seated, it was certainly an agreeable spectacle to look up
and down the long vista of earnest faces, and behold them so
resolute, so conscious that there was an important business in
hand, and so determined to be equal to the occasion. Indeed,
Englishman or not, I hardly know what can be prettier than a
snow-white table-cloth, a huge heap of flowers as a central
decoration, bright silver, rich china, crystal glasses, decanters
of Sherry at due intervals, a French roll and an artistically
folded napkin at each plate, all that airy portion of a banquet,
in short, that comes before the first mouthful, the whole
illuminated by a blaze of artificial light, without which a
dinner of made-dishes looks spectral and the simplest viands
are the best. Printed bills of fare were distributed, representing an abundant feast, no part of which appeared on the table
until called for in separate plates. I have entirely forgotten
what it was, but deem it no great matter, inasmuch as there is
a pervading common-place and identicalness in the composition of extensive dinners, on account of the impossibility of
supplying a hundred guests with anything particularly delicate or rare. It was suggested to me that certain juicy old
gentlemen had a private understanding what to call for, and
that it would be good policy in a stranger to follow in their
footsteps through the feast. I did not care to do so, however,
because, like Sancho Panza's dip out of Camacho's cauldron,
any sort of pot-luck at such a table would be sure to suit my
purpose; so I chose a dish or two on my own judgment, and
getting through my labors betimes, had great pleasure in
seeing the Englishmen toil onward to the end.

They drank rather copiously, too, though wisely; for I
observed that they seldom took Hock, and let the Champagne
bubble slowly away out of the goblet, solacing themselves

with Sherry, but tasting it warily before bestowing their final confidence. Their taste in wines, however, did not seem so exquisite, and certainly was not so various, as that to which many Americans pretend. This foppery of an intimate acquaintance with rare vintages does not suit a sensible Englishman, as he is very much in earnest about his wines and adopts one or two as his life-long friends, seldom exchanging them for any Dalilahs of a moment, and reaping the reward of his constancy in an unimpaired stomach, and only so much gout as he deems wholesome and desirable. Knowing well the measure of his powers, he is not apt to fill his glass too often. Society, indeed, would hardly tolerate habitual imprudencies of that kind, though, in my opinion, the Englishmen now upon the stage could carry off their three bottles, at need, with as steady a gait as any of their forefathers. It is not so very long since the three-bottle heroes sank finally under the table. It may be (at least, I should be glad if it were true) that there was an occult sympathy between our temperance-reform, now somewhat in abeyance, and the almost simultaneous disappearance of hard-drinking among the respectable classes in England. I remember a middle-aged gentleman telling me (in illustration of the very slight importance attached to breaches of temperance, within the memory of men not yet old) that he had seen a certain magistrate, Sir John Linkwater, or Drinkwater—but I think the jolly old knight could hardly have staggered under so perverse a mis-nomer as this last— while sitting on the magisterial bench, pull out a crown-piece and hand it to the clerk.—"Mr. Clerk," said Sir John, as if it were the most indifferent fact in the world, "I was drunk last night. There are my five shillings!"

During the dinner, I had a good deal of pleasant conversation with the gentlemen on either side of me. One of them, a lawyer, expatiated with great unction on the social standing of the Judges. Representing the dignity and authority of the

Crown, they take precedence, during assize-time, of the highest military men in the kingdom, of the Lord Lieutenant of
the county, of the Archbishops, of the royal Dukes, and even
of the Prince of Wales. For the nonce, they are the greatest
men in England. With a glow of professional complacency
that amounted to enthusiasm, my friend assured me, that, in
case of a royal dinner, a Judge, if actually holding an assize,
would be expected to offer his arm and take the Queen
herself to the table. Happening to be in company with some
of these elevated personages, on subsequent occasions, it appeared to me that the Judges are fully conscious of their
paramount claims to respect, and take rather more pains to
impress them on their ceremonial inferiors than men of high
hereditary rank are apt to do. Bishops, if it be not irreverent to
say so, are sometimes marked by a similar characteristic. Dignified position is so sweet to an Englishman that he needs to
be born in it, and to feel it thoroughly incorporated with his
nature from its original germ, in order to keep him from
flaunting it obtrusively in the faces of innocent bystanders.

My companion on the other side was a thick-set, middle-
aged man, uncouth in manners, and ugly where none were
handsome, with a dark, roughly hewn visage that looked grim
in repose, and seemed to hold within itself the machinery of a
very terrific frown. He ate with resolute appetite, and let slip
few opportunities of imbibing whatever liquids happened to
be passing by. I was meditating in what way this grisly
featured table-fellow might most safely be accosted, when he
turned to me with a surly sort of kindness, and invited me to
take a glass of wine. We then began a conversation that
abounded, on his part, with sturdy sense, and, somehow or
other, brought me closer to him than I had yet stood to an
Englishman. I should hardly have taken him to be an educated man, certainly not a scholar of accurate training, and yet
he seemed to have all the resources of education and trained

intellectual power at command. My fresh Americanism, and watchful observation of English characteristics, appeared either to interest or amuse him, or perhaps both. Under the mollifying influences of abundance of meat and drink, he grew very gracious, (not that I ought to use such a phrase to describe his evidently genuine good-will,) and, by-and-by, expressed a wish for further acquaintance, asking me to call at his rooms in London and inquire for Sergeant Wilkins— throwing out the name forcibly, as if he had no occasion to be ashamed of it. I remembered Dean Swift's retort to Sergeant Bettesworth on a similar announcement—"Of what regiment, pray, Sir?"—and fancied that the same question might not have been quite amiss if applied to the rugged individual at my side. But I heard of him subsequently as one of the prominent men at the English bar, a rough customer, and a terribly strong champion in criminal cases; and it caused me more regret than might have been expected, on so slight an acquaintanceship, when, not long afterwards, I saw his death announced in the newspapers. Not rich in attractive qualities, he possessed, I think, the most attractive one of all—thorough Manhood.

After the cloth was removed, a goodly group of decanters were set before the Mayor, who sent them forth on their outward voyage, full freighted with Port, Sherry, Madeira, and Claret, of which excellent liquors, methought, the latter found least acceptance among the guests. When every man had filled his glass, his Worship stood up and proposed a toast. It was, of course, "Our gracious Sovereign," or words to that effect; and, immediately, a band of musicians, whose preliminary tootings and thrummings I had already heard behind me, struck up "God save the Queen," and the whole company rose with one impulse to assist in singing that famous national anthem. It was the first time in my life that I had ever seen a body of men, or even a single man, under the active influence of the sentiment of Loyalty; for though we call ourselves loyal to our country and institutions, and prove it by our readiness to shed blood and sacrifice life in their behalf, still the principle is as cold and hard, in an American bosom, as the steel spring that puts in motion a powerful machinery. In the Englishman's system, a force similar to that of our steel spring is generated by the warm throbbings of human hearts. He clothes our bare abstraction in flesh and blood—at present, in the flesh and blood of a woman—and manages to combine love, awe, and intellectual reverence, all in one emotion, and to embody his mother, his wife, his children, the whole idea of kindred, in a single person, and make her the representative of his country and its laws. We Americans smile superior, as I did at the Mayor's table; and yet, I fancy, we lose some very agreeable titillations of the heart in consequence of our proud prerogative of caring no more about our President than for a man of straw, or a stuffed scarecrow straddling in a cornfield.

But, to say the truth, the spectacle struck me rather ludicrously, to see this party of stout, middle-aged and elderly gentlemen, in the fulness of meat and drink, their ample and ruddy faces glistening with wine, perspiration, and enthusiasm, rumbling out those strange old stanzas from the very bottom of their hearts and stomachs, which two organs, in the English interior arrangement, lie closer together than in ours. The song seemed to me the rudest old ditty in the world; but I could not wonder at its universal acceptance and indestructible popularity, considering how inimitably it expresses the national faith and feeling as regards the inevitable righteousness of England, the Almighty's consequent respect and partiality for that redoubtable little island, and His presumed readiness to strengthen its defence against the contumacious wickedness and knavery of all other principalities or republics. Tennyson himself, though evidently English to the very last prejudice, could not write half so good a song for the purpose. Finding that the entire dinner-table struck in, with voices of every pitch between rolling thunder and the squeak of a cart-wheel, and that the strain was not of such delicacy as to be much hurt by the harshest of them, I determined to lend my own assistance in swelling the triumphant roar. It seemed but a proper courtesy to the first Lady in the land, whose guest, in the largest sense, I might consider myself. Accordingly, my first tuneful efforts (and probably my last, for I purpose not to sing any more, unless it be "Hail Columbia" on the restoration of the Union) were poured freely forth in honor of Queen Victoria. The Sergeant smiled like the carved head of a Swiss nut-cracker, and the other gentlemen in my neighborhood, by nods and gestures, evinced grave approbation of so suitable a tribute to English superiority, and we finished our stave and sat down in an extremely happy frame of mind.

Other toasts followed in honor of the great institutions and interests of the country, and speeches in response to each were made by individuals whom the Mayor designated or the company called for. None of them impressed me with a very high idea of English post-prandial oratory. It is inconceivable, indeed, what ragged and shapeless utterances most Englishmen are satisfied to give vent to, without attempting anything like artistic shape, but clapping on a patch here and another there, and ultimately getting out what they want to say, and generally with a result of sufficiently good sense, but in some such disorganized mass as if they had thrown it up rather than spoken it. It seemed to me that this was almost as much by choice as necessity. An Englishman, ambitious of public favor, should not be too smooth. If an orator is glib, his countrymen distrust him. They dislike smartness. The stronger and heavier his thoughts, the better, provided there be an element of common-place running through them; and any rough, yet never vulgar force of expression, such as would knock an opponent down if it hit him, only it must not be too personal, is altogether to their taste; but a studied neatness of language, or other such superficial graces, they cannot abide. They do not often permit a man to make himself a fine orator of malice aforethought; that is, unless he be a nobleman, (as, for example, Lord Stanley, of the Derby family,) who, as a hereditary legislator and necessarily a public speaker, is bound to remedy a poor natural delivery in the best way he can. On the whole, I partly agree with them, and, if I cared for any oratory whatever, should be as likely to applaud theirs as our own. When an English speaker sits down, you feel that you have been listening to a real man, and not to an actor; his sentiments have a wholesome earth-smell in them, though, very likely, this apparent naturalness is as much an art as what we expend in rounding a sentence or elaborating a peroration.

It is one good effect of this inartificial style, that nobody in England seems to feel any shyness about shovelling the untrimmed and untrimmable ideas out of his mind for the benefit of an audience. At least, nobody did on the occasion now in hand, except a poor little Major of Artillery, who responded for the Army in a thin, quavering voice, with a terribly hesitating trickle of fragmentary ideas, and, I question not, would rather have been bayoneted in front of his batteries than to have said a word. Not his own mouth, but the cannon's, was this poor Major's proper organ of utterance.

While I was thus amiably occupied in criticizing my fellow-guests, the Mayor had got up to propose another toast; and listening rather inattentively to the first sentence or two, I soon became sensible of a drift in his Worship's remarks that made me glance apprehensively towards Sergeant Wilkins. "Yes," grumbled that gruff personage, shoving a decanter of Port towards me, "it is your turn next"; and seeing in my face,

I suppose, the consternation of a wholly unpractised orator, he kindly added—"It is nothing! A mere acknowledgement will answer the purpose. The less you say, the better they will like it!" That being the case, I suggested that perhaps they would like it best if I said nothing at all. But the Sergeant shook his head. Now, on first receiving the Mayor's invitation to dinner, it had occurred to me that I might possibly be brought into my present predicament, but I had dismissed the idea from my mind as too disagreeable to be entertained, and, moreover, as so alien from my disposition and character, that Fate surely could not keep such a misfortune in store for me. If nothing else prevented, an earthquake or the crack of doom would certainly interfere before I need rise to speak. Yet here was the Mayor getting on inexorably—and, indeed, I heartily wished that he might get on and on forever, and of his wordy wanderings find no end.

If the gentle reader, my kindest friend and closest confidant, deigns to desire it, I can impart to him my own experience as a public speaker quite as indifferently as if it concerned another person. Indeed, it does concern another, or a mere spectral phenomenon, for it was not I, in my proper and natural self, that sat there at table or subsequently rose to speak. At the moment, then, if the choice had been offered me whether the Mayor should let off a speech at my head or a pistol, I should unhesitatingly have taken the latter alternative. I had really nothing to say, not an idea in my head, nor, which was a great deal worse, any flowing words or embroidered sentences in which to dress out that empty Nothing and give it a cunning aspect of intelligence, such as might last the poor Vacuity the little time it had to live. But time pressed; the Mayor brought his remarks, affectionately eulogistic of the United States and highly complimentary to their distinguished representative at that table, to a close, amid a vast deal of cheering; and the band struck up "Hail Columbia," I believe, though it might have been "Old Hundred," or "God save the Queen" over again, for anything that I should have known or cared. When the music ceased, there was an intensely disagreeable instant, during which I seemed to rend away and fling off the habit of a lifetime, and rose, still void of ideas, but with preternatural composure, to make a speech. The guests rattled on the table and cried "Hear!" most vociferously, as if now, at length, in this foolish and idly garrulous world, had come the long-expected moment when one golden word was to be spoken; and in that imminent crisis, I caught a glimpse of a little bit of an effusion of international sentiment, which it might, and must, and should do to utter.

Well; it was nothing, as the Sergeant had said. What surprised me most was the sound of my own voice, which I had never before heard at a declamatory pitch, and which impressed me as belonging to some other person, who, and not myself, would be responsible for the speech—a prodigious consolation and encouragement, under the circumstances! I went on without the slightest embarrassment, and sat down amid great applause, wholly undeserved by anything that I had spoken, but well-won from Englishmen, methought, by the new development of pluck that alone had enabled me to speak at all.—"It was handsomely done!" quoth Sergeant Wilkins; and I felt like a recruit who has been for the first time under fire.

I would gladly have ended my oratorical career, then and there, forever, but was often placed in a similar or worse position, and compelled to meet it as I best might; for this was one of the necessities of an office which I had voluntarily taken on my shoulders, and beneath which I might be crushed by no moral delinquency, on my own part, but could not shirk without cowardice and shame. My subsequent fortune was various. Once, though I felt it to be a kind of imposture, I got a speech by heart, and doubtless it might have been a very pretty one, only I forgot every syllable at the moment of need, and had to improvise another as well as I could. I found it a better method to pre-arrange a few points in my mind, and trust to the spur of the occasion, and the kind aid of Providence, for enabling me to bring them to bear. The presence of any considerable proportion of personal friends generally dumb-foundered me. I would rather have talked with an enemy in the gate. Invariably, too, I was much embarrassed by a small audience, and succeeded better with a large one, the sympathy of a multitude possessing a buoyant effect, which lifts the speaker a little way out of his individuality and tosses him towards a perhaps better range of sentiment than his private one. Again, if I rose carelessly and confidently, with an expectation of going through the business entirely at my ease, I often found that I had little or nothing to say; whereas, if I came to the charge in perfect despair, and at a crisis when failure would have been horrible, it once or twice happened that the frightful emergency concentrated my poor faculties, and enabled me to give definite and vigorous expression to sentiments which, an instant before, looked as vague and far-off as the clouds in the atmosphere. On the whole, poor as my own success may have been, I apprehend that any intelligent man with a tongue possesses the chief requisite of oratorical power, and may develope many of the others, if he deems it worth while to bestow a great amount of labor and pains on an object which the most accomplished orators, I suspect, have not found altogether satisfactory to their highest impulses. At any rate, it must be a remarkably true man who can keep his own elevated conception of truth when the lower feeling of a multitude is assailing his natural sympathies, and who can speak out frankly the best that there is in him, when, by adulterating it a little, or a good deal, he knows that he may make it ten times as acceptable to the audience.

This slight article on the civic banquets of England would be too wretchedly imperfect, without an attempted description of a Lord Mayor's dinner at the Mansion House, in London. I should have preferred the annual feast at Guildhall, but never had the good fortune to witness it. Once, however, I was honored with an invitation to one of the regular dinners, and gladly accepted it; taking the precaution, nevertheless, though it hardly seemed necessary, to inform the City-King, through a mutual friend, that I was no fit representative of American eloquence, and must humbly make it a condition that I should not be expected to open my mouth, except for the reception of his Lordship's bountiful hospitality. The reply was gracious and acquiescent; so that I presented myself in the great entrance-hall of the Mansion House, at half-past six o'clock, in a state of most enjoyable freedom from the pusillanimous apprehensions that often tormented me, at such times. The Mansion House was built in Queen Anne's days, in the very heart of old London, and is a palace worthy of its inhabitant, were he really as great a man as his traditionary state and pomp would seem to indicate. Times are changed, however, since the days of Whittington, or even of Hogarth's Industrious Apprentice, to whom the highest imaginable reward of life-long integrity was a seat in the Lord Mayor's chair. People now-a-days say that the real dignity and importance have perished out of the office, as they do, sooner or later, out of all earthly institutions, leaving only a painted and gilded shell like that of an Easter egg, and that it is only second-rate and third-rate men who now condescend to be ambitious of the Mayoralty. I felt a little grieved at this; for the original emigrants of New England had strong sympathies with the people of London, who were mostly Puritans in religion and Parliamentarians in politics, in the early days of our country; so that the Lord Mayor was a potentate of huge dimensions in the estimation of our forefathers, and held to be hardly second to the prime minister of the throne. The true great men of the city now appear to have aims beyond city-greatness, connecting themselves with national politics, and seeking to be identified with the aristocracy of the country.

In the entrance-hall I was received by a body of footmen dressed in a livery of blue coats and buff breeches, in which they looked wonderfully like American revolutionary generals, only bedizened with far more lace and embroidery than those simple and grand old heroes ever dreamed of wearing. There were likewise two very imposing figures whom I should have taken to be military men of rank, being arrayed in scarlet coats and large silver epaulets; but they turned out to be officers of the Lord Mayor's household, and were now employed in assigning to the guests the places which they were respectively to occupy at the dinner-table. Our names (for I had included myself in a little group of friends) were announced; and, ascending the staircase, we met his Lordship in the door-way of the first reception-room, where, also, we had the advantage of a presentation to the Lady Mayoress. As this distinguished couple retired into private life at the termination of their year of office, it is inadmissible to make any remarks, critical or laudatory, on the manners and bearing of two personages, suddenly emerging from a position of respectable mediocrity into one of pre-eminent dignity within their own sphere. Such individuals almost always seem to grow nearly or quite to the full size of their office. If it were desirable to write an essay on the latent aptitude of ordinary people for grandeur, we have an exemplification in our own country, and on a scale incomparably greater than that of the Mayoralty, though invested with nothing like the outward magnificence that gilds and embroiders the latter. If I have been correctly informed, the Lord Mayor's salary is exactly double that of the President of the United States, and yet is found very inadequate to his necessary expenditure.

There were two reception-rooms, thrown into one by the opening of wide folding-doors; and though in an old style, and not yet so old as to be venerable, they are remarkably handsome apartments, lofty as well as spacious, with carved ceilings and walls, and, at either end, a splendid fire-place of white marble, ornamented with sculptured wreaths of flowers and foliage. The company were about three hundred, many of them celebrities in politics, war, literature, and science, though I recollect none pre-eminently distinguished in either department. But it is certainly a pleasant mode of doing honor to men of literature, for example, who deserve well of the public, yet do not often meet it face to face, thus to bring them together, under genial auspices, in connexion with persons of note in other lines. I know not what may be the Lord Mayor's mode or principle of selecting his guests, nor whether, during his official term, he can proffer his hospitality to every man of noticeable talent in the wide world of London, nor, in fine, whether his Lordship's invitation is much sought for or valued; but it seemed to me that this periodical feast is one of the many sagacious methods which the English have contrived, for keeping up a good understanding among different sorts of people. Like most other distinctions of society, however, I presume that the Lord Mayor's card does not often seek out modest merit, but comes at last when the recipient is conscious of the bore, and doubtful about the honor.

One very pleasant characteristic, which I never met with at any other public, or partially public dinner, was the presence of ladies. No doubt, they were principally the wives and daughters of city-magnates; and if we may judge from the many sly allusions in old plays and satirical poems, the city of London has always been famous for the beauty of its women and the reciprocal attractions between them and the men of quality. Be that as it might; while straying hither and thither through those crowded apartments, I saw much reason for modifying certain heterodox opinions which I had imbibed, in my transatlantic newness and rawness, as regarded the delicate character and frequent occurrence of English beauty. To state the entire truth, (being, at this period, some years old in English life,) my taste, I fear, had long since begun to be deteriorated by acquaintance with other models of feminine loveliness than it was my happiness to know, in America. I often found, or seemed to find, if I may dare to confess it, in the persons of such of my dear countrywomen as I now occasionally met, a certain meagreness, (Heaven forbid that I should call it scrawniness!) a deficiency of physical development, a scantiness, so to speak, in the pattern of their material make, a paleness of complexion, a thinness of voice, all of which characteristics, nevertheless, only made me resolve so much the more sturdily to uphold these fair creatures as angels, because I was sometimes driven to a half-acknowledgement that the English ladies, looked at from a lower point of view, were perhaps a little finer animals than they. The advantages of the latter, if any they could really be said to have, were all comprised in a few additional lumps of clay on their shoulders and other parts of their figures. It would be a pitiful bargain to give up the ethereal charm of American beauty in exchange for half a hundred-weight of human clay!

At a given signal we all found our way into an immense room, called the Egyptian Hall, I know not why, except that the architecture was classic, and as different as possible from the ponderous style of Memphis and the pyramids. A powerful band played inspiringly as we entered, and a brilliant profusion of lights shone down on two long-tables, extending the whole length of the hall, and a cross-table between them, occupying nearly its entire breadth. Glass gleamed and silver glistened on an acre or two of snowy damask, over which were set out all the accompaniments of a stately feast. We found

our places without much difficulty, and the Lord Mayor's
chaplain implored a blessing on the food; a ceremony which
the English never omit, at a great dinner or a small one, yet
consider, I fear, not so much a religious rite as a sort of
preliminary relish before the soup.

The soup, of course, on this occasion, was turtle, of which,
in accordance with immemorial custom, each guest was allowed two plates-full, in spite of the otherwise immitigable
law of table-decorum. Indeed, judging from the proceedings
of the gentlemen near me, I surmised that there was no
practical limit except the appetite of the guests and the capacity of the soup-tureens. Not being fond of this civic dainty, I
partook of it but once, and then only in accordance with the
wise maxim always to taste a fruit, a wine, or a celebrated
dish, at its indigenous site; and the very fountain-head of
turtle-soup, I suppose, is in the Lord Mayor's dinner-pot. It is
one of those orthodox customs, which people follow for half-
a-century without knowing why, to drink a sip of rum-punch
in a very small tumbler, after the soup. It was excellently
well-brewed, and it seemed to me almost worth while to sup
the soup for the sake of sipping the punch. The rest of the
dinner was catalogued in a bill of fare, printed on delicate
white paper within an arabesque border of green and gold. It
looked very good not only in the English and French names of
the numerous dishes, but also in the positive reality of the
dishes themselves, which were all set on the table to be carved
and distributed by the guests. This ancient and honest
method is attended with a good deal of trouble and a lavish
effusion of gravy, yet by no means bestowed or dispensed in
vain, because you have thereby the absolute assurance of a
banquet actually before your eyes, instead of a shadowy promise in the bill of fare, and such meagre fulfilment as a single
guest can contrive to get upon his individual plate. I wonder
that Englishmen, who are fond of looking at prize oxen in the

shape of butcher's meat, do not generally better estimate the aesthetic gourmandism of devouring the whole dinner with their eyesight, before proceeding to nibble the comparatively few morsels which, after all, the most heroic appetite and widest stomachic capacity of mere mortals can enable even an alderman really to eat. There fell to my lot three delectable things enough, which I take pains to remember, that the reader may not go away wholly unsatisfied from the Barmecide feast to which I have bidden him; a red mullet, a plate of mushrooms exquisitely stewed, and part of a ptarmigan, a bird of the same family as the grouse, but feeding high up towards the summit of the Scotch mountains, whence it gets a wild delicacy of flavor very superior to that of the artificially nurtured English game-fowl. All the other dainties have vanished from my memory as completely as those of Prospero's banquet after Ariel had clapped his wings over it. The band played at intervals, inspiriting us to new efforts, as did likewise the sparkling wines which the footmen supplied from an inexhaustible cellar, and which the guests quaffed with little apparent reference to the disagreeable fact, that there comes a tomorrow-morning after every feast. As long as that shall be the case, a prudent man can never have full enjoyment of his dinner.

Nearly opposite to me, on the other side of the table, sat a young lady in white, whom I am sorely tempted to describe, but dare not, because not only the supereminence of her beauty, but its peculiar character, would cause the sketch to be recognized, however rudely it might be drawn. I hardly thought that there existed such a woman, outside of a picture-frame or the covers of a romance; not that I had ever met with her resemblance even there, but being so distinct and singular an apparition, she seemed likelier to find her sisterhood in poetry and picture than in real life. Let us turn away from her, lest a touch too apt should compel her stately, and cold, and soft, and womanly grace, to gleam out upon my page, with a strange repulsion and unattainableness in the very spell that made her beautiful. At her side, and familiarly attentive to her, sat a gentleman of whom I remember only a hard outline of the nose and forehead, and such a monstrous portent of a beard that you could discover no symptom of a mouth, except when he opened it to speak, or to put in a morsel of food. Then, indeed, you suddenly became aware of a cave, hidden behind the impervious and darksome shrubbery. There could be no doubt who this gentleman and lady were. Any child would have recognized them at a glance. It was Bluebeard and a new wife, (the loveliest of the series, but with already a mysterious gloom overshadowing her fair young brow,) travelling in their honeymoon, and dining, among other distinguished strangers, at the Lord Mayor's table.

After an hour or two of valiant achievement with knife and fork, came the dessert; and at the point of the festival where finger-glasses are usually introduced, a large silver-basin was carried round to the guests, containing rose-water, into which we dipped the ends of our napkins and were conscious of a delightful fragrance, instead of that heavy and weary odor, the hateful ghost of a defunct dinner. This seems to be an ancient custom of the city, not confined to the Lord Mayor's table, but never met with westward of Temple Bar.

During all the feast, in accordance with another ancient custom, the origin or purport of which I do not remember to have heard, there stood a man in armor, with a helmet on his head, behind his Lordship's chair. When the after-dinner wine was placed on the table, still another official personage appeared behind the chair and proceeded to make a solemn and sonorous proclamation (in which he enumerated the principal guests, comprising three or four noblemen, several baronets, and plenty of generals, members of Parliament, aldermen, and other names of the illustrious, one of which sounded strangely familiar to my ears) ending in some such style as this—"And other gentlemen and ladies, here present, the Lord Mayor drinks to you all in a Loving Cup"—giving a sort of sentimental twang to the two words—"and sends it round among you!" And forthwith the Loving Cup—several of them, indeed, on each side of the tables—came slowly down with all the antique ceremony.

The fashion of it is thus. The Lord Mayor, standing up and taking the covered cup in both hands, presents it to the guest at his elbow, who likewise rises, and removes the cover for his Lordship to drink, which being successfully accomplished, the guest replaces the cover and receives the cup into his own hands. He then presents it to his next neighbor, that the cover may be again removed for himself to take a draught, after which the third person goes through a similar manœuvre with a fourth, and he with a fifth, until the whole company find themselves inextricably intertwisted and entangled in one complicated chain of love. When the cup came to my hands, I examined it critically, both inside and out, and perceived it to be an antique and richly ornamented silver goblet, capable of holding about a quart of wine. Considering how much trouble we all expended in getting the cup to our lips, the guests appeared to content themselves with wonderfully moderate potations. In truth, nearly or quite the original quart of wine being still in the goblet, it seemed doubtful whether any of the company had more than barely touched the silver rim before passing it to their neighbors—a degree of abstinence that might be accounted for by a fastidious repugnance to so many compotators in one cup, or possibly by a disapprobation of the liquor. Being curious to know all about these important matters, with a view of recommending to my countrymen whatever they might usefully adopt, I drank an honest sip from the Loving Cup, and had no occasion for another—ascertaining it to be Claret of a poor original quality, largely mingled with water, and spiced and sweetened. It was good enough, however, for a merely spectral or ceremonial drink, and could never have been intended for any better purpose.

The toasts now began in the customary order, attended with speeches neither more nor less witty and ingenious than the specimens of table-eloquence which had heretofore delighted me. As preparatory to each new display, the herald, or whatever he was, behind the chair of state, gave awful notice that the Right Honorable, the Lord Mayor, was about to propose a toast. His Lordship being happily delivered thereof, together with some accompanying remarks, the band played an appropriate tune, and the herald again issued proclamation to the effect that such or such a nobleman, or gentleman, general, dignified clergyman, or what not, was going to respond to the Right Honorable, the Lord Mayor's toast; then, if I mistake not, there was another prodigious flourish of trumpets and twanging of stringed instruments; and finally the doomed individual, waiting all this while to be decapitated, got up and proceeded to make a fool of himself. A bashful young earl tried his maiden oratory on the good citizens of London, and having evidently got every word by heart, (even including, however he managed it, the most seemingly casual improvisations of the moment,) he really spoke like a book, and made incomparably the smoothest speech I ever heard in England.

The weight and gravity of the speakers, not only on this occasion, but all similar ones, was what impressed me as most extraordinary, not to say absurd. Why should people eat a good dinner, and put their spirits into festive trim with Champagne, and afterwards mellow themselves into a most enjoyable state of quietude with copious libations of Sherry and old Port, and then disturb the whole excellent result by listening to speeches as heavy as an after-dinner nap, and in no degree so refreshing? If the Champagne had thrown its sparkle over the surface of these effusions, or if the generous Port had shone through their substance with a ruddy glow of the old English humor, I might have seen a reason for honest gentlemen prattling in their cups, and should undoubtedly have been glad to be a listener. But there was no attempt nor impulse of the kind, on the part of the orators, nor apparent expectation of such a phenomenon on that of the audience. In fact, I imagine that the latter were best pleased when the speaker embodied his ideas in the figurative language of arithmetic, or struck upon any hard matter of business or statistics, as a heavy-laden barque bumps upon a rock in mid-ocean. The sad severity, the too-earnest utilitarianism, of modern life, have wrought a radical and lamentable change, I am afraid, in this ancient and goodly institution of Civic Banquets. People used to come to them, a few hundred years ago, for the sake of being jolly; they come now with an odd notion of pouring sober wisdom into their wine, by way of wormwood-bitters, and thus make such a mess of it that the wine and wisdom reciprocally spoil one another.

Possibly, the foregoing sentiments have taken a spice of acridity from a circumstance that happened about this stage of the feast, and very much interrupted my own further enjoyment of it. Up to this time, my condition had been exceedingly felicitous, both on account of the brilliancy of the scene, and because I was in close proximity with three very pleasant English friends. One of them was a lady, whose honored name my readers would recognize as a household word, if I dared write it; another, a gentleman, likewise well known to them, whose fine taste, kind heart, and genial cultivation, are qualities seldom mixed in such happy proportion as in him. The third was the man to whom I owed most in England, the warm benignity of whose nature was never weary of doing me good, who led me to many scenes of life, in town, camp, and country, which I never could have found out for myself, who knew precisely the kind of help a stranger needs, and gave it as freely as if he had not had a thousand more important things to live for. Thus, I never felt safer or cosier at any-body's fireside, even my own, than at the dinner-table of the Lord Mayor.

Out of this serene sky came a thunderbolt. His Lordship got up and proceeded to make some very eulogistic remarks upon "the literary and commercial"—I question whether those two adjectives were ever before married by a copulative conjunction, and they certainly would not live together in illicit intercourse, of their own accord—"the literary and commercial attainments of an eminent gentleman there present," and then went on to speak of the relations of blood and interest between Great Britain and the aforesaid eminent gentleman's native country. Those bonds were more intimate than had ever before existed between two great nations, throughout all history, and his Lordship felt assured that that whole honorable company would join him in the expression of a fervent wish that they might be held inviolably sacred, on both sides of the Atlantic, now and forever. Then came the same wearisome old toast, dry and hard to chew upon as a musty sea-biscuit, which had been the text of nearly all the oratory of my public career. The herald sonorously announced that Mr. So-and-so would now respond to his Right Honorable Lordship's toast and speech; the trumpets sounded the customary flourish for the onset; there was a thunderous rumble of anticipatory applause, and finally a deep silence sank upon the festive hall.

All this was a horrid piece of treachery on the Lord Mayor's part, after beguiling me within his lines on a pledge of safe-conduct; and it seemed very strange that he could not let an unobtrusive individual eat his dinner in peace, drink a small sample of the Mansion House wine, and go away grateful at heart for the old English hospitality. If his Lordship had sent me an infusion of ratsbane in the Loving Cup, I should have taken it much more kindly at his hands. But I suppose the secret of the matter to have been somewhat as follows.

All England, just then, was in one of those singular fits of panic excitement, (not fear, though as sensitive and tremulous as that emotion,) which, in consequence of the homogeneous character of the people, their intense patriotism, and their dependence for their ideas in public affairs on other sources than their own examination and individual thought, are more sudden, pervasive, and unreasoning, than any similar mood of our own public. In truth, I have never seen the American public in a state at all similar, and believe that we are incapable of it. Our excitements are not impulsive, like theirs, but, right or wrong, are moral and intellectual. For example, the grand rising of the North, at the commencement of this war, bore the aspect of impulse and passion only because it was so universal, and necessarily done in a moment, just as the quiet and simultaneous getting-up of a thousand people out of their chairs would cause a tumult that might be mistaken for a storm. We were cool then, and have been cool ever since, and shall remain cool to the end, which we shall take coolly, whatever it may be. There is nothing which the English find it so difficult to understand in us as this characteristic. They imagine us, in our collective capacity, a kind of wild beast, whose normal condition is savage fury, and are always looking for the moment when we shall break through the slender barriers of international law and comity, and compel the reasonable part of the world, with themselves at the head, to combine for the purpose of putting us into a stronger cage. At times, this apprehension becomes so powerful, (and when one man feels it, a million do,) that it resembles the passage of the wind over a broad field of grain, where you see the whole crop bending and swaying beneath one impulse, and each separate stalk tossing with the self-same disturbance as its myriad companions. At such periods, all Englishmen talk with a terrible identity of sentiment and expression. You have the whole country in each man; and not one of them all, if you put him strictly to the question, can give a reasonable ground for his alarm. There are but two nations in the world—our own country and France—that can put England into this singular state. It is the united sensitiveness of a people extremely well-to-do, careful of their country's honor, most anxious for the preservation of the cumbrous and moss-grown prosperity which they have been so long in consolidating, and incompetent (owing to the national half-sightedness, and their habit of trusting to a few leading minds for their public opinion) to judge when that prosperity is really threatened.

If the English were accustomed to look at the foreign side of any international dispute, they might easily have satisfied themselves that there was very little danger of a war at that particular crisis, from the simple circumstance that their own government had positively not an inch of honest ground to stand upon, and could not fail to be aware of the fact. Neither could they have met Parliament with any show of a justification for incurring war. It was no such perilous juncture as exists now, when law and right are really controverted on sustainable or plausible grounds, and a naval commander may at any moment fire off the first cannon of a terrible contest. If I remember it correctly, it was a mere diplomatic squabble, in which the British ministers, with the politic generosity which they are in the habit of showing towards their official subordinates, had tried to browbeat us for the purpose of sustaining an ambassador in an indefensible proceeding; and the American government (for God had not denied us an administration of Statesmen, then) had retaliated with staunch courage and exquisite skill, putting inevitably a cruel mortification upon their opponents, but indulging them with no pretence whatever for active resentment.

Now the Lord Mayor, like any other Englishman, probably fancied that War was on the western gale, and was glad to lay hold of even so insignificant an American as myself, who might be made to harp on the rusty old strings of national sympathies, identity of blood and interest, and community of language and literature, and whisper peace where there was no peace, in however weak an utterance. And, possibly, his Lordship thought, in his wisdom, that the good-feeling which was sure to be expressed by a company of well-bred Englishmen, at his august and far-famed dinner-table, might have an appreciable influence on the grand result. Thus, when the Lord Mayor invited me to his feast, it was a piece of strategy. He wanted to induce me to fling myself, like a lesser Curtius with a larger object of self-sacrifice, into the chasm of discord between England and America, and, on my ignominious demur, had resolved to shove me in with his own right-honorable hands, in the hope of closing up the horrible pit forever. On the whole, I forgive his Lordship! He meant well by all parties—himself, who would share the glory, and me, who ought to have desired nothing better than such an heroic opportunity—his own country, which would continue to get cotton and breadstuffs, and mine, which would get everything that men work with and wear.

As soon as the Lord Mayor began to speak, I rapped upon my mind, and it gave forth a hollow sound, being absolutely empty of appropriate ideas. I never thought of listening to his speech, because I knew it all beforehand in twenty repetitions from other lips, and was aware that it would not offer a single suggestive point. In this dilemma, I turned to one of my three friends, a gentleman whom I knew to possess an enviable flow of silver speech, and obtested him, by whatever he deemed holiest, to give me at least an available thought or two, to start with, and, once afloat, I would trust to my guardian angel for enabling me to flounder ashore again. He advised me to begin with some remarks complimentary to the Lord Mayor, and expressive of the hereditary reverence in which his office was held—at least, my friend thought that there would be no harm in giving his Lordship this little sugar-plum, whether quite the fact or no—was held by the descendants of the Puritan forefathers. Thence, if I liked, getting flexible with the oil of my own eloquence, I might easily slide off into the momentous subject of the relations between England and America, to which his Lordship had made such weighty allusion.

Seizing this handfull of straw with a death-grip, and bidding my three friends bury me honorably, I got upon my legs to save both countries, or perish in the attempt. The tables roared and thundered at me, and suddenly were silent again. But, as I have never happened to stand in a position of greater dignity and peril, I deem it a stratagem of sage policy here to close these Sketches, leaving myself still erect in so heroic an attitude.

THE END.

APPENDIXES

4.28 impressions] Here as elsewhere a not very clear final "s" seems to have been overlooked by the compositor, and the error was not detected in proof or in preparing the copy for the book.

10.4 Cubans who professed] The MS comma after "Cubans" makes the series ambiguous, whereas the lack of a comma in I indicates clearly that the Cubans alone are to be associated with Narcisco Lopez, who was captured and executed in Havana in 1851.

13.19–14.23 The individual . . . entreaty.] The original (MS^a) form on fol. 9 was revised by two unnumbered pages (MS^b) headed "(I wish to alter this paragraph in the proof [in the proof *interlined with a caret*] as follows, in accordance with some notes (made at the time) which I have just found.)". In the line below is written, "(Page 17 Consular Experiences)". There follows the expanded text as printed in I, ending with a bridging phrase at the return to MS^a: "He had but scanty and scattered thoughts in his gray head &c." and then the notation, "(When you send the next proof, I wish you enclose one of the above.)". It is clear from the reference to page 17 of the first edition that Hawthorne had before him the proofs for gathering 2 and that he copied from this proof the beginning of the paragraph and the bridging end of the passage. This accounts for the relative exactness of the accidentals in the two parallel MS versions and offers some light on the differences.

13.25 Ninety-second street] In MS^b Hawthorne originally wrote his characteristic "street" but then, under the influence of I when he was copying out his revision from proof, altered the "s" to "S" in order to conform to what must have been the house-style capital he saw in the proof. Thereafter, in 13.32 and 14.17 in MS[b] he wrote "Street", but "street" in 14.4. Since Hawthorne's normal usage is present elsewhere in the MS (as at 5.5, in the slip at 14.4 of MS[b], and also in the continuation of the original passage at 14.27, 15.7, and 15.30, as well as later at 20.19 and so on), minuscule "s" has been retained throughout.

13.25 Philadelphia.] That the alteration in MS[b] to a period of MS[a] exclamation point was intentional is suggested by the inappropriateness of an exclamatory statement "repeated in a quiet voice". The original proof probably had the exclamation, on the analogy of its retention in 14.27 of I from MS.

28.26 this] The reading "the" in I is a misreading deriving from the wiping-out of original "the" and its alteration in MS to rather smudged "this".

35.13 my own interest and the public's] MS reads "when I am well off". That this proof-revision was made in two stages is indicated by the following Letter Book copy, Hawthorne to Fields, May 28, 1863: "In a proof-sheet of Our Old Home which I sent you to-day (page 43, or 4, or 5 or thereabout) I corrected a line thus—'possessing a happy faculty of seeing my own interest.' Now as the public interest was my sole and undivided object while I held office, I think that as a matter of scanty justice to myself, the line ought to stand thus 'possessing a happy faculty of seeing my own interest and the public's' Even then you see, I only give myself credit for half the disinterestedness I really felt. Pray, by all means, have it altered as above, even if the page is stereotyped—which it can't have been, as the proof is now in our Concord post-office, and you will have it at the same time with this." (Actually, the page was 42 in sheet 3.) Although the letter reads "seeing my own interest", I reads "knowing my own interest", which is presumably a further alteration in a revised-proof.

35.17 Pearce] Although in the English notebooks Samuel Pearce is spelled once as "Pearce" and once as "Pierce", a search of the archives by the General Services Administration confirms the spelling "Pearce".

56.30 Treeo] An owner of the "Leamington Spa" manuscript has appended the following notes:

"Note on page 18. The grave referred to is that of William Treen. The stone has been—possibly through the influence of Mr. Haw-thorne's words—carefully cleaned, and to the inscription has been added

'Blessed are the dead that Lie in the Lord.'

A. C. C.

August 5th, 1866

"2nd Note. The stone has been entirely removed. October 24th, 1870."

81.8 Nilometer] Although MS spells "Nileometer", the AM change to "Nilometer" agrees with the spelling in ENB, p. 586.

94.18 counties] Although in the eighteenth century "county" and "country" are almost interchangeable, the odds here seem to favor a misreading by the AM compositor overlooked in proof instead of a delicate authorial proof-alteration to an obscure and quite obsolete usage. For other AM misreadings passed in proof see 91.21 "-street" for "-streets"; 103.20 "its" for "his"; and 111.6 "would" for "could".

103.20 holding his hands] In MS "his hands" is interlined with a caret, but unfortunately was inscribed in the upper left corner of the page where the trimming during the binding has cut into the letters and made them uncertain. The word shows some signs of having been worked over (from what remains one might guess even that original "its" has been altered to "his", but it would be a guess only). Although the point is a fine one, the reference of the pronoun seems to have been "John a' Combe" and not "marble figure"; and it is of some interest that the statues in Westminster Abbey in "Up the Thames" are all described in personal terms. However, the central fact is the journal reading "with his hands devoutly clasped" (ENB, 133.14), and in view of this it seems likely that the AM change to "its hands" was a misreading and fancied normalization.

116.15 denied] The change to "decried" in AM, followed by I, is a misreading by Hennessy of a word not formed with perfect clarity.

133.32–33 street$_\wedge$ . . . width$_\wedge$] The "Uttoxeter" MS places commas after "street" and "width" although both *Keepsake* and *Harper's* omit them, as do MS and I. On the other hand, the addition in MS of "now", wanting in the early version, seems to change the phrase to a restrictive one and thus to justify Centenary in following MS instead of the punctuation of the "Uttoxeter" MS.

134.13 Memory . . . Remorse] The "Uttoxeter" MS has "memory . . . remorse" and at first sight it would appear that in the present MS Hawthorne simply copied the capitals from those in the *Keepsake* (and *Harper's*) print. If so, a case could be made for emendation back to the earlier minuscules; but the personification capital later in "Conscience" (137.8–9) in an added passage gives one pause, even though this in turn may have been influenced by the derived capitals earlier.

134.14 sultry] The reading "petty" in I is an obvious case of compositorial error since the MS word is not clearly written, with especial reference to the "su". However, the word "sultry" is clear in the "Uttoxeter" MS and is reproduced in the *Keepsake* and *Harper's* prints.

157.13 half-twisted] If this change from ENB and MS "half-hoisted" had been made in AM, one would have had no hesitation in labeling it a misreading. But AM also reads "half-hoisted", and the change is an unlikely error for a compositor of I working from printed AM copy. Hence this revision must be put down to Hawthorne himself. One may guess that if the skiff were drawn up on the bank as described, the owner's laziness consisted not in *hoist-*

ing the sail only halfway but in *lowering* it only halfway and leaving it when it became twisted and could not be further lowered.

168.11 close at the end] In the Randall Stewart edition of *The English Notebooks,* the corresponding sentence reads, "The park-gate of Blenheim is closed at the end of the village-street of Woodstock; and immediately on entering it, we saw the stately palace, at a distance". However, "closed" is a misreading for "close" which in the journal manuscript has been written over some other word ending in "d", this last letter of the rejection having deceived Professor Stewart in his transcription of the final reading. MS reads, "The park-gate of Blenheim stands close at the end of the village-street", which in AM becomes "close to the end". Some chance exists that Hawthorne was using "close" in the old sense of *closed,* a usage that the OED reports as late as Trollope in 1867. (Hawthorne himself may have employed the word in this sense in his journal [ENB, 264.22].) But on the whole neither the phrase in ENB nor in MS encourages this interpretation, and it is almost certain that the proximity of the gate to the end of the village street is the sole point. The seventh edition in 1858 of *A New Guide to Blenheim* remarks on page 10 that "Strangers visiting Blenheim usually approach through the Borough of Woodstock, and are admitted into the Park through a spacious Gateway or Triumphal Arch". This Triumphal Gate is quite definitely the point of Hawthorne's entrance, for he immediately remarks on the large artificial lake, the section of which called "Queen Pool" lies directly in front of the Gate. He then made the circuit of the Park, probably starting with Eagle Lodge; and passing by Rosamond's Well toward the end of the circuit came to the vista leading to the Triumphal Pillar. This Triumphal Arch is placed at the end of the main street of New Woodstock, as remarked in the *New Guide* and shown on maps. The issue, then, resolves itself quite simply into the use of the idiom "close at the end". "Close" would ordinarily take another preposition, although "at the end" is inevitable after the simple "is" of the journal; but in the journal "close at" is written as a unit over the original deleted reading and thus seems intended. In the light of other such Hawthorne idioms as "glimpses at Englishmen" (320.8) but particularly 55.31, "I first saw an example of this at Bebington churchyard", the authority of the phrase in ENB and in MS seems assured. Hence the odds favor the view that the AM change to "close to the end" is a Hennessy sophistication, normalizing a usage unfamiliar to him.

168.30 Great Duke] Except at 171.14 where all three authorities read "Great Duke", ENB persists in the form "great Duke". On the other hand, though at 168.30 MS follows ENB in the minuscule, it departs from ENB at 173.23 to capitalize "Great". Elsewhere at 176.2 and 177.33 MS seems to be influenced by ENB in reading "great". The capitalization in ENB at 171.14 seems to mark a special occasion, magnifying the Duke in connection with the Pillar erected to him. But the MS slip at 173.23, and the invariable capitalization of AM, suggest that in proof Hawthorne saw the virtues of the "Great Duke" form. The capitalization at 168.30 in AM cannot be compositorial, since this is its first appearance, although an editor may have gone back over the proof to normalize the various occurrences.

173.2 accounts] AM "account", followed by I, is a simple misreading of the ill-formed final "s" at the end of a line of MS.

178.18 stingo] This is a strong ale or beer. The compositor of AM seemingly did not recognize the word and misread it as "things", an error that Hawthorne did not catch and hence one that was transferred to I without alteration.

184.6 we] The AM reading "are", transmitted to I, is an easy misreading.

200.9 whole town] This is not an easy crux since the authority of any change of I from AM throughout the volume is relatively high, barring such misprints or sophistications as 193.21 and 194.25 in "Burns." However, the natural AM phrase, "the whole town", appears in ENB here and had already been used at 199.34. Moreover, the special reasons for altering "whole" to "old" in I are obscure, even though the age of the town, using the word "old", had been insisted on at 199.19, 34, and partly at 199.27–28. The explanation is perhaps a mechanical one. That is, in AM "whole town" ends one of the short two-column lines, and "old" of "old women" ends the next. The chance for eyeskip or memorial confusion is a good one, and may be used as a reason for rejecting a perhaps anomalous I variant.

225.10 this] The AM reading "the", transmitted to I, is a misreading of a word crowded in at the end of a line in MS.

237.17 where] Some inkspots in MS above "where" may have misled the AM compositor to misread as "while", a variant that was passed on to I.

240.14–15 Fair, . . . few∧] This punctuation seems to have been that intended by Hawthorne, but in interlining "their charms were few" he misplaced the caret before instead of after the original comma following "Fair", a not uncommon carelessness in his manuscripts.

245.34 ten] This is a curious example of Hawthorne's third thoughts. In MS he originally wrote "ten" but then deleted "ten" and interlined "two" with a caret, a reading found, of course, in AM. But on reflection, in the proof for I or in preparing AM copy for the book printer, he changed it back to the first reading, "ten".

253.34 awning] The word is ill-formed in MS and was misread by the AM compositor as "covering", an error passed on to I without Hawthorne's notice. ENB reads "awning".

270.11 Poet's Corner] In MS this reading might just possibly be "Poets' Corner" as it is throughout AM, but very likely Hawthorne was merely careless in the placement of the apostrophe, as happens occasionally. See the Textual Introduction, pp. civ–cv.

311.12 Lawrence] The MS reading is not entirely certain. AM and I read "Laurence" but probably in error since in the standard 1851 Pickering edition of Milton's works, Vol. I, the spelling is "Lawrence", as usual.

316.8 still are] MS reads "still are so" but in error AM omitted the "still" which I restored but in the process I dropped the "so".

The extreme care that enabled Hawthorne in the proof (or copy) for I to see the mistake involving "still" makes one hesitate not to adopt the further I change of excising the "so". We must consider, however, that if this change were ordered in the proof, the easiest way for the compositor to adjust the line would have been to insert "still" at the expense of the rather old-fashioned "so". But since one has no information on whether the change was made in the copy for the printer (in which case such an explanation would not hold) or in the proofs of the book after typesetting, one has no choice but to follow the general authority of I, although reluctantly, for "so" used in this manner is certainly characteristic of Hawthorne.

329.24 has] The MS "s" is not clearly formed and seems to have given rise to the AM-I misreading "had".

329.32 shirk without] MS interlines "it" after "shirk" but AM-I omit the interlineation. The choice presents itself whether the AM compositor overlooked the interlineation (although it is perfectly clear) or whether Hawthorne had second thoughts in proof. The latter seems more probable. Although the interlineation might theoretically represent a careless omission in the copying of the MS—a type of error with which its pages are sprinkled—the knotty syntax suggests instead that the interlined "it" represented an authorial effort to clarify the reference. However, we may suppose that in proof Hawthorne saw that, instead, he had further confused the matter. It would seem that "necessities" is the true antecedent of the "which" that follows, and not its dependent "office". If this is so, the next "which" in "beneath which" must be in parallel and also refer to the "necessities". It may have been that by the insertion of "it" Hawthorne was originally endeavoring to specify that his speechifying was that one of the necessities which he could not shirk; but if so the reference was by no means clear since "it" could as well refer back to "office", or even to "position" earlier in the sentence which has an "it" reference at 329.28. On the whole, then, the omission of "it" returns "necessities" as the subject of "could not shirk", a perfectly proper meaning and one that made the best of a bad job. See also the discussion of other such omissions in the Textual Introduction, pp. xcviii–xcix.

330.18 once or twice] This is the correct reading of AM. MS originally had "some-|times happened". Hawthorne deleted "some" and interlined "once" above it with a caret; he then interlined "or twice" in the left margin of the line below, with a caret, before "times", but forgot to delete "times", which related only to the rejected "some".

334.30 lights] MS final "s" though present is scarcely formed and readily gave occasion for the AM misreading "light" passed on to I without change.

344.28 his] In MS original "the" has been wiped out and "his" written over it; but the AM compositor, who set "the", must have mistaken which was the revision.

EDITORIAL EMENDATIONS IN THE COPY-TEXT

Note: The typographical appurtenances of the text have been modernized; no attempt has been made in the Centenary Edition to reproduce their original forms (as, for example, old-fashioned wide spacing of *I 'll*, or the use of periods after running titles). Except for these silent typographical alterations, this list of Editorial Emendations includes every editorial change made from the printer's copy manuscript of each chapter, when available, or from *Atlantic Monthly* text where manuscript is wanting. Only the immediate source of emendation is noted; see the Historical Collation for the complete history, within the editions collated, of substantive variants. An alteration made for the first time by the present edition, in respect to the editions collated, is assigned to CENTENARY. See the Textual Notes for discussion of all asterisked readings.

The following texts are referred to: MS (manuscript; see the Textual Introduction, pp. liv–lviii, for a complete list, by chapter, of all manuscripts located for this edition), AM (*Atlantic Monthly;* see the Textual Introduction, pp. liv–lviii), I (1863 first edition), E (1863 English edition), II (1876 Little Classics Edition), III (1883 Riverside Edition), IV (1891 Houghton, Mifflin edition), and V (1900 Autograph Edition).

When a passage in *The English Notebooks,* edited by Randall Stewart (New York: Modern Language Association of America; London: Oxford University Press, 1941), closely parallels the text, the consultive authority is noted "(ENB)". Additional texts are referred to in "Lichfield and Uttoxeter": Uttoxeter MS (The Pierpont Morgan Library manuscript), K (*The Keepsake,* London, 1857), and H (*Harper's New Monthly Magazine,* April, 1857).

In recording punctuation variants, the wavy dash ⁓ is used to the right of the bracket to represent the same word that appears to the left of the bracket. A caret ∧ indicates the absence of a punctuation mark.

To a Friend (MS,I)

3.5	an early] I; a MS
3.6	old between] I; old, without decay, between MS
3.8	of] I; of|of MS
3.17	more susceptible] I; ⁓-⁓ MS
3.20	might] I; could MS
4.15	catastrophe] I; catastrope MS
4.26	seldom] I; hardly ever MS
4.31	undeniable] I; very true MS
4.35	perfectly] I; perfect MS
5.19–34	But . . . The Wayside, July 2ᵈ, 1863.] I; Can it be, that no man shall hereafter reach that elevated seat!—that its platform, which we deemed to be so firmly laid, has crumbled beneath it!—that a chasm has gaped wide [wide *interlined with a caret*] asunder, into which the unbalanced Chair of State is about to fall! In my seclusion, accustomed only to private thoughts, I can judge little of these matters, and know not well [well *interlined with a caret*] what to hope, although I can see much to fear. I might even deem it allowable for myself [for myself *interlined with a caret*], in the last resort, to be content with half the soil that was once [once *interlined with a caret*] our broad inheritance. But you, as all men may know by the whole record of your life, will hope sted-

fastly while there shall be any shadow or possibility of a country left, continuing faithful forever to that grand idea, which, as you once told me, was the earliest that your brave father taught you; and whether the Union is to be henceforth a living giant, or a mangled and dismembered corpse, it will be said of you that this mighty Polity, or this miserable ruin, had no more loyal, constant, or single-minded upholder [upholder *interlined with a caret above deleted* 'son'], than Franklin Pierce.

THE WAYSIDE, July 2ᵈ [2 *written over* 'th']. 1863. MS

5.29   stedfast] CENTENARY; steadfast I–III,V; *prefatory letter omitted* IV

CONSULAR EXPERIENCES (MS,I)

6.21	maritime] I; maratime MS
7.3	clothing] I; cloathing MS
7.33	Tennessee] I; Tenessee MS
8.34	in] I; out of MS
9.24–25	predecessors, . . . banner,] I; $\sim_\wedge$ . . . $\sim_\wedge$ MS
*10.4	Cubans$_\wedge$] I; $\sim$, MS
11.4	Consul"!] II; $\sim$!" MS, I–E
11.16–17	sides— . . . mine—] CENTENARY; $\sim$, . . . $\sim$, MS; $\sim$,— . . . $\sim$,— I–V
13.9	Consul] II; consul MS, I–E
*13.19–14.23	The individual . . . entreaty.] *revised* MS (MSᵇ); *original* MS (MSᵃ) *reads:* The individual now in question was a patient-looking, mild old man, without energy of tone or movement, making no complaint of

his hard fortune, but only repeating in a quiet voice, with a pathos of which he was himself evidently unconscious—"I want to get home to Ninety-sixth street, Philadelphia!" He described himself as a printer by trade, and said that he had come over, when he was a younger man, in the hope of bettering himself, and for the sake of seeing the Old Country, but had never since been rich enough to pay his homeward passage. Up to the time when I saw him, he still got a little occasional job-work at his trade, but subsisted mainly on such [such *interlined with a caret*] charity as he met with in his wanderings, shifting from place to place continually, and asking assistance to convey him to his native land.

13.22	ill-fortune] I; ~‿~ MS
*13.25	Ninety-second street] CENTENARY; ~·~·~ MS; Ninety-Sixth street MS*; Ninety-second-Street MS[b]; Ninety-second Street I–V
*13.25	Philadelphia.] MS[b]; ~! MS*
13.32;14.17	street] CENTENARY; Street MS[b],I–V
14.26;15.7,30	Ninety-second] I; Ninety-sixth MS
15.15	long-remembered] I; ~‿~ MS
15.20	long-cherished] I; ~‿~ MS
15.24	away] I; way MS
16.2,25	trowsers] CENTENARY; trousers MS,I–V
16.24	smile)] I; ~,) MS
17.2–3	common sense] I; ~·~ MS
18.5	of] I; *omit* MS
18.13	"Times,"] I; ‿~,‿ MS
20.2	better—] CENTENARY; ~,— MS,I–V
20.4	advertisement] I; advertisemt MS
20.26	twentyfold] CENTENARY; twenty-fold MS,I; ~‿~ E,II–V

20.27	re-imbursement] CENTENARY; reimbursement MS,I–V
21.1	back-ground] CENTENARY; ~ₐ~ MS; background I–V
21.7	them] I; *omit* MS
21.9	predecessor] I; predecesor MS
21.26	paralleled] I; paralelled MS
23.4	government] I; govenment MS
23.20	country-seatₐ] I; ~-~, MS
23.24	government] I; Govenment MS
23.28	Oriental] I; oriental MS
24.23	him";] II; ~;" MS,I–E
27.24	*théâtre*] IV; *theâtre* MS,I–III
28.1	military] I; *omit* MS
28.22–23	Saint . . . Heaven] CENTENARY; saint . . . heaven MS,I–V
*28.26	this] *stet* MS (the I)
28.33	myselfₐ] I; ~, MS
29.11	one of] I; *omit* MS
30.32	McClellan] I; McLellan MS
31.23	Shakspere's] CENTENARY; Shakspeare's MS,I–E; Shakespeare's II–V
31.24	time,)] I; ~ₐ) MS
32.2	Captain] CENTENARY; captain MS,I–V
32.28	State, old General Cass, responded] I; State responded MS
33.10	sea-ports] CENTENARY; seaports MS,I–V
33.14	shipmaster] I; ship-master MS
34.6	expense] I; expence MS
34.22	Consul] E; consul MS,I
34.25	effect,] I; ~ₐ MS
*35.13	my own interest and the public's] I; when I am well off MS
35.16	Vice-Consul] I; ~ₐ~ MS
*35.17	Pearce] *stet* MS,I

35.17   successive arrivals] I; arrival MS

36.4   some acquaintance with] I; a smattering of MS

36.5   Statutes,] I; ~∧ MS

36.6   management,] I; ~∧ MS

36.12   Consuls] *capital uncertain in* MS

36.14   too often] I; usually MS

36.21   so,] I; ~∧ MS

36.23   unsuitable] I; inconsiderate MS

37.16   attainment] I; attaintment MS

37.17   American; there to-day] I; American, here to day MS

38.6–20   prepared, in advance of the inauguration of Mr. Buchanan . . . unreal.] I; prepared, (in advance of the inauguration of our [our *interlined with a caret above deleted* 'my'] good friend Mr. Buchanan, who, I was aware, [I was aware, *interlined with a caret*] needed [needed *precedes deleted* 'the'] appointments of this class [of this class *interlined with a caret*] for his hungry retainers, but would have been sorely grieved to turn me out) quite prepared and perfectly willing, therefore [quite prepared and perfectly willing, therefore *interlined with a caret*] to send in my resignation. [resignation. *follows deleted* 'inauguration.'] When my successor arrived,—a very genial and agreeable gentleman, an F.F.V., and, as he pleasantly announced himself, a Southern Fire-eater, who is now banquetting on his favorite diet, hot and hot, in the Confederate service—I drew the long, delightful breath, which first made me thoroughly sensible what an unnatural life I had been enduring. As soon as I was out of it, the retrospect began to look unreal. MS

38.9	breath,] *stet* MS (~ₐI)
38.14	-Eaterₐ—] CENTENARY; ~,— I–V
38.15	good humor] V; ~-~ I–IV (MS *wanting*)
39.14	English friend] I; Englishman MS
40.9–11	The . . . voyage.] I; *omit* MS

LEAMINGTON SPA (MS,AM,I)

41.0	*stet* MS] *For AM headnote see Historical Collation, p. 408.*
41.10	10] I; 16 MS,AM
42.3	cosey] II; cosy MS; cozy AM,I–E
42.22	by] I; *omit* MS,AM
42.27	again] AM; a-|again MS
43.3	necessity] AM; neces-|ity MS
43.15	indeed,] AM; ~ₐ MS
45.9	are] AM; is MS
45.20–21	yards. It seemed to me a sad emblem] I; yards; a sad emblem, it seemed to me, MS; yards, a sad emblem, it seemed to me, AM
45.23	lifetime] AM; life time MS
45.25–26	Leam—the . . . it—after] I; Leam, after MS,AM
46.8	churchyard] I; church-yard MS,AM
46.19	a diminutive] AM; a much more diminutive MS
46.32	stone-fence] CENTENARY; ~ₐ~ MS,I–V
47.4	by-and-by] AM; ~ₐ~ₐ~ MS
48.5	moustached] AM; mustached MS
48.23	¶ I have heard] I; *no* ¶ MS,AM
48.29	Western] AM; western MS
49.7	seldom] I; not always MS,AM
49.17–18	counter-injury] AM; ~ₐ~ MS

49.24	is strong, I suspect, only in] AM; is only strong, I suspect, in MS
50.34	farm-houses,] AM; ~-~ˌ MS
51.6	whithersoever] AM; whithsoever MS
51.19	Lovers'] AM; Lover's MS
51.25	high-road] AM; ~ˌ~ MS
52.4	plastered] AM; plaistered (*doubtful*) MS
52.15–16	and hidden . . . road,] AM; *omit* MS
52.21	as] AM; *omit* MS
52.24–25	unfamiliarity] AM; unfam-|iarity MS
53.2	Castle] AM; castle MS
53.8	door-ways] CENTENARY; doorways MS,AM,I–III,V; ~-|~ IV
53.12	of the] AM; *omit* of MS
53.25	battlements] AM; turrets MS
53.31	side-aisles] CENTENARY; ~ˌ~ MS,AM,I–V
54.12	distinguished a] AM; *omit* a MS
54.29	allotted] AM; alotted MS
55.9	toˌ] AM: ~, MS
55.25	Lyeth] I; lieth MS,AM
55.31	Bebington] CENTENARY (ENB); Bebbington MS,AM,I–V
56.2	historyˌ)] AM; ~,) MS
56.14	verse:—] AM; ~ˌˌ MS
56.18	cried.'] CENTENARY; ~." MS,AM,I,II–V; ~.ˌ E
56.24	endwise] AM; lengthwise MS
56.25	the headstone being within] AM (head-stone); and within MS
56.25–26	foundation-wall] AM; foundation-stones MS
*56.30	Treeo] *stet* MS
57.13	minutes'] AM; minutes MS
58.5	out into] AM; at MS
58.10	incalculable] AM; incalcuble MS
58.24	that] AM; that that MS

59.3	Old Country] CENTENARY; old country MS,AM,I–V
59.6	Wickliffe's] E; Wickcliffe's MS,AM,I
59.18	fifty] AM; a hundred MS
59.20	¶ And] I; *no* ¶ MS,AM
59.24	Western] AM; western MS
60.1	shuffling] I; scuffling MS,AM
60.10	worship∧—] CENTENARY; ∼,— MS,AM,I–V
60.17	be∧] AM; ∼, MS
60.27	the old] AM; *omit* the MS
61.1	churchyard] AM; church-yard MS
61.13–14	Stratford-on-Avon] AM; ∼-∼∧∼ MS
61.33	styled Hatton,] AM; *omit* MS
62.15	perpetrating,)] AM; ∼∧) MS
62.23	Art] AM; art MS
63.12	Bebington] CENTENARY; Bebbington MS,AM,I–V
64.12–13	a tonic] AM; *omit* MS
64.21	or a quarter] AM; *omit* MS

ABOUT WARWICK (PARTIAL MS;AM,I)

65.0	About Warwick] AM; A Sketch or two in Warwick MS
66.33	Shakspere's] CENTENARY; Shakspeare's MS,AM,I–E; Shakespeare's II–V
67.13	world,] AM; ∼; MS
67.27	well-worth] CENTENARY; ∼∧∼ MS,AM,I–V
68.3–4	than climb . . . touch] AM; instead of climbing to their summits, or touching MS
68.21	lattice-wise] AM; ∼∧∼ MS
68.29	playthings] I; play-things AM (MS *wanting*)

69.13	yeomanlike] CENTENARY (ENB); yeoman-like AM,I–II,IV–V; ~-|~ III (MS *wanting*)
69.26	High-street] CENTENARY (ENB); High Street AM,I–V (MS *wanting*)
69.33	middle ages] E; Middle Ages AM,I (MS *wanting*)
70.14	unencumbered] CENTENARY; unincumbered AM,I (MS *wanting*)
70.29	similar] AM; similiar MS
71.3–4	chimneys] AM; chimnies MS
71.25	the Eighth] CENTENARY; VIII. MS,AM,I–V
71.34	perhaps] AM; perhap MS
72.2	Saints] CENTENARY; saints MS,AM,I–V
72.24,34	Leycester] CENTENARY; Leicester AM,I–V (MS *wanting*)
72.32	Hospital] CENTENARY; hospital AM,I–V (MS *wanting*)
73.9	enclosed] I; inclosed AM (MS *wanting*)
73.10	family residence] I (ENB); ~-~ AM (MS *wanting*)
73.12	Leycester's] CENTENARY; Leicester's AM,I–V (MS *wanting*)
73.19	frame-work] CENTENARY; framework AM,I,II–IV; ~-|~ E,V (MS *wanting*)
73.28	lives_∧—] CENTENARY; ~,— AM,I–III; ~,_∧ IV–V (MS *wanting*)
73.31	dignitary_∧—] CENTENARY; ~,— AM,I–V (MS *wanting*)
73.33	old English letters] I; black-letter AM (MS *wanting*)
74.11	Hospital] CENTENARY; hospital AM,I–V (MS *wanting*)
74.32	the First] CENTENARY; I. AM,I–V (MS *wanting*)
74.34	barnlike] IV; barn-like AM,I,II–III; ~-|~ E (MS *wanting*)

75.1	brick-floor] CENTENARY (ENB); ~ˬ~ AM,I–V (MS *wanting*)
75.6	where] I; while AM (MS *wanting*)
75.8	daysˬ—] CENTENARY; ~,— AM,I–V (MS *wanting*)
75.24	fire-place] CENTENARY (ENB); fireplace AM,I–V (MS *wanting*)
75.33	enclosed] I; inclosed AM (MS *wanting*)
76.15	visitors] AM; visiters MS
76.28	crossedˬ—] CENTENARY; ~,ˬ MS; ~,— AM,I–V
76.31	field of Waterloo.] AM; *cancelled* MS
77.1	apparatusˬ—] E; ~,ˬ MS; ~,— AM,I
77.9–10	"Don't . . . talkative!"] AM; '~ . . . ~!' MS
77.13	Hospital. The] AM (hospital); Hospital; the MS
77.20–23	"And," . . . "with . . . desire!"] AM (desire?); '~,' . . . '~ . . . ~!' MS
78.4	Leycester's] CENTENARY; Leicester's AM,I–V (MS *wanting*)
78.6–7,14,23	Hospital] CENTENARY; hospital AM,I–V (MS *wanting*)
78.7,27;79.2	Porter] CENTENARY; porter AM,I–V (MS *wanting*)
78.11	other] I; private AM (MS *wanting*)
78.22	or] I; and AM (MS *wanting*)
79.8	frame-work] CENTENARY; framework AM,I–V (MS *wanting*)
79.16	Chapel] CENTENARY (ENB); chapel AM,I–V (MS *wanting*)
80.11	Castle] CENTENARY; castle MS,AM,I–V
80.14	these] AM; and these MS
80.31	Shakspere] CENTENARY; Shakspeare MS,AM,I-E; Shakespeare II-V
81.8	that] I; having MS,AM
*81.8	Nilometer] AM; Nileometer MS

82.9	twelve] I; *omit* MS,AM
83.13	Hospital] CENTENARY; hospital AM,I–V (MS *wanting*)
83.15	needle-work] E (ENB); needlework AM,I (MS *wanting*)
83.31	daytime] I (ENB); day-time AM (MS *wanting*)
84.32	Saint] CENTENARY; St. AM,I–V (MS *wanting*)
84.32	Mary's;] CENTENARY; ~: AM,I–V (MS *wanting*)
85.28	benefactor] AM; benefac-|or MS
85.30	Countess∧—] CENTENARY; ~;∧ MS; ~,— AM,I–V
86.1	long-enduring] AM; ~∧~ MS
86.9	the Sixth] CENTENARY; VI MS,AM,I–V
86.11	executed;] CENTENARY; ~: MS,AM,I–V
86.12	life-like] AM; lifelike MS
86.13	brass] AM; stone MS
86.20	anciently entombed] I; *omit* MS,AM
87.30	sole relation to] AM; only relation with MS
88.24	denoted only] AM; only denoted MS
88.25	REDFERN,'] AM; ~', MS
89.11	(all of which I have seen,)] I; *omit* MS,AM
89.12	its] AM; their MS
89.19	the money in] I; it MS; it in AM
89.24	expense] AM; expence MS

RECOLLECTIONS OF A GIFTED WOMAN (MS,AM,I)

90.11	Old Country] AM; old country MS
90.12	the wayside] I; those wayside MS,AM
90.15	is] AM; are MS
90.20	them. To] AM; them; and to MS

91.4	half-tame] CENTENARY; ~ᴧ~ MS,AM,I–V
91.29	nobler and more] AM; noblest and most MS
92.4	the] AM; one of its MS
92.28	the] AM; the the MS
93.20	has] AM; have MS
93.22	crevice;] AM; ~, MS
93.32	charm] AM; spell MS
94.2	tangled] AM; intricate MS
*94.18	counties] *stet* MS (countries AM,I)
96.1	towns,)] AM; ~ᴧ) MS
97.17	cheerful;] AM; ~, MS
97.27	up stairs] II; upstairs MS; up-stairs AM,I–E
99.23	kitchen-hearth] AM; ~ᴧ~ MS
99.32	Combe;] CENTENARY; ~, MS; ~— AM,I–E; ~,— II–V
99.32	and finally,] I; whoᴧ MS,AM
99.33	him,)] AM; ~ᴧ) MS
99.33–34	the victim of convivial habits who] I; *omit* MS,AM
100.8	this] AM; *omit* MS
100.32;101.7	churchyard] I; church-yard MS,AM
101.28	Essex-street] AM (Essex Street); Main-street MS
103.15–16	grave-stones] CENTENARY; gravestones MS,AM,I–V
*103.20	his] *stet* MS (its AM,I)
103.26	By-the-by] AM; ~ᴧ~ᴧ~ MS
103.29	' 'tis] AM (' 't is); ᴧ 't is MS
103.29	Combe!] AM; ~ᴧ MS
103.29–30	that is,] AM; orᴧ MS
103.30	My] I; my MS,AM
106.22	resistance] AM; resistence MS
106.29	phases] I; faces MS,AM
106.30	large] I; *omit* MS,AM

107.18	grave-stone] CENTENARY; gravestone MS,AM,E,III,V; ~-|~ I,II,IV
107.26	had come hither . . . here] AM; went thither . . . there MS
108.7	Farrar] I; F. MS,AM
108.11	Consul] I; consul MS,AM
109.34	in] AM; on MS
111.9	which] AM; *omit* MS
112.4	Raleigh's] AM; Raleighs MS
112.7	statesman,] AM; ~∧ MS
112.9–12	It is very . . . decisive step.] I; *omit* MS,AM
113.16	By-and-by] AM; ~∧~∧~ MS
114.14	respected,] AM; ~∧ MS
114.14	ingenuous] AM; generous MS
115.8	bruising, if they do recognize it.] AM; bruising it if they do recognize. MS
115.10–12	It was . . . poet.] I; *omit* MS,AM
*116.15	denied] *stet* MS (decried AM,I)
117.21	By-and-by] AM; ~∧~∧~ MS
118.27	half-Gothic] AM; ~∧~ MS
119.3–4	could have . . . about only by] AM; could only have . . . about by MS
119.10	Art . . . Nature] AM; art . . . nature MS
119.23–24	us what is best . . . beautifullest] I; us to see what is best, nor our poets what is most beautiful MS; us to see what is best, nor have our poets sung us what is beautifullest AM

LICHFIELD AND UTTOXETER (MS,I)

121.5	journal] I; Journal MS
121.15	chiccory] I; chickory MS
123.22–23	acknowledgement] CENTENARY; acknowledgment MS,I–V

124.8	me∧] II; ⁓,) MS,I–E
130.28;131.16	Saint] Centenary; St. MS,I–V
131.1	plaster] I; plaister MS
131.24	expense] I; expence MS
132.6	pedestal,] Uttoxeter MS; ⁓∧ K,H,MS,I
132.12	another] I; a another MS
132.21	bareheaded] Uttoxeter MS,K,H; bare-headed MS,I
132.32	burthen] Uttoxeter MS; burden K,H,MS,I
133.11–12	Lichfield; . . . distance, and,] Uttoxeter MS; ⁓, . . . ⁓; ⁓∧ K,H,MS,I
133.27	bookstall] Uttoxeter MS; book-stall K,H,MS,I
*133.32–33	street∧ . . . width∧] stet MS
133.33	it;] Uttoxeter MS,K,H; ⁓, MS,I
134.2	churchyard] Uttoxeter MS,K,I; church-yard H,MS
134.6	corner,] Uttoxeter MS; ⁓∧ K,H,MS,I
*134.13	Memory . . . Remorse] stet MS,K,H,I–V
134.14	the sultry] I; omit the MS
*134.14	sultry] stet MS (petty I–V)
135.3	two,] Uttoxeter MS; ⁓; K,H,MS; ⁓: I
135.3	Bull's] Uttoxeter MS(ENB),H; Bulls' K,MS,I
135.15	stept] Uttoxeter MS; stepped K,H,MS,I
136.5	itself] I; it|self MS
136.16	Johnson,] Uttoxeter MS; ⁓∧ K,H,MS,I
136.20–21	red brick] Uttoxeter MS; ⁓-⁓ K,H,MS,I
136.25	earthen-ware] Uttoxeter MS; earthenware K,H,MS,I
137.4	life; no] Uttoxeter MS; life! no K,H; Life! No MS,I
137.5	church; no] Uttoxeter MS; church! no K,H; church! No MS,I
137.13	pavement,] Uttoxeter MS; ⁓∧ K,H,MS,I
137.14	dript] Uttoxeter MS; dripped K,H,MS,I

PILGRIMAGE TO OLD BOSTON (MS,AM,I)

140.8	Derbyshire_∧)] AM; ~,) MS
140.20	Brontë's] E; Bronte's MS; Bronté's AM,I
140.22	these] AM; those MS
140.28	foot-paths] II; footpaths MS,AM,I–E
140.32	railway] AM; rail|way MS
141.5	Yorkshire] AM; York|Yorkshire MS
141.9–11	were . . . were] AM; was . . . was MS
142.29	court-yard] AM; ~_∧|~ MS
143.8	foot-passengers] AM; ~_∧~ MS
143.22	daylight] AM; day-light MS
143.24	Stone Bow] AM; ~-~ MS
144.18–19	West Front] CENTENARY; west front MS,AM,I–V
144.27	be] AM; were MS
145.21	West Front] CENTENARY (ENB); west front MS,AM,I–V
145.25	strong] AM; strongly MS
146.3	been] AM; *omit* MS
146.7	is vain] AM; is in vain MS
146.14	nonsense,] AM; ~; MS
146.16	Close] CENTENARY; close MS,AM,I–V
146.19	sweetest] AM; sweetiest MS
146.28	term] AM; phrase MS
146.30	had] AM; *omit* MS
147.8	bedimmed] AM; be-dimmed MS
147.9	and] I; *omit* MS,AM
147.15	Behind] I; Within MS,AM
147.19	now] AM; since MS
148.17–18	Nature . . . Art] AM; nature . . . art MS

148.29	is] AM; has been MS
149.6	tessellated] AM; tesselated MS
149.11	¶ Nothing] AM; *no* ¶ MS
149.19	arch] AM; Arch MS
150.5	proximity] AM; vicinity MS
150.6	is] AM; was MS
150.19	mould of a decaying] AM; decay of a mouldering MS
151.7	a little] AM; a a little MS
151.13	half-obliterate] CENTENARY; ∼∧∼ MS,AM,I–V
151.25	in] AM; into MS
151.28	but in this at Lincoln] I; but, here MS,AM
152.6	enough.—] AM; ∼.∧ MS
152.33	than of] AM; *omit* of MS
153.6	in] AM; into MS
153.9	by the] AM; by taking the MS
153.9	he] AM; they MS
153.17	through] AM; throughout MS
154.27–28	its consummation] I; *omit* MS,AM
154.29	striven] AM; strove MS
156.6	Wharf,] AM; ∼∧ MS
156.16,22,32	churchyard] I; church-yard MS,AM
156.19	tombstones] AM; tomb-stones MS
156.28	schoolboys] IV; school-boys MS,I–III; ∼-∣∼ AM
156.30–31	which . . . that] AM; that . . . which MS
157.11	brick-wall] CENTENARY; ∼∧∼ MS,AM,I–V
*157.13	half-twisted] I; half-hoisted MS,AM
157.19	Reverend] AM; Rev. MS
157.29	it∧)] AM; ∼,) MS
157.34	had . . . pilgrimages] AM; have . . . pilgrimage MS
157.34	he] I; *omit* MS,AM

159.5	This_∧] AM; ~, MS
160.6–7	not that . . . but] I; *omit* MS,AM
160.17	the Fourth] CENTENARY; IV. MS,AM,I–V
160.18	the Second] CENTENARY; II. MS,AM,I–V
160.27	in manuscript,] I; *omit* MS,AM
160.28	by] AM; in MS
160.33	quickly"!] AM; ~!" MS
161.4	whitlow—_∧] CENTENARY; ~—, MS; ~,— AM,I–V
161.8	antiquary] AM; antiquarian MS
161.13	the hand] AM; the own hand MS
161.15	the Fourteenth] CENTENARY; XIV. MS,AM,I–V
161.25	us] AM; us us MS
161.32	Mr.] I; *omit* MS,AM
162.3	received an invitation] AM; been invited MS
162.3	but I knew] I; but knew MS,AM
162.5	accept it] AM; *omit* it MS
162.7	five hundred pounds] AM; £500 MS
162.12	vicar] AM; Vicar MS
162.15	antiquary] AM; antiquarian MS
162.24	well-to-do] AM; ~_∧~_∧~ MS
163.10	stone-coffin] CENTENARY; ~_∧~ MS,AM,I–V
163.23–24	a yet] AM; yet a MS
163.28	re-tracing] CENTENARY; retracing MS,AM,E,II–V; ~-|~ I
164.1	landmark] AM; land-mark MS
165.9	seafaring] AM; sea-faring MS
165.10	ware-houses] CENTENARY; warehouses MS,AM,I–V
165.20	were] AM; was MS
165.23	ourselves] AM; our selves MS
165.34	well-covered] AM; ~_∧~ MS

| 166.8 | bleating] AM; bleat MS |
| 166.16 | fancied it] AM; fancied that it MS |

NEAR OXFORD (MS,AM,I)

168.4	time-worn] AM; time-word MS
*168.11	close at] stet MS (close to AM,I–V)
168.25	Nature] AM; nature MS
168.27–28	slanting] AM; aslantwise MS
*168.30	Great] AM; great MS
169.20	Art] AM; art MS
169.24	landscape-gardener] AM (ENB); ~ˬ~ MS
170.3	Ranger . . . Park] AM; ranger . . . park MS
170.14	the Second's] CENTENARY; II's MS; II.'s AM,I–V
171.1–2	Henry sometimes] AM; Henry have sometimes MS
171.4	abundant] AM; abun-|ant MS
171.8	Saints] CENTENARY; saints MS,AM,I–V
171.22	have been] AM; be MS
171.30	greatnessˬ)] AM; ~,) MS
172.14	countrymenˬ)] AM; ~,) MS
172.20	houses] AM; homes MS
173.11	elevation] I; height MS,AM
173.14	to-and-fro] CENTENARY; ~-~ˬ~ MS; ~ˬ~ˬ~ AM,I–V
173.17	make out,—] AM; make; MS
173.30	the First] CENTENARY; I. MS,AM,I–V
173.34	criticize] AM; criticise (doubtful) MS
174.3	half-lengths,)] AM; ~-~ˬ) MS
174.16	station] AM; life MS

174.28	Duke] AM; duke MS
174.30	Duke's] AM; duke's MS
175.15	door-ways] CENTENARY; doorways MS,AM,I–V
175.15	fire-places] CENTENARY; fireplaces MS,AM,I,II–III,V; ~-|~ E,IV
176.2	Great] CENTENARY; great MS,AM,I–V
176.14	by-and-by] AM; ~∧~∧~ MS
176.18	variety capable] AM; variety that can be made capable MS
177.8	ten shillings] AM; ~-~ MS
177.10	uproarious,)] AM; ~∧) MS
177.33	Great] AM; great MS
178.10	particular,)] AM; ~∧) MS
*178.18	stingo] *stet* MS (things AM,I)
178.19	be] AM; were MS
178.21	verse,)] AM; ~∧) MS
179.6	summer-weather] CENTENARY; ~∧~ MS(Summer),AM,I–V
180.5	armor] AM; armour MS
180.15–16	gentleman] AM; person MS
180.16–17	for bringing] AM; to bring MS
181.6	unpruned] AM; untrimmed MS
181.17–18	stone-floor] CENTENARY; ~∧~ MS,AM,I–V
181.33	A";] AM; A;" MS
182.12;186.32;191.10;191.18	Courtenay] CENTENARY; Courtney MS,AM,I–V
182.22	fire-places] CENTENARY; fireplaces MS,AM,I–V
182.25	wide air-holes] AM; apertures MS
182.32	stone-walls] CENTENARY; ~∧~ MS,AM,I–V
182.33	mentioned,)] AM; ~∧) MS
183.4	and all one fire-place,] I (fireplace); *omit* MS,AM
183.16	wherein] AM; when MS

183.25–26	language— . . . pathos—] CENTENARY; ~, . . . ~, MS; ~,— . . . ~,— AM,I–V
183.26	humorous] AM; *omit* MS
183.31	engaging . . . who stirs] AM; and engages . . . stirring MS
183.32	over] AM; at MS
*184.6	we] *stet* MS (are AM,I–V)
184.30	into] AM; in MS
184.33	monument] I; *omit* MS,AM
185.6	Garter] AM; garter MS
186.15	basement story] AM; *just possibly hyphenated in MS*
187.10	so] AM; as MS
187.13–14	to inhabit] AM; for a study MS
187.23	was!] AM; ~∧ MS
188.20	should] AM; shall MS
188.22	rolled] AM; rolls MS
190.3	one of] AM; *omit* of MS
190.16	Nuneham Courtenay] AM (Courtney); ~-~ MS
192.9	feature] AM; ingredient MS
192.11	fire-places] CENTENARY; fireplaces MS,AM,I–V
192.19	acknowledgements] AM; acknowledgments MS

SOME OF THE HAUNTS OF BURNS (AM,I)

193.0	BURNS] I; BURNS. | BY A TOURIST WITHOUT IMAGINATION OR ENTHUSIASM. AM
193.3	Scotland,] E(ENB); ~∧ AM,I

193.14	Shakspere] CENTENARY; Shakspeare AM,I–E; Shakespeare II–V
193.14	-street] CENTENARY (ENB); ∧Street AM,I–V
193.15–16	corner-house] I(ENB); ∼∧∼ AM
193.16	house∧—] CENTENARY; ∼,— AM,I–V
193.17	Mill Hole] CENTENARY (ENB); ∼-∼ AM,I–V
194.22–23	bed-chamber,] CENTENARY (ENB); ∼-∼∧ AM,I–V
194.26	lifetime] I; life-time AM
194.28	in∧—] CENTENARY; ∼,— AM,I–V
194.28	Shakspere's] CENTENARY; Shakspeare's AM,I–E; Shakespeare's II–V
195.7–8	Mausoleum] CENTENARY (ENB); mausoleum AM,I–V
195.9;197.27	Saint] CENTENARY; St. AM,I–V
195.9;197.27	church] CENTENARY (ENB); Church AM,I–V
195.27	foot-path] II; footpath AM,I–E
196.4	grave-stone] CENTENARY (ENB); gravestone AM,I,II–V; ∼-|∼ E
196.4	Burns∧—] CENTENARY; ∼,— AM,I–V
196.5–6	Displayed] I; Stuck AM
196.17	opened,] CENTENARY (ENB); ∼∧ AM,I–V
196.25	sons∧—] CENTENARY; ∼,— AM,I–V
197.6	clothed∧] CENTENARY (ENB); ∼, AM,I–V
197.19	demi-god] CENTENARY (ENB); demigod AM,I–V
197.22	cholera-year] CENTENARY (ENB); ∼∧∼ AM,I–V
197.32	baby-feet] CENTENARY (ENB); ∼∧∼ AM,I–V
198.29	corner-seat] I (ENB); ∼∧∼ AM
198.34	Dumfries,] CENTENARY (ENB); ∼∧ AM,I–V
199.21	mid-way] CENTENARY; midway AM,I–V

199.24	productions$_\wedge$—] CENTENARY; $\sim$,— AM; $\sim$,$_\wedge$ I–V
199.31	centuries$_\wedge$—] CENTENARY; $\sim$,— AM,I–V
199.33	beggar's] CENTENARY (ENB); beggars' AM,I–V
199.33	ale-house] CENTENARY (ENB); alehouse AM,I–V
199.34	time-worn$_\wedge$—] CENTENARY; $\sim$-$\sim$,— AM,I–V
*200.9	whole] *stet* AM (ENB); old I
200.9	town;] CENTENARY; $\sim$: AM,I–V
200.33	stopt] CENTENARY (ENB); stopped AM,I–V
200.34	wayside] I (ENB); $\sim$-$\sim$ AM
201.13	enclose] II (ENB); inclose AM,I–E
201.14	house;] CENTENARY (ENB); $\sim$: AM,I–V
201.32	stept] CENTENARY (ENB); stepped AM,I–V
201.33	cottage,] CENTENARY (ENB); $\sim$$_\wedge$ AM,I–V
202.5	sleeping apartment] CENTENARY (ENB); $\sim$-$\sim$ AM,I–V
202.6	off$_\wedge$] CENTENARY (ENB); $\sim$, AM,I–V
202.7	up stairs] II (ENB); $\sim$-$\sim$ AM,I–E
202.19	dunghill-odor;] I (ENB); $\sim$-$\sim$, AM
203.9	enough,] CENTENARY (ENB); $\sim$$_\wedge$ AM,I–V
203.15	enclosure] II (ENB); inclosure AM,I–E
203.18	daisies$_\wedge$—] CENTENARY (ENB); $\sim$,— AM,I–V
203.18	everywhere—] CENTENARY (ENB); $\sim$; AM,I–V
203.20	plough-share] CENTENARY; ploughshare AM,I–V
203.27	flower,] CENTENARY (ENB); $\sim$$_\wedge$ AM,I–V
203.31	family$_\wedge$—] CENTENARY; $\sim$,— AM,I–V
204.25	vows;] CENTENARY; $\sim$: AM,I–V
204.34–205.1	rude$_\wedge$— . . . ambitious$_\wedge$—] CENTENARY; $\sim$,— . . . $\sim$,— AM,I–V

205.6–7	the members of it] I; they AM
205.33	of Armour] I; *omit* AM
206.2	gentleman, . . . to-and-fro,] CENTENARY (ENB); ~ₐ . . . ~ₐ~ₐ~ₐ AM,I–V
206.3	Alexanderₐ—] E (ENB); ~,— AM,I
206.14	woeful] V; woful AM,I–IV
206.15	every thing] CENTENARY (ENB); everything AM,I–V
206.19–20	modern, . . . -fronted,] CENTENARY (ENB); ~ₐ . . . -~ₐ AM,I–V
206.26	stone-bridge] CENTENARY (ENB); ~ₐ~ AM,I–V
207.13	public house] III (ENB); ~-~ AM,I–E; ~-|~ II
207.16	over-scribbled] V (ENB); ~-|~ AM,III; overscribbled I–II,IV
207.21	seldom] I; never AM
207.31	birth-place] CENTENARY (ENB); birth-|place AM; birthplace I–V
207.31	Burns;] CENTENARY; ~: AM,I–V
207.33	Shakspere's] CENTENARY; Shakspeare's AM,I–E; Shakespeare's II–V
207.33	houseₐ—] E; ~,— AM,I
208.6	fire-place] CENTENARY; ~-|~ AM; fireplace I–V
208.12	birth-place;] CENTENARY (ENB); birthplace: AM,I–IV; ~-|~; V
208.19	wayside] E; way-side AM; ~-|~ I
208.28	much inspiration] I; much of his inspiration AM
208.31	monument] I; Monument AM
209.1	enclosed] I (ENB); inclosed AM
209.2,8	enclosure] I (ENB); inclosure AM
209.12	basement story] IV; ~-~ AM,I–III
209.13	templeₐ—] E; ~,— AM,I

209.17	basement story] I (ENB); ~-~ AM
209.22	pocket-Bible] Centenary (ENB); Pocket-Bible AM; Pocket Bible I–V
209.24	scripture] Centenary (ENB); Scripture AM,I–V
209.33	enclosed] I (ENB); inclosed AM
210.1	Wat_∧—] E (ENB); ~,— AM,I
210.12	sweet-briar] Centenary (ENB); sweetbrier AM,I–V
210.15	grave-yard] Centenary; graveyard AM,I–V
211.9	too_∧—] E; ~,— AM,I
212.26	of Earth's memorable sons] I; *omit* AM
214.25	Saint] Centenary; St. AM,I–V

A London Suburb (MS,AM,I)

215.11–12	purpose . . . were] AM; object . . . was MS
216.1	for] AM; of MS
218.26	that] I; *omit* MS,AM
219.10	its] AM; *omit* MS
220.8	side-walks] E; ~_∧~ MS; sidewalks AM,I
220.18	well-kept] AM; ~_∧~ MS
220.24	by a policeman] I; by policemen MS,AM
221.3–4	garden-wall] AM; ~_∧~ MS
222.6	was] AM; were MS
222.15	pleasure-seekers] AM; ~_∧~ MS
222.19	stauncher] Centenary; stancher MS,AM,I–V
222.20	railway-trains] AM; ~_∧~ MS
223.8	gateways] I; gate-ways MS,AM
223.8–9	brick-wall] Centenary; ~_∧~ MS,AM,I–V
223.25	summer afternoon] AM; ~-~ MS

224.11	too] I; *omit* MS,AM
225.8	groups] AM; groupes MS
*225.10	this] *stet* MS (the AM,I)
226.27	listen] AM; listens MS
226.33	indeed,] AM; ~∧ MS
227.20	retains] AM; has MS
228.13	dry-nurse] AM; ~∧~ MS
229.3	navigators,] AM; ~∧ MS
229.13	the Second] CENTENARY; II. MS,AM,I–V
230.5	that] AM; *omit* MS
230.7	life, yet] I; life, but yet MS,AM
230.34	an explosion] AM; a work MS
231.14	quarter-decks] AM; ~∧~ MS
233.4–7	But . . . midshipmen.] I; *omit* MS,AM
234.2	it in an] AM; it an MS
234.17	first three] AM; three first MS
235.2	Shakspere] CENTENARY; Shakspeare MS,AM,I–E; Shakespeare II–V
235.25	those] AM; these MS
236.8	Bridge] AM; bridge MS
236.32	and followed] AM; and was followed MS
*237.17	where] *stet* MS (while AM,I)
237.18	on] AM; on on MS
237.21	"Trivia";] AM; "Trivia;" MS
237.23	it] AM; *omit* MS
238.29	trollop] AM; trollope MS
239.1	hereditary] AM; heredi-|itary MS
239.2	∧Kissing . . . Ring.∧] CENTENARY; "~ . . . ~." MS,AM,I–V
239.2–7	I . . . pocket.] I; *omit* MS,AM
239.8	kinds] AM; kind MS
239.32	however—] CENTENARY; ~,— MS; ~,∧ AM,I–V
240.5	But how] AM; But How MS

*240.14–15	Fair, . . . few_∧] CENTENARY; ∼_∧ . . . ∼, MS; ∼, . . . ∼, AM,I–V
241.17	cottage-damsel] AM; cottage-girl MS
241.18	negro girl] AM; negro-wench MS
242.2	are] AM; are are MS

UP THE THAMES (MS,AM,I)

244.8–9	difficulties, added . . . picked, weigh] I; difficulties weigh MS,AM
244.17	of] AM; of of MS
244.25	one's] AM; one MS
*245.34	ten] I; two MS,AM
246.18	stone pavement] AM; ∼-∼ MS
246.34	tomb-like] AM; nun-like MS
248.15–16	and the] I; and a MS,AM
249.10	have travelled forth and re-traced] AM; travel forth and re-trace MS
249.27–30	purposes which . . . them.] I; purposes that were so poorly embodied in their most re-nowned performances. MS,AM
250.31	Government] AM; Govenment MS
251.14	maritime] AM; maratime MS
251.18	tumultuously] AM; tumultously MS
252.19	No ¶ It] AM; ¶ MS
252.22	¶ The] AM; no ¶ MS
252.27	enclosed] I; inclosed MS,AM
253.4	and_∧] AM; ∼, MS
253.5	Heaven] CENTENARY; heaven MS,AM,I–V
253.11	in_∧] AM; ∼, MS
253.30;254.1	Saint] CENTENARY; St. MS,AM,I–V
253.33–34	ornamented] AM; or-|mented MS
*253.34	awning] stet MS (covering AM,I)

254.1	Cathedral] AM; cathedral MS
254.30	Houses] AM; houses MS
255.25	the Second] CENTENARY; II. MS,AM,I
255.32	Hospital,)] AM; ~ₐ) MS
257.4	rot from] AM; rot away from MS
257.30	veteran,] AM; ~; MS
258.5	undertone] AM; under tone MS
258.9	assuage] AM; assuage MS
259.7	England"—] CENTENARY; ~,"— MS,AM,I–V
259.18–19	simulacrum] *stet* MS (simulachre AM,I)
261.1–2	pavement of the nave, afar off, falling] I; pavement, falling MS; pavement afar off, falling AM
261.6	south] AM; South MS
261.8	many-colored] AM; ~ₐ~ MS
261.26	elsewhere] AM; elswhere MS
262.3–4	full-length] AM; ~ₐ~ MS
262.10	Malcolm] I; Malcom MS,AM
262.14	a New] AM; an New MS
262.30	lifetime] AM; life-time MS
263.3	formₐ)] AM; ~,) MS
263.17	something] AM; some thing MS
263.27	small-clothes] I; ~ₐ~ MS,AM
264.4	are] AM; is MS
265.13	sepulture] AM; seputure MS
266.21	that] AM; which MS
266.24	is] AM; is is MS
267.10	I] AM; *omit* MS
268.5	sunlight] AM; sun light MS
268.12	the Fifth] CENTENARY; V. MS,AM,I–V
268.14	Shakspere's] CENTENARY; Shakspeare's MS,AM,I–E; Shakespeare's II–V
268.18	mentioned,)] I; ~ₐ) MS,AM

268.23	are] AM; is MS
268.26–27	grave-stone] CENTENARY; gravestone MS,AM,I–IV; grave-|stone V
*270.11	Poet's] *stet* MS (Poets' AM,I–V)
271.19	Fortune] AM; fortune MS
272.13	obedient] AM; *omit* MS
273.18–19	could have . . . available only] AM; could only have . . . available MS
276.4–5	arm in arm with, nay, if I mistake not, partly embraced and supported by, another] I; arm in arm—nay, partly embraced and supported, if I mistake not—by another MS; arm in arm with, nay, partly embraced and supported by, if I mistake not, another AM

OUTSIDE GLIMPSES OF ENGLISH POVERTY (AM,I)

277.13	encrustation] V; incrustation AM,I–IV
279.1	drunken∧—] CENTENARY; ~,— AM,I–V
279.32	art∧—] CENTENARY; ~,— AM,I–V
280.4	half-a-dozen] CENTENARY; ~∧~∧~ AM,I–V
280.21	side-walk] CENTENARY; sidewalk AM,I–IV; side-|walk V
280.25	oysters∧—] CENTENARY; ~,— AM,I–V
280.28	scale;] CENTENARY; ~: AM,I–V
280.33	burthen] CENTENARY; burden AM,I–V
280.33	half-a-dozen] CENTENARY; ~∧~∧~ AM,I–V
281.12	agreements∧—] E; ~,— AM,I
281.20	daytime] I; day-time AM
282.11	to-and-fro] CENTENARY; ~∧~∧~ AM,I–V
282.33	fires∧—] E; ~,— AM,I
283.33	violated∧—] E; ~,— AM,I
284.10	ears∧—] E; ~,— AM,I

285.2	re-appeared] CENTENARY; reappeared AM,I–IV; ~-|~ V
285.8	burthens] CENTENARY; burdens AM,I–V
285.9	burthen] CENTENARY; burden AM,I–V
285.11	behind∧—] E; ~,— AM,I
285.17	merchandize] CENTENARY; merchandise AM,I–V
286.13	woefully] V; wofully AM,I–IV
286.15	cosiest] I; coziest AM
286.25	footsteps] I; foot-steps AM
288.10–12	sister∧— . . . arms∧—] CENTENARY; ~,— . . . ~,— AM,I–V
288.17	Heaven] CENTENARY; heaven AM,I–V
288.24	encrusted] V; incrusted AM,I–IV
289.8	kind;] CENTENARY; ~: AM,I–V
289.20	diffusion] I; spread AM
290.18	baiòcco] CENTENARY; baiocco AM,I–V
290.26	encrustation] CENTENARY; incrustation AM,I–V
291.9	re-appear] CENTENARY; reappear AM,I–V
292.29–31	exception∧— . . . pilferings∧—] CENTENARY; ~,— . . . ~,— AM,I–IV; ~;— . . . ~,— V
293.23–24	aesthetic] CENTENARY; æsthetic AM,I–V
294.17	good nature] CENTENARY; ~-~ AM,I–V
295.3	yeomanlike] CENTENARY (ENB); yeoman-like AM,I–V
296.34	criticizable] CENTENARY; criticisable AM,I–V
297.9	them∧—] CENTENARY; ~,— AM,I–V
297.28	roundabout] CENTENARY; round about AM,I–V
297.29	began to] I; began a AM
299.4–5	Imaginative∧— . . . actors∧—] E; ~,— . . . ~,— AM,I
300.4	befel] CENTENARY; befell AM,I–V

300.22–23	face— . . . features—] E; ~,— . . . ~,— AM,I
300.22	woeful] V; woful AM,I–IV
300.26	baulking] E; balking AM,I
300.31	burthened] CENTENARY; burdened AM,I–V
301.22	concern;] CENTENARY; ~: AM,I–V
301.24	burthen] CENTENARY; burden AM,I–V
301.27	up stairs] II; ~-~ AM,I–E
301.32	to-and-fro] CENTENARY; ~∧~∧~ AM,I–V
302.17	woeful] V; woful AM,I–IV
302.20	Heaven] CENTENARY; heaven AM,I–V
302.23	matron-hen;] CENTENARY; ~-~: AM,I–V
303.11	and] I; to AM
303.29	bystanders] E; by-standers AM,I
304.20–22	remainder— . . . boy—] CENTENARY; ~,— . . . ~,— AM,I–V
304.26–27	Deluge] CENTENARY; deluge AM,I–V
304.29–32	corrupt∧— . . . a-glow∧—] CENTENARY; ~,— . . . ~,— AM,I,II–V; ~,∧ . . . ~,—E
304.32	a-glow] CENTENARY; aglow AM,I–V
306.3	pine-boards] CENTENARY (ENB); ~∧~ AM,I–V
306.28	dawns∧— . . . then∧—] E; ~,— . . . ~,— AM,I
307.17	wear;] CENTENARY; ~: AM,I
308.20	postillions] CENTENARY; postilions AM,I–V
308.20–24	One . . . -bond.] I; *omit* AM
308.28	churchyard] I; church-yard AM

CIVIC BANQUETS (MS,AM,I)

310.9	distaste] AM; distate MS
310.9	to] AM; towards MS

311.4–5	and confining . . . vegetables only because] AM; and only confining . . . vegetables because MS
*311.12	Lawrence] *stet* MS (Laurence AM,I)
311.22	staunch] CENTENARY; stanch MS,AM,I–V
312.22	table_∧] AM; ~, MS
312.34	wine_∧—] E; ~,— MS,AM,I
313.3	Coffee-house] IV; Coffehouse MS; Coffee-House AM,I,II–III; ~_∧~ E
313.12	foregoing] AM; above MS
313.18	roast-beef] AM; ~_∧~ MS
313.32	Saint] CENTENARY (ENB); St. MS,AM,I–V
313.33	mediæval] AM; mediaeval MS
314.2	stone-pillars] CENTENARY; ~_∧~ MS,AM,I–V
314.6	lighted] AM; lighed MS
314.23	Coats-of-arms] AM; ~_∧~_∧~ MS
314.28	Full-length] AM; ~_∧~ MS
314.29	the Second] CENTENARY; II. MS,AM,I–V
314.31	several royal characters are] I; more than one royal character is MS,AM
314.33	enough_∧] AM; ~, MS
315.16	the] AM; *omit* MS
315.23	reader's] AM; readers MS
315.25	steel-clad] AM; steal-clad MS
315.26	in_∧] AM; ~, MS
316.1	description] I; pages MS,AM
316.4–5	banquetting-halls] AM (banqueting); ~_∧~ MS
316.6	now] I; still MS,AM
*316.7–8	splendor still are.] I; splendor still are so. MS; splendor are so. AM
316.15;317.4	the Eighth] CENTENARY; VIII. MS,AM,I–V
316.30	silver_∧] AM; ~, MS
316.31–32	open-work] AM; ~_∧~ MS

317.5	the Second] CENTENARY; II. MS,AM,I–V
317.34	assize-time] I; ~∧~ MS,AM
318.2	Town Hall] I; (doubtful) MS; ~-~ AM
319.11	face∧] AM; ~, MS
319.31	few,)] AM; ~∧) MS
320.1	thin-visaged men] I; thin-visaged, green-spectacled men MS,AM
320.2	sallow, deeply] I; sallow with the intemperate use of strong coffee, deeply MS,AM
320.31	dining-hall] AM; dinig-hall MS
321.11;322.1	Sherry] AM; sherry MS
321.33	Hock . . . Champagne] AM; hock . . . champagne MS
323.22	roughly hewn] AM; ~-~ MS
323.26–27	grisly featured] I; ~-~ MS,AM
324.6	describe] AM; express MS
324.20	all—thorough] AM; all—which is thorough MS
325.31	His] AM; his MS
327.7	family,)] AM; ~∧) MS
327.25	bayoneted] AM; bayonnetted MS
327.28	criticizing] CENTENARY; criticising MS,AM,I–V
328.2	added—] E; ~,— MS,AM,I
328.10	Fate] AM; fate MS
329.21	well-won] CENTENARY; ~∧~ MS, AM,I–V
329.22	development] AM; developement MS
*329.24	has] stet MS (had AM,I)
*329.32	shirk without] AM; shirk it without MS
330.16	charge] I; scratch MS,AM
*330.18	twice happened] AM; twice times happened MS
331.9–10	representative] AM; representive MS
331.12–13	bountiful hospitality] AM; ~-~ (doubtful) MS

331.22	the] AM; the the MS
332.6	blue coats and buff breeches] I; blue and buff MS,AM
332.18	door-way] AM; ~∧~ MS
332.19	Mayoress] AM; May-|ess MS
334.14–15	of which] I; *omit* of MS,AM
*334.30	lights] *stet* MS (light AM,I)
335.4	consider, I] AM; consider it, I MS
335.12	dainty,] AM; ~; MS
335.17–18	half-a-century] CENTENARY; ~∧~∧~ MS, AM,I–V
335.20	worth while] AM; ~-~ MS
337.34	of generals] AM; of knights, generals MS
337.34	Parliament] AM; Parliaments MS
338.7	indeed, on] AM; indeed, one on MS
338.24	moderate∧] AM; ~. MS
338.34	another—] CENTENARY; ~,— MS,AM,I–V
339.21	earl] AM; Earl MS
339.30–33	Champagne . . . Port] AM; champagne . . . port MS
340.20	one] AM; *omit* MS
340.21	foregoing] AM; above MS
341.4	cosier] I; cozier MS,AM
341.9,12	"the literary] AM; the "literary MS
343.9	careful of their country's honor,] I; *omit* MS, AM
343.12	half-sightedness] AM; half-sigtedness MS
343.29	official] AM; *omit* MS
344.17	America] AM; American MS
344.21–23	parties— . . . opportunity—his] E; ~, . . . ~, and his MS; ~,— . . . ~,—his AM,I
*344.28	his] *stet* MS (the AM,I)
345.19	these Sketches] I; the the sketch MS; the sketch AM

REJECTED FIRST-EDITION SUBSTANTIVE VARIANTS

NOTE: Although the readings below are listed in the Historical Collation, they are given separately here since the information is of critical importance. An asterisk indicates that a Textual Note discusses the reading. The symbols used are explained on p. 359 in the headnote to the preceding appendix.

TO A FRIEND (MS,I)

*4.28	impressions] MS; impression I

CONSULAR EXPERIENCES (MS,I)

19.3	course] MS; cause I
20.8	extravagancies] MS; extravagances I
22.33	generic] MS; general I
*28.26	this] MS; the I
38.22	Ganger] MS; Gauger I

LEAMINGTON SPA (MS,AM,I)

52.3	elder] MS; older I
52.6	earthen] MS; earthern I
55.31	at] MS; in I
57.33	birds-nests] MS; birds' nests I

About Warwick (Partial MS;AM,I)

67.20	further] MS; farther I
67.23;73.20	towards] MS; toward I
85.3	tower] AM; towers I

Recollections of a Gifted Woman (MS,AM,I)

90.5	subsidencies] MS; subsidences I
91.21	village-streets] MS; village street I
*94.18	counties] MS; countries I
96.7	subtle] MS; subtile I
101.21	altar] MS; alter I
*103.20	his] MS; its I
105.16	subtle] MS; subtile I
111.6	could] MS; would I
111.10	towards] MS; toward I
112.13	round] MS; around I
114.7	further] MS; farther I
115.28	characters] MS; character I
*116.15	denied] MS; decried I

Lichfield and Uttoxeter (MS,I)

126.6	whence] MS; where I
*134.14	sultry] MS; petty I
136.20	elder] MS; older I

Pilgrimage to Old Boston (MS,AM,I)

139.18	uglinesses] MS; ugliness I
140.31	subtle] MS; subtile I

151.31	a] MS; an I
155.13	peopled] MS; people I
157.16	middle channel] MS; middle of the channel I
161.11	round] MS; around I
163.29	whence] MS; where I
165.17	in] MS; on I

Near Oxford (MS,AM,I)

168.2	bran-new] MS; brand-new I
*168.11	close at] MS; close to I
*173.2	accounts] MS; account I
174.12	further] MS; farther I
*178.18	stingo] MS; things I
179.3	sulkinesses] MS; sulkiness I
179.31	gentlefolks] MS; gentlefolk I
180.4	engraven] MS; engraved I
*184.6	we] MS; are I
188.16	hour] MS; hours I

Some of the Haunts of Burns (AM,I)

193.21	grass] AM; glass I
194.25	latter] AM; later I
*200.9	whole] AM; old I

A London Suburb (MS,AM,I)

213.18	elegancies] MS; elegances I
217.12	on one] MS; on the one I
217.20	in my] MS; on my I
*225.10	this] MS; the I

230.15	parts] MS; part I
231.25	presences] MS; presence I
234.4	sewn] MS; sewed I
237.5	sung] MS; sang I
*237.17	where] MS; while I

Up the Thames (MS,AM,I)

243.8	fishy] MS; fishing I
250.5	subtile] MS; subtle I
253.22	a] MS; an I
253.26;254.30;255.19;259.15	further] MS; farther I
*253.34	awning] MS; covering I
259.18–19	simulacrum] MS; simulachre I
260.3	when] MS; where I
266.14;267.33;268.32;*270.11	Poet's] MS; Poets' I
273.30	subtlety] MS; subtilty I
275.23	elegancies] MS; elegances I

Outside Glimpses of English Poverty (AM,I)

No rejects.

Civic Banquets (MS,AM,I)

312.10	excellencies] MS; excellences I
312.21	especial] MS; special I
312.33	foods] MS; food I
314.8	further] MS; farther I
315.11	parti-colored] MS; party-colored I
322.12	imprudencies] MS; imprudences I
327.7	a] MS; an I

*329.24	has] MS; had I
330.7	dumb-foundered] MS; dumbfounded I
*334.30	lights] MS; light I
335.8	plates-full] MS; platefuls I
*344.28	his] MS; the I

WORD-DIVISION

1. *End-of-the-Line Hyphenation in the Centenary Edition*

NOTE: No hyphenation of a possible compound at the end of a line in the Centenary text is present in the copy-text except for the following readings, which are hyphenated within the line in the copy-text. Hyphenated compounds in which both elements are capitalized are not included.

13.1	hard-|hearted	55.10	grave-|yard
14.16	Ninety-|second	55.11	grave-|stones
19.26	deep-|rooted	58.24	old-|fashioned
23.1	half-|compelled	63.16	summer-|wind
27.10	sword-|blade	63.17	half-|remembrances
30.4	judgment-|seat	63.18	side-|glance
37.17	porcupine-|quills	63.32	farm-|house
43.28	country-|houses	67.12	every-|day
46.4	garden-|side	70.31	timber-|and-plaster
47.29	well-|chosen	75.26	coal-|grate
48.2	Bath-|chairs	76.28	battle-|weapon
50.11	middle-|aged	80.8	forest-|shade
51.33	leaden-|framed	82.30	roast-|beef
52.8	house-|leeks	88.15	gew-|gaws
53.19	main-|road	88.22	what-|not
53.33	age-|long	88.29	looking-|glasses

89.12	snuff-|boxes	200.12	street-|corners
94.32	high-|road	204.1	free-|hearted
95.2	summer-|weather	216.31	hedge-|fence
99.27	deer-|stealer	220.21	village-|streets
101.10	respectable-|looking	221.5	Half-a-|century
103.33	altar-|tombs	222.19	booth-|keeper's
121.31	birth-|place	223.8	brick-|wall
122.25	clear-|sightedness	232.20	cross-|purposes
131.22	stone-|pedestal	237.1	cotton-|velvets
137.6	market-|place	238.7	sailor-|frolics
142.31	up-|and-down	238.20	world-|central
144.31	wind-|shaken	243.2	old-|fashioned
145.26	cherry-|stone	246.13	sub-|fluvial
146.10	long-|enduring	260.27	long-|enduring
147.13	east-|window	275.33	flower-|seeds
152.9	guide-|book	281.30	mud-|puddle
152.34	mason-|work	283.26	silken-|skirted
153.7	third-|class	291.17	long-|barrelled
163.24	stone-|gallery	300.11	humor-|eaten
163.32	red-|tiled	302.16	harp-|strings
164.27	Hanover-|street	304.21	rosy-|cheeked
165.32	parlor-|window	306.15	wooden-|soled
176.30	half-|obliterated	308.23	marriage-|bond
183.27	country-|house	317.3	silver-|gilt
185.2	Bosworth-|field	320.4	fat-|witted
186.1	weed-|grown	323.20	middle-|aged
188.22	to-and-|fro	332.2	city-|greatness
188.34	ivy-|grown	343.10	moss-|grown
192.13	malt-|liquor	344.18	right-|honorable

2. End-of-the-Line Hyphenation in the Manuscript

NOTE: The following compounds, or possible compounds, are hyphenated at the end of the line in the manuscript copy-text. The form in which they have been transcribed in the Centenary text, as listed below, represents the practice of the manuscript as ascertained by other appearances or by parallels within the manuscript. Other Hawthorne manuscripts of the period have been consulted when evidence was not available in the *Our Old Home* manuscripts.

3.17	more susceptible	66.4	long-established
4.17	reposited	66.8	new-fangled
6.3	smoke-stained	66.31	high-windowed
8.33	a-flame	67.31	witchcraft
11.19	well-considered	68.10	school-house
15.17	farm-house	68.14	timber-and-plaster
18.8	good-tempered	72.1	household
19.7	half-sagacity	76.3	kitchen-fire
19.33	coat-of-arms	80.5	high-shouldering
22.6	warfare	81.5	city-wall
24.30	life-long	82.33	fire-place
25.16	scholar-like	86.19	stone-coffin
29.14	tenfold	88.22	mantel-piece
33.9	off-scourings	88.26	top-light
33.11	intermixture	90.6	champaign-scenery
37.6	well-wisher	90.12	wayside
41.20	moderate-sized	92.16	foster-father
42.7	play-place	93.9	stone-fence
42.17	half-pay	93.33	boundary-fence
43.10	summer-season	94.28	cottage-walls
43.27	well-to-do	95.17	overflows
46.9	tombstones	95.30	sea-shell
46.14	iron-mongers	97.12	passage-way
46.18	shop-fronts	97.15	long-extinguished
46.24	foot-paths	98.14	side-walls
47.13	wherein	99.7	downright
47.25	second-class	99.32	boon-companion
52.11	shade-trees	102.33	foreshortened
52.24	self-respect	106.14	monomaniac
58.5	daylight	109.17	ladylike
58.9	village-green	115.23	countrywoman
61.4	nowise	120.11	court-yard
61.21	farm-houses	121.10	night-troubles
63.34	by-paths	124.6	pin-hooks

125.7	cloudlike	223.1	roundabout
127.10	stone-work	225.9	omnipresent
128.19	open-work	225.33	park-wall
130.16	angel-glimpse	226.12	wayside
130.18	court-martial	226.30	common-place
131.5	cross-street	227.29	potsherds
132.3	stone-boulder	229.6	boarding-houses
132.32	half-century's	229.26	footsteps
133.21	red-tiled	229.28	midnight
137.10	soul-substance	229.29	sea-yarns
139.13	market-square	231.30	Nine-tenths
143.6	city-gates	232.29	extraordinary
143.18	now-a-days	234.10	waistcoat
144.19	side-arches	235.6	bathing-tub
155.15	market-place	237.24	merry-maker
156.10	sunshine	238.10	mob-jammed
156.29	leap-frog	240.27	gin-shop
157.26	bookseller's	241.27	free-spoken
163.20	stone-roof	242.15	marble-polish
164.7	church-steps	244.32	prize-boat
165.10	long-boats	245.9	ware-houses
165.11	wharf-rats	249.10	re-traced (MS
165.16	summer-twilight		re-|trace)
165.18	churchyard	250.9	tallow-candles
167.20	wayside	252.1	land-sharks
168.3	stone-houses	252.13	foot-passengers
170.31	by-and-by	252.19	resting-place
173.9	entrance-hall	252.30	river-craft
179.18	overlooked	260.8	anthem-strain
179.24	grave-stones	271.5	village-street
181.3	railway	273.10	fancy-world
188.1	overflowed	312.14	dreamlike
188.4	weed-grown	316.10	wood-work
189.33	outspoken	316.31	city-grandees
190.8	pigeon-pie	317.14	sea-port
213.3	sunshine	320.4	heavy-cheeked
213.22	wine-cellar	320.31	dining-hall
216.32	brick-wall	326.4	cart-wheel
217.6	railway-train	327.6	aforethought

327.28	fellow-guests	334.24	hundred-weight
328.12	earthquake	344.29	beforehand
331.14	entrance-hall	345.13	death-grip
331.34	forefathers		

3. *Special Cases*

(a)

NOTE: In the following list the compound, or possible compound, is hyphenated at the end of the line in the copy-text and in the Centenary text.

74.19	old-|fashioned (i.e. old-fashioned)
98.1	over-|head (i.e. overhead)
133.15	market-|day (i.e. market-day)
154.6	farm-|houses (i.e. farm-houses)
158.19	counter-|pane (i.e. counterpane)
165.29	knee-|breeches (i.e. knee-breeches)
206.19	modern-|fronted (i.e. modern-fronted)
235.25	like-|wise (i.e. likewise)
252.32	water-|entrance (i.e. water-entrance)
283.34	door-|step (i.e. door-step)
285.34	upper-ten-|dom (i.e. upper-ten-dom)
295.7	good-|humored (i.e. good-humored)
295.24	west-|wind (i.e. west-wind)

(b)

NOTE: In the following cases the hyphenated compound appears at the end of the line in the Centenary text but the hyphen is an editorial emendation not present in the copy-text.

49.17	counter-|injury (i.e. counter-injury *for MS* counter injury)
103.15	grave-|stones (i.e. grave-stones *for MS* gravestones)
181.17	stone-|floor (i.e. stone-floor *for MS* stone floor)
193.15	corner-|house (i.e. corner-house *for AM* corner house)
262.3	full-|length (i.e. full-length *for MS* full length)
268.26	grave-|stone (i.e. grave-stone *for MS* gravestone)
316.31	open-|work (i.e. open-work *for MS* open work)
335.17	half-|a-century (i.e. half-a-century *for MS* half a century)

HISTORICAL COLLATION

This Historical Collation records substantive variants among editions. Typographical errors not forming accepted words are not listed after E unless they involve revision of the plates. The basis of record is the reading to the left of the bracket, which is that of the Centenary text but not always that of the copy-text manuscript or *Atlantic Monthly* text. Where "MS" (or "AM" in chapters where MS is wanting) is not specified as the source for a rejected reading, the Centenary reading is the manuscript (or AM) reading. A reading of any unlisted edition agrees with Centenary.

The following editions were collated and their substantive variants recorded: AM (*Atlantic Monthly*; see the Textual Introduction, pp. liv–lviii, for a complete list of all appearances by chapter), I (1863 first edition), E (1863 English edition), II (1876 Little Classics Edition), III (1883 Riverside Edition), IV (1891 Houghton, Mifflin edition), and V (1900 Autograph Edition). Note: "Lichfield and Uttoxeter" also includes references to the following original 1857 "Uttoxeter" texts: K (*The Keepsake*, London, 1857) and H (*Harper's New Monthly Magazine*, April, 1857). A separate "Uttoxeter" appendix records all variants among these texts.

Since the plates for the first American and English editions were the only ones that could have been revised during Hawthorne's lifetime, the intermediate printings of I and E have been cross-collated to identify variants within these editions.

See the Textual Introduction, p. lii, for a discussion of concealed printings in the first English edition.

To a Friend (MS,I)

2.6	This Volume is] These volumes are E
3.5	an early] a MS
3.6	old between] old, without decay, between MS
3.8	of] of of MS
3.8	this volume of sketches] these Sketches E
3.19	volume] work E
3.20	might] could MS
4.15	catastrophe] catastrope MS
4.26	seldom] hardly ever MS
4.28	impressions] impression I–V
4.31	undeniable] very true MS
4.35	perfectly] perfect MS
5.19–33	world. But . . . Franklin Pierce.] world. Can . . . Franklin Pierce. MS (*See Editorial Emendations in the Copy-Text.*)
5.34	The Wayside, July 2ᵈ, 1863.] *omit* E

Consular Experiences (MS,I)

6.21	maritime] maratime MS
7.3	clothing] cloathing MS
7.33	Tennessee] Tenessee MS
8.34	in] out of MS
13.19–14.23	The individual . . . entreaty.] The individual . . . land. MS ᵃ (*See Emendations for complete MS ᵃ reading.*)
14.26;15.7,30	Ninety-second] Ninety-sixth MS
15.24	away] way MS
16.2,25	trowsers] trousers MS,I–V
18.5	of] *omit* MS
19.3	course] cause I–V

20.4   advertisement] advertisemt MS

20.8   extravagancies] extravagances I–V

21.7   them] *omit* MS

21.9   predecessor] predecesor MS

21.26   paralleled] paralelled MS

22.2   archipelagoes] archipelagos E (*variant printing*)

22.33   generic] general I–V

23.4   government] govenment MS

23.24   government] Govenment MS

27.14   of last] of the last III–V

27.33   of metropolitan] *omit* III–V

28.1   military] *omit* MS

28.26   this] the I–V

29.11   one of] *omit* MS

30.20   any one] *omit* any E

30.32   McClellan] McLellan MS; M'Clellan E

32.28   old General Cass] *omit* MS

35.13   my own interest and the public's] when I am well off MS

35.17   successive arrivals] arrival MS

36.4   some acquaintance with] a smattering of MS

36.14   too often] usually MS

36.23   unsuitable] inconsiderate MS

37.16   attainment] attaintment MS

37.17   there] here MS

37.31   Mayor's] Mayors' III–V

38.6–20   prepared, in advance . . . unreal.] prepared, (in advance . . . unreal. MS (*See Emendations.*)

38.13   an] and E

38.22   called] call E

38.22   Ganger] Gauger I,II

39.14   English friend] Englishman MS

40.9–11   The . . . voyage.] *omit* MS

LEAMINGTON SPA (MS,AM,I)

41.0   *Headnote, AM Only*

MY DEAR EDITOR,—

You can hardly have expected to hear from me again, (unless by invitation to the field of honor,) after those cruel and terrible notes upon my harmless article in the July Number. How could you find it in your heart (a soft one, as I have hitherto supposed) to treat an old friend and liege contributor in that unheard-of way? Not that I should care a fig for any amount of vituperation, if you had only let my article come before the public as I wrote it, instead of suppressing precisely the passages with which I had taken most pains, and which I flattered myself were most cleverly done. The interview with the President, for example: it would have been a treasure to the future historian; and I hold you responsible to posterity for thrusting it into the fire. However, I cannot lose so good an opportunity of showing the world the placability and sweetness that adorn my character, and therefore send you another article, in which, I trust, you will find nothing to strike out,—unless, peradventure, you think that I may disturb the tranquility of nations by my plan of annexing Great Britain, or my attempted adumbration of a fat English dowager!

Truly, yours,

A PEACEABLE MAN.

41.10	10] 16 MS,AM
42.22	by] *omit* MS,AM
42.27	again] a-|again MS
43.3	necessity] neces-|ity MS
44.25	villa] villla AM

45.9	are] is MS
45.15–16	them . . . they are] it . . . it is AM
45.20–21	yards. It seemed to me a sad emblem] yards; a sad emblem, it seemed to me MS; yards, a sad emblem, it seemed to me AM
45.25–26	Leam—the . . . it—after] Leam, after MS,AM
46.19	a diminutive] a much more diminutive MS
49.7	seldom] not always MS,AM
49.24	is strong, I suspect, only in] is only strong, I suspect, in MS
50.32	stile to stile] style to style I
51.6	whithersoever] whithsoever MS
51.19	Lovers'] Lover's MS
52.3	elder] older AM,I–V
52.6	earthen] earthern I
52.15–16	and hidden . . . road] *omit* MS
52.21	as the] *omit* as MS
52.24–25	unfamiliarity] unfam-|iarity MS
53.12	of the] *omit* of MS
53.25	battlements] turrets MS
54.12	distinguished a] *omit* a MS
54.29	allotted] alotted MS
55.31	at] in AM,I–V
56.24	endwise] lengthwise MS
56.25	the headstone being within] and within MS
56.25–26	foundation-wall] foundation-stones MS
57.13	minutes'] minutes MS
57.33	birds-] birds' AM,I–V
58.5	out into] at MS
58.10	incalculable] incalcuble MS
58.24	that] that that MS
58.28	on their] on the III–V
59.6	Wickliffe's] Wickcliffe's MS,AM,I,II
59.18	fifty] a hundred MS

60.1	shuffling] scuffling MS,AM
60.27	the old] *omit* the MS
61.33	styled Hatton] *omit* MS
64.12–13	a tonic] *omit* MS
64.21	or a quarter] *omit* MS

About Warwick (Partial MS;AM,I)

65.0	About Warwick] A Sketch or two in Warwick MS
66.17	wooded] wooden III–V
67.20	further] farther AM,I–V
67.23	towards] toward I–V
68.3–4	than climb . . . touch] instead of climbing . . . touching MS
70.29	similar] similiar MS
71.3–4	chimneys] chimnies MS
71.34	perhaps] perhap MS
73.20	towards] toward I–V
73.33	old English letters] black-letter AM (MS *wanting*)
75.6	where] while AM (MS *wanting*)
76.15	visitors] visiters MS
76.31	field of Waterloo] *stet* MS (*cancelled*)
78.11	other] private AM (MS *wanting*)
78.22	or] and AM (MS *wanting*)
80.14	these] and these MS
81.8	that] having MS,AM
81.8	Nilometer] Nileometer MS
82.8	nominal] moninal II (*first printing*)
82.9	twelve] *omit* MS,AM
85.3	tower] towers I–V (MS *wanting*)
85.28	benefactor] benefac-|or MS
86.13	brass] stone MS

86.20	anciently entombed] *omit* MS,AM
87.30	sole relation to] only relation with MS
88.24	denoted only] only denoted MS
89.11	all of which I have seen] *omit* MS,AM
89.12	its] their MS
89.19	the money in] it MS; it in AM

Recollections of a Gifted Woman (MS,AM,I)

90.5	subsidencies] subsidences I–V
90.12	the wayside] those wayside MS,AM
90.15	is] are MS
90.20	them. To] them; and to MS
91.9	tree] trees IV–V
91.21	village-streets] village street AM,I–V
91.29	nobler and more] noblest and most MS
92.4	the] one of its MS
92.28	the] the the MS
93.20	has] have MS
93.31	deigned] designed III–V
93.32	charm] spell MS
94.2	tangled] intricate MS
94.18	counties] countries AM,I–V
96.7	subtle] subtile AM,I,II–V
96.11	other] *omit* III–V
97.9	still] *omit* V
97.22	huddling] huddled V
99.32	and finally] who MS,AM
99.33–34	the victim of convivial habits who] *omit* MS,AM
100.8	this] *omit* MS
101.21	altar] alter I
101.28	Essex-street] Main-street MS

103.20	his] its AM,I–V
103.29–30	that is] or MS
105.16	subtle] subtile AM,I–V
105.23	of such] for such IV–V
106.19	could] would E
106.22	resistance] resistence MS
106.29	phases] faces MS,AM
106.30	large] *omit* MS,AM
107.26	had come hither . . . here] went thither . . . there MS
108.7	Farrar] F. MS,AM
108.29	usually] actually AM
109.34	in] on MS
111.6	could] would AM,I–V
111.9	which] *omit* MS
111.10	towards] toward I–V
112.4	Raleigh's] Raleighs MS
112.9–12	It is very . . . decisive step.] *omit* MS,AM
112.13	round] around AM,I–V
114.7	further] farther AM,I–E
114.14	ingenuous] generous MS
115.3	into] in E
115.8	bruising, if they do recognize it.] bruising it if they do recognize. MS
115.10–12	It was . . . poet.] *omit* MS,AM
115.21	republished] published IV–V
115.26	that] *omit* E
115.28	characters] character AM,I–V
116.7	be] he III
116.15	denied] decried AM,I–V
117.8	a] *omit* III–V
119.3–4	could have . . . about only by] could only have . . . about by MS
119.23–24	us what is best . . . beautifullest] us to see what is best, nor our poets what is most

beautiful MS; us to see what is best, nor have our poets sung us what is beautifullest AM

LICHFIELD AND UTTOXETER (MS,I)

121.15	chiccory] chickory MS
122.24	farther] further II–V
123.15	courtesy] curtsy V
124.8	mysterious] myterious I $^{a-b}$
126.6	whence] where I–V
128.23	his] its E
132.12	another] a another MS
132.26	hands] hand III
132.32	burthen] burden K,H,MS,I–V
133.27	beside] behind E
134.14	the sultry] *omit* the MS
134.14	sultry] petty I–V
135.3	Bull's] Bulls' K,MS,I–V
135.15	hostelries] hostleries I,II–III
136.20	elder] older I–V
137.14	dript] dripped K,H,MS,I–V

PILGRIMAGE TO OLD BOSTON (MS,AM,I)

139.18	uglinesses] ugliness I–V
140.22	these] those MS
140.31	subtle] subtile AM,I–V
141.5	Yorkshire] York|Yorkshire MS
141.9–11	were . . . were] was . . . was MS

142.31	and] *omit* III–V
144.27	be] were MS
145.25	strong] strongly MS
146.3	been] *omit* MS
146.7	is vain] is in vain MS
146.19	sweetest] sweetiest MS
146.28	term] phrase MS
146.30	had] *omit* MS
147.1	Cathedral] Minster IV–V
147.9	and] *omit* MS,AM
147.15	Behind] Within MS,AM
147.19	now] since MS
147.32	dead] deae II (*first printing*)
148.29	is] has been MS
149.6	tessellated] tesselated MS
149.16	Minster] cathedral IV–V
149.18	high, peaked roofs] high∧peaked roofs II; high-peaked roofs III–V
150.5	proximity] vicinity MS
150.6	is] was MS
150.7	part] parts IV–V
150.9	Minster] cathedral IV–V
150.19	mould of a decaying] decay of a mouldering MS
151.7	a little] a a little MS
151.25	in] into MS
151.27	Cathedral] Minster IV–V
151.28	but in this at Lincoln] but, here MS,AM
151.31	a] an AM,I–V
152.33	than of] *omit* of MS
153.6	in] into MS
153.9	by the] by taking the MS
153.9	he] they MS
153.17	through] throughout MS

154.27–28	its consummation] *omit* MS,AM
154.29	striven] strove MS
155.13	peopled] people AM,I–V
156.1	not] *omit* IV–V
156.30–31	which . . . that] that . . . which MS
157.13	half-twisted] half-hoisted MS,AM
157.15	over flat] over the flat E
157.16	to] *omit* E
157.16	middle channel] middle of the channel AM,I–V
157.34	had . . . pilgrimages] have . . . pilgrimage MS
157.34	he] *omit* MS,AM
159.23	we] he III–V
160.6–7	not that . . . but] *omit* MS,AM
160.27	in manuscript] *omit* MS,AM
160.28	by] in MS
161.8	of] him III–V
161.8	antiquary] antiquarian MS
161.11	round] around I–V
161.13	the hand] the own hand MS
161.25	us] us us MS
161.32	Mr.] *omit* MS,AM
162.3	received an invitation] been invited MS
162.3	I] *omit* MS,AM
162.5	accept it] *omit* it MS
162.15	antiquary] antiquarian MS
163.21	Font] Fort AM
163.23–24	a yet] yet a MS
163.29	whence] where AM,I–V
165.17	in] on AM,I–V
165.20	were] was MS
166.8	bleating] bleat MS
166.16	fancied it] fancied that it MS

Near Oxford (MS,AM,I)

168.2	bran-new] brand-new AM,I–V
168.4	time-worn] time-word MS
168.11	close at] close to AM,I–V
168.27–28	slanting] aslantwise MS
169.24	arranger] arranges AM
171.1–2	Henry sometimes] Henry have sometimes MS
171.4	abundant] abun-|ant MS
171.22	have been] be MS
172.20	houses] homes MS
173.2	accounts] account AM,I–V
173.11	elevation] height MS,AM
173.17	make out] *omit* out MS
174.12	further] farther AM,I–V
174.16	station] life MS
176.18	variety capable] variety that can be made capable MS
177.10	be uproarious] be too uproarious II–V
177.23	without] with-|but III (*last printing*)
177.30	three] trhee E (*variant printing*)
178.18	stingo] things AM,I–V
178.19	be] were MS
179.3	sulkinesses] sulkiness I–V
179.31	gentlefolks] gentlefolk AM,I–III,V; gentle folk IV
180.4	engraven] engraved AM,I–V
180.15–16	gentleman] person MS
180.16–17	for bringing] to bring MS
181.6	unpruned] untrimmed MS
182.11–12	now has] has now V
182.25	wide air-holes] apertures MS
183.4	and all one fire-place] *omit* MS,AM

183.16	wherein] when MS
183.26	humorous] *omit* MS
183.31	engaging . . . who stirs] and engages . . . stirring MS
183.32	over] at MS
184.6	we] are AM,I–V
184.30	into] in MS
184.33	monument] *omit* MS,AM
187.10	so] as MS
187.13–14	to inhabit] for a study MS
188.16	hour] hours AM,I–V
188.20	should] shall MS
188.22	rolled] rolls MS
188.22	to] two II
190.3	one of our] *omit* of MS
190.17	belonging] belong AM
192.9	feature] ingredient MS

Some of the Haunts of Burns (AM,I)

193.0	BURNS] BURNS. │ BY A TOURIST WITHOUT IMAGINATION OR ENTHUSIASM. AM
193.21	grass] glass I
194.25	latter] later I–V
196.5–6	Displayed] Stuck AM
199.33	beggar's (ENB)] beggars' AM,I–V
200.9	whole] old I–V
200.33	stopt (ENB)] stopped AM,I–V
201.32	stept (ENB)] stepped AM,I–V
205.6–7	the members of it] they AM
205.33	of Armour] *omit* AM
207.21	seldom] never AM
208.25	of the] *omit* the III–V
208.28	much inspiration] much of his inspiration AM

212.21	pyramid] pryamid I
212.26	of Earth's memorable sons] *omit* AM
212.27	sung] sang E

A London Suburb (MS,AM,I)

213.5	nor] or IV–V
213.18	elegancies] elegances I–V
215.2	his] its E
215.2	earlier] early E
215.11-12	purpose . . . were] object . . . was MS
216.1	for] of MS
217.12	on one] on the one AM,I–V
217.20	in my] on my I–V
218.18	an] *omit* E
218.26	that] *omit* MS,AM
219.10	its] *omit* MS
220.24	by a policeman] by policemen MS,AM
221.6	token] tokens V
222.6	was] were MS
222.19	stauncher] stancher MS,AM,I–V
224.11	too] *omit* MS,AM
225.8	groups] groupes MS
225.10	this] the AM,I–V
226.27	listen] listens MS
227.13	barrows] burrows AM
227.20	retains] has MS
229.29–30	with endless . . . under famous] with their endless . . . under various V
230.5	that] *omit* MS
230.7	life, yet] life, but yet MS,AM
230.15	parts] part AM,I–V
230.34	an explosion] a work MS

231.25   presences] presence AM,I–V
231.31   tell truth] tell the truth E
233.4–7   But . . . midshipmen.] *omit* MS,AM
234.2   it in an] it an MS
234.4   sewn] sewed AM,I–V
234.17   first three] three first MS
235.25   those] these MS
236.32   and followed] and was followed MS
237.5   sung] sang AM,I–V
237.17   where] while AM,I–V
237.18   on] on on MS
237.23   it] *omit* MS
238.24   eldest] elder IV–V
239.1   hereditary] heredi-|itary MS
239.2–7   I . . . pocket.] *omit* MS,AM
239.8   kinds] kind MS
241.17   cottage-damsel] cottage-girl MS
241.18   negro girl] negro-wench MS
242.2   are] are are MS

Up the Thames (MS,AM,I)

243.8   fishy] fishing AM,I–V
244.8–9   added . . . picked] *omit* MS,AM
244.17   of] of of MS
244.25   one's] one MS
245.34   ten] two MS,AM
246.34   tomb-like] nun-like MS
248.15–16   and the] and a MS,AM
249.10   have travelled forth and re-traced] travel forth
                and re-trace MS
249.27–30   purposes which . . . them.] purposes that
                . . . performances. MS,AM
250.5   subtile] subtle I–V

250.31	Government] Govenment MS
251.14	maritime] maratime MS
251.18	tumultuously] tumultously MS
253.22	a] an AM,I–V
253.26	further] farther AM,I–V
253.33–34	ornamented] or-|mented MS
253.34	awning] covering AM,I–V
254.30;255.19	further] farther AM,I–V
256.19–20	reminiscences] reminiscenccs I
257.4	rot from] rot away from MS
257.21	illuminated] illumniated I
258.9	assuage] assauge MS
259.15	further] farther AM,I–E
259.18–19	simulacrum] simulachre AM,I–V
260.3	when] where AM,I–V
261.1–2	pavement of the nave, afar off, falling] pave-ment, falling MS; pavement afar off, falling AM
261.26	elsewhere] elswhere MS
262.10	Malcolm] Malcom MS,AM
262.14	a New] an New MS
264.4	are] is MS
265.13	sepulture] seputure MS
266.14	Poet's] Poets' AM,I–V
266.21	that] which MS
266.24	is] is is MS
267.10	I] *omit* MS
267.33	Poet's] Poets' AM,I–V
268.23	are] is MS
268.23	gives] give E
268.32;270.11	Poet's] Poets' AM,I–V
272.13	obedient] *omit* MS
273.18–19	could have . . . available only] could only have . . . available MS

273.30   subtlety] subtilty AM,I–V

275.23   elegancies] elegances I–V

276.4–5   arm in arm with, nay, if I mistake not, partly embraced and supported by, another] arm in arm—nay, partly embraced and supported, if I mistake not—by another MS; arm in arm with, nay, partly embraced and supported by, if I mistake not, another AM

Outside Glimpses of English Poverty (AM,I)

279.32   selvages] salvages E

280.31   overladen] overladened II

284.25   the less] *omit* the III–V

285.29–30   imitative] imitated II–V

287.28   witnessed in] witnessed before in III–V

287.31   nursery] nursury I

289.20   diffusion] spread AM

295.18   repetition] reception III–V

295.34   were dressed] were well dressed III–V

297.29   began to] began a AM

303.11   and] to AM

307.17   loafers'] loafer's III

308.20–24   One . . . -bond.] *omit* AM

Civic Banquets (MS,AM,I)

310.9   distaste] distate MS

310.9   to] towards MS

311.4–5   and confining . . . vegetables only because] and only confining . . . vegetables because MS

312.10   excellencies] excellences AM,I–V

312.21	especial] special AM,I–V
312.33	foods] food AM,I–V
313.12	foregoing] above MS
313.17	or] and II–V
314.6	lighted] lighed MS
314.8	further] farther AM,I–V
314.31	several royal characters are] more than one royal character is MS,AM
315.11	parti-colored] party-colored AM,I–V (party-coloured E)
315.16	the] *omit* MS
315.23	reader's] readers MS
315.25	steel-clad] steal-clad MS
316.1	description] pages MS,AM
316.6	now] still MS,AM
316.7–8	splendor still are] splendor still are so MS; splendor are so AM
317.14	English] Engligh I
319.5	farther] further E,II–V
320.1	thin-visaged men] thin-visaged, green-spectacled men MS,AM
320.2	sallow, deeply] sallow with the intemperate use of strong coffee, deeply MS,AM
320.8	at] of AM
320.31	dining-hall] dinig-hall MS
322.12	imprudencies] imprudences AM,I–V
324.6	describe] express MS
324.20	all—thorough] all—which is thorough MS
327.7	a] an AM,I–V
329.15	a] *omit* III–V
329.24	has] had AM,I–V
329.32	shirk without] shirk it without MS
330.7	dumb-foundered] dumbfounded AM,I–V
330.16	charge] scratch MS,AM
330.18	twice happened] twice times happened MS

331.9–10	representative] represenive MS
331.22	the] the the MS
332.2	the city] this city V
332.6	blue coats and buff breeches] blue and buff MS,AM
332.19	Mayoress] May-|ess MS
334.2	imbibed] inbibed AM
334.14–15	of which] *omit* of MS,AM
334.30	lights] light AM,I–V
335.4	consider, I] consider it, I MS
335.8	plates-full] platefuls AM,I–V
335.15	very] *omit* IV–V
336.26	supereminence] superemi-|ence I
337.34	of generals] of knights, generals MS
337.34	Parliament] Parliaments MS
338.7	indeed, on] indeed, one on MS
340.12	barque] bark AM,I–V
340.20	one] *omit* MS
340.21	foregoing] above MS
343.9	careful of their country's honor] *omit* MS,AM
343.12	half-sightedness] half-sigtedness MS
343.29	official] *omit* MS
344.17	America] American MS
344.23	his] and his MS
344.28	his] the AM,I–V
345.1	trust to my] *omit* to III–V
345.19	these Sketches] the the sketch MS; the sketch AM

ALTERATIONS IN THE MANUSCRIPT

NOTE: With the exceptions listed below, all alterations made in the manuscript during its inscription or review before submission (the two classes are ordinarily not distinguishable with certainty) are described here. The exceptions are as follows: (1) letters or words that have been mended or traced over for clarity without alteration of the original; (2) interlineations that repeat in a more clearly written form the identical original; and (3) deletions, mendings, or readings under alterations that could not be read. In the description, *above* means "interlined" and *over* means "in the same space." The presence of a caret is always noticed. Square brackets signify one or more illegible letters; letters within square brackets are conjectural on some evidence but not wholly certain.

Alterations in superseded manuscript passages may be read in the entries 5.19–34, 13.19–14.23, and 38.6–20 of the appendix Editorial Emendations in the Copy-Text, pp. 360–62, 364.

3.9	kind] *interlined with a caret above deleted* 'character'
3.10	inasmuch] 'ina' *altered from* 'eve'
3.16	antique] 'i' *over wiped-out* 'q'
3.16	charm] *followed by an erased comma*
3.20	sketches] *first* 'e' *over wiped-out possible* 'h'
4.4	modes] 'm' *over wiped-out possible* 's'
4.7	accomplished] *follows deleted* 'writte'
4.12	possibly] 'y' *altered from* 'e'

4.13	may] 'm' *over wiped-out possible* 's'
4.14	far] 'ar' *altered from* 'ew'
4.15	catastrophe] *precedes wiped-out comma*
4.16	afflict] *over wiped-out* 'care little'
4.16–17	room for the] 'room' *interlined above deleted* 'space' *which with* 'for the' *had been written over wiped-out* 'room for the'
4.21	of] 'o' *altered from* 'ev'
4.27	him] *interlined with a caret*
4.29	crowd] *precedes wiped-out comma*
4.32	moral] *interlined with a caret*
4.33	These] 'se' *added, below initial* 'e'
5.1	little] *over wiped-out* 'feeting' [*for* 'fleeting']
5.1	of the] 'th' *altered from possible* 'a'
5.2	Journal] 'J' *mended from* 'j'
5.5	would] 'o' *over wiped-out possible* 'h'
5.10	it] *precedes deleted* 'have'
5.10	contribute] *a final* 'd' *was deleted*
5.11	besmear] 'a' *altered from* 'e'
6.3	thus] *interlined with a caret above deleted* 'so'
6.5	corner] *interlined with a caret*
6.16	often] *interlined with a caret above deleted* 'usually'
7.2	unfortunate] *interlined with a caret above deleted* 'wretched'
7.4	wretches] *interlined with a caret above deleted* 'individuals'
7.20	difficult] *interlined with a caret*
9.4–5	part of] *interlined with a caret*
9.12	were] *interlined with a caret above deleted* 'have been' *and preceding deleted* 'ever'
9.17	it] *interlined with a caret above deleted* 'them'
9.24–25	of whom . . . banner] *interlined with a caret*
9.30	from first to last] *interlined with a caret*
10.3	from] *interlined with a caret above deleted* 'of'
10.4	Old] 'O' *mended from* 'o'
10.12	feather,] *precedes deleted* 'in hopes of at least a bit of bread'
10.21	Republic] *over wiped-out* 'own country'

10.25	pang near the heart,] *interlined with a caret above deleted* 'deadly pain in their own breasts'
10.31	by] *interlined with a caret*
11.2–3	somehow] *interlined with a caret*
11.7	servant] *interlined with a caret*
11.16	awful] *interlined with a caret above deleted* 'severe'
11.16	severe] *interlined with a caret above deleted* 'stern'
11.17	part] *interlined with a caret above deleted* 'side'
12.4	races] *interlined with a caret above deleted* 'people'
12.5	Englishman] 'man' *added later, interlined with a caret*
12.23	But] *interlined with a caret before uncorrected* 'After'
12.24	discovering] *follows deleted* 'however' *and inadvertently undeleted comma*
12.25	and ingenuous] *interlined with a caret*
13.10	profit him] *interlined with a caret above deleted* 'be profitable'
13.32	street] 'S' *mended from* 's'
14.5	Up to the] *follows deleted* 'Up to the'
14.10	falsehood] *interlined with a caret above deleted* 'tale'
14.22	any] *interlined with a caret*
14.24	gray] *interlined with a caret*
14.34	that] *interlined with a caret above deleted* 'these'
15.6	to him] *interlined with a caret*
15.28	time] *interlined with a caret*
15.29	patiently] *interlined with a caret above deleted* 'earnestly'
16.5	and] *precedes deleted* 'and'
16.15	Her] *over wiped-out* 'the Q'
16.19	his] *follows deleted* 'all'
16.22	remarkably] *interlined with a caret above deleted* 'very'
17.12–13	have been in] 'have' *over wiped-out* 'make' *and*

	'been' *interlined for clarity above* 'been in' *which was written over wiped-out* 'everything'
17.23	inexorable] *interlined with a caret above deleted* 'remorseless'
17.33	merely] *interlined with a caret*
18.5	gradually] *interlined with a caret*
18.7–8	looking . . . but] *interlined with a caret*
18.19	require] *interlined with a caret above deleted* 'request'
18.32	others,] *precedes deleted* 'the extremities of'
18.32	never] *interlined with a caret above deleted* 'not'
18.33	have been] *interlined with a caret*
19.1	as] *interlined with a caret*
19.6	the stolidity] *interlined with a caret*
19.7	invariably] *interlined with a caret*
19.18	vigor] *interlined with a caret above deleted* 'strength'
19.18	ancient strength] *interlined with a caret above deleted* 'own'
19.21	vicissitude] 'vi' *added in left margin after preceding end-line* 'vi-' *deleted*
19.26	often] *interlined with a caret above deleted* 'still'
19.28	which] *interlined with a caret above deleted* 'and'
20.1	or document,] *interlined with a caret*
20.7	lurks] *interlined with a caret above deleted* 'lies'
20.8	sober] *interlined with a caret*
20.10	most substantial] *interlined with a caret above deleted* 'wisest'
20.23	of] *interlined with a caret following deleted* 'that I should'
20.25	complete] *interlined with a caret*
21.3	otherwise] *interlined with a caret*
21.6	imagine] *interlined with a caret above deleted* 'believe'
21.7	of one or both of] *interlined with a caret*
21.8	through . . . line] *interlined with a caret*
21.28–29	eloquence] *interlined with a caret above deleted* 'effect'

22.3	his] *interlined with a caret*
22.10	matter] *follows deleted* 'therefore'
22.10	religion and] *interlined with a caret following wiped-out interlined* 'of'
22.10	they] *interlined with a caret*
22.12–13	(if men they were)] *interlined with a caret*
22.16	Ceylon] *interlined with a caret above deleted* 'Madagascar'
22.26	less ferocious and stupid ones] *interlined with a caret above deleted* 'more docile and intelligent'
22.29	losing] *follows deleted* 'forgetting their'
22.30	generally] *interlined with a caret*
22.30	greater] *interlined with a caret*
22.31	quadruped] *interlined with a caret above deleted* 'brute'
22.32	the] *interlined with a caret*
22.33	generic traits] *interlined with a caret*
22.33	race] *interlined with a caret above deleted* 'species'
23.1	that] *interlined with a caret above deleted* 'which'
23.26	establish] *follows deleted* 'fully investigate and'
23.28	do] *interlined with a caret*
23.32	rich] *interlined with a caret*
24.3	wrought] *interlined with a caret above deleted* 'made'
24.5	repent] *interlined with a caret above deleted* 'regret'
24.11	have reason to] *interlined with a caret*
24.12	Dutch gilt or] *interlined with a caret*
24.14–15	a very] 'a' *interlined with a caret*
24.26	for persons] *precedes deleted* 'for persons'
24.30	treacherous and] *interlined with a caret*
24.31	society] *follows deleted* 'his'
24.34	distant] *interlined above deleted* 'foreign'
25.4–5	when . . . shore,] *interlined with a caret*
26.2	master of the] *interlined with a caret*
26.7	police] *follows deleted* 'detective'

26.11–12   scrutinizing the affair carefully] *interlined with a caret above deleted* 'looking at the whole matter'
26.13   him] *interlined with a caret*
26.32   stolen or] *interlined with a caret*
28.11   and . . . breast,] *interlined with a caret*
28.33   warranted in] *interlined above deleted* 'to'
29.2   more] *interlined with a caret*
29.6   give] *interlined with a caret above deleted* 'have given'
29.22   sinners,] *precedes deleted* '(as I certainly shall with one that I am intimately acquainted with, and perhaps a great many more,)'
30.7   as himself] *interlined with a caret*
30.20   reasons] *interlined with a caret above deleted* 'notions'
30.21   and quite . . . neither,] *interlined with a caret*
31.11   whom] *interlined with a caret above deleted* 'which'
31.30   some] *interlined with a caret*
32.6   seem to] *interlined with a caret*
32.16–17   of murder or manslaughter,] *interlined with a caret*
32.22   took up the matter] *interlined with a caret*
32.27   prevent or] *interlined with a caret*
32.27   The American] *interlined with a caret above deleted* 'Our'
32.28   perfectly] *interlined with a caret*
32.31   quite] *interlined with a caret above deleted* 'perfectly'
32.32   that] *interlined with a caret*
33.1   time (or,] *parenthesis deletes dash and comma*
33.2   now) in] *parenthesis deletes dash and comma*
33.11   considerable] *interlined with a caret above deleted* 'large'
33.13   very] *interlined with a caret*
33.14   shipmaster] 'ship-m' *over wiped-out* 'captain of'
33.15   vast] *follows deleted* 'property'
33.20   habitually] *interlined with a caret*
33.21   irresponsible] *interlined with a caret*

33.21	often] *interlined with a caret*
33.25	enormities] *interlined with a caret above deleted* 'things'
34.10	chiefly] *interlined with a caret*
34.25	power, . . . effect,] *parentheses were deleted after* "power" *and* "effect" *but the comma after* "effect" *not added*
34.27	scarcely] *interlined with a caret above deleted* 'hardly'
34.33	acceptable] *interlined with a caret above deleted* 'agreeable'
35.9	both Englishmen,] *interlined with a caret*
35.33	eminent] *interlined with a caret*
36.4–5	some acquaintance with the United States Statutes,] *manuscript phrase interlined with a caret was* 'a smattering of the United States Statutes'
36.5–6	a tact of management] *interlined with a caret*
36.9	natural] *interlined with a caret*
36.9	and moderate acquirements] *interlined with a caret*
36.12–13	Yet, . . . accomplished.] *interlined with a caret*
36.17	especial] *interlined with a caret*
36.28	acquainted] *interlined with a caret*
37.3	far] *interlined with a caret*
37.4	to the utmost extent] *interlined with a caret*
37.25–26	as . . . saying,] *interlined with a caret*
38.4	were] *precedes deleted* 'were'
38.29	with which,] *interlined with a caret*
38.33	life-like] *interlined with a caret above deleted* 'real'
39.3	almost] *interlined with a caret above deleted* 'more than'
39.4	would] *interlined with a caret above deleted* 'do'
39.4	might] *interlined with a caret above deleted* 'could'
39.17–18	vivaciously and eloquently] *interlined with a caret*
39.30	which] *interlined with a caret above deleted* 'that'

40.3	encompassing wall, its] *interlined with a caret*
40.4	its] *interlined with a caret*
40.5	all] *interlined with a caret*
40.11	over night] *interlined with a caret above deleted* 'by night-fall'
41.10	in] *over wiped-out* 'at'
42.22	receive] *interlined with a caret above deleted* 'take'
42.30	atmosphere] *interlined with a caret above deleted* 'spell'
43.3	the ponderous necessity] 'the ponderous' *interlined with a caret above deleted* 'that', *preceding deleted interlined* 'burthen', *with* 'neces-' *interlined above* 'being' *and* 'ity' *above* 'universally'
43.8	to] *over wiped-out* 'of'
43.26	class] *over wiped-out* 'large'
44.5	rural] *interlined above* 'rural' *which is over wiped-out* 'village'
44.30	vividly] *interlined with a caret*
45.4	ostensible] 'os' *over wiped-out* 'obs'
45.22	petty] 'p' *over wiped-out* 'la'
46.23	to] 't' *over wiped-out* 'f'
46.25	tree-tops] *interlined with a caret above deleted* 'air'
47.6	malice] *over wiped-out* 'place'
47.15	all— . . . them—] *dashes delete commas*
47.17	snuggery] 'y' *altered from* 'ly'
47.27	Circus] 'ir' *over wiped-out* 're'
47.28	Clarendon-street,] *interlined with a caret*
47.33	of the scene, at a sunny noontide] *interlined with a caret*
48.15	personages] *interlined with a caret above deleted* 'figures'
48.17	Oddly] 'Od-'| *over* 'Only'
48.26	quite] *over* 'appreci'
48.32	tallow] *interlined with a caret above deleted* 'fat'
49.2–3	where she looks as if nothing could ever move her.] *interlined with a caret*
49.7	grim and] *interlined with a caret*

49.14 while] *interlined with a caret above* 'while' *over wiped-out* 'though', *the caret over wiped-out* 'yo'

49.21 actually] *interlined with a caret above deleted* 'really'

49.23 tougher] 'to' *over wiped-out* 'str'

49.24 she is] *interlined with a caret above deleted* 'they are'

50.5 damsels] *interlined with a caret*

50.14 and which make] *interlined with a caret above deleted* 'making'

50.17 wife] *interlined with a caret*

50.19 and good morals] *interlined with a caret*

50.27 particularly] *interlined with a caret*

51.14 it is] *interlined with a caret above deleted* 'they are'

51.16 well-defined] *interlined with a caret*

51.17 we] *interlined above undecipherable word*

52.10 that] *interlined with a caret*

52.10 space—] *dash deletes comma*

52.22 unhealthy] *interlined with a caret above deleted* 'unwholesome'

53.10 happy-looking] *over wiped-out* 'comfortable looking'

53.34 supporting] *interlined with a caret above deleted* 'holding up', *the* 'hold' *over wiped-out* 'supp'

55.4 is] *interlined with a caret*

55.8 ineffectually] *interlined above* 'ineffectually' *which had been written over wiped-out* 'memorialized'

55.9 and gives the bed] *interlined with a caret above separately deleted* 'to' *and* 'makes room'

55.9 to] *interlined with a caret above deleted* 'for' *and undeleted comma*

55.12 on them] *interlined with a caret*

55.16 records] *interlined with a caret above deleted* 'inscriptions'

55.18 incisions] *interlined with a caret above deleted* 'inscriptions'

55.19 shower] *interlined with a caret*

55.23	of the English sky] *interlined with a caret*
55.27	velvet] *interlined with a caret*
55.29	after the world has forgotten the deceased] *interlined with a caret*
55.30–31	It . . . friends.] *interlined with a caret*
56.2	ago] *interlined with a caret*
56.8	which was] *over wiped-out* 'elevated jus'
56.19	hard] *interlined with a caret above deleted* 'difficult'
56.25–26	foundation-] 'foundation' *followed by inadvertent mark resembling an* 's'
57.9	all] *follows deleted* 'the'
57.10	two or three] *interlined with a caret above deleted* 'mile or two'
57.26	Whitnash] *interlined with a caret above deleted* 'the village'
57.33	birds-] *interlined with a caret*
57.34	them] *interlined with a caret*
58.11	its] *the* 's' *added later*
58.11	boughs] *interlined with a caret*
58.13–14	A thousand] *over wiped-out* 'We were'
58.20	and meaning] 'and m' *over wiped-out* 'of whi'
59.10	grasping] *over wiped-out* 'catching'
59.11	effort] *interlined with a caret above deleted* 'length'
59.16	and married] *interlined with a caret*
59.16	buried] *followed by a caret but no interlineation*
59.18	race,] *comma altered from period*
60.3	modern] *interlined with a caret above deleted* 'new' *and written over* 'best' *which had been interlined with a caret before* 'new'
60.7	drone] *interlined with a caret*
60.7	through centuries] *interlined with a caret above deleted* 'drone'
61.1	long, and broad, and] *interlined with a caret*
61.2	were] *altered from* 'was'
61.3	bones.] *period altered from comma*
61.7	suggestion] *interlined with a caret above deleted* 'advice'

61.22	spacious, and] *interlined with a caret*
61.34	by-road] 'by-' *interlined above* 'by-' *written over wiped-out* 'cross' *and* 'roa' *wiped out following interlined* 'by-'
62.2	Parr.] *period altered from comma*
62.5	built] *interlined with a caret*
62.7	the bell] 'the' *written over* 'a'
62.23	mediæval] *follows deleted* 'the antique'
62.30	would be] *interlined with a caret*
63.4	simplest] *interlined with a caret*
63.6	preach] *interlined with a caret above deleted* 'speaks'; *precedes deleted* 'of'
63.8	available] *follows deleted* 'un'
63.12	were] *over wiped-out* 'seem'
64.2	disuse] 'dis' *over wiped-out* 'long'
64.4	love] *interlined with a caret above deleted* 'like'
64.6	even] *interlined with a caret*
64.13	their] *interlined with a caret*
64.29	obviated] *follows deleted* 'heretofore', *which was interlined with a caret*
64.32	revivification] 'vification' *interlined above deleted* 'vication'
64.33	Cannot] 'C' *over wiped-out* 'H'
65.8	town—] *dash was intended to delete comma*
65.11	aspect—] *dash deletes comma*
65.14	rising from among clustered roofs] *interlined with a caret*
66.3	infantile] *interlined with a caret*
66.12	At] *interlined with a caret above deleted* 'From'
66.24	along the smooth] *precedes deleted* 'along the smooth'
67.13	stream;] *semicolon altered from comma*
67.15	tread] *interlined with a caret above* 'tread', *itself written over possible* 'eart'
67.17	can] *interlined with a caret above deleted* 'could'
67.20	further] 'u' *altered from* 'a'
67.21	hospitably] 'h' *altered from* 'op'
67.29	from end] 'end' *over wiped-out word, possibly* 'one'

67.31	poetic] 'po' *over wiped-out* 'glam'
68.10	Saint] 'Sai' *over* 'the'
68.13	border] *interlined with a caret above deleted* 'line'
68.16	their . . . floor;] *interlined with a caret*
70.22	westward] *originally badly written, first* 'w' *over undecipherable letter, then whole word deleted and interlined for clarity*
70.26	Cymbeline's] 'Cy' *over wiped-out* 'Go'
71.1	crowning] *interlined with a caret above deleted* 'crowning' *mended with first* 'n' *interlined with a caret*
71.1	semi-] *interlined with a caret*
71.3–4	chimneys] *original is* 'chimnies' *in which second* 'i' *was altered from* 'e' *and* 'e' *was written over wiped-out* 'y'
71.12	sluggishly] *interlined with a caret above* 'sluggishly' *written over wiped-out* 'enjoying'
71.18	which] *interlined with a caret above deleted* 'that'
72.2	to] *interlined with a caret*
72.9	superstitious] *interlined with a caret following deleted* 'lingering'
76.11	guise] 's' *doubtfully altered from* 'z'
76.18–19	her husband] 'her hu' *over wiped-out* 'herself'
76.20	oak-panelled] 'oak' *over wiped-out* 'parlor' *and the preceding comma added*
76.31	field of Waterloo] *under spiral deletion which is in brown ink*
76.34–77.1	intervening] *interlined with a caret above deleted* 'adjoining'
79.22	representing—] *dash over wiped-out comma*
79.23	nor Angel] *interlined with a caret*
79.30	fox-glove flowers,] *interlined with a caret*
79.31	small . . . grass,] *interlined with a caret;* 'sm' *over wiped-out* 'and'
80.2	in] *interlined with a caret*
80.2	the edge] 'the' *interlined with a caret;* 'ed' *over wiped-out* 'the'
80.3	stands] *interlined with a caret*

80.5	high-] 'igh' *over wiped-out* 'o[]g'
80.12	a mass] 'a' *over wiped-out* 'the'
80.24	our] *interlined with a caret above deleted* 'my'
80.28	wandered] 'wan' *over wiped-out* 'walk'
80.29–30	and courageous] *interlined with a caret*
81.10	Parr] *interlined with a caret*
81.16	who cultivate] 'who cultiva' *over wiped-out* 'whose beans'
81.16–17	and . . . labor] *interlined with a caret*
81.17	a] *interlined with a caret above deleted* 'the'
81.27	entire] *first* 'e' *over wiped-out* 's'
82.2	a gentleman] 'a g' *over wiped-out* 'and'
82.2	independent] *originally* 'indepent' *with* 'dent' *interlined with a caret written over the original* 't'
82.7	perhaps] *interlined with a caret*
82.20	in] *over wiped-out* 'wit'
82.30	some] *interlined with a caret*
82.33	partitioned] *second* 'ti' *over wiped-out* 'o'
85.18	kindred] *interlined above deleted* 'familiar'
85.22	remarkably] *interlined with a caret following deleted* 'most'
85.27	linen] 'l' *over wiped-out* 'e'
85.30	with] 'w' *over wiped-out* 'l'
85.34	ancient Honor] *interlined with a caret above deleted* 'old integrity'
86.1	Conjugal] 'C' *mended from* 'c'
86.1	Faith] 'F' *mended from* 'f'
86.6	out] *interlined with a caret*
86.6	nobleman] *interlined with a caret above deleted* 'man'
86.9–10	On a . . . lies the] *interlined with a caret placed in the midst of deleted* 'It is a'
86.13	an image] *interlined above wiped-out* 'a fig'
86.17	any] *interlined with a caret above deleted* 'the'
86.20	among the fragments] *interlined with a caret above deleted* 'there'
86.23	to] 'o' *over wiped-out* 'e'
86.26	so that] *interlined with a caret above deleted* 'and'

87.1	render] *first 'r' over wiped-out 'm'*
87.4	other personages] *terminal 's' erased from 'others' and* 'personages' *interlined with a caret*
87.7–8	delicate] *interlined with a caret above deleted* 'pretty'
87.13	(that . . . century)] *interlined with a caret*
87.19	disgustfully] *interlined with a caret*
89.8	that] *interlined with a caret*
89.17	ransacks] *interlined with a caret above* 'ransacks' *which was written over wiped-out* 'hunts for'
89.21	at] *interlined with a caret*
89.22	more] *over wiped-out* 'chea'
90.10	that] *'th' over wiped-out 'w'*
90.17	of wood] *interlined with a caret*
90.21	English] *interlined with a caret*
91.7	freest] *altered from original* 'free' *during inscription*
91.11	Somebody] *'S' altered from 'I'*
91.12	has known] *interlined with a caret above deleted* 'knows'
91.18	similar] *over wiped-out* 'the same'
91.22	rotundity] *'r' over wiped-out 'f'*
91.25	that] *'th' over wiped-out* 'mo'
91.28	live out its] *over wiped-out* 'outlive its centu' *and then wiped out and interlined*
91.29	more majestic] 'most majestic' *interlined with a caret above deleted* 'stateliest'
91.30	patriotism] *'s' altered from 'c' and 'm' added*
92.2	and] *'n' over wiped-out doubtful 'w' and preceding 'a' added*
92.4	looks] *interlined with a caret above deleted* 'is'
92.7	nurtured] *'nur' over wiped-out* 'supp'
92.12	in England] *interlined with a caret*
92.19	outlast] *'ast' over wiped-out doubtful* 'ive'
93.17	be] *over wiped-out* 'see'
93.20	has] 'have' *altered from* 'has'
93.25	tenaciously] 'tena' *over wiped-out* 'fast'
94.3	send] *precedes deleted* 'us'
94.17	Lakes] *'L' mended from 'l'*
94.23	swallows'] *altered from* 'swallow's'
94.34	way] *interlined with a caret above deleted* 'road'

95.2	charm of the] *interlined with a caret*
95.5	little] 'litt' *over wiped-out* 'e'
95.7	seldom] *a final* 's' *wiped out*
95.7	an] *interlined with a caret*
95.8	summer-day) that] *over wiped-out* 'summer-weather', *then* 'summer-day' *wiped out and interlined for clarity*
95.11	ocean-] *over wiped-out* 'sea sp'
95.23	and surprised] *interlined with a caret*
95.25	wrought] *interlined with a caret above deleted undecipherable letters and hyphen*
95.27–28	with the] 'the' *interlined with a caret above deleted* 'that'
95.29	the house] 'the' *over wiped-out* 'a'
95.33	humorists are] *over undecipherable letters, then* 'humorists' *wiped out and interlined for clarity*
96.7	subtle] *over a blot that may perhaps have originally been* 'subtile'
96.8–9	an unseemly] *interlined with a caret above deleted* 'such disagreeable'
96.24	kept] *precedes deleted* 'there'
96.24	and that] 'that' *interlined with a caret above deleted* 'which'
97.17	cheerful;] *MS* 'cheerful,' *comma altered from semicolon*
97.19	lived] *over wiped-out* 'life'
97.29	curiously] 'curio' *over wiped-out* 'closely'
97.32	lighted] 'g' *over wiped-out doubtful* 't'; *less likely the letter is* 'h'
98.5	walls—] *dash deletes comma*
98.8–9	paces— . . . eight—] *dashes delete commas*
98.25	white-washed] 'a' *over wiped-out* 'h'
98.26	Chester] 'C' *mended from* 'c'
99.14	acknowledgement] *interlined with a caret above deleted* 'confession'
99.29	mother;] *semicolon altered from comma*
100.5	even] *interlined with a caret*
100.20	it] *interlined with a caret above deleted* 'the anathema'
100.22	mankind] *precedes wiped-out caret*

100.22–23	to muse upon] *interlined with a caret*
100.26	house] *followed by wiped-out comma*
100.30	and vast arched windows] *interlined with a caret*
100.33	way] 'w' *over wiped-out* 's'
101.10	I was] *follows deleted* 'We', *the* 'I' *added and* 'was' *altered from* 'were'
101.12	richer] *interlined with a caret above deleted* 'more lucrative'
101.21	altar] *second* 'a' *altered from* 'e'
101.22–23	addressed] *over wiped-out* 'to the w' *and then interlined*
101.24	stanza] *interlined with a caret above deleted* 'inscription'
101.29	Moreover] 'Mor' *over wiped-out* 'Unl'
102.1–2	Shakspere's] 'Sh' *over doubtful* 'h'
102.4	take] *over wiped-out* 'occupy'
102.7	grandson] 'grand' *interlined with a caret, written at a slant to join* 'son'
103.6	of] *interlined with a caret above deleted* 'with'
103.13	burgher] 'b' *over wiped-out* 'St'
103.13	doubtless] *interlined with a caret*
103.15	Shakspere] *final* 'e' *over wiped-out* 'e's'
103.19	clad] 'cla' *over wiped-out* 'in'
103.20	his hands] *interlined with a caret*
103.24	us] *interlined with a caret*
103.25	that] *altered from* 'the'
103.31	the] *over wiped-out* 'Sh'
104.7	interments] 'i' *over wiped-out* 'b'
104.8	church.] *period over wiped-out semicolon*
104.11	lie] *altered from* 'be'
104.26	only] *over wiped-out* 'nothing'
104.27	error] *interlined with a caret above deleted* 'mistake'
104.29	erroneous as they were,] *interlined with a caret*
105.5	and] *over wiped-out* 'There'
105.11	lay] 'la' *over wiped-out doubtful* 'the'
105.12	portion] *interlined with a caret above deleted* 'part'
105.13	pocket-Bible] 'B' *over wiped-out* 'b'
105.18	Miss Bacon] 'Miss Ba' *over wiped-out* 'I suspect'

105.20	been] *over wiped-out* 'read'
105.30	been] *follows deleted* 'considerably'
106.1	no] *interlined with a caret*
106.21	volition—] *dash deletes comma*
106.28	immeasurable] *interlined with a caret above deleted* 'inappreciable' *in which* 'ina' *was written over wiped-out* 'app'
106.31	discover] *interlined with a caret above deleted* 'find'
106.34	as we] 'as' *altered from* 'in' *and* 'we' *over wiped-out* 'f[]' *then interlined for clarity*
107.1–2	to Miss Bacon this] 'to Miss Bacon th' *over wiped-out* 'this explanation of her'
107.11	her] *interlined with a caret*
107.13	discovered] *interlined with a caret above deleted* 'found'
107.26	hither] *MS* 'thither' *altered from* 'hither'
107.31	faith] *interlined with a caret above deleted* 'belief'
107.32	that, too,] *interlined with a caret*
108.2–3	die. She] 'at once' *was erased following* 'die', *a period added, and* 'She' *written over* 'once'
108.4	did] *interlined with a caret above deleted* 'could'
108.5	fully] *interlined with a caret*
108.18	imagined] 'im' *over doubtful* 'con'
108.22	special] 's' *over wiped-out doubtful* 'th'
108.28	lodging-] 'd' *over wiped-out* 'an'
108.32	man] *precedes deleted* 'formerly', *which was interlined with a caret*
109.15–16	to form] 'to' *interlined with a caret*
109.18–19	in her character] *interlined with a caret*
109.27	own] 'ow' *over wiped-out* 'an'
109.34	mind,] *interlined with a caret above deleted* 'part'
110.1	faith] *interlined with a caret above deleted* 'belief'
110.22	situation] 'situa' *over wiped-out* 'place'
110.32	practitioner] *second* 't' *over wiped-out* 'o'
110.34	certainly] *interlined with a caret before* 'was'

which *had been written over wiped-out* 'never'

111.1   part. He] *period over comma and* 'He' *interlined with a caret above deleted* 'who'

111.5   and of] *interlined with a caret*

111.6–7   the edge of the grave,] *interlined with a caret which precedes deleted* 'the'

111.9   belief] *interlined with a caret above deleted* 'faith'

111.20   and as] 'and' *over wiped-out* 'as' *and* 'as' *over wiped-out* 'all'

111.21   entirely] *interlined with a caret*

112.6–7   poet, warrior, or statesman] *interlined with a caret*

112.7–8   or the Tower burial-ground] *interlined with a caret*

112.8   wherever] 'ever' *over wiped-out* 'ere'

112.32   that] *over wiped-out* 'where'

113.1   appeared] 'appe' *over wiped-out* 'once'

113.9   civil] *preceded by deleted* 'at'

113.23   fragility] 'fr' *over wiped-out* 'sh'

113.28   her] *interlined with a caret above deleted* 'this'

113.28   immense] *interlined with a caret above deleted* 'stupendous'

113.31   patient] *interlined with a caret*

114.25–27   dissertation— . . . Shakspere—] *dashes delete commas*

115.1   picked] 'pi' *over wiped-out* 'li'

115.12   scholars] 'c' *over wiped-out* 'h'

115.15   literary] *interlined with a caret*

115.17   men;] *semicolon altered from comma; precedes deleted* 'If an American had ever written a word in her behalf, Miss Bacon never knew it, nor did I.'

115.19   out] *interlined with a caret*

115.21   at once] *interlined with a caret*

115.22   most brutal] *interlined with a caret above deleted* 'bitterest'

115.23   stolen] *interlined with a caret above deleted* 'borrowed'

115.25	it] *interlined with a caret*
115.27	He] *interlined with a caret above deleted* 'who' *and preceding period added before erased comma*
115.27	was] *precedes deleted* 'likewise'
115.30	book] *over wiped-out* 'Book'
115.32	had some knowledge] *interlined with a caret above deleted* 'knew something'
116.2	that] *precedes deleted* 'that'
116.5	Player' had kept] 'had' *over wiped-out comma and* 'on the'
116.19–20	when, . . . object,] *commas delete parentheses*
116.23	friendly] 'fri' *over wiped-out* 'kin'
116.32	book] *over wiped-out* 'work'
116.35	from her] *interlined with a caret*
117.7	shadiest] *interlined with a caret above deleted* 'shadest'
117.20	that] 'th' *over wiped-out* 'wh'
117.26	vanishing] *interlined with a caret above deleted* 'glancing'
117.26	glancing] *interlined with a caret*
117.29	of their kind] *interlined with a caret*
117.35	little] *over wiped-out* 'good'
118.12	disposed] 'dis' *over wiped-out* 'dipp'
118.15	stag] *over wiped-out* 'deer'
118.18	lodge.] *period over wiped-out comma*
118.20	moat] *interlined with a caret as* 'mote' *above deleted* 'mote' *and mended to* 'moat'
118.24	on] *interlined with a caret*
119.5	improvement] 'impr' *over wiped-out* 'conven'
119.6	give] *interlined above deleted* 'add'
119.11	merely temporary one] *interlined with a caret*
119.12	rate—] *dash deletes semicolon*
119.12	yet perhaps] *over wiped-out* 'and especially'
119.15	own] *interlined with a caret*
119.19	lodging] 'lodg-|ing' *over wiped-out* 'dwel |ling'
120.1	went] 'w' *over wiped-out* 'f'
120.3	Swan.] *period over deleted parenthesis precedes deleted* 'although'
120.3	Had] 'H' *mended from* 'h'

120.6	its] *interlined with a caret above deleted* 'the'
120.7	being] *interlined with a caret above deleted* 'of which is'
120.11	with] *interlined with a caret above deleted* 'making'
120.13	a few] *interlined with a caret above deleted* 'many'
120.16	hotel] 'h' *over wiped-out* 'H'
121.22	The] *over wiped-out* 'the'
121.26	princely] *interlined with a caret*
121.26	pagan] *interlined with a caret above deleted* 'early' *and preceding* 'an' *altered to* 'a'
121.29	the legends] 'the' *over wiped-out* 'these'
122.8	it] *interlined with a caret*
122.11	personage] 'per-'| *over wiped-out* 'char-'|
122.22	was to] *interlined with a caret above deleted* 'must'
122.23	existence] *interlined with a caret above deleted* 'life'
122.24	farther] *interlined above deleted* 'more'
122.24	than to] 'to' *interlined with a caret*
122.28	generally] 'gen' *over wiped-out* 'mix'
122.30	in those] *over wiped-out* 'at that e'
123.4	great] 'g' *mended from* 'G'
123.6	an] *altered from* 'as'
123.6	-steak] *over erased* 'stake'
123.7	city] 'c' *over wiped-out* 'C'
123.19	method] *interlined with a caret above deleted* 'way'
123.19	sixpence] *over wiped-out* 'a shilling'
123.20–21	reverential and hospitable] *interlined with a caret above* 'the manners' *which is written over wiped-out* 'elder methods'
123.28	the aforesaid] *interlined with a caret*
123.30	an artificial] 'an art' *over wiped-out* 'a piece'
124.12–13	the porch of] *interlined with a caret*
124.13	in] *over wiped-out* 'of'
124.17	inscription] 'in' *over* 'st' *and preceding* 'an' *altered from* 'a'
124.22	yet] *precedes deleted* 'yet'

124.28	traces remaining] 'traces re-'| *over wiped-out* 'remaining'
124.33	a different] *interlined with a caret above deleted* 'another'
125.2	three] *interlined with a caret*
125.2–3	Thus it impressed] *over wiped-out* 'It impressed you'
125.4	lovingly] *interlined with a caret*
125.12	the beholder] *over wiped-out* 'yourself and'
125.21	appropriate] *over wiped-out* 'only ap'
126.7	here and] *over wiped-out* 'sometimes'
126.8	and extending] 'and ext' *over wiped-out* 'extending'
126.10	reddish] *over wiped-out* 'corrod'
126.11	atmosphere] 'atm' *over wiped-out* 'e[]the'
126.15	sweet] *follows deleted* 'a'
126.20	continually] *interlined with a caret above deleted* 'always'
126.21	In] *precedes deleted* 'my ignorance'
126.26	body] *interlined with a caret above deleted* 'sect'
126.29	esoteric] *interlined above deleted* 'mystic'
126.31	than] *interlined with a caret*
127.1	were venerable] *over wiped-out* 'but partook too'
127.6	noble] *interlined above deleted* 'sublime'
127.13	locally] *over wiped-out* 'only lo'
127.14–15	but two] *over wiped-out* 'only two'
127.18–19	in the grave] *interlined with a caret above deleted* 'dead'
127.34	in my fancy] *interlined with a caret*
128.1	the Departed] 'the' *interlined with a caret*
128.3	unfamiliarity] *interlined with a caret above* 'strangeness'
128.3	with] *interlined with a caret above deleted* 'at'
128.4	of an insufferable] *interlined with a caret above deleted* 'that the'
128.5	in] *follows deleted* 'is'
128.8	ceased] *interlined with a caret above deleted* 'failed'
128.17	subject] *interlined with a caret above deleted* 'one'

128.19   an open-work] 'an open-' *over wiped-out* 'a frame-'

128.23   old sculptor] 'old sc' *over wiped-out* 'sculpt'

129.8   golden] *interlined with a caret*

129.11   frock-coat] 'coat' *interlined with a caret and hyphen added after* 'frock'

129.16   magnificent] *interlined with a caret above deleted* 'sublime'

129.17   I] *interlined with a caret*

129.26   could desire] *over wiped-out* 'and a great ma'

130.8   minster] *interlined with a caret above deleted* 'Cathedral'

130.10   Johnson] 'J' *over wiped-out* 'A'

130.21   characters] 'char-' *interlined above deleted* 'per-'

130.26   They live, while realities have died.] *interlined with a caret*

130.29   Square] 'S' *mended from* 's'

130.33   A] *over wiped-out* 'In'

130.33   slanted] *interlined above deleted* 'sloped'

131.10   got] *interlined with a caret above deleted* 'found'

131.17   father's house] *interlined with a caret*

131.18   almost] *interlined with a caret above deleted* 'nearly'

131.27   himself] *interlined with a caret*

131.34   The] *altered from* 'It'

131.34   statue] *interlined with a caret*

132.3   stone-boulder] 'stone-'| *over wiped-out* 'boulder'

132.4   and sympathy] *interlined with a caret*

132.5   altogether] *interlined with a caret*

132.10   high-church] *over wiped-out* 'preaching of Dr.'

132.12   of] *over wiped-out* 'hi'

132.12   another] *interlined with a caret above deleted* 'third' *and preceding* 'a' *inadvertently undeleted*

132.21   venerable] *interlined with a caret above deleted* 'aged' *and the preceding* 'an' *altered to* 'a'

132.26   and uplifted] *interlined with a caret*

132.28   queer] 'q' *over wiped-out* 't' *of* 'st'

132.29   of living ducks] 'of' *interlined with a caret*

133.2	did] *over wiped-out possible* 'told'
133.3	the Libyan Sybil] 'the' *interlined with a caret*
133.7	purely] 'p' *over wiped-out* 'se'
133.14	Johnson] *precedes deleted* 'journeying thither a-foot'
133.19	objects] 'obje' *over wiped-out* 'thing'
133.22	A] *follows deleted* 'It is but'; 'A' *mended from* 'a'
133.22	takes you] *interlined with a caret*
133.31	his son's] *interlined with a caret above deleted* 'the'
134.15	persons] *over wiped-out possible* 'people'
134.16–17	and an absurd one,] *interlined with a caret*
134.31	their] 'ir' *over wiped-out* 'y'
134.31	great-grandfathers] *interlined with a caret*
134.32	This] *altered from* 'It'
134.32	curiosity] *interlined with a caret*
135.7	was] *interlined with a caret above deleted* 'appeared to be'
135.12–13	to indulge a solemn and high emotion,] *interlined with a caret,* 'solemn' *being an added interlineation with a caret above deleted* 'sad'
135.19	and good enough for a prince,] *interlined with a caret*
135.24–25	it . . . day.] *interlined with a caret mistakenly placed before comma after* 'dinner'
135.27	which he] 'wh' *of* 'which' *over wiped-out* 'that'
135.33	they] *interlined with a caret*
136.1	And] *over wiped-out* 'If this'
136.7	would] *interlined with a caret above deleted* 'could'
136.9	a few] *interlined with a caret above deleted* 'some'
136.10	ale] *over wiped-out* 'cup'
136.10	I] *precedes deleted* 'have somewhe' *with* 'somewhe' *over a deleted undecipherable word*
136.14	Head] 'H' *mended from* 'h'
136.25–26	shepherdesses] 'pherde' *over wiped-out* 'perdesses'
137.11	worldly] *interlined with a caret*

137.17	exact] *interlined with a caret above deleted* 'precise'
137.30	young ones] *interlined with a caret above deleted* 'children'
137.30	at] *interlined with a caret above deleted* 'round'
137.32	protect] *follows deleted* 'guard'
138.7	penance] *interlined with a caret*
138.9	I] *over wiped-out* ' "I'
138.9	circumstance] *interlined with a caret above deleted* 'story'
138.14	the old] *over wiped-out* 'it was built'
138.14	Britons] *interlined with a caret above deleted* 'Saxons'
138.16	heart] *interlined with a caret above deleted* 'imagination'
138.19	etherealized] *interlined with a caret above deleted* 'etheralized'
139.20	stuff] *interlined above deleted* 'matter'
140.7	(except] *parenthesis deletes comma*
140.12	attractive] *interlined above deleted* 'striking'
140.22	these] *MS* 'those' *interlined with a caret*
140.26	straight] 'st' *over wiped-out* 'line'
140.31	within] *over wiped-out possible* 'around'
140.34	what] 'w' *over* 'f' *of wiped-out* 'of'
140.34	anything] *interlined with a caret*
141.4	a village] 'a' *over wiped-out* 'an', 'vil' *over wiped-out* 'anc'
141.16	loved] 'love' *over* 'till' *of wiped-out* 'still'
141.23	poor lady's] 'poor' *over* 'old la' *and* 'l' *over* 'd' *of wiped-out* 'old lad'
142.8	days] 'da' *over wiped-out* 'time'
142.16	pre-conceived] *interlined with a caret*
144.5	fat] *over wiped-out* 'of f'
144.9–10	on the day] *interlined with a caret above deleted* 'on the' *and unclear* 'day', *which had been written over wiped-out* 'the Bishop asce'
144.15	an open] 'an' *altered from* 'a' *and* 'open' *over wiped-out undecipherable letters*
144.21	Close] 'C' *mended from* 'c'
144.22	looking] *over wiped-out* 'and to loo'

144.24	officers. Some] *period altered from comma;* 'Some' *over wiped-out* 'many'
144.27	Close] 'C' *mended from* 'c'
144.28	belong to] *over wiped-out* 'surrounded'
144.29	picturesque] *interlined with a caret*
144.30	Close] 'C' *mended from* 'c'
145.7	are] *interlined with a caret above deleted* 'were'; 'w' *over wiped-out* 'a'
145.15	containing] 'con' *over wiped-out* 'sho'
145.18	Christian] 'C' *over wiped-out* 't'
145.25	to look] 'to' *interlined with a caret*
146.6	that of] *interlined with a caret*
146.9	impress] 'im' *over wiped-out* 'the'
146.29	Minster] *interlined with a caret above deleted* 'vehicle'
148.29	smeared] 'sm' *over wiped-out* 'over'
149.19	red] *over wiped-out* 'ear'
149.26	inundation] 'u' *over wiped-out* 'd'
149.33	Time] 'T' *mended from* 't'
150.2	the] 't' *over wiped-out doubtful* 'al'
150.24	green] *over wiped-out* 'gray fol-'
151.22	imposing] *interlined with a caret above deleted* 'impressive'
151.31	have] *interlined with a caret*
151.32	Front] 'F' *mended from* 'f'
151.32	grand] *a preceding* 'grand' *wiped out*
152.8	rest] 'r' *over wiped-out* 'd'
153.9	voyaging by] *interlined with a caret above deleted* 'taking'
153.31	and] *over wiped-out* 'in spite'
154.12	looked] *interlined with a caret*
154.24	as] *interlined above deleted* 'as' *which had been written over wiped-out* 'as the'
155.15	into the] 'the' *interlined*
156.6	and Faneuil Hall] *interlined with a caret*
156.9	felt] *interlined with a caret*
156.31	days that had] 'days which had' *in MS;* 'which' *over wiped-out* 'that had'
157.5	have] *interlined with a caret above* 'have' *which was written over deleted* 'had'

157.6	live] *interlined with a caret above deleted* 'lived'
157.15	tower] 'r' *mended to cover final* 'e' *of original* 'towere'
157.26	went] *interlined with a caret above deleted undecipherable word*
158.5	interest] *over wiped-out* 'amuse us'
158.17	extremely] *interlined with a caret above deleted* 'very'
158.27	embroidered] *over wiped-out* 'wrought'
158.34	presented] *follows deleted* 'and'
159.4	edges and] 'an' *over wiped-out* 'of'
159.14	or] 'o' *over wiped-out* 'a'
159.16	to] *over wiped-out* 'f'
159.17	pupils] 'pu-'| *over wiped-out* 'schol-'|
159.23	relic] *interlined with a caret*
159.28	were shown] *over wiped-out* 'he showed us'
160.12	fit to] *precedes deleted* 'of such knick-knacks as were'
160.16	crowns] 'cr' *over wiped-out doubtful* 'cor'
160.25	Palace] *over wiped-out* 'Ho'
161.4	—a sort of whitlow—] *interlined with a caret placed before undeleted comma following* 'Fellon'
161.7	sipping] *interlined above deleted* 'drinking'
161.7	it] *interlined with a caret*
161.25	leading] *interlined with a caret above deleted* 'led'
162.4	incurred by an] *interlined with a caret above deleted* 'of on'
162.19	are] *interlined with a caret*
162.27	suitably] 'a' *over wiped-out* 'ed'
163.1	window is] 'is' *interlined above deleted* 'was'
163.1	but is] 'is' *interlined above deleted* 'was'
164.1	is] *interlined with a caret above deleted* 'was'
164.5	in the interior] 'in the in' *over wiped-out* 'there being'
164.6	there] *interlined with a caret*
164.16	most of] *interlined with a caret above deleted* 'all'
164.22	should] *interlined with a caret*

164.30	to suppose] 'to su' *over wiped-out* 'that the'
165.5	was] *interlined with a caret above deleted* 'am'
165.7–8	another American town,] *interlined with a caret*
165.16	schoolboys] 'schoo' *over wiped-out* 'children'
165.17	across the flat] *over wiped-out* 'a[] the flat tombst'
165.23	sunshine] *interlined with a caret above deleted* 'streets'
165.25	the] *interlined with a caret above deleted* 'the' *which had been written over wiped-out* 'that'
165.25	forlorn] *interlined with a caret*
166.8	rural] *interlined above deleted* 'rustic'
166.17	two or] *interlined with a caret above deleted* 'nearly'
167.12	mere] *interlined with a caret above deleted* 'mere' *which was altered from doubtful* 'taste'
167.17	slightly] 'tly' *over wiped-out* 'ty'
168.11	end] 'e' *over wiped-out* 'g'
168.23	nor] *interlined above deleted* 'and'
168.26	Queen] 'Q' *over wiped-out* 'the'
168.26	domain] 'do' *over wiped-out* 'D[]'
168.34	disagreeably] 'l' *over wiped-out* 'y'
170.5	door] *precedes* 'h' *or* 'k' *wiped-out before* 'for' *inscribed*
171.31	Strasbourg] 'urg' *over wiped-out* 'rg'
172.17	has] 's' *altered from* 'd'
172.25	English] *over wiped-out* 'people'
172.28	present] *interlined with a caret*
172.33	there are] 'are' *interlined with a caret*
173.1	palace] *interlined with a caret above deleted* 'grounds'
173.8	lofty] 'l' *over wiped-out* 'p'
173.10	is] *altered from* 'w'
173.25	pictures by] *interlined with a caret above deleted* 'the works of'
174.6	thin-] 'thin' *over wiped-out* 'nose' *and hyphen over wiped-out comma*
174.8	painter's] 'painte' *over wiped-out* 'pensive'
174.17	wear.] *interlined with a caret*
174.18	rather] *over wiped-out* 'pale, (as'

174.22	line—] *dash deletes comma*
174.33	a] *interlined with a caret*
175.7	with] 'w' *over wiped-out* 'f'
175.8	brighter] *over wiped-out* 'war'
175.16	floor] 'floo' *over wiped-out* 'wood'
175.26	and] *interlined with a caret above deleted* 'they'
176.25	go] 'g' *over wiped-out* 't'
177.13	noble] *over wiped-out* 'beautif'
177.16	whole] 'wh' *over wiped-out* 'rest'
177.32	from] 'm' *over wiped-out* '[]e'
177.32	offered] *precedes deleted* 'us'
178.22	jovial] *interlined with a caret*
179.8	the village] 'the vil' *over wiped-out* 'Cumnor'
179.20	one of] 'of' *interlined with a caret*
179.24	I] *interlined with a caret*
179.32	neighborhood] 'ne' *over wiped-out* 'b[]'
180.18	lightly] *interlined above deleted* 'ludicrously'
181.27–28	magnetism] *interlined above deleted* 'electricity'
181.33	The] 'T' *over wiped-out* 't'
182.3	much] 'm' *over* 'o' *of wiped-out* 'so'
182.4	a] *over wiped-out* 'an'
182.5	tincture of] *interlined with a caret*
182.14	across] 'a' *over wiped-out* 'b'
182.19	ever had] *precedes deleted* 'either a root or'
182.26	full] *interlined with a caret above deleted* 'some'
182.26	lofty] 'lof' *over wiped-out* 'openin'
183.11	seemed] 'see' *over wiped-out* 'were'
183.13	fires] 'fir' *over wiped-out* 'fla'
183.24	pieces] *interlined above deleted* 'bits'
186.11	we] *over wiped-out* 'has'
186.22	of] 'o' *over wiped-out* 'b'
187.23	little] *over wiped-out* 'crooked'
188.14	the] *altered from* 'his'
188.20	meander] 'm' *over wiped-out* 'go'
188.25	beheld] *interlined with a caret above deleted* 'saw'
188.27	voyage] *interlined with a caret above deleted* 'passage'
188.31	nunnery] *over wiped-out* 'monastery'
189.17	slipped] *over wiped-out* 'glided of'

189.25	troops] *over wiped-out* 'numbers'
189.27	Golden] 'G' *over wiped-out* 'g'
189.31	sculptors] *interlined with a caret, and comma added before caret after* 'scholars'
190.5	one] *interlined with a caret*
190.8	spread] *interlined with a caret above deleted* 'covered'
190.15	we] *over wiped-out* 'our'
190.25	it is not] 'it is n' *over wiped-out* 'I can'
191.7	as if] *precedes deleted* 'the hearts and minds of the successive owners had done all'
191.8	that] *interlined with a caret*
191.10	among] *interlined with a caret above deleted* 'one of'
191.12	new-fallen] *interlined with a caret*
191.20	many] *interlined with a caret above deleted* 'some'
191.29	better] *over wiped-out* 'dream'
191.30	-grown] *precedes wiped-out comma*
192.4	brilliantly] 'br' *over wiped-out* 'ra'
192.11	capable] 'ca' *over wiped-out* 'of'
192.12	cavernous] *interlined with a caret*
192.24	the] 'e' *over wiped-out* 'ey'
192.24	objects were] *over wiped-out* 'were presented'
192.28	his image] 'his im' *over wiped-out* 'himself'
213.4	be] *interlined above deleted* 'have been'
213.8	an impossibility] 'an im' *over wiped-out* 'a feat'
213.16	a character] *interlined with a caret*
213.19–20	warm and bright] *over wiped-out* 'warm with the re'
214.28	wearied] *follows deleted* 'already'
214.29	I] *interlined with a caret*
214.32	was] 'w' *over wiped-out* 'is'
215.7	I had sought] *interlined with a caret*
215.10	I fancy] *interlined with a caret and preceding comma added*
215.11	(in] *parenthesis deletes comma*
216.11	hunger] *interlined with a caret above deleted* 'craving'
216.22	raised in the open air,] *interlined with a caret*

216.32	concealed] *over wiped-out* 'softened or con'
217.7	discordant] *interlined with a caret*
217.32–33	in my recollection,] *interlined with a caret*
217.34	people] *interlined with a caret above deleted* 'those'
218.9	had] *altered from wiped-out* 'it' *preceding wiped-out comma*
218.17	get] *altered from* 'bec'
218.24	At] 'A' *over wiped-out* 'T'
218.29	sun-dial] 'sun' *over wiped-out* 'dial'
219.10	Tomorrow] 'T' *mended from* 't'
219.12	discerns] *interlined with a caret above deleted* 'beholds'
219.18	out of] *interlined with a caret above deleted* 'beyond'
220.3	been] *interlined with a caret*
220.11	bearing] 'bear' *over wiped-out* 'having'
220.22	take] *interlined with a caret after deleted* 'take' *which was interlined above deleted* 'have'
220.22	name—] *dash deletes comma*
221.4	or] *precedes deleted* 'or'
221.5	otherwise] *interlined with a caret*
221.7	been] *interlined with a caret*
221.8	murderer] 'mur-'| *interlined with a caret above deleted* 'crim-'| *and* 'derer' *interlined above deleted* 'inal'
221.8–9	Blackheath] *first* 'h' *over original* 'e'
221.18	was the time] *over wiped-out* 'the broad and'
221.21	view] *follows deleted* 'distant'
221.23	Houses] 'H' *mended from* 'h'
221.25	obscured a mass of things and] *interlined with a caret*
221.25–26	the objects that were] *interlined above deleted* 'whatever was'
221.33–34	exciting] *interlined with a caret above deleted* 'and excited'
222.21	made the] 'the' *over wiped-out* 'Blac'
222.25	filched away, so to speak, and] *interlined with a caret*
223.3	be] *interlined with a caret*

223.28	man] 'm' *over wiped-out* 'M'
223.32–33	because, to all appearance,] *interlined with a caret*
223.34	closer] *follows deleted* 'the neighborhood of London'
224.3	their relation] 'their' *mended from* 'the'; 'their relation' *over wiped-out* 'relation o'
224.9	when the sun shone,] *interlined with a caret*
224.17	daily] *over wiped-out* 'week'
224.34	quarrel] 'q' *over wiped-out* 'l'
225.16	horn] *precedes deleted* 'horn'
225.23	wandering] *interlined with a caret above deleted* 'straying'
225.26	might] *interlined with a caret above deleted* 'may'
225.29	erratic] *interlined with a caret above deleted* 'wandering'
225.32	divine] *interlined with uncompleted caret above deleted* 'a religious'
225.33	park-wall,] *precedes deleted* 'On a cart outside of the park-wall, (and, if I mistake not'
226.2–3	religious welfare] *interlined with a caret above deleted* 'spiritual benefit'; 'benefit' *over wiped-out* 'good'
226.3	earnest] *over wiped-out* 'loud'
226.4	gesture] *precedes wiped-out comma*
226.9	long] *interlined with a caret*
226.14	who,] *interlined with a caret*
226.19	mariner] *interlined with a caret above deleted* 'man'
226.20	which] *over wiped-out* 'that'
226.21	that] *precedes deleted* 'that'
226.21	can be expected] *interlined with a caret above deleted* 'is likely'
226.25–26	East Indian] 'East' *over wiped-out* 'India'
226.27	listen] 'listens' *over wiped-out* 'The mis'
226.33	part] *interlined with a caret*
227.1	strains] *interlined with a caret above deleted* 'songs'
227.7	Methodists] 'M' *mended from* 'm'

227.12	Methodist] 'M' *mended from* 'm'
227.15	site] *over wiped-out* 'Green'
228.4	which] *over wiped-out* 'that'
228.7	or] *over wiped-out* 'of'
228.9	sympathy] 'sy' *over wiped-out* 'pity'
228.10	sailors] 'sa' *over wiped-out* 'sol'
228.20	much] *interlined with a caret*
228.20	discontented] 'ten' *interlined with a caret above* 'disconted'
228.22	form] *interlined with a caret*
228.30	(to my] 'to' *over wiped-out* 'I'
229.2	actual] *interlined above deleted* 'genuine'
229.10	novel] *interlined with a caret above deleted* 'modern'
229.27	in a hurry,] *interlined with a caret*
230.5	element] *follows deleted* 'kind of'
230.12	painted] *interlined with a caret above deleted* 'ghastly'
230.19	truth] *interlined with a caret above deleted* 'alms'
230.19	often] *interlined with a caret*
230.21	now] *interlined with a caret*
230.33	blameless] *interlined with a caret;* 'blam' *over wiped-out* 'good'
231.12	than] *interlined with a caret*
231.14	who] *over wiped-out doubtful* 'that'
231.15	more than] *over wiped-out* 'two hundred'
231.28	in the] 'the' *interlined with a caret above deleted* 'those'
231.29	manifestation] 'ta' *interlined with a caret above* 'manifestion'
231.31	instance] *interlined with a caret above deleted* 'example'
232.7	comparative estimatc] *interlined with a caret above deleted* 'comparison'
232.8	France,] *precedes deleted* 'methinks'
232.8	methinks,] *interlined with a caret*
232.19	in his case] *interlined with a caret*
232.20	which] *interlined with a caret above deleted* 'that'

232.20	him] *precedes deleted* 'put'
232.23	usually] *interlined with a caret, following wiped-out* 'us' *above deleted* 'often'
232.31	qualities,] *over wiped-out* 'characteristics'
232.33	personage] *interlined with a caret above deleted* 'man'
233.11	adorned] *interlined with a caret above deleted* 'covered'
233.19	unexcitable] *interlined with a caret above deleted* 'pacific'
233.24	as] *precedes deleted* 'his own countrymen'
233.32	is] *interlined with a caret above deleted* 'was'
234.3	in which] *over wiped-out* 'which he'
234.13	England—] *dash deletes three dots*
234.24	festivity] *interlined with a caret*
235.8	our] *interlined with a caret above deleted* 'that'
235.9	and is occasionally as fresh as a rose,] *interlined with a caret*
235.10	or] *interlined with a caret above deleted* 'and'
235.10	habits] *interlined with a caret*
235.12	personal] *interlined with a caret above deleted* 'actual'
235.13–14	if you stop to think about it,] *interlined with a caret*
235.15	or] *over wiped-out* 'and'
235.23	so] *interlined with a caret*
235.23	completely] *over wiped-out* 'entirely'
237.3	gone] *interlined with a caret*
237.4	performances.] *precedes deleted* 'The price of tickets varied from a penny to twopence.'
237.18	on his neighbor's] *interlined with a caret above deleted* 'your' *and undeleted preceding* 'on'
237.26	characteristic—] *dash over wiped-out comma*
237.29	to-day!] *precedes wiped-out quotes*
237.30	mostly] *interlined with a caret*
237.34	shall set] 'shall' *over wiped-out* 'think'; 'set' *over wiped-out* 'I'
238.11	met] *interlined with a caret above deleted* 'found'
238.13	of them] *interlined with a caret placed over the*

	hyphen of original 'most-'| *and preceding deleted* 'ly'
238.25	teazing] *interlined with a caret above deleted* 'urging'
238.32	and an admonition,] *interlined with a caret*
239.1	hereditary] 'itary' *interlined with a caret above* 'heredi-'
239.2	Ring] 'R' *altered from* 'r'
239.25	an endless] *initial* 'e' *of* 'endless' *over wiped-out* 'f[]'; 'n' *of* 'an' *added later*
240.5	But] *interlined with a caret above unchanged* 'How'
240.7	courteous,] *interlined with a caret above deleted* 'civil'
240.9	admirable] *interlined with a caret above deleted* 'exquisite'
240.9	both] *interlined with a caret above deleted* 'it'
240.10	met] *over wiped-out* 'found'
240.10	ameliorations] *interlined above deleted* 'productions'
240.12	but] *precedes deleted* ', as a general thing'
240.13–14	though . . . male.] *interlined with a caret which covers preceding comma*
240.14–15	their charms were few] *interlined with a caret mistakenly placed before preceding comma*
240.23	chiefly] *interlined with a caret above deleted* 'mostly'
241.3	celebration . . . close] *interlined with a caret placed before semicolon and following* 'and my poor sketch' *which were deleted*
241.7	observer] *interlined with a caret above deleted* 'writer'
241.13	have] *over wiped-out* 'turn'
241.17	English] *over wiped-out* 'cotta'
241.20	men themselves,] *interlined with a caret*
241.26	refined] *over wiped-out* 'd[]'
241.27	this] 'is' *over wiped-out* 'ese'
241.30	as a] 'a' *over wiped-out* 's'
242.4	immoralities] 'ies' *over wiped-out* 'y'

242.6	with,] *precedes deleted* 'instead of turning it back'
242.7	prophaned] 'roph' *over wiped-out* 'hrop'
242.7	poison] *interlined with a caret*
242.11	we can take it as compensatory] *interlined with a caret above deleted* 'it be any consolation'
243.10	rear;] *semicolon altered from comma*
243.13	cheap] 'c' *altered doubtfully from* 'r'
244.3	of rain] *interlined with a caret*
244.7	standing-room] 'stand' *over wiped-out* 'breath'
244.14	soul] *over wiped-out* 'one'
244.15–16	struggle] 'strug-' *over wiped-out* 'contest'
244.20	stretch] 'tch' *over wiped-out* 'ech'
244.23	contain] *interlined with a caret above deleted* 'involve'
244.26	thoroughly] *interlined with a caret above deleted* 'actually'
244.28	(as . . . do)] *parentheses delete commas*
244.29	contest] *over wiped-out* 'struggle'
244.34	inferior] 'inf' *over wiped-out* 'less'
245.1	along] 'a' *over wiped-out* 'l'
245.5	seems] 'ms' *over wiped-out* 'med'
245.7	had] 'd' *over wiped-out* 's'
245.8	is] *over wiped-out* 'was'
245.8–9	buildings] 'build' *over wiped-out* 'dwell'
245.9–10	with blind windows,] *interlined with a caret*
245.17	unwholesome] 'unwh' *over wiped-out* 'turbid'
245.18	is] *over wiped-out* 'was'
245.19	displays] 's' *over wiped-out* 'ed'
245.20	a hundred] *interlined with a caret above deleted* 'innumerable'
245.27–28	at a rude landing-place] 'at a rude lan' *over wiped-out* 'on the left bank'
245.32	practical] *interlined with a caret*
245.33	inexhaustible] 'inexh' *over wiped-out* 'rever'
245.34	ten] 'two' *is interlined in the MS in darker ink with a caret above deleted* 'ten'
246.11	portions of] *interlined with a caret*
246.22	foot-] 'foot' *over wiped-out* 'eques'

246.23	and reverberate] *interlined with a caret*
246.34	interment] 'in' *over wiped-out* 'se'
247.2	read] *over wiped-out* 'detect'
247.5	magnifying-] 'magnifying' *was written over wiped-out* 'little magnifying' *and then was interlined for clarity*
247.12	partake of] *interlined with a caret above deleted* 'buy'
247.13	however,] *interlined with a caret*
247.15	contains] 's' *over wiped-out* 'ed'
247.17	serve] *second* 'e' *over wiped-out* 'ed'
247.19	people] *interlined with a caret*
247.29	proved] *interlined with a caret above deleted* 'turned out'
247.30	annual] 'annu' *over wiped-out* 'scarce'
247.34	is so great] 'is so gre' *over wiped-out* 'from the b'
248.4	larger] *interlined with a caret above deleted* 'greater'
248.13	and with] 'with' *interlined with a caret*
248.20	held] *interlined with a caret above deleted* 'accounted'
248.22	traces] 'tra' *over wiped-out* 'old'
248.23	Monthly] 'M' *over wiped-out* 'm'
248.24	enriched] *interlined with a caret above deleted* 'possessing'
248.24	with] *interlined with a caret*
248.26	(for a Yankee, at least,)] *interlined with a caret*
248.31	numerous] *interlined with a caret*
248.33	would] *over wiped-out* 'needed'
248.34	domicile] *interlined with a caret above deleted* 'habitation'
249.3	might] 'm' *over wiped-out* 'co'
249.5	chamber] 'cham' *over wiped-out* 'room'
249.6	History] 'His' *over wiped-out* 'histo'
249.12	planetary] 'plan-'| *over wiped-out* 'cycles'
249.18	comprehensive] *interlined with a caret*
249.22	solitude and] *interlined with a caret*
249.30	Noah] 'Noa' *over wiped-out* 'Rale'
249.31	peculiarities of construction] *interlined with a caret above deleted* 'qualities'

249.32   Raleigh] *interlined with a caret above deleted*
          'he'
249.34   Raleigh] *interlined with a caret above deleted*
          'he'
250.1   in his presence] *interlined with a caret*
250.1–2   this martial student] *interlined with a caret*
          above deleted 'him'
250.2   their] *interlined with a caret*
250.2   Raleigh] *interlined with a caret above deleted*
          'he'
250.3   up] *interlined with a caret*
250.4   manifest] 'manifest' *written over wiped-out*
          '[ ]significant' *then deleted and interlined for*
          clarity
250.5   Past] 'P' *mended from* 'p'
250.5   by means of] *interlined with a caret above de-*
          leted 'in'
250.5   and] *precedes deleted* 'airy music'
250.17   explore] *interlined with a caret above deleted*
          'travel'
250.17–18 successive] *interlined with a caret*
250.18   habitation] *interlined with a caret above de-*
          leted 'receptacle'
250.28   might] 'mig' *over wiped-out* 'have'
251.3   blood, (] *parenthesis covers wiped-out comma,*
          and comma was then placed before paren-
          thesis
251.3   since] *interlined with a caret over wiped-out* 'if'
251.5   crawl] *interlined with a caret above wiped-out*
          'creep'
251.6   again] *interlined with a caret*
251.7   to] *interlined with a caret*
251.12   Thames] 'Tham' *over wiped-out* 'river'
251.16   together] 'tog' *over wiped-out* 'and'
251.17–18 high and low] *interlined with a caret above de-*
          leted 'up and down'
251.19   bobbed up] *over wiped-out* '[toss]ed like'
251.30   warm] *over wiped-out* 'worse' *and then wiped*
          out and interlined with a caret for clarity
252.5   particularly] 'par-'| *interlined with a caret above*

	deleted 'espe-'| *and* 'ticularly' *interlined with a caret above deleted* 'cially'
252.6	with] *precedes deleted* 'slop-shops'
252.6	the stalls] 'the s' *over wiped-out* 'and b'
252.16	undertake] *precedes deleted* 'the'
252.16	a descriptive] *interlined with a caret above deleted* 'description of a'
252.26	This] *precedes deleted* 'is the White Tower'
252.27	enclosed] *MS* 'inclosed' *over wiped-out* 'in[circ]led'
252.28	constitutes] 'constitu' *over wiped-out* 'consitues'
252.30	Tower] 'T' *over wiped-out* 'to'
253.1	dreary kind] *interlined with a caret above deleted* 'sort'
253.4	found] *interlined with a caret above deleted* 'made'
253.6	observed] 'ob' *over wiped-out* 'no'
253.9	historical] 'hi' *over wiped-out* 'm'
253.11	amongst] *interlined with a caret placed after an inadvertently undeleted comma which is over wiped-out* 'to'
253.13	easily] *interlined with a caret*
253.13	in their minds] *interlined with a caret*
253.16	itself] *interlined with a caret*
253.18	the late] *interlined with a caret*
253.20	devouring] *interlined with a caret above deleted* 'counting'
253.20	old] *interlined with a caret*
253.22	in his life] *interlined with a caret*
253.22	Tower,] *comma over wiped-out period*
253.27	succeed each] *over wiped-out* 'accumulate so'
254.4	gaudiest] 'a' *over wiped-out* 'r'
254.5	day—] *dash deletes comma*
254.5	ones, in] 'i' *over wiped-out lefthand parenthesis and preceding comma added*
254.6	lace] *interlined with a caret*
254.8–9	after all, it might have been merely a city-spectacle appertaining to the Lord Mayor;] *interlined with a caret*
254.10	me] *interlined with a caret*

254.10	grand] *follows deleted* 'old'
254.17	cabs and] *interlined with a caret*
254.17	omnibus have] 'es' *of* 'omnibuses' *was wiped out, and* 'have' *altered from* 'has'
254.18	in hue] *interlined with a caret*
254.20	lace] *precedes erased comma*
254.24	avenues] *interlined with a caret above wiped-out* 'brick squa' *with* 'and' *over wiped-out* 'qua'
254.25	close] 'clo' *over wiped-out* 'rich'
254.25	river-] *initial* 'r' *over wiped-out* 'T'
254.27	the] *interlined with a caret above deleted* 'those'
254.27	and scattered] 'and' *interlined with a caret above deleted* 'which'
254.29	or rear] *interlined with a caret*
254.29	and] *over wiped-out* 'rise'
254.32	vast and] *interlined with a caret below deleted previously interlined* 'vast and'
254.33	effect] *interlined with a caret above deleted* 'do'
254.34	elaborately] *over wiped-out* 'in genuinely'
255.2	have] *interlined with a caret above deleted* 'catch'
255.4	palace,] *comma altered from a period*
255.4	a venerable] *follows deleted* 'in our course'
255.9	an] *over wiped-out* 'aspe'
255.12	Dome] 'D' *mended from doubtful* 'd'
255.14	because] 'be' *over wiped-out* 'that'
255.16	the world has nothing better] *interlined with a caret*
255.25	Charles] 'Ch' *over wiped-out* 'the'
255.25	bronze] *interlined with a caret above deleted* 'marble'
255.25–26	in the guise of an old Roman,] *interlined with a caret*
255.26	centre of] *precedes deleted* '[across] of'
255.27	aged] 'a' *over wiped-out* 'the'
255.30	effect] *interlined with a caret above deleted* 'result'
256.3–5	Almost . . . missing.] *originally inscribed as a separate paragraph following* 256.15 *and moved to present position, marked by inter-*

	*lined notation 'See below', with a line terminating in an arrowhead, the paragraph having the interlined notation '(*Insert this sentence above*)'*
256.5	one of these fragmentary heroes] *interlined with a caret above deleted* 'one old hero'
256.13	asked] *over wiped-out* 'asking'
256.16	great] *interlined with a caret above deleted* 'large'
256.17	is a] *over wiped-out* 'there'
256.23	world, comprising] 'world, c' *over wiped-out* 'comprising'
256.24	all] *over wiped-out* 'many'
256.26	Russian,] *interlined with a caret wrongly placed before comma following* 'Prussian'
256.28	upon earth] 'upon e' *over wiped-out* 'on earth'
257.4	that] *interlined with a caret*
257.5	unrecognized] *interlined with a caret above deleted* 'little'
257.7	imperfectly] 'y' *over wiped-out* 'I'
257.11	that] *over wiped-out* 'which'
257.14	generally] *interlined with a caret above deleted* 'often'
257.16	that] *interlined with a caret*
257.18–19	and forever.] *interlined with a caret above undeleted period*
257.21	illuminated] 'u' *over wiped-out* 'I'
257.25	stirred up] *interlined with a caret above deleted* 'wounded'
257.26	freedom and] *interlined with a caret*
257.30	mild veteran] *interlined above deleted* 'old soldier' *with a caret placed before inadvertently undeleted semicolon*
257.31	voice] *followed by wiped-out comma*
258.5	your Honor] 'r' *of* 'your' *added and* 'H' *written over wiped-out* 'know'
258.7	system] *interlined with a caret above deleted* 'life'
258.8	care] *interlined with a caret above deleted* 'care'
258.17	afar] *interlined with a caret*

258.18	structure—] *dash deletes comma*
258.19	one] *altered from* 'an'
258.24	picture] *over wiped-out* 'sketch'
258.25	try to] *over wiped-out* 'describe'
258.26	has] *over wiped-out* ', has'
258.28	Story] 'S' *mended from* 's'
258.29	continually] *interlined with a caret above deleted* 'often'
258.31	might] *interlined with a caret above deleted* 'would'
258.32	appear] *interlined with a caret above deleted* 'seem'
258.33	often] *interlined with a caret*
258.34	prophetically] *interlined with a caret*
259.2	any] *over wiped-out* 'the rea'
259.4–5	acquainted with] 'acquainted' *interlined with a caret above deleted* 'familiar' *and* 'with' *over wiped-out* 'sc'
259.7	England"—] *dash, crowded in later, intended to delete original comma*
259.11	somewhat] 'som' *over wiped-out* 'a lit'
259.13	objects] *over wiped-out* 'spectacles'
259.15	actual] *interlined with a caret*
259.16	scene] *precedes deleted* 'to the minds'
259.19	From] *interlined with a caret; follows deleted* 'As a consequence of'
259.21	longer] *interlined with a caret above deleted* 'older'
259.21–22	more eligible] *interlined with a caret above deleted* 'better'
259.28	pillared] *interlined with a caret above deleted* 'fretted'
259.34–260.1	when it came to the sermon] *interlined with a caret above deleted* 'to confess the truth'
260.4	and] 'an' *over wiped-out* 'us'
260.8	kind of] *precedes deleted* 'lofty', *interlined with a caret, also deleted*
260.9	and being] 'and be' *over wiped-out* 'the Deity'
260.11	unborn.] *period over wiped-out final* 'e'

260.15	mortal] 'mo' *over wiped-out* 'indi'
260.15–16	—and felt it no venture at all—] *interlined with a caret*
260.22	the structure] *interlined with a caret above deleted* 'it'
260.24	ancient] *interlined with a caret*
260.25	reasonably] 'r' *over wiped-out* 'b'
260.26	for] *over wiped-out doubtful* 'thence'
260.27	sweet] *interlined with a caret above deleted* 'beautiful'
260.29	received] *interlined above deleted* 'welcomed'
260.29	which] *interlined with a caret above deleted* 'that'
260.31	Sunshine] *interlined with a caret above deleted* 'It has'
260.32	seems] *altered from* 'seemed'; *precedes deleted* 'to me that sunshine is'
260.32	abbeys,] *interlined with a caret*
261.2	western] *interlined with a caret*
261.2	entrance] *precedes deleted* 'of the minster'
261.3	afforded] 'a' *over wiped-out* 'f'
261.8	orb] *follows deleted* 'circular'
261.14	almost wholly] *interlined with a caret*
261.15	time,] *comma over wiped-out dash*
261.19	once] *over wiped-out* 'famo'
261.19	but] 'b' *over wiped-out* 'L'
261.21	partly curtained] *interlined with a caret above deleted* 'almost blocked up'
261.21	the immense arch of a] *interlined with a caret above deleted* 'an arched' *perhaps later than the alteration above*
261.27	Gothic] *interlined with a caret*
261.28	overpower] 'over' *over wiped-out* 'out'
261.29	a] *over wiped-out* 'the'
261.31	most] *over wiped-out* 'best'
262.6	the First's] *over wiped-out* 'Ist's time'
262.8	the] *interlined with a caret*
262.8	record] 're' *over wiped-out* 'the'
262.13	visage] 'v' *over wiped-out* 'f'
262.14	New Englander] 'New En' *over wiped-out*

'Ameri' *and preceding* 'an' *inadvertently un-deleted*

262.16   warlike] 'war' *over wiped-out* 'ente'

262.19   guise] *over wiped-out* 'shape'

262.20   the latter] *interlined with a caret above deleted* 'it'

262.26   really] *interlined with a caret*

262.27–28   distinguished] *interlined with a caret above deleted* 'illustrious'

262.30   enveloped him like a mantle] *interlined with a caret above deleted* 'distinguished him'

262.33   illustrious] *interlined with a caret*

263.2–3   making evident a heretofore hidden dignity in the actual form] *interlined with a caret;* 'heretofore' *follows deleted* 'dignity in the actual form', *in which* 'dig' *was over* 'gran'

263.6   absurd] *interlined with a caret above deleted* 'ill'

263.8   save for the lack of color,] *interlined with a caret*

263.10   appears] *interlined with a caret above deleted* 'seems'

263.12   one] *over wiped-out* 'his'

263.12   I believe,] *interlined with a caret*

263.13   familiar] *interlined with a caret*

263.24–25   smoothe away his knowing complication of wrinkles] *interlined with a caret above deleted* 'prepare his visage'

263.25   had] *interlined with a caret*

263.26   whitened] *over wiped-out* 'been turn'

263.27   minutest] *interlined with a caret above deleted* 'smallest'

263.33–34   which would obliterate all mean peculiarities] *interlined with a caret*

264.1   the guise] *interlined with a caret*

264.3   however,] *interlined with a caret*

264.4   and form] *over wiped-out* 'is seldom'

264.7   jocose] *interlined with a caret above deleted* 'laughing'

264.12   that has] *interlined with a caret above deleted* 'who may have'

264.15–16 the roof of] *interlined with a caret; precedes interlined and wiped-out* 'its'

264.16 if] *interlined with a caret*

264.17 feel] *over wiped-out* 'like'

264.19 an] *altered from* 'a'

264.19 ordinary] *interlined with a caret above deleted* 'smaller'

264.24 be sensible] *interlined with a caret above deleted* 'acknowledge'

264.27 any] *precedes deleted* 'thing' *of original* 'anything'

264.27–28 boon from posterity] *interlined with a caret*

265.5–6 both in literature and history] *interlined with a caret*

265.6 now] *interlined with a caret*

265.17 thus] *interlined with a caret above deleted* 'so'

265.17 they] *interlined with a caret*

265.17 memorial] *interlined with a caret above deleted* 'record'

265.20 audience] 'au' *over wiped-out* 'th'

265.23 invites] 'in' *over wiped-out* '[l]'

265.24 vast] *over wiped-out* 'shad'

265.28 precinct] *interlined with a caret above deleted* 'portion'

265.28 by] *over wiped-out* 'th[]'

266.5 slumberous] *interlined with a caret*

266.13 day—] *dash over wiped-out lefthand parenthesis*

266.15 to] *interlined with a caret above deleted* 'towards'

266.25 side] *over wiped-out* 'aisle'

266.29 aloft] *precedes erased comma*

266.31 as yellow as old parchment] *interlined with a caret above deleted* 'yellow with time'

267.1 else] *interlined with a caret above deleted* 'otherwise'

267.1 been] *over wiped-out* '[]lla'

267.11 other] *follows deleted* 'any'

267.16 aspiring for] *interlined with a caret above deleted* 'possessing'

267.17 long-enduring] *interlined with a caret*

267.20	flit] *over wiped-out* 'glide'
267.31	or beyond] *interlined with a caret*
267.33	into the chapels] *interlined*
268.10	because] *interlined with a caret*
268.18	gigantic] *interlined with a caret above deleted* 'colossal'
268.27–28	lines to his memory] *interlined with a caret above deleted* 'epitaph'
269.2	At best] *interlined with a caret above deleted* 'After all'
269.2	only a] *over wiped-out* 'it is but'
269.4	artist-] *interlined with a caret above* 'breed'
269.5	pursuits] *interlined with a caret above deleted* 'kinds of eminence'
269.8	lifetime] *precedes erased comma*
269.9	official personages] *interlined with a caret above deleted* 'men of office'
269.13	greatness] *follows deleted* 'this'
269.13	dimly lighted] *interlined with a caret above deleted* 'obscure'
269.21	a spiritual] 'a spir' *over wiped-out* 'his[]'
269.24	period] *interlined with a caret above deleted* 'time'
269.26	horizontal] 'hor' *over wiped-out* 'flat'
269.28	humblest] *over wiped-out* 'meanest'
269.28	companions. And] *period altered from semicolon, and* 'A' *from* 'a'
269.34–270.1	leaning out of the sky, and] *interlined with a caret*
270.3	notion] 'not' *over wiped-out* 'idea'
270.5	reverberations] *interlined with a caret above deleted* 'vibrations'
270.8	as] *over wiped-out* 'of'
270.17	even] *interlined with a caret*
270.19	bust] *interlined with a caret*
270.21	the judgment] 'the judg' *over wiped-out* 'an English'
270.23	if] *interlined with a caret*
270.23	verse,] *precedes deleted* 'perhaps'

270.24	yet] *interlined with a caret above deleted* 'but'
271.1	sketching] *interlined with a caret above deleted* 'describing'
271.3	was] 'w' *over wiped-out* 'th'
271.5	prospect] *interlined with a caret above deleted* 'view'
271.5	that of] *interlined with a caret*
271.7	or] *over wiped-out* 'out'
271.7	opened] *altered from* 'openened'
271.10	quietly] *over wiped-out* 'alive all'
271.15	external] *interlined with a caret*
271.17	remarkable] *interlined with a caret above deleted* 'distinguished'
271.30	white] *over wiped-out* 'gr'
272.1	more] 'm' *over wiped-out* 'ea'
272.3	gleam] *interlined with a caret above deleted* 'glow'
272.3	his sprightly] 'his' *interlined with a caret above deleted* 'the play of', *then* 'sprightly' *interlined with a caret following* 'the play of'
272.6	transformation] *interlined with a caret above deleted* 'change'
272.7	trusting] *follows deleted* 'I'
272.8	difficult] *interlined with a caret above deleted* 'hard'
272.8	his] *interlined with a caret*
272.10	agreeable—] *interlined with a caret above preceding deleted* 'perfect', *above which* 'pleasing' *had been interlined and then deleted; the dash deletes a comma*
272.11	natural] *over wiped-out* 'growth'
272.12	disposition] *interlined with a caret above deleted* 'nature'
272.12	else] *interlined with a caret*
272.15	eyes] 'ey' *over wiped-out* 'we'
272.18	surrounded] 'surroun-'| *over wiped-out* 'immediately'
272.18	him] *interlined with a caret*
272.18	of the vicissitudes] *interlined with a caret*

272.22	not from any] *interlined with a caret above deleted* 'from no'
272.24	to] *over wiped-out* 'a'
272.28	within] *over wiped-out* 'in him'
272.32	was] *over wiped-out* 'is'
273.3	was] *over wiped-out* 'is'
273.5	entered] 'ed' *over wiped-out* 's'
273.6	given] *precedes deleted* 'many'
273.12	one.] *period over erased comma*
273.13	I beheld him . . . robes.] *interlined with a caret following erased comma and added period*
273.16	timid man] *interlined with a caret above deleted* 'coward'
273.21	generally] *interlined with a caret above deleted* 'in other respects'
273.23	declining] *interlined with a caret above deleted* 'old'
273.27	the latter] *interlined with a caret*
274.10	long] *interlined with a caret above deleted* 'great'
274.17	himself—] *dash deletes comma*
274.20	is] *interlined with a caret following deleted* 'it'
274.23	vulgar] *interlined with a caret*
274.24	was] *interlined with a caret*
275.1	probably] *precedes deleted* 'had'
275.3	attaining to] *interlined with a caret above deleted* 'winning'
275.12	anticipations] *interlined with a caret above deleted* 'hopes'
276.4	arm . . . not] *in MS dashes after these words delete commas*
276.6	minstrel] *interlined with a caret above deleted* 'poetic'
276.6	a week-day one] *interlined with a caret above deleted* 'another'
276.8	whose] *mended from* 'who'
276.8	kind introduction] *interlined with a caret*
276.9	Leigh Hunt.] *follows deleted* 'his friend'

310.4   Dinner] 'D' *altered from possible* 'F' *or* 'T'
310.12   kindest] *written over* 'better'
310.14   majestic] *interlined with a caret after deleted*
             'stately'
311.2   and consolatory] *interlined with a caret*
311.2   hope] *precedes deleted* 'and consolation'
311.12   proposing to] *interlined with a caret above deleted* 'inviting'
311.13   a] *follows deleted* 'to'
311.13   series of nice little] *interlined with a caret*
311.13   dinners] 's' *added later*
311.14   untasted] *interlined with a caret*
311.16   indeed,] *interlined with a caret*
311.34–312.1 to appreciate] 'to' *altered from* 'its'
312.6   ruggedness] *interlined with a caret above deleted*
             'rougness'
312.12   coarseness,] *comma altered from semicolon by scratching*
312.33–34   and to . . . wine] *interlined with a caret with following comma*
313.2–3   the . . . Coffee-house,] 'the . . . Coffe house,'
             interlined with a caret above deleted 'Parker's'
313.8   guest's] *originally appeared* 'guests' *but final* 's'
             written over to follow the apostrophe
313.14   partially public] 'public' *interlined with a caret*
313.18   these] 'se' *over* 'y'
313.19   festivities] *interlined with a caret*
313.32   church] *precedes deleted* 'which is'
314.2   low stone] *interlined with a caret*
314.3   well-worn] *interlined with a caret*
314.17   Henry the] 'the' *interlined with a caret*
314.31   characters] 'character' *in MS interlined above
             deleted* 'personage'
314.32   their] *interlined with a caret after deleted* 'his'
314.33–34   for a person . . . such,] *interlined with a caret
             placed before undeleted comma following*
             'enough'
315.4   ceiling] *over wiped-out* 'roofing'
315.6   seen.] *period replaces erased comma*

315.6   At] 'A' *mended from* 'a'; *follows deleted* 'though' *and wiped-out comma*

315.7   they] *over wiped-out possible* 'it a'

315.12   faintly] *interlined with a caret*

315.13   is] *over wiped-out* 'are'

315.15   untouched] *over wiped-out* 'undescribed'

315.17   Countess] *interlined with a caret above deleted* 'Dame'

315.18–19   if she had no ampler garniture,] *interlined with a caret,* 'had' *being inserted with a separate caret*

315.21   at] *over wiped-out* 'of'

315.22   scene] *interlined with a caret above deleted* 'picture'

315.27   long-forgotten] 'l' *over wiped-out* 'f'

315.28   mouldy] *interlined with a caret above deleted* 'dusty'

316.2   this reverence] 'this' *over wiped-out* '—this'

316.10   walls.] *period added after a comma following* 'walls' *was deleted and written over with a caret*

316.10   It is] *interlined with a caret above deleted* 'and'

316.10   also] *interlined with a caret*

316.12   all portraits] *interlined with a caret*

316.15   the Eighth.] *in MS* 'VIII.', 'V' *altered from possible* 'I', *and a following period wiped out*

316.20   monarchs] *over wiped-out* 'Kings and'

316.28   sphere.] *follows deleted* 'sphere.'

316.29   state] *over wiped-out possible* 'estate'

316.34   hundreds] *interlined with a caret above deleted* 'scores'

317.1   punch-bowl] 'w' *over wiped-out* 'ol'

317.3   Loving] 'L' *mended from* 'l'

317.4   one] *over wiped-out possible* 'whi'

317.10   a long] 'a' *over wiped-out* 'l'

317.17–18   his Worship] 'h' *of* 'his' *over wiped-out possible* 'H'

317.18   most of] *interlined with a caret above deleted* 'all'

317.20   during] *over wiped-out* 'in all'

317.20   and] *interlined with a caret*

317.25–26   than ours] *interlined with a caret*

317.32   accords] 'ac' *over wiped-out* 'they'

318.1   Judges] 'J' *mended from* 'j'

318.1   the prominent] 'the' *interlined with a caret*

318.3   and he] *interlined with a caret above deleted* 'who'

318.6   resemblance] *interlined with a caret above deleted* 'resemblance' *and written over wiped-out* 'transmissions'

318.7   transmissions] *interlined with a caret above deleted* 'repetitions'

318.14   invariably] 'ably' *over wiped-out* 'al'

318.18   in a critical spirit] *interlined with a caret which covered comma after* 'company'; *a comma then added*

318.19   apart] *interlined with a caret*

318.19   silent] *interlined with a caret*

318.29   clad] *interlined with a caret*

318.30   rapier] *over wiped-out* 'dress'

318.33   that] 'th' *over possible* 'wh'

319.16   glance,] *interlined with a caret above deleted* 'part'

319.16   take] *over wiped-out possible* 'and'

319.24   entirely] *interlined with a caret above deleted* 'quite'

319.28   such] *interlined with a caret*

319.33   an] *interlined with a caret*

320.2   sallow] *in MS, precedes* 'with the intemperate use of strong coffee', *of which* 'the . . . coffee' *is interlined with a caret*

320.4   -paced] *interlined with a caret*

320.5   would] *over wiped-out possible* 'will'

320.13–14   thorough] 'th' *over wiped-out* 'gen'

320.16   has] *interlined with a caret*

320.22   measure] *interlined with a caret above deleted* 'judge'

320.25   conformity] *interlined with a caret above deleted* 'accordance'

320.26	went] 't' *over wiped-out* 'th'
321.1	richly] *over wiped-out* 'well'
321.5	vista] 'v' *over wiped-out* 're'
321.27	Panza's] *interlined with a caret which covers an original* 's' *of* 'Sancho's', *the apostrophe being likewise covered by first* 'a' *of* 'Panza's'
321.27	out of] *interlined with a caret above deleted* 'into'
321.30	betimes] *interlined with a caret above deleted* 'early'
321.32	rather copiously] *interlined with a caret above deleted* 'abundantly'
321.34	away] *interlined with a caret*
321.34	goblet] *over wiped-out* 'glass,'
322.23	yet] *interlined with a caret*
322.25	knight] *interlined with a caret above deleted* 'fellow'
323.1	Crown] 'C' *mended from* 'c'
323.18	in order] *interlined with a caret*
323.23	seemed] *precedes deleted* 'capable'
324.10	retort] *interlined with a caret above deleted* 'response'
324.13–14	at my] *over wiped-out* 'before []'
324.14	subsequently] *interlined with a caret above deleted* 'afterwards'
324.15	prominent] *follows deleted* 'most'
325.1	Loyalty;] *semicolon possibly altered from period*
325.3	life] *interlined with a caret*
325.14	Mayor's] 'M' *over wiped-out* 'L'
325.20	this party of] *interlined with a caret above deleted* 'these'
325.21	drink] *interlined with a caret above deleted* 'wine'
326.6	in] *interlined with a caret above deleted* 'to'
326.6	swelling] *the* 'ing' *added later*
326.7	Lady] 'L' *mended from* 'l'
326.18	institutions] *second* 'i' *altered from* 'u'
326.21	me] *interlined with a caret*
326.31–32	his countrymen] *interlined with a caret above deleted* 'they'

327.5	often] *interlined with a caret*
327.8	necessarily a public] *interlined with a caret*
327.11	whatever] 'what-'| *interlined with a caret above deleted* 'at' *and* 'ever' *interlined with a caret above deleted* 'all'
327.13	been] *interlined with a caret*
327.16	rounding] *interlined with a caret above deleted* 'turning'
327.22	except] *interlined with a caret above deleted* 'unless it were'
327.22–23	who responded] 'who re' *over wiped-out* 'for the'
327.24	hesitating] *interlined with a caret above deleted* 'interrupted'
328.11	such a misfortune] *interlined with a caret above deleted* 'it'
328.14	inexorably—] *dash deletes comma*
328.18	impart to] *interlined with a caret above deleted* 'give'
328.21	I] *interlined with a caret*
328.22	there] *interlined with a caret*
328.26	not an idea] *over wiped-out* 'nor, which'
328.33	at] *over wiped-out* 'to'
329.9	long-expected] *interlined with a caret*
329.12	and should] *interlined with a caret, and preceding comma added*
329.14	most] *precedes wiped-out comma*
329.30	beneath which] *interlined with a caret above deleted* 'which'
329.31	by] *interlined with a caret above deleted* 'without' *which followed deleted* 'under'
329.31	no] *interlined with a caret above deleted* 'any'
329.32	shirk] *in MS followed by* 'it' *interlined with a caret*
330.8	talked] *interlined with a caret above deleted* 'met'
330.8	with] *interlined with a caret*
330.12	perhaps] *interlined with a caret*
330.18	once or twice] 'once' *interlined with a caret above deleted* 'some-'| *and* 'or twice' *interlined with a caret above undeleted* 'times'

330.25	many] *over wiped-out* 'most'
330.26	amount] *interlined with a caret above deleted* 'deal'
330.31	who] *interlined with a caret*
330.31	out] *interlined with a caret*
330.32	that] *interlined with a caret*
330.33	knows that he] *interlined with a caret*
331.3	dinner] *interlined with a caret above deleted* 'feast'
331.8	nevertheless] 'neverthe' *over wiped-out* 'however,'
331.13	so] *over wiped-out possible* 'as'
331.27	Easter] 'E' *mended from* 'e'
332.5	In] *altered from* 'At'
332.5	-hall] 'h' *over wiped-out* 'H'
332.7	wonderfully] 'w' *altered from* 'l'
332.16	friends] *follows deleted* 'English', *which was interlined with a caret*
332.18	in] *over wiped-out* 'at'
332.23	two] *interlined with a caret*
332.24	of] *added in margin*
332.26	nearly or quite] *interlined with a caret*
332.32	correctly] 'cor-'| *over wiped-out* 'rightly'
332.34	found] *interlined with a caret*
333.8	literature] *follows deleted* 'and'
333.8	and science,] *interlined with a caret misplaced before preceding comma*
333.15	mode or] *over wiped-out* 'principle of'
333.15	principle] 'le' *over wiped-out* 'al'
333.25	doubtful] 'd' *over wiped-out* 'ab'
333.31	satirical] *interlined with a caret*
334.8	it was my happiness to know] 'it was my hap-'| *interlined with a caret above deleted* 'I used' *and undeleted* 'to', *and* 'piness to know' *interlined with a caret above deleted* 'be familiar with'
334.9	often] *interlined with a caret*
334.9	or seemed to find,] *interlined with a caret*
334.12	deficiency] *interlined with a caret above deleted* 'lack'

334.15–16   resolve . . . sturdily] *commas following these words were wiped out*

334.18   from] 'fr' *over wiped-out* 'p'

334.20   could] *follows deleted* 'be'

334.33   damask] 'dam' *over wiped-out* 'table-' *and second* 'a' *over wiped-out* 'cl'

334.34   set] *over wiped-out* 'the'

335.2   implored] *interlined with a caret above deleted* 'asked'

335.5   relish] 'r' *over wiped-out* 'a'

335.7   was] 'w' *over wiped-out* 'a'

335.13   but] *interlined with a caret above deleted* 'only'

335.18   to drink a sip] *over wiped-out* 'always to drink'

335.23   an] *the* 'n' *added later*

335.23   arabesque] *interlined with a caret*

335.26   themselves] 'themselves' *was deleted, but later interlined with a caret above the deletion*

335.27   guests] *precedes added period and deleted* 'themselves'

335.27   and honest] 'and' *interlined with a caret*

336.1   generally] *interlined with a caret*

336.1   estimate] *the first* 'e' *over* 'ae'

336.5   widest] 'w' *altered from* 's'

336.10   bird] 'b' *over wiped-out* 'f'

336.20   reference] *interlined with a caret*

336.20   disagreeable] *over wiped-out* 'solemn'

336.30   romance;] *precedes deleted* 'but being so singular and distinct an ap-|parition, she seemed like-lier'

337.5   outline] *over wiped-out* 'profile'

337.7   to put] 'to' *interlined with a caret*

337.9   and darksome] *interlined with a caret*

337.12   Bluebeard] 'b' *over wiped-out* 'B'

337.32–338.2   (in . . . ears)] *parentheses delete commas*

338.2   ending] *interlined with a caret above deleted* 'and ended'

338.7   the tables—] *over wiped-out* 'all the tables'

338.24   moderate] *precedes deleted* 'sips' *and undeleted period*

338.26   doubtful] 'dou' *over wiped-out* 'ques'

338.29	be accounted] 'be a' *over wiped-out* 'result'
338.29	repugnance] *interlined with a caret*
338.31	important] *interlined with a caret*
339.1	poor] *interlined with a caret above deleted* 'thin'
339.4	could] *interlined with a caret above deleted* 'was'
339.4	have been] *interlined with a caret*
339.7	table-] 'ta' *over wiped-out* 'di'
339.11	happily] *interlined with a caret above deleted* 'successfully'
339.11	thereof] 'reof' *over wiped-out* 'refrom'
339.23	including,] *interlined with a caret*
339.23	the] *follows deleted* 'to'
340.9	imagine] 'im-'| *interlined with a caret above deleted* 'fan-'| *and* 'agine' *interlined with a caret above deleted* 'cied'
340.16	, a few hundred] ', a few hun-'| *over wiped-out* 'for the sake of'
340.18	sober] *interlined with a caret above deleted* 'bitter'
340.19	thus] *interlined with a caret*
340.23	interrupted] *interlined with a caret above deleted* 'disturbed'
340.27	English] *interlined with a caret*
340.28	my readers] 'my' *over wiped-out* 'the' *and* 's' *added to* 'reader'
340.30	are] *over wiped-out* 'were'
341.3	not had] 'had' *interlined with a caret*
341.15	eminent] *interlined with a caret*
341.16	were more] *over wiped-out* 'are stronger'
341.20	inviolably] 'invio' *over wiped-out* 'sacred'
341.21	now and] *interlined with a caret*
341.27	thunderous] *interlined with a caret*
341.31	on] *over wiped-out* 'by'
342.15	right or wrong, are] *interlined with a caret, and comma inserted after preceding* 'but'
342.26	whose normal condition is savage fury,] *interlined with a caret misplaced before preceding comma*
343.2	periods,] *interlined with a caret above deleted* 'times,'

343.3	talk] *precedes a possible wiped-out comma*
343.6	nations] 'na-'| *interlined with a caret above deleted* 'coun-'| *and* 'tions' *interlined with a caret above deleted* 'tries'
343.7	world— . . . France—] *dashes delete commas*
343.10	of the] 'the' *interlined with a caret above deleted* 'their'
343.11–12	consolidating] *first* 'i' *altered from* 'o'
343.12	(owing] *parenthesis deletes comma;* 'o' *altered from* 'f'
343.17	international] 'inter' *over wiped-out* 'politic'
343.27–28	in which] *over wiped-out* 'with the f'
343.29	their] *precedes deleted* 'own'
343.31	indefensible] 'de' *interlined with a caret*
344.1	indulging] 'indul-'| *interlined above deleted* 'affording' *and* 'ging' *interlined with a caret above* 'them'
344.1	with] *interlined with a caret*
344.3	probably] *interlined with a caret*
344.4	War] 'W' *mended from* 'w'
344.16	chasm] 'c' *over wiped-out* 'g[]'
344.17	England] *over wiped-out* 'countries' *following deleted* 'the'
344.22	have] 've' *over* 's'
344.28	his] *over wiped-out* 'the'
344.32	knew to possess] 'knew to poss' *over wiped-out* 'knew to be poss'
345.13	Seizing] *interlined above deleted* 'I seized upon'
345.17	I] *interlined with a caret*

SPECIAL APPENDIX: ORIGINAL
1857 "UTTOXETER"

Note: The text of "Uttoxeter" is here edited according to the principles of all Centenary texts, from the copy-text manuscript in the Pierpont Morgan Library, with emendations from the published appearances in *The Keepsake* (London, 1857), pp. 108–13, and in *Harper's New Monthly Magazine*, XIV (April, 1857), 639–41.

For a physical description of the manuscript, see the Textual Introduction, p. lvi. Following the text are appended Editorial Emendations, Word-Division, Historical Collation, and Alterations in the Manuscript.

Uttoxeter

By Mr. Hawthorne, "Author of the Scarlet Letter" &c.&c.
[*in another hand*]

At Lichfield, in Saint Mary's Square, I saw a statue of Dr. Johnson, elevated on a stone pedestal, some ten or twelve feet high. The statue is colossal (though perhaps not much more so than the mountainous Doctor) and sits in a chair, with a pile of big books underneath it, looking down upon the spectator with a broad, heavy, benignant countenance, very like Johnson's portraits.

The figure is immensely massive—a vast ponderosity of stone, not finely spiritualized, nor, indeed, fully humanized, but rather resembling a great boulder than a man. On the pedestal, are three bas-reliefs; in the first, Johnson is represented as a mere baby, seated on an old man's shoulders, resting his chin on the bald head which he embraces with his arms, and listening to the preaching of Dr. Sacheverell; in the second tablet, he is seen riding to school on the backs of two of his comrades, while a third boy supports him in the rear. The third bas-relief possesses, to my mind, a good deal of pathos. It shows Johnson in the market-place of Uttoxeter, doing penance for an act of disobedience to his father, committed fifty years before. He stands bareheaded, very sad and woe-begone, with the wind and rain driving hard against him; while some market-people and children gaze awe-stricken into his face, and an aged man and woman, with clasped hands, are praying for him. These latter personages, I fancy, (though, in queer proximity, there are some living ducks and dead poultry,) represent the spirits of Johnson's father and mother, lending what aid they can to lighten his half-century's burthen of remorse.

I never heard of this statue before; it seems to have no reputation as a work of art, and very probably may deserve none. Yet I found it somewhat touching and effective, perhaps because my interest in the character of that sturdiest old Englishman has always been peculiarly strong; and especially the above-described bas-relief freshened my sense of a wonderful beauty and pathos in the incident which it commemorates. So, the next day, I left Lichfield for Uttoxeter, on a purely sentimental pilgrimage, (by railway, however,) to see the spot where Johnson performed his penance. Boswell, I think, speaks of the town (its name is pronounced Yute-oxeter) as being about nine miles from Lichfield; but the map would indicate a greater distance, and, by rail, passing from one line to another, it is as much as eighteen. I have always had an idea of old Michael Johnson journeying thither on foot, on the morning of market-day, selling books through the busy hours, and returning home at night. This could not well have been.

Arriving at the Uttoxeter station, the first thing I saw, in a convenient vicinity, was the tower and tall grey spire of a church.

It is but a very short walk from the station up into the town. It had been my previous impression that the market-place of Uttoxeter lay immediately roundabout the church; and, if I remember the narrative aright, Johnson describes his father's bookstall as standing in the market-place, close beside the sacred edifice. But the church has merely a street, of ordinary width, passing around it; while the market-place, though near at hand, is not really contiguous, nor would its throng and bustle be apt to overflow their bounds, and surge against the churchyard and the old grey tower. Nevertheless, a walk of a minute or two would bring a person from the centre of the market-place to the church-door; and Michael Johnson might very well have placed his stall, and have laid out his literary wares, in the corner, at the tower's base,—better there, perhaps, than in the busy centre of an agricultural market. But the picturesqueness and full impressiveness of the story require, that Johnson, doing his penance, should have been the very nucleus of the crowd—the midmost man of the market-place—a central figure of Memory and Remorse, contrasting with, and overpowering the sultry materialism around him. I am resolved, therefore, that the true site of his penance was in the middle of the market-place.

This is a pretty spacious and irregular vacuity, surrounded by houses and shops, some of them old, with red-tiled roofs, others wearing a pretence of newness, and probably as old as the rest. In these ancient English towns, you see many houses with modern fronts; but if you peep or penetrate inside, you often find an antique arrangement, old rafters, intricate passages, balustraded staircases, and discover that the spruce exterior is but a patch on some stalwart remnant of days gone by. England never gives up anything old, as long as it is possible to patch it. The people of Uttoxeter seemed very idle, in the warm, summer day, and stood in little groups about the market-place, leisurely chatting, and staring at me, as they would not stare, if strangers were more plentiful. I question if Uttoxeter ever saw an American before. And, as an American, I was struck by the numbers of old persons, tottering about, and leaning on sticks; old persons in knee-breeches, and all the other traditional costume of the last century. Old places seem to produce old people, as by a natural propriety, or perhaps the secret is, that old age has a tendency to hide itself, when it might otherwise be brought into contact with new edifices and new things, but comes freely forth, and meets the eye of man amid the sympathies of a decaying town. The only other thing that greatly impressed me in Uttoxeter, was the abundance of public-houses, one at every step or two, Red Lions, White Harts, Bull's Heads, Mitres, Cross Keys, and I know not what besides. These are probably for the accommodation of the agricultural visitors on market-day. At any rate, I appeared to be the only guest in Uttoxeter, on the day of my visit, and had but an infinitesimal portion of patronage to distribute among so many inns.

I stept into one of these rustic hostelries, and got my dinner— bacon and greens, and a chop, and a gooseberry pudding, enough for six yeomen, besides ale—all for a shilling and sixpence. This hospitable inn was called the Nag's Head, and, standing beside the market-place, was as likely as any other to have entertained old Michael Johnson, in the days when he used to come hither and sell books. He, perhaps, had eaten his bacon and greens, and drunk his ale, and smoked his pipe, in the very room where I now sat; a low, ancient room, with a red brick floor, and a white-washed ceiling, traversed by bare, rough beams, the whole in the rudest fashion, but extremely neat. Neither did the room lack ornament, the walls being hung with engravings of prize-oxen, and other pretty prints, and the mantel-piece adorned with earthen-ware figures of shepherdesses. But still, as I sipped my ale, I glanced through the window into the sunny market-place, and wished that I could honestly fix on one spot rather than another, as likely to have been the holy site where Johnson stood to do his penance.

How strange and stupid it is, that tradition should not have marked and kept in mind the very place! How shameful (nothing less than that) that there should be no local memorial of this incident, as beautiful and as touching a passage as can be cited out of any human life; no inscription of it, almost as sacred as a verse of Scripture, on the wall of the church; no statue of the venerable and illustrious penitent, in the market-place, to throw a wholesome awe over its traffic, its earthliness, its selfishness! Such a statue, if the piety of man did not raise it, might almost have been expected to grow up out of the pavement, of its own accord, on the spot that had been watered by Johnson's remorseful tears, and by the rain that dript from him.

Well; my pilgrimage had not turned out a very successful one. There being no train till late in the afternoon, I spent I know not how many hours in Uttoxeter, and, to say the truth, was heartily tired of it; my penance being a great deal longer than Dr. Johnson's. Moreover, I forgot, until it was too late, to snatch the opportunity to repent of some of my own sins. While waiting at the station, I asked a boy who sat near me, (a school-boy, some twelve or thirteen years old, whom I should take to be a clergyman's son,)—I asked him whether he had ever heard the story of Dr. Johnson, how he stood an hour, doing penance, beside that church, whose spire rose before us. The boy stared, and answered —"No." I inquired if no such story was known or talked about, in Uttoxeter. "No," said the boy; "not that I ever heard of!" Just think of the absurd little town, knowing nothing of its one memorable incident, which sanctifies it to the heart of a stranger from three thousand miles over the sea! Just think of the fathers and mothers of Uttoxeter, never telling their children this sad and lovely story, which might have such a blessed influence on their young days, and spare them so many a pang hereafter!

But, personally, I had no right to find fault with these good people; for I myself had felt little or no impression from the scene; and my experience has been similar in many another spot, even of far deeper consecration than Uttoxeter. At Stratford-on-Avon—even at Westminster Abbey, on my first visit—I was as little moved as any stone of the pavement. These visits to the identical scenes of poetical or historic interest inevitably cause an encounter and a shock of the Actual with the Ideal, in which the latter—unless stronger than in my own case—is very apt to be overpowered. My emotions always come before, or afterwards; and I cannot help envying those happier tourists, who can time and tune themselves so accurately, that their raptures (as I presume from their printed descriptions) are sure to gush up just on the very spot, and precisely at the right moment!

> (Proof to author
> Mr. Hawthorne
> American Consul
> Liverpool) [*written in another hand*]

EDITORIAL EMENDATIONS IN THE COPY-TEXT

482.18   poultry,)] H; ⁓ₐ) MS
483.18   Memory and Remorse] K; memory and remorse MS
484.20   ceiling] K; cieling MS

WORD-DIVISION

1. *End-of-the-Line Hyphenation in the Centenary Edition*

482.10   market-|place   483.11   church-|door

2. *End-of-the-Line Hyphenation in the Manuscript*

482.13   woe-begone   484.15 market-place
484.12   gooseberry   484.35 market-place

3. *End-of-the-Line Hyphenation in the Manuscript and in the Centenary Edition*

482.14   awe-|stricken (i.e. awe-stricken)
484.19   white-|washed (i.e. white-washed)

HISTORICAL COLLATION

482.31–32 Lichfield; . . . distance,] ⁓, . . . ⁓; K,H
482.35   -day] -days K,H
483.22   pretty spacious] ⁓, ⁓, K,H
483.35   numbers] number H
484.3   amid] amidst H
484.6   Bull's] Bulls' K
484.10   among] amongst K
484.24   sipped] supped H
485.25   of] on H
485.29   afterwards] afterward H

ALTERATIONS IN THE MANUSCRIPT

482.1   stone] *precedes deleted* 'not fully humanized,'
482.1–2   not finely] *over wiped-out* 'nor finel'

482.4   a mere] *interlined above* 'a mere' *which was written
             over wiped-out* 'seated on'
482.15   with] *over wiped-out* 'clas'
482.36   home] *interlined with a caret*
483.9   bounds] *interlined above deleted* 'bonds'
483.12   placed] *interlined above deleted* 'had'
483.12   his] *over wiped-out* 'sta'
483.25   many] *over wiped-out* 'modern'
483.25   houses with] *interlined with a caret*
484.1   otherwise] *interlined with a caret*
484.20   the whole] *interlined with a caret*
484.26   rather] *over wiped-out* 'more'
485.7   some] *interlined above* 'some' *which was written over*
             'of some'
485.14   town] *over wiped-out* 'know'
485.14   nothing] 'n' *over wiped-out* 'kn'
485.24–25   as little] *over wiped-out* 'li'
485.27   Actual] 'A' *mended from* 'a'
485.27   Ideal] 'I' *mended from* 'i'

CROSS-REFERENCES WITH
THE ENGLISH NOTEBOOKS

The following list shows some of the substantive relations between entries in *The English Notebooks* and matter in *Our Old Home*. The numbers listed are those of the pages of the Centenary Edition of *Our Old Home* and the Randall Stewart edition of *The English Notebooks* on which corresponding passages will be found.

Consular Experiences

Our Old Home	English Notebooks	
7–9	4	Description of Liverpool consulate
10–11	4–5	Deputations calling on U.S. consul
13–15	562	Beggar trying to return to Philadelphia
15–18	117–18, 154–55	Connecticut shopkeeper trying to see Queen Victoria
20–21	43	U. S. claimants to British property
25–30	113–14	The New Orleans clergyman
39	3	Henry Bright

LEAMINGTON SPA

Our Old Home	English Notebooks	
41–47	565–67	Leamington
48–50	27–28, 88–89	Personal "beauty" of English women (See also pp. 333–34 of the Centenary Edition.)
50–51	191	English footpaths
51	122	Bypaths—protected by English—an American farmer would plough and plant
51–53	123	Laborers' cottages
53–54	123–24	Country church
55–56	20	Gravestone in Bebington churchyard
56	124	Gravestone under eaves
57–61	125–26, 589–90	Whitnash
61–63	582	Dr. Parr's preaching

ABOUT WARWICK

65–66	127	St. John's School
68–69	127–28	Warwick main-street architecture
70–78	141–43, 583	Leycester's Hospital
78–84	588–89	Leycester's Hospital revisited
84–85	127–29	St. Mary's Church
88–89	587	Warwick Old Curiosity Shop
89	548	Signet ring of Pharaoh, etc.

RECOLLECTIONS OF A GIFTED WOMAN

Our Old Home	English Notebooks	
90–91	124–25	General remarks on tameness of English landscape
91–92	121	English and American trees compared
92–93	160	Parasitic growth on trees; hedges and fences
92	51	English flowers brought to America by pilgrims
95	121–22	Warm weather
95–96	130	Stratford houses, old people
96–100	131–32	Shakespeare's house
100–104	132–34	Shakespeare's tomb in Church of the Holy Trinity
104–17	386–89	Miss Delia Bacon
117–19	134–36	Charlecote Park and Hall

LICHFIELD AND UTTOXETER

120–33	147–51	Lichfield
133–38	152–53	Uttoxeter
133–34	152	Dr. Johnson's penance in Uttoxeter

PILGRIMAGE TO OLD BOSTON

139–66	474–80	Boston, England
161	421	Relics recollected

PILGRIMAGE TO OLD BOSTON—*Continued*

Our Old Home	*English Notebooks*	
161	306	Drop of King Charles's blood visible in his prayer-book
165	130	English old people

NEAR OXFORD

167–78	405–10	Blenheim (*Our Old Home* closely follows the *Notebooks*.)
178	413	Arch Deacon (ale)
192	399	Spiers ("Spires"), former Mayor of Oxford
178–92	415–22	Oxford environs
183	416	Description of kitchen at Stanton Harcourt

SOME OF THE HAUNTS OF BURNS

193–212	499–511	Burns country (*Our Old Home* closely follows the *Notebooks*.)
207–8	131	Allusion to Satan's hoof's breaking flagstones

A LONDON SUBURB

214	22–23	Hawthorne's "first English fireside" in Rock Park
216	7–8	Poor fruit-growing

A London Suburb—*Continued*

Our Old Home	*English Notebooks*	
216–19	390	Warm summer day in Bennoch's garden
220–21	384	Blackheath
221	374	Parliament House seen from Blackheath
224–27	390–91	Greenwich Park
225–27	375	Greenwich Park—Sunday crowds, outdoor preaching
227	375	Greenwich Park barrows
227	242	British Museum artifacts
228–34	216–17	Greenwich Hospital
228–29	233	Rotherhithe—remembers Gulliver
234–40	289–91	Greenwich Fair
234, 236–37	115–16	Greenwich Fair (Tranmere Fair)
239–42	197	Fineness/coarseness in British character

Up the Thames

245	216	Shipping on the Thames
245–51	232–33	Thames Tunnel
251	233	John Taylor—"water-wit"
251–52	233–34	Wapping
253–55	248–49	Up the Thames to Chelsea
254	249	Westminster Bridge and the Houses of Parliament
255	249	"builded better than they knew"
255–58	250–51	Chelsea Hospital

Up the Thames—*Continued*

Our Old Home	*English Notebooks*	
259–64	212–13	Westminster Abbey
262	224	Statue of Lord Mansfield in Westminster
263–64	595	Statue of Wilberforce
266–70	218–20	Westminster Abbey: Poet's Corner and chapels
271–76	254–56	Leigh Hunt

Outside Glimpses of English Poverty

277–78	13	General squalor (no precise details used in *Our Old Home*)
278–79	17	Spirit-vaults and beds
279–83	17–18	Butcher's shop, milkmen, infants, etc.
280–81	40	Coals fall off cart
284–85	36	Woman saving shoes in bad weather
285–86	116–17	Lower-class girl described
288–89	38	Ballad singer and policeman
289	104	Patient starvation of the poor
290–92	43	Liverpool beggar without legs
292–93	35	Begging subscriptionists (treated generally in the *Notebooks*, in detail in *Our Old Home*)
292	95	Ruined tradesman for whom subscription is sought
293–306	273–78	West Derby Workhouse
306–8	456	Wedding of poor couples in Manchester Cathedral

OUTSIDE GLIMPSES OF ENGLISH POVERTY—*Continued*

Our Old Home	*English Notebooks*	
308–9	557	Another wedding in Manchester Cathedral
308–9	103–4	Hereditary privilege may one day be challenged

CIVIC BANQUETS

313–16	578, 138–39	St. Mary's Hall, Coventry
315	139	Lady Godiva (The leaf from the *Notebooks*—presumably the original from which Hawthorne drew—has been cut out.)
316–17	287–88	Barber Surgeon's Hall
317–30	12	Mayor of Liverpool's official dinner
322	266	Story of the Liverpool magistrate, Linkwater or Drinkwater, who fined himself
323–24	56	Sgt. Charles Wilkins
326–27	91, 440	"ragged and shapeless" British oratory
327	457–58	Lord Stanley—well-meaning, poor delivery
329	90	Likens oratory to being under fire
331–45	319–23	Lord Mayor's dinner, London
333–34	27–28	Attractiveness of English women (The notebook passage is heterodoxy, pointedly modified in *Our Old Home*, admitting American scrawniness in contrast to ampler English physique.)

Civic Banquets—*Continued*

Our Old Home	*English Notebooks*	
333–34	88–89	Physical unattractiveness of English women (See also pp. 48–50 of the Centenary Edition.)
336–37	321	The brother and sister-in-law of Lord Mayor David Salomons described
340–41	282	Three English friends: Francis Bennoch, and Mr. and Mrs. S. C. Hall

OUR OLD HOME

Volume V of the Centenary Edition of the Works of Nathaniel Hawthorne.

Published by the Ohio State University Press, Columbus.

The text is set in eleven-point Fairfield, with Caslon initial capitals. Chapter headings are set in fourteen-point Caledonia capitals.

Composition, presswork, and binding by the Kingsport Press, Inc., Kingsport, Tennessee.

Paper for the Centenary Edition is sixty-pound Olde Style Antique Wove, manufactured by the S. D. Warren Company, Boston, Massachusetts.

Binding cloth for the Edition is Colonial Linen, manufactured by the Columbia Mills, Inc., Syracuse, New York.

Preliminary pages designed by Turck and Reinfeld, Inc., New York City.